THE BEAST OF THE CAMARGUE

Also by Xavier-Marie Bonnot

The First Fingerprint

Xavier-Marie Bonnot

THE BEAST
OF THE CAMARGUE

Translated from the French by
Ian Monk

MACLEHOSE PRESS
QUERCUS · LONDON

First published in Great Britain in 2009 by MacLehose Press
This paperback edition published in Great Britain in 2010 by

MacLehose Press
An imprint of Quercus
21 Bloomsbury Square
London
WC1A 2NS

English Translation Copyright © 2009 by Ian Monk

The Beast of the Camargue by Xavier-Marie Bonnot © Editions L'Ecailler du sud,
Published with original French title: La Bête du Marais
The Beast of the Camargue is published by arrangement with L'Ecailler du sud,
care of Agence litteraire Pierre Astier & Associés
ALL RIGHTS RESERVED

This book is supported by the French Ministry of Foreign Affairs,
as part of the Burgess programme run by the Cultural Department
of the French Embassy in London.

A CIP catalogue reference for this book is available
from the British Library

ISBN 978 1 906694 79 1

10 9 8 7 6 5 4 3 2

Printed and bound in Great Britain by Clays Ltd, St Ives plc

To my father, who first told me the story
of the Tarasque when I was his little boy.

AUTHOR'S NOTE AND ACKNOWLEDGEMENTS

The characters and situations in this novel are the product of my imagination, and are not based on reality.

Some sections will probably bring a smile to the lips of specialists in prehistory or members of the Marseille murder squad. I have intentionally altered places, transformed research laboratories, shifted around hospitals, upturned hierarchies and metamorphosed the murder squad's offices. I have also taken liberties with a number of official procedures.

Without asking a single word of permission . . .

My sincere thanks go first to Maurice Georges and Jérôme Harlay, two friends who spent many hours correcting this text and who have enriched it with their always pertinent remarks. My gratitude also to Michel Emerit, formerly professor of animal ecology at the University of Montpellier and correspondent for the Museum of Natural History, who was of great assistance thanks to his knowledge of the environment of the Camargue, and the documentation he supplied about its flora and fauna.

TRANSLATOR'S NOTE

In the original French, a large amount of Marseille slang is used. No attempt has been made to imitate its probably inimitable presence.

. . . Alabre
De sang uman e de cadabre,
Dins nòsti bos e nòsti vabre
Un moustren, un fléu di diéu, barruolo . . . Agués pieta!

La bèsti a la co d'un coulobre,
A d'iue mai rouge qu'un cinobre;
Sus l'esquino a d'escaumo e d'àsti que fan pòu!
D'un gros lioun porto lou mourre
E sièis pèd d'ome pèr miés courre;
Dins sa cafourne, souto un mourre
Que domino lou Rose, emporto ço que pòu.

. . . Thirsty
For human blood and corpses
In our woods and our ravines
Roams a monster, a scourge of the gods . . . Have mercy!

The beast has a dragon's tail
And eyes redder than cinnabar;
On its back, its scales and spikes are terrifying!
It has the muzzle of a great lion,
And six human feet, to run faster;
Into its cavern, under a rock
Overlooking the Rhône, it carries all it can.

Frédéric Mistral, *Mireille*

1.

Last night, the mistral had stopped suddenly, just after nightfall. There had then been a moment of delirium, the bars had turned into bodegas full of heady music, gleaming faces and sleepless eyes.

The police patrols cruised around in second gear, laid back and bored to tears. A few brawls broke out between gypsies, Arabs and gorillas from the town hall outside a gaudy fairground. But the national police force turned a blind eye – no treading on the toes of the boys from the municipal brigade.

The last crackers had exploded far away, in the hidden nooks and crannies of the town, before the sun came up: the last fireworks of a party that weariness had now put to bed.

That morning, liquid heat poured down from the sky.

The man was lying on the riverbank, in the foetal position, arms wrapped round his knees. He opened his eyes and, through his twitching eyelids, saw the white shape of the towers of the castle above him, melting into the saturated light.

The man was drenched in sweat, his raven hair stuck to his forehead like strips of cardboard. In the distance he could hear vague noises, presumably the last party animals stumbling home. But he very soon changed his mind: it was the baying of an angry crowd that was echoing off the walls of the fortress.

The clamour made his head spin. He closed his eyes again.

The man had hardly slept for three days. Three days of solitude. A taste of acid bile twisted his lips and flared his nostrils. The pastis he had drunk had now worn off. Time to get going.

He sat up. In front of him, the Rhône flowed calmly by. A few crooked roots scratched at the placid surface like monsters, as though trying to hold back the river's regal progress. He tried to stand, but then realised that his legs would not hold him for a while, so he lay back on the warm, dry grass and stared at the powerful branches of the acacia that clawed at the sky above him.

It was time to think, to go over the past three days.

On the first day, as soon as the sun rose over the Camargue, he had started watching out for white spoonbills, spending hours hidden like a crocodile in the rock samphire across the marshland, a few metres from the Redon lagoon.

He had been waiting for months for the spoonbills, since March, when thousands of grey mullet gather in the placid waters of the delta, within easy swimming distance of the empty beaches, still shivering with cold; the time of year when the cormorants and herons come to gorge themselves on the surface fish.

For some time he had been studying the habits of spoonbills, and the places where they came to rest on their way back from Africa. This was often at the foot of clumps of tamarisks. He wanted to be able to observe them in the dawn's golden light, but spoonbills are capricious as well as rare. That year, he had had to make do with the gluttonous antics of the cormorants and herons.

That morning, those large birds had still not appeared. He had waited until noon before finally deciding to change his vantage point and heading further west, towards the Capelière nature reserve. He had exchanged a few words with the keeper. Chitchat, nothing more.

During the afternoon, he wandered around for some time, his loaded camera in one hand and his binoculars in the other, stopping now and then to observe.

He had walked to the ends of the earth. Then the first spoonbill appeared, immaculate, stretching its long neck through the reeds, at the edge of the marsh. A second came to rest on a half-submerged tree trunk, in the middle of the dark waters. The ground, cracked in places and spongy in others, led away towards the setting sun, the flat horizon and the sea, which the mistral was furrowing.

The spoonbills had then flown back into their mysterious habitat, and night fell on the tip of the Camargue. In the distance, beyond the straight lines of the marshland, the flames of the great Fos oil terminal rose red into the dark sky, like proud banners. At one in the morning, he went back to his car and drove home, further north in Provence.

Day two was the day of the beast.

He had decided not to take his car and to hitchhike instead. He had waited a good hour for a friendly driver to pick him up at the Tarascon exit. It was a solitary tourist, an Englishman burned by the wicked sun, who had said, in perfect French:

"I've been living in Mouriès for three years now."

"Really?" he had replied, pretending to take an interest in his driver. "I come from Eygalières."

"I'm going to Marseille today . . . taking the boat to Corsica," the Englishman went on, waving a hand through the hot air towards an imaginary sea.

"You have a good journey," he had said, for want of anything better.

The Englishman's Land-Rover, an old model, about as comfortable as a church pew, made one hell of a din. By the time they reached the turning that led to the Thibert farmhouse he had fallen into a sort of torpor, before pointing to a lay-by on the long straight stretch of Route Nationale 568, between Arles and Martigues.

"You can drop me off there."

The Englishman braked abruptly, without asking any questions. The man got out and waited for the Land-Rover to fade into the distance. Then he slipped off through a barrier of reeds, careful to avoid their long leaves, which were as sharp as razors.

He walked straight on, like a bush hunter, across the huge flat expanse covered with scrawny grass and partitioned in squares by barbed wire: an hour's walk, perhaps more. Behind him, in the distance, rose the dark crests of the Alpilles hills and the peak of Les Opiès, bleached by the sun's last gleams.

Far off, in the direction of the rank of cypresses, the sheep of Méril farm were just visible. Not pausing for a moment, he leaped over a fence and found himself in the middle of some heifers, presumably belonging to the Castaldi herd. He walked straight on, keeping

3

close enough to the pitch-black calves so as not to be spotted by chance passers-by, but far enough away so as not to spook them. A couple of times, his gaze met their empty eyes.

But he knew them too well to be afraid.

The day was fading by the time he reached Départementale 35, which marked the eastern border of Vigueirat national park, just a few kilometres away from Thibert's farm. He decided to spend the night on that strip of the Camargue. The end of the day was luminous, as thousands of stars came out over Provence. Before nightfall, he was back at the beach and had crept through the ruddy clumps of samphire, without being noticed. Then he waited, as he usually did, flat on his stomach among the pink sea daffodils, white sand camomile and yellow sandy everlastings.

Then he sang, and the beast came. He told it of the Festival marvels and then took his leave.

When darkness fell on sea and land, he unrolled his sleeping bag in a warm hollow of a dune, sheltered from the wind. He slept for a few hours. In the depth of his sleep, he toyed with his craziest dream: to liberate the beast on the Festival of Saint Martha.

On the night of July 29.

He would talk about it with the master. But, in any case, he didn't give a damn for his advice. The monster listened only to him.

The Rhône flowed on, heavy with late spring rain. Beneath the walls of King René's Castle, some children had climbed onto a little promontory over the green waters of the river by clinging to the ivy that snaked its way along the rocks.

The man had completely recovered his spirits. He stood up, slung his jacket over his shoulder and walked towards the cries of the crowd.

It was Monday, June 30. The third day.

The last bull race had just finished, and with it, the grand festival of la Tarasque.

2.

The bell of the Opéra Municipal of Marseille echoed brightly from the gallery stairway to the marble of the main function room. It stopped abruptly when Michel de Palma burst into the Reyer Hall. Félix Merlino, the ancient cloakroom attendant, patted down the few locks of curly hair which still fringed his gleaming scalp.

"Ah, Michel! You're the last!"

Merlino grimaced, making his massive chin rise and his pale lips droop.

"Hello, Féli, has it started?"

"Oh yes, it's started! For the last time this year. Come on, Baron, get a move on . . ."

The Baron. Commandant Michel de Palma's nickname. The idea had come from Jean-Louis Maistre, his blood-brother on the *Brigade Criminelle*, who had started calling him that one evening, as a joke after a few too many drinks. He thought it suited the "de" of his surname, his slender build and melancholy aristocratic manner.

The Baron pushed open the padded doors that led to the first balcony, paused for a moment, then glanced around at the audience, as he had always done ever since his father had initiated him into serious theatre when he was still a little boy.

The auditorium was bathed in velvet, and crammed from the first row of stalls up to the gods. The air was laden with sour breath, musky perfumes and the dust of face powder. From the orchestra rose a riot of trills, scales and snatches of melody twisting around each other like superheated atoms. De Palma spotted Capitaine Anne Moracchini of the *Criminelle* and nodded to her discreetly. He was at least an hour late. In the ten years that they had been working

5

together in the *Police Judiciaire*, this was the first time that he had invited her to the opera; at the very last moment, too, because this was the final performance of *La Bohème* that season.

Darkness had fallen when he sat down beside her.

The first few minutes passed by. Moracchini seemed totally wrapped up in the music, which trembled in the air around them. Then the old man in the gods who for years had been coughing at the start of each performance suddenly stopped. An electric sigh ran through the opera house and silence descended.

Rodolfo walked towards the front of the stage:

"Che gelida manina
Se la lasci riscaldar
Cercar che giova? Al buio non si trova."

Instead of looking at Mimi, Rodolfo never took his eyes off the conductor and stood on tiptoe each time he hit the middle register and compressed his diaphragm.

"Chi son? Sono un poeta.
Che fascio, scrivo . . ."

In the end, Rodolfo didn't do too badly for an end-of-season show, but de Palma felt disappointed. Under the cover of the applause, he crept out of the auditorium. In the Reyer Hall, Félix Merlino was pacing up and down, lowering his heels in slow motion so as not to make the parquet creak.

De Palma turned on his mobile. Two messages had been left that day, Saturday, July 5. The first had arrived at 7.58 p.m., just before he had entered the opera house, and the second at 8.37 p.m., presumably while Rodolfo had been sounding off in his garret in Montmartre.

"Good evening, Commandant de Palma. Maître Chandeler speaking. I'm a lawyer. The person who gave me your number would prefer to remain anonymous, but I'm taking the liberty of calling you. We don't know each other, but I should very much like to meet you so as to discuss a case . . . as soon as possible would be best, if

6

that's alright with you. Say Monday the 7th? See you very soon, I hope."

It was a male voice that made its nasal consonants sing slightly, both deep and smooth at the same time. The second message was also from Chandeler, leaving a different mobile number and begging him not to give it to anyone else.

Félix Merlino came up to the Baron and pointed at the phone.

"Turn that thing off at once. If ever I hear the damn thing ring, I'll . . ."

"Don't fret, Féli. In any case, there's no need to worry considering the warblers on stage this evening."

"You should have heard the first cast. Then you'd have really heard something . . ."

"Oh really? Because this lot sound like the mistral rattling the shutters in my ex-mother-in-law's house."

"That's right! It's a disaster tonight."

"But they're still applauding . . ."

"People clap anything these days. Not like before . . . You remember?"

De Palma raised his eyes to the ceiling and waved his right hand over his shoulder in a sign of shared nostalgia with Merlino.

"When things were as bad as tonight, they even had to call in the police sometimes to calm the audience down!"

Félix Merlino shook his head and, with his foot, swept away a scrap of lace which must have been torn off a gown.

"We haven't seen you for ages, Michel. The other day I was talking to the pianist Jean-Yves, you know, the singing coach, and he asked after you . . ."

"You know I had a bad accident?"

"I read about it in the paper. But you look better now."

De Palma did not reply, but looked at the square tiles of the parquet. Applause could be heard coming from the auditorium, muffled by the padded doors. Merlino walked reverently over to the varnished doors of the dress circle and opened them in the manner of a sacristan with a cathedral doorway.

Anne Moracchini tapped de Palma on the shoulder.

"Well, for a night at the opera it was quite a success!"

"I'm sorry, Anne. I did try to get seats for . . ."

She looked at his mobile and pulled a wry face.

The police capitaine was wearing a black pencil skirt that revealed her knees, and a silk purple top onto which her dark hair tumbled down. Her legs were clad in sheer stockings that clung to the curve that rose from her fine ankles to her knees. When his cheek brushed against hers, he recognised the peppery notes of Gicky, and felt a thrill.

"You left before the end! Didn't you like it? I thought it was really good," she said, laying a hand on his forearm.

He did not want to disappoint her on their first night at the opera together by telling her what he thought of the cast.

"Yes, yes, it was fine," he replied, with a wink at Merlino.

He had never seen her look so beautiful, so elegant. Usually she wore trainers or flat shoes, jeans, and a bomber jacket over a T-shirt or pullover, depending on the season. And of course the Manurhin revolver that she wore in the small of her back, to keep it inconspicuous.

"Come on, let's have a drink," said de Palma at last, rousing himself from this trance of admiration. He ordered two glasses of champagne and they went back to the main hall.

"It's marvellous here! All this art deco stuff. What's that on the ceiling?"

"A painting by Augustin Carrera, *Orpheus Charming the World* . . ."

"I sometimes wonder what the hell you're doing in the force," she said, with a sideways glance.

"So do I. But I have my reasons."

"I hope you do."

Moracchini gazed at the huge Carrera fresco, before examining the details of the metalwork and gilt masks along the cast-iron balconies. The Baron's mobile rang.

"Change that ring tone, Michel. It grates!"

"M. de Palma?"

He knew the voice at once.

"Speaking. One moment please."

The Baron sat down on a purple divan, set a little apart from the crowd.

"This is Yves Chandeler. I'm a lawyer."

De Palma paused for a moment, taking control.

"Yes?"

"Um . . . did you get my message?"

"I did."

"I hope I'm not disturbing you."

He did not like the way this plummy voice prolonged each open vowel it came across. It suggested a childhood spent in Marseille's best private schools, in a society that de Palma knew nothing about, but tended to despise.

Again, he imposed a moment's silence.

"Not at all."

"I'll get straight to the point. When can I see you?"

He felt like saying that people seldom asked him questions that were more like barely concealed orders, that he had no idea why this man was calling him and that he did not want to see anyone except Anne Moracchini. Instead he replied perfunctorily:

"Monday, 4 p.m. in your office? Does that suit you?"

"Today's Saturday so . . . yes, that will be perfect. I'm at 58 cours Pierre-Puget. I suppose you know where that is."

"Indeed, not a very original address for a lawyer."

"No, you're right. Next door to the high court!"

"See you on Monday, then."

He hung up without a goodbye. Moracchini walked over to him, holding her glass of champagne.

"I suppose that horrible ringing means that the interval's over? And are you planning to let me go back to seat number 35 all on my own?"

"No, Anne, certainly not!"

He slid a hand around her waist.

It was 2 a.m. when de Palma drew up in front of the little house Moracchini owned in Château-Gombert, at 28 chemin de la Fare, the last remainder of her marriage.

9

"How about a nightcap?"

The air was alive inside the car. She looked at him hard. He lowered the window for a breath of air.

"No, I'm going home . . . I need to sleep. I don't feel so good. In fact, I've . . ."

"You've got another of your migraines. Come here and I'll give you a massage."

She laid her long fingers on his temples and rubbed gently.

"What does your doctor say?"

"He says he doesn't know, like all the doctors!"

Moracchini continued her massage, tracing small circles above his eyebrows, then she withdrew her hands like a caress, took hold of his temples and squeezed them gently.

"Do you remember, Anne?"

"Yes, I do, but I don't want to talk about it . . ."

"Nowadays, I think about it less, but a month ago I kept on playing the film in my head like a loop from hell. Non-stop."

She pressed the top of his skull softly and raked through his hair with her nails.

"I can still see myself going into the Le Guen cave and reaching the bottom. I've never told anyone, but if you only knew how frightened I was. Guts in a knot, balls on the ground."*

"That's pretty . . ."

"So to speak."

He breathed deeply and shut his eyes.

"I can still see those marvellous paintings, how impressive they were. I can't describe how I felt, seeing the hands of prehistoric men. And then I saw her. And he was behind me. I turned . . ." De Palma's breathing speeded up. He closed his eyes and turned his head in a circle. "I can see myself spinning round on my left leg, and firing at him . . . Then he hit me smack on the forehead. It was like being struck by lightning."

"It's made you into a top cop, with a medal and accolades and

* De Palma is relating the conclusion of his previous investigation in *The First Fingerprint*.

10

all. Plus a good deal of jealousy. Well done. And I might add it's not done away with your charm."

"His strength was superhuman. I often think about that. My aim was straight, I can see myself lining it up . . . I'll never get it out of my mind that he managed to dodge a bullet. He had the reflexes of a great prehistoric hunter, I'm sure of it. He was stronger and quicker than a normal man. Compared with him, we're all degenerates."

"You're talking as if you admired him!"

"He dodged a .38 bullet! Lightning versus lightning. At incredible speeds. You can't help respecting something like that. Do you see?"

"What I see is that he's going to go down for life, and that it's thanks to you."

"You could also say that I missed him!"

"I've never said that."

"In any case, I didn't arrest him on my own."

"Thank you, from all the little cops like me, Michel."

Almost imperceptibly, she drew him against her breasts. He sensed that they were tense beneath the thin fabric. She stroked his forehead tenderly, just where the man who called himself "the Hunter" had hit him with his tomahawk.

"I'm going home, Anne."

"As you want, boss."

She moved her hands down to the nape of his neck, and met his mouth with lips swollen with desire.

Isabelle has just had her third child.

The Baron has received an invitation.

A pale blue card with a photo of the little fellow.

He is called Michel, just like him.

Isabelle wanted that. In memory of that firebrand policeman who crossed her path.

Isabelle has always been a friend to him.

And it is true that he has never let her down.

NEVER.

He has always prized the memory of the beautiful teenager he loved.

ALWAYS.

How could he ever forget her?
Isabelle wants Michel to be her third child's godfather.
He is not sure if he will accept.
But he is thinking about it. He's already refused twice.
She will end up thinking that he doesn't care about her any more.
Poor Isabelle.
If only she knew how much the Baron thinks about her.
Night and day.

Day and night.

The paper had yellowed with the years.

It was written in the muscular hand of Commissaire Boyer, the father of police headquarters. Boyer the magnificent, who made people grow up in a single burst.

De Palma was naked on his bed. He still had Anne's perfume on his lips. He could hear Boyer's voice: "Bring him to me. Bring him in. Right here. I want to see him before the big farewell. De Palma, you go to the crime scene with Maistre. I think she's still there. You'll see about all that with Marceau. I want your opinion. You young people sometimes have new ideas."

And Boyer the boss had written across the sheet of paper, with his big fat pencil, one end blue, the other red:

RAPE AND MURDER, in red.

And at the bottom, in blue: CASE UNSOLVED.

Name: Isabelle MERCIER.

Fair hair, 16 years old. 1m 63cm. 56 kilos.

28 rue des Prairies. 20th arrondissement.

Date of discovery of the body: 20 December, 1978, at 9.56 p.m.

Case followed by Inspectors de Palma, Marceau and Maistre.

"Case unsolved," the Baron repeated, smoothing the sheet between his thumb and index finger. The letters U.N.S.O.L.V.E.D. burned into his eyes.

"Bring him in!"

In his first notebook, the Baron had written: Isabelle Mercier. And that was all.

*

At the top of the page, Isabelle's photograph is stuck on with a paper-clip.

It is an identity shot.

Black and white.

Isabelle is sixteen.

She is smiling shyly.

Her hair makes two commas on her velvet cheeks.

Maistre and de Palma arrive at 28 rue des Prairies.

It is the first time that Boyer the Terrible has entrusted them with a case.

And this one seems to mean a lot to him.

Isabelle is lying on her stomach.

Jean-Claude Marceau is looking out of the window.

The official photographer is staring at her, the corners of his mouth trembling.

"Maistre and de Palma . . ."

"Hello, lads. The old man is throwing you in at the deep end. Take a look. I've never seen anything like it."

De Palma bends down.

He raises a lock of hair caught in the coagulated blood.

It is like a piece of caramel.

Beneath it, an eye stares at him dumbly.

An eye in the middle of nothing.

An eye without a face.

Jean-Claude turns round.

"To do that to a face, you really have to hit it hard. Fucking hard. Never seen anything like it, lads."

Jean-Louis Maistre has gone to throw up.

De Palma swallows back his saliva.

He wants to keep the horror inside him.

And the horror is inside him.

Never forget.

"Hello, Maistre?"

"Have you seen what time it is, you bugger?"

"She's back, Le Gros."

"Isabelle?"

"Yes."

"She's never been away . . ."

"I dreamed she sent me a card for the birth of her third child."

"That's funny, Baron. I had a dream just like that, too."

3.

La Capelière, two old buildings standing side by side, belonged to the *Société nationale de protection de la nature*. In 1979 this ancient property, hidden away among the tamarisks that skirted the lagoon of Le Vaccarès had become the information centre for the National Reserve of Camargue.

At the entrance, a notice on the ramshackle dry-stone wall displayed a pair of flamingos, face to face, and the acronym S.N.P.N. in the middle. The paint was wrinkled by the rising damp from the stagnant water, and baked into strips by the sun.

On the ground floor there was a small museum, the administrative offices and a laboratory. The first floor held a dormitory for students who were in residence, as well as the flat of the institution's head, Dr Christophe Texeira, a researcher and lecturer at the University of Provence. He was forty-five; his hair was speckled with grey and his face was dominated by his prominent chin and two dark eyes that kept in perpetual motion beneath his bushy eyebrows. His thick lips brought him great success with his female students. He seemed the happiest of men.

That evening, alone in the office that was also his laboratory, Christophe Texeira was finding it hard to concentrate: a report on the latest survey of the insects of the Reserve of Vigueirat, on the far side of the Rhône, had raised a tide of weariness inside him.

Texeira had come to the Camargue for its birds, but for the past two years he had been regularly asked to count its mosquitoes and spiders, not to mention the frogs and toads. That night, he was pacing up and down and occasionally glancing out of the window.

The moon was setting.

On the surface of the reed bed, the tips of the rushes were quivering in the lingering brightness. In the gusts of the salty breeze they intermeshed like lines of silver blades.

He peered through his binoculars, then slumped into his chair. What intrigued him that evening were the photographs laid out on his desk, beside the pink and green files of reports.

The pictures were magnificent.

A walker who had called by the previous weekend had managed to photograph some white spoonbills: two near Grenouillet and another which had strayed into the grass that runs between the canals towards Sambuc, near the stud farm at Loule.

It was incredible! This hiker had taken several pictures of these mythical birds while he, the head of the nature reserve and with a doctorate in biology, had hardly seen any on this side of the delta. Usually they gathered on the south bank of the Vaccarès, near La Gacholle. But not always.

"I'm looking for white spoonbills," the visitor had said.

"That will be difficult," Texeira had replied.

"They need to be told of love and marvels."

Marvels!

The man looked distinctly eccentric: shoulder-length black hair, smooth face, as stocky as a prop forward, with the air of someone who doesn't know what to do with all his muscles. What was more, he was dressed like something the cat had dragged in: Viet Cong sandals, a heavy wool sweater despite the heat, scuffed jeans and a patched-up haversack.

On the other hand, the Zeiss binoculars, the 200 mm narrow aperture zoom lens and the Nikon digital camera that hung around his neck made the biologist green with envy. Not to mention the pair of periscopic binoculars he glimpsed in the man's bag.

These rare photographs had arrived through the letter box of the S.N.P.N. and had been postmarked: Tarascon, July 1.

The biologist could not remember the walker's name, otherwise he would have telephoned to congratulate him.

In fact, had he ever got his name?

Texeira went into the entrance hall of the centre, turned on the lights and glanced at the bulky visitors' book on the table, beside the till.

Each page was divided into six columns, in which the visitors could note down the species they had observed, the places, dates and of course their names, and their addresses and jobs as optional extras.

On the page for Saturday, there were a good ten names, but they were just tourists, who had wanted to leave a trace of their visit and find something witty to say.

He looked at his watch again. It was nearly 1 p.m. He decided to get down to work and polish off the figures in his insect survey.

A few minutes later, he noticed that his new assistant had made yet another mistake: he came across a *Cassida viridis* and a *Cassida sanguinolenta*, two larvae, beside a *Polistes gallicus*, a variety of wasp. He would have to go back over the whole thing, label by label. He decided that it was high time to sleep on the problem and go up to his flat on the first floor.

As he closed the shutters in his bedroom, he noticed that the gate of the reserve was open. Grumbling, he pulled on his trousers and trainers, then went out into the grey night air.

He could have sworn he had closed the gate before going into his office. This gave him pause for thought: his memory was utterly infallible. He could see himself lifting the latch and could even remember thinking once again that he really should get it fixed because for some months now the accumulated rust had been making it ever harder to close.

So someone had entered the park after 7 p.m.

He decided to check, took the torch from the cupboard and set off down the path that ran alongside the Fournelet canal – the only practicable route for a visitor to this miniature bayou.

After five minutes spent weaving through creeks overgrown with ash trees and monstrous brambles, he came to a halt beside the observation hut of Les Aulnes, overlooking the swamp. He listened to the night air. At first, there was total silence, then, as the seconds crept by, the little sounds of nature swelled again.

A short while later, he felt everything stirring around him: there

17

was a gentle slapping of stagnant water nearby, the scurry of tiny rapid feet among the clumps of rock samphire; no doubt a rodent fleeing some pressing danger.

Like a wild cat, he sprang up the wooden steps of the hut. The quiet waters gleamed like old silver beneath the moon. In the middle, a dead oak had slumped into the mud, poking its branches out of the filthy water like a drowning man waving for help. Up on its trunk, a little wader was sitting up for the night, surveying the glittering pond around it.

It took him a moment to realise that the song of the frogs had stopped. He was so used to their incessant racket that he hadn't been paying attention. But now, Texeira pricked up his ears: he could still hear them, further off, by the Vaccarès, but not in his immediate vicinity. Experience told him that some other presence was close.

Then he heard the sharp sound of footfalls and snapping reeds on the far side of the swamp, in the direction of the salt meadows. In fact they were coming from the old warden's hut, which lay about two hundred metres away, beyond the reed bed.

With all of his senses alerted, Texeira listened. The sounds of footsteps stopped. His first thought was of some big game, a wild boar perhaps, or a roebuck escaped from a hunting reserve, or else a bull which had managed – as they quite often did – to break through the barbed wire around the Loule estate.

But that would not explain the open gate! It must be a human presence, maybe the type of keen birdwatcher who came to take up position long before the sun rose over the marshes so as to admire the dawn ballet of the birds of the Camargue.

He went down from the observation hut, crossed the last few metres of the path beneath the trees, and stopped at the edge of the clump of samphire. At the far side, the bright walls of the shed and its pointed, churchlike roof stood out clearly against the dark grey of the tamarisks.

The sound of footfalls had started again, in fits and starts, as though someone were looking for something beside the reed bed, at the far side of the swamp.

Then came a splash and movement in the water.

And footsteps. Massive, weighty ones.

It reminded Texeira of the big game animals he had tracked in eastern Africa. He threw himself flat behind some samphire to get a better view.

Then a strange high voice, like a counter tenor, like a tinkle of crystal, arose from the surface of the stagnant water:

"*Lagadigadeu, la tarasco, lagadigadeu . . .*"

Then a second, more virile voice, as deep as an organ's bass notes, joined the first one, becoming a scream of terror ripping apart the shadows.

"*Laïssa passa la vieio masco . . . Laïssa passa que vaï dansa . . .*"*

The two voices mingled.

"*La tarasco dou casteu, la tarasco dou casteu . . .*"†

Then utter silence fell. Texeira emerged from his hiding place and aimed his torch in the direction of the voices. But he saw nothing. He searched through the darkness, playing the light across the black surface of the swamp. Nothing.

To build up his courage, he shouted: "I am Christophe Texeira, the head of the reserve. You're trespassing, and I'm asking you to leave now . . . Immediately! The joke isn't funny any more."

* "Let the old witch go by, let her go so she can dance . . ."
† "The Tarasque of the castle . . ."

4.

Monday, July 7.

De Palma rang the doorbell of Chandeler & Associés, 58 cours Pierre-Puget, just a stone's throw away from the high court, in a desirable residence guarded by a pair of brawny telamones.

A female voice husky with years of smoking emerged from the intercom.

"Chandeler & Associés, can I help you?"

"Michel de Palma. I have an appointment with Maître Chandeler."

"He's on the first floor. Come on up."

De Palma climbed slowly up the huge staircase flanked by cast-iron banisters that led up towards the light streaming in through a glass roof.

He knew Chandeler by name: a youngish lawyer specialising in the most lucrative cases, a squeaky-clean, US-style brief, whose clients included shipowners and thrusting promoters of the tourist business that was flourishing along the coasts of the city.

Earlier that year, in spring, Chandeler had been shaken up by two incorruptibles from the drugs squad during an investigation into one of his clients: a big name in the export–import business, a king of the container trade, who had finally been put away behind the bars of Baumette prison for smuggling cigarettes and cocaine. The drug squad reckoned that Chandeler had been in it up to his ears, but couldn't make it stick.

"Please do take a seat," said the voice from the intercom, a tall blonde secretary, painted like a Sicilian puppet, who pointed to a sofa upholstered in buffalo hide. "I'll tell Maître Chandeler that you're here."

Chandeler & Associés had huge premises, full of period furniture and collector's items: an eighteenth-century sedan-chair, antique ship's compasses, a few Ambrogiani paintings, a harbour scene of Algiers by Bascoulès.

All that wealth on display must have excited the boys from the drugs squad, who would still have in mind the several other famous lawyers who happened to have figured prominently in recent trials of underworld bosses.

From the hall, the Baron could hear plaintive telephones in the neighbouring offices, as well as deeper voices punctuated by the tap of a computer keyboard.

A huge man appeared through the double doors. In two strides, he was standing in front of the Baron and sketching a ferocious smile.

"Monsieur de Palma, I presume. I'm so pleased you're here," Chandeler said, shaking the policeman's hand with a vice-like grip.

"I was rather at a loose end today," the Baron replied, shrugging awkwardly.

"How lucky!"

Chandeler invited de Palma to sit, then flung himself down on a leather-upholstered armchair.

"First, allow me to thank you for agreeing to see me. I suppose you must be wondering what this is about?"

The Baron trained his eyes on the lawyer, who was now swivelling ninety-degree arcs back and forth on his chair, as though an axis ran through his body and up to the crown of his skull.

"So, why are we meeting?"

"It's rather delicate. Here it is. My client, Madame Steinert, believes that her husband has been murdered. Unfortunately, the police have concluded that he has simply gone away, and so of course there's nothing as yet they can do."

"And how long has her husband been gone?"

"Thirteen days."

"Is that all?"

"I see what you mean, but his wife, my client, is convinced that he is dead! She has good reason to think so: her husband is not in

21

the habit of going off. He's not exactly footloose, if you see what I mean."

"Yes, I do see. But what I don't see is what I can do for you."

Chandeler stopped fidgeting. He placed his elbows on his desk and joined his hands in mid-air, as though about to pray.

"Well, the point is that my client is not just anybody. Have you heard of Steinert-Klug Metals?"

"No."

"Never mind. And does the name William Steinert mean anything to you?"

"No, I'm sorry."

"Evidently you do not read the papers!"

"You know as well as I do that hacks write a load of nonsense."

"But they do repeat things they've been told," Chandeler said, tightening the knot of his tie. "There was an article about his disappearance, as well as an article that drops me in the shit!"

De Palma sized up this lawyer, who met his gaze for a few seconds before looking down and starting to rummage around on his desk.

"Here," he said, handing him a press cutting. "William Steinert was one of the most powerful magnates of the German metal industry. Imagine what a fortune that means!"

"I can," de Palma said, nodding.

"And this is the man who has disappeared. Of course, his family would like the investigations to be carried out as discreetly as possible for the time being."

De Palma put the cutting down on the desk without reading it, and instead glanced at the blue file that lay in front of Chandeler. He read, upside down: "William Steinert Case. SK Metal." Nothing else.

"I see you're already calling it a case. What makes you think that he hasn't just dropped out of sight for a few days, as people like that often do?"

"I'd so like to agree with you. But I think that what we have here is at best an accident or a kidnapping, and at worst a murder."

De Palma uncrossed his legs and rubbed his chin.

"O.K., Chandeler. There's plenty of money in the family. Millions, if I get your drift."

The lawyer nodded and swivelled again on his chair.

"They can afford whatever they want. Including the best services that the French police force has to offer."

Chandeler leaned heavily on his elbows and clasped his hands together.

"I can easily imagine what you're thinking," he said, flashing de Palma a smile. "But I must say that you now belong to the police aristocracy, given that the hacks you despise so much have been talking about you for so long. I have even heard that you are to be decorated shortly."

De Palma raised a hand, as though chasing away such flattery.

"And then, surprising as it may seem, there are very few private detectives who know the region really well, its criminal culture, the underworld, that sort of thing . . . and you know all that like the back of your hand. To be quite honest, I was the one who suggested you. I only knew of you from the media and your reputation at the high court. So I know that you're a brilliant officer, even if you don't like being mentioned in such terms! You have a career full of big cases and high-profile prosecutions. Most important, you go all the way. You have the courage to do that. And it's you who knows the local underworld best. All of your former colleagues agree about that. And I think that the underworld is involved in this business. There you have it."

"What makes you think I'll be interested in this case?"

"Nothing. It's just that my client . . ."

"I don't follow you."

"Of course, you will be paid for what I'm asking you to do. And, believe me, you won't regret it."

"And you know perfectly well that I can't accept! I may be on sick leave, but I'm still on the force and intend to stay there till I retire."

"I know, I know . . . all I'm asking for is a few days' spare time. In any case, the affair will become public knowledge in a few weeks' time. We won't be able to keep it secret as long as we should like to. This article has done us considerable harm. I don't know where their information came from . . . Well, never mind."

"What do you mean?"

23

"What I mean is, officially, or at least up until today, William Steinert has gone off on a little jaunt to the tropics. But you know as well as I do that there's no fooling people in a scene like this one. Last Friday, questions were already being asked. When this article comes to the right people's attention, I hate to think what will happen. At the next board meeting, the wolves will be baring their teeth. I suppose I am making myself clear?"

"Loud and clear. But once again, I don't see what I can do to help."

"What I want you to grasp is that I'm ready to do all I can so that, in a week's time, the theory of a kidnapping can be ruled out."

"So what you want to know is whether a ransom is in the offing or not."

The lawyer tightened his lips and nodded.

"And perhaps you'd also like to know if Steinert is still alive?"

"You are reading me like a book! So, yes, we quite understand one another, M. de Palma."

"I still haven't said yes."

Chandeler clenched his jaws several times and focused on a point in front of him.

"Do you know where he disappeared?"

"In Tarascon."

De Palma smiled: the emperor of the machine tool disappearing in the town of Tartarin . . .

"I know, it might seem funny to you, but that's how it is. William Steinert hasn't been heard from since June 24."

For the Baron, Tarascon was an unlikely name and place, with a castle adorned with beautiful towers and spanking new arrow slits. The home of the true-blue Provençals, in the heart of their eternal land, a white town at the top of the vast Rhône delta.

"His wife wasn't worried for the first few days. In those circles, people don't see each other all the time. But then she made some phone calls to Germany, and then to his Paris office, and she had to face the truth: her husband had indeed vanished somewhere between his office in Tarascon and the farmhouse where they live a few kilometres away, between the villages of Maussane and Eygalières."

Maussane: part of the golden triangle of Provence, the home of snobs, fading artists, and natives proud of their stuffy traditions. Everything that the Baron most detested.

"So what do you think, M. de Palma?"

He took a deep breath then curled his lip sceptically.

"I think that you suspect someone, or some organisation, and that you don't know how to contact them . . . I mean, you don't want to contact them. That's why you thought of me and were given my phone number. Probably by some retired old bastard who keeps going on about what a great cop he used to be. How he arrested gangland bosses . . . never mind.

"And it's true that there are not many private detectives in this town, and I'm one of the last policemen able to recite the local mafia's phone book without getting a number wrong. I've taken liberties with official procedures, but the times required it. The old bastards you know aren't up to date. They are a murder or two in arrears. And that's what matters! I can tell you quicker than anyone else when someone in the mob catches a cold or steps out of line. It's a hobby of mine. Some people bet on horses, I keep up with all the files on serious crime. Which means that I've got my informers out there and can find out quite a lot."

Chandeler coughed slightly and fiddled with the Steinert file. De Palma laid his palm on the lawyer's desk.

"Chandeler, you know that I know a lot about the underworld, but I've always stayed as straight as a die. Both feet in the gutter, but straight. I'll be able to write a book about it when I'm an old bastard too . . . Just like all the old coppers who think that they've served some purpose on earth."

"I can see that there's no getting round you . . ."

"I'm sorry, Monsieur, but policemen like me aren't there to help men like you . . ."

"What do you mean by that?"

"I don't like your furniture, or your secretary, or your shoes . . ."

Chandeler took the blow manfully. He stayed sitting, completely understanding the barely veiled threat that had just been made.

"I'm sorry, M. de Palma, I thought that we could reach an understanding. Never mind."

De Palma stood up and stretched, without taking his eyes off the lawyer.

"If you should change your mind, de Palma, don't hesitate to call me, even late in the evening. I suppose you have made a note of my mobile number!"

When he pushed open the door of the La Rivière bookshop in the middle of Tarascon, he pretended not to notice the bookseller who was smiling broadly at him. She was pretty, with her milk-white teeth and big shy eyes.

He went over to the Provence section, which took up all the space beside the window and which thus provided a view of the Bar des Amis, on the other side of the rue de la Mairie.

He took down a huge coffee table book that covered Provence from Palaeolithic times to the present, taking in the glory of Rome as well as all its major and minor conflicts, its parades and traditional flim-flam. It contained some beautiful photos: Arlésiennes in their ancient costumes, the fields of lavender around Sénanque Abbey, gypsies on the pilgrimage to Saintes-Maries-de-la-Mer, white manes and long bracket-shaped horns in the Camargue half drowned by salty water, rare birds . . . But no white spoonbills. What a shame.

Over the road, the owner of the Bar des Amis went out onto the pavement and waved his large hairy arms about as if to chase the unhealthy air of his premises from his tarry lungs.

The man replaced the book, then looked for another title on the shelves, without taking his eyes off the comings and goings across the street.

"Are you looking for anything in particular, sir?"

"Um, no," he said, still staring at his objective. "It's for a present. And I haven't made up my mind yet."

"Maybe I could help you?"

"No, don't worry. Thanks anyway."

The pretty bookseller gave him a thin smile and disappeared among the shelves of paperbacks.

Then he saw the person he was looking for. Christian Rey was going into the bar. A second man, whom he had never seen before, arrived less than a minute later. He was tall, with a swaying gait and grey hair. He might well be no more than a normal customer.

"Can I take this please?" the man asked the bookseller, handing her *Mémoires et récits* by Frédéric Mistral.

"Do you need it gift-wrapped?"

"No, no, I'm in a bit of a hurry in fact," he said, giving her the exact amount.

He placed the book at the bottom of his bag and went out. The first tourists had now appeared. He walked fast, turned down the first alley to the right and stopped in a doorway, as though following a pre-rehearsed route, then from his bag he took a cotton jacket and a baseball cap. He added a pair of light sunglasses and took out his Nikon with the 200 mm lens.

He retraced his steps and stopped for a moment to examine his appearance in the chemist's window: his disguise looked convincing enough to confuse any potential witnesses. Whatever happened, he would be the man in a cap with sunglasses and a camera – a commonplace sight in the streets of Tarascon in midsummer.

A minute later, he went into the Bar des Amis and ordered a beer at the counter by pointing at the tap of Leffe. That way, he would be the man in the cap who did not even speak French.

The owner, a big Corsican with a grey complexion and smiling eyes, set the beer down and went on shining the zinc bar in silence, occasionally glancing at the television screen, which was showing highlights from that year's football championship.

All at once, Christian Rey emerged from the back room like a shadow, accompanied by the man with grey hair. The two exchanged a few words. As they did so, he paid and left the bar.

Rey and the man with grey hair . . . this was something new. But, it did not disturb him, and did not unduly complicate the mission he had set himself. Maybe he would have to eliminate Grey Hair too? It did not matter much. One more or one fewer. He took a couple of photographs in front of the bar, as Rey turned left, and Grey Hair right.

Then he had to change once again, quickly at the corner of rue de la Mairie. He knew that Rey was cunning, and he did not want to take any risks. He took off his jacket and glasses and put on a red polo shirt.

Rey stopped at Chez François, then opposite the town hall at Le Narval, and finally at the Bar de la Fontaine, not far from the ramparts of King René's Castle. Each time, the scenario was the same: he went inside, shook a few hands, then came out again a few minutes later with a package concealed in a supermarket bag. And each time, the man took some photographs.

Rey then headed for the castle car park and got into his Kompressor convertible. The man watched as he drove off, and only stopped looking when he took the bridge that crosses the Rhône towards Beaucaire.

The morning had been well spent. He now knew exactly where he would capture Christian Rey.

Then he would take him to see the beast.

It was time.

5.

De Palma saw her as he passed the war memorial commemorating the dead of the wars in the Far East. She was standing on the other side of Corniche Kennedy, looking out to sea from the bridge of white stones that arches above the stream in the valley of Les Auffes.

From that distance, he couldn't make out her face, but she looked beautiful and blonde, with a slender figure. Probably a foreigner making the most of the last light of day to take a photograph of the sea.

Just like thousands of other tourists.

But the woman had neither a camera nor a camcorder, just a black bag slung over her shoulder. And she seemed to be observing him.

De Palma stopped for a moment and leaned on the cast-iron railing in front of the war memorial. Rain was on the way. At the far side of the port, the housing estates of the northern suburbs were fading into the dingy nightfall.

A customs boat emerged from the Passe Sainte-Marie, slipping across the calm sea. The customs officers had recently decided to dismantle the cigarette-smuggling networks, so they were pulling in all the boats that came from North Africa. Instinctively, de Palma glanced to his left and, through the grey light, could make out the *El Djezaïr* in the distance as it slid calmly between the Château d'If and the Frioul archipelago.

The din of cars along the harbour road rose above the railings then spread out across the sea. De Palma stopped in front of the Grand Bleu bar, looked inside and signalled to the waiter to serve him a beer on the terrace outside.

He sat down facing the sea, turning his back on the roar of the

29

traffic. A migraine was starting up. He closed his eyes and breathed deeply, as if to open the jaws of a vice.

"Good evening, M. de Palma."

He opened his eyes. A violent rush of adrenalin pinned him to his chair. The creature he had seen near the war memorial was standing in front of him. It was Isabelle Mercier, with her almond eyes.

For a few seconds, de Palma wondered if he wasn't suffering from one of his now familiar hallucinations. His hands shook slightly. He hid them beneath the table.

"Forgive me for introducing myself in such an abrupt manner . . . My name is Ingrid Steinert."

After his appointment with Chandeler, he had supposed that this business of the German billionaire was well and truly over. But he took Ingrid Steinert's proffered hand, and its soft touch made him feel ill at ease.

"Good evening, Mme Steinert . . . please, do sit down. Can I offer you a drink?"

She was wearing a huge diamond ring on her middle finger. The sort of luxurious gem that can be seen either in jewellers' windows on place Vendôme in Paris, or among the hauls from famous burglaries.

"Mmm . . ." she said, pursing her lips. "I'd really like a pastis . . ."

Mme Steinert trained her eyes on the Baron. Her resemblance to Isabelle Mercier was striking. She had large eyes of a pure blue that fondled whatever they looked at. Big blue eyes that shifted to turquoise when her mood suddenly changed.

She produced from her bag a cigarette case of leather and gold and opened it delicately.

"Cigarette?"

"No thanks, I've quit."

He saw in her eyes that he was failing to conceal his discomfort. He cleared his throat, and his curiosity was drawn by the wedding ring on Ingrid Steinert's finger, which matched her diamond and her earrings. An absolute fortune.

"What can I do for you, Madame Steinert?"

Her eyes clouded over, and she ran the tips of her elegant fingers through her hair. De Palma realised that he had upset her, and immediately felt sorry about his brusqueness. He felt awkward, and she noticed.

"My lawyer met you and he told me that you refused to help me. So today I've come to see you myself."

"You haven't wasted time! You're not used to people refusing you, is that it?"

"You're quite right. But that's not why I'm here."

"How did you find me?"

"It wasn't hard," she said, and glanced at a man who stood across the avenue.

De Palma spotted the bodyguard, then another: two heavies, probably Germans, who were trying to blend in among the kids of Malmousque who were kicking a ball about.

"And you never go out without your two bruisers?"

"Not since my husband died. There are three of them, actually. It's the price I have to pay to feel safe."

De Palma swallowed a mouthful of beer, then slammed his glass down so hard that its contents shot over the rim and splashed her cigarette case.

"I'm sorry, Mme Steinert, but I'm going to have to repeat what I told your lawyer. I can't and won't do anything to help you."

She did not reply, but merely raised her glass of pastis to her lips, without taking her eyes off the Baron. A yacht was moving almost imperceptibly towards the old port, its main jib swollen by the dying wind. For the first time in months, de Palma felt a stab of fear. He observed Ingrid Steinert and realised that something was happening, a game that he couldn't control.

"Does it surprise you," she said mockingly, "that a woman should make contact directly?"

"It does, when it's a woman like you."

"Why?"

"Because you're extremely rich and you can pay for men like me just as you please, and not have to stir yourself!"

"You think so? Don't put yourself down! Money can't buy everything, and *Es ist höchste Zeit!* as we say in German – we're out of time."

She opened her cigarette case again. Her fingers were shaking slightly. She looked towards the islands.

"You have to help me, M. de Palma."

The tone of her voice had darkened. Her whole body was tense. De Palma felt sorry for her.

"You have heard of my husband, William Steinert, haven't you?"

"No, sorry, I haven't."

Ingrid Steinert's expression hardened, and her chin jutted out as though to stress her determination. She clasped her hands on the table. In the distance, the hills of L'Estaque were fading into the twilight. In Mourepiane, the lights from the gantries glittered on the ro-ro ships bound for North Africa or the Black Sea.

"My husband has been murdered," she said calmly. "And I want to find the person or persons who did it."

"Look, I understand how upset you must be, but I can't help you. Really I can't. I'm just not allowed to."

"You tell me what's allowed? The Tarascon police are shelving the case. So far as they're concerned, my husband has gone off some-where and there's nothing they can do about it! No-one will believe me. What does it all mean?"

She kept her hands clasped tightly together, which gave even more strength to her bearing.

"All I can advise you to do is to go to the authorities, to the public prosecutor, and try to have them open an investigation. That's what Chandeler should have told you to do. The *Brigade Criminelle* in Marseille has some very good people, the Tarascon section too. I've an old friend I could phone up if you want. You could . . ."

"There are things that I can't tell you here. We'll have to meet again." Then she added: "If you want to, that is. And don't forget that money is no object."

De Palma remained silent for some time. His migraine was returning and he gently massaged his temples. Ingrid Steinert was observing his slightest reactions. He looked up and met her steady gaze.

"O.K., tomorrow, I'll try to get to know your husband's case."

The lights of the cargo boats heading for Corsica lit up one after the other. The wind had turned again, barely a breath of air.

"Thank you."

"Let's get this straight, I am promising you nothing."

A voice inside told him he'd just been snared by Ingrid Steinert. He wanted to say something spiteful, but swallowed it back. The woman in front of him wasn't just trying to clear up her husband's death. In fact, all through their conversation she had spoken his name just once, and hadn't shown the slightest sign of sadness. Anxiety, yes, but not sadness.

"Here's my card," she said. "It has all of my addresses and phone numbers, personal and professional. You can contact me whenever you want."

She smiled and raised her glass. He had the impression that she was about to propose a toast to their unlikely collaboration.

"Try the mobile numbers first," she said in a strangely muted voice. "They're the most reliable."

The moment she stood up, a Mercedes 500 with German number plates drew up at the pavement. De Palma had no idea how Ingrid had summoned her watchdogs. The driver got out and opened the door. She disappeared behind the smoked-glass windows.

A few sailing boats were roaming around the port of Marseille, propelled by their outboard motors. As it passed by the seawall, the *Danièle-Casanova* gave two blasts of its siren, filling the sky.

He strolled for a while in the little quartier of Malmousque before returning to his new acquisition: a vintage red and chrome Alfa Romeo Giulietta coupé, which he had haggled for with an old collector in Mazargues, a few days after coming out of hospital.

Ten minutes later, he found his legendary car where he had left it in traverse de la Cascade and, not for the first time, had to admit to himself that he was suffering from lapses of memory.

Reversing dangerously, he crossed traverse de la Cascade and turned onto Corniche Kennedy. The traffic was getting heavier, in fits and starts in some places and total gridlock in others. Most of the

Marseillais who worked in the middle of town went home to the southern suburbs by way of the Corniche.

The Giulietta was heating up. The Baron clenched his jaws, and kept an eye on the dashboard thermometer. His nerves were as taut as steel cables, no doubt because of going on the wagon. Since his accident, alcohol affected him physically as never before, hacking away at his nerve endings.

In the distance, at the far side of the harbour, the day's last ray of sunlight crossed the greyness hanging over Ile Maïre. It came like a sign from the elements: it was there, years before, that he had first kissed Marie, his ex-wife. Now and then, on days of nostalgia, he would stand in front of Maïre to count the waves. For some time the island's tip had been his navel, the centre of his existence, but now he was not so sure. He needed a new centre.

At the end of the Corniche, he drove around the statue of David and left the calm of the sea behind him. The long traces of the cars' brake lights drenched the view of Le Prado in blood red and created the impression that they were rising up to the hills of Saint-Loup. He slipped a C.D. into his walkman and put on his headphones: Mozart, or Boche music, as Jean-Louis Maistre used to say, who preferred the full and brassy melodies of the Italian masters.

"I'm the bird-catcher,
Ever joyful, hooray!
I'm known as a bird-catcher
By the young and old in all the land."

Mme Steinert's face settled in his mind, the sheerest fact, above the traffic jams, with its perfectly oval shape, straight nose and azure eyes that could pierce sheet metal.

Isabelle Mercier.

The real world up to its tricks again.

A cop at the end of his tether.

Dark thoughts his constant visitors.

A slight prickling made his brows crease. Another migraine. He chased away the images of the two women.

"I'm known as a bird-catcher
By the young and old in all the land.
If I wanted girls, I'd trap them by the dozen!"

He headed towards Rabateau, overtaking the entire rank of cars that seemed glued to the tarmac, before driving into the industrial estates around La Capelette.

"If all the girls were mine,
I'd barter them for sugar,
And all my sugar I would give
To the one I liked best."

In front of the half-demolished old sulphur plant, he avoided the mattresses and wrecked washing machines on the paving stones. Then he lowered the window to feel the air on his face; there was still that same electric smell as when he had been a boy, when he used to bring girls to these dead streets to fondle them, while his friends were at home groaning over Euclidean geometry.

When he got home, the Baron drew the curtains across the French window overlooking the gardens of the Résidence Paul Verlaine. Night was falling; the orange light of streetlamps spilling out across the grey and black bark of a tall sea pine.

Jean-Louis Maistre rang the doorbell. De Palma could not remember having invited him round.

"Sorry, Le Gros, my brains are jelly at the moment."

"No matter," Maistre said, sitting down on a chair. "Any news of your medal?"

"No, why?"

"Because it's supposed to be soon."

"I couldn't care less . . ."

"Come on, don't play the romantic cop. A bit of recognition never did anyone any harm!"

Maistre was the exact opposite of de Palma: short and stocky, with a bright face beneath a black mane of hair. Always ready to laugh at anything, even the dirtiest tricks. The two friends had met in the *Brigade Criminelle* at 36 quai des Orfèvres in Paris, the sanctum of the *Police Judiciaire*. Their friendship had been cemented during long evenings spent over packs of beer instead of their guns.

When the Baron returned to Marseille, Jean-Louis had followed him. Now he had a wife and children, and had abandoned the *Police Judiciaire* for the quieter pastures of the *Sécurité Publique*.

"Tell me, Le Gros, does the name William Steinert ring any bells?"

"You should move to a real police office, Baron, that way you'd be up to date – we know our stuff in the *Sécurité Publique*! We've got a missing person's alert for him. It arrived this morning. You do mean the German billionaire who lives in Provence?"

"That's him. Do you know anything else?"

"No, sir. Nothing apart from the notice dated today."

Maistre's face was covered with fine wrinkles announcing imminent old age, and tiny pink veins ran across his fleshy cheeks.

"Why are you interested in Steinert?"

"Good question! His wife has asked me to find him."

"Just like that?"

"Just like that!"

Maistre burst out laughing. He crossed his arms over his stomach.

"I wouldn't mind playing at private eye myself."

De Palma sighed.

"There's something that's bothering me."

"What's that?"

"She looks like Isabelle."

Maistre fell silent. He was thinking, trying to find the right thing to say. The Baron interpreted this silence as a sign of mistrust: his friend had doubts about his mental health.

"When will I see you next, Baron?"

"Dunno."

"How about next weekend? The children haven't gone on holiday yet. They'd love to see you."

"I'm fine for this weekend."

Maistre stood up, took a C.D. down from the shelf beside him and pretended to read the cover.

"Come to think of it, in fact it's the boys in Tarascon who are on the case at the moment. At least they're the ones who put out the alert. But I reckon it will all end up with the *Police Judiciaire*."

"Do you think Marceau is in the know?"

"I reckon so. He's always the one who deals with this kind of thing."

"How do you get on with him?"

"I haven't seen him for ages. But things were O.K. the last time I did. We had a good chat: two old-timers going down memory lane."

"It's odd that he should be mixed up in all this as well."

Maistre opened his eyes wide and shook his head.

"It's a coincidence, Michel. It's true that Marceau was with us when we got stuck with the Mercier case, but that's as far as it goes."

"He worked very hard on it . . ."

"We were three young officers from the same year at the police academy, and we happened to end up on a case that affected all of us. We were marked by Isabelle. Marceau maybe more than we think."

"You're right, Le Gros. I'll look him up in Tarascon."

"He'd like that."

The Baron ran his index finger along the line of C.D.s and picked out *The Court of the Crimson King*. He slid it into the player, poured himself a shot of Aberlour and slumped into the armchair.

"You're into pop music now?"

"You made me listen to it on stake-outs, don't you remember?"

"Like it was yesterday. We used to smoke the evidence as well."

Maistre pulled a face and knitted his eyebrows. He scratched the tip of his nose and shrugged.

"I think I've found a boat, Baron."

"For fishing?"

"Affirmative. It's a lad from Pointe-Rouge who's selling it."

"Then we'll go fishing with King Crimson on full blast."

At night in La Capelette, the factories stood in dark rectangular clusters, ruins of pitiless time.

It was in front of the huge wall of the pith helmet factory that the local boys used to fight with the lads from Pauline or Saint-Loup. With bicycle chains and hobnailed broom handles.

De Palma was generally the last to get into a fight, but he was also the most violent – a violence he had now locked up behind bars of alcohol and music, and, when he was young, doggerel verse as well.

The Marseille that the Baron knew could turn the sweetest children sour; it fed them neither folklore nor good intentions, but rather violence and the lure of money.

In La Capelette, the role models were the local gangsters, who drank in the Bar de l'Avenir under the bridge of the railway that ran through the neighbourhood and ended up in the municipal dump. The hard nuts of l'Avenir were the only ones with even a shred of prestige, a success that stuck like shit to a blanket. They all had Italian roots, but were proud to be from Marseille, despite the great white city's record of injustice.

The others, that seething mass of proles, worked like nobodies. After their shift was over the smartest of them used to go and rack their brains at the offices of the Communist Party, reforming the world with Stalinist slogans.

The Baron had been born in this area, but had never belonged to it. He was not raised with his feet treading sawdust in the bars or cafés, talking too loudly and waving his hands around the way the plebs do on T.V.

But when he bumped into a childhood friend in the street, who had been in and out of prison, he would greet him as a friend. Their eyes would meet, and commonplaces rained on the tarmac. Nothing more. The true Marseillais is a silent man.

6.

On Friday, July 11, at 5.50 a.m., a fine drizzle was blowing in from the bay.

From the dual carriageway overlooking the harbour, you could see the flickering yellow lamps on the bellies of freighters streaming with rain. Anne Moracchini and Daniel Romero were driving in silence, their mouths bitter from the day's first cup of coffee and their eyes still puffy with sleep.

Capitaine Moracchini, the only woman in the *Brigade Criminelle*, did not like the rain. It reminded her of her early years with the *Police Judiciaire* in Versailles.

"Daniel, did you remember the blotting paper?"

"Yes, Anne," Romero sighed. "It's in the bag."

Daniel Romero was wondering whether his boss's explosive mood was going to cool down, or if she was always like this when she went to grab a gangster while the milkman was still doing his rounds. He did not know that Moracchini could not bear rain, especially not at 6 a.m. when they were about to make a difficult arrest in a lane in the village of Saint-André. It was enough to make you think that criminals had a guardian angel out to ruin the best-laid plans.

"What's your aftershave, Daniel?"

"*Habit Rouge.*"

"Tomorrow morning, try *Pour un Homme* by Caron. It's just as virile and doesn't get up my nose so much."

Lieutenant Romero had just arrived on the brigade. With his good looks and relaxed, feline gait he looked perfect in his new part. He kept his cool in all circumstances, had a brain that still sparked and a true belief in his mission. He had been with the *Brigade Anti*

Criminalité, before taking the officers' exam and joining the *Criminelle* in Marseille – his deepest wish come true.

On the church square of Saint-André, Moracchini looked at the clock on the Xsara's dashboard.

"Jesus, what are the B.R.I. boys up to? They're not here yet! And it's six already!"

"Maybe they're lost?"

"That's not funny, Daniel . . ."

At the top of rue des Varces, a Mégane appeared, with its headlights off, followed by a 306.

"Just look at them," Moracchini said, mechanically checking her Manurhin. "Aren't they just wonderful?"

"They're on time, you can say that for them. On the dot of six . . ."

"Yeah," she said, spitting her chewing gum out of the window.

A third unmarked car drew up behind the Xsara.

"How many are we altogether, Anne?"

"Eleven . . ."

She got out and shook hands with Capitaine Bonniol, of the *Brigade de Recherches et d'Intervention*.

"It's there," she said, pointing at number 32, which was half erased.

It was a ramshackle maisonette, set back from the rest of the street. A rusty fence, mended with reinforcings for concrete, stood in front of a small garden of irises and scrubby rose bushes. To the left was a prefabricated garage, and at the far end the house itself, with its bedroom under the rafters; one of those prewar shacks put up by Italian labourers in one weekend, using materials nicked from building sites. A first step out of their shanty town.

Moracchini drew her 357, signalled to the B.R.I. hard cases to hang back and gave four violent kicks that almost demolished the door.

"This is the police, M. Casetti!" she shouted loud enough to crack her voice. "Open up!"

More kicks, then she nodded to her team-mate.

"This is the police." Daniel Romero, in a voice that was almost soft. "Come quietly, M. Casetti."

"Shall we break the door down, Anne?"

"Why not bring in the anti-terrorist squad and T.V. reporters while you're at it! Are you joking or what? We'll do it the old-fashioned way. He'll come down and open up like a good boy."

"My arse he will," said Bonniol.

At that moment, a light shone through the bedroom shutters. A shotgun barrel gleamed in the air.

"This is Capitaine Anne Moracchini, of the *Brigade Criminelle*. I have a judge's warrant . . . You know me, Jean-Luc . . . come on, open up!"

Events unfolded just as the two had imagined from the start. The door was pulled ajar, a figure appeared and a pair of eyes shone in the half-light. Romero kicked hard at the bottom of the door and Moracchini aimed her revolver at Casetti standing ashen-faced in his underpants.

"No messing now, Jean-Luc. And no sudden moves. Put your hands where we can see them and turn round."

Jean-Luc Casetti, a crook used to the routine, turned and offered his wrists to the police officer. Bonniol turned on the kitchen light, and a greenish glare came down from the neon on the ceiling.

"Not too tight, please," Casetti begged.

"Don't worry, Jean-Luc. We've been here before!" Moracchini grabbed hold of Casetti and sat him down on the kitchen table.

"We've got a warrant . . ."

Casetti shook his head and looked skyward.

"We're here because you're suspected of taking part in a raid on a security van. So, as of now – and it's ten past six – you're in police custody. If you want, you can see a lawyer, and also a doctor. How are you, no problems at the moment?"

"No, I'm fine."

Jean-Luc Casetti was short, with bright eyes that darted around in all directions. A gypsy called Bagdad de la Cayolle had fingered him as the gunman in the double murder of the Ferri couple. After two lean years in a post in Nice, the *Criminelle*'s new boss, François Delpiano, had jumped at the chance of solving his first big case in Marseille. But Moracchini was sure that the tip was a phoney. She had said as much to Delpiano, but he wouldn't listen. All he had agreed was to bring in Casetti for a hold-up, so as not to put the wind up the people who had taken out the contract on the couple.

"Casetti, the security van raider ..."

"Please Inspector, not in front of the children. Don't say a word."

"No, Jean-Luc, I'm a Capitaine now!" Moracchini said, to cool things down a little.

A little girl wearing a blue-flowered dressing-gown over her bony shoulders and foam slippers on her feet was standing in the kitchen doorway.

"Hello," Moracchini said, as simply as possible, smiling at the wide-eyed girl.

"Hello, Madame."

"What's your name?"

"She's called Marion," Casetti butted in proudly.

"You had a son too, no? A big lad ..."

"Christophe? He's in jail."

"Why?"

"Because he takes after his prick of a father."

"For a long stretch?"

"Ten years."

"Jesus, ten years, Jean-Luc! That's no life."

Despite her years on the force, it still riled her when a crook spoke so coolly about his family's troubles. The verdicts seemed to rain down on the Casetti family without ever teaching them anything. They went in and out of prison and seemed to accept these return trips between the free world and "inside" as if they were the terms of a contract. A contract often settled by a bullet.

"We're going to search the house, Jean-Luc. Have you got anything to tell me before we begin, and find it ourselves?"

"There's nothing here. Zilch," he said, gesturing at the corridor from which his wife had just emerged, with the family's latest addition in her arms.

"Here's our youngest – Pierre. He's just turned three."

Moracchini and Romero looked at each other in silence. Casetti's

42

wife, her eyes still red with sleep, put her son down. The child immediately went over to his father and grabbed him by the handcuffs, beaming widely. Romero looked away.

"O.K., Jean-Luc. We're going to have you spit on some blotting paper, so as to take your genetic imprint. You know, your D.N.A. . . . Then you'll come along with us, and if you're clean you'll be back home tomorrow morning. O.K.?"

"Jesus, you turn up mob-handed with all that artillery! It's like the Napoleonic wars in here. That one over there's got a pumpgun loaded with buckshot, and you ask me if I'm O.K.?"

"That's right!" Madame Casetti almost screamed, raising her hand towards Bonniol. "The last time you turned up, there were just two of you. With that big copper, the one who was in the paper. What's his name again?"

"Commandant de Palma."

"Yes, him. He's a real man. He risks his life. Everyone knows that. He's got respect for people. No need to come with a squad. I've got nothing against you, Madame. I know you're on the level. But him" – she pointed at a guard from the B.R.I. – "aren't you ashamed of pointing a gun at children?"

Bonniol made to open his big mouth, but Moracchini glared at him.

Five years ago, on the orders of a nervy magistrate, she and de Palma had come to fetch Casetti on suspicion of murder, but nothing had come of it. Forty-eight hours later, they had taken back home "Casetti the Gangland Killer" as an inspired sub-editor had dubbed him.

"In fact, we nearly brought the T.V. cameras along," she said, to lower the pressure.

"That's all we need! The last time, for the lad, we had those local telly shitheads round. I thought it was just the new police procedure to film everything. Then two months later, they showed the boy on T.V., and everyone knew. Fuck the lot of them!"

Moracchini's mobile rang. She went out into the garden.

"Anne? It's Michel."

"What's up with you? Insomnia?"

"I'm not waking you up, am I?"

"Thanks for the kind thought. It's six thirty, and you'll never guess where I am."

"Go on."

"At Casetti's. Don't pretend you didn't know."

"For the Ferri murders? What a prick that magistrate is. Every time there's a hit he's going to send us to Casetti's!"

"No, this time it was the new boss."

"Delpiano! Good, now I feel better off on leave."

"What's more, we've picked him up on a Friday, which means we'll spend all weekend questioning him."

"That triple bastard."

"And I wanted to see you a little!"

One of the B.R.I. team came close, so she went out into the alley.

"O.K., so what's up? You're going to pop the question?"

"Um, no, but I'll have to think about it . . ."

"We're made for each other, Michel, but only after ten in the morning."

"I can imagine those nights of passion."

"Hmmmm . . ."

"Tell me, does the name Steinert mean anything to you?"

"You never change. I talk love to you, and you talk job. Who do you mean?"

"A guy who's disappeared. I found the case interesting and . . ."

"And you want me to ask around! O.K., Baron. But right now I'm going back to Casetti. Who told you that it was the Ferri murders?"

"I know everything, you should know that."

She went back into the house. Casetti had spat conscientiously onto the blotting paper that Romero had handed him – so conscientiously that the two from the *Criminelle* realised at once that he must be in the clear. Or at least over the Ferri affair. The rest was quite another story. De Palma had always suspected him of doing jobs for the one-armed-bandit racketeers. Before running his own amusement arcade, Casetti had been a top bank robber. Not the sort who screws up and gets pulled in by the *Brigade de Répression du Banditisme* every time he fails to make ends meet. But between that and becoming a gangland trigger man lay a gulf that a magistrate fresh in from Lyon was too quick to cross. The credo was to apply constant pressure on the big boys of organised crime. To dig for information constantly, whenever official procedures gave them enough leeway. The police might drag their heels, but the magistrate took himself very seriously.

Moracchini glanced at Casetti's daughter. She was born during his first spell out of prison. A child of the visiting room, which explained the great difference in age between her and her elder brother. The little girl had the look of a weary Madonna, despite the sparks that occasionally lit up her eyes.

"It's half-past seven. Are you going to school soon, Marion?"

"Go to school while you take my daddy to prison?"

"If it isn't him, he'll be home tomorrow."

"The last time, the magistrate put him in prison anyway! For my daddy, even when it's not him, it's still him!"

"Don't talk to the police like that," Casetti said. "They're doing their job."

At ten o'clock that same morning, de Palma was driving slowly along Route Nationale 568, north-westward from Marseille, in heavy rain. Visibility was down to about twenty metres, which did not improve his mood.

The thirty-year-old radio in the Alfa Romeo was crackling. De Palma took out his walkman, put on the headphones and swore when he realised that he had forgotten the box set he had bought the day before: a legendary version of the *Götterdämmerung* with Astrid Varnay and Wolfgang Windgassen, conducted by Clemens Krauss. He wanted to compare it with the ten other versions of *The Ring* he already owned.

So now he would have to be content with reflecting on the day he was going to spend far from Marseille. That night, he had made the decision to investigate the Steinert case. It had been neither the billionaire's wife's money, nor his unhealthy curiosity that had clinched the decision; but rather the simple fact that this woman looked like Isabelle Mercier. De Palma saw it as a sign, something that had risen up from the chaos in order to drive him forward. He

45

was also intrigued by the fact that she had personally sought him out, after the blunt refusal he had made to Chandeler. Something in her story rang false, and de Palma could sense the turbulence in these big-money cases like a weather radar.

The rain redoubled, and he suddenly had the impression of being inside the belly of a snare drum during a parade on July 14, which made him slow down even more, and thus increased his irritation.

He hated this long road, as straight as an American freeway, punctuated with chip vendors, sellers of melons and other local produce, and whores in caravans who serviced truck drivers by the edge of meadows as flat as the sea.

Each time he took the R.N. 568 it was always for some shady affair: bar owners murdered by slot-machine racketeers, or some settling of scores among the gypsies of Arles and its outskirts. All he needed now was a migraine to ruin his day completely.

When he reached Tarascon, by now on Route Départementale 99, the rain stopped abruptly. He parked on rue du Viaduc in front of the commissariat, in one of the spaces reserved for police officers. Straight away the security guard, wrapped in his royal blue outfit, hurried over.

"De Palma, Marseille P.J.," he said, flashing his tricolour card. "I'm here to see Jean-Claude Marceau."

"Oh, right. Talk to my colleague then."

The second security guard behind the grille was not so bad: brunette, about twenty, with an angular build, an inviting smile and big dark worried-looking eyes. The first hint of charm on this gloomy morning.

"Capitaine Marceau? Yes, stay there; I'll see if he's free," she said, poring over her list of telephone numbers.

The hall of the commissariat smelled of stale tobacco and the sour breath of its hundreds of visitors. A winding staircase, pockmarked with chewing gum and cigarette burns, led up to the first floor, where the departments of investigation and public safety lay in a curving corridor with a low ceiling and brick walls. Voices broke out from behind the wall of the drug squad.

"On my mother's life, it wasn't me . . ."

"Fuck your mother, arsehole. We've been tailing you for six months. Can't you see yourself in the fucking photos?"

"On my mother's life . . ."

That morning, in the Cité des Rosoirs, the drugs squad of the *Service d'Investigation et de recherches de la sécurité publique* had nabbed a housing estate baron with 40 kilos of dope in the boot of his car, some of it in his son's cot and the rest in his wife's vanity case.

De Palma arrived at the door to the investigation rooms.

"Hide everything! The P.J.'s here!" a voice wrecked by filterless Gitanes yelled from behind the half-closed door.

De Palma shoved it open.

"Hi, Jean-Claude, sounds like things are heating up next door!"

"Really? It's never them, you know how they are . . ."

Marceau greeted the Baron with a hug and took a long look at him.

"Jesus, Michel de Palma. The Baron . . . you can't imagine how pleased I am to see you. It's been ages."

"You haven't changed."

"And you've still got just as much imagination! How are things?"

Jean-Claude Marceau was a year younger than de Palma, and had kept the look of an eternally melancholy teenager, into hard rock and dope. Of course he was into neither, just an excellent police officer who was now rotting in a small commissariat after a brilliant start to his career with de Palma and Maistre in Paris. It had all been down to a fit of nostalgia.

In the early 1990s, Marceau had decided to go back to Tarascon, his home town. He wanted to find his roots again, to unlock the Provence that lay deep inside his body and soul. He had started with the *Brigade de Répression du Banditisme* in Marseille, before asking to be transferred to the *Sécurité Publique*.

Through the partition, the din was growing louder.

"I've got out of touch with the drug squad," said de Palma, pointing at the wall with his thumb.

"We've got that guy by the short and curlies. His wife and two brothers-in-law are involved in smuggling and they've just coughed. Starting with 40 kilos this morning, we've now reached one ton. He's a wholesaler."

Marceau swivelled round his computer screen, which showed a black-and-white picture of a stairwell.

"This is a live webcam! You can see the stairs of a building in Les Rosoirs, just beside the other bastard's flat. And it can pivot, and zoom . . . Look!"

Marceau clicked his mouse and the camera moved.

"We hid it in an air vent. We're expecting another delivery any day. According to our grass, there'll be 150 kilos."

"You're rolling in it these days in the commissariats."

"What's more, it records the whole lot on D.V.D. – it picks out the places when there's movement. The highlights of these arseholes' lives."

Marceau occupied the current investigations office. In practice, he dealt with everything.

"You came here specially to see me?"

"No, I wanted your recipe for fake pastis."

"Come on then, out with it."

"William Steinert?"

Marceau pointed to the missing person's notice which was pinned to the wall.

"You're with missing persons now?"

"I want to do someone a favour. So they can clarify the situation. It isn't all that clear."

"Same old de Palma, still the big boss with the know-nothing air . . . You remind me of a hack I used to give stories to from time to time. He always used to play the ignoramus."

"Steinert disappeared on the 24th, is that right?"

"That's what his wife says . . . it's not the official account. But there is no official account."

"What do you know about it all?"

"He's loaded," Marceau said, opening his arms. "And he's been missing since at least June 24. I say that because no-one really knows. It could easily have been the 22nd or 23rd."

"Yeah, I suppose he's not the sort who goes home from work every evening at the same time. I can just picture all that money."

"Then multiply by ten and you're probably closer."

"Have you seen his wife?"

"Yes. She came here with two heavies and her lawyer."

"Chandeler?"

"That's right."

De Palma's expression suddenly changed. He stared at his fellow officer sadly.

"It's a striking resemblance, isn't it?"

"The case isn't closed for you either?"

"Not that one."

"And yet when you look at it, Michel, it's just a case like any other."

"Yeah."

A long silence fell in the room. From the neighbouring office, quiet sobs could be heard.

"O.K. I just wanted to know what you made of it. Then I'll call her, tell her the case is closed, and that's an end to it."

"Michel, the guy has disappeared, that's what I make of it. And nothing is going to be closed before he breaks surface again, dead or alive! The problem is that I can't do anything about it! If you only knew the amount of work that lands on me day after day: drugs, rapes, muggings, a fucker who's swindled his wife . . . it's all the time the jackpot! And I'm a jack of all trades, my friend!"

Next to Steinert's missing person's notice, there were some press cuttings covering the few good results achieved by the local police in Tarascon: mostly about drugs, smack sold by Tunisians from Beaucaire, who regularly got rumbled; there had also been a network of stolen car dealers, with faked number plates on identical models that were chopped by a gang in Paris before being passed on by gypsies during their pilgrimage to Saintes-Maries-de-la-Mer.

It was nothing to get excited about, but there were little signs of improvement in the area: for the older locals, a stylish house with a swimming pool in a Provençal village; for the younger, a dwelling of the same sort in an estate by the highway. It would always be better than council housing in Marseille, or worse, the Paris suburbs . . . De Palma respected this sort of police work. He knew that it was as hard to arrest a middle-league drug dealer as it was a mad-dog killer.

"What's your feeling about the Steinert case?"

"There are two possibilities. Either he's dead, or he's off galli-vanting for a few days. There'd be nothing surprising there, with this kind of customer. In the latter case, we don't give a shit. In the former, we wait to find the body and the cause of death. That's all."

"You're right, Capitaine. In fact, you can't get any righter. But apart from that, do you know anything about our client?"

"Yes, a couple of things . . ." Marceau slid his right hand beneath a file and produced a packet of filterless Gauloises. "I know that he's been buying up land left, right and centre, and not everybody likes that. I also know that he's often been seen in the company of local personalities."

"What sort?"

"The sort that have been under investigation for decades . . ."

"For example?"

"Mayors, deputies, a couple of well-known Greens . . . but only the sort who have friends among the magistrates."

"That doesn't mean anything!"

"Of course not, but you asked me what I knew. So I'm telling you!"

Marceau's grey eyes were sparkling.

"Talking of pastis, I think it's time."

"And you leave your magic camera on all day?"

"Twenty-four-seven, my friend. This is real police work here."

"That's what Maistre says too, since he started work with the *Sécurité*."

"How's Le Gros doing?"

"He's fine."

Outside, now that the rain had stopped, a peppery smell was creeping through the white streets of the old town.

Marceau drew de Palma through the maze of paved sidestreets that glittered in the blue light. The shopkeepers were taking back out their revolving displays of postcards, until the next shower arrived. On place de la Mairie, the owner of the café/tobacconist was sticking his nose outside to inspect the sky, while drawing on a cigarette gripped between thumb and index finger.

The two officers sat down on the terrace of the Guardian, a discreet bar between two plane trees, just opposite King René's Castle. Marceau surveyed the area several times, before leaning closer to de Palma.

"Michel, in fact there is something that's been bothering me about this business."

"I'm listening."

"Those public figures I mentioned. All of us have already seen or heard their names somewhere, in police reports or files, during phone taps or else in real estate deals. There aren't many of them, but they are the ones who pull the strings around here. This isn't Marseille, you know, everything comes out sooner or later."

"O.K., O.K., but I don't see what's so surprising about a businessman like him hanging out with their sort."

"Steinert isn't from around here . . . How can I put it, people here . . ."

"I see, I see . . ."

"He's bound to have upset some of the local big boys. In his neck of the woods, by Maussane, there are some big landowners who are well known for their shady deals . . . and the price of land has shot up, these last few years, if you see what I mean."

"So you think he's been whacked, one way or another?"

"I don't think anything for the moment. These are just possibilities that shouldn't be ruled out. You can't imagine what's at stake financially in little rustic villages round here!"

From the way Marceau slumped back into his wicker chair, de Palma understood that the confidences were now over. Maybe he did not in fact know anything else. In any case, the time had now come to pay a call at the Steinert residence.

Marceau read his mind.

"I thought you were still convalescing, Michel . . ."

"I am, more or less . . ."

"Wait till you're given the case before getting your hands dirty."

"Given the case! I'll never be given this case. No, I'm just out for a little information, that's all. I couldn't give a damn about the rest of it."

"Since when have you been coming out to Tarascon about cases you couldn't give a damn about?"

De Palma looked up towards the walls of King René's Castle. On the ramparts, a few tiny tourists were waving energetically at anyone who chanced to look up at them. Instinctively, the policeman waved back.

Christian Rey had no time to react, or to do anything at all. Stuck in traffic on the far side of the pont de Beaucaire, he saw a man coming towards him and soon spotted the automatic concealed under his T-shirt. The man asked him to unlock the door, then he sat down on the rear seat.

"Give me the gun you keep in the glove compartment," he barked, pressing the barrel of the automatic into the nape of Rey's neck.

He did so, handing over his snub-nosed Smith and Wesson.

"Good. Now turn round and head for Marseille."

"Look, I don't know who you are, but I swear to you that I never touched Nono!"

The man slapped his neck.

"Who mentioned Nono, you lump of afterbirth?"

"Fuck . . ."

"From now on, keep it shut."

They left Tarascon heading south, and turned onto the R.N. 568. At the Mas-Thibert junction, the man told him to stop and park behind an abandoned caravan, which must have been used for some years by a whore.

The sea breeze whistled gently in the cypresses, rolling dried grass and strips of greasy kitchen roll along with it. There was a smell of warm car oil, hay and melting tarmac.

"Now get out and put your hands on the bonnet."

With a violent kick, the man spread his captive's legs.

"Hands behind your back!"

"But . . ."

"I told you to shut up. Stick your conk on the bonnet and put your hands behind your back."

Trembling, Rey did so. He almost felt reassured when he felt handcuffs being closed round his wrists.

They got into another, smaller car and drove on endlessly along the tracks and roadways of the delta. Rey realised that the man was trying to disorientate him in this maze of byways.

At the tip of the delta, they turned back towards Arles and the sea, crossing the Salin-de-Giraud and passing alongside the huge mounds of white salt that rose up towards the blue sky like chalk pyramids.

They came to a halt on a lane that swerved between clumps of saltwort, lost among the samphire at the end of this world of wind and salt. The man put a blindfold over Rey's eyes and tied it tightly around the back of his head.

"Now walk."

They went on for some time. To Rey, it seemed like hours, first on a hard, flat surface, then across a reed bed and finally through a swamp with water up to their waists.

Rey supposed that they were heading more towards the interior of the delta, through an incomprehensible mass of marshland and wild vegetation. At the beginning, there was a smell of sea air, laden with hints of marine plants and oxygen. Then came the stenches of saline earth and stagnating swamps, warm with sun and maceration.

The driveway of La Balme farmhouse was lined with old free stones and described a large S through groves of olive trees. It was an ancient property in the foothills of the Alpilles, with a fine solitary dwelling for the owners and large buildings for the farm workers.

De Palma had had to scour the region to find it. In Mouries, he was told to take the road to Les Baux, but then he had driven too far. So two bends before the entrance to the village he had turned back and asked the way once more from a labourer who was tinkering with the motor of a chainsaw in the shade of an olive tree. The man, as knotty as the tree he was threatening with his saw, shot him a suspicious look.

"La Balme? Go straight down towards Maussane, then turn left onto R.D. 78." The man gestured broadly, the better to indicate the direction. "Then, after about two kilometres, you'll see three pine trees, three tall ones that is – round here we call them the Fairy Pines. Then take the track that leads towards the mountain. You can't miss it."

"Thank you very much."

"Don't mention it," the man mumbled, leaning back over his chainsaw.

From the Fairy Pines, a few metres off R.D. 78, the Steinert place looked like something from Tuscany. A few sunbeams broke through the ceiling of the sky which was muffled in darkness, and cut the gloom with broad, gilded shafts.

The property covered over 100 hectares, smoothly sloping down at first, then rising gently up towards the buildings that stood with their backs to the Alpilles. This solid earth, with stones as large as fists, had been constantly ploughed through the centuries; it was never sticky or black, and rose in dust beneath the stifling sun.

The homestead of the farm was thirty metres long by fifteen wide, and stood at right angles to the outbuildings. Four huge plane trees framed a fountain and stretched their pollarded branches over what used to be the stables.

From a distance, the sight was impressive, but only the turquoise rectangle of a swimming pool almost as large as the stables suggested that the owners had greater means than the soil would usually support.

As it happened, the Steinert family had maintained most of the buildings in their original functions: the barn door was open on a giant tractor, parked like a crab in its hole; next to it there was a vine tractor, which looked like a scale model with its narrow chassis.

De Palma parked his car beneath a plane tree. To his right, he could see the pool, which was a good twenty metres long, and, beyond it, a green artificial tennis court complete with changing rooms.

Further on, where a green meadow stretched as far as the first white rocks of the Alpilles, three horses were killing time by chasing off the flies that pestered them.

There was no gate or fence. And apparently no bodyguards. If the farmhouse was under surveillance, then it was highly discreet.

Ingrid Steinert was in the midst of three groups sitting around like obedient schoolchildren at small tables on a vast paved patio half covered over by climbing vines and flowering wisteria.

The lady of the manor was radiant, passing from one group to the other, making her light dress swirl with its Provençal motifs. Each group was gathered in front of small phials full of olive oil. The various members were holding tasting glasses and scribbling on notepads.

When she noticed de Palma, Madame Steinert did not look surprised. She gave him a formal smile and graciously beckoned him to join her.

"We're defining the new collection of our oils," she said, shaking his hand energetically. "We taste them again and again. They're last year's oils."

"You're . . . you're tasting oil?"

"Of course . . . it should be savoured like a fine wine! In fact, let me introduce you to Eric Bartel, one of France's greatest wine experts."

Bartel, a little fellow with a turned-up nose, barely glanced at de Palma before he grimaced and bent back over his glass.

"We taste each variety so as to decide which one we're going to send to the miller, and which ones we're going to dilute and flavour, such as Salonenque, Lucques or Grossane, and then sell in bottles. A lot of it goes abroad, especially to the U.K. and Germany."

Bartel suddenly came alive. He wriggled on his seat, his eyes flashing.

"This one is more mature," he said, raising his glass in front of his animated eyes. "It has notes of toast and hints of rosemary. Just enough, no more. It's extremely fine . . . And beautiful, just beautiful."

He twisted his glass, while the other tasters adopted serious expressions and confirmed the chief expert's diagnosis.

"We're aiming to get an *appellation d'origine controlée*," Ingrid said. "That would bring us some sizeable business opportunities."

De Palma felt about as relaxed as a young actor struck by amnesia.

55

Madame Steinert went over to him, laid a hand on his forearm and said softly:

"I think that we have a lot of things to talk about. If you have the time, of course. As a matter of fact, I was expecting you."

She turned back towards the tasters, delivered a few remarks, cutting the air with a swipe of her right hand, and arranged to meet them later that afternoon to continue their deliberations. She then beckoned discreetly to de Palma to follow her indoors.

The farmhouse living room was huge and worn by time. Four narrow windows looked out over the terrace and, in the distance, rows of olive trees.

"My husband never altered anything," she said, with a sweeping gesture. "At least, not in this part of the house. He was rather mystical . . . He used to say that we shouldn't change the old ways. Hence the lack of luxury. Simplicity, always more simplicity. Practically the whole place is the same, apart from the few rooms I dealt with myself and decorated as I wanted."

The whitewashed walls were hung with a hunting rifle, a set of battered copper saucepans and a few paintings, presumably by Provençal artists, which slumbered in the darkness alongside a couple of abstract canvases. These were the only touches of wealth in this decidedly peasant décor.

"William finally agreed to putting up these pictures, after years of arguing . . . As you might imagine, there were no works of art here originally. People just worked and had no leisure time at all."

"But you also have a tennis court, horses and a swimming pool!"

"Oh, you noticed?" she said with a broad smile. "But it was I who wanted them, not my husband. Although he did take a dip sometimes, when it was really hot."

The entire place created an odd impression. Why had Steinert left everything as it was? Why hadn't he wanted to leave his stamp on it?

De Palma could not help thinking about the former owners. How long had the same family lived in this farmhouse? There were probably still some descendants.

She disappeared for a moment, then came back with a massive

photograph album, which she put down on the table before inviting him to sit down beside her.

"I'd like to show you some pictures of my husband. I think it might help you to get to know him better."

She opened the first page of the album delicately, as though it were an ancient grimoire. De Palma leaned forward and saw a typical marriage photograph: William Steinert, wearing a pearl grey morning jacket, stood to the left, a top hat in the crook of his right arm, and a rather carnivorous grin on his face; to the right, Ingrid, wearing a diadem set with diamonds, and holding a bouquet in her left hand, was pouting at the photographer. The whole thing looked highly conventional.

The second shot she lingered over was a portrait of a young Steinert, with a John Lennon haircut from before the hippy era. He looked like a nice young man, and his long pointed nose gave him a sad and blasé look, which might have seemed pessimistic or melancholy, but which de Palma judged as revealing an excitable, fiery nature.

"This is my favourite photo," she said, placing her open hand on the portrait.

For the first time, he noticed that she had extremely long fingers, with trimmed nails perfectly lacquered with transparent varnish.

"It's absolutely him. That blend of strength and melancholy, and you can see the intelligence in his eyes."

"It's funny, he doesn't look German at all."

"*Provenzale* . . . How true. He almost looks Provençal."

She showed him more photographs of Steinert, posing amid the machinery in a factory in Munich. He was born in 1942 and had inherited a majority holding in Klug-Steinert Metal, one of the largest tool manufacturers in Germany.

"A year ago, my husband handed over most of his responsibilities to his younger brother, Karl Steinert. You can see him here, in this family portrait. He has the same forename as his grandfather, the founder of the company. William had the same name as his great-grandfather . . ."

"How old is Karl Steinert?"

"Forty-eight."

"Ten years younger than his brother."

"That's right. But the youngest brother is Georg, who was born in 1962. He's an eternal Bohemian, and revels in it."

With an agitated gesture, she turned over the page.

"Between Karl and Georg there's Isabella, who's forty-two. She was artistic when she was young and started out a career as an actress. But now she deals with part of the family business."

She gave a scornful look and sat back.

"She never comes here . . . I mean, very rarely. She has an office in Paris and looks after the watchmaking business – Klug Steinert also makes mechanisms for brands of luxury watches, like the one you are wearing, M. de Palma."

"Is Karl married?"

"Yes, to the family's worst enemy. She's French and comes from an aristocratic family. Her name's Ann-Sophie de Bingen. Quite a ring to it, no? I find it *wirklich lächerlich* . . . absolutely ridiculous."

"What, the aristocracy?"

"No, I mean . . . never mind, M. de Palma. What about your name . . . ?"

"I'm from an old Italian family. But my grandfather was just a plain seaman in the merchant navy. My father too . . . And I'm just a plain policeman."

"I didn't mean to offend you, I do apologise."

A ray of sunshine lit up the room. Through the window, two rows of olive trees were just visible as they disappeared into this fresh stream of light.

"Forgive my asking you this, but your accent . . . I mean, you don't have a German accent!"

"My mother's French, and I've spent much of my life in France, in Paris. A good family and a good education . . ."

Her fingers were drumming on the table. She opened her cigarette case, took one out and turned it between her thumb and index finger.

"And how do you find life in Provence?"

She lit the cigarette and flexed her mouth, which for the first time made her look unrefined.

"You can ask me that again some other time."

"Sorry, but I'm a police officer, not a confidant. I'm trying to understand certain things."

De Palma stood up abruptly and walked over to the window. The garage door was open, revealing a brand-new black Mercedes, a metallic grey 4×4 B.M.W. and the latest Porsche convertible, also grey. They all had Bouches-du-Rhône number plates.

"Is there a car missing?"

"Yes, the one my husband used every day. A Range Rover."

"Do you know its registration number?"

"It's 8526 VM 13."

She knew it off by heart, which de Palma found unusual for a woman, especially for a woman of that class.

"I have to leave you now, M. de Palma. The tasters' meeting will be over in a few minutes' time, and we have to make our choices by this evening."

They went out onto the patio and strolled towards the tennis court and swimming pool. A damp, slightly sour smell hung in the air. A tractor appeared at the far end of the drive, pulling a huge chrome-plated tank.

"By the way, why did you go to see the police in Tarascon instead of the local gendarmerie?"

"Because the last time I saw my husband was in Tarascon, not far from his office. In fact, I just followed Chandeler's advice. He doesn't have much time for the gendarmes."

"His office?"

"Yes, he has a huge one, just by the theatre. I was going to suggest showing it to you, if it isn't too late."

"I don't think that's essential. I . . ."

"You don't believe me when I say he's dead, do you? I suppose I don't seem sad enough for you . . ." she said, drawing out her words.

He ignored her remark.

"William doesn't sound very German. It's more of an English name."

"Yes, in German it's Wilhelm . . . My mother-in-law was English." She moved closer to him.

"We should talk about your payment. I thought that a sum of . . ."

"I don't want anything, Mme Steinert."

He spoke so firmly she was left speechless.

A sound of tinkling bells echoed off the walls of the barn. In the hills just above the farmhouse, a shepherd was leading his flock to pasture, shouting incomprehensible instructions to his dog.

"Look, M. de Palma, my meeting will be over at about six o'clock. We could meet at seven in front of the theatre in Tarascon. If you agree, of course . . ."

"I . . . alright."

The shepherd came to a halt. De Palma could have sworn that he was observing them.

"So you have neighbours?"

"That's Eugène Bérard, an old shepherd. You wouldn't guess it from looking at him, but he's ninety-two and he's a poet, a real, very traditional Provençal poet."

De Palma took his eyes off the hills and went over to his car. On the way, he noticed a huge rectangular container carved from lime-stone. He stopped to look at what he first supposed was an old water trough.

"What is this thing?"

"It's a genuine Roman sarcophagus. My husband discovered it in the Downlands."

"The what?"

"Some fields we own on the other side of the main road. Nothing of any real interest, apart from their size. About thirty hectares, if you include the woods and hills. We grow a bit of lavender there, that's all."

By the Fairy Pines, de Palma turned left then drove towards Eygalières, away from Maussane. He went far enough to be out of sight from any curious eyes in the farmhouse and parked his car in a hollow in the road.

In front of him was a tiny valley, dug out by wind and rain storms, a mineral chaos in which only green scented grasses, a few stubborn mastic trees and oaks could survive.

He plunged into this network of pathways and corridors that usually ended in limestone gulches, overhung with rock faces pitted with skulls of stone, their empty eye-sockets staring out to the void.

From the far side of one such block, de Palma could hear the bells of Bérard's sheep, but the echo stopped him placing them exactly. He clambered over a large ledge overgrown with brambles and at last emerged from the canyon. An arid slope dotted with charred tree trunks led up to the foothills of the Alpilles.

Suddenly, a sharp whistle and a booming voice echoed off the rock face. De Palma spun round, with the feeling that someone was playing a trick on him.

"*Matelot, toque lei.*"

He saw nothing and could hear only the rhythm of the bells that was speeding up as though on an infernal merry-go-round.

"*Toque lei.*"

De Palma turned round once more and, two metres further down, saw a huge mongrel dog, its fur ruffled by the vegetation, and its canines bared.

"Matelot, it's a friend," the voice said.

The dog started wagging its tail, and the shepherd emerged at last from behind a bush. He was a short man, gnarled by the years, and wore an ancient black hat, with a ribbed velvet waistcoat of the same colour over a grey shirt. Beneath his aquiline nose, his thin, almost white lips were quivering, dropping down in a half-moon over a slightly protruding chin. His extraordinarily bright, jade eyes danced below bushy eyebrows, constantly shifting from his flock to de Palma.

"Good day to you, M. Bérard."

Bérard gave no reply, but just stared intently at the police officer, leaning his knotty hands on the top of his stick.

"So she told you my name, did she?"

"You mean Mme Steinert, I suppose . . . there's no hiding anything from you, at least! You're highly observant."

"Good lord no, I can scarcely see anything any more . . . not at my age."

"Well enough to have watched me just now."

Bérard turned towards his sheep which, driven by some whim or another, suddenly formed a file and vanished behind a rock.

"*Matelot, toque lei, aqui, ah . . . Aqui.*"

"Did everything burn here?"

"Yes, three years back. Some business about hunting, and rivalry between federations. That's the fashion around here, they burn everything down if you won't toe the line."

The shepherd sat down and his stare became calm, almost engaging. He took off his hat to reveal steel-grey hair which was still curly above his broad, deeply wrinkled forehead.

"How many head do you have?" De Palma asked, gazing round in the direction of the flock.

Bérard plucked a piece of yellow grass and chewed it.

"Good lord, almost none. Forty-odd. But only old ewes. The young ones are up in the mountain pastures with my grandson."

The animals came back, driven once again by some unfathomable instinct, and continued to graze, in time and hurriedly. The sound of tearing grass rose up between the two men.

"In the old days, there used to be lots of flocks in the area, but now there's no money in it. Except down there, on the plain of La Crau. But not up here in the hills . . . Anyway, they all think of nothing but making oil."

Bérard stared down at the Steinerts' fields of olive trees. From there, the property looked huge.

"It's because the land's got expensive. Young people can't afford to start out here nowadays."

"How much does a farm like La Balme cost?"

Bérard looked at his stick with a cunning air.

"There's a farm on sale like this one, with its land and machines, over by Mouriès . . . Say a price, just to see."

"No idea."

"Over a billion, young fellow."

"You mean in centimes . . ."

"Yes, in old francs!"

"Who can afford such a place?"

"Some Americans are interested. But the youngsters are trying to organise something with the local authorities so that they can turn it into a cooperative."

"What about the Steinerts?"

Bérard looked at the Baron for a few seconds, knitting his eyebrows, then he turned back towards La Balme.

"That's not the same. William was a real man, a master, with fine manners. I taught him how to prune olive trees and many other things about the land. I'm going to miss him."

Bérard licked his lips with his pointed tongue and swayed gently back and forth. Then he nervously slashed at the grass in front of him with the tip of his stick.

"Why do you say that William was a good man? What about his family?"

"They're not the same. No-one knows his wife, and she never speaks to anyone. His brothers are worse. Poor old William! And poor old me, I'm all alone now."

"All alone?"

"Some things you can't talk about . . ."

"Why are you so sure that he's dead?"

Bérard stood up and walked towards his sheep. De Palma followed him.

"Everything to do with La Balme is cursed."

"Why do you say that?"

"There are evil stones, from the old days . . ."

"Evil stones?"

"Goodbye, Monsieur. My sheep are waiting for me."

The old man vanished into the scrub, just as he had arrived, followed by his sheep, with his huge dog bringing up the rear.

Going back down into the valley, the light changed, becoming greyer and more uniform. The bushes in the rugged rocks looked darker. As he walked, de Palma had the feeling that he could hear a voice. He stopped and listened. It was like a complaint, an ancient vibrato recitation in a language unknown to him, words arising from some mysterious place he could not locate, from behind one of those countless rocks:

> *". . . Alabre*
> *De sang uman e de cadabre,*
> *Dins nòsti bos e nòsti vabre*
> *Un moustren, un fléu di diéu, barruolo . . . Agués pieta!"**

Anne Moracchini had taken advantage of the perfect calm that reigned in the offices of the brigade to look through some files. At 6.15 p.m. she called de Palma on his mobile.

"Michel, I've got some info about your fellow, William Steinert."

"Go ahead, but don't ask me to take notes. I'm driving and it's starting to pour again. I can't wait to get back to Marseille."

"I dropped in on the S.T.I.C.,† and they have him on file. Nothing much, just some business about financing a political party . . ."

"Was he convicted?"

"Just formally questioned, by the boys in Tarascon."

"Which party?"

"Jacques Chirac's R.P.R."

"Really? I would have imagined him more as centre left, the champagne socialist type, someone who cares about paupers like you and me."

"Hang on a minute, that doesn't mean he was *in* the R.P.R. What's more he's German. Anyway, it was all based on phone tapping and town hall rumours. The sort of thing that smells decidedly fishy."

Suddenly arriving at a roundabout that he had forgotten existed, de Palma had to brake abruptly. To his right, a brand-new sign indicated the Abbaye de Montmajour and Fontvieille. A truck from a cellulose factory on the banks of the Rhône was concealing the exit for Tarascon. He drove all the way round the roundabout, now breathing heavily into his telephone.

"Are you still there Michel?"

"Shit, I nearly took the road to Montmajour!"

---

* " . . . Thirsty
   for human blood and corpses,
   In our woods and our ravines
   Roams a monster, a scourge of the gods . . . Have mercy!"
† Service de Traitement de l'Information Criminelle.

"It's for holidaymakers . . . So, as I was saying, he was questioned for corruption."

"O.K., I'm not deaf! So what had our dear William done?"

"Nothing at all, apparently, he was completely cleared!"

"Hmm. Listen, don't worry about all that, I'm going to see what I can find out today, and then I'll let it drop. Maybe he's the sort of man who vanishes like that, only to reappear a few days later."

"You think so?"

"It's possible. He might be a billionaire who likes to treat himself to a little adventure from time to time. He could be sunbathing in the Caribbean while I'm getting drenched in Provence."

"Whatever, Michel, you should still get some rest."

"Yes, *chérie*, I know. What happened with Casetti by the way?"

"He's here, in Daniel's office. We're waiting for the D.N.A. tests to come back from Nantes. He'll be home tonight or tomorrow morning. That's all. See you later, Commandant."

The clock-tower of Saint Martha's church was ringing the angelus when Ingrid Steinert got out of her B.M.W. in front of the Tarascon theatre and adjusted the strap of her sandal.

From the far end of the street, de Palma was watching her. As she approached him, he observed the mane of dishevelled hair that fell over her bare shoulders.

"Excuse me," she said contritely. "I'm a little bit late."

She had changed her clothes, and was now wearing a yellow cotton dress that fluttered over her body. She had also removed her big diamond and now just a fine gold chain hung around her neck while discreet earrings were hidden by her blonde hair.

When she was just a metre away from him, he smelled the perfume that she was wearing on her neck. At that moment, the policeman's head was about as much in order as a jigsaw violently shaken in its box.

"Let's go," she proclaimed, with a hint of anxiety in her voice.

William Steinert's office was on the second floor of an old nineteenth-century building. She produced a huge set of keys and, as she went over to the door, he could not help admiring the hem of her dress as it swung against her sumptuous legs.

The door was reinforced, as were both sides of the walls, enough to keep out the most determined of burglars.

"I think it's the round key, the yellow one."

"Really? If you say so."

"There's maybe an alarm. You should be careful."

"We'll see."

She eventually found the right key, which was indeed the one that de Palma had suggested.

"It's the first time I've been here . . . It's very upsetting. Please, go in first. I'm feeling rather apprehensive."

She pronounced the final word with a slight accent, rolling the "r" and aspirating the "h". De Palma noticed this tiny detail at once. He stopped on the threshold and groped for the light switch.

No alarm went off, even though William Steinert had furnished his office with the latest in security equipment. The detective at once deduced that either the industrialist had forgotten to switch it on – which seemed strange for someone who took such precautions – or else somebody had disconnected it and couldn't put it back into action. Why not Ingrid Steinert herself? But that didn't square with the emotion that showed in her gaze.

"Does your husband employ a cleaner, or anyone else who looks after his office for him?"

"I don't know."

"You'll have to find out."

Steinert's office was in fact a large flat, presumably dating back to the same period as the theatre, and it was made up of three huge rooms that communicated directly one into the other, without a corridor. The ceilings were unusually high, with decorative mouldings, like Bavarian cream cakes.

The owner could not have opened the windows for some time: a smell of scented tobacco and accumulated dust filled every nook of the first room, which served as a hall, and was furnished with a coffee-table and four old-fashioned upholstered chairs to take up the space.

Why this furniture? Was it a waiting-room? Did Steinert receive clients in this office?

She crossed the room without stopping. She was worried and seemed to be looking for something in particular.

The second room was very much more spacious. The two high windows and the shutters were closed, and also reinforced. The dying yellow gleam of evening filtered through the blinds. Ingrid turned on the light.

It was a library, with genuine rococo shelves in massive walnut, each shelf crammed to bursting with books, some displaying their spines, others piled up anyhow. The fine layer of dust that covered them showed that they had not been touched for some time, presumably since Steinert's disappearance.

"My husband used to read a lot," she said with emotion. "My God, all these books . . ."

For the first time, de Palma sensed that she felt sad when she thought about her husband.

He glanced at the spines of the books. Steinert did not seem to have arranged his books by subject, or by author, and still less in alphabetical order. Many of them were in German.

On the shelves facing the windows, the books were arranged more neatly, a sign that they had been considered more important, or maybe read less often than the others. However, the layer of dust was thinner than elsewhere.

The Baron's lips formed the titles on the worn covers: *Le musée de sorciers* by Grillot de Givry; *Sciences occultes et magie pratique*; *Les admirables et merveilleux secrets du grand et du petit Albert*; *Le matin des magiciens* by Pauwels and Bergier; *Les arts divinatoires*; *Orthodoxie maçonnique* followed by *La maçonnerie occulte et de la tradition hermétique* by Jean-Marie Ragon; *La science des mages* by Papus . . .

De Palma gingerly took down the *Traité de l'apparition des esprits*, a tome written by Noël Taillepied and published in Paris by Guillaume Bichon in 1587. Although knowing nothing of the occult arts, he realised that this must be a very rare work, most probably owned only by initiates.

"Your husband seems very interested in the occult!"

"I didn't know that. But I can see that most of the books here in

German are on the same subject. Do you know much about it your-self?"

"Far from it," he said, opening *Les états multiples de l'être* by René Guénon, the most renowned French mystic of the nineteenth century. "Some of these books seem extremely general, and not a high level, while others are far more specialised. This one, for example."

De Palma was thinking hard. Every time he discovered something, it felt as though he were sinking deeper into molten tar, with nothing to stop this slow and progressive suffocation.

The third room was William Steinert's actual office. Expensive paintings on the walls: a Léger, a De Staël, a couple of Bascoulès . . .

What a strange combination, de Palma thought. There was nothing symbolic in all this. But he understood the point of the alarm. On a shelf, there were several statues of Greek gods, which he was inca-pable of identifying, and two bulky Egyptian ushabtis, funerary figures, standing on a metal mounting; all of this must have been worth a fortune.

On the table lay a disordered pile of manuscript notes, mostly concerning Provençal myths and legends. On one page, Steinert had jotted down in his very fine, neat hand details about the mythical monsters found in the region of Tarascon.

The Drac, an amphibious dragon, used to spirit away big-breasted washerwomen to feed its young . . . Less interesting than the Tarasque, the heroine of Tarascon became a star of regionalist marketing . . . A hideous beast that consumed everything in its path . . . Tamed by Saint Martha shortly after Christ's death. See monuments and abbey.

"Your husband writes?"

"Yes, he loved writing. Part of the reason why he'd partly retired from business was to devote more time to his passion."

"A book about the myths and legends of Provence . . ."

"I didn't know that."

De Palma went round the office once again, examining the pictures. He lingered in front of a Bascoulès canvas, a scene of boats being loaded in the port of Oran. For a moment, he had the impression that the tugs were busy pushing at the huge black hulls of the freighters of the Paquet company, while blowing columns of smoke into the burning sky.

He went back into the library and examined every surface. Mentally, he photographed the exact layout of the furniture and of various books that seemed important to him, then he returned to the office to do likewise. He noticed that there was no computer or telephone. But there was a telephone socket on the wall.

"Curious for a man of such importance. I don't see him carrying a laptop around and only using his mobile . . . Still less, doing without the Internet."

He took a long look at the office. The placing of the notes didn't look natural. The pen lay well to the left, while Steinert was definitely right-handed, you could tell from his handwriting. Things had been moved about and then wiped clean.

Beside the pen, there was a feather measuring a good thirty centimetres, which was thin and extraordinarily white. De Palma picked it up carefully, stared at it for a moment, then put it back down where it had been.

"I don't think that our visit has taught us anything of significance, apart from getting to know your husband's character better. And first of all, that he was hiding some things from you."

Ingrid did not reply, and felt ill at ease. Was it because of the presence of this police officer in her husband's personal space, she wondered. Was it the discovery that he had hidden whole aspects of his life from her? She remembered that once, after the theatre, her husband had invited her to visit his den, but she had refused, saying that she felt too tired. It had been one of the few occasions when they had made love late into the night. She felt swamped by emotion and decided to bring this visit to an end.

De Palma waited for her to go back into the hall before unbolting the shutters and the office window and wedging them open with two wads of paper – in case he had to come back, without coming in through the front door . . .

"Did your husband have any enemies?"

"Of course. In his position, you always have enemies!"

He noticed a hammer on the desk, of the sort used by auctioneers, with a black handle and ivory head. It had a rare beauty and looked very old. He picked it up and made to hit out at something in mid-air.

"I mean people capable of taking his life . . . Had he received any threats? Was he worried the last time you saw him?"

"I'll think about those questions, M. de Palma."

He knew from the tone of her voice that she was lying. But as yet he did not know to what extent or for what reason.

As they left, de Palma told her that it was standard procedure to carry out a neighbourhood enquiry. But it would not be done by him, and for two reasons: first because he wasn't allowed to, and second because he thought it wiser not to make things public. A neighbourhood inquiry would happen, or it wouldn't. But he sensed that in the end it would serve no purpose.

On the R.N. 568, he drove straight towards the big refineries at Fos. Two clouds darker than night had risen in the distance, above the flares of the oil terminal.

Several questions beset him. Why had Madame Steinert gone out of her way to show him her family photographs and her husband's office? Why just those two things? Why not the rest of the farmhouse? And the family?

Why did she always talk about her husband in the past tense, as though she was sure he was dead? She could just as easily have said nothing to him at all. So what was going on? He would take care not to ask her these questions for some time.

Third point: he was almost certain that Steinert had a computer and that it had been removed from his office. Was this for no particular reason, or because someone wanted to get at his hard drive? Maybe Steinert had removed certain objects himself, because of some threat or fear?

When he got home, he phoned Moracchini.

"Good evening, my lovely. Where are you at with your hold-up?"

"We've just got the D.N.A. results. They're negative. But Delpiano wants us to squeeze him anyway. I don't like that."

"You'll always be a sentimental girl."

"It's because of his kids that it gets to me. I don't give a damn about him . . ."

"So what about me, in all this?"

"What? You're not going jealous on me, are you?"

"I'm asking you to dinner this evening."

"I can't, Commandant . . ."

"You put your suspect inside for the night, then tell Delpiano that you've got a migraine and come and eat with me."

"Michel, you know perfectly well that I can't do that."

He hung up and gazed round his three-room flat. His ex-wife, Marie, had left with the walnut bookcase she had inherited from her mother, who had had it from her own mother, and so on for generations. As a result, the Baron's criminology books were now piled up on the carpet in two stacks a metre high. On top of one was *Précis d'analyse criminelle*, and on the other *Crime et psychiatrie*, which he must have read a good twenty times.

In place of the bookcase and sofa, which had also disappeared in the divorce, two big rectangular patches divided the space like archaeological remains. They were just about all that was left of ten years of marriage. Two rectangular marks and a few poorly framed photos.

Only the C.D.s and unobtainable vinyl had been given new shelves. Dozens and dozens of bootlegs of opera greats sung in marvellous theatres: Del Monaco and Callas in Verona in a superheated *Aïda*, Flagstad and Melchior in a forgotten *Tristan* . . . Then the collector's albums of the Stones bought in London in his carefree youth; all of Muddy Waters which he had brought back from the States; Jimi Hendrix . . . they all meant as much to him as his .45, the legendary piece concealed behind the boxed sets of the Beatles and of Rossini, whom he disliked and never listened to.

He slipped Strauss's Four Last Songs into his C.D. player and sat down in front of it, his eyes fixed on the crystal display. Tomova-Sintow's vibrato flowed over his tired skin. He remembered that

Marie had given him this record on a wedding anniversary. He could picture her with her brilliant smile revealing her extraordinarily white teeth, as she waved the little package at the end of her long fingers. That night, they had made love several times, and she had admitted that she had not used any form of contraception for a month. But nothing happened. The child de Palma wanted and dreaded had not arrived. He would never arrive.

He lay down on the carpet, his hands clasped behind his neck, and fell asleep before the third song, his mouth bitter with alcohol, with a deep crease down his forehead, alongside a faint scar shaped like a question mark.

A scar that hours of surgery had reduced.

A few months before, the Baron had been disfigured, his fine features split open.

Luckily for him, his nose had not been totally demolished and the bone of his forehead had mended. For the rest, the surgeon had removed strips of skin from his backside and stitched him back together patiently, over several hours, like an old granny patching some workaday jeans.

Looks wise, things had not turned out too badly: a remodelled nose that took a few years off him, and a scar ringed with pale purple streaks on his forehead which made him look dangerous when he scowled.

Inside, it was a different story. Migraines that wouldn't stop any more and that made him fear the worst of his demons, crude blood-red snapshots of agonies that came back more and more.

In Le Guen's cave, he had been afraid, with this fear he could no longer expel from inside him. It was a fear that invaded the hazy zone of his awareness, the zone he hardly ever dared to enter. If the Baron had never thought about revenge, it was no doubt to avoid transgressing his own prohibitions, gambling with his own taboos. The incubation time for revenge was far too long. He was a man of anger and storms, not a sneaky obsessive with no statute of psychic limitations.

In the middle of the night, a nightmare caught de Palma in the depths of sleep.

15 September 1982. 9.30 a.m.

The first anonymous call. A raucous voice.

A supermarket bag hung from a green oak on the hill of Notre Dame. Inside the bag, a head.

The neck has been severed just under the chin.

He and Maistre examine it: there is a trace of sperm on the forehead, like a diabolical unction, the signature of Sylvain Ferracci, or the "Dustman", as a hack on Paris-Match *called him.*

11 a.m. A second call.

A woman's voice. The trail will now begin.

In a dustbin in Rabatau, some clothes: a woman's severe houndstooth suit, flesh-coloured stockings stained with blood.

12 a.m. A third call.

A child's voice.

Behind it, "Us and Them" by Pink Floyd.

On the jetty of La Pointe Rouge, the torso and legs. The belly has been opened from the pubis to the sternum.

A whirlpool.

Maistre, the crack shot, withdraws a Beretta from the armoury.

He weighs the clip in his hand and slips it into the butt.

De Palma watches him stroke the automatic's black breech.

He is a certified marksman and can bring a man down firing blind at twenty metres.

Maistre wants to get this over with. His eyes are red with fatigue and misery, and his brains a grenade with the pin pulled out.

De Palma hardly feels any better.

If they catch sight of Ferracci, he's a dead man.

Everything happens so fast.

A street corner, a chase.

A cellar.

De Palma sticks the barrel of his gun into the Dustman's mouth and shuts his eyes.

He's going to press the trigger.

He will if this creep doesn't stop screaming.

Maistre approaches.

De Palma's whole body is trembling.

Slowly, his friend withdraws the barrel of the Manurhin from the predator's mouth.

Streaks of light enter the Baron's head, they hit him, again and again.

Thick blood runs down over his eyes.

It's Marie's head in the bag.

No, it's Isabelle–Ingrid who's winking at him.

An obscene peekaboo from the hereafter dark dreams.

He got up, swallowed two aspirins and stood in front of the bathroom mirror.

He looked long and hard at his face, made younger by the summer sun and the knife of the surgeon who had spent half a day refashioning his features. He pushed back his hair and examined the scar at the top of his forehead. Then he leaned closer to the mirror and looked at his nose, the only part of his face he had ever liked.

His nose had changed, and now looked like something moulded out of plastic: it was an intruder in the picture, a part of himself torn away from him for ever. He lowered his eyes and splashed water over his face, as if to purify himself.

7.

At 6 a.m., Christophe Texeira left his office in La Capelière. He wanted to be at his observation post before sunrise and, most of all, to make himself scarce as soon as the first tourists showed up.

The day before, he had told Nathalie, his new assistant, that he would be out for most of the morning.

"How am I supposed to cope with all those groups and families?" she had protested timidly. "Do you realise?"

"You give them their tickets then escort them to the start of the green track. Then let them get on with it. Anyway, they aren't at risk. If there's an emergency, call me on my mobile. I won't be far away. I'll be in the reed hut, just by the samphire meadow, the place I showed you yesterday."

Nathalie had adopted a sulky look which rather appealed to Texeira.

"I hope the ghost in the hut doesn't gobble you up."

"No, he only moves at night."

The two of them had discussed at length the voices he had heard in the night. Nathalie had made fun of him at first, then they had ended up deciding that the world was full of waifs and strays and that there was nothing they could do about it. There was no peace to be had anywhere, not even in the marshes of the Camargue.

There was no point sending for the gendarmes from Le Sambuc.

That morning, the biologist made his way rapidly along the straight path that led to the hut. The grassland and nearby marshes were silent. Only the *oup-oup-oup* of a hoopoe could be heard across that brown vastness.

The heat of the previous day still weighed down on the baked ground.

When Texeira reached the edges of the marsh, he noticed that the cracks in the earth had widened again. Some greenish samphire, impervious to thirst, still survived in that tiny Sahara.

Panting, he put down his bag, checked that his mobile was off, then took out his Zeiss binoculars and Reflex camera and hung them round his neck in case a rare bird happened to pass by.

A mauve gleam spread over the flat, salty waters. The level of the marshes had fallen again in the heat wave. He heard a faint noise: a little egret, completely white, emerged from the reed bed and advanced into the pond in search of its first meal of the day, making little plops with every step.

This bird was not very rare at that time of year, but he still took two photographs, pleased with this first encounter. The thought of the tourist who had sent him those shots of spoonbills crossed his mind.

The light was changing fast; the salt marsh was turning pink. In less than an hour, the sun would start its torrid trajectory, indifferent to nature's torments.

Texeira picked up his bag and strode towards the reed hut, with its whitewashed walls, in the only clump of trees on the reserve at the far end of the little canal.

He stopped twice to observe a redshank that seemed to be following him along the other side of the canal. He knew this nesting pair. His former assistant had pointed them out to him last spring, before going to join the team in Vigueirat. This specimen didn't look afraid, it must have got used to tourists and other lovers of high-class bird life.

Once at the hut, he put his bag onto a table half consumed by earwigs, took out his thermos and poured himself some coffee.

The window provided a discreet view over the entire marsh. He raised his binoculars and made a slow panoramic scan of its greenish waters. Nothing. Just plain solitude, slightly disturbed by a soft morning wind that ruffled the occasional tufts of reeds.

He would have to wait, perhaps for an hour, for the insects to come out of their hide-outs and offer themselves to the neighbourhood's gourmet beaks. Making the most of the calm, he placed his

Zeiss on a tripod. Just at that instant, a black stork, an extremely rare bird, landed thirty metres from the hut, just below the haggard tree that had been sinking slowly into the swamp since time immemorial.

The large bird was so close that he could hear the heavy beat of its wings stirring the humid air. He did not have time to grab his Nikon before the stork flew off again, ponderously, towards the east.

Its sudden departure surprised him. He had been so careful not to make a sound.

Two squadrons of rooks landed behind a tamarisk and started squabbling over what was presumably a scrap of carrion lying there. The rooks' verbal jousting was disturbing his morning observations. He had to put a stop to it.

In less than two minutes, he had covered the distance. The rooks flew off to the far side of the marsh. At first he saw nothing unusual, and looked for their feast for some time among the twisted roots, wary of the deepish mud around the area.

Near the tree, there was nothing to be seen, but looking up he noticed a round shape, like an old leather football, just emerging from the water about three metres in front of him, out of reach.

He went back to the hut, fetched a long herdsman's pole and returned to the scene.

It took same effort not to sink into the muddy slime. The stick glanced off the surface of the object, so he tried to get at it from beneath and the pole caught onto what he took to be a bit of bone or a piece of a large bird's wing. Then, slowly, he dragged the thing back towards the edge.

At first, its weight surprised him. It wasn't a bird, but perhaps it was some big game animal, a boar maybe, which had drowned in the marsh.

Suddenly the object turned over in the water, in a peculiar slow motion. Texeira tried to step backwards, but the warm mud sucked at his boots and kept him glued to the bank.

A nervous shudder captured him, before he finally dragged himself free.

The stringy weeds receded and the face of a man appeared, swollen, with empty eye-sockets and jutting teeth, as though smiling at his terrible end.

At 2.30 p.m., the offices of the Tarascon gendarmerie were deserted. All that could be heard was the purring of computers awaiting the next rounds of questioning.

Marceau was alone, busy typing out the final report of an unpleasant case: a man who had been stabbed to death outside a bar by a gypsy after some row about slot machines. He had reached his final sentence when Commissaire Larousse rushed in, his tie askew, with a haggard look and rumpled hair.

"Marceau, I've just had a call from the boys in Le Sambuc. They've fished a dead man out of the marsh. It might well be our guy, what's his name again . . . ?"

"Steinert, William . . . Could be."

"O.K., I'm coming with you. Give me a couple of minutes and we'll take your car. Mine's had it."

Marceau had always been fascinated by the way his boss could suddenly shift gear in response to events: but it had to be worth his while, he had to feel certain.

Conclusion: it really was Steinert who was floating somewhere in the Camargue surrounded by a squad of gendarmes in combat dress.

When the two officers parked on R.D. 36b, the sun was a white ball dancing over the Vaccarès lagoon. The air tasted of rusty metal, laden with rancid mud and the scent of hyacinths.

Marceau already felt nauseous.

Capitaine Nicolaï shook hands with his two colleagues.

"Hello, Larousse. It's Steinert alright."

Nicolaï was a real military type, with a three-braided kepi screwed onto a shaved head, and a paratrooper's badge pinned to his camouflage jacket. It was all a bit over the top. He had a piercing stare, cheeks hollowed by the strains of combat and a jutting nose like a Gothic hero, which made him seem stern all the time.

"How do you know that?"

"Gendarmes know their job," said Nicolaï, working his smile.

"Give us a break, Capitaine," Marceau butted in. "That's just state prosecutor bullshit."

Larousse twisted his mouth into a grimace, which might mean any number of things that his men still had problems working out. He squeezed his nose between his thumb and index finger. Marceau had already noticed during other investigations that this implied that he was worried.

"As a matter of fact, the prosecutor is already on the scene, gentlemen. Come with me."

"If that's an order," said Larousse, shifting in the damp heat.

The gendarmes had done a decent job: there was a taped-off safety area, with technicians in waterproof body suits, down on their knees examining the marshland with scrupulous attention. Plus an inflatable dinghy, divers, a helicopter . . .

The prosecutor was standing beside the red tape that sealed off the area, talking to Colonel Audouard, the gendarmerie commander, who had come especially from Marseille to supervise the forensic teams.

Larousse coughed gently when he spotted the prosecutor, adjusted his tie and walked over with his hand extended.

"I came as soon as I got your message, sir. This is Capitaine Marceau. He took Mme Steinert's statement."

"Very good, Commissaire. I was talking with the Colonel here while waiting for you, and I told him of my wish to have your unit deal with the case. After all, you've practically started working on it already! What do you think?"

"I think that will be fine. We . . . we still have enough men available. I would even suggest appointing Marceau as chief investigating officer."

"O.K. No objections, Colonel?"

"None. It will allow me to put more men onto the Vidal case in the Var."

"Good, for once the gendarmerie have no complaints . . . I must leave you now, gentlemen. Forgive me if I remind you of a few extremely important points. I don't want any journalists poking around, either from the T.V. or the press. Given the identity of the victim, I don't want to take any chances. I shall be paying close attention to the case, and I won't conceal the fact that the chief state prosecutor rang me up earlier to have a word about the matter."

The prosecutor raised his hand and pointed a finger skyward.

"There's no need to tell professionals like you that the Steinert family has a long arm. And when I say long, I do mean long . . ."

He paused for a moment and rolled his eyes behind his square glasses. The policeman and the gendarme both nodded.

"Commissaire Larousse, all I can do now is to wish you luck. And let's all just hope that it was simply an unfortunate accident."

Larousse and Marceau were unsure how to interpret this final point but, knowing the prosecutor, they took it as a covert order.

"There's a spare seat in the helicopter, sir," the colonel quickly added, with a broad smile. "If you want, it's all yours."

Larousse watched the blue lark rise into the sky, and could not help saying to Marceau, through clenched teeth:

"What a tosser that prosecutor is. As soon as he sees a blue uniform he goes weak at the knees. It's as if they turn him on."

"That's normal enough. His father was a gendarme."

"Well, you certainly are in the know. I thought he was more into gay S&M."

"Anyway, we can really thank him for this case. Any more rotten and you die!"

"Come on, let's go and see our customer."

Before he uncovered the corpse, the gendarme who was guarding the bodybag said to Marceau:

"I warn you, it's not a pretty sight."

"Really?" he replied. "Thanks, it's the very first time I've seen a stiff . . ."

The gendarme swiftly unzipped the bag and pushed its two halves apart.

William Steinert's face was swollen, and still splattered with mud and little brown weeds; a liquid that looked like white dribble was oozing from between his teeth.

The small carnivores of the marsh had already started devouring the tenderest parts: the lips, parts of the cheeks and the eyes had already vanished. But Steinert was still recognisable.

Marceau bent over the body. The smell of decomposition was unbearable, and there was a stink of lukewarm sludge.

"The back of the neck and head don't seem to have been touched. There are no traces of a struggle on his hands, and no broken fingers. On the abdomen, there are no apparent wounds. Nothing to speak off on a superficial level. Neither on the back nor on the legs. The stomach is bloated. He must have drunk quite a lot of water."

"I think he must have drowned," the gendarme said.

Marceau did not answer, but looked towards the marsh. A few bubbles rose from the silt and burst on the surface.

"Where was the body?"

"Right here, in front of us. According to Christophe Texeira, he was about three metres away from the edge. In fact, the pole used to drag him in is just that length, so he could even have been nearer."

"Who pulled the body up onto the bank?"

"Some colleagues."

"And who put it in the bag?"

"Some colleagues."

"And where's the forensics report?"

"Um, there isn't one for the moment."

"Great, that makes three foul-ups in one. You've beaten your own record, lads. Congratulations. Where are his belongings?"

"We found a rucksack with a wallet, purse, car keys, cash . . . the usual stuff you find in a bag. Then there was some photographic equipment, binoculars and a folding spade."

"A folding spade?"

"Yes, like the ones commandos carry. But we're not sure if it was actually his. We'll have to check the fingerprints, if there are any. In fact, we found it by the hut. If you come with me, I can show you everything."

"Later, later."

"Can I close the bag again?"

"O.K., and put him on ice at once. He stinks like hell."

Marceau moved away from the group and called de Palma on his mobile. The Baron answered at once.

"We've got him, Michel."

"Who, Steinert?"

"Yeah, in the marshes, just by a dump called La Capelière, in the Camargue. Stone dead, and in an advanced state already."

"How long?"

"About a fortnight, I reckon. That also fits with the dates."

"Thanks for telling me so soon . . ."

"Listen, Michel, I only heard an hour ago. Ever since then, I've had Larousse on my back, so sorry if I couldn't call you in secret. We also had to deal with the gendarmerie."

"Don't worry, my boy!"

"I've got the case."

"Why you? That's the gendarmes' patch!"

"It's a funny business. The prosecutor was out here in person earlier."

The Baron whistled.

"Speak to you later, Michel. We'll have to inform the widow. I'll go as soon as they give me the green light."

A 4×4 B.M.W. appeared on the road, followed by a cloud of dust.

"It looks like I won't have to bother, Michel. I'll bet you anything you like that she's just showed up. Thanks again, the gendarmerie."

The B.M.W. drew up next to the group of vehicles and Ingrid Steinert got out, along with a man in a suit and tie, presumably the family's lawyer. A brigadier went over to her. They exchanged a few words, then shook hands. Jean-Claude Marceau's expression changed, and the veins in his neck tensed slightly. He frowned, took a step forward, but Nicolaï held him back.

"Leave it, Jean-Claude. Let the brigadier handle the widow. He's used to it. We'll see about her later."

Marceau went back to the body and tried to imagine its last moments of life in the slime of this outlandish place.

From what the gendarme had told him, the body had had its back to the bank, as if it had fallen into the water head first.

"That's one hypothesis," the officer said to himself. "But I don't see why he would have thrown himself flat on his face into this shitty pond. There's no reason at all. Unless the body moved over time . . . But there's no current in this marsh. Unless it was the wind. Or some animal."

He looked for traces in the earth and mud beside the bank, but all he found was a mass of boot and shoe prints, presumably left by the investigators. Nothing else. He walked over to the clump of reeds, parted a few canes and noticed that a couple were broken.

"A man did this. And longer ago than yesterday . . ."

Marceau kneeled down amongst the reeds. The earth here was particularly dry and cracked in places, even though barely a metre from the marsh.

He thought of Boyer, the guru of the force back in Paris: "Move outside the problem, lads. Go and stick your nose where no-one else would stick it. Even at random. Widen the circle. There's bound to be something. Remember Locard's exchange principle. They always leave something behind and always go away with something."

Just as he was about to rejoin Larousse, he saw the print of a shoe, deeply encrusted in the dry earth. He spread his fingers wide in the hollow of the print and saw that it measured almost two spans long. It was a fairly big man's shoe and he must have been running, to judge by the deep impact of the heel and the smearing at the toe.

Marceau had done enough mountaineering and hiking to recognise at once a Vibram sole, as used on a large number of walking boots. He followed the direction of the step and noticed a second, half-formed print, as if the walker had been perched on the tip of one foot. It was almost outside the reeds, close to Steinert's supposed place of death.

Marceau went back along the path and found two more prints on the way to the hut. The way they were pointing showed that they came from the hut.

"He walked this way without stopping," he murmured to himself. "Otherwise somewhere or other there would be two prints practically side by side. He walked, then he jumped into the water. As though he was running away from something. Try turning that into an accident!"

He called to the gendarme and asked to see William Steinert's shoes. They had Vibram soles. Of the right size.

"Mme Steinert has just identified her husband's body," Nicolaï said. "I spoke to her for a few seconds. It looks like she's getting over the shock."

"Yes," said Marceau vaguely, still lost in his thoughts.

"She's just gone, look."

"She gets over things quickly, you're right. I'll go and see her soon."

Commissaire Larousse arrived, flapping his arms and staring into space.

"Finished, Marceau?"

"Nearly, boss."

"Stop calling me 'boss'. We went to the academy together."

"Yes, but I'm not a Commissaire Divisionnaire."

"Commissaire or not, I'm still getting devoured by mosquitoes. Found anything?"

"Nothing at all. Anyway, we got here when the party was already over."

"I talked with widow Steinert. She's extremely beautiful and a pain in the arse. She could make trouble. She wanted me to know that she knows people who know people. I wouldn't have minded leaving this business to the gendarmes. To be honest, with just a few days to go before the holidays, it looks decidedly iffy to me."

When the two policemen left the Camargue, the sun was beginning to ripple its twilight colours across the surfaces of the ponds: the pale pink of the horizon, the gold of the reeds burned by its beams, the dark grey of the endless Vaccarès.

A hint of coolness settled on the sleeping waters.

Marceau had just dropped Larousse by his Golf when his mobile rang.

"You don't waste time, Michel. How did you guess I was in my car?"

"Turn round and you'll see."

De Palma was standing a few metres away, in front of the Tarascon commissariat.

"You're back for a breath of Provençal air?"

"I was looking up an old colleague . . . Can we talk for a few minutes?"

"Let's take a stroll around the block. I need some fresh air."

They walked for some time without saying a word. The roads in the centre of Tarascon were lit by reddish streetlights.

"Do you know what this street used to be called, Michel?"

"No idea."

"The rue des Juifs. There used to be a Jewish ghetto here."

"They can't have had much fun in the days when the pope lived in Avignon," de Palma remarked.

"Unhappily, the worst was yet to come."

They passed some tourists, the heels of their camel-leather sandals clacking on the still-warm paving stones: a couple of old English-women, their noses raised, scrutinising the façades.

On place de la Mairie, they ordered two double whiskies. Marceau knocked his glass back in one and ordered another.

They swapped small talk. Marceau looked rather on his guard, as though the thread of their friendship had not stood up to the frictions of life and the horrors of their profession.

Marceau sank his second glass just like the first. He was a man who rarely displayed his inner troubles, and this trait had always impressed the Baron; he seemed to stow away the worst things he experienced in his career on the force in some part of himself that was insensible to emotions, like an attic where people store what they no longer want to see and will end up throwing out.

But this was merely a front. De Palma knew how deeply violence affected him and how he had to work on himself so as not to look troubled. He knew about Marceau's real need to regain his inner calm.

They paid and strolled off again through the night towards the Rhône.

"Still, there were a couple of things that bothered me just now." Marceau was speaking in a monotone.

"There were traces of footsteps. Tomorrow I'll go and take moulds with a boy from the lab. They lead from the hut and head straight to the place where Steinert was found. I don't know why, but they looked really odd to me . . . The kind of thing that looks as though it can't have got there by chance."

"Why do you say that? Lots of people visit the place."

"Yes, but not the edge of a stinking marsh!"

"You mentioned a hut . . ."

"Yes, it's just nearby. That's where the spade was found."

"What spade?"

"The gendarmes think it was Steinert's, but they're not sure. Anyway, that's not hugely important, or not for the moment."

Lit by the town lights, King René's Castle stood out as an imposing white mass in the darkness of the night. At the foot of the ramparts, some kids were playing football.

"We'll have to wait till tomorrow to get a clearer idea. Did Ingrid Steinert phone you?"

"Yes, just now."

"Well?"

De Palma breathed out long and hard to drive off the enveloping heat. The ball came to rest at his feet. He kicked it back and heard a distant thank you.

"It was as if she felt nothing and wanted to declare war on the entire world, she is so utterly convinced that her husband was murdered."

"For now, apart from a few footprints, it looks like a drowning. We'll see after the autopsy tomorrow."

"It's funny all the same . . ."

"You find this funny?"

"The shepherd I told you about . . . he said that La Balme farm-house was cursed."

"If you start believing all the stories told by old peasants in

Provence, you won't get very far. They're all completely crazy out there."

There was a hint of hostility in Marceau's voice, mixed with a growing curiosity which he was failing to conceal.

"We'll go and see later, if the autopsy doesn't last too long. What's more, I'm going to have to see the director of the reserve, Christophe Texeira. He's the one who found the body."

Marceau shook his head, as though trying to chase away an unpleasant mental picture.

"Then I'll try and find out a bit more about our William."

"How?"

"For once, I might be in luck. I've got an old school friend who didn't go the same way as me. He had a brilliant university career and ended up as a big businessman round here. Sometimes, when I need to find out about the local rich kids, I go and see him. He knows a thing or two."

Marceau headed off again towards the Rhône. From afar, in the direction of Saint Martha's church, T.V. sets could be heard, filling the air with the last programmes of the evening.

"You'd better wait for the results of the autopsy before doing anything, Michel. In my opinion, the forensic surgeon is going to say that he drowned in forty centimetres of water and the prosecutor will close the case."

Marceau was staring at the wall of the house across the street. He seemed hypnotised by a rectangle of light and the murmur of the street.

"It sounds like you're dying to close this café."

"If we keep on delving, we'll come up with a pile of shit. Just wait for the press to get hold of the story, and you'll see."

"The press is in the know already, Jean-Claude, you must realise that."

"How the hell should I know that?"

The Baron gestured vaguely. It crossed his mind that it might well be Marceau himself who had tipped off a local Tarascon hack about this disappearance.

*

When he got back into his car, at about 1 a.m., summer lightning was brightening the darkness. De Palma looked for a C.D. in the glove compartment and realised once again that he had forgotten his discs.

Wearily, he pressed his temples between his fingers to ease a nascent headache.

8.

Billionaire's body found in marshland in the Camargue

The body of William Steinert, 57, has been found by a scientist in the nature reserve of La Capelière, in the Camargue. The man, a wealthy German industrialist, lived for most of the year in his farmhouse near Maussane. His love for the land of Mistral and Daudet . . .

De Palma folded *La Provence* in four and tossed it irritably onto the living-room table.

The article about Steinert was brief and said nothing particularly precise; neither the gendarmes nor Marceau had given any information to the local news hound.

A photograph to the left of the article showed Steinert amid a jungle of milling machines and lathes. The caption read:

In the 1960s, William Steinert became one of the top German machine-tool magnates.

De Palma rubbed his chin and glanced at the photograph. His morning stubble was itchy and an unpleasant taste of coffee clung to his palate. He went into the bathroom and examined himself in the mirror. The wrinkles around his face seemed to have been dug deeper by a malicious designer who had pressed hard with his pen during the night.

He cleaned his teeth, gargled for a long time then spent a quarter of an hour in a scalding shower.

At 10 a.m., he got a call from Ingrid Steinert. She asked him to come and see her as soon as possible, but he dodged her invitation by claiming a doctor's appointment. That would give him time to wait and see what the results of the autopsy turned up.

He put on some jeans and his last clean T-shirt, and telephoned Yvan Clergue, his contact among Marseille's most powerful financiers.

"Michel, my old mate, how are you?"

"Not so good. I still get these damned pains in the head."

As usual, his friend was in a hurry. He went straight to the point.

"How can I help you, Michel?"

"How about lunch? We could . . ."

"I'll stop you right there. I'm off to Tokyo in an hour's time."

"I just wanted to ask you something."

"Go ahead. I'm on my own, my secretary's out."

"Do you know a man called William Steinert?"

"He was in *La Provence* this morning. Of course I know him."

"Joking apart, do you know anything about him?"

"A big wheel, a real captain of industry – 'they don't make his sort any more.' But as far as he was concerned, business was secondary. Just to pay the rent, as it were. What mattered to him was creativity. I'm just giving you an idea of his personality. He was rich, and when I say rich I mean immensely rich. A family fortune and so on and so forth. But he wasn't at all into being a celebrity or being stuck in a rich man's ghetto."

De Palma rummaged for his notepad and pen.

"I met him once, maybe twice. I can't remember exactly. He was a true enthusiast. Not the sort of person you often meet in our field. People said that he was capable of talking to you for hours on end about something quite different from what you came to see him for."

"What was he doing here in Provence? Business?"

"Not at all! At least not to my knowledge. I think he had a farmhouse, but I'm not sure where."

"Near Maussane."

"Maybe. In industry, he was highly respected. He was primarily an engineer, the sort who was able to roll up his sleeves and literally go back to the drawing board . . ."

"What I don't understand is why the two of you met."

"I was waiting for that. Here I am, talking to you about the poetry of industry, and you stay the copper right to the end! O.K., to put it briefly, I was contacted by some financier colleagues to look into starting up a leisure park. That was two years ago. They wanted to open a sort of Provençal-style Disneyland. If I remember correctly, the people involved were the Tarascon town hall, the *département*, region, local villages and so on and so forth . . . But it never got further than the planning stage."

"And so?"

"And so Steinert was involved . . . I don't know why exactly, but he was involved. Anyway, when they organised a drinks party over a model for the park, he came along. But when it came to the subject in hand, he was rather cold, hostile even."

"Hostile?"

"These are only hazy memories, but I think he was against the idea."

"So why go to this party?"

"That's just what I'm wondering about now . . ."

De Palma clamped the receiver between cheek and shoulder and poured himself some coffee.

"I see. And what happened then?"

"As a matter of fact, I don't really know. I heard that they then started prospecting around the Camargue. But I didn't get involved because it was a real hornets' nest."

"Why do you say that?"

"As if you didn't know. Imagine a huge leisure park in the middle of Provence, then imagine all the wolves coming out of the woods!"

"Yes, I see. Can you give me any names?"

Clergue was about to speak, then fell silent. De Palma could hear his secretary's voice before his friend placed his hand over the receiver.

"No, I can't help you any more there! Look at the local authorities I mentioned. Especially in Marseille. There aren't that many politicians over there. They're all from the same family, if you get my drift."

"Loud and clear. Thanks, my friend. Next time, lunch is on me."

"No problem, Michel. *Ciao*."

Clergue had said "all from the same family", which translated as "freemasons". There was nothing unusual about local businessmen or politicians belonging to the masons. De Palma had even found a hammer, a Masonic artefact, on Steinert's desk.

Oddly enough, what intrigued him the most about all this was Steinert's attitude during the drinks party to launch the project. Clergue had said cold and hostile. But that did not square with the image he had of the German billionaire. He tried to piece together a scenario based on the few elements at his disposal, but nothing fitted.

At 11.30 a.m., he arrived at the front desk of the archives of the Marseille Chamber of Commerce. The director, an indolent forty-something, welcomed him by looking at his watch.

"Do you have a reference number or something?"

"No, but I do have this."

The Baron produced his police identity card.

"That hardly solves the problem of the reference. But I'll see what I can do."

Michel watched him disappear behind the shelves. The air conditioning was cool and through the building's large windows you could see La Bourse shopping mall and the remains of ancient Massalia.

The archivist returned with a spiral-bound folder of forty pages.

"Here you are. That's all I can find for now. The rest of it is closed because it's industrial property. I don't even really have the right to give you this," he added, waggling the folder.

"Listen, my friend, I can always come back with a warrant from the judge. But I wouldn't want to bother him about such a trifling matter. All I want to do is check a couple of things."

De Palma removed the brochure from the archivist's grip.

The Big South
The first leisure park where culture is a pleasure

The title was printed over a series of photographs of white beaches, Camargue landscapes at sunrise, and historic sites, overprinted with the outline of the castle of Tarascon, a portrait of Taven the Witch, and a depiction of the Tarasque that took up a good part of the image.

De Palma glanced through the first pages, which were mainly taken up with words of introduction from each of the politicians involved in the project: the presidents of the departmental and regional councils, the mayors of Maussane, Tarascon, Arles . . .

On the second page, the authors had written a note outlining their plan and their ambitions to found "an alternative" to Disneyland:

> . . . The accent will be placed on ludic and cultural activities that will plunge the visitor interactively and transgenerationally into the heritage of Provence, and more generally into the cultures of the lands of the northern Mediterranean.
>
> As regards Provence, we have selected certain strong cultural markers: a reconstruction of Le Guen's cave (a prehistoric site beneath the sea), Greek remains, Roman antiquities, literature (Mistral, Daudet . . .), and, of course, various aspects of the particularly rich legendary heritage of Provence: the Golden Goat, Taven the Witch and the Tarasque seem to us to be especially interesting subjects for the creation of a theme park . . .
>
> With this in mind, a study will be carried out so as to select the mascot for The Big South. So far, Taven the Witch and the Tarasque have been chosen as focal points for activities in the park.

The company in charge of the feasibility study was S.O.D.E.G.I.M. (*Société d'étude et de gestion immobilière*), whose C.E.O. was a Philippe Borland. De Palma jotted down his name and his company's on his notepad. Then he flicked through the rest of the brochure, skipping the details of the financial set-up, since they were too complicated to be analysed rapidly.

On page 21, he came across a more detailed description of the ludic and cultural activities: they had planned a legendary journey, rather like a ghost train, with a reconstruction of Taven the Witch's den, a rather complicated merry-go-round consecrated to the

Tarasque, and presented as the linchpin of the show; and a criss-crossing of roller-coasters with a "super splash" in a pool set in the middle of the park.

On his notepad, de Palma wrote in block capitals: TARASQUE. Then he looked for what interested him most: the planned site for the project. The idea was to set it up in a triangle between Maussane, Les Baux and Fontvieille. Just where Steinert owned land. A lot of land.

On the next page, there was a surveyor's plan and map showing the various holdings. De Palma pointed at the photocopier behind the counter.

"Could you copy this page for me?"

"Sorry, sir, but that isn't allowed."

"Look, one more time, we won't quarrel, you'll just copy it for me and no-one will be any the wiser. After that I'll leave you in peace."

The archivist glanced at his watch, then placed page 29 on the Xerox glass.

At 12 p.m., the Baron double-parked his Alfa Romeo in front of a kebab shop on avenue de la République. He ordered a doner and chips, with cream sauce, tomatoes, onions and lettuce. His mobile rang.

"Michel? It's Marceau. The autopsy leaves no room for doubt: death by drowning."

"He drowned!"

"Yeah. They've been at it since seven this morning, and it's just what I expected."

"Who performed it?"

"Mattei, as usual."

De Palma trusted Mattei's verdicts completely.

"I think the case will be closed any time now," Marceau said, "and there's nothing I can do about it. There's no evidence at all."

"There are your footprints!"

"Are you joking? Are you expecting me to go down on my knees in front of the prosecutor and tell him that I've found some

94

traces of boot-marks in the dry mud in the Camargue? Wake up, Michel!"

"Did you get moulds made?"

"Yes, this morning. There's a team of technicians on hand. So it will be the last time we have to drag our feet over to that stinking place!"

De Palma tried to concentrate. The case was going to be out of the police's hands before long. He was torn between his desire to believe in the forensic scientist's conclusions and his own instincts.

"I'm going back to the commissariat to see what's going on. How about you, Michel?"

"I don't know. Maybe I'll go and see Ingrid Steinert, a courtesy call."

"Did she call you this morning?"

"Yes."

"So, see you later. I hope she won't stir things up for us. She'll have to accept that there's nothing more that I can do."

After the Fairy Pines, the air shimmered as if emerging from a wood stove; the trees were cracking under the blaze of the sun.

De Palma looked at the photocopy of the surveyor's plan from the Chamber of Commerce. He climbed a hillock that overlooked the whole of the valley, then orientated the chart.

To the east lay La Balme farmhouse, its buildings rippling in the noon day sun. Then, standing out against the pure blue sky, the white lines of the chalk hills of the Alpilles contrasted with the brown, scrub-covered mounds and rust-red slopes that led to the legendary cliffs and viewpoints.

The Baron turned south, in the direction of the Camargue, and observed the plain. He selected a few landmarks from the map and noticed that, broadly speaking, the planned site for the park occupied what Mme Steinert had called the "Downlands": woods of little agricultural interest, close to the main roads and far enough away from La Balme farmhouse so as not to disturb the billionaire's seclusion.

Why had Clergue mentioned Steinert's hostility?

It was one of those places soaked in history, where people have been living since time began, fragile sites which have become retreats for billionaires and snobs of all descriptions, loaded with money and pride. The smallest plot of land could fetch a fortune. So de Palma supposed that an amusement park, which was bound to attract a lower-class clientele, would not have appealed to most of the people who had chosen to live in this luxurious ghetto.

Along the road between Aix and Tarascon, thousands of cypresses were swaying heavily in the thick air. De Palma thought he could hear the din of Marius's Roman legions.

Then his mind went back to William Steinert, a man from the north and its winters of snow and greyness, a descendant of the very Teutons who Marius had cut to ribbons not far from the Via Domitia.

Steinert was the sort of billionaire that Michel would have liked to have known. He himself knew next to nothing about the Provence next door to his native Marseille, nothing except for a familiarity with its murder cases, the memory of a school trip to Saint Rémy Museum on the far side of the Alpilles, and the name of Marius, the saviour of Rome who gave independence to Marsiho, here at the foot of these modest peaks.

The name of Marius had long dwelt in the Baron's imagination; he could still clearly remember his primary school teacher showing him the image of the soldier's trophies, engraved in the stone of Saint Rémy.

The promoters of the future park must have thought of making Marius into one of the heroes of their tourist amusements. And they had already chosen the Tarasque of Tarascon as the mascot of "The Big South". As he got back into his Giulietta, it seemed to de Palma that this was not such a bad business idea. He could imagine shelves full of cuddly Tarasques in the stores as souvenirs . . . the Tarasque and the Tarasquettes . . . two thousand years of oral tradition transformed into bar codes. He also sensed that this monster of the marshes had not cropped up in this investigation by chance. Everyone was interested in it, and this was starting to worry him.

Mme Steinert was alone on the patio. He felt he was looking again at Isabelle Mercier, as she had been in the Super 8 films that her father had loaned to the police.

She did not stand up when he closed his car door and gave her a clumsy wave.

"At least you'll believe me now," she called out, in a tinny voice. "I'm really sorry."

She lowered her head, her face disappearing behind the golden veil of her hair.

"The hardest thing of all was seeing him, recognising him even when he was – what is the word? *Verstümmelt*! Completely disfigured . . . It was . . . *Unerträglich*, unbearable."

She jerked her head back to toss her hair over her shoulders and spoke without emotion, as though she were reciting a text, focusing as she did so on a piece of Provençal cloth that presumably came from one of her new collections.

"I've been trying to wipe that image since this morning . . ."

"If you'd like me to leave," de Palma murmured, "I can always come back tomorrow, or another day . . ."

"Stay, take a seat. I've sent everyone home today. Even the three 'thugs' as you call them, who take care of my safety. I didn't want to see anyone. Except for you. How odd."

She gazed at the Baron. Her eyes, usually azure, had turned turquoise, making them look hugely empty. He coughed so as to avoid having to say anything.

"Have you heard the results of the autopsy?" she said, without taking her eyes off him.

"Yes, and I think they can be trusted. The forensic surgeon is the best I know. No doubt about it."

"And you? What do you think?"

De Palma sat down in front of her.

"I think there's no reason to look any further. It was just an accident. A stupid one, as all accidents are. If he had been murdered, the pathologists would have found something."

She kept on gazing at him, but her expression had changed. It had become familiar, even teasing.

"You don't believe a word you've just said, but I'm not blaming

97

you. Not at all. It's simply some problems between different police authorities, and hierarchies, something like that, that are worrying you or holding you back. But you know full well that my husband didn't drown in fifty centimetres of water, or was it eighty . . ."

"You know, sometimes . . ."

"My husband was the best swimmer in his year at the engineering school in Munich. He was one metre ninety tall."

De Palma lowered his gaze and allowed a silence to settle between them.

The facts were there and he could not deny them. No one could deny them.

The sky gleamed like blue silk. It suddenly seemed to him that the stink of the swamp was sticking to his skin like a wet shirt, along with a smell of fish sauce and rotting seaweed.

He looked back up towards her.

The wind had blown a lock of her hair over the corner of her mouth, just where he had noticed two beauty spots. She looked dreamy, as though asking herself questions before providing the answers.

"You know, we'd been out of love for ages . . ." she said, drawing out her words. "Not long after our wedding, he started to become strange. He read peculiar books, and had passions not readily shared with a young woman. He was much older than me. Our marriage was a mistake that I made, but I still had enormous affection for him. And respect, too. Immense respect . . . it's more a friend I've lost than a husband."

She pointed towards the property then glanced around, as though trying to take it all in in a single sweep.

"It's for him that I'm going to stay here, and that I won't touch anything for now. His soul is still here. At night, I can sense him roving around the buildings and up there on the hills. He loved the hills so much. Have you read *Wuthering Heights*?"

"Heathcliff and Cathy . . ."

"It was his favourite novel. He could talk about it for hours . . . hours on end."

De Palma felt as if he had just been bled dry. At that moment, he no longer knew who he was exactly, or what he was supposed to be doing there. Some dark force held him close to this woman.

She stood up and went into the kitchen, then returned with two bottles of apple juice and a jug of cold water on an olive-wood tray.

"I'm being a terrible hostess. You must be thirsty?"

"A little, I must admit."

"Have you eaten?"

"No, but I don't want to abuse your hospitality."

"You're a strange man, M. de Palma. It's as if you're afraid of me, or else you mistrust me. I'm a woman like any other woman. All I'm doing is fighting to know the truth about my husband's death. And it will be known, believe me."

"Indeed," said de Palma, feeling vexed.

"Don't get angry."

He swallowed his glass of apple juice and poured himself another at once. Ingrid watched him, missing none of his gestures, which duly increased his irritation.

"I must explain something very important to you if you want to understand my husband."

She breathed deeply, her chest swelling as if she wanted to draw out of herself something that had been weighing on her for far too many years.

"You must understand that my husband's father was here, during the German occupation."

She stared at the swaying lines of olive trees, as though memories that were not her own had come to haunt her.

"And when I say he was here," she went on, tapping the table with the nail of her index finger, "I mean here, in this farmhouse."

She fell silent for a moment. A warm breeze, scented with pine and scrub, blew down from the Alpilles and subsided beneath the huge plane trees.

"It was my father-in-law who dug up the sarcophagus you saw over there. And many other things, too. I suppose that you must now be beginning to understand the particular associations that connected my husband with this place. I want you to understand that he was not like the other rich residents who live around here!"

The questions clamoured at de Palma. What role had William Steinert's father played during the war? If he was in the Nazi party . . . Why had he, a great industrialist, buried himself in this hole?

She guessed what he was thinking, and did not wait to be asked.

"At the start, the industrialist wasn't him. It was his elder brother, who died during the Dresden bombing in 1945. As there were only two children, my father-in-law took over the business. But he was no manager. He had trained to be an archaeologist and got his doctorate in 1939. In the spring of that year, just before war broke out."

"But . . . how did he end up here?"

"The Nazis sent him to this region because during the two years before war broke out, he'd spent his winters here, studying old stones."

"So it was him who carried out the dig in the 'Downlands'. Then, in 1939, he was obviously forced to leave France. But soon afterwards the Nazis sent him back. It must have been good propaganda for them. And let me tell you that he was clearly very well received by the people in the village since he came back on a number of occasions after the war. One of the few Boches not to be seen as the devil incarnate."

"When did he die?"

"In 1980. He was seventy-six. He's buried in a discreet grave in the cemetery of Eygalières."

She sat up in her chair and poured herself a glass of water. Her expression seemed less stern. De Palma noticed that the vengeful expression he had observed on arriving at the farmhouse had vanished. The colour of her eyes had changed again.

"Of course, I'd rather you didn't mention all this to anyone. It's *unter dem Siegel der Verschwiegenheit*, a well-kept secret in these parts, and no-one mentions Karl Steinert. When my husband bought the lot in the graveyard, he had his father's remains transferred there with the greatest discretion. He had the necessary money. So I'm counting on your discretion too."

She placed her hand delicately on de Palma's forearm; instinctively, he laid his hand on hers.

*

100

For the past three days, Rey hadn't drunk a drop of water or had anything to eat.

For three days, he had been in a black hole, left there by the man he had taken at first for a policeman. The only thing Rey had managed to keep was a vague notion of time. In his prison, he could feel the variations of temperature when the sun rose or set.

That was all he knew about the outside world.

Despite the darkness, his eyes were burning in their sockets. His tongue was thick and hard with thirst, and his hands were shaking.

The day before, when he had had his first visions, he had thought he had come down with a fever. Then the visions had gone, the same way they had come. It must have been his thirst playing tricks.

First, he had seen his mother, with her nasty little eyes, saying to him in her sour voice: "Your father won't come back, your father won't come back . . . son of a bitch."

Then he had walked down a long corridor leading to a round room. In the centre was an armchair with its back to him. He knew this room well. A hand as dry as dead wood emerged from the chair and beckoned him to come over. He approached slowly, with fear in his guts, his mouth twisted in disgust, before walking around it. Father Morand was sitting there, his weak neck propped up on a mauve cushion and twisted like a loin of veal. The man of God stared at him with his wicked eyes: "Come and kiss me, my son. Only you can kiss like that . . . Nearer, yes, like that . . ."

He had woken up and chased away this image of his boarding school with a blast of insults bellowed into the night. He had howled like an animal for some time, then his howling had dwindled into a groan, from which two syllables occasionally emerged: "Pa . . . Pa."

Then sleep had overtaken him by surprise, suddenly, as if an invisible hand in the shadows had injected him with morphine.

The final image that he had retained of the outside world was of a hut with a thatched roof, in the middle of a marsh. He was incapable of saying where it was.

The man had taken off the blindfold near some rushes, then made him walk on, with a .45 dug in his back. They had crossed the reed bed along an unseen path before emerging onto a dry marsh, with

101

stars of salt spangling its mud. On the far side, he had made out a hut, half concealed by some poplars and ash trees.

And then, there had been a heavy blow on his head. Everything had wavered and turned white, just like when he used to shoot up.

After that, he had found himself in darkness and had felt round the cellar where he was being kept prisoner, like a mole sniffing out the nooks and crannies of its little underground world. He had also yelled out.

How long now? He was no longer sure. But he could remember yelling during the first two days. No-one had come. He had heard nothing, and it was this utter silence that was now driving him crazy. He could cope with the darkness, but this almost total absence of sound was unsettling him and affecting him physically.

The temperature was rising. Soon his body was going to be covered with a layer of salt water, that seeped out inexorably from every pore of his exhausted skin, and his thirst would grow even more unbearable. He wondered how many days he had left to live: two, or maybe three.

Maybe less.

From what he had read about survival, Rey knew that you couldn't last long without water. He knew that madness would take hold of him and not let go until his body had dried up like a corpse in the sun.

He had counted the days. Tomorrow it would be Tuesday, July 29. The festival of Saint Martha.

He almost smiled. It brought back old memories. The snapshots of his childhood and the pleasures of his life as a man before it had all fallen apart and he had ended up underground.

He scratched his face several times as if to punish himself for all his errors.

The mayor of Eygalières was still on duty when de Palma requested an appointment with him from his secretary, a chubby brunette with false nails that turned the tips of her fingers into claws.

"And you are Monsieur . . . ?"

"De Palma, I'm a journalist."

"O.K., I think he'll see you when he's through. He shouldn't be long."

The Baron walked over to a revolving display decked with brochures about the town and browsed through some of them.

"Has M. Simian been mayor for long?"

The secretary looked up from her register and gave him a challenging look.

"This is his fifth term of office, and I think he'll be standing again."

"So he's popular here!"

"Very," she said nodding her head and whistling. "He gets re-elected every time, with a landslide."

"Is he right or left wing?"

The secretary swayed her hand.

"In the centre, more like. But officially the right, the U.M.P."

The office door opened. The mayor was a small man, balding, with bifocal glasses perched on the tip of his nose. He held out his hand to de Palma and looked him straight in the eye.

"My secretary tells me that you're a journalist?"

"Yes, I'm freelance. At the moment I'm working with *Villages* magazine, we're doing a report about the mayors of small towns in Provence which have become the country retreats of the rich."

"Then you've come to the right place! But I must point out that the rich people you're talking about are extremely discreet, and rely on me to maintain that discretion."

"Don't worry, that's not what it's about."

Simian walked round his desk, sat down in his chair and opened his arms to invite de Palma to take a seat too.

"So? I'm listening."

"We're trying to see how it works out for the local people, those who want to stay here and can't afford a single patch of land any more. How do they cope?"

"For me that's a constant problem. I am a farmer's son myself, and my father used to be mayor of Eygalières . . . what I mean is that we've seen how things have changed. I must admit that there's not much the town hall can do. Land is bought and sold at the prices agreed on by the various parties. It's the law of the market."

"But you could issue some decrees about how the land is to be used, or something like that?"

"Yes, but that wouldn't change the property prices."

The mayor discoursed on various aspects of the problem. De Palma simply took notes while waiting to get to the heart of the matter. The man in front of him was clearly a wild old bird, an expert at sounding sincere.

"Have you heard anything about plans for a leisure park in the region?"

"Not a thing. Who told you about that?"

"Someone who said they worked for S.O.D.E.G.I.M., I can't remember their name."

"Never heard of it. You must be misinformed."

The Baron searched through his notebook.

"Here it is: Philippe Borland . . . he's the chairman of S.O.D.E.G.I.M."

The mayor twisted his mouth to express his ignorance. Then he stood up and walked over to the map of the district on the wall.

"We have zones that can or cannot be built on, for various reasons, as you know. I try to keep a harmony between the residential areas and the more traditional rural environment. And I must tell you that it's a peculiarly difficult balancing act."

He pointed at various plots of land and circled his finger around them.

"The people who live here have considerable means . . ."

"By the way, one of your residents has just passed on! Did you see the papers?"

"William Steinert? Yes, I read about him. It's sad."

"Did you know him?"

The mayor's attitude changed. Clearly the question upset him.

"We had very little to do with him. He was very discreet. Like all the big landowners we have here."

Anne Moracchini had discovered in police records that William Steinert had been questioned about the illegal funding of the local right-wing party, though the case had subsequently been dropped. But it did mean that Steinert must have known the mayor of Eygalières, as well as the other politicians in the area.

"A colleague told me that he owned half the district."

"Half would be an exaggeration. Let's just say that he owned a lot of land."

"Indeed," de Palma said, looking at the map. He placed his index finger on the Downlands. "And what's this zone here?"

The mayor took off his glasses and nibbled one of the side-pieces.

"It's called the Downlands. It's woodland. We need a bit of greenery."

"An old boy in the village told me that there are Greek or Roman remains there. Is that true?"

"No, it's not! That's just an old story, nothing more."

"And can this land be built on?"

"I . . . I'd have to check the zoning regulations. There might be some available plots there. I can't remember. You know, our district is quite large!"

Simian put his glasses back on and looked at his watch.

"There is a small problem, Monsieur Simian . . . you tell me that you've never heard of S.O.D.E.G.I.M., but I know that you were contacted by this development company, just over a year ago . . ."

The mayor went back to his desk and tapped his nose several times.

"Indeed. I did hear about that project. But, as you surely must realise, the town hall of Eygalières cannot take part in a . . . an amusement park. You should go and see the people in Maussane. The land is there, in fact."

"But it would be a good thing for the district, wouldn't it?"

The mayor looked once more at his watch and stood up, his hands pressed on his desk.

"I'm sorry, M. de Palma, but I have a meeting with the inter-municipal steering committee. I shall have to leave you."

The dark waters of the Rhône merged with the night. From Beaucaire bridge, beyond King René's Castle, the restless tips of the trees sketched out a shadowy silhouette.

De Palma left his Giulietta in the castle car park. Before going out into the darkness, he waited for a municipal police patrol to disappear behind the church of Saint Martha. He walked for some time through the streets of Tarascon, drinking in the atmosphere of the old town centre with its inevitable pots of flowers at each corner and its paving stones polished by the tourists' heels.

When he was just a few metres away from the theatre, he stopped and listened to the sounds of the evening. Most of the inhabitants were at home in front of the evening's film or talk show.

A few tourists were still wandering around. Two of them, apparently Dutch, were standing in front of the baroque façade of the theatre. A salvo of flashes lit the darkness.

He waited for a while, pretending to read the theatre's programme: they were performing *Mireille* with some star unknown to him.

As soon as the tourists had vanished into the humid night, he walked towards the door of Steinert's building. He gave a last glance around, then climbed up the drainpipe that ran down from a neighbouring house.

Trying to make as little noise as possible, he arrived on a terrace roof made of old tiles and crouched down for a moment to get his breath back. His temples were pounding and he wiped his forehead with a nervous gesture. He was thirsty; *like a carpet slipper in your mouth*, as Maistre put it.

Slowly, he stood up. No-one could have seen him.

He crept forward like a cat, being careful not to disturb the terracotta tiles. After a few metres, he arrived below the window of Steinert's office. The hardest part was still to come. He had to hand himself upwards, open the window, get a foothold and find his way inside.

For the first time in his life, he paid homage to the skills of the *Groupe d'Intervention* of the national police force. He decided to proceed a stage at a time.

He leaped up, gripped on with one hand and opened the shutters with the other. Then he slumped back onto the roof, exhausted by his efforts.

Now for the window. During his visit with Mme Steinert, he had wedged it open with a piece of paper folded in four, so there should be no problems.

He waited to get his breath back, braced himself again, slid one elbow over the sill, then the second, and pushed the doors open with a sudden jerk of his head, making them bang against the inner walls of the office. The noise alerted a neighbourhood dog, which started howling into the night.

With a single leap, de Palma vanished into Steinert's office and then closed the shutters and window behind him.

Once inside, he flopped into the armchair and gathered his wits. His shirt was soaked with sweat and stuck to his back. He had scratched his forearm against the roughcast on the wall and cut one of his fingers while climbing up the drainpipe. It was nothing to be proud of.

Gently, he slipped on his surgeon's gloves, took out his Maglite and, without moving from the chair, played the beam methodically around the room, metre by metre.

Nothing had been touched, or at least nothing that he had mentally photographed during his first visit. There was still that dominant fragrance of fine tobacco, tinged with honey; presumably a special pipe blend.

De Palma got out his notebook and jotted down this detail, then went into the library to examine each shelf thoroughly.

Among the dozens of books about the occult sciences, his attention was drawn to some files that were yellow with age, bound in thick cardboard and tied up with blue ribbons. He took down three of them and laid them on the central table.

He opened the first folder. One by one, he turned over the pages, which were covered by a very fine, very regular handwriting with occasional sketches of vases appended with captions.

Some of the captions were in French: Massaliots, Mouriès, canopic jar, aquamanila . . . and after each one there was a date: 525, 480 . . .

The second file also dealt with vases from Mouriès, while the third was about bronzes and contained a large number of drawings.

He went back into the office and checked all of the surfaces that might hold fingerprints. Nothing. Which meant that someone had wiped everything off after their visit.

"Not very smart," he thought to himself. It was better to wear gloves rather than clean everything up. This was an amateur job . . . They should have realised that a place like this should at least contain its owner's dabs.

He returned to the library and checked the other surfaces. Nothing. The only conclusion he could draw from all this was that someone skilled enough to open a reinforced door had then wiped the whole place behind him. Why?

"Unless the person in question had the keys," he thought. "That would be quite a different story . . ."

Going back into the office, he sat down in Steinert's chair and leaned back. A migraine was on its way, no doubt triggered by the exertions he had just made. He massaged his temples for some time and at last took in the scale of what he had done.

But, in fact, it was not the first time that he had broken into someone's place, and presumably not the last. He closed his eyes as though to evade his guilty conscience.

When he opened them again, he at once saw three objects on Steinert's desk: a white feather, the ebony and ivory hammer and a large pen of the Omas brand. This rarity lay beside a pile of notes, photographs of sculptures and reproductions of ancient engravings. He picked up the pen and turned it round under his eyes. Not a single fingerprint on this either.

"Things are looking more professional," he mumbled. To make sure, he dismantled the bakelite handle of a drawer with his Swiss army knife and checked inside. Nothing. The cleaner had clearly not missed a thing.

"Someone came here, certainly several times . . . then came back to remove all the fingerprints and any clues he might have left behind. Someone who doesn't want to be traced . . ."

De Palma picked up the hammer and tapped it several times on his palm. "But it's not necessarily Steinert's murderer." He put it back and began to examine the papers, which had to be Steinert's. They were written in perfect French:

The oldest and most horrible representation of terror is a man-

eating monster, called the Tarasque by the Provençals.

There are countless depictions of the Tarasque in paintings, sculptures and drawings: the most impressive example is without doubt the 140-centimetre sculpture in the Musée Lapidaire in Avignon.

It is an expression of what the Salluvii, or more precisely the Cavari, found most terrifying.

The Tarasque is depicted holding two severed bearded heads in its lion's claws, while devouring a human torso in its mouth. It would seem that the Greeks, who were widely present in the region of Tarascon, were inspired to make such a representation of horror by various barbarian customs: head hunting etc. For these Greeks, it would also seem that the civilised world stopped at the summit of the Alpilles . . .

The British scholar Moore saw in it the murderous aspect of the gods and compared the Tarasque to other man-eating monsters that can be found in Ireland and throughout Northern Europe (cf. Crom, the idol struck down by Saint Patrick).

According to art historians, this tradition seems to have been initially Italian, essentially Etruscan, and then Greek. It can thus be supposed that the monster followed the routes of colonisation. In my opinion, the myth's origin lies in the sedentarisation of mankind during the Neolithic period.

Previously, the natural world that surrounded hunter-gatherers was magical (cf. the depictions in painted caves). With the emergence of notions of ownership, the Neolithic farmers began to experience fears of the future: worries about drought, or extreme weather . . . They answered the questions that tormented them by inventing gods and monsters . . . These forces of chaos could be tamed only by being depicted, and no doubt by being offered human sacrifices to satisfy their appetite . . .

The text ran on for another three pages. He set it down and glanced at the photographs. There was an old picture of a flagon with the caption: "Bronze from Durenberg, Austria, with monster devouring a human head." There were also amateur shots of the papier-mâché

Tarasque that the inhabitants of Tarascon paraded in the streets during the town's festivities, and a picture of a stone monster eating a man, reproductions of other sculptures on the same theme . . . after that he found ten sheets of paper, the first of which was headed in the right-hand corner by a title written in black felt-pen:

Heracles, the civilising hero of Provence.

Then some notes:

His life was a series of senseless murders . . . [There followed a list of massacres carried out by Heracles]. *In the Crau, he stoned to death the monster Albion (personification of the Albigues of Upper Provence) and Lusis (eponym of the Ligures). BUT* [word underlined in red] *a civilising aspect:*
- *he forbade human sacrifice*
- *by killing the thousand-armed Lysis, he overcame the dangers of the Rhône, thus making it navigable*
- *he taught weaving*
- *he taught house building*
- *he taught how to organise a city*
- *etc . . .*

Cf. the release of the cosmic cattle [two words underlined in red]. *The guardian corresponds to the forces of chaos, the cattle to life . . . By freeing the red, divine kine from Geryon's control, Heracles effects a change in his nature: he abandons brute force and becomes a civilising hero . . . WORLD HARMONY.*

And, at the foot of the page:

See the digs in Maussane and Mouriès. Especially, Art strt/37-10B and Art strt/38-11A.

Finally, written in large letters he read:

DOWNLANDS.

De Palma lingered for a while over that last sentence. It presumably indicated two library reference numbers – the last thing Steinert had noted before his death. He noted them carefully, and beside them wrote the names of the Tarasque and Heracles and underlined them twice.

It was two in the morning. He decided to search William Steinert's den with a fine-tooth comb, like a forensic scientist. This took him longer than he expected, but he was careful to miss nothing.

At three thirty, he leaned out of the window, checked that no-one could see him and let himself slide down the wall until his elbows were resting on the sill.

Just as he was about to brace himself to close the first shutter, he heard a faint metallic click that he recognised immediately. It was the safety catch being taken off an automatic, somewhere in the darkness.

In an instant, he turned round and saw a figure on the opposite pavement taking aim at him. He only just had time to drop down onto the roof before he heard the "plop" of a silencer. Intense pain held him pinned to the tiles. Instinctively, he curled up in the darkness to get out of the sniper's sight.

His entire body was shaking, each of his muscles twitching uncontrollably. This was not the first time that he had been fired at, but it still took some time to collect himself.

Then he analysed the situation.

Someone had just shot him.

Using an automatic with a silencer.

The bullet had hit his right shoulder, that was all.

The person knew where he was.

The person must have followed him from La Balme farmhouse, or even before.

Perhaps he'd had orders to follow him.

He touched his wound and found that the bullet had just left a shallow graze. He took out a paper handkerchief and pressed it onto the gash. He closed his eyes as his fingers made contact with the sticky blood.

This was the second time in less than a year that someone had tried to kill him.

"It's amateur work . . ." he said to himself. "The guy's a bastard, but not a professional one. Otherwise he would have waited for me to come down the drainpipe and taken me out without any problem."

He let fifteen minutes go by and listened to the night. All he could hear was a T.V. set somewhere up above him and some more distant music.

A car drove by. He went over to the edge of the roof and looked down into the street, his face pressed against the tiles. It was empty.

Suddenly, loud voices and laughter echoed off the walls; apparently a group of young people were leaving a party in the building across the street. De Palma made the most of the situation and threw himself down onto the pavement, his Bodyguard pressed against his chest.

When he hit the ground, he rolled over to take cover behind a delivery van, just as he had learned during his commando training course in the army. Then he stood up, pretended to be getting out of the van and stayed as close as possible to the group . . .

An hour later, he parked on a lay-by on the R.N. 568 in the middle of the vast plain of La Crau. His hands gripping the wheel, he stared into space. Far, very far in the distance glowed the flames of Fos-sur-Mer.

9.

The weather had been stifling all day. At the end of the afternoon, as the temperature went down, a light wind had risen out to sea, stirring the air as gently as a fan.

De Palma was leaning on his balcony rail and sipping a beer. He had spent the morning at the emergency admissions of La Timone hospital, waiting for a houseman to sew up his shoulder. Nine stitches.

The doctor had been skilful and hadn't asked too many questions. De Palma had simply told him that he had torn his shoulder on a car-park fence while getting out of his vehicle.

The telephone rang. It was Jean-Louis Maistre reminding him that they had arranged to meet at the yachting harbour of Pointe-Rouge.

De Palma put on a light jacket, slipped his Bodyguard into its holster and also took the .45 that he kept hidden behind a pile of C.D.s. He checked the clip and slipped the automatic behind his back. Then he changed his mind and replaced it, telling himself that he would not let paranoia get to him yet.

In any case, the Bodyguard with its six .38 special rounds was good enough to deal with the most desperate situations.

Half an hour later, Maistre and de Palma were strolling along the quays of Pointe-Rouge.

In the shipyard of Plaisance Plus, a whole row of hulls stood on a set of huge shelves, waiting for a lick of paint. There were also small speedboats and a fishing vessel half corroded by the sea. A workman in blue overalls started up a sander. Maistre had to shout:

"I think it's here, Michel. He said the fourth ring after the electricity meter. I think he must have meant that one."

113

A dilapidated boat was bobbing up and down on the sluggish swell. Maistre gave it a long affectionate look, then walked slowly towards it, like a child encountering his wildest dreams made real.

"Yes, this is the one, Michel. There's a bit of wood missing from its bow."

De Palma stared blankly in the opposite direction.

"Hey, Michel, are you listening to me or daydreaming? Don't forget that we're here to look at a boat, not just for a stroll on the quays."

"Sorry, I was miles away."

Maistre pulled on the mooring rope to bring the boat nearer, then clumsily clambered aboard.

"You coming, Michel?"

The manager of Rouge Plaisance, a ship chandler, came out at once, wiping his hands on an oily rag.

"Excuse me, gentlemen. But do you know this boat's owner?"

De Palma gave him a chilly look.

"We've got an appointment with him. He's late."

"And why do you want to see him?"

"We want to buy his boat."

"What, is it for sale?"

De Palma remained silent. The man from Rouge Plaisance turned on his heel and went back into his store.

"O.K., Jean-Louis, is your comedian going to show up or isn't he?"

Maistre came back onto the quay, still staring at the object of his dreams.

"I don't get it, Michel. We've talked about buying a boat a hundred times. You agreed to it and now you've got cold feet."

"I've not got cold feet."

"If you could only see yourself, you'd scare away a sea snake. Just think about the boat and going sailing in her."

"We haven't bought it yet."

"And if our man doesn't show, we certainly won't be able to."

Maistre's mobile rang. It was the boat's owner to cancel the meeting. He had decided to keep the boat for his son.

"Fuck him," Maistre said as he hung up. "The bugger's called it off."

"It doesn't matter, Jean-Louis. We'll find another one."

"Sure, but I could just picture myself in this one already. Behind Maïre making soup, just like two and two make four."

"That's for later."

"Yeah . . . but when I think of all these boats that just stand here idle, it really gets me down . . ."

"I'm deep in shit, Jean-Louis."

Maistre looked his friend up and down, while searching for something in his pockets.

"What's going on?"

"A nasty business. Something serious happened to me yesterday evening. I mean, last night."

Maistre opened a packet of cigarettes, removed one, lit it and dragged on it nervously, swaying on his feet.

"What happened is that someone shot me . . ."

Maistre closed his eyes, exhaled loudly and stared at the boats that were rocking gently in the port. After a long silence, de Palma added in a flat voice:

"I was coming out of Steinert's office, and someone took a shot at me. I've got a fine scar on my left shoulder. I had it stitched up this morning."

In a fury, Maistre threw his barely started cigarette onto the ground and stamped on it.

"Nothing serious, just a scratch. But . . . I was scared out of my wits, Jean-Louis . . ."

Maistre sniffed and looked his friend straight in the eye.

"And can I ask what the fuck you were doing in the middle of the night in Steinert's office? I thought I heard he was dead!"

"I wanted to . . ."

Maistre wanted to shout, but he spoke quietly, through clenched teeth.

"Don't tell me you broke in, then the landlord or someone took you for a burglar in the heat of the moment!"

"Something like that."

"Jesus, I was sure of it. Now, out with it all."

"I got into Steinert's office through the window, and when I came out someone was waiting for me on the pavement opposite and tried to whack me. Now you know everything."

"And that's all? And you tell me this, just like that? In Pointe-Rouge! You should have called me at once!"

"I must admit that didn't occur to me."

"And all because of this investigation you're undertaking into this sodding billionaire, even though everyone says he drowned in twenty centimetres of stinking water!"

"You've got it, Le Gros."

Maistre produced a second cigarette and stuck it in his mouth without lighting it.

"And don't tell me that all this proves you're right, Baron. I don't want to hear it."

The sun disappeared behind the harbour wall of Pointe-Rouge, so that the sea turned violet and tinged with pink on the surf around the rocks. At the end of the jetty, a boy was playing with a puppy. Maistre stopped and finally lit his cigarette.

"I'm sorry, Le Gros."

"What's there to be sorry about? Some fucker is out to whack you. The problem is that he won't let it drop. Have you got that into your sorry head?"

"I . . ."

"And if that's so, he's there ahead of us. Have you got a description?"

"No. Just an automatic with a silencer."

"Classic. But not with a silencer. I don't want to give you the wind up, but this sounds like a contract."

"I don't think so. If it had been, he would have waited for me to reach the street. That would have been easy."

"Get your car and come back and stay at my place. Then we'll see."

"Not this evening."

"Drop it, Michel."

"Not this evening, I've got an appointment."

"Go fuck yourself, Baron. One day, you'll be beyond anyone's help."

He tried to make his words sound as forceful as possible, but the

Baron had already taken out his car keys. He was no longer listening. His face was set.

The Majestic was at the corner of boulevard Banon and traverse Casse, in the quartier Montolivet. It was a shabby bar that had seen its moments of glory in the days of the French Connection: it was there, over a formica table, that the smuggler, Constant Ribellu, and the greatest chemist of them all, Jo Cesari, had discussed the next shipments of heroin to New York and Italy. All under the observant eyes of the boys from the drug squad.

From behind the bar, Paul Brissonne was staring at the Baron. A worried furrow formed an S shape between his pale grey eyes.

"You should lay low for a while, boss. Otherwise they'll end up nailing you once and for all."

"Don't worry, Paulo. If he'd wanted to get me . . ."

Brissonne blinked several times, which for him was a sign that he felt nervous. Suddenly, he slammed his fat hand down on the counter, palm turned upwards.

"Don't talk shit, Michel. Some guy tails you without you noticing, then takes a potshot at you using a silencer . . . so this guy had really thought out what he was doing, no question."

De Palma took a swallow of his beer and drew imaginary forms in the condensation on the cold glass.

"But what I don't get is that he could have taken me down in the street!"

"Maybe he missed you on purpose! I mean, sorry to put it this way, but it's one of our guys. I've no idea who, but someone from our side of the fence. And if I ask around, I'll find out."

De Palma had known Paul Brissonne for ages. He had arrested him during a police round-up after a settling of old scores, one more in a long series of killings between rival clans. Brissonne was not part of any team or family, just a good fellow, half gypsy and half Italian, as dangerous as a big cat and at home in any kind of water, even the filthiest.

He was almost sixty but still very much alive. In Marseille it was said that he feared no-one. His record was perfect: the social services,

117

borstal, the attempted murder of his own father, a good thirty hold-ups, Poissy prison and a few other stretches inside before coming back to the old port.

Brissonne had become de Palma's friendly informer during a spell in police custody. The gangster had been beaten up all day, and been passed to the Baron for questioning at around eight p.m. He was like a beast chained to the wall and had been thirsty for the past twenty-four hours. De Palma had ordered a crate of beer and the two of them had talked for several hours. The crook then laid out his life story like a bad poker hand, full of fishy runs and busted flushes. He described beatings and more beatings until the day when he had decided to stop taking it and punch before being punched.

That day, he had grabbed the man who claimed to be his father by the neck and squeezed with an iron grip. He would have killed him if the neighbour had not come by.

"I'm vicious, chief. If you only knew how vicious I am," he added in tears.

At the end of the night, the Baron had torn up his statement and typed out another, which Brissonne dictated to him. And at eight in the morning, Brissonne had left police headquarters with a debt of honour to the Baron.

"I'll ask around, Michel. By the way, if I find out who did it, do I ice him or not?"

"Don't touch him, Paulo. I want him for myself."

"Any ideas?"

"There's some real estate deal which is going to be signed around Eygalières and Maussane, down in Provence. Serious dosh . . . for an amusement park with all the trimmings. And maybe someone got in the way, a man called William Steinert. For now, that's all I know. They're burying Steinert tomorrow, and I'm going to be there."

"Do you want me to come with you, or send someone along?"

"No thanks, Paulo, but I'll keep my eyes peeled."

Brissonne clicked his signet rink on the zinc of the counter.

"It's only the boys from Aix who could take on a score like that . . . I know them. Last year Morini, Le Grand, wanted me to open a bar with him. It was going to be Lulu, the Chink and Paulo. Not forgetting Le Grand, of course. If it's them who've taken out the contract, I'll know by tomorrow. But it'll be bad news if it is. They're crazies up there."

"What about S.O.D.E.G.I.M., ever heard of it?"

"Fuck it, yes! You've hit the nail on the head. It's one of Morini's covers. He's got a guy called Philippe Borland to run it. They're involved in the buildings going up in the new suburbs around the port."

"Morini controls all that?"

"Yeah, I'm telling you, Le Grand is no slouch."

"What about this Borland?"

"Don't know him. He's never much in view. But that's normal for a figurehead."

With the back of his thumb, the thug massaged the white scar on his lower lip.

"No later than tomorrow. I'll call you around four."

"Thanks, Paulo."

"My pleasure."

"Come on, let's get some pizza."

"Have you seen the time? Are you mad, Baron?"

"There's Vincent's place. He's open late."

Brissonne took his .45 from under the bar and they went out into the night.

10.

William Steinert was buried early the next morning.

Ingrid had made it known that her husband had always wanted his funeral to be as private as possible: family members, a few people who had frequented the farmhouse, and no-one else.

A very simple farewell ceremony was conducted among the olive trees, with Steinert's body facing the Alpilles. Madame Steinert did not weep, and looked very dignified in a black silk dress with her hair tied back.

She read out a beautiful text which she had written for her husband the day before: a few simple words, which summed up their shared life, the year that they had loved each other, and then their rather solitary existence in Provence which he had made his second fatherland.

> "Ich hatt' einen Kameraden,
> Einen bessern findst du nit,
> Er ging an meiner Seite
> In gleichem Schritt und Tritt."*

No-one noticed the tiny black figure, sitting on a bump of wind-swept rock. It was Bérard, the solitary shepherd in the middle of the hills and burned trees.

The old man, his head bare, had not taken out his flock that morning and was murmuring some verses by a distant relation, the Master of Maillane:

* *I had a friend, You will never find a better one, He walked by my side, step by step.* (Ludwig Uhland)

*"O belli Santo, segnouresso
De la planura d'amresso,
Clafissès, quand vous plais, de pèis nòsti fielat;
Mai à la foulo pecadouiro
Qu'à vostro porto se doulouiro,
O blànqui flour de la sansouiro,
S'es de pas que ié fau, de pas emplissès-la."**

Steinert's body was then taken to the cemetery of Eygalières, where the industrialist would now sleep beside his father.

As the cortege passed in front of the chapel of Sainte-Sixte, at the entrance to the village, it halted for a minute. This was Mme Steinert's decision. She remembered that the first thing her husband had spoken to her about, when they had first met in Munich, was this simple chapel which had since become a symbol of Provence for tourists.

He had said: "Sometimes, I feel as if I had been born there. I don't know why, but I really feel at home . . . I belong to that land."

The procession then set off down the avenue lined with Florentine cypresses which led to the graveyard.

De Palma hung back, beside a plane tree a good ten metres from the Steinert burial vault. He watched as the little crowd gathered and he mentally photographed as many faces as possible. He looked for resemblances to the figure who had fired at him, and noticed that about a dozen people had similar builds.

There were a few village elders, who never missed a burial while awaiting their own. They stayed for a few moments, then vanished behind the tombstones.

The mayor of Eygalières also attended. He shook a few hands, then offered his condolences to the widow. They exchanged a few words and, from his expression, de Palma deduced that he knew her well. So Simian had lied to him.

---

* *"O beautiful, sovereign saints/Of the plain of bitterness,/You fill, when you so wish, our nets with fish;/But for the crowd of sinners/Who lament at your door,/ O white flowers of our salt moors,/If it is peace they need, then fill them with peace!"* – Frédéric Mistral, *Mireille*, Canto XII.

Behind her stood two men, as stiff as church candles, whom de Palma had noticed at the farmhouse. One was about forty, and the other twenty-something; they were both Provençal, at first glance country people who were ill at ease in their black suits. The two of them looked as though they were on guard duty behind their mistress. They seemed so alike that de Palma would have sworn that they were father and son. The elder of them stared hard at the policeman, as you do at an intruder, or someone whose face and appearance you want to remember.

The close family, from Germany, stood in front of her. From the photographs he had seen, the detective recognised Karl, the younger brother, and his wife. To his right stood the second brother, plus a few friends or cousins. He looked at them intently. Their grief was sincere, and he eliminated the family hypothesis completely. Nobody here could help him in any part of his investigation.

A prayer in German rose up, like a murmur from between the graves. He had the impression that the stones around him were shivering.

The prayer came to an end. The family and close friends formed a line to say a last farewell to William Steinert. De Palma waited for the widow to be alone before offering his condolences.

"That's curious," she said in a thin voice. "You look sad as well."

He did not answer and gazed into the blue of her eyes, washed pale with grief.

"Death always affects me. And today more than ever."

He waited for her reaction, and that of the two men behind her, but she seemed not to have heard.

"Come to the house. The custom is to get together and eat something in memory of the dead."

"I can't. I have to go back to Marseille this morning."

De Palma went over to the grave and stared at Steinert's coffin. He picked up a handful of earth and threw it down. As it fell on the pale oak, it set off a hollow echo.

He had just glimpsed the truth behind this murder, which he had so far refused to see.

*

At 3.50 p.m., the Baron's telephone flashed up a number withheld.

"Good day, my man. Can we meet?"

He recognised Paul Brissonne's voice.

"Whenever you want."

Brissonne sounded slightly strained, as though out of breath.

"As usual, then?"

"O.K., five o'clock."

De Palma thought for a moment about the boys from Aix. For some time now, they had been involved in all the deals from Nice to Marseille, including all of the small towns in between.

The man who ruled this empire was obese, a huge tub of lard: Marc Morini, a.k.a. Le Grand. He was a vicious thug de Palma had watched climbing since the end of the 1980s.

Le Grand had done time, just four years for pimping, and had escaped by the skin of his teeth from the killers of the Marseille clan as he emerged one night from The Funk House, a nightclub in Aix.

That was in 1995. The *Brigade Criminelle* had counted 69 bullet holes in the crime boss's car, mainly double zeroes, 9 mm rounds and the inevitable 11.43s.

Le Grand had had the presence of mind to lie flat in his Merco Coupé and drive blind before piling into the car of a tipsy student girl. In fact, he owed his life to his lieutenant, who had opened fire to cause a diversion before taking a burst from an Uzi in the chest.

When Laurent Le Gulvinec, the brigade's commander, had caught up with Le Grand in the pine forest, panting and with blood pouring from his forearm, the sun was rising over the steaming countryside.

The gang boss had stared at the cop like a child scared by the dark. He had pissed himself. This was a story that did the rounds of the dark corridors of the *Brigade Criminelle* for some time: "Le Grand had pissed his pants." But the story had gradually faded from memory as the pisser had risen in the ranks of the underworld. Nowadays, in criminal circles, not even the police dared to speak of it.

So there was nothing surprising about Marc Morini taking an interest in plans for an amusement park. He had put money into the new opportunities in Marseille: theme bars, rum dives, karaoke joints blazing with neon, techno clubs ... So he was not about to go back to bourgeois jazz haunts in the centre of Aix. So it was natural that he wanted to expand a little, and the Provence of Mistral must have seemed to him to be the best investment in the world. Especially because Morini was a local boy, born in Tarascon and jailed for the first time in Arles.

De Palma took the sun-bleached R.N. 568. The road was littered with vegetable crates and melon packaging, left there by greengrocers' vans and blown by the wind.

On the horizon, the tarmac shimmered in the light laden with benzene and carbon monoxide. The huge storage tanks of the oil terminal were barely visible.

Paul Brissonne was sitting on a cube of limestone facing the wall of Crinas, in the only scrap of shade in old Marseille: the Centre Bourse, at the feet of the huge commercial exchange designed by some Vauban of the age of money. It vaguely resembled an enormous concrete hand with some fingers missing, laid on the four remaining walls of the Greek Phocea, Lacydon's old port. Now, the harbour lay between lawns browned by the sun and dog piss, not to mention turds and litter.

Beside Brissonne, an old Algerian was reading the latest edition of *Al Watan*, a sandal dangling off the tip of his foot.

The gangster was starting to feel that he wouldn't mind taking advantage of the air-conditioning in the Centre Bourse, if he had not been armed to the teeth.

The Baron's hand slapped his shoulder.

"Good day, Paulo. So you're contemplating the marvels of Greek Massalia?"

"This was a wasteland when I was a kid. But now, Jesus, it stinks of dog's piss ..."

"Who knows, maybe it stank like that in Greek cities!"

"Let's go for a stroll."

They took a few steps across the huge paving stones of the Phocean roadway then came to a halt beside the harbour.

"Le Grand doesn't take kindly to you sticking your nose into Mme

Steinert's business, but he says that it wasn't him who sent round the boy with the silencer. It's not one of his guys. That's for sure."

"Can you arrange a meeting between me and 'Piss-pants'?"

"Who?"

"Piss-pants. That's what we used to call him at headquarters. Because, one fine morning, a friend of ours from the brigade found him in some woods near Aix with his pants wet."

Brissonne glanced round him.

"Don't fuck with him, Baron, because he could really take you for a ride, one of these days. Cop or not, Le Grand couldn't give a toss."

"All I want is a meeting."

"Every day, he goes to the Café des Deux Mondes, on place de l'Hôtel de Ville . . ."

"Thanks, Paulo."

"You're welcome."

"You're the big man, Paulo, not him."

When Brissonne looked up, de Palma had already vanished behind the Crinas wall.

11.

As he parked his Alfa Romeo alongside a mud-spattered Range Rover, de Palma glanced at the clock on the dashboard: 10 a.m. exactly. The time of his appointment with Texeira.

La Capelière was deserted, an odour of dried mud and dead weeds rising as the sun heated the air. Mosquitoes were dancing crazily over the reed beds. De Palma wiped his hand over his forehead, which was beaded with sweat, and headed straight for the museum.

Texeira was talking with the student who was in charge of welcoming the visitors; he turned round quickly as soon as the police officer came in.

"Step this way, M. de Palma," he said, over a vigorous hand shake. "Let's go into my office."

On entering the lab where Texeira worked, de Palma noticed the prevailing smell of alcohol. Several test-tubes full of water and containing the shoots of various plants had been placed on a draining board. Beside the microscope, tiny insects were soaking in flasks full of preserving fluid.

A number of species had been pinned onto a polystyrene strip, each with its label:

Scarabeus laticollis
Le Sambuc (dep13), 3/05/2003 CT rec

Texeira warmed to the Baron's interest in his work.

"They're the results of samples we took a few months ago . . . Scarabaeid beetles are very important animals for us, because they eat cattle dung. It's a good job they do, otherwise . . ."

"Your job is really fascinating!"

"My main subject is birds. But these days, it's the dung-beetles that are in the limelight. There are nearly 700 species of coprophages like them! There we are. We can't always do what we want."

De Palma simply shrugged to show his agreement. For the moment, he was trying to soak up the atmosphere, the smells and sounds of a universe totally alien to him, certain that he would uncover scraps of the truth in such a place.

"M. Texeira, did you know, in any way whatsoever, William Steinert, the man you found in the marsh?"

"I spoke to your colleague about that – I can't recall his name . . . Anyway, yes, I used to know Steinert during the time when he often used to come here."

De Palma bent over the microscope.

"And how did you get on?"

"Very well. Really. He often stayed for lunch."

"And you say that he hadn't been back for a while?"

"Not for about two years. He preferred birdwatching either round Méjanes way, or by the Fangassier and Grand Rascaillon lagoons. He said there were fewer tourists. And it's true that there's quite a crowd here in the summer."

"And what did he do when he used to come here?"

"Well, he arrived early in the morning, before sunrise, and he waited for nature to awaken. A bit like everyone who's a real enthusiast."

"And did you ever go with him?"

"No, I think the two of us preferred making our observations alone."

"When did you see him last?"

"Last winter, quite by chance at the market of Tarascon. We bumped into each other and exchanged a few words. He promised to come back and see me in the spring."

"Nothing else?"

Texeira looked at de Palma for some time, while jangling some keys in the pocket of his lab coat. He seemed suddenly to be on his guard, suspicious even. De Palma realised that he was not going to get everything he wanted to know out of the scientist that morning.

"I don't quite understand the reason for your visit, M. de Palma. I've already told all this to your colleague. What was his name . . . ?"

"Marceau."

"That's right."

"Don't worry, this is just a routine check," the Baron said, handing him his card. "If anything else comes to mind, call me on my mobile. Sometimes, days later, witnesses remember details . . . I'll just go and take a look at the scene, so as to wrap up the investigation."

Texeira examined his police card.

"I'll come with you, there are places that are better avoided. You could come back covered in mud from head to toe. Or even fall into quicksand."

"That's all I need!" the Baron said, opening the lab door.

They walked for some time between the ash trees and alders, which made the scene look like a mangrove swamp, as did the dead trees rotting slowly in creeks covered with pondweed and duckweed.

The muggy heat stilled everything, drawing a stench of decay from the canals and creeping brambles.

This path, christened "Nature and Observation", was a complex circuit, winding between pools and crossing some streams before reaching a vast expense of dried mud. Texeira stopped and pointed at a hut some fifty metres away.

"I was in that hut you can see over there, at the end of the scrub."

The hut was shaped roughly like a teepee, with low walls which must once have been white and a thatched conical roof that took up almost two-thirds of its height.

"The body was on the other side of the reeds, in the marsh."

"That morning, did you come exactly the same way to get here?"

"That's right . . ."

"And you didn't notice anything?"

"No, nothing. It was still dark."

The scrubland, partitioned into thousands of diamonds, was running a temperature and the samphires were curling themselves up as small as possible in their beds of parched mud. When they went inside the hut, de Palma felt as though he had burst into a lost paradise.

"The body was over there, by that clump of rushes. As I explained to your colleague, the first thing I saw were some rooks circling around in that direction. I thought at first that they'd found some carrion . . . Boars sometimes drown there. But I would never have imagined that it was a man."

De Palma gazed round the hut. He saw nothing that could tell him a thing about Steinert's death. He went back out into the heat and headed slowly for the place where the body had been found.

Dozens of footprints were set hard in the dried mud, presumably left by gendarmes and various onlookers.

"Great job," he murmured. "Now we can't make sense of it."

He walked several times around the grove, but found nothing. He hunkered down for a moment, as though to make contact with the past and reconstitute the scene as it must have happened. He searched for images, but none came.

"The body was lying in the water, is that right?"

"Just in front of where you are. It was face down."

De Palma stood up. Something did not fit.

Ingrid Steinert was right. Her husband could not have died with his nose in the slime of this stinking marsh by accident. Either he had been thrown into the water, or else he had thrown himself in. Texeira had drifted away, so he took the opportunity to call Marceau on his mobile. He got the answering machine. Then he tried Mattei, the forensic surgeon.

"Good day, Doctor Death, it's Michel."

"What's up, Baron? Are you asking me out to lunch?"

"No, I just wanted to know if you found any diatoms on Steinert."

"I did indeed, super-sleuth. And you aren't the first person to ask."

"Shit."

"What's the problem? You too would like him to have been murdered? Well he wasn't. He drowned."

"And that's all you found?"

"Yes, that's all. And it's already quite a lot."

"Nothing else."

Mattei sighed into the telephone.

"No, except for his adrenalin level . . . which had gone crazy . . . He'd pumped a ton of it into his heart before dying. I'll leave the conclusions up to you."

"O.K., doc, never mind. I'll drop by and see you some time."

"It'll be a pleasure, as always."

De Palma was still in the dark, but he was sure of two things: Steinert had drowned, hence the presence of diatoms, and he had been utterly terrified before he died, hence the high level of adrenalin.

And that was absolutely normal. The billionaire had been scared before his death.

He looked again at the stagnant waters. A few bubbles rose from the slime before popping on the surface. Further off, a fish leaped out of the water to plunge back down into the murky depths.

"M. Texeira, is there only a single path that leads to this hut?"

"No, there's at least one more, if you go round the other side of the reed bed. In fact, this track is circular, you can go all around it if you want. On the other hand, you can also get here over the grassland you can see over there . . . so long as you're not afraid of bulls."

De Palma turned around and behind a fence saw some dark forms that stood out against what was left of the greenery.

"Are those bulls really dangerous?"

"It's better to be careful . . ."

Texeira went back to his office. De Palma decided to go all the way round the circuit.

He crossed the rest of the scrubland, then walked beside the barbed wire along the meadows before reaching the edge of a drying marsh. A grey heron on the waters headed straight into the rushes as soon as it spotted him.

Right in the middle of the marsh, a turtle as big as a calabash was sunning itself on a log rotten with damp. He realised that it was the first time he had seen one in the wild and stopped for a moment to savour the spectacle.

The path continued into a sodden reed bed, and the heat enveloped him. The plants grew so close together that no-one could push their way through.

"If somebody carried Steinert here to drown him," he said to himself, "then he certainly didn't come this way. Given his size and weight, even the footpath wouldn't be wide enough. No, he came over what Texeira calls the grasslands."

When he got back to La Capelière, Texeira was talking with a group of tourists dressed in camouflage gear, with boots on their feet, and binoculars and zoom lenses hung around their necks. They had just come back from a morning's observation.

Texeira left them for a moment to speak to him.

"What else can I do for you, M. de Palma?"

"You've already done a great deal. Just a reminder: if you remember the slightest detail, anything at all, even if it seems of no interest to you, then please inform me."

"No, I don't think there's anything."

Texeira gave the impression of hiding something.

He might be lying, the Baron thought. If Steinert pumped up that much adrenalin, then he must have cried out before dying . . . or at least, that is a real possibility. And Texeira would have heard him from here . . .

"Really," he insisted, staring into his eyes. "Don't hesitate to call me."

Texeira came up to him, scratching the back of his neck.

"Well, there is one thing I didn't tell your colleagues."

"What's that?"

"One evening, I heard voices. People singing on the far side of the marsh."

"Is that unusual?"

"Extremely. It's the first time I've ever heard such a thing."

"And what were they saying, these voices?"

"Something in Provençal, or else Italian . . ."

"Do you remember any of the words?"

"Sorry, no . . ."

"It doesn't matter. When was that?"

"The night before Steinert died."

131

"And could you pinpoint where these voices were coming from?"

Texeira looked very embarrassed.

"From the far side of this reed bed."

"And what time was it?"

"About midnight."

"And was it far from the place where Steinert was found?"

Texeira shook his head and pursed his lips.

"No, not very far."

De Palma decided not to pursue his questions, and simply trust Texeira. He had hidden a few things to spare himself trouble. The Baron had seen it thousands of times. He just shrugged his shoulders.

"Oh well, it was probably just a coincidence, nothing more."

Instead of heading towards Tarascon, he turned left on leaving La Capelière and tried to drive around to the other side of the reserve.

He found himself on the road to Le Sambuc and noticed that both sides of the marshes of La Capelière were only accessible by foot. And even then you would have to scale the barbed wire and avoid the marshes and perhaps quicksand too.

To find a way through that succession of stagnant waters, clumps of white poplars and brambles, ghost trees and impenetrable reed beds, you would have to know the place like the back of your hand.

To go and howl at the night in such a location meant making a real effort. And probably more than that. He was now sure that William Steinert had drowned in the marshes after being terrified out of his wits.

At the end of the morning, he parked his car between two plane trees, beside the old army recruitment centre in Tarascon.

Five minutes later, he was in rue du Théâtre Municipal, just a few metres from Steinert's office. He let a municipal vehicle go by, then a driving-school car which seemed to be grazing on the sweltering paving stones as it crept along. He examined the scene around him closely, then leaped up the drainpipe which he had climbed two days before.

When he was back on the roof, the tiles burned his hands. He stood and walked on as far as the office's window-ledge.

He looked at the shutters: they had been carefully closed from inside. He bent down and looked down the street, trying to imagine the trajectory of the bullet that had hit him. It took him barely a minute to spot the tiny impact in the cement on the façade.

The bullet had ricocheted.

"Shit," he said to himself. "Why couldn't it have got stuck in the fucking cement?"

He looked around the tiles, but found nothing.

He tried to imagine the bullet's trajectory after the ricochet, then he headed towards the far end of the roof. There it was, clearly visible between two tiles. De Palma picked it up and put it in a plastic bag.

"You've just made your first mistake, idiot," he muttered between his teeth. "I wouldn't be in your shoes if this bullet tells me what it knows."

12.

On Tuesday morning in the ballistics department, de Palma gazed at the weapons on their pegs: quite a lot of .45s, CZs, a row of Herstals . . . He paused in front of a Walther P38, one of the favourite guns of the old-time gangsters, the ones who had fought in the war and stayed in business until the 1980s. He had even met a superstitious old boy from Le Panier who never went into a hold-up without his P38.

"It's a 9 mm. A good old number 9."

"What about the weapon?" the Baron asked.

Pierre Diaz looked up over his rectangular glasses, which were perched on the tip of his turned-up nose, leaned on the test barrel and looked resigned.

"Instead of saying 'Thanks Pierrot', you do my head in with stupid questions. Come on now, Michel!"

The Baron raised both hands in a sign of apology.

"It was a SIG, my friend. A SIG 29. A precision weapon, often used by marksmen who take part in competitions. I've got quite a few colleagues who go to clubs who use one. A nice gun."

"How do you know it's a SIG?"

"There are two very fine grooves, there, on the sides. All the SIG 29s do that. It's their signature!"

"Don't take me for an idiot, Pierrot. I know you're good, but don't push it too far. Without your machines, you're no better than me. A 9 mm is a 9 mm."

"In your opinion, Baron, does your gun talk, yes or no?" De Palma felt a wave of heat climb up from the tops of his thighs to his stomach. Diaz looked at him, pleased with the effect.

"It talks like a jackass, as a matter of fact. The barrel says it all: two grooves, and no more. This SIG has been used once before, for a hold-up." Diaz picked up the notebook that lay next to him. "I'm bored stiff at the moment . . . there's really fuck all to do," he cursed, staring at his cross-ruled notepad. "So, I found out a few things on the side. And here we go: the Ben Mansour case. The hold-up of a lousy Arab grocer's on rue de Lyon. Jesus, using a SIG on a corner store! You've either got no religion or you're a fucking idiot, take my word for it!"

"You're certain of this?"

Diaz whipped off his glasses.

"I'm not even going to answer that . . ."

He beckoned to de Palma to come and look at the screen of the comparator: on the right was the image of the projectile that he had collected on the roof in Tarascon; on the left, the comparison. The grooves were a perfect match. Diaz tapped on the top of the left-hand screen, where the words "Incriminated Bullet" flashed up.

"The guy who used this gun is a real jerkoff."

"Have you had the boys from criminal records round?"

"Yeah, but their computer is down, they've been waiting to have it changed since June, and now it's the end of July. So no records. No nothing, for that matter."

"Shit."

"So go back upstairs, you lazy sod . . ."

"Yeah."

"The best thing you can do is go and see Le Gulvinec. He was the one who looked into the Ben Mansour heist. He was on a crusade to put the whole lot of them in the slammer, all those little buggers from the northern estates who were holding up late-night grocery stores."

Diaz tapped the Baron's forearm.

"There's no more respect . . . they even shoot each other now."

"What can you do? They're allowed to be as dumb as we are!"

Anne Moracchini had put both feet up on her desk and was staring into space while chewing the end of her ballpoint.

"Hello, my lovely."

She stretched and offered the Baron her cheek.

"Well, what a surprise! The opera, a great night out, then zilch. Nice work, Michel!"

"I . . . I was up to my eyes in it. Plus, I did call you . . ."

She threw her pen onto the desk.

"Stop right there, Michel. People could get away with that before the invention of mobiles and electronic address books and all that. You're getting past it, my friend."

"I came to ask a favour."

"Fancy that!"

De Palma could hardly meet her eye. He felt like a shit. He had told her nothing, had not answered her calls and did not know how to talk to her.

"I'd like you to talk to Le Gulvinec."

"Why go through me? You afraid of him?"

"It's not that. But officially, I can't."

"Then try being unofficial."

"Anne, this is important."

"What's this all about, now? You turn up just like that, all of a jitter, like a schoolboy going to his first party, and then you ask me to do you a favour without even telling me why?"

De Palma pulled over a chair and sat down beside her.

"The other day, someone shot at me," he blurted out.

She immediately pulled her feet off the table and leaned towards her colleague.

"WHAT?"

"You heard me."

She ran a nervous hand through her hair and stood up.

"And now you tell me!"

At first, she looked at him tenderly, then her expression hardened. De Palma shook his head in surrender.

"I found the bullet and showed it to Diaz, he . . ."

"Just a second, Michel, just a second. You're telling me that you were shot, you found the bullet, you showed it to Diaz and . . ."

Moracchini was worried. She walked round the desk to sit down opposite the Baron.

"Michel, look at me. We've known each other for fifteen years. You're the only cop I admire in this fucking profession. You're the man who . . . Anyway, I think you've seriously lost the plot and you need a good head doctor plus a few months of R and R."

She let a long moment of silence go by, then moved close enough to touch him.

"Show me."

He uncovered his shoulder. A piece of lint with two strips of plaster made a white square on his brown skin. She placed a kiss delicately on the dressing.

"'The little kiss that cures everything', as my father used to say."

He realised that he had not felt the least touch of affection for days.

"I spoke to Maistre yesterday. We talked about you a lot, but he didn't mention that. There's male solidarity for you. How touching."

It was difficult for de Palma to hide his emotions. His temples had tightened and were pressing on his eyes. He wanted to hold Moracchini in his arms, even for a moment. But he stopped himself.

"Le Gulvinec isn't here at the moment," she added in a sombre voice. "He's on leave back in Brittany. Lucky him. It's baking here. A real scorcher."

De Palma rubbed at his forehead.

"What did Diaz tell you?"

"He said that the bullet came from a SIG and that the gun had already been used in a hold-up. He also told me that Le Gulvinec had caught the case. Young thugs from the north suburbs robbing the local Arab grocers."

"Why don't you call Maistre? It's his section, after all! If they're his local thugs, then he must know them. Also, he'd love you to call him. I bet he hasn't slept since you told him your story."

Daniel Romero came into the office and came up to the Baron.

"M. de Palma, I have been so much wanting to meet you!"

"So you're the new recruit?" De Palma said, shaking Romero's hand. "How's old Casetti?"

"Fine. Listen, I'm really pleased to . . . I mean, to get to know you, Michel. I've heard so much about you."

De Palma kept his eyes fixed on the floor. Romero caught Moracchini's eye.

"When I was in the B.A.C., Maistre was always telling us that there was only one good officer on the force . . . and it was you. The 36, the French Connection, the works."

"That's nice for the rest of us!" Moracchini said.

De Palma stood up, holding the small of his back as though nursing lumbago.

"Tell me, Daniel, what if I said the name Ben Mansour?"

Romero sat down, propped his chin in his hand, and flicked his lips with his index finger.

"Ben Mansour . . . Shit, that does ring a bell . . . But in the B.A.C. you see so many of them! Ben Mansour . . ."

"A grocer, on rue de Lyon."

"Ah right . . . a hold-up in a corner store. It was the gang from La Paternelle, with a few boys from Bassens. Arabs and gypsies who'd teamed up."

Romero was waving his hand in the air.

"Seriously mean bastards, I can tell you. They'd put a bullet in you for the slightest reason. In Ben Mansour's place, they shot up the bottles of plonk. Poor old bastard."

"Is he still alive?"

"No. He died shortly afterwards, just like that. It was really sad."

"And then?"

"Some bigshot in your office took over the case. We gave him everything we'd found out, but it didn't do any good."

"Why do you say that?"

"Well, in the B.A.C. you know no-one can spell their own names!"

"Leave it out, Daniel, don't start that crap."

"The man in the *Criminelle* . . . I can't remember his name, something weird, with a Breton ring . . . anyway, he never got back to us."

"Le Gulvinec. He's a good cop. When was all this?"

Romero looked up at the ceiling and wrung his hands, as though to rack his memory.

"1988. In the winter and spring. I'm sure about that. The year my daughter was born."

De Palma studied Romero for a while. He was in very good shape. An athlete's physique and square features, which suggested a straight character, but with considerable abilities beneath his rather rugged look.

"We questioned one of those bastards once. It was some years later, in 1991 or thereabouts. A little routine I.D. check at the McDonalds drive-in on the roundabout, and who do we come across? Jérôme Lornec."

"The gypsy?"

"Spot on. In an Audi A6 and everything. The bugger was straight. With his papers, and all. But he wasn't insured. And that was enough to drag him down to the station. The fucker was furious."

Moracchini was tense, concentrating on what her new colleague was saying.

"The problem with people like Lornec is that they have an answer to everything."

"What happened?"

"We knew he was involved, because we chased them once. They'd just done a grocery in the town centre, the one next to the station, when you go down . . ."

"Rue de la Grande Armée", said Moracchini.

"That's it. So we went down boulevard des Dames then the dual carriageway towards L'Estaque. We caught up with them near the petrol station. A real race! All of us were breaking two twenty, with them in front with their foot down, driving like crazy! And they could have kept going! But then they turned off towards Saint-Henri, and so we were sure to nab them."

Romero was gesticulating wildly, his left hand imitating the getaway car, and his right the pursuers.

"First roundabout, by Saumaty, they go straight across. Second, they mount the pavement. For a couple of seconds, they stop . . . Jesus, I had the window open . . . I remember it as if it was yesterday, it was poor old Jacky who was behind the wheel . . . Believe it or not, I emptied my clip. Six 38s in the driver's door. Jesus fucking Christ!"

Romero stood up, gripped by a sudden excitement.

"My whole clip, it had never happened to me before."

"I remember that business. Maistre told me about it. He misses you, you know."

"Poor old Maistre, he had a lot of reporting to do about those six 38s. Me too, for that matter."

"And what about Lornec?"

"Jesus, you don't let up! Lornec was the driver. I put one in his shoulder."

Romero slapped his left side.

"We found out because we heard tell that they were looking for a nurse later that night. At the time, they weren't too careful with mobiles. But that's over now!"

"What about the motor?"

"We found it at the bottom of Plan d'Aou. Classic."

Moracchini tidied away a file that was lying on her desk, making as much noise as possible.

"And Lornec?" said de Palma. "What happened when you nabbed him at McDonald's?"

"I got him to take off his shirt, and bingo! He had a lovely scar on his left shoulder."

"Nice one," said de Palma with a whistle.

"That day, I cracked. I stood right in front of the fucker and said: 'I'm the one who got you in the shoulder. The next time, it'll be one in your head.'"

Romero sat down, lost in his memories.

"All he answered was: 'I don't understand a word you're saying.' End of story."

"And what became of Lornec?"

Moracchini closed the cupboard door, making a sound of buckled sheet metal.

"He does odd jobs," she said. "He's a big boy these days. In fact, he's just out of prison. He did a year for gun possession. Apparently, security vans are his thing."

"That doesn't surprise me. I told you, they were a gang of real bastards. You should see the boys in records to check if there's anything new."

140

"You haven't got any other names?"

"No, none," Romero said, gazing at de Palma as though he wanted to question him in turn.

"I've found a bullet that comes from a gun used in a hold-up by that gang. The Ben Mansour case."

Romero literally jumped backwards.

"Fuck me! Show!"

The Baron stuck his hand in his jeans pocket, removed the plastic bag and placed it daintily on the table. Moracchini looked at him sharply.

"I shouldn't think it was them . . . after all this time. They must have passed on the piece, though it's surprising they didn't junk it."

"Not that surprising. Such things happen. Especially with gangs like that. They aren't great thinkers. They aren't about to take a PhD in logic, if you see what I mean."

"So, if I'm getting it right, you're back on the team?"

"Soon, soon. A month from today."

Romero was longing to ask where the bullet came from, he could sense it.

"That bullet almost killed me a few days ago."

Moracchini looked daggers at the Baron. Romero didn't know what to say. A few seconds later, he walked out of the office.

"I'll have to check. But I reckon I know how to get hold of your Lornec," Moracchini said.

She walked over to the Baron. He realised that she needed to hold him, to feel him against her. He hugged her waist and nestled his face in the hollow of her breasts. They stayed like that until the ringing of the telephone parted them.

Casetti looked around in all directions when he saw Moracchini draw up beside him and lower the window of her Xsara.

"Jean-Luc, I dropped by at your place, and your wife told me that you'd taken the car. So I drove round the block, and here I am. Can we talk for a minute?"

The gangster glanced at his rear-view mirror.

"I'm alone, Jeannot, so don't worry. I just want to ask you for some information. You're not scared of a woman, are you?"

"Follow me, I don't want to be taken for a grass."

"O.K., except you follow me."

She drove towards L'Estaque along the coast road, keeping Casetti's Volvo in her mirror. Once they had reached the village, she took the chemin de Cézanne up towards the hills that overlooked the whole of the port of Marseille, with its huge sea wall, the Sainte-Marie pass and further away the white heights of the city.

Glancing around him, Casetti got out of his car. Moracchini checked her clip, undid the leather strap of her holster and walked over towards him.

"I'm here as a friend, Jean-Luc. There's nothing to fear."

"Don't worry about me."

"I'm trying to connect Lornec and Le Grand. Do you know how?"

The gangster swayed from one foot to the other, his hands stuck deep into his jeans pockets.

"Le Grand you say?"

"Don't pretend you don't know. Morini!"

"Lornec is at home, in Les Tourettes, you know where! But for Morini, it's more complicated . . ."

Casetti was panting as though he had just performed some feat of acrobatics.

"Does he carry a gun for Le Grand?"

"Who, Lornec?"

"No, the Pope!"

"People say a lot of things . . . anyway, what I've heard is that Le Grand spreads the good word whenever he can."

"He's a saint!"

For the first time, he looked straight at her.

"I swear it, he always spreads the good word."

"And it's best to listen."

"I think so."

She shifted so that she was looking at him in profile. In the underworld there are things that aren't said face to face.

"I closed the case yesterday. But I'd advise you to change your mobile. Understand? Change it at once."

"Thank you, Madame."

"And if you hear about a SIG 9 mm lying around there, you phone me, O.K.?"

"O.K., Madame. I'll ask around for you, but don't think I'm turning into a grass. This is just returning a favour."

She lowered her head and whispered:

"And if you want my advice, drop Le Grand. It's starting to smell bad for him."

She turned on her heel and went back to her car. By radio, she notified Mélina, the centre of all Marseille's police, of her whereabouts just in case Casetti changed his mind and lost his cool.

Lornec was sitting on a low wall outside a building. He looked to be rehearsing his prison career to a couple of teenagers who were hanging on his words.

"What shall we do, Jean-Louis? Jump him?"

Maistre dropped his binoculars onto his stomach.

"This is a gypsy camp, my old mate. You can't barge in just like that! We'll go round the block and in from the other side. After that, let me handle it."

Maistre started up the unmarked Clio and drove round Les Tourettes: two rows of shacks lined with the wrecks of cars, standing back from the coast road, between Saint-André and L'Estaque.

The Clio pitched across the bumps on the only road. Maistre stopped in front of the second house and got out. A little old man, bearded and wrinkled like a piece of old fruit, raised the curtain over the entrance and shook the officer's hand. They exchanged a few words, then Maistre returned to the Clio.

"It's O.K. We're expected."

Lornec had not moved. He stood up and waved away the teenagers when he saw the Clio approaching.

"Jérôme Lornec?"

"That's me."

"I'm Commandant Maistre of the north section and this is Commandant de Palma of the *Brigade Criminelle*. Can we ask you a couple of questions?"

"Anything you want, boss!"

Lornec was more than 1.80 metres tall, lean and wiry. His face was pockmarked, his hair black, and his green eyes flashed with energy. He kept tensing the muscles of his jaw while he gazed from one policeman to the other.

"We've found a weapon," said Maistre, "a SIG that belonged to you and your gang a few years back. Does that ring a bell?"

"I've never had a gun, boss."

"Bullshitting already! Look, Jérôme, you're going to change your tune, because you and I haven't got any time to waste. This weapon, we're not trying to pin it on you, because we know you've got nothing to do with this business. Only it's killed somebody, and it used to belong to you. So, as we're decent people, and know that you're a real man, we've come along to talk to you respectfully."

Maistre walked over to the gangster.

"Respect, Jérôme! But if you mess me around, you'll be explaining yourself to the magistrates."

"O.K., boss! Respect. It's just I don't get why you've come to see me. Because the guns from back then were captured."

Maistre and de Palma glanced at one another for a second.

"I was even questioned about that SIG. It had my prints on it. You should look in your own house, boss!"

Maistre took a handkerchief out of his pocket and wiped his brow. He nodded to de Palma to indicate that he could now join in.

"They say that you're working off and on for Le Grand. Is that true?"

Lornec's expression changed at once. He was angry, and bristling with violence.

"I don't know who you're talking about."

"Are you taking us for idiots? Don't try and be smart. Does the 421 ring any bells?"

Lornec scuffed up the street dust with the tip of his shoe.

"You know where I mean? The nightclub, near Marignane, with the dice-shaped neon lights on the front."

"I go there sometimes."

"I know, and once you were seen with a certain Morini. You know who I mean."

"Don't know him," Lornec said, shrugging.

"The snag is, kid, that we've got photos."

De Palma walked into the middle of the road. It was deserted. He kicked a tin can hard, making it bounce against the wall.

"In your opinion, how many people know that you're talking to the pigs? How many, apart from your tribe?"

"I couldn't give a fuck, boss! Everyone knows I'm no grass."

"For now they do, Lornec. For now. But I'd advise you to watch out in the future. Because I'm going to put the word around."

Lornec clenched his teeth. His eyes looked as though they were going to pop out of their sockets. The veins in his arms stood out.

"What do you want from me? For me to tell you I'm with Le Grand? Everyone's with him these days, you prick. You know that as well as I do!"

"O.K., cool it! Just try and understand what we're after."

De Palma took out his notepad.

"The scene is the northern suburbs. The three boys who might have used that SIG are in the same gang. Their names are Lornec, Vandevalle and Santiago. They're travellers. Vandevalle was nailed in 1988 for armed robbery, he went down twice, including five years for pimping. He died in 1997 in the scrubland round Carpiagne – it was the start of the barbecue season. Santiago: done for armed robbery in 1990. He was the youngest. Three sentences: possession of a weapon, robbery and criminal conspiracy. Died in April 1998."

"A work accident?" Maistre asked.

"Exactly."

"Still nothing to say, Lornec?"

"No, not about that gun. I've told you everything."

"So what's Le Grand up to at the moment?"

"No idea, boss. Honest."

"Try and find out, my son," Maistre said. "We're not here to hassle you. Respect, O.K.? Respect. But Le Grand is playing the fool right now. Tell us what you know, or else the shit will hit the fan. If we're talking like this, it's because that SIG was used to shoot someone."

"Who, boss?"

"One of ours," said de Palma. "And that's really not good news."

"I don't shoot cops, boss."

When they were back in the car on the motorway that passed by the port, Maistre and de Palma remained silent. Lornec had put them in their place. If he was telling the truth then a SIG had vanished either from police headquarters or from the clerks' office after it had been seized. Apart from the enormity of the event, there was also the difficulty in following up this sort of lead.

"I'm on duty at 5 o'clock, Michel. I'll have to drop you off in town."

"Wherever you want, Le Gros."

"I'll deal with the SIG."

13.

Voices were rising from out in the darkness. Christian Rey could hear them intermittently. When he had completely woken up, the voices had melted into the reality that forced itself back once again.

How many days had he spent without eating or drinking?

His mouth was now no more than an open wound. His lips had split open from thirst. The stench of his guts filled his mouth, as if he'd swallowed barrels of putrid wine.

His tongue had shrunk. He was sure of it. It felt like a little piece of black horn, as hard as a knife handle. It clattered against his palate each time he moved it.

His eyes burned in their sockets, the final flames of life in his battered body; a timid blaze rising from the warm embers of a fireplace. He remembered how in his last dream he had called on death, but death had not come.

Death does not come just like that. He had been its delivery boy often enough, too often, to know that.

How many people had he killed? Gangland small fry, and bigtime chisellers too. How many?

Faces appeared. Faces compressed by the forceps of memory, distorted as though pressed behind a window. He remembered the number twelve. No more, no less. He obeyed the law of the jungle. There was no fixed price, despite what was said in the press and by experts on the box. He killed to order, and his rate ranged from nothing to a hundred thousand.

The police had never found out about him. They just had their suspicions. Nothing more. All they knew about was the machines.

"A big hello from uncle" – that was what he used to say before pressing the trigger of an anonymous .45. "A big hello from uncle."

"SAY HELLO TO HIM FROM US!" the voices out of the void seemed to yell back.

He wanted to shout, release a little suffering from his guts, from the rubbish chute of his memory. But sounds no longer came: his throat was like a red-hot exhaust pipe.

Half dead, he listened to the shadows that were smothering him.

Someone or something was moving a few metres away. On the other side of his prison wall. A panting sound and banging. As though a heavy object was being dragged across the ground and a door or a cover being closed. It made a dull crack. He analysed the sound and found nothing in his memory that might fit it. The sound was not sharp, like two objects banging together.

Rey moved around as much as possible in order to make a noise: so someone might hear and bring help. He crouched on the ground like a limbless saurian and tried to wriggle over to the wall.

But he could not. And behind it, just metres away, the sounds continued. Something was moving more and more. He thought he could even hear a human voice.

There was a furious shifting and snuffling. Like the sound of an animal. He was sure of it now. It was long breaths coming from a huge maw, interspersed by the sound of feet running over what sounded like damp earth, possibly mud. A heavy, sucking sound.

One last time, he tried to cry out.

Then he flopped on the floor, beaten.

He thought again of his childhood. He said to himself that so long as he had a spark of consciousness left, he should remember what had been sweet in his young life. But the images rebounded off each other, visions from nowhere, faces he had never seen, situations he had never imagined. Everything jumbled together, in close-up, behind his half-closed eyes.

He realised that his mind was playing magic tricks on him before making its bow and allowing death to do its job.

It felt as though he were appearing before the god of mobsters, the one who counts the ill deeds and buggers you if you interfere.

The god of thugs, who had lost his place on the Capitol and was now doing overtime in the corridors of pain. The god of the lightless.

For days now, Rey had been wondering when exactly things had gone wrong for him. He supposed that it must have been after his mother's death.

He was seventeen. Prison had followed. Then the years of pimping, of slapping around his meagre herd and fucking them fast at night, after everyone else. The pimp always comes after everyone else.

He had dipped his dick in the come of the customers of the two fat whores who worked for him. That was when things had started to go wrong. Really go wrong.

The evening when Betty the brunette had told him about missing her periods, he had roughed her up more than usual. He remembered having got drunk and starting all over again. It wasn't right, he knew it, but it had not bothered him. He had dumped Betty in a disused well between Maussane and Eygalières and then gone back to his bar and stuffed himself with khemia and pastis.

The gendarmes had found the body, but that was all. Impossible to identify.

Death was in him now. That would not really bother him, but he wanted to know WHO and WHY.

On the other side of the wall, the din kept up. He heard a long clanking of iron and sheets of metal clashing together. It was a sound he knew, the kind that the door of the barn made on the farm where he had spent the only holidays of his youth. A big door mounted on a rail was being opened. He was sure of it. It brought back memories.

Images surged up from his agony.

And then a voice rose in the darkness. A high-pitched voice.

"*Lagadigadeu, la tarasco, lagadigadeu . . .*"

Then a second, deeper one:

"*Laïssa passa la vieio masco . . . Laïssa passa que vaï dansa . . .*"

The two voices joined together.

"*La tarasco dou casteu, la tarasco dou casteu . . .*"

Rey recognised that song from his distant childhood.

*

De Palma and Maistre made their way through the tourists who were congesting the rue Boulegon. When they reached place de l'Hôtel de Ville, it stank of melting sandals, redheads' armpits and pavement deposits. De Palma spotted Le Grand in his lair: the Café des Deux Mondes.

Standing a few metres from the entrance, he analysed the scene with precision: minimal risk. Marc Morini alias Le Grand was quietly sipping a beer, his back to the door, with his bodyguard facing any possible danger. Just like all gangland bosses. And this morning, no-one was expecting any danger. In Aix, the underworld feels at home.

De Palma approached. The bodyguard stood up.

"What's your problem?" he said, taking off his Ray-Bans.

De Palma produced his warrant card and stood in front of Le Grand. Maistre arrived behind him.

"Police, sir," said Maistre, his hand on his Beretta. "Keep your hands on the table and identify yourself."

"Vincent Lopez."

"L.O.P.E.Z.?"

"That's right."

Morini's lips were blue and taut. He took a gulp of beer and put the glass back down firmly on the table.

"Not in front of the customers, gentlemen," said Morini.

Maistre stared at him then told the three customers drinking at the bar to get lost.

"And who are you?"

"Marc Morini, the owner."

"O.K., so do like your pal. Hands on the table."

De Palma went round the table and searched the bodyguard.

"Just a second . . . lucky-dip time . . . and we win a Glock! This gentleman has taste. A brand-new 9 mm."

The Baron pushed Lopez down onto the table and slipped on the handcuffs.

"How are things, Morini?"

"I don't know who you are, sir . . . or why you're talking to me like that," the mobster said, his cheeks and double chin wobbling. "Do you have a warrant?"

150

"No-one mentioned any warrant," said Maistre, raising his hand. "Start by shutting the fuck up or I'll blow your balls off."

Morini lit a cigarette and exhaled the smoke like a bull about to charge.

The Baron checked that the toilets were empty and that there was no-one in the kitchen, before closing the door of the bar and drawing the curtains. He then went behind the counter and opened the drawers one by one. Just below the till he found a second gun: a loaded C.Z. 9 mm, with a bullet in the chamber.

"Well now, Jean-Louis, this is starting to look like criminal conspiracy here, with the arsenal and all. Do you think we'll find a little powder, or shall we wait a while longer?"

"Why, have you got some with you?"

De Palma went over to Morini and stared straight into his eyes.

"So you're the big boy round here! A simple bar owner in the centre of Aix. The same old story: a little café, to justify the earnings, no messing . . . Look, Jean-Louis, there's even a fruit machine!"

"Yes, but then there's everything behind it, and we're no fools."

"So, now, all together, we're going to the back of the bar. We've got things to talk about, lads. And you, the thug, we'll put you in the kitchen."

Marc Morini mumbled something incomprehensible as he sat down on the plastic upholstery on the bench at the far end of his bar.

"I'll be brief," said de Palma calmly. "Either you tell us a bit about your projects in the Camargue, or else we dip you seriously in the shit. I'm sure if we look hard enough we'll find some dope. We're here informally, but our friends at the commissariat will join us if we call them. And they'll find whatever we choose to show them."

Morini's head had sunk into his shoulders, like a boxer who knows that this round is not going his way.

"Does S.O.D.E.G.I.M. mean anything to you?"

Le Grand shook his head and exhaled through his nose.

"What, lost your memory?"

De Palma put two sachets of what could well have been heroin down on the table. Morini pulled back.

"What do you think you're doing?"

"It was a commissaire from Paris who taught me this trick. It goes back to the French Connection. In the report, these two bags will be what I found behind the bar, just next to the gun."

"Bastards . . ."

The Baron shoved a finger into the flesh of Morini's cheek.

"No swearing, Morini, or things could turn nasty."

Maistre heard a noise from the kitchen. He stood up and drew his Beretta.

"What's all this about S.O.D.E.G.I.M? It doesn't exist any more!"

"There we go. And what about Philippe Borland?"

Morini breathed in sharply then glared at the Baron, his tiny bright eyes full of fury.

"O.K., O.K . . . he was a manager. I wanted to invest a little money, but as I can't do it officially, I took him on."

"Fine. So nothing belongs to you, but everything is yours. Now tell me about that park in Provence, the Big South."

"I . . . dunno. What's that?"

"Don't fuck with me, Marco. The amusement park in Provence. How about a little cooperation?

"It's completely on the level, boss. There's nothing behind it, I swear."

"Nothing except your dosh, which stinks at long distance."

Maistre came back holding a mobile.

"The little shit was trying to call his friends. So I gave him one. He's sleeping now."

Morini had clasped his hands in front of him. He was looking towards the door of the bar and rocking his head from side to side, as though carrying out a clever calculation between what he could say and what he should conceal.

"O.K., let's continue. It was on the level, nothing behind it. Right?"

"Exactly," Morini said, without taking his eyes off the door.

"The trouble is that there are people who get in the way. And I have the feeling that you decided to dissuade them from continuing. Have you been felling a few trees to get a clearer view by any chance?"

"I don't know what you mean."

152

"Does the name William Steinert ring any bells?"

"Yes, but I don't know him and he has nothing to do with all this."

"Have you ever met him?"

"No, never."

"I know that he was at the drinks party for the launch of the Big South."

"But I wasn't."

De Palma stepped back and examined Morini, who had his chin cradled in his hands, and his elbows on the table. The gangster had his predatory senses on red alert. He only answered when the question concerned him personally. As for the rest, he knew he was running no risk.

"For that business, I put up some cash, and that's all. I don't deal with anything, my name doesn't appear. A real ghost!"

"And you can say that honestly?"

"I'm telling the truth, that's all."

De Palma was beginning to have doubts. He sensed that Morini was stalling, and knew that he was capable of doing so for hours on end. But time was short.

"O.K., I'm not going to beat about the bush. Steinert's dead. Contrary to what was announced, an investigation is ongoing, and you're right in our sights."

"You've got nothing on me!"

"Oh yes we have. We dropped in on your pal, Jérôme Lornec, the gyppo."

Morini's lips stretched so far that they finally formed a smile on his flabby face.

"What's he got to do with all this?"

"It's a long story. When he was a little thug, he used to use a SIG. And then this SIG vanished for several years. Then it suddenly resurfaced and took a shot at me while I was checking out William Steinert's place. What do you say to that?"

"I don't follow you. The last time I saw Lornec was in prison, I think."

De Palma stood up and went behind the bar to pour himself a whisky. Maistre kept his eyes on Morini.

"Right. I'll tell you this one thing. I intend to find out who killed William Steinert, and I advise you to keep your filthy paws off my investigation. Otherwise it will be war. A war that you will lose."

"Now you listen to me, officer. I'm not at war with you. You can investigate Steinert all you want, but it wasn't me or one of my lads. It's quite true that I put a load of cash into that proposition for a theme park. I was born in Tarascon. It's my region and I love it. I want to give it something beautiful. I'm ready to pay whatever it takes."

Morini banged on the table then lowered his head.

"You're almost touching when you try hard!"

"You're just trying to scare me with all this hoop-la," Le Grand said, raising his stubby fingers in the air. "And to get me talking. But you've got it all wrong, lads. I've heard of Steinert because I live in Maussane, otherwise I couldn't give a fuck about him."

Maistre moved towards the gangster, who instinctively recoiled into his seat.

"Don't play the wise guy with us, Morini. Or else I stick shit on your arse and tonight you'll be sleeping in the can. Get me?"

Morini only stared back at him with the eyes of someone who had not been scared for years.

14.

Tarascon was waiting for the feast of Saint Martha. That year, the day of the patron saint of housewives fell on a Tuesday. Tuesday, July 29.

Out of the sun, between the panelled walls of the sacristy, Father Samuel Favier was putting the finishing touches to his sermon.

From time to time, street noises reached him and broke his concentration. He was looking for an ending, a real conclusion that would make the faithful think. But all he could find were commonplaces, the kind of liturgical clichés he'd been taught in the seminary.

On the cork noticeboard on the wall, next to the schedule of services, he had pinned up a simple drawing by a child in catechism classes. It was the picture of the week: Saint Martha as Terminator, overcoming a terrifying Pokemon. It was the version that he preferred of the miraculous Lazarus's young sister, who had arrived on the beaches of the Camargue two thousand years before with a band of apprentice saints, ready to get to grips with the prevailing paganism.

Martha, the patroness of housewives, but also of Tarascon.

Martha, inseparable from the monstrous Tarasque, which was half man and half reptile. The saint had delivered the people of Tarascon from this spawn of the devil, quite simply by speaking to it. Martha had sweet-talked the beast with a few kind words and the help of the Holy Ghost. Then she had tied her belt around the monster's neck and led it to the Rhône, where she made it promise never to terrorise the people again. The Tarasque had promptly vanished beneath the rock that now bears King René's Castle.

In his past life, Samuel Favier had been an emergency doctor, until he had met God on the battlefields of the former Yugoslavia.

Saint Martha was his first parish, and his sermon about the Tarasque the first real obstacle that the Almighty had placed in the young priest's path.

He was trying to find something edifying to say about this legend dressed up as a religious thriller. The ex-doctor in him wanted to be high-brow, and talk about man's reptilian brain, about the Tarasque that survives in all of us, ready to gobble up morality and common sense at the slightest disturbance of the ego. The Tarasque, that colourful version of the instinctive, raw, terrifying violence of the human race. That was what Favier wanted to highlight.

And yet his predecessor, old Father Bessodes, as he gave him the keys to his church, had warned him not to risk a schism: "Don't go too far with the Tarasque . . . they don't like that! You'll be taking a big risk. They're very sensitive about their tale of a monster, and can't stand it if you diverge from the official version. All that matters in this town is tradition. They'd be lost without their monster. If you tell them that the Tarasque is more a symbol than anything else, and that it never existed, you'll expose yourself to the fury of good society, the mayor and the bishop. Remember that they're all more or less cousins or friends, and they're the people that run the place."

During the service the previous Sunday, he had announced that he would be saying a grand mass on Tuesday evening at 8.00 p.m., so that all the townspeople could attend.

It was now Monday. He was rereading the opening passage of his text when he heard the church door creak. The big sacristy clock indicated 10.00 a.m. precisely. The *Tarascaires*, the Knights of the Tarasque, were early.

"Good morning, Father. I've come to fetch her."

"Really? I thought you'd come to confess, you wicked sinner."

Favier warmly shook the powerful hand of Marc Gouirand, the leader of the Knights.

"Tell me, Marc, how long have you been taking care of this creature?"

"The last festival made it twenty years."

He whistled with admiration. Marc Gouirand was a solid fellow, forty-something, muscular, with a jutting chin and the look of a cheeky brat who had strayed into the world of adults.

"So, why do you look after the Tarasque?"

"My wife says that she's my mistress . . . It's a tradition, Father. And without traditions, we're nothing."

"There's always Him up there," said Father Favier, pointing towards the top of the church.

"Yes, true. But . . . I've been seeing the Tarasque ever since I was a little boy," he replied, rubbing his chin. "When I was a child, all I dreamed of was being able to push her. And now here I am, right behind her."

"I've been told that it was you who repaired her."

"If you'd seen her, twenty years back when I took her over . . . she was in a real mess. Like a hippy, or a tramp. Good grief! No-one had given her the slightest lick of paint since the end of the First World War. Think of it . . . since 1918 . . . She was hideous, really hideous."

"Why, do you find her beautiful then?"

"She's magnificent! Come and see."

Marc Gouirand led Father Favier into the depths of the nave. The Tarasque was there, its bulging eyes wide open, both menacing and familiar, motionless in its special chapel. In the half-light, its huge Jurassic reptilian body could be made out, with its scales still filthy from the weeds of the Camargue and its red crest raised.

A gold and mauve ray of light lit up its face on the slant, making it look like a moustachioed villain. The Tarasque had the face of a turn-of-the-century wide boy or an Apache battered by fate.

"There she is, our famous beast," Gouirand murmured, instinctively standing back.

"Is it a male or a female in your opinion, Marc?"

Its jaw drooping, the monster stared derisively at the entrance to the crypt that contained the tomb of Saint Martha.

"A big question, Father. La Tarasque is a female name, but it's a monster. For me, she's female, but people see her as they want."

Favier went over to the legendary reptile and stroked its mane. He noticed that some chips of wood were missing from its face, especially on the right cheek and ear. A piece of moustache had also been broken off.

"Whatever happened to this poor monster?"

"We hit a car. Someone was double-parked just in front of the castle. It's hard to stop her sometimes."

The Knight raised the beast's heavy head and made the fearful white teeth in its jaws clack together. Their massive impact echoed through the vaults of the church.

Favier glanced at the crypt of Saint Martha, hoping that the din of monstrous teeth would not rouse the holy lady in her marble sarcophagus.

Gouirand kneeled down in front of the reptilian mouth.

"It's going to be a pain in the . . . to stick back the missing bits of wood. We'll have to make repairs . . ."

The priest went over and bent down to look at the extent of the damage.

"You'll have to find a wood carver. And a good one!"

"That's no problem. For the Tarasque, everyone pitches in."

Gouirand walked around it, examining the fabulous creature's scales which were highlighted with gold and grey, as well as its bright red spikes. He finished with its tail, which was tied in a knot and tipped with the blade of a lance.

"And maybe a lick of paint on her tail . . ."

"And how about a little blood on the teeth?"

"Why not? She loves blood. If she could eat a couple of towns-folk before Saint Martha's day, then she would."

"Yes, but don't forget Saint Martha herself!"

"Don't you worry, Father. We're not about to forget your lady friend."

With surprising ease, Gouirand pulled the Tarasque towards him, taking care that the tail did not damage the altar behind it. The jaws clacked again as he turned it towards the church's main door.

"How much does this contraption weigh?"

"Six hundred kilos, and she's five metres long."

"And you're just going to walk it through the streets of Tarascon like that?"

"I'm used to it. She listens to me."

Father Favier opened wide the double doors of the church and let out the Tarasque, led by its most loyal knight. A raw light invaded the transept, and the priest closed up again fast, raising a din that made the entire Gothic façade tremble.

Inside, quiet footfalls were echoing in the apse. Probably the first tourist of the day. Even though it was not yet visiting time.

Father Favier crossed the choir and went round the ambulatory to ask the visitor to come back in the afternoon. But he saw no-one. He searched the house of God from top to bottom, including the crypt of Saint Martha. No-one.

Yet he was sure that he had heard footsteps.

He went back to his sermon, with the unpleasant sensation of suffering from auditory hallucinations. And also with the certitude that he should not upset cranks like Gouirand. Especially since his parish was full of them.

A warm breeze was rising from the sea and blowing along the dirt track that led up to the sparse meadows of the Alpilles. Eugène Bérard's sheep were sheltering from the heat of the sun beneath a limestone overhang.

The shepherd kept his eyes fixed on the Baron. His luminous stare was analysing each gesture and each expression.

"Have you hurt your hands?"

"Can't hide anything from you!"

"You look as if you've been fighting the whole earth."

De Palma smiled, rubbed his hands together, then stuck them into his jeans pockets.

"Last time, you told me about the Downlands. Do you remember?"

"That's the land on the other side of the Maussane road. It's called the Chemin de Galibert. On the top, there are vines and some lavender. It belonged to poor old William."

"And this land is cursed?"

"Those are ancient beliefs . . . In the old days, people used to say that there was the statue of a Roman god there. I can't remember his name."

159

"Hercules, or Heracles."

Bérard glanced at the Baron, a flash of fire in his eyes, like a flame from a canon's mouth. His voice grew harsher.

"Who told you that?"

"I looked up a few archaeological records that mention it."

Bérard was now on his guard. He took a step backwards and leaned on his stick.

"I didn't know there was anything about that in the books."

"And you? Why don't you tell me a little bit of what you know about the Downlands."

"Oh, they're not worth much. They're full of stones as big as houses. There's nothing to be done with them."

"So why did they mean so much to William Steinert?"

"I can't answer that."

"I'm sorry, but you'll have to."

Bérard just whistled to his dog.

"You'll have to, M. Bérard. Steinert was murdered."

The shepherd stood up, like a bamboo rod that had stayed bent too long. De Palma had not been expecting this reaction. In the old man's face, he read an expression of great sadness.

"I think you ought to tell me the truth. There are powerful forces at work that are threatening everything and everyone around here."

"Oh, those forces won long ago, M. de Palma. All the land now belongs to outsiders."

Bérard turned back towards the valley and fell silent for a moment.

"Outsiders like the Steinerts?"

"William was different."

"Could you tell me a little about him?"

The shepherd bent down and plucked a blade of grass which he split between his nails and stuck in his mouth.

"Do you have time?"

"I'm at your disposal."

"I'll have to take the animals back. Come with me to the farm. It's not far. Then we'll talk."

Eugène Bérard lived in the farmhouse of Les Fontaines: two buildings, one for him, the other for the sheep, formed an L in front of a large barn, in which slept a 1960s Massey-Ferguson, a harrow and a haymaker, all of them covered in rust.

His flock pushed its way through the entrance to the fold. Lambs that had lost their mothers were bleating. The shepherd went up into the barn to fetch some hay for the mangers, then he gave the lambs their ration of barley.

"Goodness, they're hungry! With this heat, there's nothing left to eat in the pastures."

"You take good care of them."

"I certainly do!"

Despite his great age, he still moved among his jostling charges without losing his balance.

"William often used to come here. Sometimes he gave me a hand. But he didn't want anyone to know that. It reminded him of his childhood, when he helped with the harvesting or haymaking."

A last ray of dusty sunshine came in through the double doors. The air was charged with the animals' vitality and the grinding of their jaws as they quickly reduced their hay to a fragrance of mint and thyme.

"Come on, we've earned a drink."

The farmhouse living room was plunged in total darkness. Bérard opened the shutters to let in the evening light. He placed a jug of water, two glasses and a bottle of pastis on the table. Then he disappeared.

The room was partly taken up by a huge table covered with oilcloth. At the far end, there was a large freestone fireplace and a modest grandmother clock. The only other piece of furniture was a tall, dark, walnut cupboard.

Bérard returned with a small package under his arm.

"I knew William when he was very young. His father came here, before the war."

He poured two pastis and raised his glass.

"Your health, sir."

The old man rummaged through his papers, careful not to let de Palma see anything.

"William's father carried out digs in the region. He was looking for sarcophagi and old stones. One day, I bumped into him not far from here, just as I did with you, and the two of us got on. Look, here's a photo of him."

Steinert senior was standing beside Bérard, his hand on his shoulder. Both of them were smiling at the photographer.

"That was the day when we found the statue of Hercules. I was the only one who knew where it was."

The old man sat down in front of the Baron.

"William's father was a good man. His name was Karl. He'd studied archaeology back in Germany."

"Archaeology?"

"He was interested in the ancient Greeks and Romans who came to this region. And as the people round here knew that I was interested too, they sent him to see me. That's how we got to know each other."

The old man pushed his cap back, freeing a lock of silver hair which stuck onto his damp forehead. He took a swig of pastis.

"And then the war broke out. Round here, we didn't see much of the Germans. Just a few patrols. After all, nothing much happens in the countryside! Then, in 1942, Karl came back with a whole gang of Boches. They were students from Munich University. They started digging again . . . this was the time of the Vichy government. They worked with some students from France."

He let his big hand drop onto the tablecloth. The mechanism of the clock started up, and seven chimes filled the room with sound.

"And did they find anything?"

"Nothing much . . . but they all stayed at La Balme, except for William's father, who refused to live in the farmhouse. So, you see, he lodged at the central hotel in Maussane, while the youngsters slept in the barn! But all went well. I mean, this wasn't a crowd of Nazis. I can still picture them all in the farmyard. They were nice and helpful. But then, in 1942, the Wehrmacht turned up, and everything changed. Some of the students left, while others put on army uniforms."

Bérard showed a photograph from the war years. To judge from the various people's dress, Steinert was surrounded by local worthies.

"That's the old mayor of Maussane, and this is the father of the present mayor of Eygalières."

De Palma waited for the old shepherd to resume the conversation of his own accord. Bérard stood up, walked over to pat his dog's head, then took a packet of tobacco down from the mantelpiece.

"At the end of the war, we were visited by bogus members of the Resistance from Marseille, Arles, Tarascon and round here. They were real thugs. Especially the ones from these parts . . ."

Bérard paused. He clenched his teeth and seemed to be short of breath.

"I must tell you that I was in the Resistance and Steinert knew it. I was in the Vincent network. It was a small organisation that we set up with some local lads. Steinert even helped me out a couple of times. But try and explain that to a load of lawless ruffians."

"What happened?"

"They shaved the head of Mme Maurel, the owner of the farmhouse, and they shot one of her brothers. If you go into the farmyard, you can still see the bullet marks in the barn wall, to the right of the door."

Bérard thumped down his empty glass and stared into space. The clock chimed the half-hour. He removed a deckle-edged photo from the pile. It showed a young woman of about twenty, with a beautiful face lit up by rather a fixed smile and tender eyes.

"This is Simone Maurel . . . I could do nothing to help them. Not a thing. Poor old Emile. His body had been torn apart by the time I got there."

"What about Mme Maurel?"

"She died shortly afterwards. Of shame . . . How can you live with that?"

The shepherd sat back down. His figure had shrunk once more. Through the window, he watched the dust in the yard rise up towards the sun.

"You'll have another one, won't you?" he asked, pouring out a fresh glass without waiting for a reply.

"What about the other brother?"

163

"He died too. But much later . . . A tractor accident. He'd got a job on the Janson farm."

The shepherd finished his sentence with a gesture that de Palma did not understand. Evoking the past had evidently upset him. He was an emotional man concealing a long-standing anger.

Outside, the two tall olive trees in the yard were changing colour in the evening light. The dog went out and growled.

"In 1946, a man came to see me. I never learned his name. He simply told me that Steinert had sent him and that he was going to buy La Balme. Then he asked me if I'd agree to look after the land. And I did so for several years. I don't have much in the way of land myself! After my wife died, in the 1980s, they bought the Downlands. William arranged the purchase. His poor father was already dead."

"And you knew there was this real estate scheme?"

Bérard's eyes filled with anger.

"If they ever do that . . ."

"So long as the Downlands aren't for sale, they won't be able to do anything!"

"Don't you believe it! I own part of it, and I'm very old. I'd left everything to William. But now he's dead and they could turn us out if they want. They make the laws, and adapt them as they want. And now William's gone. He knew what he was doing, plus he had money and lawyers. No-one argued with him! But poor people like us . . . we count for nothing!"

"And is the mayor of Eygalières in on this?"

"Of course he is! All the big cheeses are in the know. Anyway, I'd rather not say any more. There's no-one left to save our little corner of Provence."

"There's still William's wife! She's very rich too, and the Downlands are hers now."

"I don't know if she'll stay. I don't think so, without her husband . . ."

Bérard had spoken as though he was expecting an answer.

"His wife intends to stay."

"I don't know if William told her."

"Told her what?"

164

"William was Simone Maurel's son. He was born in 1942. It was poor Simone's only sin: having the child of a man she had loved during the war."

De Palma was lost for words. The light had changed. In the cooler air, the birds were starting to sing, while the sheep had fallen silent. There was a smell of sweat, rancid wool and strong milk.

"She died and left her son behind . . . When she was shamed like that, she sent him to his father, in Germany . . ."

Bérard shivered. These memories were exciting his heart. For a moment, his features changed; his face emptied of the remnant of life that had been driving him on just a few minutes before.

"What I've just told you, no-one else knows. William found out when he was much older. I told him. When his mother died, he was only three. He didn't remember her."

Bérard blew his nose loudly.

"William was like a son to me."

On the road that led down towards Fontvieille, de Palma tried to put his ideas in order. The day before, he had learned nothing from Morini, except for the confirmation of what he already knew: the mob in Aix was laundering money in business deals such as this amusement park. There was nothing surprising about that. The only detail that provided any progress was Morini's origins: he came from Tarascon. One day, that could turn out to be relevant.

On the other hand, this meeting with Bérard had sent his mind into a panic. He had been expecting anything but that, and suddenly whole sections of the mystery had fallen. He now understood why La Balme farmhouse had meant so much to Steinert and why he had changed nothing in most of its rooms.

He stopped beside the vines that grew along the Downlands. To the right, between the white crests of the rocks that rose up as far as the fortress of Les Baux, the sky was still red from the sun. In the valley, a silvery light flattened out the contours.

The Baron went in among the pines, took a few steps, then stopped. There was a smell of warmth and roots. As far as the eye could see, there were the twisted trunks of oaks and stumps rotting on a bed of needles. As the night fell, the pines and mastic trees stood like threatening sentinels.

The Baron retraced his steps. In the distance, he could hear cars driving up to Les Baux, and a solitary cuckoo among the creaking branches.

It must be warm on the beach.

The sand is golden with pink and violet glints.

The image is slightly hazy,

Stippled by time.

Isabelle is in her swimsuit.

She's fifteen and a half.

She's walking across the sand like a clown.

Close-up. A smile at the camera.

She's just been for a swim. Her swimsuit is taut.

Her breasts are hard.

She has sand on her calves and the tops of her thighs.

Her grandmother is watching her and waving at the lens.

Then the letters and numbers stand out on the white background.

Maistre turns off the projector.

Marceau stands up.

De Palma doesn't move.

He's turned round his chair and leaned his forearms on the back rest.

He yawns.

"What's the time, Jean-Claude?"

"Three o'clock. I'm knackered."

"Me too," Maistre adds.

"You coming, Michel? Let's go and get a bite to eat at the Pied de Cochon."

The Baron grimaces.

"You want to eat after what we've just seen?"

"Yes, Michel, I still want to eat. Because we have to keep our strength up if we want to find that fucker."

That night, de Palma leafed through the pages of his notebooks, looking for a truth that was receding a little more each day. Isabelle Mercier had been his only failure. He had found answers to all the other investigations, even if the courts had not always delivered the verdicts he was hoping for. There were policing certainties and then there were judicial truths.

He had sent to prison a countless number of people who had committed bloody crimes. Most had received maximum sentences: a life behind bars, as well as few executions when he was a young officer.

Each time, the truth had emerged, and that was what really mattered for him.

Except for Isabelle Mercier.

He remembered the feeling of powerlessness that had gripped him and which he had shared with Maistre and Marceau. He felt the same way now. He did not understand why Steinert had died. The little voice that whispered to him that it was for a few hectares of land did not satisfy him. Morini did not kill people without knowing the whys and wherefores of his action. That much he was sure of.

On the day of the billionaire's funeral, he had glimpsed a truth: Steinert had died accidentally. Yet he knew that the context of this accident had not been natural. Around the edges of that accident he could vaguely discern a meshing of events that went beyond the harshnesses of life and had made death inevitable.

15.

Marceau was the first on the scene. He was alone, having intercepted an urgent message on the Homicide frequency. The call had mentioned the cleaning and maintenance depot of the town of Tarascon. The operator had then specified: "In the municipal garage".

A patrol was on its way.

The first thing Marceau saw was the Tarasque, then Marc Gouirand and, sitting beside him, Father Favier, who had raised the alarm. The monster had been placed amidst a stack of equipment, in the very place where Gouirand had left it the day before to treat it to a wash and brush-up. In front of its maw lay a horribly mutilated body: a torso, a head and an arm caught in its wooden teeth.

Like a barbaric offering to the hideous creature.

"Have you touched anything?"

Father Favier advanced towards him.

"No, nothing, sir. I was a doctor before I became a priest. I know the police's methods."

"What about you, sir?"

Gouirand did not respond. He was sitting on a low wall, his head in his hands.

Favier took Marceau by the arm.

"I think it would be better to wait. He's still in shock."

A patrol arrived and started to trample over the scene of the crime, before coming to a halt at the sight of the corpse. Marceau shooed them away at once. He did not approach the body straight away, but stood for some time in silent observation. Then he took out his mobile, asked for the forensic unit in Marseille, hung up and turned towards Favier.

"O.K., Father. Can you tell me exactly what happened, between the moment when you discovered this horror and now?"

Favier took a deep breath.

"I was about to go through my sermon for this evening's mess one last time, when I got a phone call: it was Marc Gouirand, to tell me . . ."

"What did he say precisely?"

"Not much."

"Try to remember."

"He was having trouble speaking. All I understood was Tarasque and municipal garage. That's all."

"But you realised that something was wrong?"

"I used to be an emergency doctor. I'm very familiar with accidents and tragedies."

"And then?"

"Then, I came here. Marc was sitting just as you see him now. He hasn't moved since. I saw the corpse and called the police. Three minutes later, you got here."

Marceau looked at his watch. It was now 10.20 a.m. Favier's version of events fitted perfectly. He looked at Gouirand, who still had not moved. In a few minutes' time he would question him.

Meanwhile, he went back to his car and radioed to ask where the Marseille forensics team was.

"On their way," yelled the voice on the radio.

At 10.45, Larousse arrived, accompanied by the deputy public prosecutor: a pretty and slender brunette with square glasses and a little upturned nose decked with freckles. Marceau had never seen her before.

Larousse introduced them.

"What do you think, Marceau?"

He scratched his head.

"A real act of barbarism. The work of a lunatic. I haven't seen anything this vile for ages. This is Father Favier, who alerted us."

The young deputy prosecutor tried to move closer to the body, but Larousse held her back by the arm.

169

"We'd best stay here in case we disturb something. Let's wait for the technicians. They should be here soon."

Marceau glanced at Gouirand. He noticed that he had now raised his head and was staring into space. The detective decided that it was time to ask a few questions. He went and sat down beside him.

"How do you feel?"

Marceau held out his hand, but Gouirand took no notice.

"That's Christian in front of the Tarasque."

"Christian who?"

"Rey. A former knight."

Marceau offered him a cigarette, but he refused with a shake of his head.

"And did you know this Rey well?"

"He's a childhood friend."

Marceau drew a little nearer to Gouirand.

"And you said he was a knight?"

"A Knight of the Tarasque! One of those who push her and attend to her."

Gouirand raised his eyes and looked at the corpse which was just a few metres away. A smell of panic and death hung over the municipal garage.

"What happened when you got here earlier?"

"I discovered him, just as you see him now. I didn't touch anything. Can you imagine?"

Gouirand buried his head back in his hands. Marceau saw that he was not going to get anything more out of him. He stood up, gave him a friendly pat on the shoulder, and went back to Commissaire Larousse.

"You know who that is in front of the Tarasque?"

"No."

"Rey."

"Christian Rey?"

"That's right."

"Can you explain?" the deputy prosecutor butted in, a hint of authority in her voice.

"An old acquaintance of ours," Larousse replied. "Christian Rey:

170

pimping and illegal gambling machines. We also long suspected him of being the local mob's executioner. That's who."

"Do you think this could be a settling of scores?"

"Why not? That would be the classic scenario."

"I don't think so," Marceau replied.

"Really?"

"Yes, really."

"Well, we'll see," Larousse concluded coldly.

The team arrived from Marseille. Marceau gave them a very brief run-down, then he put on some gloves and overshoes before following the technicians towards Rey's body.

After each step, the technician in charge placed a yellow marker on the ground with a big black number written on it. Behind him, his colleague took a photo of each one.

A couple of minutes later, they were two steps away from the corpse and bent down to catch their breath.

A chest. Arms without hands. And a head, which was weirdly intact. The body had been severed across the torso.

Gaping wounds. Bones sticking out. Marceau noticed a vertebra and a rib, cut clean through by what he supposed must be a machine.

The face gave out a ghastly impression. The cheeks were phenomenally hollow, as though there was nothing left but leather over the jaws. The teeth stuck out, while the eyes seemed to be still biting into what remained of the visible world.

Marceau had rarely experienced such a sensation of animal terror. It felt like being transported years back, to Paris, when he was a young inspector and doing his apprenticeship in horror.

Rey's skin was still pink. There was no trace of decay, while the blood had already coagulated on the surface of the wounds.

The police officer examined the skull, but saw no wound. There was no round hole, the sign of a bullet. No ecchymoses or haematomas either.

Marceau took a step back.

"I'll leave you to it," he said to one of the team. "We'll see during the autopsy."

He carefully retraced his steps and went back the way he had come.

"So?" Larousse asked.

"So, you'd have to be a genius to say what exactly Rey died of. Whatever it was, it wasn't a good old 11.43."

"You're thinking of something in particular?" the deputy prosecutor said.

"Yes. A machine. Only a machine could amputate a body like that. Something like a huge pair of shears."

"And that's not going to happen in the context of a gangland killing?"

"That's not what makes me wonder. Because they don't always gun each other down."

"So what's the problem?"

"The Tarasque."

"The what?"

"The Tarasque."

"Oh right, that nasty great thing over there."

"Michel? Jean-Claude here. I've got a stiff on my hands. A Christian Rey. Does that ring any bells?"

"Jesus, Christian Rey. There's definitely a time and a place for everything. And some people will be saying that it was high time."

"Yeah, but there's a catch."

"What's that?"

"He was found practically in the mouth of the Tarasque. This morning."

The Baron let a silence pass by.

"And what are you thinking?"

"I'm thinking it's more than just a gangland killing. What about you?"

"I don't know. It's all news to me. Have you got anyone who's talking?"

"The one who discovered the body. He told me that Rey was a Knight of the Tarasque."

"A what?"

"One of the people who push the thing when they take it out for the carnival."

"The Tarasque, you say!"

For a few seconds, the Baron hesitated. Ideas were spinning through his mind.

"Is the prosecutor there?"

"His deputy. A skirt. She's new and she looks to me as thick as they come."

"And where are you at with Steinert?"

"The case has been closed. I've just heard the news. Officially, there's no more Steinert case."

"But I still think he was killed."

"The only thing that's certain about it is that the prosecutor's closed the case."

"O.K., we need an urgent talk, Jean-Claude."

"Why urgent?"

"See you later, my lad. I'll be there this afternoon."

Marceau's office stank of stale Gitanes and sweat. He was sitting in front of his computer, with his feet on the table. De Palma was standing in front of him, staring intently, his face tense.

"And you're telling me that you went to see Morini, just like that, with Maistre?"

The Baron did not respond.

"And then you tell me that it won't be the last time. That you've been shot at and you've got some names!"

"Affirmative," de Palma said, his voice slightly muted.

Marceau suddenly stood up.

"Affirmative, my arse! I reckon that you're operating more and more like a cowboy and that you're putting your fellow officers in danger. You have an influence on Maistre, don't abuse it! He's a father. I thought I'd just remind you of that, in case you'd forgotten."

De Palma relaxed.

"I hope you still have a scrap of conscience left, to show you the possible consequences of your foul-ups."

"I needed to know. That's all there is to it."

"What did you expect Morini to tell you? In the police we don't always know everything. That's the way it is."

"And you can live with that?"

"For ages now, I've learned to live with small truths and big lies. And with more and more unknowns in this big equation of shit."

De Palma folded his arms over his chest. He glanced at the missing persons notices stuck up on the walls. Steinert's was still there.

"Does Morini come from Tarascon?" he asked, opening his pad.

"He was born in rue des Archives, and he's still got plenty of friends in the neighbourhood. What's more, he does a lot of business round here. I'd advise you to watch your back in these parts. Tarascon is a bit like his manor."

"Born in 1943 in Tarascon, Bouches-du-Rhône," de Palma said laconically. "Arrested for armed robbery in 1963, then for procuring and so on and so forth. The irresistible rise of an arsehole. A big lie, as you put it, on legs."

"What do you expect me to do about it? They say that he lunches with the mayor and mixes with freemasons as casually as you go to the barber's . . . People say a lot of things about Morini."

"Do you know where he lives?"

"He's got a huge villa in Maussane, just in front of the village. And land all around it. Enough to spot an enemy coming."

"That must make a change from his lousy little bar in Aix. Because he can't spot an enemy coming there. Can you show me on the map where the fucker lives?"

"I've got it on my machine."

Marceau clicked his computer mouse to open a file.

"Here, that's where it is. On the road to Eygalières. Just by this big forest to the right on the way up."

De Palma suddenly realised that he meant the Downlands. In other words, Steinert and Morini had been neighbours of a sort.

Marceau sat down again.

"They say that he runs all the one-arm bandits from Nîmes to Toulon, including all the small towns to the north as far as Valence, and maybe even Lyon. Plus the whores, and the nightclubs. He's not much into drugs, as far as I know. Morini's thing is gambling. Christian

Rey was one of his men, by the way. He used to be the local debt collector."

Marceau lit a Gitane and watched its blue smoke rise towards the ceiling.

"Him and another guy, an ex-cop called Bernard Dominguez."

"I know him," said de Palma. "He was a good officer until he started screwing whores all day long."

"I'd just love to nail him . . . Anyway, apart from that, there isn't much to say about Morini. In the end, he's a classic godfather. He's got a hell of a reputation, but in fact he's just like the rest of them."

He stubbed out his half-smoked cigarette.

"Which is bad enough already!"

Marceau suddenly looked tired. He seemed sad and empty. He closed the windows on his computer screen and lit another Gitane.

"I haven't forgotten Isabelle either. Sometimes I realise that I haven't thought about her for the past two or three days and I feel guilty. Jesus, do I feel guilty."

That day, there was a space between the two men that nothing could fill, not even their memories.

"It was you who gave Chandeler my number."

Marceau simply raised a hand and lowered his eyes, while trying to look indifferent.

"I'm not holding it against you, Jean-Claude."

A long silence.

"And Maistre, what does he say?"

"You know Jean-Louis. It all goes on inside. He's not much of a talker."

There was quite a crowd on place de l'Hôtel de Ville in Aix. It was market day. Marc Morini was sitting on the terrace of his bar, with his bodyguard in front of him. The man took out his 200 mm and took two photographs.

Just like last time, the man noticed that the nearest stall to Morini's bar was an Italian cheese seller. He went over and ordered five hundred grams of parmesan and a chunk of mozzarella. From there, he had a three-quarters view of Morini. He took a third photograph.

The clock chimed eleven in the town hall belfry.

The last time he'd come, he had seen some policemen he did not know go into the bar. They had stayed for a good fifteen minutes and then had come out with stern faces. Some time later, a bunch of shady characters turned up.

So Morini wasn't easy to get at.

This seemed to be the same situation. Morini was sitting in the same position.

He picked up his portions of parmesan and mozzarella and went back into the centre of the market. One more anonymous face.

He bought some candied almonds and was opening the box when he saw Morini's bodyguard stand up and go inside the bar.

Le Grand was alone. Still with his back to the street. The man did not wait a moment longer. He felt buoyed up by all the wonders that the Beast had revealed to him. He got out his Colt .45 and made straight for his prey, his gun pressed against his right thigh.

Morini did not have time to say or do anything at all. His predator's instinct deserted him the moment the Beast's servant stuck the barrel of the .45 into his fat neck.

"On your feet, shit-face. And quick."

Morini did so in silence. Lucky for him, or the man would have had to finish him off there and then.

"Hands behind your back."

"But you can't do this. Who are you?"

"I'm the police," the man said, flashing a tricolour card.

They walked some thirty metres along the square then ducked into an old 406 estate.

When Morini saw a parking ticket was stuck behind the left-hand windscreen wiper, he knew instinctively that there would be no official questioning or police custody at the end of this journey.

This was the end of the line for his life as a predator. He had been expecting it for a long time, but not like this.

Marceau's clearest memory of Christian Rey went back to his time with the *Brigade de Grand Banditisme* in Marseille. Rey had been questioned about a gangland killing. He was suspected of having offed the rebellious owner of Le Nain Jaune, a bar in central Avignon. Judge Bonnardi wanted the gangster questioned, and the gangster had been questioned. Nothing had come of it.

Today, Rey had been half eaten by some infernal machine and was lying on the chrome-plated dissection table of the forensic surgeon at La Timone hospital.

With Dr Mattei in charge. The doctor of the dead.

"There's not much left of our friend."

"What do you make of this wound?" Marceau asked.

"Hard to say."

"Could it be from a machine, such as a grinder or something of that sort?"

"Maybe yes, maybe no . . . it looks to me more like a bite."

"Hang on, Mattei. I might have told you that it was found in front of the Tarasque, but there's no need to start telling stories."

"I mean it, Jean-Claude . . . I really do."

Mattei stood back from the table, both arms raised, a scalpel in his left hand.

"I saw this kind of bite wound when I was working in Mauritius, just after I'd qualified. It was a fisherman who'd been attacked by a shark, in the lagoon. He'd been half eaten. Just like this."

Marceau ran his hand over the nape of his neck to wipe away the sweat that was dripping down his back.

"Leave it out, Mattei. There aren't any sharks in Tarascon. What else have you found?"

"Lots of interesting things: algae, traces of earth under the fingernails, and so on . . ."

"You said algae?"

"Yes, and silt. But from fresh water, I'd say. There are no traces of salt or anything that might suggest sea water."

"So what are your conclusions?"

"That our customer spent some time underwater. Stagnant water probably. A bit like the one the other day."

"William Steinert?"

"Spot on. Except that Steinert drowned."

"You're sure about that?"

"Of course I am! There can't be any doubt about it. Steinert died of drowning just as surely as this one died of being eaten by something. Got it?"

"Loud and clear, boss."

Marceau looked at Rey's body. He tried to recall the mobster he had encountered when he was in custody: his face had shrunk, it no longer looked the same, Marceau was sure of it. In his memories, Rey had been fairly chubby, though without a belly, tall, and built like a prop forward. The half man that they had in front of them must have suffered horribly, suffered a gangster's Passion, followed a scumbag's stations of the cross.

"He was tortured before being finished off," he said, as though throwing a card down on the table.

"What do you mean by that?"

"Tortured. No water or anything else for days. Look at his cheeks."

Mattei turned towards Marceau.

"You'll end up getting my job one of these days, Jean-Claude!"

"Not yet, doctor death. But I'm working on it."

Mattei pointed out traces of burns on Rey's wrists. One or two old scars. A tattoo on his shoulder.

"Nice tattoo," he said.

Marceau leaned over to see.

"What is it?"

"An impossible monster: a Tarasque. That fits with what Gouirand told me."

With a twirl of his scalpel, Mattei drew a circle around Rey's skull and asked his assistant for the saw.

"I don't think I'll find out much more today. We'll have to wait for the D.N.A. results and chemical tests."

"How long?"

"For the chemistry, tomorrow at the latest. It's being done in Marseille. But I'm sending the D.N.A. to Nantes, so it could take some time."

"Why didn't you go with Bordeaux?"

"We don't work with them any more. Too many foul-ups."

"So let's wait for the labs. They're the real police these days."

The skin of Marceau's face was so taut that his skull protruded clearly. He went over to the corpse while Mattei was lifting its scalp. As he pondered, he clenched his teeth, and his jaw muscles bulged when he did so. A cold gleam glazed his eyes.

16.

It had been raining since the middle of the night. The water had gathered black trails of dust on streets and pavements overheated by the sun.

The day before, de Palma had had the stitches removed from his shoulder wound. Apart from a slight tugging on his skin, he no longer felt a thing.

As soon as he emerged from the automatic gate of Résidence Paul Verlaine, he felt the touch of eyes from across the street.

He could not tell where the danger lurked, but he could sense it. For the coming night, he had decided to sleep at Maistre's place. After that, he would see.

If he was sure of one thing, it was that Morini would not let up. He had gone too far: his visit to Lornec and then the threats he had made in Aix were too much to swallow. But it was a long step from there to taking out a contract, even if Morini had built his empire on the basis of incredible violence. Even if he had wiped out rival gangs like a butcher. He was a psycho who enjoyed just two things: getting himself invited to the orgies of the great and good, and offing someone. All the same, he never did so without a good reason.

As he turned into rue Laugier, he looked in his rear-view mirror and saw a Scenic following him. He made out the driver's face, and he had seen enough gangsters in his life to realise that the man on his tail was no part-timer.

He accelerated suddenly, putting a good fifty metres between them, then found himself face to face with the number 18 bus that was coming up avenue de la Capelette. Behind him, the Scenic's driver picked up his mobile.

De Palma turned off the avenue and drove the wrong way up rue Saint-Jean. The car was no longer there in his mirror. He stopped, checked the clip in his Bodyguard, picked up his .45, racked the slide and laid in on the passenger seat.

Was he succumbing to hallucinations again?

He was still wondering about that when, thirty metres away, he saw a motorcycle heading straight for him with two men in the saddle.

De Palma floored the pedal and drove straight at them. They swerved to avoid him.

In front of Saint John's church, he just missed a couple of kids who were kicking a football.

He wrenched the wheel to the left, like someone on a stunt-driving course, then drove along the railway track, the Alfa hugging the tarmac.

Left again, in a screech of tyres.

On the pavements of the old industrial estate there were holes, burned-out mattresses, wrecked fridges, a blind T.V.

The old pith helmet factories, scheduled for demolition for years, were still standing. A glance in the mirror: no-one.

The Baron parked his Giulietta in front of the watchman's hut, by a time clock now swollen with rust.

At that moment the motorbike braked. De Palma threw himself out of his car, rolled over and stood up, legs bent, aiming his Colt at the target, his left palm bracing the butt.

The gun jumped in his hands, like a toy with a mind of its own.

The first two bullets made little volcanoes of dust in the walls of the electric plant.

The driver tipped his bike over and crouched behind it. The other ran in a circle to outflank de Palma.

A third shot. A direct hit. Under the impact of the 11.43, the bike shuddered.

One hit. Two. The shells hit metal. CLANG. CLANG.

And then a great BOOM.

Heat everywhere. Hydrocarbons and benzene combined.

181

The black leather-clad body rose into the sky and bounced off the grey stones of the wall. Then it fell back, one leg over its head, disjointed by the explosion.

The Baron bent double and scurried behind the watchman's hut.

A pile of rubble hid him from the old works canteen. It smelled of tramp shit and dog piss. The fetid stench started to crawl over his skin and invade each pore.

A T.V. set wobbled under a burst of fire. The Baron felt the first kiss of death. Right in the shoulder. In the same place as last time, but deeper. He fell to the ground and saw the blood oozing between his fingers. Drops of life on his finger nails.

One bullet. Two. Three. And click.

Shit, the spare clip was in the car.

He pulled out his Bodyguard.

A .38 special. The famous police issue.

He moved forward, his pistol in his left hand. Nothing.

He waited in the silence.

How much time had gone by? Hours. An eternity. Just a few seconds. De Palma knew how time dilated.

He cocked an ear. Someone was running down the slope away from the factory, fleeing towards the ruins of the sulphur plant.

De Palma went back to the driver. With the tip of his gun, he lifted up the helmet's visor. The right eye was puffy. Vincent Lopez. Final contract.

Suddenly, he heard sirens toiling through the traffic down below, in La Capelette.

He took a few steps and sat down on the pavement. There was a smell of melted leather and petrol fumes.

When his colleagues zoomed in, de Palma stood up on his long legs, produced his police card and put his hands up.

Anne Moracchini came into the hospital room with Maistre just behind her.

"How's it going, Michel?"

She planted a kiss on his forehead. She was wearing the same musky perfume as on their night at the opera.

"It hurts, but the quack says it's nothing and I can go home tomorrow if I want."

"In any case, you shouldn't stay here, as long as this hasn't been sorted. I'm afraid the hacks have not only mentioned your name, but also the hospital where you're being treated."

"Kind of them. I hope they've also published the room number."

"You're staying at my place," Moracchini said.

"Don't take advantage . . ."

She took a chair and drew it up next to him. Delicately, she placed her hand on his.

"As soon as we found out, we went on a little trip to Aix," she said softly. "Maistre, Romero and I."

"He was there?"

"No," Maistre murmured.

"And?"

Moracchini lowered her eyes.

"His thug told us that he hasn't been seen since yesterday."

"The poor lad must be worried!"

"And so he should be," Maistre said. "Just imagine, you're sitting talking to someone, you get up for a slash, you hang around a bit because you're taking a dump as well, and when you come out again, no Morini!"

"You're kidding me!"

"You heard correctly," Moracchini said. "The heavy's name is Serge Mondolini, remember him? He's one of our regulars."

The Baron frowned.

"So, he goes to the crapper, and when he comes back Morini has vanished in a puff of smoke. He's making it up."

"I don't think so. Really I don't. He even told us that he feared the worst and would give us all the help we needed."

"I'll go and see him, in a few days' time."

"That's right, go and put your oar in," Maistre said, glancing out of the window. "Tell us where you'd like to be buried."

"Next to my father."

Moracchini stood up.

"Michel, you're going to have to choose between your friends and your bullshit. When you get out of here, you're coming to my place. And I don't want to see you hanging around La Capelette. As for Morini, we'll deal with him."

"Who knew that I lived at 102, boulevard Mireille Lauze?"

"They know lots of things."

"No, there are very few people who know that. Very, very few. Except for my close friends."

"They simply tailed you, you dummy."

"Except that, since going to see Morini, I've been really careful. I go home via traverse de la Barnière by jumping over the wall. After that, no-one can see me. So what do you think?"

"I . . . I don't know."

"Well, I do! Some fucker has been out for my blood ever since I took an interest in this case."

De Palma stopped for breath. An arrow of pain pierced his shoulder.

"This is serious, Anne. Very serious. It goes deeper than just the no-good local mob."

"Obviously what you're saying fits in with the first attempt too."

"No it doesn't."

"Why not?"

"When you use a SIG, you don't miss."

"What do you . . ." Maistre stammered.

"The first time was to scare me. This time it was to kill me."

"That's all very well, Michel, but you haven't even asked who's in charge of your case."

"And so?"

"I am," Moracchini said, with a glint of defiance in her eyes.

He looked at Maistre, who seemed lost in very distant memories.

"And our initial investigations have turned up a bullet from a SIG."

"Where did you find it?"

"On that pile of rubble, in a big lump of plaster. It had been fired in a south–north direction. In other words, it came from the one who got behind you. Not the driver, but the passenger!"

"That's the news of the day."

He took the remote control in his good hand and raised his bed to the sitting position. The doctor on duty came in.

184

"How are you feeling?"

"Fine, it just tugs a bit."

"That's normal, it's the stitches."

The doctor raised the dressing and adjusted his glasses.

"Is there anyone at home who can change dressings?"

"Yes," Moracchini said. "I've had experience."

"O.K., so you can go home if you want. I'll take out the stitches next week."

Moracchini's living room led out to a cool garden with two huge oaks at the bottom, on the bank of an old irrigation canal. She had planted some rambling roses and wisteria, as well as strewing potted plants all around it.

De Palma felt good. He watched his colleague and realised that it was the first time that he had seen her at home and entered her personal space.

She sat down next to him, with some lint and gel. As she changed the dressing, he felt her breath on the nape of his neck.

"He shot you just where he hit you the first time. He's a maniac."

She put on the lint and two strips of plaster, then rolled down his sleeve.

"Do you want a drink?"

"Yes, something strong, I've earned it."

She mixed a jug of Mojito, with crushed ice and fresh mint. They drank in silence, savouring the chilled liquid.

She had bunched her hair up over her neck, which highlighted her features and made her look like a young girl. De Palma said so, and she smiled with affection.

She told him about her father, who often paid her compliments. He was a man of few words and unfinished sentences. She had spent much of her teenage life trying to make sense of this man, whom she adored more than anything, and what he meant by the words he left hanging. He was a lawyer, born in Algeria, who reserved his eloquence for the courts.

So she came to realise that she was a woman destined for silence and contemplation.

185

"It's strange that you're now telling me about your father!"

She slapped him on his good shoulder.

"It's because you impress me, M. de Palma! So I have to defend myself as best I can."

"I impress you, do I?"

"Yes, and sometimes you should realise that."

She stood up and winked at him.

"Come on, let's go back inside. We'll be more comfortable."

She lay back on the sofa, propped up on her elbows.

"Now, you can tell me something about yourself."

"There's nothing to tell."

"What were you like as a little boy?"

De Palma rarely thought about his childhood and what he had been through with his brother. It plunged him into unending sadness. His brother had died of leukaemia, and he had nursed a sense of guilt that still had not left him: guilty of failure to help, a terrible feeling, and one that haunted him. He had never spoken about it to anyone.

"There's one memory I have of those days, it was when we used to come out of the conservatoire on place Carli after our music lessons. Our heads were full of demi-semiquavers. I don't know why, but in my memories, the sun is always setting . . . Anyway, we'd walk down to the opera house with our friends. It was magic. We went by the Gare de l'Est and bought slices of pizza from the Italian place that used to be on the corner of the Canebière. Then we'd eat them as we went through the red-light district, staring at the whores in thigh boots who would wink at us."

"Why did you go to the opera?"

"I was an extra."

"You used to sing?!"

"Extras don't sing, Anne. They're just part of the crowd, priests, guards or pages, or whatever. They play no part, but without them the show lacks sparkle. They're magnificently pointless. Can you imagine *Aïda* without the soldiers? I was a high priest with a ropy wig and foundation all over my face, standing right next to Radames. On another occasion, we executed Mario in *Tosca* . . ."

186

He fell silent. In the half-light, he was looking for an attitude of pride, something to hide behind while his feelings had time to subside.

He regaled her with tales from the stage: the terrible flops, when screwed-up programmes and loose change would rain down on the boards like drops of humiliation, and the splendid successes that made the lines of velvet seats explode.

He had spent more than eleven years on the boards of the municipal theatre; eleven years of electric warmth in the dark, secretive wings; in the white lights of the Svobodas; the warm shadings of liquid blue and ochre in the distance, stage left or right, or else on the proscenium, the only place where the gleaming, serious, anonymous faces of the audience can be seen.

Eleven years of interpreting the anxieties of opera stars during the long minutes of waiting before going on stage, the suffering that sends voices wafting above the violins and carries them right to the end, up there in the heights of the big theatre.

Moracchini suddenly realised just how much a man like this must suffer in the Marseille police force. With a gesture as soft as a sigh, she stroked his shoulder. The Baron shrank into himself.

"The world is divided in two: those who love Callas and those who love Tebaldi."

"What about you?"

"Tebaldi in *Aïda* and Callas in *Norma*."

"Trying to have it both ways are you?"

He stretched and poured himself a glass of water. She moved closer.

"When I was a kid, there were Stones fans and Beatles fans. Two different schools."

"I remember that. And so?"

"All of them were often complete idiots. Some were even top of the class, the sort who understand nothing and feel nothing unless you can stick a label on it. But luckily enough, there are also people who love music."

She drew him towards her, kissed him maternally on the lips and forehead and smiled into his eyes. He buried his face in her hair, and moved down the suntanned length of her neck.

With a heave, she turned onto her back, and a violent stab of pain in his shoulder made him cry out.

Slowly, he undid her fine silk top, freeing her heavy breasts, which he took into his hands and covered with kisses. Then, he lost himself in the hollow of her stomach and breathed in her pepper-scented closeness.

17.

De Palma gave his temples a long massage. For the past two days he had been convalescing at Jean-Louis Maistre's place, on the heights of L'Estaque. He had left Moracchini's house to avoid settling into a relationship that still scared him.

He stood up straight and breathed in deeply. The breeze was blowing the sea air up to the houses on the side of the hill.

The sky was azure as far as the eye could see. The city in the distance was white, the colour of precious shells. The seawall cut its way through the waves, looking like a huge exclamation mark at the end of a long sentence of tiny patches of land, with burning roofs and hills.

"How's life, Baron?" Maistre asked. "You haven't been too bored all day long?"

"I slept a lot. The boss wants to see me, tomorrow."

"Oh," Maistre said, pouring two pastis.

"I couldn't give a toss what they say. Anyway, they can't touch me."

"Especially when your 11.43 shells are lying in a drawer in my office."

The Baron turned towards his friend.

"Anne really loves you, I'm telling you. Between you and me, she's washed you whiter than white. If you feel you're looking like a fridge door or an aspirin, then it's down to her."

De Palma sat down on the low stone wall that Maistre had built last winter to keep in place the little earth his garden possessed.

"She even put a few shells from your piece on the scene of the crime. Not bad, don't you think?"

"I . . ."

"As far as I'm concerned, I could beat you senseless . . . What the fuck are you still doing with your 11.43? Throwing it away might have been a good idea after what happened."

When he got angry, Maistre's proletarian Parisian accent came back. He had never really lost it.

"If you're just going to get in my face, Jean-Louis, then I'm off!"

"Alright, don't get into a sulk. Anne will be here soon."

"I'm going to need another piece."

Maistre disappeared for a moment into the shade of the house, and emerged with a black box which he handed to de Palma.

"This is clean?"

"Of course it is, you idiot. It's mine, I bought it with my police pay."

"So what am I supposed to do with it?"

"It's a last resort, Michel. It's never been used, but it's been around. A Corsican sold it to me. What's more, I had the barrel and hammer changed. Not bad, eh?"

It was a snub-nosed Colt Cobra. A marvellous gun. As black as death and as slim as a dream. De Palma weighed it in his hand. He liked its bulk and its varnished wood grip. Both sober and classic.

He clicked open the cylinder and slipped in six .38 shells.

When Moracchini arrived on the patio, she glared at the Cobra while placing a soft kiss on the Baron's neck.

Just then, his mobile rang.

"M. de Palma, Ingrid Steinert here."

"Hello," he answered, moving to one side.

"I'm very worried. I read in the papers that you've been shot. And that you killed someone . . ."

"You shouldn't believe everything you read in the papers, you know."

He noticed that Moracchini was watching him and seemed to be trying to lip-read what he was saying.

"I don't know . . . I mean . . . were you wounded?"

"Nothing serious."

"When will we meet again?"

"I'll call you tomorrow. Right now, I need some rest."

"O.K., speak to you tomorrow then. Take care."

As he hung up, he felt Moracchini's gaze on his back. He turned round. She was standing just behind him.

"Was that Ingrid Steinert?"

"Yes, I must admit that I'd rather forgotten . . ."

"What did she want?"

"She'd seen in the papers that I'd killed someone and been wounded. That's all."

"We're going to have to sort a few things out with her."

"As you say . . ."

Morini lost his balance. He fell flat on his face and it took him some time to get to his feet again.

Since being locked up in total darkness, this was the second time he had fallen. First his head spun, as though he no longer knew which way was up and which down, then his huge body collapsed.

The last memory that he had of light was a flat expanse half covered in water and a white-walled hut in the background. What struck him was that his kidnapper had blindfolded him, and had only restored his sight when they arrived in this marsh.

And then pitch darkness. Not the slightest gleam of light came in from outside. He had now lost any sense of day and night. Hunger gnawed at his stomach. He was terribly thirsty.

He felt his way around the walls of his prison and located the door. He hammered on it. Several times. Just as he had done when the judge had put him in solitary in D block of Les Baumettes prison.

"Open up!"

The only answer was the enormous silence.

"Open up!" he screamed, before he broke down sobbing.

In the car, he had tried to negotiate with his abductor. He was sure he'd seen him before somewhere. Tall, with greying hair around his temples. Well into his forties. With an odd accent. This accent did not match the man's appearance. Morini had initially supposed that he was a police officer, then he wondered if he might be a mobster from a rival gang. This thought process had lasted for about a minute.

He had tried to sweet-talk him, then he had got irritated and turned to threats. Until the man gave him a thunderous slap and gagged him.

Jesus! He'd been caught like a baby. That thought tormented him even more than the thirst. He had mistaken a gangster for a cop. Even worse: he had failed to distinguish between a gangster and a raving lunatic.

His instinct had deserted him.

He told himself that he no longer deserved to live.

18.

Above La Balme farmhouse, the last glimmers of day were covering the limestone crests of the Alpilles with red lace.

Maistre's 205, covered with dust and with wrecked shock absorbers, bounded over the last rock in its path. But it was better than the Alfa Romeo, which everyone now seemed to recognise.

That morning, de Palma had gone to see Brissonne. His grass had not been very reassuring. Morini had lost it after their visit and had almost killed Lopez with his bare hands. The underworld was buzzing with their meeting. But the contract had been put out by Lopez, not Morini.

Brissonne also had a warning for de Palma: Morini had well and truly vanished, and people were wondering who was behind his disappearance. The big guns were going to start doing the talking in a few days' time if he did not resurface. A mob war was going to break out. It was inevitable.

"You should make yourself scarce, Paulo. Take a few days off!"

"I'm going on a trip to Italy. I've got a few friends there."

The mobster frowned at the Baron.

"Watch out for yourself, Michel. There's a storm brewing, and you know what that means."

Madame Steinert was alone, wearing a black blouse and a thin floral skirt that clung to her slim figure. She was walking slowly beside the pool, with bare feet.

De Palma got out of the 205. Instinctively, he checked that the Cobra was there on his hip, then glanced all around before going towards her.

She waved and came to meet him.

When they were close, she extended her cheek to him. For the first time.

"It's good to see you, Michel. Those journalists are idiots. The way they put it, it sounded as though you were at death's door. It's *furchtbar* . . . awful."

"It was just a flesh wound."

"I hope so."

Her voice was deeper than usual and she did not look straight at him. Instead, she gazed at the turquoise surface of the pool.

"I asked to see you because I think I've got something new to tell you."

"Really?"

"Yes, but first, let's have a little drink. What do you say, Michel?"

He felt awkward and simply nodded.

On the patio, she rang a small bell and a young woman emerged from the kitchen. She said something in German to her, and de Palma realised that this was the first time that he had heard her speak the language. He found it rather pleasant.

"I'd like you to try the white Muscat that we make here. It was William's idea. He had preserved an old vine behind the pool house over there. I must say that it's really good. It's my favourite."

The Baron's throat was dry. He drank back half of his glass at once. The sweet wine filled his mouth with a bouquet of honey. She winked at him.

"You're my guest this evening. Do you know the Val d'Enfer?"

"No."

"It's a mysterious place below Les Baux. Taven the Witch is supposed to have spent time there."

"My father used to tell me stories about witches."

"Was it him who introduced you to Cathy and Heathcliff?"

The Baron put down his glass, and clumsily knocked an olive onto the ground.

"Yes, it was him. How . . ."

"I'm good at guessing things. William was always impressed by my gift."

"You also have a good memory."

194

"Yes, sometimes. When people interest me."

She raised the Muscat to her lips.

"I wanted to invite you to have dinner with me in a restaurant near Val d'Enfer. What do you say?"

"I don't know if I should accept!"

"Unless you'd prefer to eat here. Our cook, Robert, has made a pistou soup which is like nothing you've ever tasted before. So what will it be: gastronomy or simplicity?"

"Simplicity," he said.

"I'm touched by your tastes."

She stood up and went into the living room. He watched her supple sway and thought that fate had played a hell of a trick on him between the shanty town of La Capelette and the farmhouse of La Balme.

He filled his lungs with air full of the fragrance of olive trees and ripe grapes. The image of his mother placing the tub in the kitchen to give him his evening bath crossed his mind. He could picture himself again in that soapy water with his grazed knees and black hands after playing knucklebones in the primary school playground on rue Laugier. The tub and coal stove had four rooms to heat.

He stood up and walked over to the pool. A cricket was picking out a melody somewhere in the clump of lavender.

A delicate hand was placed on his forearm.

"I'd like to show you something, if you wouldn't mind."

"No, not at all."

She had changed and was now wearing a very simple pale pink dress that revealed her shoulders and stopped above her knees.

They went into the building through the main entrance. De Palma recognised the reception room where she had welcomed him the first time he had visited the farm. Then he followed her to the first floor up a broad white-stone staircase of a quite surprising sobriety. No decorations, no frills. The whitewash smelled old.

Here, too, William Steinert had not wanted to change a thing. No doubt to preserve the memory of the mother he had never known.

"I want to show you a few documents that I found this week while I was sorting through William's things."

195

She opened the door of a large room which had been furnished as a lounge or reception room, with a billiard table in the middle, settees upholstered in Marseille piqué, and knick-knacks all around: a chess set on an occasional table, an old pinball machine and a 1950s Wurlitzer jukebox. There were oil paintings everywhere.

She noticed that he had paused for a moment.

"Do you like the style?"

"It's one hell of a mixture!"

"They're all collector's pieces. William used to call it his museum. Everything you see here was picked up in markets across the world. They're real rarities. I wanted you to see them so that you could understand what sort of man he was."

In a glass case, he noticed some wax cylinders, a letter signed by Blaise Cendrars and some Egyptian and Greek antiquities. There was also a statue measuring about a metre high.

"It's a marble kouros."

It was smiling into eternity, its lips raised at the corners of a stone mouth.

"It's from the end of the archaic period. It's magnificent. There are many museums that envy us."

"The line is simple, but perfect. It looks like the Rampin Horseman."

"Are you a connoisseur, Michel?"

"An old memory from history at university. I loved Greek art."

"Oh, I see . . ."

She drew nearer to him, as though seeking greater closeness.

"Would you like another glass of Muscat?"

"Yes please," he replied, without taking his eyes off the kouros.

"Come and sit down. Laura will bring us the necessary."

She sat down in an armchair and crossed her legs. Slightly embarrassed by her stare, which never left him, the Baron sat down opposite her.

"Why did you join the police, Michel?"

"It's funny. Every time I trot out the little culture I possess, I'm asked the same question."

"That's fair enough, isn't?"

"Yes, perhaps . . ."

"But you still haven't answered."

"Because I come from a poor neighbourhood in Marseille, and I didn't have much choice."

"I think we always have a choice."

"Maybe. But you may have to be more courageous than I am."

"It isn't a question of courage. But why did you stay?"

It was an ordinary question, but it took him unawares.

"Perhaps because of a girl who looked strangely like you."

"Could you explain?"

"I can't."

"She's dead, isn't she?"

Laura arrived carrying a tray with two glasses of Muscat. De Palma took one, and took his chance to stand up.

"She's dead and you never found her killer. Am I right?"

"I . . . I'd rather not talk about it. If you don't mind."

"I quite understand. Come on, I'll show you something."

At the far end of the room, there was an art deco-style table with curved legs, on which Ingrid had placed a whole pile of papers and photographs.

The photographs were shots of the Camargue. De Palma saw lagoons that disappeared over the horizon in the light of dawn or dusk. There were also some shots of birds: raptors, herons, and other species he did not know.

He paused over some photographs of large white birds.

"They're white spoonbills. The last pictures he took, as far as I know. Laura went to fetch them from Tarascon today."

"They're magnificent."

"Yes they are, aren't they?"

"Did the photographer say which day your husband dropped the film off?"

"The day he disappeared. June 24. I thought that might tell you things."

"And you're quite right. So we're now sure that he vanished on the 24th. What are these documents?"

"They're notes he left in his car. The police didn't take them away."

De Palma read:

1 – *La Capelière. At the far end of the large meadow? Turn left then right towards the dead tree in the water. Ten metres to the left. In the coppice.*
2 – *From the guardian's hut, towards the marsh.*

"They look like directions, don't they, Michel?"

"One of them gives the exact place where he was found."

"I hadn't noticed that."

On another piece of paper, which was folded in four, Steinert had written:

Rush hut number 2, well hidden after the reed bed. A good place for sunrise. Mention it to Christophe.

"Did your husband often make notes like this?"

"All the time. His memory wasn't very good, he was always forgetting things, so he kept notes."

"Do you know this Christophe?"

"It's Texeira, the director of the reserve. We've met once or twice."

She put the photographs back into their envelope.

"There, that's all I wanted to show you. The rest is just snippets of his existence, nothing of any great interest."

"In a life, everything is of interest."

She stared at him with a little girl's eyes.

"Come on, Michel. Let's have some of that famous pistou soup. We'll talk about something cheerful. William wouldn't have liked us to be sad."

19.

Maistre's investigations into the career of the SIG had so far not been conclusive, except in discovering that the proper series number had not been recorded on the list of exhibits from the grocery hold-up. That was why he'd had trouble locating it. The number recorded by the police differed from that used in court. In the paperwork of criminal justice and the police, the weapon no longer existed. Maistre had never seen such a disappearing act.

This was also why he had decided to take his time, and avoid arousing colleagues' suspicions. Because one of them was involved in this story, and sooner or later he knew that he would find him.

Late in the afternoon, the Baron was driving through the sweltering heat of the Vaccarès reserve. Texeira had called him: the voices had returned.

Along the banks of the lagoon, there was an overwhelming smell of dead algae and dried-up slime. Every available space along the road was occupied by a mobile home or caravan. Some holiday-makers were Dutch, others were German, with red thighs and faces consumed by the sun.

He turned onto the road to La Capelière before parking the 205 between two tourist coaches.

The reed bed was rustling in the furnace. The tips of the reddened canes swayed almost imperceptibly, moved by an invisible breeze.

Texeira was standing in the middle of a group. He was handing out brochures and visitors' guides to the reserve. When he looked up, he saw de Palma waving at him.

"I'm coming, I'm coming . . ."

De Palma signalled him to take his time, before retreating from the sun into the ecology museum. Texeira joined him a few minutes later.

"Good afternoon, M. de Palma. I'm up to my neck right now. But come to my office in five minutes' time and we can talk."

The Baron decided to explore the museum a little. He had a good look at an exhibit showing the composition of the flora in the marshes. He had had no idea that there were so many different species of plants, and especially algae.

When he had finished, he bought a plan of the reserve, a brochure about the birds of the Camargue and an ordnance survey map of the area.

Texeira was in his office looking through his binoculars when the Baron appeared in the doorway.

"We've now got all the time we need. I suppose you're here about the voices."

"That's right."

The biologist stowed away the Petri dishes that were scattered over the draining board. Then he placed both his hands on his binoculars.

"I heard voices. It was past one o'clock. They were coming from the far side of the marsh, from around the old hut. There were voices and footsteps."

"And what were they saying, these voices?"

"It's very hard to say!"

"Why?"

"Because I think it was in Provençal, or something like that."

"Provençal?"

"Yes, they said: *La Tarasco, la Tarasco . . . Lou Castéou*. The Tarasque, in other words. That much I understood. And it does sound like Provençal, don't you think? The rest, I can't tell you. I just can't remember."

"One voice or several?"

"I think there were two, because one was high and the other lower."

"Did Steinert mention these voices to you?"

"No, why?"

"Just asking."

Texeira sat down on a swivel-chair. He folded his arms and raised his shoulders.

"I did say I'd keep you informed. But I don't see what can be important about all this. There are just some idiots who come here to kick up a din at night. There are so many loonies around these days."

"Another thing: why didn't you tell me right away that you knew Steinert well?"

"I was cross with myself afterwards. I was being selfish. I didn't want any trouble, that's all. Anyway, what I know about him is quite irrelevant."

The Baron gestured broadly to tell him to stop making excuses.

"Tell me about him instead. What was he like?"

Texeira took off his glasses and started to clean the lenses with the lapels of his white coat.

"He was a very impressive character, even if you didn't quite know who he was. When he turned up here in the evening, before bivouacking in the marshes, he used to speak about all sorts of things and – how can I put it? – he was radiant. He had a presence, with quite exceptional magnetism. A great, very great man . . ."

"You seem to have respected him."

"We had the same opinions about ecology, the protection of animals . . ."

"Meaning?"

"He thought, like me, that we can't ignore the human factor, that ecology is a whole, and that protecting nature also means protecting a region's cultural and human heritage. I know that he fought hard for that, especially when it came to archaeology. He was always up in arms against this or that mayor of some town in the backwoods of Provence. If wanted to, he had the means to make their lives difficult, but he always preferred to negotiate. He was a good listener. When I spoke to him, he attended to what I said as though he was a student. It was rather impressive when you bear in mind that he was a real capitaine of industry in his country."

"Do you know his wife?"

"No. In fact, he never mentioned her."

"But she says that she's met you!"

"Honestly, I don't remember that."

"You mentioned his campaigns. Could you tell me anything more about that, or give me some examples?"

"That will be hard, he was quite discreet about his concrete actions. But I do know that he forced the gendarmes to investigate the world of seasonal workers. There are loads of illegal immigrants around here. It's a real form of slavery."

De Palma leaned against the bookcase, and a dark gleam lit up his face.

"Did he come here alone?"

"Yes, always alone. He would park his huge 4×4 beside my car then come up to see me. But he never came here when there was a crowd."

"Did you ever wonder why?"

"I asked him and he told me that he didn't like the company of tourists. They were what he hated the most."

De Palma went over to the window and looked out at the marshes.

"M. Texeira, do you still have my phone number?"

"Yes, of course. It's in my diary."

"If you ever hear these voices again, call me at once."

"O.K. As you want. Is it that important?"

"I don't know. But I do think that it's far more important than you imagine."

The Baron wiped his forehead with his handkerchief.

"Are you here every night at that time?"

"Yes, usually."

"And are you asleep then?"

"I never go to bed before about half-past one or two."

"Now, could you show the place where these voices were coming from?"

"Follow me."

On the path that ran beside the reed bed, the earth was as hard as old cement, and covered in cracks despite the recent rain. Texeira strode ahead rapidly. From time to time, he glanced towards the creek.

"The level is going down," he said, pointing at the water which was frothing like detergent.

They entered a clump of ash trees. Texeira turned left, went up some wooden steps that were hidden among the trees and vanished into a hide. Panting, de Palma did likewise.

"Here we are. The voices came from the far side of the marsh. Over there, in that large reed bed."

"What exactly did you hear?"

"As I told you, two voices, some words in Provençal, and some noises."

"What sort of noises?"

"Splashing, the sound of feet in water . . ."

"And then?"

"That's all. They sang, then everything stopped."

"They sang?"

Texeira looked annoyed by the officer's avalanche of questions.

"Yes, so what?" he said with a sigh.

"Look, M. Texeira, you hear voices in a place where no-one can go, then you tell me that people were singing, and after that, that there were sounds of splashing . . . and all this subsequent to someone being found dead on your reserve in extremely suspicious circumstances. You also forget to tell me that you knew this person. Do you see now why I'm asking questions?"

"I'm sorry, M. de Palma, really I am, but I thought these kinds of detail wouldn't really interest you, and then I didn't want to have to deal with you."

"How can someone get over there?"

"Actually, I've never been there and don't see how anyone could without getting soaked."

"In a boat, perhaps?"

"We'll take the reserve's punt."

The marsh was a good hundred metres wide by two hundred long. It lay amid practically virgin territory, which seemed to be returning to life as the sun set.

At the far side of the pool, an egret took flight, slapping the surface of the water with the tips of its wings.

Texeira stood up in the flat-bottomed punt and pushed with a long pole, which sank deep into the silt, making wide brown stains in the greenish water.

In under five minutes, they arrived at the edge of the reed bed. De Palma made to stand up, but Texeira stopped him short.

"Watch out, there's quicksand around here. Let's look for a patch of solid earth then move slowly. If you see any birds on the ground, try not to frighten them. They've taken up their quarters for the night."

They crept around the reed bed in a northerly direction. Texeira tested the ground on the bank, metre by metre. It was only after a hundred metres that the punt touched bottom.

Texeira prodded a few more times, then nodded: they were now on a sand bank that emerged from the water in the middle of the reed bed.

When they leaped over board, de Palma laid his hand on Texeira's shoulder.

"Thanks for all this. Now we'll have to keep our eyes peeled. The slightest thing you find unusual, please show me."

"No problem."

"I'll follow in your footsteps. Take your time, because you'll probably notice things that I wouldn't. I'm counting on you."

Texeira advanced slowly. Soon they were standing in about ten centimetres of water. All around, the Baron observed hordes of creatures that were unknown to him. All around him, the marsh was crawling with life.

Suddenly, Texeira stopped.

"There are some footprints here."

De Palma walked over and saw on a strip of earth that rose above the water the trace of a footprint: a man's, with size eight or nine shoes. There was just one, because the person who left it must have walked through the water, just as they were doing now. A footprint made by a sole with crampons, and which was easily recognisable to a knowledgeable eye – Vibram soles.

"This is a real surprise," Texeira said. "You can't come here unless you really know the place well."

De Palma regretted not having brought a camera with him. He removed a piece of paper from his pocket and stuck it on a reed stalk. Then he produced his notepad and made a rough sketch showing the direction of the foot: just about due north, according to Texeira's indications.

"Let's go on."

"We can't be that far from the hut."

They walked on a few metres further. The reeds grew less dense and opened out onto a second marsh, smaller than the first. In the distance, a reed hut with rather dingy white walls stood on a mound of earth between two poplars.

"How many huts are there like this one?"

"Just two."

"And have you ever been inside this one?"

"No, I must admit I haven't. It's silly, but that's the way it is. One of my students went in last year. And he told me that there wasn't much there. It's just another hut. Also, it's not in a very good position for observation. Ever since they've dammed the stream you saw earlier, the water has risen here and you can't get to it by foot."

"O.K.," de Palma said. "Let's try it anyway."

"In that case, we'll go back to the punt and carry it to here."

Half an hour later, de Palma and Texeira set foot on the mound and went over to the hut. They walked all around it before going inside.

It was an oval room. In the middle stood an old table gnawed by wood lice. There were three chairs with broken straw seats, an ancient haversack and some glasses full of dust.

De Palma scrutinised every nook and cranny. The only thing of interest that he found were traces of a recent presence. Very recent, judging by the marks that could be seen, especially in the dust on the table.

The earth floor had been swept, and then the traces of the broom removed. When he bent down, he saw that it had been cleaned recently.

No more than three or four days ago, he thought.

Texeira called him from outside.

"Look."

On the bank, the earth had been turned over and the sand below the water ploughed up by someone or something.

"It's as if a large animal has been blundering around."

"Which would explain the sounds of splashing," Texeira said, pointing at the marks.

"And you heard that noise the second time?"

"No, probably because I was further away. Or maybe because I didn't pay attention."

The traces on the bank were also recent. They went down into the water and vanished into the silt. And yet some hollow, wedge-shaped marks could still be seen. The water of the marsh had dug deeper around the marks.

De Palma noticed that on the bank everything that might have been recognisable had been wiped away. That much was clear.

A heron landed on a dead tree which was rocking on the grey waters. At that moment, the natural world quivered. On the tips of the reeds, a pink light glittered briefly. The sun was setting, in the distance, on the far bank of the Vaccarès.

"No, Michel, I can't answer that! I don't know if William was a freemason or not. He was very discreet about his private life. And don't imagine that I was part of his private life."

Mme Steinert was agitated. Her hair was still damp. She had tied it up over her neck, and secured it with an ebony chopstick.

After leaving the Vaccarès, de Palma had gone to see her at La Balme. He had warned Maistre that he would be back late that night. Maistre had grumbled, Moracchini had thrown a fit of jealousy, and the Baron had done as he pleased.

"I'm sorry to disturb you for so little reason. I'll go."

"You're not disturbing me, Michel. I want you to stay to dinner."

"I'm afraid of upsetting you with all my questions."

"Not at all. Don't forget that I was the one who put you in this position."

De Palma squirmed in his chair.

"Have you heard from Chandeler?"

"No, not since I decided to dispense with his services."

"And may I ask why you decided to fire him?"

"Quite simply because he was too greedy. Too voracious. In fact, he only handled a tiny part of the family's business."

From her frown, de Palma guessed that Chandeler had probably tried his luck with her and had been turned down.

"Can you tell me more about the Downlands?"

"We could go for a stroll there."

"But it's nighttime!"

"Then we'll go tomorrow."

"Tomorrow?"

"That is, if you agree to sleep over at the farmhouse. There's plenty of room to spare, you know."

All the Baron did in answer was to gaze up at the white drystone walls pierced by little windows. The house had three floors. On the top one, a few of the windows glowed in the darkness. They must be the servants' quarters.

"Did you ever wonder why your husband was so determined to keep this place as it is?"

"I'm sorry?"

"Why he didn't want to change anything, or hardly anything?"

The question had caught her unawares. She seemed almost upset, as though he had just made her realise that she had never really worried about her husband's strange behaviour.

"I don't know. I think that he was very concerned about authenticity."

"There was more to it than that."

Her turquoise eyes peered at him cautiously. Then, slowly, she picked up a cigarette, placed it in her lips and flicked open her lighter.

"It's because William was the son of the house's former owner, Mme Maurel."

Ingrid put her lighter down slowly, and looked at him hard. Clearly, she had not known the truth. She looked away. He saw that her eyes were shining.

"I didn't want to shock you, but I think I owe you the truth."

She undid her hair and let it tumble down, still damp, onto her golden shoulders. Then she folded her hands over her chest with a gesture of self-protection and squeezed hard.

"I'm not blaming you. That was the real problem with William. He hid so much from me. I think you can now understand . . . life with him wasn't easy."

She stood up and paced towards the swimming pool. Her dark shadow undulated over the blue surface.

"It was Bérard who told you that, I suppose?"

"Yes."

"He knows a lot of things about my husband."

"Yes, it would seem so. I think you should go and see him."

Suddenly, she looked fragile. She trembled. A wrinkle appeared on her forehead. She stubbed out her cigarette.

"I . . . stay here tonight, Michel. This . . . this isn't an invitation, it's a demand. Do me this service . . ."

"I don't want you to consider it as a service."

"In my world . . . I mean, in my . . . Um . . . I feel really clumsy this evening."

She put her hand back onto her cigarette case and took out another, which she lit and dragged on deeply. De Palma realised that he did not like seeing her smoke. It made her seem too familiar. He looked away.

"One day, I was summoned to what we call the scene of the crime. It was years ago. When I'd just joined the force. I was in Paris. And I can remember it like it was yesterday.

"Her name was Isabelle Mercier. She was sixteen. Blonde . . . a beautiful girl. Or rather, I didn't know that till later, if you see what I mean. When I saw the photos and films that her father agreed to show us.

"I've searched for a long time. A very long time. Without ever letting up. I have entire books full of notes and statements. Ever since, I've been out to get the person who made her suffer what she went through . . . And I might die like this! But I'll never stop searching. I'll construct a thousand different scenarios. I may never find the right one, but that's just too bad. You know, it's rather like an endless quest."

She drew heavily on her cigarette then stubbed it out in the ashtray.

"She looked like you, Ingrid. The resemblance is terrible. Terrible."

"Stop it, Michel, you're scaring me."

She crossed the living room then stopped in a doorway that presumably led to what she called her "private domain".

"Goodnight, Michel. You'll find your room on the first floor, opposite the lounge you're already familiar with. I'll see you tomorrow."

She let her arm drop down beside her, then vanished into her own quarters.

Morini tried to lift himself up on his arms, but failed. His muscles had melted away. His legs were barely responding any longer.

He remembered the voices that he had heard the day before, or just now. This morning or last night. It made no difference.

The voices had been so distant it was as if they were being filtered through thick layers of cotton. He remembered yelling out, but he wondered if his voice had not remained stuck to his lips, or in the depths of his burning throat.

After that, he had drunk his urine and his thirst had eased off for a while. But only for a while. Before long, an acidic slime had built up in his mouth and on the edge of his tongue.

But he could clearly remember the voices. One had said: "Everything's been cleaned up here", or something like that. And the other one: "There are still some traces in the water." They were two men who did not know each other very well, to judge by the way they spoke.

Of that he was sure.

He fell asleep, exhausted by this effort of recall. An enormous racket woke him up. A sound of splashing in the water, just on the other side of his prison wall.

And then a song surged up into the darkness. As high-pitched as a child's voice.

"*Lagadigadeu, la tarasco, lagadigadeu . . .*"

And then a second, far deeper voice. Like the cry of a farmer calling in his herd.

"Laïssa passa la vieio masco . . . Laïssa passa que vaï dansa . . ."
The two voices then blended into a strange duet:
"La tarasco dou casteu, la tarasco dou casteu . . ."
This chant brought back fond memories. It was the song that the Knights of the Tarasque sang when pushing their papier-mâché monster through the streets of Tarascon, before charging the terrified crowd.

And him, Morini, in the pure white uniform of the Knights, with a musketeer's hat. He had been a little boy the first time he had seen the Tarasque, raised on tiptoe, his chin resting on the windowsill.

He swore that if he ever got out of this alive, then the amusement park would be named after the Tarasque. He was Le Grand. The person everyone listened to. Whom everyone obeyed.

He would have liked to remain a Knight of the Tarasque . . . if prison hadn't interfered with his fate. Since he had left the monster, there had been a void in his life. That was why he had put so much effort into the Big South.

The park must carry the stamp of the monster. Or at least its image. With entertainments wholly devoted to it. His father would have liked that idea. Not his mother, but he did not care about that.

The ceiling of the prison opened suddenly. Earth fell down onto his face.

A fierce light struck his eyes like a slap. A superhuman force seized him and dragged him up into the dark sky.

De Palma woke early. The farmhouse was deserted. He went out onto the patio and savoured the fading freshness of the morning. The farm workers had gathered around a huge tractor in the garage and were discussing the coming day's work.

An intense light surged up between the breasts of the Alpilles. In under an hour, La Balme would be inside the furnace.

He looked at his watch and found that it had stopped during the night; it still said 11.30, the time he had gone to bed.

He took out his mobile, switched it on and found that he had nine messages. The recorded voice told him that the first message had been left at eighteen minutes past midnight.

"M. de Palma, Christophe Texeira. I'm sorry to bother you so late, but the voices are back again. Call me back as soon as you get this message."

He cursed himself for having turned off his telephone while in Ingrid's company.

He listened to the others. They were all from Texeira, who had tried to contact him all night at various times; the last message had been at 2.19 a.m.

He telephoned him back at once.

"I heard them around midnight."

"Midnight?"

"Yes, that's right. The same routine in Provençal again. But this time I had a great idea: I recorded them."

"How's the result?"

"Come and listen!"

De Palma did not wait to say goodbye to Mme Steinert. He got into the 205 and made straight for La Capelière.

There was thunder in the air. Clouds were drifting up from the sea and gathering over the vast meadows of La Crau and the swamps of the Camargue.

When he turned into chemin de la Capelière, heavy drops exploded onto the Peugeot's dusty bonnet.

Texeira was waiting in the little museum's doorway. De Palma ran over to him.

"Good to see you, M. de Palma!"

"Good to see you too!"

"Let's not waste any time, come inside."

Texeira placed a small tape recorder on his desk, of the kind the Baron had often seen in old-fashioned listening devices.

"It's a Nagra," Texeira said with a hint of pride in his voice. "And here's the magic microphone."

He showed him a long mike, rather like the ones used by the police during stake-outs. It had SENNHEISER printed on its body in chrome letters.

"It's old, but when used with this parabola the results are quite extraordinary. We use it to record birdsong."

211

"Great," said de Palma, who was losing his patience.

"An ancient piece of kit, but effective! And here's what I recorded."

He pressed 'play'.

The first sounds were of footfalls and breathing. Like someone in a big hurry.

"That's me, running to get as near to the voices as possible."

Then, suddenly, the footsteps stopped . . . Texeira's panting could still be heard, then nothing. The biologist had presumably turned the mike in the opposite direction.

"Here we go."

At first, there was the sound of a heavy tread through fairly deep water. Someone or something was going through the marsh at a distance that de Palma couldn't estimate. Then the sound stopped, just a faint splashing before the first voice started up. It was so sharp and strange that de Palma recoiled from the machine:

"Lagadigadeu, la tarasco, lagadigadeu . . ."

There was a loud noise of water, as though something was stirring in the depths of the swamp, followed by a second far deeper voice:

"Laïssa passa la vieio masco . . . Laïssa passa que vaï dansa . . ."

The two voices joined together like a terrifying choir in the middle of the night and the marshes.

"La tarasco dou casteu, la tarasco dou casteu . . ."

There were other sounds that de Palma could not really identify. It sounded like footsteps in mud, but he wasn't sure.

The two voices rose again in the night.

"La tarasco dou casteu, la tarasco dou casteu . . ."

De Palma noticed that the two men had apparently moved; their voices had grown muffled. They had moved away from the mike, either going into the undergrowth or behind a wall.

"They went into the hut," he exclaimed.

"You think so?"

"It's a possibility."

"Hang on, the worst is yet to come."

Texeira turned up the volume.

"This microphone can often pick up things that are inaudible to the human ear."

There was a strangled cry. It was barely discernible, but de Palma knew it at once: the last screams of a man being put to death.

Texeira stopped the tape. His hand was trembling.

"That's all. There's nothing after that."

"Can you play the last minute again?"

The Baron listened with his eyes closed. He mentally reconstructed the scene, as captured by the mike in the darkness of the swamp.

"Christophe, have you been back to the hut?"

"No, I remembered what you told me."

"I think that you've just saved your life."

"Really?"

"One hundred per cent sure."

Texeira looked him up and down.

"I suggest we take a look at the hut. Do you have time?"

"Not really. But I must admit that I'm dying with curiosity."

For over an hour, the sea breeze had been driving the stink of the cellulose factory on the Rhône back up towards Tarascon.

Despite the few drops of storm rain, it was still hot. The heat seemed trapped in a bag that nothing could penetrate.

When he saw the crowd that had gathered, Marceau quickly wiped the sweat from his forehead. He had some trouble making his way through the onlookers before finally reaching the heavy doors of Saint Martha's church.

The officer who opened them for him was looking suitably grim. Once inside, an old veteran whom Marceau had known from the territorial brigade pointed to where the action had happened.

At the far end of the apse, the forensic team had stretched a yellow tape across and placed a few markers. The gate leading to the crypt was open. Marceau noticed blue glimmers rising from the underground depths of the church: the technicians were using a CrimeScope to scan the scene on wavelengths invisible to the naked eye.

Marceau kept his distance, allowing the forensics team to finish its painstaking work.

"Oh, you're here!" Larousse said, looking as rough as he always did when something important had happened. "We've managed to limit the damage in the press."

"What have you told them?"

"That a visitor had discovered the lifeless body of a tourist, and for the moment the police are pursuing their investigations."

"Why, isn't that true?"

"You mean you don't know?"

"I was on leave yesterday."

Larousse took Marceau by the arm and drew him to one side.

"It's the same scenario as last time."

"Christian Rey?"

Larousse nodded.

"The body was discovered by a visitor, just after opening time. A Danish tourist called Thomas Nielsen. But this time we've got a really big fish on our hands. Morini. How does that grab you?"

"Morini!"

"Indeed. After Rey, his lieutenant, we now have the boss himself. Who's going to be next?"

"So you think we've got a serial killer on our hands?"

"What would you call it?"

Marceau glanced round at the crypt. Larousse turned towards him.

"Where are you at with Rey?"

"We've got the D.N.A. results."

"And?"

"Unknown D.N.A. on the wounds."

"And so?"

"So we have some totally unknown D.N.A."

"What do you mean by that?" Larousse snapped.

"I mean that it is traces of saliva that were found."

Larousse stared up towards the ceiling of the church. He took a deep breath.

"And you have made all the necessary comparisons with other D.N.A. . . . I don't know, say . . ."

"Saliva on a wound generally indicates a bite."

"Do you realise the size of the wound, Marceau?"

Jean-Claude raised his hands before letting them drop again.

"I called Nantes last night. They do very good work, but this time they have no idea. No idea at all."

"What about the genetic records?"

"Nothing doing either. D.N.A. unknown."

A member of the forensic team appeared in the entry to the crypt. He took off his gloves and mask and threw them into a yellow box. After that, he beckoned to Larousse and Marceau.

"Hi, Jean-Claude, how are things?"

"I'm getting by. How about you?"

"It's not a pretty sight down there. Jesus, I've never seen anything like it!"

"Can we go down?"

"Right away. We've just finished."

Larousse and Marceau put on their gloves and overshoes then walked through the Gothic door.

As they went down the steps, Marceau felt the stench grip his throat. He stopped and put on the gasmask that the technician held out to him.

"What a fucking stink."

Larousse was behind Marceau and squinting over his mask, which gave him a pig's snout.

A little lower down, the photographer was taking several pictures of a bloodstain on the railings of the tomb of the chevalier Jean de Cossa.

When they got to the crypt, Marceau stopped dead.

Morini's body was placed in front of the sarcophagus that contained the remains of Saint Martha. His head lay with its left cheek pressed against the flagstones, looking towards the monument with bulging eyes. The bottom of his torso and his legs were missing. Marceau's gaze was liquid and brimming with anger.

"Have you got anything to tell me?" he asked the technician.

"Sure, where would you like me to begin?"

"Tell me about the wound. I'll read the report for the rest of it."

"It's the first time I've ever seen a wound like that," the technician replied, shaking his head. "Just look."

They bent over the body.

"You get the impression that the flesh has been torn away. The inner organs have gone. It's a completely empty torso."

Marceau pointed at a whitish gleam on the blood.

"And what's that?"

"It looks like either saliva or semen, I can't tell yet. But I'd say it was saliva."

Larousse was standing to one side and looking away from the body. Marceau stood up slowly and stared at Saint Martha laid out on her deathbed: her fine, delicate figure draped in marble. Her face was spattered with blood and her body crisscrossed with brown marks, as though the madman who had desecrated the shrine had tried to scratch the stone.

"The death certainly occurred last night. I think the body was left here early this morning. Probably between eight and nine o'clock."

"Are you sure?"

"Almost. Some of the bloodstains aren't quite dry yet."

"Not coagulated?"

"Yes, coagulated, but not completely dry."

"Which means that the body was brought here just after the murder. At most thirty or forty minutes later. Otherwise, the blood would already have coagulated and there wouldn't be all these stains."

"I completely agree."

"Also, he transported it in a bag or something like that. There are no traces anywhere else."

"Good point," said Larousse. "So what's your conclusion?"

"I don't have one," Marceau said, gravely. "Nothing at all. Morini must have been slaughtered not far from here, then his body was brought here and staged like this. Where's the priest?"

"He's in the sacristy. Delmastro is questioning him."

"I want to see him at once."

Above the saint's head, the inscription *Sollicita non turbatur* had been crossed out with several streaks of blood.

"*Sollicita non turbatur*?" Marceau read. "Does anyone know what that means?"

"I lost my Latin years ago," Larousse replied.

"But it seems to have meant something to him. Look at how he crossed out the words."

"Whatever happens, not a word to the press for now," said Larousse. "I don't want to see a single hack in the vicinity."

The Commissaire turned on his heels and went back upstairs. Marceau stepped back and observed the entire scene. This was a vision like none he had ever witnessed before. Morini had been left like a sacrifice at the feet of a saint who was particularly loved in Tarascon. This staging must contain the answer to this slaughter.

Back on the surface, Marceau tore off his mask and gloves.

"I've just had a call from the prosecutor," Larousse told him. "This case is being given to the *Police Judiciaire*. There's nothing more for us to do here."

"I was expecting that." Marceau cursed as he threw away the gloves.

"They'll be here any moment now."

"Who's on it?"

"Moracchini. Plus someone I don't know called Romero."

"I know Moracchini, but not the other."

"Sorry, Marceau, but this is too big for us. This is the second gangster we've found half eaten. We don't have the resources for this kind of thing. The prosecutor's right. It's a case for the P.J. At least that way we're in the clear."

De Palma took an initial photograph of the sandbank, then a second of the thin band of earth that wove through the reed bed.

Texeira had lent him the digital camera that belonged to the reserve. The Baron checked the image, then walked on.

"Same principle as last time, Christophe. The slightest detail could be important. Even the smallest."

Texeira stared at the ground and frowned. A quarter of an hour later, they were standing in front of the footprint they had discovered the day before. No-one had touched the marker de Palma had left there.

He took three more photographs, then he placed the measuring

217

rod that Texeira handed him next to the print and took another snapshot.

After a further fifteen minutes, they reached the stretch of water that lay between them and the reed hut.

There was not the slightest breath of air. The only sounds being made by the rotting life of the swamp came from bubbles rising from the depths of the silt and bursting on the surface.

The Baron signalled to Texeira to crouch down.

"Look closely," he said. "Has anything changed?"

Texeira gazed towards the hut. He took his time before answering.

"The door," he said.

"Exactly."

"Last time, it was closed. I shut it, in fact."

Half an hour later, they set foot on the mound of earth that the hut stood on. The Baron took out his Cobra and motioned to Texeira to hang back.

He walked on gingerly, almost in slow motion, as tense as a big cat.

The ground around the hut had been meticulously cleaned. On the bank, he found the same traces as during their first visit. He decided not to linger over such details and instead go straight inside.

Gently, he pushed the door open with his foot, pointing his gun into the gloom of the hut. The door creaked loudly. Texeira followed him inside.

On the table, he noticed some finger marks. He looked closer and saw that the person who had left them had taken the precaution of wearing gloves. The dirt floor had been swept.

"I don't understand," Texeira said.

"Well I'm starting to get an idea."

"Lucky you!"

"On the tape, you can clearly hear that the voices fade away, or they're muffled."

"That's right, just before the scream."

"So let's picture the scenario: two men come in here with a third person. They are on the bank when they're singing, then they come inside."

The Baron gestured to illustrate his version.

"Why two men?"

"It's very clear on the recording, when the scream is heard. So there are three voices."

"That's true, you don't hear the third one before."

"No, you don't hear . . ." the Baron repeated thoughtfully.

"What you say is perfectly obvious when you think about it."

"Before . . . Jesus, the third person was already here!"

"Are you sure?"

"It seems the most likely scenario."

The Baron retreated to the door, took several paces outside, then came in again.

"They come in singing, then, at that moment, they strike down the person who's in here."

"Strike down?"

"And maybe killed him. Look, they've cleaned everything up."

He gazed around the floor. Then he bent down to peer beneath the table. The ground was marked with what looked like wide sweeps of a broom. He retreated again to the room as a whole, then moved closer again to peer at the traces from different angles. He took the measuring rod and scratched the floor in several places.

"It's really odd," he said. "Really it is."

Texeira observed him tensely. He didn't miss one of the policeman's gestures.

"Weird . . ."

All at once, the Baron drew some long lines in the dirt. He did it several times in all directions, and lifted some earth. He kept going until the tip of the rod hit an obstacle. Then he kneeled down and rubbed at the place the rod had hit. In less than thirty seconds, he had uncovered a trapdoor.

He stood up abruptly and pushed the table aside.

"Help me lift this thing up. Or rather, lift it up in front of me, while I keep my gun trained on what's inside. You never know."

Texeira raised the panel of wood. A fetid smell invaded the room. De Palma recognised the stench of decomposing human excrement.

Texeira produced a torch from his pocket and handed it to the Baron.

The trapdoor led to a long tunnel about a metre wide. In the torch beam, de Palma could see the entrance to an underground room at the end of the tunnel; a sort of cellar dug out of the raw earth.

"Can you see anything?"

"Nothing that exciting. We'll have to go down and see. But we won't be doing that for the moment."

He retreated, and took two snapshots. Then he photographed the interior of the passage, while Texeira held open the trap.

"We're going to leave everything as we found it, so that no-one will guess that we've been here."

Ten minutes later, they crossed back over the stretch of sleeping water. De Palma stared at the reed hut, which danced before his eyes each time Texeira pushed with his pole.

In the humid light, a buzzard emerged from a clump of stunted ash trees and poplars; it beat its wings heavily then glided above the surface of the reed bed before vanishing behind the curtain of rushes.

The bells of Saint Martha's church were ringing the angelus when Anne Moracchini and Daniel Romero parked their unmarked Xsara in front of the building.

They presented their tricolour cards to the guard on the door, who was looking increasingly confused.

"Commissaire Larousse?"

"He's just left."

"Commandant Marceau?"

"They left together in fact."

"Perfect," Moracchini said. "The P.J. always gets a warm welcome. How nice."

She went inside the church and headed straight for the entrance to the crypt.

The forensic team had put away their equipment, and the clean-up teams were ready to start.

"Where's the body?"

"It's been taken away, just five minutes ago."

"I see," Moracchini said. "They haven't heard the last of this."

She went down the crypt steps, followed by Romero. It was Romero's first real investigation with the brigade, and the squabbles had already begun.

When Moracchini saw the bloodstains on the statue of Saint Martha, she paused for breath, went over slowly and tried to picture the placing of Morini's body.

As the technicians had removed their powerful lamps, the saint's burial place had returned to its sepulchral gloom. The smell of the corpse had practically vanished.

A brigadier from the Tarascon commissariat arrived in the crypt.

"Who took the body away?"

"The emergency services. They took it to Marseille for the autopsy."

"I mean, who gave the order to move it?"

"It was Marceau, he . . ."

"O.K., O.K. . . . What time was that?"

The brigadier walked over to the light to look at his watch.

"Just half an hour ago."

The two officers looked at each other in silence.

"Pick up all the details you can, Daniel. I'm going to try and get hold of Michel. I'd like him to have a look."

"O.K., Anne. Do you want me to take some photos?"

"In this light?"

"I've got flash."

"Try it, and if not you ask them to put the juice back on."

The team of cleaners appeared in the doorway, two black figures in the blue gleam.

"Don't touch anything," Moracchini said, pointing at them. "Go back upstairs at once."

"Commandant Marceau . . ."

"I don't give a shit about your Commandant Whatsisname. We're from the P.J. and I've been mandated by the prosecutor of Tarascon, clear? And I'm ordering you to go back upstairs."

The two officers did not wait to be told twice.

"Do you want me to call Marceau, Madame?" the brigadier asked.

"I'll have him sent for . . . if he wants to play games like this, then I'll get him summonsed by the magistrate as soon as possible. He's going to see who's in command here!"

Moracchini found a quiet spot in the car park in front of Saint Martha's church, just a few metres away from King René's Castle, and dialled de Palma's mobile. In vain. She tried his home and got the answering machine but did not leave a message.

Furiously, she stuffed her mobile into the back pocket of her jeans and went back inside Saint Martha's.

Father Favier was pacing around the sacristy, utterly bewildered. From time to time, he stopped, opened drawers that contained various sacred objects, then closed them again with a nervous twitch.

"Try and calm down, Father," Romero said. "We need you to tell us everything you know."

"Sorry, but I don't know anything at all. Nothing! During my ten years on emergency wards, I never saw such viciousness. It's unspeakable."

"I know," Moracchini said, glancing over at Romero. "We're just trying to put your movements together. After that we'll leave you be, alright?"

The priest came to a halt.

"Alright."

"What time did you discover the body?"

"I didn't. It was a visitor."

"Never mind! We'll get his statement later."

"It must have been about nine o'clock. But I'm not sure."

"What time did you call the police?"

"Straight away."

Romero noted down all these answers carefully, as well as any details that seemed important to him, such as Favier's attitude on being asked each question.

"Did you hear a noise or anything earlier?"

"No, not that morning."

"But yes, you did before?"

222

"Two days ago. I had the impression that someone had slipped into the church. But there was nobody there."

"You mean that you heard sounds suggesting an alien presence, or something unusual, is that it?"

Father Favier nodded then started pacing up and down once more.

"We'll leave you in peace, then talk to you again later, O.K.?"

Favier muttered something that neither of the officers could hear.

The judge immediately sent a warrant to the offices of the *Brigade Criminelle* in Marseille, giving permission to search Morini's residence. Moracchini and Romero arrived just after the gendarmes, who had surrounded the gangster's house.

"I'm Commandant Bonin, of the Tarascon company," said the gendarme, shaking the capitaine's hand. "We were expecting you."

Morini's wife had just been informed of her husband's death. She was hysterical. Moracchini made her sit down in the living room. Without waiting for reinforcements from Marseille or the local boys from Tarascon, she started the search.

"It's 14.00 hours, Daniel. Note down: Began search in the presence of Mme Morini."

The two floors of Morini's home must have measured a good three hundred square metres.

On the ground floor, there was a huge entrance hall, decorated soberly, with white walls, a few paintings by minor Provençal artists, two classical sculptures and green plants everywhere. To the right, it led into a vast living room with pale green walls, several leather sofas of different styles, padded armchairs and heavy curtains with huge pastel flowers.

On the walls, the crime boss had hung a series of photographs of old Tarascon featuring the centre and the castle before the reconstruction work had been done on the river and the town. Above one of the sofas hung a poster for the Tarascon carnival, dated 1932. Beside that, a sepia photograph depicted the Tarasque surrounded by its Knights. A Regency glass case contained a set of miniature bronze or ceramic Tarasques, as well as a collection of various monsters made of terracotta or copper.

At the back of the room, there was a bar of real zinc, which the gangster must have picked up somewhere shady. An antique one-armed bandit stood beside it.

The bay window looked out on a twenty-metre pool and a neoclassic-style pool-house. Further on, there was a forest of pines and oaks: the part of the Downlands that belonged to Morini.

On the first floor, seven bedrooms were laid out as suites complete with jacuzzi and desk each in a different style.

"We'll start with the bedrooms, Daniel. Let's get going."

Only two of them were used regularly: one contained Morini's personal belongings, the other his wife's.

"So the two of them didn't sleep together!" Romero said.

"You know, mobsters aren't people like the rest of us!"

The two officers went through everything in the wife's room. They found nothing except a collection of lingerie that made Romero blush.

Then they searched Morini's study, where they came across a few telephone numbers jotted down on Post-its. Moracchini placed them in a plastic envelope. The four mobile phones that lay on the bedside tables were also seized, as well as Mme Morini's address book.

Moracchini went back downstairs to the entrance hall. She gave instructions to the reinforcements that had just arrived, then went to see Morini's widow. The young woman was sitting on a thick leather sofa, her eyeliner running down her cheeks. She smelled distinctly of gin.

"Can we speak to you Mme Morini? Are you feeling any better?"

She must have been a good twenty years younger than her husband. Her black hair was tied up over her fragile neck by a knotted velvet ribbon. She wore a white dressing-gown, over her suntanned skin, and beneath it a bikini with bright red and yellow flowers.

"You can ask me whatever you like. I know nothing. He never told me anything . . ."

She spoke with a slight Marseille accent.

"What's your name?"

"Stéphanie. And that's practically all I can remember about myself!"

She looked up at Moracchini and stared into her eyes. She was quivering with rage.

"Anyway, I suppose it had to happen sooner or later."

Moracchini sat down next to her.

"Had he received any threats?"

"He seemed more nervy than usual, but you never really knew with him. It depended on what business he was doing."

"When did you see him last?"

"About a week ago. I can hardly remember, in fact! It's a bit like living in a parallel world. He said he was going to Aix and would be home in the evening. He never came back."

Moracchini guessed that Stéphanie must have been taking large quantities of some sort of dope to put up with a pig like Morini.

"Did he phone you to tell you he wouldn't be home?"

The young woman pouted cynically.

"Are you joking or what? When he didn't come home, he never said anything. But, this time, he said he'd be home."

"I mean, since his disappearance, have you received any calls from him, or anyone else?"

"No, Madame, nothing. But I do remember, on the day before he disappeared, he wasn't in his normal state of mind. He stayed for ages in his bedroom whispering into his telephone."

"And that wasn't usual, if I understand you correctly?"

"Exactly. But, you know, when you live with someone like that, you soon learn to be like the three little monkeys: you hear no evil, speak no evil, see no evil . . ."

Moracchini could not stop herself from looking scornful.

"O.K. You stay here. I'll be back to question you again later. In the meantime, get dressed."

She then went out into the garden and made a long telephone call to de Palma.

It was just after midday when the Baron turned into the driveway of La Balme farmhouse. The heat was stifling and he had problems keeping his grip on the steering wheel of the 205.

For the first time in a while, he noticed one of the young woman's bodyguards, who vanished behind one of the buildings when he approached. Mme Steinert must have seen him coming, because she was waiting for him on the patio, with a stern expression on her face.

"We missed you this morning for breakfast."

"I'm sorry I had to leave you like that. But I had to make a trip to the Camargue."

"Oh really?" she said, crossing her legs.

"Yes, one or two routine checks, as they say."

"And ideas like that suddenly grab you! I know, I'll go and check some details in the Camargue . . ."

As she spoke, she snapped her fingers in the air. Her voice had grown metallic.

"You've arrived at the right time, Michel. I've sent my chauffeur Georg to go and fetch M. Bérard for a lunchtime drink. And here he comes."

The Mercedes 4×4 steered a wide circle in the courtyard. The Baron recognised Georg. He was the bodyguard he'd spotted the first time he had seen her in Marseille. He was wearing sunglasses.

Bérard would not let the bodyguard help him out of the car. Bent double, he then came to shake Ingrid's hand. When he saw the Baron, who was standing to one side, he whistled softly.

"So the policeman is here too!"

"A policeman, but above all a friend," Ingrid said, still clutching his hand. "Come on, we're going to have something to drink."

"Oh, I can't stay long. Especially in this weather. You know, my charges are waiting for me. *Quand plòu en Avoust, tout òli e tout moust.*"

"What does that mean?" Ingrid asked with a smile.

"When it rains in August, all is oil and grape must."

"That's good news, isn't it?"

He stared at her, then twitched his head with a twist of his lips.

"Don't you think so?" she asked.

"It's the beginning of August. And there was thunder this morning. Good God! *Quand trono lou matin marco d'auro.* You don't understand!"

She raised her hands then let them drop to her sides.

"When there's thunder like this morning, it's often a sign of wind. Sweet Jesus, I'm afraid it'll start blowing, and what with all those fires around here . . ."

"*Fängt der August mit Donnern an, er's bis zum End' nicht lassen kann*: if it thunders at the beginning of August, it will continue to the end of the month," she replied.

Bérard lowered his eyes and stared at his feet for a moment. Then he adjusted his beret, uncovering a lock of silver hair.

"Goodness, William understood patois."

"It's true, he had learned Provençal."

"He spoke it better than I do," said Bérard with a whistle. "He had really studied our language."

"Come on, M. Bérard. Let's have a drink in the shade. You'll feel better."

"Oh, don't worry. The sun doesn't bother me."

Bérard was feeling embarrassed. He was glancing around darkly. De Palma was impressed by the vigorous aura given off by this man who was almost a hundred years old.

"So you asked me to come to tell you about the former owners?" He looked at the Baron.

"I thought it preferable for Mme Steinert to know what you told me when we last met. But it wasn't me who asked you to come today."

Bérard gave Ingrid a long stare.

"It's all ancient history. Especially now the poor soul's dead."

"Did you know his father?" she asked.

"Oh yes. In the prewar days, before everything fell to pieces. He used to come here in search of antiquities and, as I knew a lot about such things, he used to ask me questions. Sometimes, we went for a walk together and I showed him places."

"Such as the Downlands," de Palma said.

"Yes indeed. We went there . . . I remember as if it were yesterday. He was walking behind me, on a day like today. Really muggy! We started on the Fontvieille road then went as far as the big oak up there. That's where I showed him the old stones, as we call them."

"That's where the statue of Hercules was?"

Bérard looked up at the Baron.

"He called him Heracles. That's the Greek name. Because in fact the stones came from Greece. The Romans only arrived later. I read that in books."

Bérard wetted his dry lips with his pastis. Then he took an olive.

"Ah, Carpentras black. They're excellent!"

"We're going to plant some more."

"Wait for the spring then put them in that large plot you have by the road up there. It's neither too damp nor too dry."

Bérard took a good swig of pastis, then looked with interest at Ingrid.

"If you mean to plant, does that mean you're going to stay?"

"Why, were you afraid that I'd leave?"

"Yes, after William's death, I was really afraid of that."

"No, we're staying."

"Well, in that case . . ." Bérard said, flapping his hand.

De Palma waited for a moment.

"What do you mean by that, M. Bérard?"

"Some people aren't going to be best pleased."

Mme Steinert was about to say something, but the Baron motioned to her to stay out of this.

"Who do you mean?"

"The ones who want to open the park. They came to see me the other day. I told them that I wouldn't sell them an inch of land. That they'd have to wait till I was gone. And that anyway, I'd left everything to William."

"Can you describe these men to me?"

"They looked very respectable. One of them told me his name. It sounded German or something. Not like a name from these parts."

Ingrid started.

"Not M. Chandeler, by any chance?"

"What was that?"

"Chan – de – ler."

"It could well have been that."

"What did he look like?"

"Tall, very tall. With nicely combed hair. Forever smiling, like a salesman. Like, like . . . the people who work in banks. Know what I mean? They're always trying to sell you something. But don't worry, they left me a calling card. I'll show it to you. But I reckon it was the same name as the one you just mentioned."

"And the other?"

"The other man was fat. He was a tall man too, but fat. And he looked like a real crook."

"Did he give you his name?"

"No, no. He didn't say much. And outside there was another one waiting in the car."

De Palma's head was racing. There was nothing surprising about Chandeler being there. He was simply a lawyer who was trying his luck. But who was he working for? And who was the fat man who came with him?

"Tell me, M. Bérard. Do you remember what day this was?"

"Goodness, no. I sometimes lose track of time a bit. I might tell you something wrong."

"But it wasn't yesterday?"

"Definitely not," he replied, raising his hands. "It was a few days after poor William's death."

"It doesn't matter."

The shepherd took another swig of pastis, then stood up.

"I must go back, my flock is waiting."

Ingrid took both his hands. She looked at him affectionately.

"Can I come to see you one of these days?"

"Oh, my house is a poor place, you know! Only William used to come by, he didn't mind. My wife's dead and gone these twenty years now. So things aren't kept as they should be."

"It doesn't matter . . . Or else I'll come to see you while you're watching your sheep."

"Alright. I'll be by the rocks a little later, when it's not so hot."

The Baron's mobile rang.

"Where are you, Michel?"

"In Provence, Anne."

"Still with Ingrid?"

"There's no hiding anything from you."

"Go straight away to the forensic unit in La Timone."

"Why?"

"They've taken Morini there. But we're on the case."

"I'm on my way."

"But don't go inside, Michel! Remember, officially you're not involved in this investigation."

"O.K. I'll join you in a couple of hours' time."

He arranged to meet her in a café on boulevard Baille, just by the hospital.

Bérard sat back down on a wicker chair. De Palma noticed that Ingrid's eyes were wet with emotion.

"See, what did I tell you? The wind's rising. That's not good."

A greenish light fell from the neon lamps in the dissection room. Moracchini and Romero, dressed in green overalls and with masks on their faces, were standing behind Doctor Mattei and his assistant.

Mattei looked at Moracchini and pointed his scissor's at Morini's injuries.

"There's saliva on the wounds. The same saliva as last time, at least I think so."

The doctor of the dead indicated a dangling strip of flesh.

"Look, his dermis, epidermis and muscles have been completely ripped apart! As if something had bitten him, then pulled to remove the piece."

Moracchini looked at Romero. Above her white mask, her eyes looked anxious.

"Any ideas, Doctor?"

"None."

"I think that the D.N.A. will help us out once again. And I'm ready to bet we'll find the same as last time."

"So?"

"He's been fed to something. That's how he died. What do you think, Mattei?"

"I can't think of anything at this level. I can't imagine jaws that powerful. Unless there were several animals at the same time."

Mattei bent down once more to examine Morini's wounds, almost touching them with his nose. He frowned and held his breath.

"The spinal column has been bitten in two by jaws. It's not possible otherwise. It's just like a dog bite, but ten times bigger. And it reminds me of men I saw in the tropics, who'd been attacked by sharks . . ."

Mattei had slit open the thorax and neck up to the chin. He had levered the thoracic cage open before removing the lungs and heart.

"There was adrenalin in the heart and water in the lungs. I also found some algae on the body."

"So it's just the same scenario as with Christian Rey. Exactly the same . . . The guy is dropped in water, then he gets eaten."

"And it's fresh water, too. So no sharks . . . A crocodile maybe . . ."

"Why not a Komodo Dragon? What a headache! I just don't get it."

She looked at Romero and noticed that his eyes had glazed over. She had not known her new colleague very long, but she had worked out that this was the sign of intense mental activity.

"The Tarasque," de Palma murmured.

Moracchini's eyes were red with fatigue and disgust. She had picked up the Baron and was driving down the motorway towards Château-Gombert.

"What are you muttering about?"

"The Tarasque. That's all."

"You wouldn't be starting to lose it, by any chance?"

"No, no . . ."

"But the Tarasque doesn't exist!"

"Perhaps not. But someone is crazy enough to play the monster for us."

The overhead metro overtook them. She noticed a group of youths horsing around in the last carriage.

"Someone is staging a scenario? Now that's more like it!"

"The bite, the algae . . . it all fits together. There's someone somewhere who wants to resurrect the Tarasque."

"That's one possibility. But what might also have happened is that

Morini and Rey were quite simply snuffed by their little chums in gangland. There wouldn't be anything very surprising about that either."

"Not the right modus operandi."

"How can you be sure, Michel? They're getting crazier and crazier, you know that as well as I do."

The Baron waved away her suggestion and pursed his lips. His face was almost ashen and a headache was starting to grow at the base of his forehead.

"Romero's gone back to Tarascon to pick up Marceau's report. The bastard, he couldn't bear us being given the case. He'd had our friend removed before we got there."

"It doesn't really matter, Anne."

"What are you talking about? We've got nothing and he's maybe hiding things to keep us slaving away like idiots."

She drove under the metro line and accelerated suddenly, as though she was fleeing something. Her hands were clenched on the steering wheel and the headlamps of the cars on the other side of the road glittered in her damp eyes.

The next evening, at 7 p.m., the Baron leaped over the surrounding wall of the Résidence Paul Verlaine, drew his Cobra and made a panoramic scan.

He let a neighbour from the third floor go by, holding his son by the hand. Then, when no-one else was in sight, he went along the path leading to his building, careful to stay close to the pines and the shrubs that bordered it. The Cobra was tight against his thigh. In case of sudden danger.

It was the first time he had been home for three days. It smelled musty and full of bad memories.

The answering machine flashed up ten messages. Two of them were people hanging up, while the other eight were from his mother, whom he had not called for a week.

Without wasting any time, he went into the bedroom, grabbed a travelling bag and threw in two pairs of jeans, a pair of trainers, a few T-shirts and a drawer-full of boxer shorts and socks. In the wardrobe, he noticed the box in which he kept a hoard of souvenirs. He looked inside and found a notebook that contained a photograph of Isabelle Mercier. He examined it for a moment, before noticing something that had hitherto escaped him, despite the scores of times he had stared at it: she had a beauty spot shaped like the ace of spades just between her ear and the angle of her jaw.

He had spotted this detail only today. And he knew why. Because he had also seen it somewhere else. On Ingrid Steinert's cheek.

He lay down on the bed and sank into the dark waters of his memories. As ever, all he could see was a face that no longer existed, and a body already stiffened by death. A single eye that still stared at him over all those years and sleepless nights.

For a long time, he stayed in the shadows of his bedroom, watching the daylight gradually fade away between the slats of the shutters. Isabelle had been the first victim, but how many more corpses had he seen since then in his life as a detective?

At least three hundred. Maybe more.

The number made his head spin.

At the beginning, he had thought that he should hang on to all of them and hold them in his memory. It was his debt to the dead, because the dead know that they exist so long as someone pictures them. And if they are forgotten, it is all over.

As a little boy, he would sometimes walk in the alleys of Saint Peter's cemetery. He liked to read the names of the deceased on the slabs of granite and to invent their life stories, little novels in a nutshell telling of their vanished destinies, instant dramas in which love and wonders played leading roles.

Starring roles.

He jumped up, closed his bag and headed for the door.

Outside, the night had stretched its canvas. He waited for there to be nobody near his building, for the stairwell and hall to be plunged in darkness, then he walked out into the gloom of Marseille.

Thirty minutes later, he was bounding up the stone staircase that led through the prickly pears to Maistre's patio.

He served himself a kir then sat down on the low wall that overlooked the little houses of L'Etraque. In the distance, the sea was like a vast black slick running from the harbour wall as far as Maïre and then to the flickering star of the Planier lighthouse.

Maitre was browsing through a boat supplies catalogue. The murmur of the city could be heard from afar.

"Do you think we'll ever find our fishing boat, Michel?"

The Baron answered with a grunt.

20.

Controller General Lamastre had been regional head of the P.J. in Marseille for five years. He was rather a stylish man, he was in the town hall's good books, and didn't like disciplinary scandals.

That morning, Lamastre was getting impatient. He picked up the F.B.I. special agent badge which he always kept on his desk; it was a souvenir from his stay in Quantico years before, when he had decided to try to adapt the American super-cops' profiling techniques to French procedures. The badge had been given to him by James Lehane Jr, one of the best manhunters in the U.S.A.

"Take a seat, Michel. I don't like having to talk to you like this, but I have no choice. How are things?"

"Fine, sir. I've completely recovered. And I'm longing to get back to work."

"You knew Lehane too, didn't you?"

"Yes. He was a great guy. I've read both of his books and must admit that I've used his ideas a lot."

"Indeed," Lamastre said, putting down the badge. "Quite a detective. Let's drink to his health before I give you a scolding."

Lamastre came from Normandy. His blue deep-set eyes, perpetual three-day beard and a complexion fired by alcohol did not undermine his natural elegance. He produced a bottle of Jim Beam and two glasses from his desk drawer.

"The news isn't good," he said as he poured out the bourbon. "Certain people around here want your balls on a plate, Michel."

"I know."

"In this country, cops like you are becoming a rare commodity . . .

and certain people like that fact. To be quite honest, I'm seeing what can be done to avoid your being charged."

"They've got nothing against me, I've done nothing wrong."

"The problem is that you were seen having a rather physical conversation with that bastard Morini, just a few days before he passed on. Do you follow?"

"Of course I do, but . . ."

"Don't try to explain yourself, Michel. I know full well that it wasn't you who cut him in half and I've already rejected any such insinuations. Don't forget, however, that they exist. But the snag is that we have a statement from a customer of Morini's bar. He saw you and he's willing to sign, with his elbows if need be."

"I don't follow you . . ."

"Leave it out, Michel. I'm not out to get you."

Lamastre handed him the official report.

"They want your arse, and they'll get it if you carry on like this. Our friend here apparently saw everything. Just read the statement! It's highly detailed."

"O.K., so I talked with Morini and I handcuffed his bodyguard."

"And both of them died within the next few days . . ."

The Baron sat back in his chair. Lamastre picked up his badge again.

"I need to know why, Michel."

"It's a bit complicated. I don't know where to begin."

"I've got all the time in the world, and there's plenty of bourbon left. This is a friend asking, Michel!"

Caught in the trap, the Baron stayed silent for a while. He was going to have to talk, but first he wanted to find out exactly how much his boss knew. When he reached out his hand to take the report, Lamastre gripped it.

"Don't play silly buggers now. The report is mostly about Lopez. The man you blew to pieces not far from where you live. It's all rather messy, isn't it? As for the rest, I honestly couldn't give a damn!"

He raised his hand.

"Who cares if you put the shits up that fucker Morini? But for two magistrates who specialise in organised crime to try to pin the death of good old Lopez on you – that I can't abide. So I need your version of the truth. And it had better be truer than that of our learned friends. Message received?"

"Loud and clear."

De Palma knew that Lamastre was extremely rigorous, absolutely honest and quite ready to stick his neck out for his men. So he had to play it straight while also hiding both his strengths and his weaknesses. Otherwise, the trap might close on him for good.

"This customer's statement is a tissue of lies," he said.

"That's not what I want to hear, Michel."

"Between you and me, boss, this is pure perjury. But, O.K., I'll tell you everything."

He started at the beginning: the meeting with Mme Steinert, the shot in the dark . . . He also mentioned the grass who had put him on the track of Morini.

Lamastre listened, still clutching his badge.

"You're in it up to your neck," he said. "You know what being charged means for a police officer?"

"I know, Chief."

The Controller General threw his badge down on a file marked "De Palma".

"As far as I'm concerned – I mean the Marseille P.J. – I'm going to give you a clean slate. When do you start work again?"

"Next Monday."

"O.K., let's say that de Palma's great return is going to be postponed slightly. Get yourself another month or so of sick leave. Time enough to let things run their course. We'll see how things stand when autumn comes. And I'm going to visit your friend the prefect later today."

"Say hello from me."

"It's lucky for you that you've been friends these twenty years."

"We go back to our days on the *Brigade Criminelle*."

"I know, I know, the pests in Paris. There's more to life than Maigret, you know."

"He was a young Commissaire at the time."

"Stop, you're bringing tears to my eyes."

Lamastre poured out two more shots of Jim Beam.

"So, Steinert you say?"

"Yes, boss."

"That case stinks, don't you think?"

"It isn't a case. I mean, everything possible has been done to turn it cold."

"Yes, I heard they'd decided he drowned."

"It was a murder. As sure as two and two make four. And someone big was behind it: property deals and so forth!"

"I'm ready to believe you, but it won't wash. People are judged on the facts, not on intellectual constructions."

Lamastre knocked his glass back in one and grimaced as he felt the burn go down.

"There are hundreds of poor bastards who get murdered and are put down as suicides. Do you know why?"

The Baron shrugged and picked up the F.B.I. badge.

"Because there's a two-gear justice – everyone knows that. And a two-gear police system. A D.N.A. test costs between 300 and 800 euros, do you follow me, de Palma?"

"Of course . . ."

"I know, I'm stating the blindingly obvious . . ."

He poured himself another shot.

"And I advise you to lay off the Steinert case during the month on sick leave you're going to take."

When he emerged into the courtyard of police headquarters, de Palma tried in vain to contact Marceau on his mobile. So instead he telephoned the commissariat, only to be told that his old colleague had gone on holiday abroad two days before.

The Baron was about to pull away in Maistre's 205, when Romero's head appeared at the window.

"Good day, boss. How are things?"

"I've just seen Lamastre. He'd rather I stayed ill for a while."

"No surprise there. You're much talked of right now, and not all of it good!"

"That's nothing new."

"Things are drifting up to the surface."

"Who cares?"

Romero stuck his head into the car.

"I went to see Maistre yesterday. As we got nothing out of Lornec, we took a little trip to the Belle de Mai to see what we could find out about those old hold-ups."

"Anything new?"

"Not much. But there's one thing of interest. At the time, it was Marceau who was in charge of the investigation. You should give him a call."

"That's right. He was on the B.R.B.* at the time. I should have thought of that. The snag is that he's on leave right now. The bugger's abroad and no-one knows where. We'll have to wait for the end of August."

"Shit, that's a shame."

"That's one way of putting it. Anyway, nothing is panning out at the moment."

"Anne's here. Do you want to speak to her?"

"No, my lad. I feel as though I stink of something dead right now."

"Come on, Michel, forget it!"

"You don't know them. They're as jealous as divas."

"Whatever. Let's try and get together as soon as possible. O.K.?"

"No problem. See you around."

The Canadair banked over the summits of the Alpilles before swooping towards the Downlands, barely thirty metres above the ground.

With tears in his eyes, Bérard watched it fly in line with the lavender fields, which were half hidden by the black smoke. Madame Steinert had taken the old shepherd by the arm because he could not keep still.

Once past the Route de Maussane, the Canadair dropped its tons of water over the burning torches of resin and oak, before vanishing into the blue sky smeared with black.

* *Brigade de Répression du Banditisme.*

239

"M. Bérard, you can't stay here. The firemen are telling us to leave."

The old man did not move. He murmured something inaudible, like an incantation, as he watched the inferno advance on a turret of limestone.

A quartermaster of the Marseille fire brigade shouted above the tumult and the cracking of tree trunks torn apart by the flames.

"You can't stay here," he called, unrolling a hosepipe. "Move away! This is no place for you."

Madame Steinert guided the shepherd to the other side of the road. The wind drove the smoke towards them. In a swirl of fury, everything grew dark and sparks danced in the scorched air. She took him by the shoulder and led him towards her car. It was at that moment that she saw de Palma emerge from behind a fire engine.

"You've got to go," he said. "Get into the car, M. Bérard, you'll make yourself ill. The air is toxic."

The Baron motioned to Ingrid to take the driver's side, then he sat Bérard down in the passenger seat. The old boy was like a puppet. He no longer reacted to what was going on around him.

The Baron sat in the rear of the Mercedes 4×4, and they drove off towards Eygalières. The firemen had set up their command post in front of Morini's house and were fighting the blaze just a hundred metres away from the façade.

"Let's take M. Bérard home."

She nodded and overtook a Maussane firemen's ambulance.

"Where is your flock, M. Bérard?"

The old man did not reply. De Palma saw that he was crying, his eyes wide with terror.

When they arrived in the courtyard of Les Fontaines, Matelot the sheepdog didn't move. De Palma realised that something terrible had happened before or during the fire. He motioned to Ingrid to stay in the car.

"Drive off as soon as I'm out."

Ingrid had her hands clamped on the wheel. Bérard was staring ahead, as though what was happening no longer touched him.

The Baron threw himself out of the car and ran over to the dog's kennel, his Bodyguard drawn. Ingrid pulled away at once.

Matelot had been shot in the head. His skull had exploded, scattering brain matter all over the kennel.

De Palma went into the barn and listened. He heard the Mercedes leave the farmhouse turning and head towards Eygalières. Then there was silence.

Les Fontaines was in a state of stunned suspense. Flies were buzzing around in the heavy air. The sheep were gone. The gate of their pen was wide open. On the ground, the straw had been disturbed and scattered over the yard. It made a long yellow track that led towards the fields. The herd had been stampeded. Behind a manger, a lamb was breathing feebly, its back broken when the herd had trampled over it in panic.

He pushed open the front door of the house and pointed his gun inside. He smelled the old man's odour, newly mingled with the smell of wood ash that clung to the ancient furnishings. The overwhelming stillness had something disturbing about it. The only sign of life was the ticking of the clock.

He walked slowly inside, still on his guard.

The pantry door was open and a tin of biscuits had been spilt over the floor. Beside it lay some papers which looked like bills and a few carefully folded ten-euro notes.

The Baron glanced into the cupboard. It contained three shelves. The top one contained a line of bottles of liqueur and empty jars. Beneath it, a pile of dishcloths had been ransacked, leaving an empty space beside it; presumably where the tin had been. On the bottom shelf there were some cans and bars of chocolate, which had also been turned over.

He went all around the room then headed for the only door, which was in the far wall. It was closed. He turned the handle but could not open it. It was either locked or jammed. He tried again, and gave it an angry kick, but it wouldn't budge. He realised that it must be locked from the inside.

A meow broke the silence. A cat appeared in the front doorway, no doubt the only surviving witness of the terrible scene that had played out in the farm.

The big clock chimed six p.m. Outside, the air smelled scorched. The wind had risen and was blowing the smell of the fire towards Les Fontaines.

The Baron was about to leave when he heard the sound of a body hitting the ground. He just had time to duck when two gunshots rang out. A window shattered. Then there was a sound of rapid steps. A man was running towards the far side of the buildings. The Baron stood up and took aim.

It seemed to happen in slow motion. He fired once and saw the .38 bullet hit the ground. When the man turned round, he corrected his aim and pressed the trigger. The shot hit the man in the left leg; he made to fire back but the Baron put a second round into the same place.

The man fired once, and then again. The Baron just had time to duck before another window blew apart. When he stood back up, the man had vanished. De Palma ran out after him.

He stopped dead when he heard a powerful motorbike roar away on the dirt path.

The farm was still vibrating from the shots and there was a reek of burned powder. Most of the sheep had taken shelter in the field just behind the barn, a few more were lingering in the garden.

De Palma went back to the dining room. The lock on the door that led to the bedrooms was an old model, easy to open. In the farm's stock of tools he found a length of thick wire and fixed up a makeshift key. Thirty seconds later, the lock gave way.

The walls of the shepherd's bedroom were covered in a faded yellow wallpaper dotted with pale blue and pink flowers. To the right of the window, a huge wardrobe occupied all of the space; to the left was a single chair, with a black suit jacket draped over its back. The brown walnut bed was covered with a thick eiderdown and a hand-knitted bedcover.

He opened the wardrobe. On the upper shelf, there were some piles of ironed shirts and below that some carefully folded black corduroy trousers. An old hunting rifle lay in front of the pair of trousers. He opened the breach. It was loaded with two Tunet double zero cartridges.

The rest of the room told him nothing. There was a Christ made of yellow metal mounted on ebony on one of the walls, and a dried olive branch nailed up above the bedstead.

At the far end, a door led to another connecting room. When he opened it, it felt as though something invisible had been released, as if an impalpable form passed by him and fled outside.

There were a few dusty sticks of furniture and some old photographs hung on the walls: sepia portraits of past generations; a group of people in a glass-fronted frame; a papier-mâché Tarasque with a man in a costume like a musketeer's, with knee breeches, buckled shoes, frilly shirt and broad hat. It was Bérard, posing beside the monster as a Knight of the Tarasque. Other knights were standing behind him.

To the left of the beast stood several officials, no doubt from the Tarascon town hall, and two taller men in Nazi uniforms.

The Baron remembered what Bérard had told him about the Resistance and the protection old Steinert had given him. He took the photograph down and turned it over. Behind it, Bérard had written in a fine hand: Festival of the Tarasque, 1942.

He hung it back up, then looked around the room. He saw at once that it had been ransacked. The chest of drawers had been searched. There were two dog-eared breviaries, a copy of the Provençal edition of Frédéric Mistral's *Mireio*, a *Trésor du Félibrige* and a few books by Roumanille and Daudet. As he closed one of the drawers, his foot struck some object. He bent down and picked up an ancient tome from the floor: Agrippa's *La philosophie occulte ou la magie*. The preface stated that this edition dated from 1911, but that the text had been written in 1540. It was a work for an initiate.

He sat on the bed and thought for a moment. Someone had come to search the place and had been disturbed. What had he been looking for? A book about magic?

De Palma reconstructed the scenario: on seeing him arrive, the man had locked the door leading to the bedrooms and had escaped through the rear window, which was not very high. So he probably had not had enough time to find what he had come for.

De Palma searched both rooms meticulously, but found nothing unusual apart from that book about magic. He thought of the tomes he had seen in Steinert's office and tried to make connections, but he had to give up: he did not know enough about the occult arts to take this line of inquiry further.

He took down the framed photograph again and studied it closely: 1942, the festival of the Tarasque, with the Nazis in attendance . . . But it was just a picture like thousands of others.

All the same, Bérard had gone out of his way to tell him about that period. It had been the childhood of Steinert, the Boche's son, as they called him after the war. William's father had saved him from that shame, but his mother, Simone Maurel, had had her head shaved and her brother had been shot in the yard of the La Balme farmhouse.

He replaced the photograph and stepped back. The men and women posing beside the Tarasque were staring at the camera, their smiles fixed for posterity, not realising that they were covering themselves with shame by consorting with the enemy.

They all seemed to belong to a single family, gathered around a ridiculous monster. One of them had placed his hand on a Nazi officer's shoulder. Bérard was puffing out his chest.

De Palma was sure that it was all there, in that photograph, but he was incapable of decoding it. Only Bérard could do that. The south wind pushed the black smoke of the blaze towards Les Fontaines.

The sheep had returned to the yard and were bleating for their missing master. De Palma let them into the pen and tipped some bundles of hay into the mangers. As he closed the doors again, he realised that he was going to have to return to the scene of the fire on foot.

On the road from Maussane to Fontvieille, several fire engines were parked end-to-end on the kerb. Groups of firemen were talking, their faces running with sweat, their white hoods lowered round their necks.

When de Palma arrived, he saw that a gendarme officer was conferring with the commandant of the brigade.

"Good evening, Capitaine. I'm Michel de Palma from the Marseille P.J. Can I ask you a couple of questions?"

"Have you got your papers?"

He produced his tricolour card and brandished it under the gendarme's nose.

"So how can I help you?"

"I just wanted to know whether you consider this to be arson or not."

"It was arson," the head fireman replied. "No doubt about it."

The gendarme glared.

"Look," he said. "I want to know what you're doing here."

"I'm investigating. On my personal initiative."

"Initiative my arse."

"Listen, Monsieur, I have every reason to believe that this fire is connected with a case that we are investigating. Now, you can always refuse to talk, but I'll mention that fact in my official report. What do you say to that, Capitaine?"

"Piss off," the gendarme replied, and turned on his heels.

"He's had a hard day," the fireman said. "He's got his knickers in a twist."

The capitaine slammed the door of his 406.

"As I just told you, this was definitely arson. A classic technique: an insecticide spiral, a wick on the end, and petrol in a container. You light it then walk away. The spiral burns down, and the fire starts several hours later."

"I thought so," de Palma said. "If you find out anything else, could you give me a ring?"

"No problem," the fireman answered, taking the card that the Baron handed him.

Ingrid had put her arm through Bérard's and was walking him up and down the patio of La Balme, like a nurse.

"How is he?" the Baron asked.

"I've been expecting you for some time . . . I think he should be taken to hospital," she whispered. "He seems to have lost his reason."

Bérard's face was still just as listless. He looked as though he was staring into an unknown world, and had lost the spark that kept him so bright.

245

"Can you hear me, M. Bérard?"

The shepherd did not answer.

"I'm the police officer from the other day. Do you remember me?"

"I'm sure that he's in a state of shock, and should be hospitalised. I called the mayor of Eygalières. He told me that Bérard has no family, and that no-one there will have the time to deal with him until tomorrow."

"And you think it can't wait till then?"

"Not only think. I'm sure it can't! And you can't expect him to go home by himself in that condition."

An ambulance from Tarascon came to fetch Bérard at 8 p.m. Ingrid and the Baron decided to go with him.

At 10.32 p.m., the old shepherd died. The doctors at the hospital failed to make any real diagnosis. They just mentioned his great age and the psychological shock.

That evening, Ingrid took de Palma's hand and squeezed it tight. She put up her hair, which had tumbled down over her shoulders. Her profile stood out against the crude light of the neon lamps. Between her cheek and the lobe of her ear, there was a beauty spot shaped like an ace of spades.

At two in the morning, de Palma dropped Ingrid off at La Balme. He told her about the photograph he had seen on the shepherd's bedroom wall and realised how hard it would be to use it now that Bérard was dead.

He left the farmhouse, drove up towards Eygalières and parked Maistre's 205 by the entrance to an olive grove, where the road to Maussane met the sunken track that led to Les Fontaines. No-one could see the car from the main road.

He took a torch from the glove compartment, closed the car door quietly and headed off down the path, keeping the beam of light fixed on the ground.

To the right, the dark ranks of vines looked like ridges of coal in the shadows. There was a fragrance of ripe grapes and warm pine resin. Each footstep crunched in the sharp little stones along the

246

track. Suddenly, the Baron dived in among the trees and advanced into the darkness.

Les Fontaines farmhouse was about forty metres away, out in the open. He switched off the torch and felt his way forward in the moonlight. Five minutes later, he was crossing the yard.

The flock was calm. He slipped into the doorway, used his wire in the lock and went straight up to the bedrooms. Everything was eerily silent. He found the photograph, took it down and played his torch over the faces of the people around the Tarasque.

It was at that moment that he sensed he was not alone.

The photograph comes to life.
   The crowd surges with clamour.
   "La tarasco, la tarasco . . ."
   The crowd opens like a wound.
   Before the papier-mâché monster that is rushing towards it.
   "La tarasco, la tarasco . . ."
   Bérard is holding on to the monster's tail.
   He steers it with precise gestures.
   "La tarasco, la tarasco . . ."
   Bérard calls out: "Laïssa la passa . . . Laïssa la passa . . ."
   The knights join in: "La tarasco dou casteu . . . Lagadigadeu . . ."
   The children run away screaming.
   The monstrous mouth clacks its teeth.
   One of its knights finds a girl in the crowd.
   She is beautiful and dark, like a gypsy virgin.
   The beast's servant captures her.
   Two other knights force her up onto the animal's neck, chanting:
"Lagadigadeu . . ."
   The virgin roars and wriggles her bare legs.
   "La tarasco, la tarasco . . ."
   Bérard grips the beast's tail so as to make a seasaw movement.
   The entire crowd sings: "La tarasco, la tarasco . . ."
   The neck rises.
   The virgin bounces upwards.
   "La tarasco, la tarasco . . ."

She straddles the Tarasque.
Her thighs are half naked.
She grabs at the hideous monster's mane.
"La tarasco, la tarasco . . ."
People are laughing and giggling.
People are sparkling, their eyes lit up with pastis.
Glasses clink.
On the terrace of the Café du Centre, people are chatting in German.
In German and in Provençal.

De Palma spun round and pointed his torch at the window. A livid face stared at him from outside, its features carved out by the beam of light.

He drew his Bodyguard. The face vanished at once, and he heard the thud of a body landing on the ground. He ran to the window, opened it and played his torch over the farmyard. It was empty. In the pen, the sheep were jostling each other, barging against their mangers.

21.

The temperature had dropped. The muggy heat of the past few days was over. Breezes were blowing between the clumps of rushes, making wrinkles on the smooth waters.

Moracchini and the two forensic technicians jumped off the punt that Texeira had lent them. Just behind them, de Palma and Romero were sitting in an inflatable dinghy, making a first reconnaissance tour around the reed hut. At each push, Romero's pole splashed loudly in the water.

Richard, a forensics veteran, entered the hut first. He stayed there for half an hour before emerging carrying an armful of bags which he placed in a plastic crate.

"We'll put the seals on later, when we get back to the office," Romero said. "I'll just note down what they are."

"There's quite a lot of stuff," said Richard. "It looks rich."

"That's good news," Moracchini said, looking at the packets.

Richard had listed the contents of each sample and the number of the marker.

"I'm just going to take a couple more shots, then we'll go down into the hole."

"As you like."

De Palma and Romero examined the bank that ran around the hut. They didn't see much, apart from bird tracks in the sodden earth. They were all over the place.

But no traces of human feet.

They went back to the place where de Palma and Texeira had noticed, some days earlier, that the bottom of the marsh had been disturbed.

249

The water level had risen slightly and there was nothing usable. But the Baron still wanted to explore in the northerly direction given by the footprint he had found. He advanced through the reeds, but the vegetation grew so dense that he had to concede defeat: it was impossible to go this way.

"Let's see if Richard's finished with the hut. I want to be there when they go down into the hole."

Richard was finishing taking photographs. His colleague, Patrick, hadn't found much around the hut except for a few feathers.

"Michel's right. Someone has cleaned up. And I must say the guy has talent. You'd think they belonged to our team."

"Don't tempt fate."

"No really, it's as if they'd had police training."

Richard came out of the hut and put his camera down on its case. He wiped his forehead and took off his gloves.

"We'll wait for Michel, then down we go."

The smooth slope that led down to the underground room was about two metres long. The room itself measured two by three metres – high enough to stand up. It had been dug out of the earth, which was quite hard here, and then the floor had been crudely concreted over. The walls had simply been smoothed down, like cob.

It all formed a proper room, which, in its shape and conception, recalled the underground hides of the Viet Cong.

"It stinks down here," Moracchini said.

"Yeah," said Richard. "Shit and piss. Human, and not that old. It's like being in a lair. I'll put the CrimeScope over it, but at first sight there isn't much to find."

Moracchini pulled herself up out of the tunnel and sat down next to the Baron. She produced a packet of cigarettes and offered him one. He waved his left hand to say no.

"You've really stopped smoking, Michel?"

"It's bad for migraines. So I'm trying to stay stopped."

"What do you think about all this?"

"I don't understand a thing. We're finding a new piece of jigsaw every day. On the one hand, there's a lunatic wiping out mobsters one after the other. Then there are voices, here, in the arsehole of the world. Voices talking about the Tarasque in Provençal. Plus a billionaire who drowns in the same patch. Add to that the bastard who's trying to shoot me, then you have the entire picture. If you can find the least bit of logic in all this, then let me know."

"Maybe not everything's connected. O.K., they intersect, but they're not necessarily linked. It's happened before."

"I'd put it differently: there is a connection, but no logic. That's what makes it all so hard."

"And what's the connection?"

"The Tarasque."

She looked up at the ceiling.

"You really believe in all that?"

"I don't believe, I'm making an observation. Steinert was interested in the Tarasque, Christian Rey was a Knight of the Tarasque, so was Morini, who was even born in Tarascon. Plus he was a neighbour of Steinert and had an interest in the famous Downlands. I also found out that he knew Rey, who worked for him collecting his slot machines takings. Is that a link, or isn't it? Then there's the fact that the corpses are found in places or next to places that have something to do with the Tarasque."

"O.K., so this isn't all coincidence. Steinert was into the Tarasque. O.K. Everyone in Tarascon is into the Tarasque. Voices have been heard here. O.K. Steinert died nearby. Right. But what tells you that there's a link between the two bodies?"

"The adrenalin."

"What?"

"Adrenalin. This blasted adrenalin. It's in every body. Loads of it. Mattei is adamant. The people who died around here had the fright of their lives before they died. That's the only true, definite link. And it's a good scientific one. The rest is still hazy, I quite agree, and I must admit that it's been messing with my head for days now."

In the series of hold-ups involving Lornec and his gang, Marceau had signed most of the statements and almost all of the reports. Just a few of them bore the signature of Alexandre Vander, a capitaine in the B.R.B.

Maistre leafed through scores of pages trying to get to the essentials. There were statements by Lornec, Vandevalle and Santiago. The last two had been killed. Only Lornec was still of this world.

The reports were uninformative. Everyone had denied everything and had provided bogus alibis: Lornec was supposed to have been at his sister's place, Santiago had gone to see a friend in Nîmes, while Vandevalle claimed that he had been watching the semi-final of the European Cup.

According to the list of exhibits, some weapons had been seized at Lornec's house. But a SIG automatic pistol was not among them. Maistre flicked through Marceau's conclusions, closed the file with a sigh and returned it to the secretary of the records department.

On his way back to his office, he dropped in on the B.R.B. Vander was there, typing up some phone-tapped conversations made during an investigation into stolen cars.

"How are you, Vander?"

"Fine, except that I'm spending all my time tapping phones. Jesus, that's no job for a real policeman!"

"I need your help, Alex."

"Are you inviting me to join the *Sécurité publique*?"

"No, I want you to think back to the case of Lornec, Santiago and Vandevalle. They did hold-ups during the Nineties."

Vander rolled his chair backwards and placed his huge hands on his thighs.

"That was the crew in the north. And they go back quite a way. We never got any real results. Two of them have been iced since then. But as far as I know, Lornec is still alive."

"Did you work with Marceau at the time?"

"Jean-Claude? Yes, we collared them together, but the case fell through."

"Were there some guns?"

"Yes."

"Do you remember the models?"

"Hang on, I'll have to get back in the mood . . . There were some hunting rifles, maybe a couple of revolvers. I can't remember. That's quite a poser you've asked me."

"Try and remember! An unusual weapon."

"Just a second. Wasn't it then that we found something a bit odd . . ."

Vander gripped his chin and closed his eyes.

"A SIG. Yes, I think there was a SIG. You don't often find a piece like that."

"Even nowadays?"

"No, absolutely not . . . it's the only time I've seen robbers using a SIG. They generally prefer big pieces, like an 11.43, and not fine artillery like that."

"And you don't know what became of it?"

"It was taken as an official exhibit, of course! What do you imagine? Get out the file and you'll find it. But if you're looking for the actual piece, I'm not so sure. It may be downstairs in records or still at court."

Vander glanced at his computer screen, clicking twice on "Save".

"You've got one hell of a memory, Alex."

"Haven't I just! You know, sometimes I can recall the phone numbers of people we were tapping three years back. Just imagine that!"

"You've always impressed me."

Maistre slapped him on his bulky shoulder. Vander pretended to wince.

"Tell me, why are you interested in all that ancient history?"

"I just wanted to check something out in a case. We've got a gun that's talking, and it's the same one."

"That's odd. Because at the time, it had never been used. It was brand-new."

"Are you sure?"

"Definite. No doubt about it. You remember the guns that mobsters use. They're like miracles at Lourdes! Just ask Marceau, and you'll see!"

"Thank you, my man."

*

Maistre waited until he was in his car and stuck in a jam on the northbound motorway before telephoning the Baron.

"This business about the SIG is starting to look funny. Vander tells me that he saw the gun and that it was officially recorded, but there's nothing in the file. What's more he says that the weapon had never been used."

"It's more than just strange. Have you checked out the chronology?"

"What do you mean?"

"The date when the exhibits were sealed, and the date when they picked up the bullet."

"I don't have the date on me. I meant to get it."

"The exhibits have the wrong number, but the date must be the same as for the statements!"

"Sorry, Michel. I don't think as fast as you do."

"Check the day they found the casing in the old grocer's shop against the day when Marceau and Vander pulled in the three little sods. If it's before, then there's no problem. If it's afterwards, then you'll have hit the jackpot. And you know what I'm hoping . . ."

"I'll call you back in five minutes."

Maistre pushed his knees up to steady his steering wheel and opened the file. It took him just five minutes to work out that there was a period of no less than two years between the two dates. This revelation gave him the heaves.

"Bingo Michel! The bullet was discovered later . . ."

"What's your conclusion?"

"That the weapon disappeared from our nice safe haven. And that some people are so cocksure that they leave things as gross as this behind them."

"And after all that, it wound up in the hands of the man who tried to kill me."

"Three times."

"Exactly. Well done. But we need to know more than that. Have you mentioned this to anyone?"

"Yes, Vander."

"There's no risk with him. But don't tell anybody else. Otherwise, we could really end up in hot water."

"O.K."

"And then, we mustn't look for links when there aren't any, if you see what I mean."

"Right."

"It's Lornec who provides the link. Lornec, then Morini. Lornec was working for him right up till his death."

"How do you know that?"

"I'm psychic."

"Leave it out, Michel."

"All the same, Lornec has nothing to do with this. He was just unlucky enough to be in the right place at the right time. But I'm sure he's not behind it all. A piece arrives at headquarters or the court, then it leaves. That's the real problem. And there are only two people who could have done it."

"Stop it, Michel. You're giving me the shivers."

"Either a magistrate or an investigator."

"Marceau!"

"Obviously. The judge had no interest. Too dangerous for him, and anyway they know the ground. In those days, the magistrate was probably Alonso; she was certainly not the kind to give a gun back to a mobster with a letter of apology."

"Why Marceau?"

"I have no idea. To be honest, I'm at a loss. This comes as a bomb shell to me."

"But, Michel, just imagine, we've known him for ever! Really, I can't believe it."

"I realise that. But if I remember right, four or five years ago there was a big shortage of guns on the market. That might explain it. Marceau has always had money problems. The Inspector General's office has already bawled him out on a couple of other occasions for similar reasons."

"I hope we're wrong about this!"

"I'd like us to be, Le Gros. I really would."

The Baron took a long look at the map. He wanted to avoid the area of the fire so that no-one would spot him. To approach from the north, on the Fontvieille–Maussane axis, was impossible. The same applied to the direction from Eygalières. He would have to go from the south, even if that meant cutting through private property.

The map showed several paths through the forest. The hardest part would be avoiding any fire patrols or the local police. He would leave the car as far away as possible from the place he was aiming for.

In Marseille, he had rented a 4×4 Nissan Patrol. It had cost him a fortune and he wouldn't get it back.

He folded up the map and drove as far as Raphële, where he took the road that led straight to the Alpilles. A quarter of an hour later, he was going down a track that led away from the main road into the wilds.

He drove for some time between two rows of barbed wire, then the road climbed through the first wood of pines and stunted oaks. The 4×4 gobbled up the steep slope and started to pitch like a boat. Then the road began to snake along increasingly rugged hillsides.

In the distance, the plain of La Crau melded into the sky, the sea, and the marshlands of the Camargue. It was a huge, flat expanse, hazy in the evaporating dew.

When he passed the final bend, which formed a pass, the first charred trees appeared. The landscape changed suddenly. Nature had been blowtorched; dark stumps stuck up from the earth like charcoal claws. The limestone formed a few white patches that stood out from a blanket of soot.

From afar, the Baron glimpsed the white turret that he wanted to see. From here, it looked like a big limestone cube jutting up from the ground, with four pine trees at its feet, twisted by the agony of fire.

He parked the Nissan Patrol in the shelter of two rocks, then set off on foot, moving at a trot. He knew that there would soon be helicopter patrols in the sky, checking that the fire had not been rekindled.

Fifteen minutes later, he arrived at the base of the rock in a sweat and started his explorations.

Bérard had mentioned old stones, and he could more or less recall the topographical charts he had seen in Steinert's study.

Above all, he had the few translations that Ingrid had made for him. All of the notes he had read spoke of this "white tower", a clear landmark in the valley, and of the village that was supposed to have existed at its feet during the first century B.C. According to Ingrid, this was where the large sarcophagus which now stood in the farmyard of La Balme had originally come from.

De Palma knew that he was going to have to act quickly to determine if the land ravaged by the blaze still contained any Greco-Roman ruins which might have blocked, or at least delayed, certain real estate projects.

He soon found what the shepherd had called the old stones. The fire had in fact revealed what had previously been hidden by the forest's undergrowth: perfectly carved blocks of varied dimensions, half buried in the earth.

They formed something like a limestone wall that led away towards La Crau before disappearing into the ground.

Old Karl Steinert had been right. There had been dwellings here. The text translated by Ingrid read:

. . . According to Canon Malvan (the digs date from the nineteenth century), in the place called "La Tour Blanche" there are houses and a line of large stones which could well have been a boundary wall, but this has not been proved.

The houses are not organised according to an orthogonal plan, but instead scattered around in complex plots, all quite different from each other. Presumably the initial construction was relatively recent, dating back to 30 or 40 B.C., and it was a house arranged around a courtyard with a portico . . .

Towards the south, there was perhaps a large garden or a vast area set aside for games and displays. But its current state does not allow us to say more, because the rather dense vegetation precludes the possibility of taking samples . . .

The text then described several ceramics which had been found in the vicinity, some of which went back to the second century B.C.

... On a limestone block there is a carving of a quite unusual monster: half man and half crocodile, it looks strangely like the Tarasque of Tarascon ... This stone is situated at map reference 26 N / 84 E ...

... This discovery, or rather rediscovery, was made by Monsieur Bérard, a farmer living in Eygalières, who owns the land. Monsieur Bérard has told me on a number of occasions that this land used not to be wooded, at least not as it is today.

Furthermore, I have Monsieur Bérard's agreement to make this land available if ever a dig were to be carried out.

Steinert, 23 October 1938.

Brambles and shrubs covered the edges of the ancient walls. It was impossible to get near them without pruning them back. The Baron took several photographs. Most of the stones were swamped by tree roots and scorched bushes. He walked once more around the rock, but saw nothing else of interest. It was only when he gained a little height that he saw the lines in the ground: squares, rectangles, and a few curves.

He took another set of photographs and decided to return home.

As he got back into the Nissan, he suddenly realised why the wood had been burned down, and above all who had done it.

At that very moment, the whirr of a helicopter arose above the Alpilles and spread out across the plain of La Crau.

22.

Marceau came out of his house, at 10 rue des Halles, at 11.45. It was his fifth day on leave, and he still had a few details to sort out before going abroad. This year it was Mexico.

He bought his newspaper from the kiosk over the road then went to the Café du Globe, where he ordered a coffee, just as he had done every day since being posted to the commissariat in Tarascon.

Motionless, the man observed him, the 200 mm in his right hand. If all went according to plan, Marceau should emerge again in less than fifteen minutes, time enough to drink his coffee and perhaps order another, as he had done the day before yesterday. There'd be time to take one or two snapshots.

But, today, Marceau was not working. The man had known this since last night.

"The commandant is on leave. You can contact him at the end of the month," a young female voice had said on the telephone.

He approached the stationer's opposite the bar, and pretended to be choosing a postcard in case the cop decided to change direction and move faster, as he sometimes did for no apparent reason.

Marceau emerged after just one coffee. He took a single snapshot, face on. Then the cop turned left at once and, instead of going home, walked up rue de l'Hôtel de Ville towards the theatre.

The man followed him. He was certain that his prey could not escape him.

On arriving at the theatre, Marceau looked around in all directions. He did not see the man who had just had time to slip into a doorway. Marceau stood still for a while before producing a bunch of keys and going inside the building which housed William Steinert's office.

This was unexpected. But never mind, the man knew how to improvise. He gave himself a few minutes' thought, and finally made up his mind to wait. Marceau was a daunting target.

It took a good half an hour before the door opened once more and Marceau reappeared. They both walked off.

The man told himself that today was not the day. Definitely not. The day seemed to be full of surprises. Unless luck smiled at him.

And that is what happened.

Instead of going home, Marceau stopped to make some photocopies. Then he returned to put back the documents he had taken from Steinert's office. Another thirty minutes went by. Marceau came out and threw into the gutter what looked to the man to be a pair of gloves. This was not important.

After that, for some unexpected reason, Marceau decided to take the ring road. When he had almost reached the place where the man's car was parked, its owner came up next to him.

Everything speeded up. The man pulled his automatic on Marceau and forced him to put his hands behind his back. Then he put the cuffs on and removed the gun from his target's belt.

Thirty minutes later, he was driving through the byways of the Camargue.

Moracchini was savouring the fruits of her work. In less than forty-eight hours, she had managed to obtain the D.N.A. results, using charm and the promise of more.

And the tests were talking: the traces of saliva found in the wounds of Christian Rey and Morini came from the same source.

The fragments of D.N.A. found in the reed hut matched Rey and Morini. In this case, it was the genetic records department that had made the match, as both of the mobsters already featured there among the police's bar codes and alleles.

The conclusion was that both of the gangsters had spent time in that hole. She could almost reconstruct their last days: no water, no food and total darkness. The forensic report was definite.

Furthermore, Mattei was equally definite: both bodies had been bitten by a pair of outsize jaws, such as those of a crocodile. He recommended comparing them with any animals that the two men might have come into contact with. This seemed surprising, but it was his department's expert opinion.

Moracchini and Romero had then gone to grill Lornec about his possible connections with Marceau. The gangster had told them nothing, but had seemed put out. Moracchini was never wrong about that. Nor was her team-mate.

Gouirand, the head of the Knights of the Tarasque, had been questioned twice. But both sessions had been disappointing. Moracchini had been expecting a lot, especially when she had discovered Gouirand's CV in police records: he had been caught twice red-handed during hold-ups with his pal Rey. The two men had been friends. But the trail stopped there. Still, she remained optimistic.

"We've made pretty good progress, haven't we?"

Through the bay window of the department's photocopying room, de Palma stared at the dome of La Major which was glowing in the sunlight.

"Yes, great! Now I think we should go through the names of the characters involved in property deals with S.O.D.E.G.I.M. around Maussane, Eygalières . . . even as far as the Camargue. I mean projects such as entertainment parks, leisure centres and so on."

"Is that all?"

Moracchini had put her hair up and pinned it with a ballpoint pen. She was wearing a light dress and strappy sandals.

"Yes my dear, we're going to have to get down to it!"

"We've got time."

"In the force, we never really have time."

"I know, but when it comes to the Steinert affair, no letter rogatory has been issued to allow us to take evidence. In fact, we're working on the fringes of legality. I could claim it to be a personal initiative, but I don't hold out much hope there."

"It's tricky. We're dealing with village secrets here, things that go on behind our backs that are unbeknown to us. It would be logical enough for Morini to take out Steinert so as to get hold of his land.

But then there's Bérard. Was it necessary to kill him, too? Why didn't Morini's henchmen go and see the old man and talk him into selling? It's all pretty weird, isn't it? And why not do the same with Steinert? I can only wonder if we'll ever find out."

Moracchini untied her hair and shook it back.

"So you think these are family secrets?"

"Not only that! Do you have Gouirand's phone number?"

"Yes."

"Call him and ask if he knew Morini."

Moracchini picked up her mobile and telephoned Gouirand. She spent less than a minute on the telephone, but, from the expression on her face, he guessed that he had been spot on: Morini had been a Knight of the Tarasque in the 1980s, at the same time as Rey.

Marc Gouirand was standing in front of the town hall, cleaning the windscreen of the mayor's Safrane. He was wearing dark glasses, cotton trousers and a flowery shirt that opened to reveal his chest. Moracchini had been watching him for some time, sitting over a coffee in the Bar du Centre.

When he put down the chamois, she got to her feet and went over to him.

"Monsieur Gouirand, do you recognise me? I'm Anne Moracchini, from the Marseille P.J."

The head of the Tarascaires straightened and looked her up and down.

"I wanted to ask you a few questions about the death of Christian Rey."

"Now?"

"If it's possible."

Gouirand glanced at his watch.

"The mayor's still in a meeting. It should take about another three quarters of an hour. Is that enough?"

"It's up to you to make yourself available to the police, sir, and not the other way round. Are we clear?"

Gouirand's smile vanished and he lowered his gaze.

"Perhaps you'd rather come to the station in Marseille with me?"

"No, no, it's alright!"

"Fine, so tell me, when exactly did you first meet Rey?"

"That's easy: in primary school. We'd known each other as long as I can remember."

She pretended to note this down.

"And what about Morini?"

"The same goes for him. We were all the same age."

"You know he's dead?"

Gouirand simply nodded before giving the windscreen of the Safrane another wipe with the sponge.

"And they both used to be Knights of the Tarasque, like you?"

"Yes, we all started together."

"Then what happened?"

"I don't really know. After that, we all went our separate ways. They became crooks, and I got a job at the town hall."

She stared up at the building: it was very old, made of dressed stone that dated back to the Middle Ages, and covered with mullions, diamond-shaped stained-glass windows and extravagant sculptures.

"And have you been working here long?"

"Since 1987."

"Can I ask you what you do exactly?"

"I'm the mayor's chauffeur."

"I know that, but I've also heard that you organise the distribution of election posters and can use your fists a bit."

Gouirand shrugged. She glanced at the back seat of the Safrane and saw the handle of a blackjack sticking out of the pocket of an evening jacket.

"What's the blackjack for, opening bottles?"

"It's just in case the mayor gets into danger."

"So you're also his bodyguard?"

"Not really, but you never know."

"I think you'll be called in for questioning in a few days' time. So stay in Tarascon, O.K.?"

"Very well, Madame."

"De Palma, I'm a police officer."

The blonde at the door of Chandeler & Associés blinked, and her lips formed a pout.

"Do you have an appointment?" she said at last, observing the visitor over her glasses.

"Is Maître Chandeler seeing a client?"

"No, I mean yes . . ."

De Palma opened the door, the secretary followed him in.

"Sir, this gentleman . . ."

"That's alright, that's alright . . . you can leave us. I know M. de Palma."

She had barely closed the double doors when she heard a slap and a cry resound behind her.

Chandeler was on his knees, his spectacles in his hands. He paused for a moment, sniffed back the blood that was pouring from his nose, and got to his feet. The Baron stepped back and gave him a kick in the guts that bent him in two.

Chandeler rolled over before standing up again. He was about to call out when he noticed with terror that the Baron was holding a gun on him. A handsome Cobra with a cold, gleaming barrel, just two metres away from him.

"Sit down, you piece of shit."

Chandeler raised his hands in a gesture of appeasement and walked over to his chair.

"No, not there, here," de Palma barked, pointing at the seat intended for clients.

"Think about what you're doing, Commandant. You've already committed an action that will have serious consequences for you. Don't make matters worse."

The Baron went over to Chandeler and scrutinised his adversary's every tic. When he came in reach of the lawyer he let fly a punch that knocked his glasses back off.

"You're going to pay for that."

"You know that the old shepherd's dead?"

"I don't know what you're . . ."

Another slap shot out.

"Listen to me. We've got everything we need on you. We've even got a photo of you in Bérard's place with your pal Morini."

Chandeler doubled over.

"So either you start singing or I'll put the word out that I roughed you up a bit and you gave up all the others. To look at you now, I reckon that they'll all believe me."

"I'm only a cog in the machine."

"And a Knight too, as I see."

"Just a cog. There are big interests at stake, very big . . ."

"A Knight who is also an intellectual!"

"They're . . . it's a financial group . . . with . . ."

The Baron came over to him. He hunched up even more.

"A group of people with . . ."

"With Morini among them."

"Yes, that's right."

"You know that you're starting to get on my tits, telling me things I know already!"

The telephone rang.

"Answer and tell your secretary to go home. Anyway, it's time."

Chandeler did so, while drying the blood that was dripping from the corner of his mouth.

"O.K., let's try again. Morini isn't a scoop. I hope you've got something better . . ."

The Baron decided to play a card he wasn't sure of. He made a gesture, a simple gesture: he ran his index finger over his belly as though he was cutting through his torso with an imaginary weapon.

Chandeler opened his eyes wide and started to tremble all over.

"The problem is they don't want to sell, and in the region it's the only place where such a project can be carried out."

"What's all this nonsense? You can build a park wherever you want."

"Check out who owns all the land around the site, and you'll understand."

"Names, Chandeler, I want names . . . You know them, they're your clients."

"If I tell you, I'm a dead man."

The Baron grinned.

"And also if you don't," he half murmured.

"Why not do a deal . . ."

"A man has just died. He has to be avenged."

"O.K., there are some people from around here, then some Italians and Americans . . ."

"I want a list."

Chandeler went over to his desk, opened a file and handed a sheet of paper to de Palma.

"It's all there," he said, looking away.

"You see, where there's a will . . ."

He looked at the list of names. Morini's was not on it, but he recognised one or two cronies amenable to laundering his money.

"I just hope that the beast doesn't eat you, too!"

"I too have received the mark."

The Baron nodded as though he knew what he was talking about.

"Show me," he said.

Chandeler stared at the Baron with his eyebrows raised. He slowly opened a desk drawer and removed a plain white feather. It was just like the one de Palma had seen in Steinert's office.

"Who else received this mark?"

"We all have."

"All the rich bastards on your list?"

"Yes, that's right."

"Pray to the god of swine like you that the police you despise get him before he gets you."

The Baron backed away to the door, opened it and left.

Maistre was standing bolt upright facing the sea. It looked as though he were savouring infinity. After a while, he came alive again and poured red wine into a plastic cup.

"I've got the truth at last . . . or at least, part of it."

Maistre did not turn round. He kept his eyes fixed on the horizon which was still red with the fury of the sun. The siren of a roll-on roll-off boomed in the terminal of Mourepiane.

"If I'm not mistaken, the whole business was actually quite banal."

"That's often the way it goes, Baron. You think you're up against exceptional villains who are pulling off incredible capers, and generally you end up with a couple of pricks not worth getting up in the morning for."

Maistre looked at his watch. Moracchini appeared at the end of the patio. She was wearing a linen dress that revealed her shoulders and slender ankles. She took off her sandals and walked barefoot across the limestone tiles.

"Delpiano already knows that you've given Chandeler a pull."

"Why, are they in the same chapel, I mean lodge?"

"He's just told me about it on the phone. He wants your hide, Michel. I have no idea why he's got it in for you so much, but it scares me."

She sat down just beside him. De Palma sensed his body turn electric from the stealthy contact with her dress. He quickly stood up, removing the sheet of paper Chandeler had given him from the rear pocket of his jeans. Moracchini took it and read it carefully.

"There are some people I know in here!"

"Yes, and some others you don't. It doesn't matter! But they all have a point in common."

"What's that?"

"Someone has sent them a feather like this."

"And what does it mean?"

"Not much for the moment, except that when I mentioned bodies that had been sliced in half to Chandeler, he practically shat himself."

Maistre picked up the paper and stared at the list.

"Jesus, there are two or three here that the financial brigade would like to nab: Grimaud, Landrace, Rossi . . . fuck me!"

"They're the ones who wanted to buy up Steinert's land, the patch they didn't want to sell, the famous Downlands. It belonged to his father, and Bérard presumably sold it to him before the war."

"You mean the woods that burned down yesterday?"

"That's right. But they weren't involved in the arson."

"Who was it then?"

"Bérard himself. He wanted everyone to know that there are Greco-Roman ruins in the forest so that no-one could build anything there."

Moracchini was rubbing her forearms as if she was cold.

"And you think that's why they killed Steinert?"

"It might look that way, but I don't think so. The problem is that I'm not sure we'll ever get to the bottom of this business. Unless we get a stroke of good luck at last."

Maistre lit a cigarette and drew on it nervously.

"There's something I don't understand," he said. "These people have got enough dosh to build their damned park where they want."

"You're right, Jean-Louis. But I think there are one or two things we're still missing. Around here, it was just about the only viable site. There are lots of tourists, and everyone had something to gain. The people selling the land could name their price. A plot where you can get planning permission in this Bermuda Triangle is worth a fortune: as much as 4,000 euros per square metre! Did you realise that?"

"Maybe so, but there's still the coast and everything. I mean, it's the back of beyond out there."

"I reckon that there's subsidy on offer, but above all it was a group of guys who'd known each other since childhood. A sort of clan. Morini and Rey were old pals!"

"Yes, but one was the godfather and the other the stooge!"

"You're right, Le Gros. We've now got to uncover their connections with the others."

Maistre stood up and got out two bottles of wine. He put three glasses on the table and uncorked the first bottle. The roll-on roll-off which was sailing out of Mourepiane gave another blast of its siren.

"Some guys who are rolling in it get rid of a troublesome billionaire. That works. Especially when you see the names on the list. But still you say that it's something else!"

"Yes, something else."

23.

Moracchini nearly spun off the road to avoid hitting a tourist. The Xsara swerved to the left and collided with the pavement. Romero laid his hands on the dashboard.

"Jesus, Anne, watch out. I've got kids, you know."

"Put the lamp and siren on the roof. We'll be more visible."

In front of the castle of Tarascon, she took the wrong turning, going towards the church instead of the ring road. She reversed back, then shot off the wrong way along the outside lane.

Just after the castle, a traffic cop appeared in the middle of the road and pointed left, towards the car park by the banks of the Rhône.

She parked the Xsara just in front of the security cordon.

"Ah, there you are, Moracchini. Jesus, what a mess. And you knew him, I think?"

Larousse's face was creased, his eyes almost hanging from their sockets.

"I'm sorry, I don't know the identity of the . . ."

"It's Marceau."

"What?"

"He's down there, on the rocks. He's like the others. It's . . . it's hideous."

She climbed down to the edge of the river, walked among the clumps of grass that grew just beside the water, then halted. Larousse pointed in the direction of the castle.

"He's there, can you see him?"

"Yes, quite clearly. Now get rid of those idiots who're trampling around all over the place. The forensics team will be here in a minute."

269

Larousse turned on his heels without replying. He made do with yelling at some onlookers.

"Daniel, call de Palma again. Tell him to get out here. We need him. Too bad if that prick Delpiano kicks up shit, we'll find an excuse. He and Marceau were friends, I think."

"O.K., I'll deal with it."

"Then we'll have to go and search his place. At once. In two minutes' time, I want there to be three officers turning over his house."

Marceau had been laid at the foot of the ramparts, on the rock often used by the kids of Tarascon as a diving board. It was a fisherman who had discovered him. His first thought was that it was someone who had fallen from the ramparts.

"Anne? Michel here. I'm not going out there. It's too late, anyway . . ."

"Up to you."

"I'm sorry, Anne, but it'll take me an hour to drive there. Do you see?"

She hung up and took a good look at the people who were watching what was going on. Way up in the ramparts, over 80 metres from the ground, there were several faces framed in the crenellations.

She noticed a brigadier from the local police section and asked him for some binoculars. He disappeared among the horde of police cars, then came back with a pair of 8×30s. She aimed them at the castle and made out some tourist heads, all of them fair, probably English or Dutch, out on a family excursion. Then she panned left and saw three little boys leaning over the wall and gesturing at the corpse.

"And their parents leave them to it," she said to herself.

She scanned along the walls of King René's Castle. There was no trace of blood or anything out of the ordinary. At last she reached Marceau's body, which shone in the sunshine like a pool of nail varnish.

"The first time, it was in front of the Tarasque," she muttered to herself. "The second in the crypt of Saint Martha, and now on this rock."

She was about to lower the binoculars, when a taller figure appeared behind the boys. She peered upwards and saw a man with a cap on his head. The outline remained for some time in her field of vision. Then she had the feeling that their eyes met. The figure disappeared, all at once.

She immediately grabbed Romero by the arm and whispered to him:

"There's a man up there acting suspiciously. I don't know if I'm imagining things or what, but I think we should take a look. And be quick about it."

"O.K., but no running otherwise he'll spot us."

In less than two minutes, they were both standing in front of the castle's postern. As they went through the door, Moracchini flashed her card at the janitor.

"Close the entrance and let nobody out, except for children."

The local official, who was bulky and half asleep, struck a pose of importance and carried out the order without a word.

"How many stairways lead up to the roof?"

"Today just one. The other one's closed."

She drew her Manurhin and entered the castle courtyard.

A few tourists stared at her and backed off whispering when they saw a revolver's black steel in the policewoman's hand. She stared at them one after the other. Mentally she compared each face and form with the capped silhouette on the ramparts. None of the men in the castle courtyard matched the image she had engraved on her memory a few minutes before.

Romero took up position on the far side of the courtyard and scrutinised the arrow slits and windows around him.

Some tourists in shorts and sandals emerged from the Gothic staircase, clearly surprised to see an armed man and woman looking at them. It was the family that Moracchini had spotted earlier, with the three little boys who had been leaning over the battlements.

Romero asked them if there was anybody left at the top, but no-one understood what he was saying. He moved them out of the courtyard and told the doorkeeper to hold on to them while they searched the castle.

"Shit, Anne, we don't have a radio."

"Too bad. We can't waste any time. Let's go up."

She dived into the half-lit stairwell, climbing fast and trying not to let her Converse shoes clack against the cold stone.

After two L turns to the right, the steps came out in a vast room hung with tapestries. Romero entered behind Moracchini, then ran across to the far side, before entering a second room and emerging again at once. To her right, Moracchini noticed a wooden arrow against the wall, indicating the route for the visitors in three different languages.

A staircase as broad as the first led to another room as vast as the previous one, but better lit. A tourist was reading an information display inside it. She aimed her gun at him, and he turned pale. He put his hands up and stammered something in German. She motioned to him to leave by the stairs. He did not need telling twice, but walked crabwise as far as the door without taking his eyes off the threatening gun.

A second arrow pointed to the upper floors of the castle. Moracchini saw that the staircase was a spiral one, narrower than the others. A real rat trap. She gestured to Romero to cover her, before starting upwards as quietly as possible, two steps at a time. He followed a metre behind.

The roof was deserted. She headed for the place where she had spotted the man in the cap and leaned out over the void. It certainly was the best vantage point for observing what was going on below. She could see the two forensic scientists who were busying themselves around Marceau's body and, beside them on the riverbank, Larousse gesticulating wildly as he talked into his telephone.

Meanwhile, Romero was pacing around the roof.

"We've missed him, Anne. He must have gone down at top speed and we missed him."

"Shit, shit and shit!"

"Can you describe him?"

"He was quite tall, with a white cap over his eyes. Like half the population of this fucking town."

She leaned on the ramparts, trying to think out a strategy. Beneath her feet, the Rhône flowed peacefully on towards the delta of the Camargue. Its huge green curve seemed almost motionless in its bed.

"Let's go down and take a longer look. Then we'll see."

The room on the second floor told them nothing, nor did the next one down. King René's Castle was completely deserted. As they went down the second staircase, Romero stopped dead. He had heard something.

"Did you hear that?"

Moracchini shook her head.

A second rattle reached them. It came either from below them or from behind one of the walls. The two officers dashed down the stairs and stopped at the place where the stairs gave on to the courtyard, through a doorway carved with stone flowers.

More banging echoed through the silence of the castle.

"It's that way," Moracchini said. "On the river side."

They emerged from the stairwell and headed towards the possible source of the noise. At first, all was silent, then after twenty seconds that seemed like an eternity, a song rang out:

"*Lagadigadeu, la tarasco, lagadigadeu . . .*"

The voice was imprisoned inside a room of the castle. But it was impossible to say exactly where it might be coming from. Its owner must be somewhere behind the walls, in a place that communicated with the outside world by some such means as an arrow slit or narrow door.

"*Laïssa passa la vieio masco . . . Laïssa passa que vaï dansa . . .*"

There was a long silence. And then, plainly from further away:

"*La tarasco dou casteu, la tarasco dou casteu . . .*"

Moracchini searched in all directions. She almost glued her ear against the walls. On his side, Romero went back up to the large room on the first floor and leaned out of one of the windows. He saw nothing but the Rhône and, over to his right, Marceau's body drying in the sun. The voice had gone for good.

After twenty hours' work, the technicians came back with over two hundred samples. From some of these, the scientists sometimes

273

removed a good twenty different specimens. In all, over eight hundred items were sent to the biology laboratory at Nantes.

The next day's *Provence* was headlined: 'Police Officer Brutally Murdered'. The national papers picked up the A.F.P. reports and added their own not always welcome comments. The Provence of Mistral was shown in a variety of unflattering lights. Not a single article refrained from mentioning Tartarin and the Tarasque. It was the headline story early in August. It lasted ten days, and no longer.

In mid-August, the first forensic results arrived on the desks of the police and of Marie-Paule Garcia, the investigating magistrate. The scientists had found dozens of unknown D.N.A. traces, but the only one that made any sense was the sample taken from Marceau's wounds, which matched those taken from Rey and Morini.

Moracchini, Romero and the other officers who had searched Marceau's house found photocopies of documents, letters, and plans from archaeological digs, some of them in German. Moracchini at once made the connection with the papers de Palma had seen in Steinert's office. She decided to place them under seal while waiting to see what else would turn up.

On Marceau's bedside table, next to the telephone, the police found an address book with the contact details of regional politicians and businessmen. In the wardrobe they collected another, thicker note-book with names and numbers. Once all of this information had been put together, what emerged was a huge network of illegal gambling machines organised by Marceau and Christian Rey on behalf of Morini. The policeman covered up the racket and got twenty per cent of the profits. Rey took thirty and Morini fifty, protection included. This told potential competitors: "Lay off Le Grand's slot machines." Now that the notice was out of date, the one-arm bandit war was going to start all over again. The B.R.B. and illegal gambling boys were going to have their hands full.

But the most interesting discovery was made during the subsequent search of Marceau's private parking lot. Several handguns turned up: two CZs, two Colt .45s and a 9 mm Beretta. Hidden above the control box for the opening mechanism of the garage door, they also found a box of 9 mm shells wrapped up in a chequered towel and a full SIG 29 clip. The gun itself was nowhere to be found.

The Timone forensics unit released Marceau's body after two weeks, like a beast letting go of its prey after feeding on it.

The Baron and Maistre attended the funeral alongside Marceau's elderly aunt. No-one else came. Their former team-mate was incinerated at the Tarascon crematorium at 9 o'clock on a Thursday morning.

As he watched the coffin disappear into the mouth of the furnace, Maistre crossed himself.

"I can still see him as he was the first time we met in Paris. He was looking for Boyer's office. He wasn't a bad guy."

"He could have killed me but didn't," the Baron said as he turned away.

Isabelle Mercier's name was not spoken.

Twenty days after the discovery at Tarascon Castle, things still stood as they were. The links between Rey, Morini and Marceau were known at last.

Moracchini had examined the police officer's career in great detail, and certain grey areas appeared, particularly in financial terms. Marceau had been fixing up a ruined family house in Baux-de-Provence, a property inherited from his mother. The work had cost around a million francs, a sum that was far beyond his means.

She noticed once again that their investigations were centred inside a perimeter that stretched between Baux and Mouries and between Eygalières and Maussane.

For a few days, the Baron distanced himself from their inquiries and from everybody else. He spent his days fishing, either on the burning pebbles of the Baie des Singes, just opposite Maïre, or at the far end of the snaking tarmac of Les Goudes, or else around the creeks of Morgiou and En Vau, snug in a hired Zodiac inflatable dinghy, alone and tiny on the waves that washed over the limestone's fantastic shapes.

The Baron had chosen this retreat so as to withdraw into himself, to delve inside his soul; his only companions in sadness were the great opera singers in the headphones of his Walkman: Renata Tebaldi, Carlo Bergonzi, Mario del Monaco, Montserrat Caballé . . . in well-worn versions of *Aïda, Turandot* and *I Pagliacci*. Real Italian opera full of heavy emotions and flawless melodies. His personal favourites, as a child of the sun.

He had not caught much, either on the languid sea or in the music of his fathers.

He only understood when he changed to Wagner and Strauss, to Melchior, Varnay, Rysanek and Flagstad. When he folded away his rods and returned the Zodiac. His other half was far away. For weeks now, Isabelle Mercier had not called on him from the far side of the known world.

Ingrid Steinert had gone back to Germany for an indefinite stay. Settling her inheritance from her husband was causing her endless problems. She was now the owner of a large stake in Klug-Steinert Metal, which raised the hackles of many of her in-laws. She telephoned the Baron several times. Late in the evening, after spending endless hours in the offices of lawyers and notaries in the four corners of Germany.

When de Palma emerged from his torpor, he immersed himself in books about the German occupation of Provence. He spent whole days at the Méjanes library in Aix-en-Provence, amid students about to retake failed exams in September, soaking up dissertations, theses and symposium papers.

Not once did he see the name of Steinert appear. On the other hand he learned how many of the region's powerful families had consorted themselves with the occupiers after 1942, the year of William Steinert's birth. But most of the studies remained extremely discreet about the names of those involved and the fortunes amassed during that period.

It was when he opened a dissertation about the region of Tarascon entitled *L'épuration en Provence: 1944–1946* that the Baron came across the names of Steinert and Maurel. The account had been written in 1966 by a Gilbert Sicard, and in his preface the author warned the reader that he would cite no names of witnesses or victims without the express permission of those concerned or of their families.

... In the months that followed the liberation of Provence, between August 1944 and January 1945, old scores were settled in the region of Les Baux, and in particular in Maussane and Eygalières.

According to the witnesses we have questioned, the most sordid event took place at a farmhouse called La Balme, where Emile, the eldest son of the Maurel family, was shot dead and his sister Simone had her head shaved ... Yet from various statements it would appear that the Maurel family had never collaborated with the occupiers and that this was in fact a settling of differences between powerful inhabitants of the region, fed by old rivalries and jealousy ... Etienne, Emile's younger brother, had even been part of the Vincent Group, a particularly active resistance network commanded by a farmer in Eygalières named Eugène Bérard.

Henri Bayle, the head of the F.F.I. in Tarascon, claimed that none of his men was mixed up in this affair. At least, this is what emerges from the statement he made to the gendarmerie of Tarascon during the investigations into the case that were carried out in 1952, after a complaint had been lodged by Simone Maurel's brother, Etienne ... As often happened, the case was quickly closed and no charges were made. Cited in the statements and Maurel's accusation are the names of the region's most powerful landowners. Henri Bayle declared that he had never heard it said that resistance fighters had shot Emile Maurel. This is confirmed by the records of the F.F.I ...

According to oral testimony, Simone Maurel's head was shaved in the village square of Eygalières, where she was then exposed to public condemnation. It is easy to imagine the degree of humiliation experienced by a young woman whom people spat upon (statement of a man who witnessed the scene) ...

277

She was accused of having had a liaison with a German, a certain Karl Steinert, who was neither an army officer nor in the police . . . According to the same oral sources, nothing was proved, but it seems that Simone Maurel was judged by a kangaroo court made up of the same people who had had her brother shot . . .

De Palma made a few notes on his pad. At the foot of the page, he wrote in capital letters: REVENGE.

France Telecom came up with three Gilbert Sicards, one in Fontvieille, one in Arles and one in Tarascon. De Palma tried them all. The first two were dead ends. When he dialled the Tarascon number, he got an answering machine which informed him that Gilbert Sicard would be away until the beginning of September. He left a message.

He picked up Bérard's photo and examined it closely. Once again, he had the impression that a door was slowly closing. That hope was forbidden.

It was now late August.

The first of a new wave of gangland killings occurred in the centre of Aix: nine 11.43 bullets took the life of François Lomini, one of Morini's lieutenants. Three days later, it was the turn of Jérôme Lornec, shot down in front of the 421, the nightclub Morini had put him in charge of.

Jean-Luc Casetti was taken out by three bursts from an Uzi in a bar on avenue de la République, over a glass of pastis.

Gangland abhors a vacuum.

24.

It had been raining all morning. The flagstones leading to Saint-Blaise's church were gleaming with water and misery. It was twenty-two years to the day since de Palma had last been there.

And some years since he had returned to Paris.

He could still picture the white coffin carried by the undertaker's assistants from Porte de Bagnolet, and the hundreds of bouquets of flowers and naïve drawings from the neighbourhood children.

That day, he had parked his service car, an unmarked R8, in rue des Prairies. Maistre and Marceau were with him, stiff in their too-tight dark suits. Maistre's straight black hair fell down over the collar of his shirt, giving him the look of a romantic Napoleon. Marceau was curly-headed, his adolescent features marked with sadness and disgust.

De Palma walked slowly up the steps of Saint-Blaise's church then stopped in front of the door. He did not enter. A force held him outside. He angled to the left, and climbed the few steps that led to the local graveyard. An old woman was filling a green plastic watering can from a tap in the central alleyway.

He passed in front of Brasillach the Collaborator's tomb and was amazed to find it in perfect condition. Isabelle's sepulchre lay one lot further on. Some fresh flowers had been laid there, presumably that very morning. There was a plaque with the photo of the girl. She was smiling.

Beside her name, there were also the names of her parents: her father who had died eight years later, and her mother a year after that.

He put down the bunch of violets that he had bought at the

florist's on rue Belgrand. He wanted to say a prayer, but he did not know any for the dead. The old woman came over to him.

"Did you know her?"

"Yes, I did."

"She was a pretty little thing, wasn't she?"

De Palma bent down and straightened the violets, which had slipped down onto the granite.

"She always winked back when people looked at her," he said, standing up. "A little smile in the corner of her mouth and a wink."

"Are you a family member?"

"You could say that."

A few drops of rain splashed on the tombstone, making a dry slapping sound. De Palma looked up. Heavy clouds were advancing from the east ring road towards Porte de Bagnolet.

"And the police never caught the one who did it!"

"No, never."

"If you want my opinion, they can't have looked very hard."

"Do you think so?"

"Definitely."

"Maybe you're right."

"Are you really a family member?"

"No, not really."

"I see."

"Why do you ask?"

"Because that's where they should have looked. In her family."

In a flash, de Palma pictured again the long nights spent going through statements. Everything had gone through the mill. The slightest testimony. The smallest clue. All the forensic evidence had been gathered, but in those days the police scientists new nothing about biological sampling.

"You're not from around here, are you?"

"No, I'm from Marseille."

"I didn't know they knew people from Marseille."

"You don't always know everything about everybody."

His face clouded over, and she realised that she was intruding. He was thinking about Marceau, his old team-mate in Paris who had ended up in trouble. He did not blame him. He alone knew that Marceau had been a decent man right up till the end, despite the corruption, despite the tortured soul. Marceau had been an excellent marksman; he had won prizes. He could have killed de Palma three times. But he had not done so, no doubt in memory of Isabelle and this tragedy which had bound them together for ever.

De Palma took a long look at Isabelle's face stuck there on the marble of her grave. She looked so like Ingrid that he felt shaken to his very roots. Isabelle and Ingrid, years apart. Almost a lifetime.

A violent pain shot across his forehead and spread out in his skull. He massaged his temples until the migraine abated.

Because that's where they should have looked. In her family. He repeated the sentence to himself several times.

The old woman had disappeared at the far side of the cemetery, towards rue des Prairies.

He turned on his heels and walked back down rue de Bagnolet.

At the Saint-Michel terminus, a few steps away from police headquarters, he ordered a beer and telephoned Judge Brivet. A secretary answered and told him to call back. He gave her his number, name and rank. She promised to pass on his message.

Nowadays, Gilbert Brivet worked in the financial section in Paris. Twenty years before he had had the duty – a crushing one for a young magistrate – of dealing with the Mercier investigation. De Palma wanted to have a word with him, one old hand to another. Brivet must have almost reached retirement age.

The Baron had just ordered a second beer when his mobile rang.

"Michel? Gilbert here. How are you?"

"Fine, fine, and you?"

"Up to my neck in it as usual. But I can't complain. Can we meet?"

"That's why I called you."

"Jesus, Michel, it's good to hear from you!"

"Same here."

"Let's meet up at Les Chauffeurs, how about that?"

"It still exists?"

"Etienne's gone. He doesn't run the restaurant any more, but it's still really nice. And, this evening, there shouldn't be too many people."

Gilbert Brivet still looked like a choirboy. At over fifty, he had kept his youthful features despite his greying hair and life's little dramas. He was neither married nor divorced: no woman would stay with this eternal adolescent caught in the corridors of power.

From his student past, he had retained the manner of a scholar who knows everything about anything, capable of listing all the records he had ever listened to and the hundred of detective novels he had devoured. Although the hard knocks of destiny had given him a rather weatherbeaten appearance, which only added to his charm. As a magistrate he was fearsome and feared, one of the few who could make the political microcosm tremble with his accusations and sly leaks to the press.

When the Baron appeared in the doorway of Les Chauffeurs, Brivet stood up, almost knocking over the bottle of red wine in front of him.

"Well, well, well, Michel. What a turn-up!"

"Good evening, Judge."

Brivet still had the same deep comma-shaped furrow that divided his forehead in half when he was happy or worried.

"While I was waiting, I did my sums. The two of us go back nearly twenty-five years now."

"The Americans were leaving Vietnam. I remember it as if it was yesterday. With Maistre, we introduced you to a certain Marcel Gouffé. It was 8.45 and the end of his time in custody. He had admitted everything, the murder of his wife and the rest. During his questioning, we also watched shots of the chopper over the American embassy in Saigon. Yes, just like yesterday, my man!"

"Back then, you, Maistre and Marceau were a team of aces. What's become of them?"

"You haven't heard?"

"Heard what?"

"Marceau is dead."

"Shit. But how was I supposed to know?"

"It was in all the papers. A month ago."

"Fuck. I was on holiday in Africa."

"It wasn't a happy end . . ."

The Baron took a menu from their waiter.

"He'd gone wrong, you know. He was up to his ears in dodgy deals. Not a pretty story."

"Jesus fucking Christ!"

"Yes, quite. They killed him. But not in a decent way. Very indecent, in fact."

Gilbert Brivet laid his pale eyes on the Baron, who was studying the menu. He weighed him up, as though trying to gauge the force of the knocks that his friend had received and those he had returned.

"What you're telling me is awful, Michel. He often used to come and see me. In fact, every time he came through Paris. He always called and we would meet up."

"He shot at me."

"What?"

"Three times. He shot at me three times."

The Baron pronounced this last sentence rather like a suspect in custody, releasing some of the guilt that was weighing down on him.

"Hang on there, you're telling me that Jean-Claude Marceau took a shot at you . . . But . . ."

"You heard right."

"Fuck."

The Baron ordered a veal cutlet in a cream sauce with fries, just as he had done during all his years with the Paris police. He raised his eyes, and could almost see Marceau and Maistre in front of him. Marceau with his long locks and moustache like the singer Georges Moustaki, his idol at the time. Marceau who had been a socialist despite it all, a master at stake-outs, and capable of orchestrating an interrogation as if it was a dialogue scripted by Godard.

"It's odd to see you again like this, Michel. You turn up out of the blue, with your news of death . . . It makes me . . ."

Brivet's eyes misted over with misery and nostalgia. He trembled on his seat, like a young tree bracing its strongest branches against the north wind.

"But now you're with the finance squad, you're out of all that!"

"Yes, I am. But sometimes I miss the old days. I'm sorry we don't see more of each other."

"That's my fault. I got married. Then I wanted to forget about Paris and my old life."

"I think we've all been running away from the same thing."

De Palma ordered two pastis.

"I visited her grave this afternoon."

Brivet placed his elbows on the table and laid his chin on his interlaced fingers.

"And I wondered if . . ."

"Stop, Michel. There's no point going back over that now. Life just played us one of its rotten tricks that evening. On you, Maistre, Marceau and me. And as rotten tricks go . . ."

Brivet closed his eyes.

"If you only knew how many times I've played that thing over in my mind: usually it's not me who's on duty that night, usually I don't deal with cases like that. Jesus, it's the first time, and I'm too young. And instead of calling in an old hand to help me out, I decide to play magistrate . . ."

He gulped his pastis, put his glass on the table and spun the ice around for a moment.

"That's all you can say about the matter. We were there when we should have been somewhere else."

"True. But the worst of it is that after that – well I've seen my share of cold meat, believe me. But, I don't know why, I've never been able to get her out of my head."

The Baron trained his eye on his friend, who kept his own eyes fixed on the ice cubes he was still swirling in his glass.

"I went to check out the exhibits."

"And?"

"They're still there. In the courts, they throw nothing away, odd as it might seem. I wondered if we might be able to get something out of the D.N.A."

The Baron gestured to the waiter for two more glasses of pastis.

"That will be difficult! Both for the tests and for the comparisons.

The boys in the genetic labs are a pain in the arse."

The magistrate's face was sad, his eyes humid.

"I don't know," he said. "I'm no longer involved in that kind of case and I never need them. In finance, all we deal with are figures."

"But I can ask for comparisons to be made."

"Even if you're not officially on the case any more?"

"Hang on, am I a cop or aren't I? All we have to do is justify opening the case again."

"But that's the problem. Plus there's the fact that the bastard probably isn't even on record."

"Who knows? More and more are getting caught like that."

"Hmm," said Brivet, sipping his pastis.

The magistrate concentrated on the menu for some time. The waiter came over. The Baron looked at his friend, who was hiding behind a list of dishes, prices and culinary descriptions.

"I'll have the same as you, the veal cutlet."

"It's funny. They haven't changed the menu."

"No, when the old boy left, they decided to keep the same style. And they were right. The place is packed every night."

"I have the impression that it's still the same tablecloths . . ."

"They repainted the walls once. But with the same colour. As for the tablecloths, I think it's nostalgia making you see things as before."

"After that we used to go to Le Bus . . ."

"If only they'd known about that at court!"

"They knew, of course they did."

"We once bumped into a lawyer there. Just once. Their sort didn't go to Le Bus because it was full of druggies. They preferred more upmarket joints."

"Yes, Le Bus was full of gangsters . . . And boys from your home town too."

The Baron turned his palms up towards the ceiling.

"And we didn't smoke only tobacco!"

The two cutlets arrived at the same time. The Baron stared at his fries swimming in cream.

"In fact, why on earth did we start eating here?" Brivet asked.

"It was my cousin who recommended the place. It was the last real wine and coal merchant in Paris. That's why."

"It's a shame Jean-Louis isn't here."

"He's a real Parisian, but you won't get him out of Marseille."

"What about you, Michel?"

"I've asked to be transferred back here."

Brivet put his knife and fork down on the wrong side of his plate, as though he was left-handed.

"You did what?"

"You heard me right! Last week, I asked to come back to the *Brigade Criminelle* in Paris. And I got Gégé to back up my request."

"He's the chief of police now."

"It helps to have friends."

Brivet picked up his knife and fork.

"You're still the craziest person I've ever met," he said, waving knife and fork in front of him.

25.

Moracchini put down the headphones beside her Toshiba, the service laptop.

She read back the sentence she had just typed, then she frowned and blinked.

The beast is coming . . . The old witch will dance . . .

The number dialled belonged to Chandeler, to his office line. And the call had been made from a telephone box in the centre of Tarascon.

The lawyer had absolutely insisted on his telephone being tapped and an investigation opened. The first call he had received was on Thursday, August 28, and the second on the 30th. The message which had just been recorded by the police computer was dated 3 September.

The three calls had been made from boxes located within the triangle formed by Maussane, Tarascon and Arles. Moracchini had turned everything there upside down and examined everyone who was on police records for even the slightest misdemeanour: nothing.

The receivers of the telephones used had been sent to the forensics lab in Marseille for D.N.A. sampling. In theory, she should get the results the next day.

She had then sent a tape of the man's voice on 3 September to be analysed by the scientific team in Ecully. The sound lab had taken its time before sending the following report:

The voice belongs to a person of male gender, aged from forty to fifty.

The individual in question does not present any vocal

287

particularities or difficulties of pronunciation which would indicate an alien or someone of foreign origin. French is thus his mother tongue.

The man tries to conceal his accent, but characteristics remain which would indicate that he speaks with a natural southern and more particularly Marseille accent; the manner of stressing the nasal consonants being typical of that region.

We add that this person proves to be particularly clever at concealing his voice . . .

She put down the report, chose a lock of her hair and started plaiting it without taking her eyes off her computer screen.

That morning, she had called up de Palma. He was still in Paris and had not said when he would be back. He had sounded cold on the telephone, which had made her both sad and furious with herself. So she had decided to distance herself from him as much as possible. It had become obvious that she missed de Palma, and this growing dependency scared her.

She went down to the surveillance centre and came back with another C.D. of tapped calls which she slipped into her computer. The three telephone boxes were not among the numbers used. There were a whole lot of mobiles, far too many for her mood that day. She decided to give Chandeler a call.

"Maître Chandeler?"

"Maître Chandeler didn't come to work this morning."

"Really?"

"And I must say I'm extremely worried. Usually he phones if he hasn't come in in the afternoon."

She looked at her watch. It was 3 p.m.

"If he doesn't phone in the next hour, call me back. Ask for Capitaine Anne Moracchini of the Marseille P.J."

She stared at the long list of mobile numbers and set to work. Romero was taking a day off.

The first thing she did was eliminate all the numbers that appeared more than three times, reasoning that the man would certainly not have used the same telephone that often. This removed over half of them, or thirty calls over a period of twenty-nine hours. Then she excluded all the female voices. This left a total of twenty-one calls.

Four of the remaining people had hung up at once. Eight of them were clients, but one of these drew her attention: the man on the telephone sounded panicked and was talking in a disjointed way about property investments. She decided to listen in more detail later.

The thirteenth call filled her with fright. The number used belonged to Bouygues Telecom.

First there was a long silence, during which just a few meaningless sounds could be heard. Apparently, the person on the telephone was in a very quiet place: there was no noise of traffic or passersby. Then, ten seconds later, came the song:

Lagadigadeu, la tarasco, lagadigadeu . . .

The voice stopped.

A few seconds later, a second voice, as deep as a bass note from an organ, struck up the same melody. At the end of what Moracchini called the couplet, the first voice joined in:

Laïssa passa la vieio masco . . . Laïssa passa que vaï dansa . . .

She put down the headphones. Her hands were trembling. She called de Palma at once and got his voice mail. She hung up with a curse. Romero was unavailable too.

She had to know at once where this call had come from. There was a chance that one of the singers had used his personal telephone. The chance was a slim one, but it was worth chasing up. She tried Romero again, and he finally answered.

"O.K., Anne, I'll be there straight away."

Commissaire Delpiano was on holiday. His deputy advised her to apply to the investigating magistrate. She called him and summed up the situation.

"I think this recording should be analysed at once," he replied.

"We'd have to go to Lyon!"

"I think you'd better go yourself."

"I'll leave right now."

"Fine. I'll sort out the red tape and send a fax to Ecully. Speak to you later."

*

The north-bound motorway was gridlocked. She put the siren on the roof of her car and set off down the hard shoulder, passing by the line of cars that shimmered on the hot tarmac.

De Palma called.

"I'm on my way to Ecully. I should be there by seven this evening."

"Anything new?"

"You're a pain in the arse, Michel. That makes three times I've called you!"

She explained the situation.

"O.K., I'll try and join you there. I should be able to make it by about eight. We'll have dinner and talk this over."

"Hang on, I don't come from Lyon, you know!"

"Neither do I. We'll sort something out."

His words brought a smile to her lips. She looked at the passenger seat. There was only her shoulder bag and the file of tapped calls. She had not brought anything with her for the night . . .

At six p.m., most of the officers and staff who worked in the various departments of the scientific centre at Ecully were finishing their shift. Moracchini crossed the gardens and walked up the side of the large building that contained the national genetic fingerprint records and biological analysis laboratories.

She had driven like a creature possessed, at an average speed of over 160 kph, which meant peaks that topped 200. Her official Xsara was boiling by the time she stopped it in the visitors' car park.

It was the first time that she had been to this strange place, secluded from outside disturbances. Amid a park planted with cedars and pines, the police had set up some cutting-edge laboratories in Bauhaus-style buildings of two or three floors, all right angles, made of glass, metal and wood.

At the end of the main drive, she turned towards the computer, sound and video laboratories.

"The sound department, please?"

The doorkeeper, a blond lad immaculately dressed, looked up over the reception counter.

"You want to see Leila Hamdi?"

"That's right."

"Second floor. The lift's over there, to your left."

Hamdi was deep in the middle of a conversation between two mobsters. *On my mother's life*, one of them said. *You're dead, I swear*, yelled the other. Behind the voice that kept on repeating *On my mother's life*, she had identified the sound of a bus stopping and then pulling off again. One of the two men had called from somewhere close to a bus stop.

The scientist spun round on her chair when she saw Moracchini appear at the door and knock on the frame.

"Hello, Leila, I'm Anne Moracchini."

Hamdi stood up.

"Yes, I've heard a lot about you. We get news from all over France around here."

Moracchini shook her hand.

"So this is an emergency, you say? It's the same guy from the other day, I suppose."

"That's right. And it's red-hot!" she replied, handing her the C.D. "Did you get the fax from magistrate Laurence Modiano?"

"No, that's not my department," she replied, shrugging. "Anyway, I couldn't care less about all that red tape."

Along the wall behind her there was a row of recording equipment: a Revox with enormous tapes, a Nagra and a large number of machines with VU metres, ranging from the simplest mini-cassette player to the very latest digital model. To the left of the door, two large computer screens were displaying the curves and graphics of sound sequences.

"Impressive kit!"

"It's the best there is," the scientist replied, stroking her computer keyboard. "Most of the software comes from Russia . . . it was invented in K.G.B. times and perfected later. I've also got some programmes from the F.B.I., but they don't work so well. It always surprises visitors when I tell them."

Most police officers had problems understanding what she did. There was a world of difference between fieldwork and a doctor of physics capable of identifying the origin of a sound that was inaudible to their cloth ears. Yet Hamdi had worked on several famous cases and made vital contributions.

"Is it long?" she asked.

"No, just a couple of minutes."

"We'll proceed as usual. I'll listen to it first in my headphones, then we'll talk. You can go and get some coffee if you want, the machine's down the corridor, turn left then left again. Come back in five minutes."

On one side of the lab, big picture windows looked out over the adjacent corridor. Moracchini saw a commissaire pass by whom she had known for ages. She went outside while Hamdi slid the C.D. into her digital player.

Five minutes later, Moracchini was back. The scientist still had her headphones on and was thinking, her elbows on the desk, one index finger tapping on her mouth.

"This is weird," she said, taking off the headset. "Really weird."

"Why's that?"

"Was it picked up from a mobile?"

"Yes."

"What time?"

"At 20.34."

Hamdi looked at the computer screen and pointed at a window displaying some green clouds, denser in some places than in others.

"This is the sound spectrum of what we're about to listen to. It gives us the profile."

She clicked her mouse and the profile started to scroll. Moracchini heard a whole lot of new noises, sounds she hadn't heard in her office.

"That," the technician said, pointing with her finger, "is your caller's breathing. He thinks before he speaks. I'd say he was an anxious sort. Those little traces are the noises around him. They're barely audible because he's inside what I think is a car or a small room. The sounds are all muffled and there's no echo. But we can still clearly hear bird calls, and what you see there is a frog. If I isolate it, look what we get."

A couple of adjustments, and the sound of croaking became clear.

"But there are loads of them!"

"Your customer is next to a pond or a lake, anyway a place where there are plenty of frogs."

"How about a marsh?"

"Why not indeed!"

She let the sounds run on then paused on a spike in the profile.

"That's the call, or even the grunting, of a bird I don't recognise. There are several of them. Your guy could have been in a zoo. In any case, close to a bird I don't know. And I know quite a few!" she added with a grin.

Moracchini said nothing. She was completely fascinated by her colleague's equipment and know-how.

"Now, as for the voice, it's the same guy as last time. I told you he was clever, but now he really impresses me. I've only seen this once in my life. In Vietnam."

She peered at Moracchini, over her thick glasses.

"It's someone who can produce two voices at the same time."

"You mean that both voices on the tape belong to the same person?"

Hamdi nodded a big yes.

"Look, those are the A and the R of the high voice when it says *tarasco*, and here are the same letters pronounced by the deeper voice. They're identical. But it's practically impossible to find two people who have exactly the same A and R. The same goes for the other vowels. They're pronounced identically, but on different registers."

"That's amazing. How is it done?"

"The Vietnamese guy I met told me that he used his stomach, a kind of ventriloquism! I could hardly believe it, but he managed to produce two different sounds in that way. I can't tell you any more, except that your customer is a rare case. Extremely rare."

Moracchini's mobile rang.

"It's Michel. I'm at the train station in Lyon."

"Already?"

"It's nine o'clock!"

"Can you make it to Ecully?"

"No, there's no point. Tell me about it later. I'll try and find a couple of hotel rooms and I'll call you back."

"If you find just one, I wouldn't mind . . ."

Hamdi stared at her intensely.

"Was that a colleague?"

"De Palma. Do you know him?"

"Everyone knows de Palma. He was one of the first people to ask me for a voice analysis, and one of the first to trust me. Is he coming here?"

"No, he doesn't think he can make it. But if we go out for a bite to eat, do you want to come along?"

"Sorry, this evening I can't. I have a date. We'll work on for a while then stop before my head explodes."

She sat down in front of her computer and listened again to the same extract. Then she picked out a particular sound and clicked on several windows.

"I've got to identify this damn bird. It's the key to the whole thing. Can you hear it?"

It was like a slight grunt, at first in a middle register then deeper, like an "r" ending with a sort of "wou" then an "a". The call came back at frequent intervals: *rrwouaa, rrwouaa . . .*

"It's the sort of thing you don't pick up with your own ears. It was the software that identified and amplified it."

Rrwouaa, rrwouaa . . .

"I think you've already been a great help, Leila."

"No problem. That's my job!"

She turned towards a second computer and went online. Then she made two telephone calls.

"Shit, all I'm getting are answering machines," she said with a sigh.

She tried yet another number. In vain. Then she stood up, removed the C.D. from the player and replaced it in its box.

"Can you come back tomorrow, around ten?"

"Do you think that . . . ?"

"It's essential. I'll try to identify the bird and all the rest. Right now, I can't do anything more. Everyone's shut up shop. But tomorrow I'll contact some colleagues or scientists in France who may recognise this sound. This evening, it's not possible."

"O.K. I'll see you then."

"But I'll give it a go again later, in my place. If I find out anything, I'll give you a ring."

It was now 10 p.m.

De Palma had taken a room in the Hotel Ibis by the station. When they got back, it was past midnight and they tossed a coin to see who would sleep on the street side of the bed. The Baron won.

"Let's have a night cap. I've got a couple of things to tell you."

She took two individual bottles of vodka from the minibar and mixed them with orange juice. As she did so, she told him about the events of that day.

"A groaning bird?" he said, puzzled. "I'd never have thought that a bird could groan."

"But that's what comes out of the machine."

"Leila is almost never wrong. So this is big news. And if our friend Chandeler hadn't started shitting himself, we'd never have thought of birds."

"Chandeler hasn't been heard of since this morning."

"I'm afraid he'll end up like the others. It's the same rationale. And we can't do a damn thing about it!"

"This isn't the first time we've been in this kind of situation, and it won't be the last. In cases like this, it always takes several corpses before you find a pattern. This time, I think we've made good progress and I don't have a sense of feeling helpless."

The Baron was tense. He ran his fingers through his hair several times, blinking nervously as he did so.

"It's because I'm completely self-centred and reckon I should solve everything in record time! De Palma the protector of his fellow human beings . . . So when I fail, I blame myself and feel I should take on the universe. I've been thinking things through, Anne – life in general and myself in particular. And I realise that I'm arrogant and selfish. On this case, you've done as much as I have, you keep me up to date with what you do. I tell you hardly anything. I'm really sorry."

"Sorry isn't bad!"

He sipped at his screwdriver, running the sweet, cool liquid down his throat.

"Texeira also made a recording of the voice. I forget to tell you about that and I didn't even send it to the lab. Sometimes I think I'm the king of jerks. Wrapped up in myself."

She sat down next to him and massaged his neck.

"And I haven't told you about the Liberation either, and Steinert's connections with La Balme."

"You'll have time enough tomorrow, in the car."

"More and more often, I wonder what I'll do after leaving the force. Have you ever thought about that?"

"Don't take this badly, but I've got a good few years on you."

She caressed his cheek and drew him towards her, sliding a hand beneath his shirt. She kissed his chest, and drew his leg between her own. He felt her firm body, tense with desire, her breasts crushed against his torso. She undid his belt and laid him back.

Much later, in the middle of the night, he woke up. Moracchini was asleep. The red light from the street was coming through the cracks in the shutters. His mind was empty.

It was the first time in a long while.

Leila Hamdi was waiting for the two of them beside the coffee machine. She had tried to conceal the signs of a sleepless night under a thick layer of make-up, and had varnished her nails a bright red that stood out against the white plastic of the cup in her hand.

During the night, she had consulted two colleagues in the U.S.A. and one in Germany about the strange bird calls. The Americans had come up with answers that sounded implausible: the species they credited with the sound was a type of moorhen found only in the swamps of the Mississippi delta. The German had owned up his ignorance at once, but suggested an obvious lead: websites run by birdwatchers.

For hours, she had surfed the net looking for sites with sound recordings, and at around two in the morning, with eyes red from staring, she hit the jackpot: ornithopedia.com had one of the most extensive archives of bird-call recordings imaginable. All she had to do was to find the right one. It took her another couple of hours to download all the grunts that sounded more or less like the one on the tapped telephone call. In the early hours, she went to bed with a single name clear in her mind: the white spoonbill.

On arriving at the lab, she immediately compared the two profiles: they were identical. So when she saw Moracchini and de Palma arrive on the second floor, she threw herself at them.

"I've got good news for you," she said as she kissed them both. "It's a white spoonbill. And apparently, they're extremely rare."

De Palma said nothing until the lab door closed behind them.

"A white spoonbill, you say?"

"Stone-cold certain."

He telephoned Texeira at once.

"Have you got white spoonbills in your sector?"

"Of course, but they're rare. They're a sort of mythical bird for lovers of the Camargue."

"Mythical?"

"What I mean is that they're quite hard to observe. They're extremely picky migrators."

"Are there any here at the moment?"

"Theoretically speaking, yes. But I haven't seen any since the end of spring."

"Any chance you can clue yourself up?"

"Perhaps, but I don't see how."

"Neither do I, but you have to try, Christophe. And as fast as you can . . . right now, I mean! I can't explain why, but you have to."

"O.K., I'll get on it. I'll call up all my birdwatching friends."

Moracchini and de Palma left Ecully at about 10 a.m. Moracchini took the wheel. For a long while, until they had left the traffic jams around Lyon, the Baron kept his eyes pinned on the rear of the cars in front of them. It looked as if he was sailing in murky waters.

She did not even try to lift him out of this strange torpor. On the other side of the Lyon tollbooth, it was her mobile that broke the silence.

". . . the phone used to call Chandeler was reported stolen at the commissariat of Tarascon on July 19th at 10.15. That's all I can tell you."

"Thanks, Daniel . . ."

Chandeler gathered his strength. It had now been over a day since he had drunk or eaten anything. It felt as though his lips were coming off in shreds, and his tongue and throat were growing as rough as sandpaper.

He groped around in the darkness until his hands climbed a groove in the wall. At the top he found a right angle, a horizontal line, and another right angle. This must be a door. He was sure of it. He gauged its size and changed his mind. It was more like a trapdoor.

It was the only way out of the place where he now was.

Trying not to make a sound and holding his breath, he stuck his ear against the panel of the trapdoor and made out a noise on the other side of someone rummaging in what might be a drawer or a piece of furniture. Whatever it was, the movements sounded agitated and were accompanied by a deep voice that kept repeating, in a loop, as if chanting a mantra:

Lagadigadeu la tarasco, lagadigadeu dou casteu . . .
Lagadigadeu la tarasco, lagadigadeu dou casteu . . .

Suddenly, the voice moved away and he heard a door slam shut. His jailer had left. Feverishly, he felt around the panel and discovered, on the right-hand side, a hole. There was a lock but no handle. He put an eye to the hole. It was blocked, but a tiny ray of light came through it. This beam, as fine as a needle, brought him a joy such as he hadn't felt for ages. Small as it was, this hint of day gave him hope.

He sat down on the floor of his prison without taking his eyes off the source of light. After a moment the point was as large as the sun.

298

26.

Ingrid Steinert was standing in the shade of the mauve wisteria that spilled down over the patio, between the rambling roses which were back in bloom. She was wearing a tight cotton dress, stretched by her thighs and breasts and fastened with a knot behind her back.

When de Palma came over to her, she took a final drag of her cigarette before flicking it into the garden. She held a limp hand out.

She had cut her hair quite short, like a schoolgirl's from the 1940s. That gave her a curl over each ear and a straight fringe, which made her look extraordinarily young. De Palma remembered that Isabelle had exactly the same haircut in the last known photograph of her.

"How are you, Michel?"

"I must admit that I'm happy to see you again . . . and a little embarrassed too."

She gazed at him as if to examine his conscience. In the distance, a tractor could be heard coming and going across the fields. On the road from Eygalières, he had noticed a group of grape-pickers in a vineyard that must belong to La Balme. Because of the heat wave, the harvest was early that year.

He raised his eyes and peered at the hills of the Alpilles, looking for Bérard's sheep.

"What an awful way to go, don't you think so Michel?"

Weighed down by memories, he did not reply. He simply nodded and waved a hand in the air.

"So the grape-picking has started?"

"Not today. It rained last night, a heavy thunderstorm. The farmers have gone to inspect the vines to see if there hasn't been too much damage. We'll start in a few days' time when it's all dried out."

The noise of the tractor stopped. Everything turned calm again. A cool breeze, still charged with the vicious mood of the storm, caused the heavy leaves of the plane trees to flutter.

"I'll have to go back to my autumn collections," she said. "My life's in a terrible mess. I'll also have to deal with the olive trees. Nothing has been done for months."

Laura, the housekeeper, came out of the living room.

"I'll have to do some shopping in Arles, Madame. Do you mind being left on your own?"

"No, not at all."

The sky above the Alpilles was turning red, with blue flames piercing the clouds like blasts from a blowtorch.

"Are your husband's papers here?" De Palma asked.

She hesitated. Her eyes scanned his face.

"Quite a few of them. As a matter of fact, I was wondering when you'd ask if you could look at them."

"I think the time has come."

"What exactly are you looking for?"

"Everything."

"I've been through them and tried to sort them out. I've set all his letters aside, and what you call his papers in a big box. It's upstairs. If you want, we can go and take a look."

There were documents dating back over many years. De Palma tried to organise them chronologically. The oldest came from the Sixties and read like everyday thoughts in a diary kept by a foreign tourist in Provence. There were also some poems and a lot of notes about birds. De Palma read through them in detail. He had in mind the white spoonbill that the wiretap had revealed.

"Do you remember William ever talking about a bird called the white spoonbill?"

"Particular memories, no. He said it was very rare, and getting rarer. He was always very glad when he managed to photograph them. You know, he adored the birds of the Camargue."

De Palma dipped back into the ornithological notes. They included precise accounts of nesting locations and maps to show observation points, but none concerned the places he had already located. Steinert had inserted photographs with descriptions written on the back: velvet scoter, red-breasted merganser, great skua, yellowhammer . . . William Steinert had been a gifted photographer.

She came over to him, he could almost hear her breathing. A second bundle included a notebook on recycled paper. On the first double spread, Steinert had jotted down a date, 1990, which was no doubt the start of its use. Overleaf, there was a picture of a water rail lurking in the quiet of the marshland, its red beak brilliant against the green and gold of the rushes. On the facing page, Steinert had written:

Water rail. Rallus aquaticus.
    One nest with 5 eggs on 23 March 1990. Samphire field north of Le Vigueirat, thirty metres from observation point 18.
    One nest and two chicks on 14 March 1997. Samphire field of La Sigoulette, 43°30/4°28.
    The chicks will not be flying in August.

On the fourth page, there were the same kind of notes about a common crane, taken the following year. De Palma flicked through the book rapidly, then stopped about halfway through.

White spoonbill. Platalea leucorodia.
    Two specimens. 17 August 1995. 07.30. Marshes of St Seren.
    One specimen in flight on 28 June 1999. 18.20. Redon salt marsh.
    In Delachaux: observed quite frequently. Around 51 sightings between 1957 and 1979. Quite common in July and August. Very few in winter.

There was something unreal about the photograph. It showed a white spoonbill gliding in the summer heat, borne up on the thermals, its snow-white wings spread wide in the sunlight.

"He also used to mention the black stork. He said that with the white spoonbill it was the most beautiful bird in the region. It's also very rare. Look at the next page."

There was a stylish shot of the big bird, strangely majestic in the middle of a meadow in the Camargue, where it seemed to have strayed. De Palma had never seen one before and found it magnificent.

Steinert had noted:

1 specimen. 19 May 1998.
If Texeira is to be believed, this is the first photo taken since 1987! Anyway the only one known.

He leafed through the rest of the book but found nothing else of interest. The only thing that stuck in his mind was Texeira's name. He telephoned the biologist.

"Any news of white spoonbills?"

"No. Nobody's seen any for months. At the start of the summer, there was someone who sent me some shots he had taken. I must admit I was rather jealous."

"Do you know this person?"

"No, I'm afraid not. Why?"

De Palma let a moment's silence pass by, while he changed gear.

"Have you ever met this visitor?"

"Yes, in fact I have. We'd spoken together, a few days before I got the photos."

"Do you remember him?"

"Quite clearly. I'm observant."

"Go on."

"He's tall, about 1m 85. Hair chestnut or black. Aged around fifty. With the look of an old globetrotter, if you see what I mean – scruffy trousers, and a combat jacket . . . A bit of a hippy, or a dreamer. There are quite a few people like that in the world of birdwatchers. They're often highly intelligent with it."

"Describe his clothes . . ."

He motioned to Ingrid to hand him a piece of paper and a pen.

"Jeans rather grubby, army jacket khaki, and sandals like the leftist militants used to wear in the Seventies."

"Viet Cong sandals?"

"That's right."

De Palma made a note.

"On the other hand his kit was terrific. You could say it was the classic photographer's kit, but at prices that only the keenest amateurs or professionals will pay. Also he had periscopic binoculars."

"What are they?"

"They're like a periscope . . . you know, as in a submarine: see without being seen. Not many people have those!"

He jotted down this detail in block capitals and underlined it twice.

"And have you seen him since?"

"No, but while we've been talking, I've been downstairs to check the observation log. The day was June 28th. I received the photos a few days later."

"And how does that fit with the voices?"

"Well . . . Jesus, it was practically the same day, or somewhere close. Do you think that . . ."

"I'm not thinking, Christophe. I'm observing! It could mean nothing."

"Hang on, you're starting to scare me!"

"Oh, you're in no danger. No danger at all!"

Ingrid had stood up and was staring intently at de Palma. Her cotton dress filtered her tall, firm figure in the morning light that slanted through the windows.

De Palma thought hard. All this was not really taking him anywhere, but it had him so excited that gusts of heat were rising inside him. He wanted to act and was desperate for the means to do so, or concrete lines of investigation. He had to admit the truth: he was standing on the threshold of a room in total darkness, and didn't know how to turn the light on. But another door had just opened.

Ingrid came over, sat down beside him and opened another notebook, which had cardboard covers and was bound like a real book. Their shoulders touched. He was hypnotised by her long fingers as they turned over the pages.

"I looked at this one yesterday," she murmured. "I think you should look at it, Michel."

She turned over another three pages and passed him the notebook. He felt her breast lie gently on his forearm for a second.

"When I found this last night, it really scared me."

She laid her hand on his shoulder.

"Read it, Michel."

It has been said that the Tarasque, half-human and half-reptile from the Jurassic, symbolises the Roman dominator settled in Provence over a long period.

For the Vokae who lived on the right bank of the Rhône and the Salluvii who were spread out between Monaco and Marseille, Rome could be symbolised by a monster. It is something one can easily imagine: a beast emerging straight out of the imagination of peoples subjected to the Pax Romana. *This monster could symbolise this domineering Rome. But there is more to it than that.*

The Tarasque is a reptile. Some have seen in it a representation of mankind's basest instincts (the reptilian brain), others have seen it as the gods of paganism tamed by Saint Martha.

But can it not also be viewed as the representation of a bane that really existed? Bérard says that the truth lies there and that tarasques existed. Back to Roman times: the Roman legion that occupied and administered the region of Tarascon was based in Nîmes. Its emblem was . . . a crocodile.

Bérard says that the Romans brought with them those huge reptiles captured in the Egyptian Nile. They are said to have used them as mascots. What is much more certain is that they used them in the arenas of Nîmes and Arles . . .

What is more, the crocodiles of the Nile could readily adapt to the climate and habitat of the Camargue, in many ways similar to that of the banks of the Nile.

From this point on, Steinert had written fast, his hand so fine and spidery that it was barely legible.

This could explain the spoor I saw yesterday in the marshland of La Capelière. I had never seen anything so big and so impressive. It was not made by an animal listed among the fauna of the

Camargue. I mentioned this to Bérard. He told me: "She's back, I called her and here she is." The look in his eyes was frightening . . .

I'm going back into the marshes tomorrow at nightfall to check these marks. I don't want anyone to spot me. After that, I'll show it all to Texeira.

NB: Bérard seemed out of his mind.

De Palma looked up from the notebook and let his mind wander through the maze of clues that now lay before him.

He had just read what must be William Steinert's last words. Ingrid had laid her hand on his arm.

"I don't know why, but I've made the connection with what I've been reading in the press. You know, those mutilated bodies. The crocodile, the Tarasque . . ."

"It's the presence of Bérard that worries me most. I think we're in great danger."

De Palma concentrated. He wanted to burst his head open, the ideas were hurting so much. He mumbled, pointing his index finger at some imaginary point on the table.

"Bérard, the Tarasque, William . . ."

He wanted to add: "and the Germans", but restrained himself.

"Bérard, the Tarasque, William, the birds . . . The Tarasque, the birds . . . Bérard and the Tarasque."

She put a hand on his shoulder and gently squeezed the muscle that bulged beneath his shirt.

"Bérard and the Tarasque . . ."

He looked for an unusual detail. Boyer, his father figure on the murder squad, had taught them that technique: an element that does not seem to fit into the jigsaw and that finally completes it. He rapped his hand on the table.

"Was the shepherd interested in the occult arts?"

She searched in his face.

"I think he was. William used to say that he was a bit of a *Zauberer* . . . a sorcerer! He nursed his sheep with plants that he alone knew about. Sometimes he told William about impossible things . . . William even told me that he had had some incredibly intense esoteric experiences with Bérard."

"Why haven't you told me this before?"

She moved even closer to him.

"I don't know. I never took it very seriously. William was a mystic about nature, I have trouble believing in God."

De Palma put his arm round her shoulder and hugged her hard. She let her body lean against his chest.

"I believe you, Ingrid."

He relaxed his embrace.

"Can I offer you something to drink?"

Through the window, he stared at the spectacle of trees under the sun. She smiled at him gently, then produced two glasses.

"I've opened another bottle of Muscat, Michel. I know how much you like it."

They drank the sweet white wine and spoke at length, first about William Steinert, then about the few notions of magic that de Palma possessed. Then the conversation drifted on for over an hour. She opened a second bottle. The wine came from the old vines alongside the Downlands.

They played at exposing their lives, taking care never to say everything, until their minds ran out and a strange sensation of joy arose between them.

She was standing beside the window, and it seemed that the forms of her body had suddenly been highlighted by a watercolourist's brush. Irresistibly he went over to her, and took her hands. She did not resist and offered him her lips. He lost himself in the warmth of her face. It was as if she had been born from the sun.

Her breasts were hard under the cotton of her dress. He raised his hands along her sides and then her back; her skin was bathed in her woman's heat.

306

27.

The sultry humidity had been rising for some time.

Chandeler reckoned that the sun must be approaching its zenith or possibly past it. The sounds of drawers and cupboard doors being opened and closed reached him through the wooden slats of the trapdoor.

Suddenly, he heard a door slam with a heavier noise, different from the others. The man who was keeping him prisoner must have just gone out. This was not the first time. On each occasion, the lawyer had noticed that his jailer returned after a period he reckoned at over an hour.

He went over to the trapdoor, guided by the tiny point of light that glinted through the shadows, then he started to bang on the wood, first with his shoulder, then with his heels. His keeper gave no sign of life, which gave him courage.

He braced his hands on the floor for maximum support, then drew his knees up to his chin and kicked out hard. A violent pain shot from the tips of his toes to his spine. He slipped his nails between the edges of the door and noticed that there was now a little give. He crouched back down and kicked, again and again.

The pain in his feet and legs was becoming unbearable.

He clenched his teeth. Tears were in his eyes.

Another blow.

The trapdoor gave way.

He threw himself at the aperture.

He was free. Blinded by light.

On a desk in front of the trapdoor was a huge computer with a screensaver showing large white birds. The cries of birds emerged from the loudspeakers. On the other side of the room, to either side of the window, stood two stuffed white birds the size of storks, the same as the ones on the monitor.

On the walls there were photographs pinned up. In snapshots taken with a zoom lens, Chandeler recognised Morini, his former client, taken at a three-quarters angle, sitting in his bar. In two other shots, a man was walking in the street. Above it a Post-it read: Jean-Claude Marceau.

Chandeler began to tremble. Thirst was constricting his throat, but he did not take the time to look for water. He gathered the little strength he had left and headed towards the door. It was locked from the outside. A huge bunch of keys hung from the door jamb. His fingers shaking, he tried the keys one after the other. Twice the bunch fell from his hands. His feet hurt as if they had been beaten by canes. About a dozen keys later, he found the one that turned.

The door opened out onto a narrow path that retreated through a reed bed. He walked as fast as he could, trying not to scream each time his feet touched the ground. Most of the rushes had to be over three metres high. He turned round and saw that his prison was no more than a tiny farmhouse, half engulfed by ivy, concealed in a grove of ash trees and reeds. It was absolutely invisible in its jungle sanctuary.

Father Favier's fingers were long and gnarled, as though one-euro coins had been slipped in between the phalanges. His hands were in constant motion, which Moracchini read as a sign of nerves.

"You're telling me that just before the death of Christian Rey you spoke to Gouirand in your church!"

"That's right, yes. But why are you asking me these questions again?"

She ignored the priest's reply, went over to him and tossed her hair back provocatively. Favier did not even notice her gesture.

"Never mind about your discussion. You then state that once Gouirand had left your church, you heard some noises, is that right?"

"As I've already explained several times: Gouirand had come to fetch the Tarasque to clean it. When he had gone, I closed the door behind him. Everything seemed quiet, then I heard those noises. I couldn't find out where they came from, but I'm sure I heard them! Someone was there, and then that someone left. I'm sure of it!"

"As if with the help of the Holy Ghost?"

The priest smiled with mild disdain.

"You could put it like that."

She stood up and stretched. She was wearing tight jeans and a T-shirt she had won at the police marksmanship competition.

"So what do you think about all this, Father?"

"I don't know what to reply. Of course, I don't believe all these stories that are going around in Tarascon! Just imagine it, only yesterday some more people came to ask me to say masses to fend off the evil spell. Masses to fight the Tarasque . . . Some people believe in a curse, others are asking for processions through the places of the legend of the Tarasque. Do you see me telling the bishop that I'm off on a procession to the castle of Tarascon or in the marshes of the Camargue? Not to mention what the journalists would have to say."

"Yes, I can quite understand!"

"Oh no you can't! I've had official requests addressed to me to go and bless the waters of the marshlands. It's as if the people in the town were possessed by this demon. Even the young lads from North Africa are talking about the Tarasque, can you believe that? I mean, it's not even part of their culture . . . My predecessor did warn me, but I never thought it would go this far."

She continued to stare at him, trying to catch his attention with female wiles, which had to be bothering him, but he did not show it.

"Each to his own monster. You have the Tarasque, we have the city football team."

She pointed at the window.

"And do you know where this Gouirand is right now?"

"No, honestly, I don't," he replied, turning his hands up towards the ceiling. "I think he may have simply gone away on holiday."

She turned back towards her computer and clicked on the criminal records file.

"O.K., I don't see any reason to detain you. Thanks for coming in."

"I have nothing to add except to say that this is the work of a madman!"

De Palma appeared in the doorway and tapped on the frame.

"Come in, Michel. I think you know Father Favier."

De Palma held out his hand. Moracchini placed herself between the two men.

"I just wanted to check a few details again with the priest of Saint Martha," she said. "But I'm through now."

The priest got to his feet and picked up an old battered leather briefcase, which he had placed on her desk.

"Your colleague in Tarascon also questioned me twice."

"The Tarasque ate him too!"

The priest stopped playing with his fingers and stared back at de Palma. He was wearing a curious expression, both eyebrows raised at a slant.

"It isn't funny to say that, sir, really not funny."

De Palma placed a hand on the priest's back and guided him gently to the door.

"You're absolutely right, it's no joke."

The man of God slipped out like a shadow and disappeared down the green corridor.

"We've got to lay hands on Gouirand. I'll have him brought in."

"Bérard too was a Knight of the Tarasque."

"Really? I'm going to end up wondering who wasn't."

He handed her a sheet of paper, on which he had made a series of notes:

White spoonbill (Platalea leucorodia).

   Shape and size of a pure white heron. Long black bill, shaped like a spoon at the end. The adult has an orange strip on its chest and, in spring, a long orange/yellow head crest. Immature: no strip, black wing-tips, pink bill. Silent except during the breeding season when it produces a groaning call.

Shallow fresh and coastal waters, nests in colonies in trees, bushes and reed beds on marshy ground.

86 centimetres.

Can be observed in the Camargue in spring and autumn. Nests in North Africa. Groaning sound from nests (not in Camargue). Occasional clicking of bills.

Long neck, long feet. Flies with neck extended.

Feeds on aquatic invertebrates and small fish.

"Very interesting, Michel. But it doesn't tell us much."

"I copied it from a birdwatcher's guide for the Camargue. Take another look."

She read back through the notes, murmuring each word.

"Jesus, so it sings only when nesting, and that happens only in North Africa."

"So the recording was a sound montage. A very clever one, but a montage all the same. I think we really are up against a madman of a kind we've never imagined before."

"Any ideas?"

Moracchini had sat down on the edge of her desk; she was examining her nails and frowning.

"We'll have to investigate the ornithology freaks. All those obsessed with our little feathered friends. You never know . . ."

"Yeah, but in the meantime Chandeler is out there in the wilds, with the psycho."

"What can I say?"

"Nothing. Just say nothing."

As he emerged from the reed bed, the man knew at once that his prisoner had given him the slip. Without knowing why, he felt it, but he had had to prepare the beast. And that was not an easy thing to do. He had been making it fast for a while, and the storms that span in the sky above the delta had swamped the air with electricity.

The beast was more uptight and dangerous than ever before.

He took out his knife and ran inside the house. Inside it was quiet.

311

He stopped, his arms flailing in front of the staved-in trapdoor. In the late afternoon shadows, the white spoonbills were watching him with their glass eyes. They seemed to be laughing at the strange trick that fate had played on him.

He stayed still for some time. His mind was so clouded that he felt as if his cerebral convolutions were muddled together.

From the computer came the clicking of beaks and groaning. It was the spoonbills' song of love and grace during their nuptial display. He smiled as though emerging from his torpor. The recording was on a loop. It dated back to the days when he had worked for an Algerian oil company.

After a moment, it seemed to him that the stuffed birds were coming to life on their varnished wooden stands. He walked over to them on tiptoe, uttering little cries, like quiet groans.

Tears filled his eyes. He wiped the sweat that was running down his temples. His hands were trembling, his guts churning. He tried to get hold of himself, but shakes and painful spasms were knotting his entrails. He went closer to the birds, and stopped less than a metre away. With the tips of his fingers, he stroked their marvellously white plumage. He sank his fingertips into the down of their long graceful necks.

He asked the spoonbills to give him the strength to fight through the crisis that was now submerging him, but the trembling soon turned to convulsions, and he collapsed.

He came round some time later, unable to tell how long the attack had lasted. The spoonbills were still there, he could hear the dry clicking of their long, spoon-shaped beaks and the groaning of the males.

Mad with rage, he went outside and headed for a lean-to beside the house. He returned a few minutes later with a jerry-can of petrol. His eyes were red with fury, and saliva was dribbling from his lips, twisted downwards by an unknown pain.

He went inside the house and methodically spread fuel at strategic points. Then he nervily struck a match and rushed outside, pursued by the fire's hot breath.

He stopped running a long time later, when he found himself on the road to Salins-de-Giraud. A column of smoke was rising in the distance, a huge exclamation mark above the marshes.

At that moment, he thought of the beast. Only at that moment did he realise that she would be furious and that nothing could stop her.

28.

Chandeler felt a bony hand shake him vigorously. He half-opened his eyes and saw a weather-beaten face with slanted eyes staring at him, its lips twisted upwards in a grin that revealed two rows of ivory teeth.

"Wake up, sir! . . . Wake up . . . Can't stay here."

Chandeler squinted and saw that two Asians were looking down at him nervously.

"Wake up, sir! . . . Not possible . . ."

He gathered the last of his energy to mumble a few words:

"Must . . . call . . . the police. I . . ."

"We not police, sir . . . We work in fields. Workers!"

Chandeler heard a torrent of onomatopoeias flooding his weakened mind. He thought for a moment that he was hallucinating again. Since being kidnapped, he had constantly been wandering between the real world and nightmare visions.

He tried to stand up, but immediately felt powerful arms catch hold of him and raise him from the ground to carry him to a trailer coupled to a vineyard tractor. All at once he found himself lying in the middle of some crates that smelled of raw earth and greenery, with the sun blazing in the sky up above him.

Four people sat beside him in the cart. Four Asians to whom he gave a smile of gratitude. Then the procession crossed a field that was out of his line of sight and turned down a sunken lane bordered by ash trees and poplars.

It must be quite late in the day, the blue sky was becoming tinged with pink and orange. A smell of diesel and smoke enveloped him,

314

the tractor almost stopped and the engine shifted up a gear: now they were driving down a tarmac road.

He gradually recovered his spirits as he exchanged glances with his saviours. After escaping, he had walked for some time until, exhausted, he had found a stream, where he had drunk his fill of water, and a place in a curly bush, away from prying eyes. It was next to a field, maybe a vineyard, he could no longer remember. What did it matter? He had fallen asleep.

For some time, he observed the men who had rescued him, and realised that they must be illegal migrant workers. He had heard tell of this sort of workforce trafficking in the Camargue. Several big landowners had been caught red-handed using modern-day slaves. They generally came from Thailand or Cambodia, and worked like coolies for a handful of euros.

The man who greeted him in the farmyard of La Fraysse must be foreman, or something like that. The Asians vanished into the buildings.

"The workers found you just as they were finishing work. I am Fabrice Luciano, I'm the manager here."

"Chandeler, member of the bar in Marseille."

The foreman recoiled.

"How did you come to be in such a state, on the edge of a strawberry field?"

"I . . . I . . . it's too long and too crazy to explain. I must speak to the police."

"I can take you to Marseille if you like."

"No, no, I must call the police!"

"Listen, sir, I . . . how can I put it? The workers who brought you wouldn't like the police to know that they were working here . . . if you see what I mean."

"I must speak to the police. Let me call them."

"So long as you don't tell them what happened here. I don't want to see any policemen or gendarmes around here."

"O.K. I'll call a friend."

At 7.12 p.m. de Palma's mobile rang.

*

It all went very quickly. Less than an hour later, de Palma arrived at La Fraysse with Moracchini and Romero. Chandeler was sitting at the big dining-room table and finishing the meal he'd been given.

When he saw the police officers, he stood up and wrung their hands for some time.

"It's the first time in my life that I'm glad to see a policeman."

"There's a first time for everything," de Palma replied. "Now, tell us about it all."

Chandeler's expression changed abruptly, a veil of terror covered it. It was only after a long silence that he started the tale of his kidnapping: on leaving the court in Marseille, where he had been defending an industrialist accused of bribing civil servants, a man had approached him then discreetly stuck a gun in his belly.

"He was forty-five to fifty years old. A metre eighty, maybe more . . . He was about my height in fact, and I measure one metre eighty-five. Dark, shoulder-length hair, small blue eyes and bushy eyebrows. A thin nose . . . Unshaven. He was wearing a safari jacket, jeans and sandals."

Chandeler had not argued with this man's orders and had got into a nearly new Ford Scorpio. This detail had struck him: it must have been a hire car. Then they had driven towards Martigues, Fos and the Camargue.

De Palma produced a map of the Rhône delta and unfolded it on the table.

"Try hard to remember. We're on the long straight line of the R.N. 568. At some moment you turn left. Is it this road?"

"Yes, that's it. Beside it, there's an old caravan and a wrecked fridge."

"Then you drive on."

"We drive for quite a while down the same road. There are mown fields on both sides . . . I mean, there's nothing in them . . . We continue and arrive at a junction, there's a signpost pointing to Sambuc. We drive . . ."

Chandeler reflected, his eyes closed, rerunning the journey in his mind.

"On the right, there was a large expanse of water, and on the left reeds everywhere. And then . . ."

Chandeler plunged back into his memories. He frowned.

"I want to remember, but I can't."

"Did you drive for long in that direction?"

"No, not at all."

"How many minutes," Moracchini asked.

"No more than five."

She looked at de Palma.

"It sounds like it was near La Capelière."

"There's been a fire there!" the foreman said.

"A fire?"

"An old farmhouse has just burned down. It nearly set light to the entire region."

"Could you take us there?"

"No problem."

De Palma looked at Chandeler, he seemed completely wrecked.

"I suggest you stay here for the moment. We'll come back soon and drive you to Marseille. O.K.?"

Chandeler simply nodded in reply.

Astride the main branch of an old ash tree, he watched two cars pass by on the road to Sambuc. The first was a Japanese 4×4 of a make he didn't know, the second a Peugeot 406. Cops, he thought.

Previously, he had observed the dance of the fire engines and the vehicles of the gendarmerie converging on the blaze.

The sun, still heavy with light, was sinking into the silver of the Vaccarès. There were flamingos, non-migrants, pecking in the depths of the water before disappearing into their secret reed beds.

Cops won't find anything, he thought. Nothing. Except for Chandeler, who would no doubt give his description. And the lawyer would provide a host of useful details to the police. The second car, that was it: not gendarmes, but cops from Marseille, the P.J. and perhaps even that damned plainclothes detective he'd seen in Morini's bar and then spotted again in the lawyer's office the other evening. That one, he knew by instinct he had to beware of. The same type as Marceau, violent but gifted with sensitivity. That said, he had nothing against him and would do nothing as long as this officer did not interfere with the beast's designs.

He turned towards the fire. There was no more smoke, the firemen and gendarmes must now be combing through the house. But everything must have burned.

Why had he set it ablaze? Was it a fit of folly, as uncontrollable as it was unforeseeable?

In fact, he had no idea. It was not the first time that his nature had overcome him. He saw marvels and then all at once everything would collapse, at the slightest snag, the smallest detail that spoiled the whole. It was like a blot of pollution in the midst of nature. A flower of dishonour in the vastness of his pride. He had to destroy, even if it meant losing everything.

The memories of the past few months returned to him. He had the feeling of having accomplished a good part of his mission. The Tarasque had accomplished what was expected of it. The park would never exist. That was the main thing. He had eliminated one of the brains, Morini, and some of his best soldiers. A pity about Chandeler.

He sincerely regretted the death of Steinert. It had made him sad, truly: they had shared so many things together.

Steinert had wanted to see the beast.

And he, the Knight, had always refused to show it to him. It was Bérard who had made the decision. Steinert had not been initiated. Or not sufficiently.

But Simone's son had been more stubborn than a mule, he had wanted to see all the same. So he had looked for it. Until the day when he had found it. You always end up finding what you look for.

How had he done it? He didn't know. He supposed that Steinert must have followed him. And the beast would have eaten him if he had not run like a thing possessed.

Unfortunately, it was dark, and William had not seen the marsh. And he hadn't been able to save him, otherwise the beast would have escaped.

He had had trouble bringing it back into its lair, among the rushes. Several times, he had sung the song of the servants of the beast to calm it down and, finally, it had consented to follow him.

Sadness filled him. William would never know the end of the story. He would never know that everything had been achieved.

The Vaccarès was completely absorbing the sun. Like a tranquil monster that methodically swallows its prey before slowly digesting it. A light wind rustled the parched leaves of the tree. He sniffed the air like a wild animal gauging the danger. Just as Bérard had taught him, the old man, the chieftain.

Bérard the magician.

Wisps of charred wood and scorched tiles tickled his nostrils. The face of the old shepherd surged up again, as though his old master had returned across the river of death to give him strength.

He stayed in his tree until nightfall. Then he climbed down, as agile as a wild cat which decides that the hunting hour has arrived. It must have been past nine o'clock when he disappeared into the rushes, dry and sharp as sickle blades.

It smelled of burned grass and sugary wood. The heat of the blaze was still rising from the ground and from the stones fallen from the wall.

Moracchini was questioning a fireman from Le Sambuc, who was doing his best to explain, by pointing at the remains of the farmhouse, that the fire must have started inside the building.

De Palma wandered onto the path and walked for about a hundred metres. The reed bed had been caressed by the flames; close to the house, the tips of the canes were singed.

Along the path recent footprints could clearly be seen; some soft green herbs had been broken, what looked like a water hyacinth had been crushed.

He turned round. He was in the middle of the reed bed and the ruins of the house had vanished from sight. All that was left was the smell impregnating the heavy air.

For a hideout, you couldn't find better, he thought. Just a few paces from the road.

He took a few more steps and saw that the vegetation had been disturbed. Some young rushes, lower than the others, had been broken and prints were clearly visible in the sandy soil and in beds of moss. "This must be Chandeler's escape route," the Baron thought.

He retraced his steps and saw Moracchini searching in the ruins of the farmhouse.

"We need a forensics team," she said when de Palma reached her. "Try finding anything in this mess!"

She kicked out at the carcass of a half-melted computer.

"According to the firemen, he set fire to the place with petrol. He must have spread it around then lit a match."

"Simple and effective," de Palma replied, lifting up a still-smoking joist.

The fire brigade captain approached and handed them a black object: it was the bowl of a pipe that had resisted the flames. De Palma shifted it in the palm of his hand. He suddenly remembered that the first thing that he had noticed on entering Steinert's office was a strong smell of aromatic pipe tobacco.

He remembered too that Mme Steinert had assured him that her husband never smoked. De Palma was a man who believed in signs, and he sensed that the genie of the police had just sent him one. All that remained was to interpret it.

Moracchini came over.

"Interesting?"

"Maybe. Let's go on searching. This could be our lucky day."

Beneath a pile of stone which had fallen from the walls, they found a carbonised mass and, beside it, a singed white feather.

"A white spoonbill," the Baron said.

Digging deeper, he found a plaster base with wires sticking out of it. After a moment's reflection, he realised that it must be the framework of a stuffed bird.

They learned nothing from the rest of the house. A sea breeze had risen and blown the strong smell of the blaze away across the Vaccarès.

Because that's where they should have looked. In her family. That sentence, pronounced by an old woman in a Paris graveyard, suddenly struck his forehead like a rubber bullet. *Because that's where they should have looked. In her family.* He felt old, incapable of catching balls on the bounce, a washed-up player with a lousy backhand. He had not even asked for the old woman's name. Pain entered at the top of his skull and descended between his eyes.

A fireman raised his helmet. The black smoke had given him the face of a miner. He placed his axe against a section of the wall and lit a cigarette.

The next day, Gouirand reported to the offices of the *Brigade Criminelle* at ten o'clock exactly. Moracchini questioned him for over two hours and learned nothing new except for a few details about Morini's youth and some of his friends in the police force. She thus discovered that Morini had quite simply grown up with an important regional politician. Christian Rey had been part of the same network.

"What about Bérard, did you know him?"

"I often used to see him during the traditional festivals, at Christmas or the festivals of the Tarasque. He would come and recite poems and tell us legends in Provençal. People said that he was a member of the *Félibrige* and that he was a descendant of Frédéric Mistral."

"He was also a Knight of the Tarasque!"

"I know that he had been one once, but long before I started taking care of the Tarasque. I spoke to him about it a couple of times. He even gave me some advice when I wanted to make some new costumes."

"So you knew him?"

"Only vaguely."

"What about Steinert?"

"Never met him. Nor heard of him, till I read about him in the papers."

That morning, de Palma had debriefed Chandeler.

The lawyer explained that S.O.D.E.G.I.M. had been dissolved and Philippe Borland had dropped out of sight long ago. Shortly before dying, Morini had been busy starting up a second company, a kind of gasworks based in Monaco and Luxembourg, and whose capital consisted of cash coming in from every imaginable tax haven.

"Morini was with me when we went to see Bérard. We wanted to buy his stake in the Downlands, but he refused."

"What happened then?"

"He told us that he was going to see to it that we'd never be able to build on that land."

"And you threatened him!"

"That was Morini. He got annoyed and wanted to scare him. I guarantee you that I tried to intervene, but I couldn't do anything."

De Palma knew the rest of the story.

"When did you first receive the mark?"

"One or two days after we went to see Bérard."

"And did it arrive at your home?"

"Yes, it did. Why?"

"Because very few people know your personal address!"

Chandeler had started. He realised that he would never sleep in peace again until the police laid their hands on the man who had tried to murder him.

"Maybe it's time you told me everything."

"Yes, I think it is."

Chandeler had picked up his telephone and asked to be sent up a packet of cigarettes. Two minutes later, a young woman had opened the door and had placed on the occasional table a tray with a pack of filterless Craven-A, a box of matches and an ashtray.

"I need to think things through and get some sleep," he said. "Could you come back at the end of the afternoon?"

He had lit a Craven-A and drawn on it greedily. The lawyer was in such a state of agitation that de Palma could smell the rancid odour of his fear.

"We all knew each other . . . That's what you have to understand. I'm a local boy, too."

After four pulls on his cigarette, he stubbed it out and coughed slightly.

Gouirand glanced nervously at de Palma when he saw him enter Moracchini's office. He had never come across him before, and he read such determination on the officer's face that he instinctively recoiled.

"We're getting to know all the family at last, Michel. I get the impression that everyone knows everyone else!"

"More than you think," the Baron said.

Gouirand's gaze kept on shifting from one officer to the other. Moracchini noticed this and sat down behind him to unnerve him.

"M. Gouirand, I have the impression that the Tarasque is bringing bad luck all round."

"I don't see what you mean."

"Rey and Morini were Knights of the Tarasque, weren't they?"

"It's true, I knew them back in the days when they were part of the team. I've already told that to your colleague."

De Palma massaged his wounded shoulder. He stared at the chief Knight intently.

"And what about Marceau?"

Gouirand's expression changed, his lower lip drooping slightly. It made him look suddenly old and pathetic.

"I don't know what you mean . . . I've already answered all your questions."

The Baron's face relaxed, and his eyes sparkled.

"You see, M. Gouirand, in crime there is always a logic. People kill one another for thousands of reasons, and it often happens that these reasons have no apparent logic. Yet that logic is always there, in front of us. Our job is to understand it. Always, do you understand? It's a duty. I knew Marceau for years. We were colleagues at police headquarters in Paris . . . They were the best years of my life. Then I came back to Marseille, and Marceau to Tarascon."

De Palma stood up and passed his hand over his forehead.

"For months, I've been telling myself that Marceau was in Tarascon because the force had sidelined him and that he wanted to return home, just as I wanted to come back to Marseille. Quite simply. Then I learned that he'd been topping up his pay by doing odd jobs for the mob. Quite simply. So far, so logical."

Moracchini stared at the Baron. She noticed that the muscles of his face were stiffening and the veins in his arms standing out.

"And then Marceau gets eaten by your cursed animal: there, there is no more logic. Why?"

He suddenly turned his back to Gouirand.

"Because there are certain things I don't know ... and what can I possibly not know about a friend of twenty-five years' standing?"

He spun round and darted his feverish gaze into Gouirand's eyes.

"M. Gouirand, I've spent all night thinking about this. And I've noticed something stupid. Really stupid. Marceau was born in Tarascon. He came from an old-established family. Just like you, like Rey, like Morini, like most of the knights. It's as stupid as that. Except for this: you and Marceau are from Tarascon. But not your parents, who were born in one of those dismal surrounding villages, like hundreds of the town's inhabitants. Logic, do you understand me? As for the rest, I must say that I used my imagination a little and I think I've got it right."

The Baron picked up a chair and sat down in front of Gouirand. He sized him up for a few seconds.

"Why didn't you say that you'd known Marceau for ages and that he too was a Knight of the Tarasque ... Why?"

"I don't know ..."

Gouirand hid his face in his hands. De Palma observed him.

"Did you also receive the warning?"

The Knight's head sank even lower.

The Baron stood up and motioned to Moracchini to come aside and talk to him. They spoke in whispers.

"The best thing for him is to go into hiding, and straight away. We haven't caught our psycho yet, and he could well change his M.O. and start blowing away whoever's left before we can get to him."

"We could even put him behind bars if we want to. We've got enough on him. All I'll have to do is phone up the magistrate."

"Good idea. Put him in custody. We'll see clearer tomorrow."

"How did you work that out about Marceau?"

"I was bluffing. Chandeler told me that they all knew each other, so I improvised from there. I'll have to go back and see him soon. Ask our friend the same questions now. He'll wind up thinking we know everything."

324

They went back to Gouirand. De Palma resumed his place in front of him.

"I think you can tell us his name," said Moracchini harshly. "I think it's time! Enough people have died. Do you realise what your silence can cost you in court?"

"If I knew his name, I'd have told you a long time ago. But I don't."

She pursed her lips and tried to make eye contact with the Baron.

"I believe you," de Palma said. "But, I only half believe you . . . I think you're hesitating between several people. Am I mistaken?"

"No, sir."

"What if I tell you that he's a keen birdwatcher, crazy about our feathered friends, and spends most of his time in the Camargue? A metre eighty-five tall, looks a bit like a hippy . . ."

Gouirand stiffened on his chair. He wiped away the drops of sweat that were beading on his forehead.

"It's Vincent Soubeyrand," he murmured. "It can only be him."

"He was Steinert's best friend, wasn't he?"

"That's right. Soubeyrand from the Clary domain."

"Does he still live there?"

"No, there's only his mother, Mireille, and some farm workers."

Moracchini jotted down the address and summoned an officer to take Gouirand down to the cells. De Palma looked at the road maps. Clary lay beside the road between Maussane and Eygalières, just a few kilometres away from La Balme.

"There's a telephone, shall we try?"

"Why not?"

She plugged the loudspeaker into the telephone and entered the number, without taking her eyes off the keyboard. A man answered. She frowned.

"Am I speaking to Monsieur Lebel?"

"You've got the wrong number."

"Sorry, I must have made a mistake."

They looked at each other in mutual thought: a man's voice in a house where a woman was supposed to be living alone. It might mean nothing, but it had to be checked.

"How funny," said de Palma. "Vincent and Mireille."

"What's so funny about that?"

"They're the heroes of Mistral's masterpiece."

"Right. And then there's an unhappy ending in the Camargue."

An hour later, de Palma and Moracchini drew up in their police Xsara in a sunken track bordered by oak trees, a few metres from the turning that led to the Clary farmhouse. From a distance, the unmarked car was quite invisible.

De Palma drew his Bodyguard and walked into the copse beside the road. The baking air buzzed with the song of the cicadas. At each footstep, scraps of dead wood and dried grass crackled beneath his feet. After fifty metres, he stopped in a sweat. The Clary farmhouse was in front of him, on the other side of a vineyard that still smelled of ripe grapes.

Moracchini came to a halt beside him and took out her binoculars.

"There's nobody outside the building."

"Let's go."

"The only problem is the dog. There's always a damn dog in this kind of place."

The Baron mopped his forehead.

"There's a chance in a thousand that he's here," she said. "That's all. And if we do anything stupid, we get ourselves demolished by our learned friends."

Moracchini's hair was full of long pine needles. She drew her Manurhin and hefted it in her hands.

"You're probably right, Anne, there's very little chance that he's here. But we still have to go. No two ways about it."

"If you say so," she replied, watching him push forward under cover of the vines.

She let him go on for a few metres and headed for the drive so as to block any possible escape route.

She had not reached her objective when a first shot rang out. The bullet ricocheted in front of her, raising a clod of earth. She dived down onto the dusty path, and rolled over to take cover behind a row of vines.

"Are you O.K., Anne?" De Palma cried out.

She just had time to reply before a second shot hit the drive at random. She realised that the sniper could not see her and concluded that he must be in the house and firing from a first-floor window, just behind the pine tree that must be blocking his line of sight.

The Baron had crawled towards the farmhouse, flattened to the ground. A breeze blew sour stenches that came from the pens, and the smell of oil from the farming machinery. Black flies danced in the air around him, and mocked his jeopardy. There was dust in the sweat of his forehead and his clothes were covered with dirt.

When he was no more than ten metres from the buildings, he stood up and studied the windows. Everything was still. Despite Moracchini's fears, there was no dog. He concluded that the herd had gone out and that the dogs were guarding the animals.

He decided to move on to where he could flatten himself against the wall, when he heard the characteristic sound of a motorcycle starting up. It was coming from the garage he had noticed when he was at the far end of the drive.

"The car, Anne!" he shouted. "Get to the car!"

The double doors of the garage banged against its walls and a big motorbike rocketed out. De Palma stood up and fired. The driver bent down over the handlebars and started weaving to right and left. De Palma fired again and again, fanning his shots. When the clip was empty, he threw down his gun, drew his Colt .45 and ran after the bike. A single bullet hit the motorcyclist, who jerked in his saddle.

Thirty metres further on, Moracchini braced herself in firing position and aimed at the motorcyclist. Three shots rang out. None of them hit their moving target. The bike slalomed once more, then swerved left into a field and disappeared.

When de Palma came over to her, fury was still gleaming on his face. She said nothing, but flicked open the cylinder of her Manurhin, removed the still-warm casings and filled the empty chambers with three new .38 shells.

"We have to search the house," she said, frowning.

"Forget it. I think we'd better go and see Chandeler. He's expecting me."

Chandeler was sitting in his chair, a glass of Islay, his favourite whisky, in his hand.

Moracchini and de Palma walked towards him. Both of them had seen enough dead men to know that the killer had been there just before them. A trickle of blood still glistened on the grey-veined marble of the living room, sketching its Chinese calligraphy as far as the lawyer's luxurious Persian rug.

Chandeler had looked death in the face. He had probably even talked with his executioner. Vincent Soubeyrand had put a bullet in his head, a hollow-point which had left a neat round hole in his forehead and blown apart the back of his skull. Pieces of brain were stuck to the armchair.

She put a hand on the corpse's forehead.

"This happened less than an hour ago," said de Palma, leaning over the body.

"It was a nine-millimetre, for sure. And I'll eat my hat if it wasn't a SIG that killed him."

Chandeler's murderer had folded his victim's hands over his stomach and placed a white feather between his fingers.

"Jesus, all of this really gives me the creeps," Moracchini said, taking a step backwards.

De Palma picked up the feather and took a long look at it.

"The signature hasn't varied from the start; but he can't take them to the Camargue any more for the creature to eat them. He's panicking, Anne. He no longer knows where to turn and he's going to start shooting in all directions."

"Do you have any idea of the place where he's hiding?"

"No. Chandeler was our last chance to find out. He's crafty and he's been observing us for some time now. He knows how we operate. He's always at least one move ahead of us."

"And we can't even give out his description."

29.

Saint Joseph's was a private secondary school whose surrounding wall took up a large part of one side of rue de Beaucaire, just a few metres away from Tarascon town hall.

It was 5 p.m.

In front of the gates, children were running in all directions, excited by their first day back at school.

The Baron spotted Gilbert Sicard, who was watching them come out. Two days before, Sicard had replied to the message de Palma had left on his answering machine. The former history student had become a teacher and was now headmaster of a Catholic school.

"Good evening, M. de Palma. Come into my office."

They crossed a concrete playground planted with three ancient plane trees. The classroom windows looked out over a shadowy courtyard, and a grey door led to the headmaster's office at the far end.

"This is all very sad . . ." Sicard said, weighing in his hands a copy of his dissertation, before putting it down on his desk.

"You're just about the last chance I've got."

Sicard had an odd-looking face: round, with eyes like marbles and thick oval glasses perched on an aquiline nose.

"I must tell you that I myself come from those very same villages. My mother was born in Maussane and my father came from Fontvieille."

Sicard opened his thesis and riffled through the pages with his thumb.

"There are things missing from my version," he said. "But you must understand that I wrote it in 1966. I was very young at the time."

329

He knew the history of his native village thoroughly. He spoke at length about the period of the Occupation, and named one after the other the families that had collaborated with the Nazis. The Reys had been the most involved. One of their sons, Christian's uncle, had died in Pomerania in the SS uniform of the Charlemagne Division. The Reys had consolidated their fortune and had not been among the families investigated during the subsequent purge. Christian Rey's grandmother had even been part of the kangaroo court that had judged Simone Maurel.

"These are very painful stories," he said, closing the cover.

He then spoke of the bogus resistance fighters who had shot Simone Maurel's brother. De Palma noted the names of Gabriel Morini and Sébastien Marceau. Emile Maurel had been shot down without any semblance of justice. Gabriel Morini and Sébastien Marceau had gone to La Balme and had killed him in the guise of belonging to the resistance.

"Why do you think they did that?"

"For money, Monsieur! Or rather, for land. The Maurel family was the richest in the region and it has to be said that Simone's parents hadn't always been very straight when they bought land. Just before the war, they had got their hands on the Downlands by paying off old Morini, an Italian lumberjack who had married a girl from Eygalières, a girl called Bérard . . . Justine Bérard. He was an old drunk who had sold the land to Maurel for a song. The Maurels wanted it all, and for that the younger members of the Morini family could never forgive them! That transaction ruined them in fact, do you see?"

De Palma saw the jigsaw coming together. *Because that's where they should have looked. In the family.* He opened his bag and took out the photograph he had found in Bérard's house. Sicard took it and stared at it for some time, as though running a magnifying glass over each person in the shot.

"Where did you find this picture?" he asked with a frown.

"I'd rather not say."

Sicard put the photograph down and folded his hands. A glint of bitterness turned his eyes cold.

"It's the Tarasque," he said, still staring at the picture. "The Knights of the Tarasque who are standing round the monster are descended from the most powerful families of Tarascon and its vicinity. You can see Bérard, Emile Maurel, Lucien Soubeyrand . . . At the end of the fifteenth century, King René codified the brotherhood of the Tarasque in such a way that the sons of the great families of the region came together instead of fighting duels. In those days, it was only the sons of the powerful who had the right to serve the monster. Before the war, this tradition was still in force and that must have made a lot of people jealous. Especially because these families are very traditional. The Bérards descended from one of Mistral's daughters, and I think that the Soubeyrands were connected with Roumanille. In this part of Provence, let me tell you that is quite something!

"Let me tell you also that during the war they had quite a problem choosing a side, because most of them were Catholic fascists. But they were also patriots, Bérard and Soubeyrand above all. Etienne Maurel, too. They formed the Vincent network and were in the resistance right from the start. They were also members of the *Félibrige*, that famous literary circle . . . Bérard was even its laureate once."

Sicard opened his hand and pointed a thumb towards the ceiling.

"So here we have tradition, jealousy, revenge . . . In the series of murders that happened last summer you can find all of that. According to what you told me earlier, it was a conflict between two conceptions of Provence: traditionalists and those who wanted to use its folklore for more commercial ends. It's more complex than that. I know nothing about the plans for the leisure park that you mentioned. I do know that the real motive was revenge."

Control of the Tarasque had changed hands, and Vincent Soubeyrand, the heir to an epoch, could not bear that fact. In the middle, there was Bérard, the former head of the Knights and the master of them all. Old man Soubeyrand had died in the 1950s after his fall from fortune, and his son Vincent was badly unbalanced. He was notoriously violent, and from what Moracchini had managed to unearth so far, he had been jailed several times for assault and wounding during village dances and election campaigns.

"What about Steinert?"

"As a matter of fact, I don't know much about him. I always thought it odd that he bought the La Balme farmhouse. I don't know why, but I said to myself that there was a secret behind all that."

"He was the son of Simone Maurel and Karl Steinert."

Sicard stared at the photograph. His eyes were wide, and shone like a mirror reflecting flames from a fire.

"If there is anyone who should have been out for revenge, it was him. And he didn't do it. That will be the final truth of this tragedy."

He uttered this last remark in a murmur that lost itself in the silence of the empty school.

30.

It appeared on the front page of *La Provence*.

Giant Crocodile Shot in the Camargue

After the panther of the creeks, this might have sounded like another hoax, if the farmers of the Camargue had not been finding the carcasses of bull calves and colts in the swamps of the delta . . . Completely devoured by jaws of an exceptional size . . .

. . . According to the first examinations carried out by specialists from the Natural History Museum of Marseille, the creature was a Nile crocodile, a species increasingly rare. It is now extinct in Egypt itself, where the animal once symbolised the god Sobek. Only a few specimens of this formidable predator have been identified recently, but further upstream, in the region of the great African lakes.

This crocodile had already ravaged flocks of sheep and had devoured a wild colt. It was the local farmers who decided to organise hunts which resulted in the finding of the reptile . . .

How did such a creature come to be living wild in the Camargue? That is the question which the gendarmerie of Tarascon are now looking into . . .

Moracchini put down the newspaper and rubbed her eyes.

Daniel Romero arrived in the office, three parallel wrinkles marking his forehead. His gestures were nervous. The day before, he had been given a dressing-down by a magistrate and he was worried already about the appointment he had at 11 a.m. with Delpiano, the head of the squad.

"Have you seen the news?"

Romero shrugged his shoulders without even glancing at the paper.

"Have we got the D.N.A. results?"

"Yes, they arrived not an hour ago."

"And?"

"It's certainly the monster they killed yesterday. It devoured the bodies of Christian Rey and the others. We're on the right track."

Romero muttered something then looked at his watch.

"Have you called Michel?"

"I've been trying for an hour, he can't be found. Neither on his home number nor on his mobile."

"Yesterday, he told me that he was going to take a trip to the Camargue. He wanted to check a few things out."

Moracchini picked up *La Provence* again and crumpled its pages as she turned them.

It was the end of October. Over the delta, clouds had gathered and were weighing on the sky still red from the sun.

The Baron was alone, barefoot, on the long beach of Beauduc.

All day long he had been searching the reed beds around the observation hut once again, with rage in his heart. He had found precisely nothing.

Texeira had joined him late that morning and had told him about the black stork he had spotted, not far from the buildings of La Capelière. They had then called up the memory of William Steinert, and the hunt which the farmers had organised since the previous week to find the crocodile.

The sea breeze was shifting the sand across the surface of the beach. It made his ankles itch. He sat on the ground and leaned back against a breakwater. In front of him, the grey black trunk of a poplar lay like a huge carcass on the golden sand. The next storm would probably roll it out to sea, or deposit it further along the delta.

He closed his eyes and breathed deeply. The air that came from

334

the vastness of the sea made him feel better and unknotted his stomach.

The day before, he had received in his letterbox a light envelope marked 'By Air'. The postmark showed that it had been sent from the central post office of Annaba, Algeria, on 26 October.

The letter it contained was brief; it was a man's handwriting, fine and harmonious.

Michel

I shall keep, as a memory of you, a pistol bullet. The odd farewell gift that you gave me on our last meeting at the farmhouse of Clary. A surgeon friend of mine told me that it was an 11.43 shell and that I was lucky to be still alive.

You nearly killed me, Michel. And I'm almost sorry that you did not succeed. But that is the way things go. Do you know that, at William's funeral, I was standing behind Ingrid and our eyes met?

I know that you have been seeking your truth for some time by investigating the murky world of real estate in Provence. That was a good idea, but it made no sense, even if it might have seemed to . . .

The story reads differently.

There were twelve who served the Tarasque. Twelve who seemed to form a single person and whom the war was to separate. Some did their duty as men, others were like crows on carrion. I saw my lands change hands, my lands burn. My father destroyed.

Ai jamai descata lou plat davans moun paire* . . . As we say in Provençal. And my father died of grief and misery descended upon us.

When the smallest parcel of our Provence began to cost millions, I saw yesterday's swine sell the land of the immortals. After the death of my father, I was compelled to sell the fields that my family had tilled for ever so as to pay the death duty. On the death of my mother, our house will be sold for the same reason. Thus does our eternity change hands.

* I never looked at my food before my father.

335

William was my friend, the best I had. Perhaps you remember the poem that Ingrid read over his grave:

Ich hatt' einen Kameraden,
Einen bessern findst du nit,
Er ging an meiner Seite
In gleichem Schritt und Tritt . . .

William did not want that vengeance. Not like that. He never knew about what I was planning. What I did, I did for the honour of our two families and that of my master Bérard.

I owed you this fragment of confessions. The rest has no importance and I have trust in your intelligence.

The first white spoonbills arrived yesterday. They are magnificent, aren't they?

Vincent

Soubeyrand had enclosed with his letter two photographs of spoonbills taken during a mating display. The big birds had their wings spread and their necks were intertwined.

The Baron stood up, crumpled the letter into a ball and threw it to the wind that lurked between the hillocks. He thought of Isabelle Mercier and looked for her image of innocence. Beyond the dunes, there was only the blur of the foam that the sea was stirring.

Prague Fatale

Philip Kerr

W F HOWES LTD

This large print edition published in 2014 by
W F Howes Ltd
Unit 4, Rearsby Business Park, Gaddesby Lane,
Rearsby, Leicester LE7 4YH

1 3 5 7 9 10 8 6 4 2

First published in the United Kingdom in 2011
by Quercus

A CIP catalogue record for this book is available
from the British Library

ISBN 978 1 47127 493 0

Typeset by Palimpsest Book Production Limited,
Falkirk, Stirlingshire

Printed and bound in Great Britain
by TJ International Ltd, Padstow, Cornwall

Once again, to Jane

PROLOGUE

Monday–Tuesday 8–9 June 1942

It was a fine warm day when, together with SS-Obergruppenführer Reinhard Tristan Eugen Heydrich, the Reichsprotector of Bohemia and Moravia, I arrived back from Prague at Berlin's Anhalter Station. We were both wearing SD uniform but, unlike the General, I was a man with a spring in my step, a tune in my head, and a smile in my heart. I was glad to be home in the city of my birth. I was looking forward to a quiet evening with a good bottle of Mackenstedter and some Kemals I had liberated from Heydrich's personal supply at his office in Hradschin Castle. But I wasn't in the least worried he might discover this petty theft. I wasn't worried about anything very much. I was everything that Heydrich was not. I was alive.

The Berlin newspapers gave out that the unfortunate Reichsprotector had been assassinated by a team of terrorists who had parachuted into Bohemia from England. It was a little more complicated than this, only I wasn't about to say

1

as much. Not yet. Not for a long time. Maybe not ever.

It's difficult to say what happened to Heydrich's soul, assuming he ever had one. I expect Dante Alighieri could have pointed me in the approximate direction if ever I felt inclined to go and search for it, somewhere in the Underworld. On the other hand I've a pretty good idea of what happened to his body.

Everyone enjoys a good funeral and the Nazis were certainly no exception, giving Heydrich the best send-off that any psychopathically murderous criminal could have hoped for. The whole event was mounted on such a grand scale you would have thought some satrap in the Persian Empire had died after winning a great battle; and it seemed that everything had been laid on except the ritual sacrifice of a few hundred slaves – although, as things turned out for a small Czech mining village called Lidice, I was wrong about that.

From Anhalter Station Heydrich was carried to the Conference Hall of Gestapo headquarters, where six honour guards wearing black dress uniforms watched over his lying-in-state. For a lot of Berliners it was a chance to sing 'Ding-Dong! The Witch Is Dead!' while sneaking a wary tiptoes look inside the Prinz Albrecht Palace. On a par with other semi-hazardous activities like climbing to the top of the old radio tower in Charlottenburg or driving on the bank at the Avus Speedway, it was nice to be able to say that you'd done it.

On the radio that night the Leader eulogized the dead Heydrich, describing him as 'the man with the iron heart', which I assume he meant to be a compliment. Then again, it's possible that our own wicked wizard of Oz might simply have confused the Tin Man with the Cowardly Lion.

The next day, wearing civilian clothes and feeling altogether more human, I joined thousands of other Berliners outside the New Reich Chancellery and tried to look suitably gloomy as the whole ant's nest of Hitler's myrmidons came bursting out of the Mosaic Hall to follow the gleaming gun carriage as it bore Heydrich's flag-draped coffin east along Voss Strasse and then north up Wilhelmstrasse toward the General's final resting place in the Invaliden Cemetery, alongside some real German heroes like von Scharnhorst, Ernst Udet and Manfred von Richthofen.

There was no doubting Heydrich's bravery: his impetuous part-time active service with the Luftwaffe while most of the top brass stayed safe in their wolf's redoubts and their fur-lined bunkers was the most obvious example of this courage. I suppose Hegel might just have recognized Heydrich's heroism as the incarnation of the spirit of our despotic times. But for my money heroes need to have a working relationship with the gods, not the Titan forces of darkness and disorder. Especially in Germany. So I wasn't in the least bit sorry to see him dead. Because of Heydrich, I was an officer in the SD. And pressed into the tarnished silver cap

3

badge that was the loathsome symbol of my long acquaintance with Heydrich were the hallmarks of hatred, fear and, after my return from Minsk, guilt, too.

That was nine months ago. Mostly I try not to think about it but, as another famous German lunatic once observed, it's hard to look over the edge of the abyss without the abyss looking back into you.

CHAPTER 1

September 1941

The thought of suicide is a real comfort to me: sometimes it's the only way I can get through a sleepless night.

On such a night – and there were plenty of them – I used to dismantle my Walther automatic pistol and meticulously oil the metal jigsaw of pieces. I'd seen too many misfires for the want of a well-oiled gun, and too many suicides gone badly wrong because a bullet entered a man's skull at an acute angle. I would even unload the tiny staircase that was the single-stack magazine and polish each bullet, lining them up in a rank like neat little brass soldiers before selecting the cleanest and the brightest and the keenest to please to sit on top of the rest. I wanted only the best of them to blast a hole in the wall of the prison cell that was my thick skull, and then bore a tunnel through the grey coils of despond that were my brain.

All of this might explain why so many suicides go wrongly reported to the cops. '"He was just

5

cleaning his gun and it went off," said the dead man's wife.'

Of course guns go off all the time and sometimes they even kill the person holding them; but first you have to put the cold barrel against your head – the back of the head is best – and pull the damned trigger.

Once or twice I even laid a couple of folded bath towels under the pillow on my bed and lay down with the firm intent of actually going through with it. There's a lot of blood that leaks out of a head with even a small hole in it. I would lie there and stare at the suicide note that was written on my best paper – bought in Paris – and placed carefully on the mantelpiece, addressed to no one in particular.

No one in particular and I had a pretty close relationship in the late summer of 1941.

After a while, sometimes I would go to sleep. But the dreams I had were unsuitable for anyone under the age of twenty-one. Probably they were unsuitable for Conrad Veidt or Max Schreck. Once, I awoke from such a terrible, vivid, heart-stopping dream that I actually fired my pistol as I sat bolt upright on the bed. The clock in my bedroom – my mother's walnut Vienna wall clock – was never the same again.

On other nights I just lay there and waited for the grey light to strengthen at the edge of the dusty curtains and the total emptiness of another day.

Courage was no good anymore. Nor was being

brave. The endless interrogation of my wretched self produced not regret but only more self-loathing. To all outside eyes I was the same man I had always been: Bernie Gunther, Kriminal Commissar, from the Alex; and yet I was merely a blur of who I had been. An imposter. A knot of feelings felt with gritted teeth and a lump in the throat and an awful echoing lonely cavern in the pit of my stomach.

But after my return from the Ukraine, it wasn't just me that felt different, it was Berlin, too. We were almost two thousand kilometres from the front but the war was very much in the air. This wasn't anything to do with the British Royal Air Force who, despite Fat Hermann's empty promises that no English bomb would ever fall on the German capital, had managed to put in irregular but nonetheless destructive appearances in our night skies. But by the summer of 1941 they hardly visited us at all. No, it was Russia that now affected each and every aspect of our lives, from what was in the shops to how you occupied your spare time – for a while dancing had been forbidden – to how you got around the city.

'The Jews are our misfortune' proclaimed the Nazi newspapers, But nobody really believed von Treitschke's slogan by the autumn of 1941; and certainly not when there was the more obvious and self-inflicted disaster that was Russia with which to compare it. Already the campaign in the East was running out of momentum; and because of Russia and the overriding needs of our Army, Berlin felt more like the capital of a banana republic that had run out of bananas, as well as almost everything else you could think of.

There was very little beer and often none at all. Taverns and bars closed for one day a week, then two, sometimes altogether, and after a while there were only four bars in the city where you could regularly obtain a pot of beer. Not that it tasted like beer when you did manage to track some down. The sour, brown, brackish water that we nursed bitterly in our glasses reminded me most of the liquid-filled shell-holes and still pools of No Man's Land in which, sometimes, we had been obliged to take cover. For a Berliner, that really was a misfortune. Spirits were impossible to come by, and all of this meant that it was almost impossible to get drunk and escape from oneself, which, late at night, often left me cleaning my pistol.

The meat ration was no less disappointing to a population for whom the sausage in all its forms was a way of life. Allegedly we were each of us entitled to five hundred grammes a week, but even when meat was available, you were just as likely to receive only fifty grammes for a hundred-gramme coupon.

Following a poor harvest, potatoes disappeared altogether. So did the horses that pulled the milk wagons; not that this mattered very much as there was no milk in the churns. There was only powdered milk and powdered eggs, both of which

8

tasted like the masonry dust shaken from our ceilings by RAF bombs. Bread tasted like sawdust and many swore that's exactly what it was. Clothing coupons paid for an emperor's new clothes and not much else. You couldn't buy a new pair of shoes and it was almost impossible to find a cobbler to repair your old ones. Like everyone else with a trade, most of Berlin's cobblers were in the Army.

Ersatz or second-rate goods were everywhere. String snapped when you tried to pull it tight. New buttons broke in your fingers even while you were trying to sew them on. Toothpaste was just chalk and water with a bit of peppermint flavouring, and there was more lather to be had in queuing for soap than in the crumbling, biscuit-sized shard you were allocated to keep yourself clean. For a whole month. Even those of us who weren't Party members were starting to smell a bit.

With all of the tradesmen in the Army, there was no one to maintain the trams and buses, and as a result whole routes – like the Number One that went down Unter den Linden – were simply done away with, while half of Berlin's trains were physically removed to help supply the Russian campaign with all the meat and potatoes and beer and soap and toothpaste you couldn't find at home.

And it wasn't just machinery that went neglected. Everywhere you looked, the paint was peeling off walls and woodwork. Doorknobs came away in your hand. Plumbing and heating systems broke down. Scaffolding on bomb-damaged buildings became more or less permanent, as there were no roofers left to carry out repairs. Bullets worked perfectly of course, just like always. German munitions were always good; I could testify to the continuing excellence of ammunition and the weapons that fired it. But everything else was broken or second-rate or substitute or closed or unavailable or in short supply. And tempers, like rations, were in the shortest supply of all. The cross-looking black bear on our proud city's coat of arms began to look like a typical Berliner, growling at a fellow passenger on the S-Bahn, roaring at an indifferent butcher as he gave you only half of the bacon to which your card said you were entitled, or threatening a neighbour in your building with some Party big-shot who would come and fix him good.

Perhaps the quickest tempers were to be found in the lengthening queues for tobacco. The ration was just three Johnnies a day, but when you were extravagant enough actually to smoke one it was easier to understand why Hitler didn't smoke himself: they tasted like burnt toast. Sometimes people smoked tea, that is when you could get any tea, but if you could, it was always better to pour boiling water on the stuff and drink it.

Around police headquarters at Alexanderplatz – this area also happened to be the centre of Berlin's black market, which, despite the very serious penalties that were inflicted on those who got caught, was about the only thing in the city that could have been described as thriving – the scarcity of petrol hit us almost as hard as the tobacco and alcohol shortages. We took trains and buses to our crime scenes and when these weren't running we walked, often through the blackout, which was not without hazard. Almost one third of all accidental deaths in Berlin were a result of the blackout. Not that any of my colleagues in Kripo were interested in attending crime scenes or in solving anything other than the enduring problem of where to find a new source of sausage, beer and cigarettes. Sometimes we joked that crime was decreasing: no one was stealing money for the simple reason that there wasn't anything in the shops to spend it on. Like most jokes in Berlin in the autumn of 1941, that one was funnier because it was also true.

Of course, there was still plenty of theft about: coupons, laundry, petrol, furniture – thieves used it for firewood – curtains (people used them to make clothes), the rabbits and guinea pigs that people kept on their balconies for fresh meat; you name it, Berliners stole it. And with the blackout there was real crime, violent crime, if you were interested in looking for it. The blackout was great if you were a rapist.

For a while I was back in Homicide. Berliners were still killing each other, although there wasn't a moment passed when I didn't think it risible that I should continue to believe that this mattered

11

very much, knowing what I now knew about what was happening in the East. There wasn't a day when I didn't remember the sight of old Jewish men and women being herded toward execution pits where they were dispatched by drunken, laughing SS firing squads. Still, I went through the motions of being a proper detective, although it often felt like I was trying to put out a fire in an ashtray when, down the road, a whole city was the scene of a major conflagration.

It was while I was investigating the several homicides that came my way in early September 1941 that I discovered some new motives for murder that weren't in the jurisprudence books. Motives that stemmed from the quaint new realities of Berlin life. The smallholder in Weissensee who drove himself mad with coarse, home-made vodka and then killed the postwoman with an axe. A butcher in Wilmersdorf who was stabbed with his own knife by the local air-raid warden in a dispute about a short ration of bacon. The young nurse from the Rudolf Virchow Hospital who, because of the city's acute accommodation crisis, poisoned a 65-year-old spinster in Plotzensee so that she might have the victim's better-appointed room. An SS sergeant back on leave from Riga who, habituated to the mass killings that were going on in Latvia, shot his parents because he could see no reason not to shoot them. But most of the soldiers who came home from the eastern front and were in a mood to kill someone, killed themselves.

I might have done it myself but for the certainty that I wouldn't be missed at all; and the sure knowledge that there were many others – Jews mostly – who seemed to soldier on with so much less in life than I had. Yes. In the late summer of 1941 it was the Jews and what was happening to the Jews that helped to persuade me against killing myself.

Of course, the old-fashioned sort of Berlin murders – the ones that used to sell newspapers – were still committed. Husbands continued to murder their wives, just like before. And on occasion wives murdered their husbands. From where I sat most of the husbands who got murdered – bullies too free with their fists and their criticism – had it coming. I've never hit a woman unless we'd talked about it first. Prostitutes got their throats cut or were battered to death, as before. And not just prostitutes. In the summer preceding my return from the Ukraine a lust-killer named Paul Ogorzow pleaded guilty to the rapes and murders of eight women and the attempted murders of at least eight more. The popular Press dubbed him the S-Bahn Murderer because most of his attacks were carried out on trains or near S-Bahn stations.

That is why Paul Ogorzow came into my mind when, late one night in the second week of September 1941, I was called to take a look at a body that had been found close to the line between the S-Bahn stations at Jannowitz Bridge and Schlesischer. In the blackout nobody was quite

13

sure if the body was a man's or a woman's, which was more understandable when you took into account that it had been hit by a train and was missing its head. Sudden death is rarely ever tidy. If it was, they wouldn't need detectives. But this one was as untidy as anything I'd seen since the Great War, when a mine or a howitzer shell could reduce a man to a mangled heap of bloody clothes and jagged bone in the blink of an eye. Perhaps that was why I was able to look at it with such detachment. I hope so. The alternative – that my recent experience in the murder ghettoes of Minsk had left me indifferent to the sight of human suffering – was too awful to contemplate.

The other investigating detectives were Wilhelm Wurth, a sergeant who was a big noise in the police sports movement, and Gottfried Lehnhoff, an inspector who had returned to the Alex after having retired.

Wurth was in the fencing team, and the previous winter he had taken part in Heydrich's skiing competition for the German Police and won a medal. Wurth would have been in the Army but for the fact that he was a year or two too old. But he was a useful man to have along on a murder investigation in the event that the victim had skied onto the point of a sword. He was a thin, quiet man with ears like bell-pulls and an upper lip that was as full as a walrus moustache. It was a good face for a detective in the modern Berlin police force, but he wasn't quite as stupid as he looked.

He wore a plain grey double-breasted suit, carried a thick walking stick, and chewed on the stem of a cherrywood pipe that was almost always empty but somehow he managed to smell of tobacco.

Lehnhoff had a neck and head like a pear, but he wasn't green. Like a lot of other cops he'd been drawing his pension, but with so many younger officers now serving in police battalions on the eastern front he had come back into the force to make a nice cosy corner for himself at the Alex. The little Party pin he wore in the lapel of his cheap suit would only have made it easier for him to do as little real policing as possible.

We walked south down Dircksen Strasse to Jannowitz Bridge and then along the S-Bahn line with the river under our feet. There was a moon and most of the time we didn't need the flashlights we'd brought, but we felt safer with them when the line veered back over the gasworks on Holtmarkt Strasse and the old Julius Pintsch lighting factory; there wasn't much of a fence and it would have been easy to have stepped off the line and fallen badly.

Over the gasworks, we came across a group of uniformed policemen and railway workers. Further down the track I could just make out the shape of a train in Schlesischer Station.

'I'm Commissar Gunther, from the Alex,' I said. There seemed no point in showing him my beer-token. 'This is Inspector Lehnhoff and Sergeant Wurth. Who called it in?'

'Me, sir.' One of the cops moved toward me and saluted. 'Sergeant Stumm.'

'No relation, I hope,' said Lehnhoff.

There had been a Johannes Stumm who had been forced to leave the political police by Fat Hermann because he wasn't a Nazi.

'No, sir.' Sergeant Stumm smiled patiently.

'Tell me, Sergeant,' I said. 'Why did you think that this might be a murder and not a suicide or an accident?'

'Well, it's true, stepping in front of a train is a most popular way to kill yourself these days,' said Sergeant Stumm. 'Especially if you're a woman. Me, I'd use a firearm if I wanted to kill myself. But women aren't as comfortable with guns as men are. Now with this victim, all of the pockets have been turned inside out, sir. It's not something you'd do if you were planning to kill yourself. And it's not something that a train would normally take the trouble to do, either. So that lets out it being an accident, see?'

'Maybe someone else found him before you did,' I suggested. 'And just robbed him.'

'A copper maybe,' offered Wurth.

Wisely Sergeant Stumm ignored the suggestion.

'Unlikely, sir. I'm pretty sure I was the first on the scene. The train driver saw someone on the track as he started to gain speed out of Jannowitz. He hit the brakes but by the time the train stopped it was too late.'

'All right. Let's have a look at him.'

'Not a pretty sight, sir. Even in the dark.'

'Believe me, I've seen worse.'

'I'll take your word for that, sir.'

The uniformed sergeant led the way along the track and paused for a moment to switch on his flashlight and illuminate a severed hand that lay on the ground. I looked at it for a minute or so before we walked on to where another police officer was waiting patiently beside a collection of ragged clothes and mangled human remains that had once been a human being. For a moment I might have been looking at myself.

'Hold the flash on him while we take a look.'

The body looked as if it had been chewed up and spat out by a prehistoric monster. The corrugated legs were barely attached to an impossibly flat pelvis. The man was wearing a workman's blue overalls with mitten-sized pockets that were indeed inside out as the sergeant had described; so were the pockets in the oily rag that was his twisted flannel jacket. Where the head had been there was now a glistening, jagged harpoon of bloody bone and sinew. There was a strong smell of shit from bowels that had been crushed and emptied under the enormous pressure of a locomotive's wheels.

'I can't imagine what you've seen that could look worse than this poor Fritz,' said Sergeant Stumm.

'Me neither,' observed Wurth, and turned away in disgust.

'I dare say we'll all see some interesting sights

before this war is over,' I said. 'Has anyone looked for the head?'

'I've got a couple of lads searching the area for it now,' said the sergeant. 'One on the track and the other down below in case it fell into the gasworks or the factory yard.'

'I think you're probably correct,' I said. 'It looks like a murder all right. Quite apart from the pockets, which have been turned out, there's that hand we saw.'

'The hand?' This was Lehnhoff talking. 'What about it?'

I led them back along the track to take another look at the severed hand, which I picked up and turned in my hands like it was an historic artefact, or perhaps a souvenir once owned by the prophet Daniel.

'These cuts on the fingers look defensive to me,' I said. 'As if he might have caught the knife of someone trying to stab him.'

'I don't know how you can tell that after a train just ran over him,' said Lehnhoff.

'Because these cuts are much too thin to have been inflicted by the train. And just look where they are. Along the flesh of the inside of the fingers and on the hand between the thumb and the forefinger. That's a textbook defensive injury if I ever saw one, Gottfried.'

'All right,' Lehnhoff said, almost grudgingly. 'I suppose you are the expert. On murder.'

'Perhaps. Only of late I've had a lot of competition.

There are plenty of cops out east, young cops, who know a lot more about murder than I do.'

'I wouldn't know,' said Lehnhoff.

'Take my word for it. There's a whole new generation of police experts out there.' I let this remark settle for a moment before adding, very carefully, for appearance's sake, 'I find that very reassuring, sometimes. That there are so many good men to take my place. Eh, Sergeant Stumm?'

'Yes sir.' But I could hear the doubt in the uniformed sergeant's voice.

'Walk with us,' I said, warming to him. In a country where ill-temper and petulance were the order of the day – Hitler and Goebbels were forever ranting angrily about something – the sergeant's imperturbability was heartening. 'Come back to the bridge. Another pair of eyes might be useful.'

'Yes sir.'

'What are we looking for now?' There was a weary sigh in Lehnhoff's voice, as if he could hardly see the point of investigating this case any further.

'An elephant.'

'What?'

'Something. Evidence. You'll certainly know it when you see it,' I said.

Back up the track we found some blood spots on a railway sleeper and then some more on the edge of the platform outside the echoing glass-house that was the station at Jannowitz Bridge.

Below, someone aboard a river barge that was

quietly chugging through one of the many red-brick arches in the bridge shouted at us to extinguish our lights. This was Lehnhoff's cue to start throwing his weight around. It was almost as if he'd been waiting to get tough with someone, and it didn't matter who.

'We're the police,' he yelled down at the barge. Lehnhoff was yet another angry German. 'And we're investigating a murder up here. So mind your own business or I'll come aboard and search you just because I can.'

'It's everyone's business if the Tommy bombers see your lights,' said the voice, not unreasonably.

Wurth's nose wrinkled with disbelief. 'I shouldn't think that's very likely at all. Do you, sir? It's been a while since the RAF came this far east.'

'They probably can't get the petrol either,' I said.

I pointed my flashlight on the ground and followed a trail of blood along the platform to a place where it seemed to start.

'From the amount of blood on the ground he was probably stabbed here. Then he staggered along the platform a ways before falling onto the track. Picked himself up. Walked a bit more and then got hit by the train to Friedrichshagen.'

'It was the last one,' said Sergeant Stumm. 'The one o'clock.'

'Lucky he didn't miss it,' said Lehnhoff.

Ignoring him, I glanced at my watch. It was three a.m. 'Well, that gives us an approximate time of death.'

I started to walk along the track in front of the platform and after a while I found a greyish green passport-sized book lying on the ground. It was an Employment Identification Document, much like my own except that this one was for foreigners. Inside was all of the information about the dead man I needed: his name, nationality, address, photograph and employer.

'Foreign worker's book is it?' said Lehnhoff, glancing over my shoulder as I studied the victim's details under my flashlight.

I nodded. The dead man was Geert Vranken, aged thirty-nine, born at Dordrecht in the Netherlands, a volunteer railway worker; living at a hostel in Wuhlheide. The face in the photograph was wary-looking, with a cleft chin that was slightly unshaven. The eyebrows were short and the hair thinning to one side. He appeared to be wearing the same thick flannel jacket as the one on the body, and a collarless shirt buttoned up to the neck. Even as we were reading the bare details of Geert Vranken's shortish life, another policeman was coming up the stairs of Jannowitz Station with what, in the darkness, looked like a small round bag.

'I found the head, sir,' reported the policeman. 'It was on the roof of the Pintsch factory.' He was holding the head by the ear, which, in the absence of much hair, looked as good a way to carry around a severed head as any you could have thought of. 'I didn't like to leave it up there, sir.'

21

'No, you were right to bring it along, lad,' said Sergeant Stumm and, taking hold of the other ear, he laid the dead man's head carefully on the railway platform so that it was staring up at us.

'Not a sight you see everyday,' said Wurth and looked away.

'You want to get yourself up to Plotzensee,' I remarked. 'I hear the falling axe is very busy these days.'

'That's him all right,' said Lehnhoff. 'The man in the worker's book. Wouldn't you say?'

'I agree,' I said. 'And I suppose someone might have tried to rob him. Or else why go through his pockets?'

'You're sticking to the theory that this is a murder and not an accident then?' enquired Lehnhoff.

'Yes. I am. For that reason.'

Sergeant Stumm tutted loudly and then rubbed his stubbly jaw, which sounded almost as loud. 'Bad luck for him. But bad luck for the murderer, too.'

'What do you mean?' I asked.

'Well, if he was a foreign worker, I can't imagine there was much more than fluff in his pockets. It's a hell of a disappointing thing to kill a man with the intent of robbing him and then find that he had nothing worth stealing. I mean, these poor fellows aren't exactly well paid, are they?'

'It's a job,' objected Lehnhoff. 'Better a job in Germany than no job back in Holland.'

'And whose fault is that?' said Sergeant Stumm.

'I don't think I like your insinuation, Sergeant,' said Lehnhoff.

'Leave it, Lehnhoff,' I said. 'This isn't the time or the place for a political argument. A man is dead, after all.'

Lehnhoff grunted and tapped the head with the toe of his shoe, which was enough to make me want to kick him off the platform.

'Well, if someone did kill him, like you say, Herr Commissar, it'll be another of them foreign workers that probably did it. You see if I'm wrong. It's dog eat dog in these foreign-worker hostels.'

'Don't knock it,' I said. 'Dogs know the importance of getting a square meal now and again. And speaking for myself, if it's a choice between fifty grammes of dog and a hundred grammes of nothing then I'll eat the dog anytime.'

'Not me,' said Lehnhoff. 'I draw the line at guinea pigs. So there's no way I'd ever eat a dog.'

'It's one thing saying that, sir,' said Sergeant Stumm. 'But it's another thing altogether trying to tell the difference. Maybe you haven't heard, but the cops over at Zoo Station are having to put on night patrols in the zoo. On account of how poachers have been breaking in and stealing the animals. Apparently they just had their tapir taken.'

'What's a tapir?' asked Wurth.

'It looks a bit like pork,' I said. 'So I expect that's what some unscrupulous butcher is calling it now.'

'Good luck to him,' said Sergeant Stumm.

'You don't mean that,' said Lehnhoff.

'A man needs more than a stirring speech by the Mahatma Propagandi to fill his stomach,' I said.

'Amen,' said Sergeant Stumm.

'So you'd look the other way if you knew what it was?'

'I don't know about that,' I said, getting careful again. I might have been suicidal but I wasn't stupid: Lehnhoff was just the type to report a fellow to the Gestapo for wearing English shoes; and I hardly wanted to spend a week in the cells removed from the comfort of my warm, night-time pistol. 'But this is Berlin, Gottfried. Looking the other way is what we're good at.'

I pointed at the severed head that lay at our feet.

'You just see if I'm wrong.'

CHAPTER 2

About a lot of things I'm not always right. But about the Nazis I wasn't often wrong. Geert Vranken was a voluntary worker and had come to Berlin in search of a better job than the one that was available to him in Holland. Berlin's railway, which was experiencing a self-inflicted crisis in recruiting maintenance staff, had been glad to have an experienced track engineer; Berlin's police was less keen to investigate his murder. In fact, it didn't want to investigate the case at all. But there was no doubting that the Dutchman had been murdered. When eventually his body was given its grudging, cursory examination by the ancient doctor brought back from retirement to handle forensic pathology for the Berlin police, six stab wounds were found on what remained of his torso.

Commissioner Friedrich-Wilhelm Lüdtke, who was now in charge of the Berlin Criminal Police, wasn't a bad detective. It was Lüdtke who had successfully headed the S-Bahn murder investigation that led to the arrest and execution of Paul Ogorzow. But as he himself explained to me in his newly carpeted office on the top floor of the Alex, there was an important new law coming down the pipe from the Wilhelmstrasse, and Lüdtke's boss, Wilhelm Frick, Minister of the Interior, had ordered him to prioritize its enforcement at the expense of all other investigative matters. Lüdtke, a doctor of law, was almost embarrassed to tell me what this important new law amounted to.

'From September 19th,' he said, 'all Jews in Germany and the Protectorate of Bohemia and Moravia will be obliged to wear a yellow star inscribed with the word "Jew" on their outer garments.'

'You mean like in the Middle Ages?'

'Yes, like in the Middle Ages.'

'Well, that should make them easier to spot. Great idea. Until recently I've found it rather hard to recognize who is a Jew and who isn't. Of late they do look thinner and hungrier than the rest of us. But that's about it. Frankly I've yet to see just one who looks anything like those stupid cartoons in *Der Stürmer*.' I nodded with fake enthusiasm. 'Yes, this will certainly prevent them from looking exactly like the rest of us.'

Lüdtke, looking uncomfortable, adjusted his well-starched cuffs and collar. He was a big man with thick dark hair neatly combed off a broad, tanned forehead. He wore a navy-blue suit and a dark tie with a knot that was as small as the Party badge in his lapel; probably it felt just as tight on his neck when it came to speaking the truth. A matching navy-blue bowler hat was positioned on the corner of his double-partner's desk, as if it was hiding something. Perhaps it was his lunch. Or just his conscience. I wondered how the hat would look with a yellow star on the crown. Like a Keystone Kop's helmet, I thought. Something idiotic, anyway.

'I don't like this any more than you,' he said, scratching the backs of his hands nervously. I could tell he was dying for a smoke. We both were. Without cigarettes, the Alex felt like an ashtray in a no smoking lounge.

'I'd like it a whole lot less, I think, if I was Jewish,' I said.

'Yes, but you know what makes it almost unforgivable?' He opened a box of matches and bit one. 'Right now there's an acute shortage of material.'

'Yellow material.'

Lüdtke nodded.

'I might have guessed. Mind if I have one of those?'

'Help yourself.' He tossed the matches across the desk and watched as I fished one out and put it in the corner of my mouth. 'I'm told they're good for your throat.'

'Are you worried about your health, Wilhelm?'

'Isn't everyone? That's why we do what we're told. In case we come down with a dose of the Gestapo.'

'You mean like making sure Jews wear their yellow stars?'

'That's right.'

'Oh sure, sure. And while I can see the obvious importance of a law like that, there's still the matter of the dead Dutchman. In case you'd forgotten, he was stabbed six times.'

Lüdtke shrugged. 'If he was German it would be different, Bernie. But the Ogorzow case was a very expensive investigation for this department. We went way over budget. You've no idea how much it cost to catch that bastard. Undercover police officers, half the city's rail workers interviewed, increased police presence at stations – the overtime we had to pay out was enormous. It really was a very difficult time for Kripo. To say nothing of the pressure we came under from the Propaganda Ministry. It's hard catching anyone when the newspapers aren't even allowed to write about a case.'

'Geert Vranken was a rail worker,' I said.

'And you think the Ministry is going to be happy to learn that there's another killer at work on the S-Bahn?'

'This killer is different. As far as I can tell nobody raped him. And unless you count the train that drove over him, nobody tried to mutilate him either.'

'But murder is murder, and frankly I know exactly what they'll say. That there's enough bad news around right now. In case you hadn't noticed, Bernie, this city's morale is already lower than a badger's arse. Besides, we need those foreign workers. That's what they're going to tell me. The last thing we want is Germans thinking that there's a problem with our guest workers. We had enough of that during the Ogorzow case. Everyone in Berlin was convinced that a German couldn't possibly have murdered all those women. A lot of foreign workers were harassed and beaten up by irate Berliners who thought that one of them must have done it. You don't want to see any more of that, do you? Christ, there are problems enough on the trains and the underground as it is. It took me almost an hour to come to work this morning.'

'I wonder why we bother to come in at all given that the Ministry of Propaganda is now deciding what we can and what we can't investigate. Are we really supposed to find people who look Jewish and check to see if they're wearing the right embroidery? It's laughable.'

'I'm afraid that's just how it is. Perhaps if there are any more stabbings like this one then we can devote some resources to an investigation, but for now I'd rather you left this Dutchy alone.'

'All right, Wilhelm, if that's the way you want it.' I bit hard on my match. 'But I'm beginning to understand your twenty-a-day match habit. I guess it's easier not to scream when you're chewing down on one of these.'

As I stood up to leave I glanced up at the picture on the wall. The Leader stared me down in triumph but, for a change, he wasn't saying very much. If anyone needed a yellow star it was him;

and sewn just over his heart, assuming he had one; an aiming spot for a firing squad.

The Berlin city map on Lüdtke's wall told me nothing either. When Bernhard Weiss, one of Lüdtke's predecessors, had been in charge of Berlin Kripo, the map had been covered with little flags marking the incidents of crime in the city. Now it was empty. There was, it seemed, no crime to speak of. Another great victory for National Socialism.

'Oh, by the way. Shouldn't someone tell the Vranken family back in Holland that their major breadwinner stopped a train with his face?'

'I will speak to the State Labour Service,' said Lüdtke. 'You can safely leave it to them.'

I sighed and rolled my head wearily on my shoulders; it felt thick and heavy, like an old medicine ball.

'I feel reassured already.'

'You don't look it,' he said. 'What's the matter with you, these days, Bernie? You're a real bat in the balls, do you know that? Whenever you walk in here it's like rain coming in at the eaves. It's like you've given up.'

'Maybe I have.'

'Well, don't. I'm ordering you to pull yourself together.'

I shrugged. 'Wilhelm? If I knew how to swim I'd first untie the anvil that's tied around my legs.'

CHAPTER 3

Prussia has always been an interesting place to live in, especially if you were Jewish. Even before the Nazis, Jews were singled out for special treatment by their neighbours. Back in 1881 and 1900, the synagogues in Neustettin and Konitz – and probably several other Prussian towns, too – were burnt down. Then in 1923, when there were food riots and I was a young cop in uniform, the many Jewish shops of Scheuenviertel – which is one of Berlin's toughest neighbourhoods – were singled out for special treatment because Jews were suspected of price-gouging or hoarding, or both, it didn't matter: Jews were Jews and not to be trusted.

Most of the city's synagogues were destroyed of course in November 1938. At the top of Fasanenstrasse, where I owned a small apartment, a vast but ruined synagogue remained standing and looking to all the world as if the future Roman emperor Titus had just finished teaching the city of Jerusalem a lesson. It seems that not much has changed since AD 70; certainly not in Berlin, and it could only be a matter of time before we started crucifying Jews on the streets.

I never walked past this ruin without a small sense of shame. But it was quite a while before I realized there were Jews living in my own building. For a long time I was quite unaware of their presence so close to me. Lately, however, these Jews had become easily recognizable to anyone that had eyes to see. Despite what I'd said to Commissioner Lüdtke, you didn't need a yellow star or a set of callipers to measure the length of someone's nose to know who was Jewish. Denied every amenity, subject to a nine o'clock curfew, forbidden 'luxuries' such as fruit, tobacco or alcohol, and allowed to do their shopping only for one hour at the end of the day, when the shops were usually empty, Jews had the most miserable of lives, and you could see that in their faces. Every time I saw one I thought of a rat, only the rat had a Kripo beer-token in his coat pocket with my name and number inscribed on it. I admired their resilience. So did many other Berliners, even some Nazis.

I thought less about hating or even killing myself whenever I considered what the Jews had to put up with. To survive as a Jew in Berlin in the autumn of 1941 was to be a person of courage and strength. Even so it was hard to see the two Fridmann sisters, who occupied the flat underneath my own, surviving for much longer. One of them, Raisa, was married, with a son, Efim, but both he and Raisa's husband, Mikhail, arrested in 1938, were still in prison. The daughter, Sarra, escaped to France in 1934 and had not been heard of since. These two sisters – the older one was Tsilia – knew I was a policeman and were rightly wary of me. We rarely ever exchanged much more than a nod or a 'good morning'. Besides, contact between Jews and Aryans was strictly forbidden and, since the block leader would have reported this to the Gestapo, I judged it better, for their sake, to keep my distance.

After Minsk I ought not to have been so horrified at the yellow star, but I was. Maybe this new law seemed worse to me because of what I knew awaited those Jews who were deported east, but after my conversation with Commissioner Lüdtke I resolved to do something, although it was a day or two before I figured out what this might be.

My wife had been dead for twenty years, but I still had some of her dresses and sometimes, when I'd managed to overcome the shortages and have a drink or two and I was feeling sorry for myself and, more particularly, for her, I'd get one of her old garments out of the closet and press the material to my nose and mouth and inhale her memory. For a long time after she was gone that was what I called a home life. When she'd been alive we had soap, so my memories were all pleasant ones; these days things were rather less fragrant, and if you were wise you boarded the S-Bahn holding an orange stuffed with cloves, like a medieval Pope going among the common people. Especially in summer. Even the prettiest girl smelled like a stevedore in the dog days of 1941.

At first I figured on giving the two Fridmann sisters the yellow dress so that they could use it for making yellow stars, only there was something about this I didn't like. I suppose it made me feel complicit in the whole horrible police order. Especially since I was a policeman. So, halfway down the stairs with the yellow dress draped over my arm I went back to my flat and fetched all of the dresses that were in my closet. But even this felt inadequate and, as I handed over my wife's remaining wardrobe to these harmless women, I quietly decided to do something more.

It isn't exactly a page from some heroic tale as described by Winckelmann or Hölderlin, but that's how this whole story got started: if it hadn't been for the decision to help the Fridmann sisters I'd never have met Arianne Tauber and what happened wouldn't have happened.

Back inside my apartment I smoked the last of my cigarettes and contemplated putting my nose in some records at the Alex, just to see if Mikhail and Efim Fridmann were still alive. Well, that was one thing I could do, but for anyone with a purple J on their ration cards it wasn't going to help feed them. Two women who looked as thin as the Fridmann sisters were going to need something more substantial than just some information about their loved ones.

After a while I had what I thought was a good

idea and fetched a German Army bread-bag from my closet. In the bread bag was a kilo of Algerian coffee beans I'd purloined in Paris and which I'd been planning to trade for some cigarettes. I left my flat and took a tram east as far as Potsdamer Station.

It was a warm evening, not yet dark. Couples were strolling arm in arm through the Tiergarten and it seemed almost impossible that two thousand kilometres to the east the German Army was surrounding Kiev and slowly tightening its stranglehold on Leningrad. I walked up to Pariser Platz. I was on my way to the Adlon Hotel to see the maître d' with the aim of trading the coffee for some food that I could give the two sisters.

The maître d' at the Adlon that year was Willy Thummel, a fat Sudeten German who was always busy and so light on his toes that it made me wonder how he ever got fat in the first place. With his rosy cheeks, his easy smile and his impeccable clothes he always reminded me of Herman Göring. Without a doubt both men enjoyed their food, although the Reichsmarshal had always given me the impression that he might just have eaten me, too, if he'd been hungry enough. Willy liked his food; but he liked people more.

There were no customers in the restaurant – not yet – and Willy was checking the blackout curtains when I poked my nose around the door. Like any good maître d' he spotted me immediately and quickly came my way on invisible casters.

'Bernie. You look troubled. Are you all right?'

'What's the point of complaining, Willy?'

'I don't know; the wheel that squeaks the loudest in Germany these days usually gets the most grease. What brings you here?'

'A word in private, Willy.'

We went down a small flight of stairs to an office. Willy closed the door and poured two small glasses of sherry. I knew he was seldom away from the restaurant for longer than it took to inspect the china in the men's room so I came straight to the point.

'When I was in Paris I liberated some coffee,' I said. 'Real coffee, not the muck we get in Germany. Beans. Algerian beans. A whole kilo.' I put the bread bag on Willy's desk and let him inspect the contents.

For a moment he just closed his eyes and inhaled the aroma; then he groaned a groan that I'd seldom heard outside a bedroom.

'You've certainly earned that drink. I'd forgotten what real coffee smells like.'

I hit my tonsils with the sherry.

'A kilo, you say? That's a hundred marks on the black market, last time I tried to get any. And since there isn't any coffee to be had anywhere, it's probably more. No wonder we invaded France. For coffee like this I'd crawl into Leningrad.'

'They haven't got any there, either.' I let him refill my glass. The sherry was hardly the best but then nothing was, not even in the Adlon. Not any more. 'I was thinking that you might like to treat some of your special guests.'

'Yes, I might.' He frowned. 'But you can't want money. Not for something as precious as this, Bernie. Even the devil has to drink mud with powdered milk in it these days.'

He took another noseful of the aroma and shook his head. 'So what do you want? The Adlon is at your disposal.'

'I don't want that much. I just want some food.'

'You disappoint me. There's nothing we have in our kitchens that's worthy of coffee like this. And don't be fooled by what's on the menu.' He collected a menu off the desk and handed it to me. 'There are two meat dishes on the menu when the kitchen can actually serve only one. But we put two on for the sake of appearances. What can you do? We have a reputation to uphold.'

'Suppose someone asks for the dish you don't have?' I said.

'Impossible.' Willy shook his head. 'As the first customer comes through the door we cross off the second dish. It's Hitler's choice. Which is to say it's no choice at all.'

He paused.

'You want food for this coffee? What kind of food?'

'I want food in cans.'

'Ah.'

'The quality isn't important as long as it's edible. Canned meat, canned fruit, canned milk, canned vegetables. Whatever you can find. Enough to last for a while.'

'You know canned goods are strictly forbidden, don't you? That's the law. All canned goods are for the war front. If you're stopped on the street with canned food you'd be in serious trouble. All that precious metal. They'll think you're going to sell it to the RAF.'

'I know it. But I need food that can last and this is the best place to get it.'

'You don't look like a man who can't get to the shops, Bernie.'

'It isn't for me, Willy.'

'I thought not. In which case it's none of my business what you want it for. But I tell you what, Commissar, for coffee like this I am ready to commit a crime against the state. Just as long as you don't tell anyone. Now come with me. I think we have some canned goods from before the war.'

We went along to the hotel storeroom. This was as big as the lock-up underneath the Alex but easier on the ear and the nose. The door was secured with more padlocks than the German National Bank. In there he filled my bread bag with as many cans as it could carry.

'When these cans are gone come and get some more, if you're still at liberty. And if you're not then please forget you ever met me.'

'Thanks, Willy.'

'Now I have a small favour to ask you, Bernie. Which might even be to your advantage. There's

38

an American journalist staying here in the hotel. One of several, as it happens. His name is Paul Dickson and he works for the Mutual Broadcasting System. He would dearly like to visit the war front but apparently such things are forbidden. Everything is forbidden now. The only way we know what's permitted is if we do something and manage to stay out of prison.

'Now I know you are recently returned from the front. And you notice I don't ask what it's like out there. In the East. Just seeing a compass these days makes me feel sick. I don't ask because I don't want to know. You might even say this is why I went into the hotel business: because the outside world is of no concern to me. The guests in this hotel are my world and that's all the world I need to know. Their happiness and satisfaction is all that I care about.

'So, for Mr Dickson's happiness and satisfaction I ask that you meet with him. But not here in the hotel. No, not here. It's hardly safe to talk in the Adlon. There are several suites of rooms on the top floor that have been taken over by people from the Foreign Office. And these people are guarded by German soldiers wearing steel helmets. Can you imagine it. Soldiers, here in the Adlon. Intolerable. It's just like 1919 all over again but without the barricades.'

'What are workers from the Foreign Office doing here that they can't do in the Ministry?'

'Some of them are destined for the new Foreign

Travel Office, when it's finished. But the rest are typing. Morning, noon and night, they're typing. Like it's for a speech by the Mahatma.'

'What are they typing?'

'They're typing up releases for the American press, most of whom are also staying here. Which means that there are Gestapo in the bar. Possibly there are even secret microphones. I don't know for sure, but this is what I heard. Which is another source of grief for us.'

'This Dickson fellow. Is he in the hotel right now?'

Willy thought for a moment. 'I think so.'

'Don't mention my name. Just tell him that if he's interested in a bit of "Life Poetry and Truth", I'll be beside the Goethe statue in the Tiergarten.'

'I know it. Just off Herman Göring Strasse.'

'I'll wait fifteen minutes for him. And if he comes he should come alone. No friends. Just him and me and Goethe. I don't want any witnesses when I speak to him. These days there are plenty of Amis who work for the Gestapo. And I'm not sure about Goethe.'

I hoisted the bread bag onto my back and walked out of the Adlon onto Pariser Platz, where it was already getting dark. One of the only good things about the blackout was that you couldn't see the Nazi flags, but the brutal outlines of Speer's partly constructed Foreign Travel Office were still visible in the distance against the purpling night sky, dominating the landscape west of the Brandenburg

Gate. Rumour had it that Hitler's favourite architect, Albert Speer, was using Russian POWs to help complete a building that no one other than Hitler seemed to want. Rumour also had it that there was a new network of tunnels under construction connecting government buildings on Wilhelmstrasse with secret bunkers that extended under Herman Göring Strasse as far as the Tiergarten. It was never good to pay too much attention to rumours in Berlin for the simple reason that these were usually true.

I stood by the statue of Goethe and waited. After a while I heard a 109 quite low in the sky as it headed south-east toward the airfield at Tempelhof; and then another. For anyone who'd been in Russia, it was an instantly recognizable and reassuring sound, like an enormous but friendly lion yawning in an empty cave and quite different from the noise of the much slower RAF Whitleys that occasionally ploughed through Berlin skies like tractors of death and destruction.

'Good evening,' said the man walking toward me. 'I'm Paul Dickson. The American from the Adlon.'

He hardly needed the introduction. His Old Spice and Virginia tobacco came ahead of him like a motorcycle outrider with a pennant on his mudguard. Solid footsteps bespoke sturdy wing-tip shoes that could have ferried him across the Delaware. The hand that pumped mine was part of a body that still consumed nutritious food. His

41

sweet and minty breath smelled of real toothpaste and testified to his having access to a dentist with teeth in his head who was still a decade off retirement. And while it was dark I could almost feel his tan. As we exchanged cigarettes and conversational bromides, I wondered if the real reason Berliners disliked Americans was less to do with Roosevelt and his anti-German rhetoric and more to do with their better health, their better hair, their better clothes and their altogether better lives.

'Willy said you've just come back from the front,' he said, speaking German that was also better than I had expected.

'Yes, that's right.'

'Care to talk about it?'

'Talking about it is about the only means of committing suicide for which I seem to have the nerve,' I confessed.

'I can assure you, sir, I am nothing to do with the Gestapo. If that's what you're implying. I dare say that's exactly what someone who was a Gestapo informer would tell you. But to be quite frank with you there's nothing they have that I want. Except perhaps a good story. I'd kill for a good story.'

'Have you killed many?'

'Frankly, I don't see how I could have done. As soon as they know I'm an American most Berliners seem to want to hit me. They seem to hold me personally responsible for all the ships we've been giving to the British.'

'Don't worry; Berliners have never been

interested in having a navy,' I said. 'That kind of thing matters more in Hamburg and Bremen. In Berlin, you can count yourself lucky that Roosevelt never gave the Tommies any beer or sausage, or you'd be dead by now.' I pointed toward Potsdamer Platz. 'Come on. Let's walk.'

'Sure,' he said and followed me south out of the park. 'Anywhere in particular?'

'No. But I need a few minutes to address the ball, so to speak.'

'Golfing man, huh?'

'I used to play a bit. Before the Nazis. But it's never really caught on since Hitler. It's too easy to be bad at it, which is not something Nazis can deal with.'

'I appreciate your talking to me like this.'

'I haven't told you anything yet. Right now I'm still wondering how much I can tell you without feeling like – what was his name? The traitor. Benedict—?'

'Benedict Arnold?'

'That's right.'

We crossed Potsdamer onto Leipziger Platz.

'I hope we're not headed for the Press Club,' said Dickson. 'I'd feel like a bit of a fool if you took me in there to tell me your story.' He pointed at a door on the other side of the square where several official-looking cars were parked. 'I hear all kinds of bullshit in that place.'

'You don't say.'

'Doctor Froehlich, the Propaganda Ministry's

liaison officer for the American media, he is always summoning us in there for special press conferences to announce yet another decisive victory for German forces against the Red Army. Him or one of those other doctors. Brauweiler or Dietrich. The doctors of deceit, that's what we call them.'

'Not forgetting the biggest deceiver of them all,' I said. 'Doctor Goebbels.'

Dickson laughed bitterly. 'It's got so bad that when my own doctor says there's nothing wrong with me I just don't believe him.'

'You can believe him. You're American. Provided you don't do anything stupid, like declare war on Russia, most of you should live for ever.'

Dickson followed me across to Wertheim's department store. In the moonlight you could see the huge map of the Soviet Union that occupied the main window, so that any patriotic German might look at it and follow the heroic progress of our brave armed forces. It wasn't like there was anything else in the store to put in the window. When the place had been owned and run by Jews it had been the best store in Germany. Now it was little better than a warehouse, and an empty one at that. The shop assistants spent most of their time gossiping and ignoring the spectators – you could hardly call them customers – who wandered around the store in search of merchandise that simply wasn't there. Even the elevators weren't working.

There was no one on the sidewalk in front of

the window and it seemed as good a place as any to tell the American radio journalist the truth about our great patriotic war against the Russians and the Jews.

'Give me another one of your cigarettes. If I'm going to cough up the whole story I want something inside me to help it along.'

He handed me an almost full pack of American cigarettes and told me to keep it. I lit one quickly and let the nicotine go and play in my brain. For a moment I felt giddy and light-headed like it was the first time I ever smoked. But that was how it should have been. It wouldn't have been right to have told Dickson about the police battalions and resettlement and special actions and the Minsk ghetto and pits that were full of dead Jews without feeling a little sick inside.

Which is exactly what I told him.

'And you saw all of this?' Now it was Dickson who sounded sick inside.

'I'm a captain in the SD,' I said. 'I saw it all.'

'Jesus. It's hard to believe.'

'You wanted to know. I told you. That's how it is. Worse than you could possibly imagine. When they don't let you go somewhere it's because they can't boast about what they're doing. You could have worked it out for yourself. I'd be there right now but for the fact that I'm a bit particular about who I pull the trigger on. They sent me home, in disgrace. I'm lucky they didn't send me to a punishment battalion.'

'You were in the SD?' Dickson sounded just a bit nervous.

'Correct.'

'That's like the Gestapo, isn't it?'

'Not exactly. It's the intelligence wing of the SS. The Abwehr's ugly little sister. Like a lot of men in the SD, I came in through a side door marked No Bloody Choice. I was a policeman at the Alex before I was in the SD. A proper policeman. The kind who started out helping old ladies across the road. Not all of us make Jews clean the street with a toothbrush, you know. I want you to know that. Me, I'm a bit like Frankenstein's monster with the little girl at the lake. There's a part of me that really wants to make friends and to be good.'

Dickson was quiet for a moment. 'No one back home is going to believe this,' he said, eventually. 'Not that I'd ever get it past the local Press Censor. This is the trouble with radio. You have to clear your copy in advance.'

'So leave the country. Go home and buy a type-writer. Write it up in the newspapers and tell the world.'

'I wonder if anyone would believe me.'

'There is that. I can hardly believe it myself and I was there. I saw it. Every night I go to bed in the hope that I'll wake up and find that I imagined the whole thing.'

'Perhaps if you told another American besides myself. That would make the story more believable.'

'No. That's your problem, not mine.'

'Look,' said Dickson, 'the man you should really meet is Guido Enderis. He's the chief of the *New York Times* Berlin office. I think you should tell him what you just told me.'

'I think I've talked enough for one evening. Odd but it makes me feel guilty in a whole new way. Before I only felt like a murderer. Now I feel like a traitor, too.'

'Please.'

'You know there's a limit to how guilty I can feel before I want to throw up or jump in front of a train.'

'Don't do that, Captain – whatever your name is. The whole world needs to know what's happening on the eastern front. The only way that's going to happen is if people like you are willing to talk about it.'

'And then what? Do you think it's going to make a difference? If America's not prepared to come in to the war for the sake of the British I can't believe they're going to do it for the sake of Russia's Jews.'

'Maybe, maybe not. But you know, sometimes one thing leads to another.'

'Yeah? Look what happened back at Munich, in 1938. One thing led to absolutely nothing at all. And your lot weren't even at the negotiating table. They were back home, pretending it was nothing to do with the USA.'

Dickson couldn't argue with that.

'How can I get in contact with you, Captain?'

'You can't. I'll speak to Willy and leave a message with him if I decide I'm ready to puke another fur ball.'

'If it's a question of money—'

'It's not.'

Instinctively we both glanced up as another 109 came rifling in from the north-west and I saw the moon illuminate the anxiety on Dickson's smooth face. When the sound was just a footnote on the horizon I heard him let out a breath.

'I can't get used to that,' he confessed. 'The way these fighters fly so low. I keep expecting to see something blow up on the ground in front of me.'

'Sometimes I wish it would. But take my word for it: a fighter tends to buzz a little louder when it decides to sting.'

'Talking of things blowing up,' he said. 'The Three Kings. You hear anything? Only, the doctors of deceit have been giving us the runaround. Back in May they said they had picked up two of the leaders and that it was only a matter of time before they got their hands on the third. Since when we've heard nothing. We keep asking, but no one says anything, so we figure that number three must still be at liberty. Any truth in that, you think?'

'I really can't say.'

'Can't or just won't?' A cloud drifted across the moon like something dark over my soul.

'C'mon, Captain. You must know something.'

'I'm just back from the Ukraine so I'm a little

48

behind with what's been happening here in Berlin. But if they'd caught Melchior, I think you'd have heard all about that, don't you? Through a megaphone.'

'Melchior?'

'And I thought it was just the Germans who were a godless race.'

I walked away.

'Hey,' said Dickson. 'I saw that movie, *Frankenstein*. And I remember that scene, now. Doesn't the monster throw the little girl in the water?'

'Yes. Sad isn't it?'

I strolled south, down to Bülowstrasse, where I turned west. I might have walked all the way home but I noticed there was a hole in my shoe and at Nolli I decided to get on the S-Bahn. Normally I would have taken the tram, but the thirty-three was no longer running; and since it was after nine o'clock the only taxis around were those that were called by the police for the service of the sick, the lame, the old, or travellers from railway stations with heavy bags. And senior Nazi Party members, of course. They never had a problem getting a cab home after nine.

Nolli was almost deserted, which was not uncommon in the blackout. All you could see were occasional cigarette ends moving through the darkness like fireflies, or sometimes the phosphorescent lapel badge of someone keen to avoid a collision with another pedestrian; all you could hear were the trains as they moved invisibly in and out of the art nouveau glass dome of the station overhead, or disembodied voices, snatches of passing conversations as if Berlin was one big open-air séance – a ghostly effect that was enhanced by infrequent flashes of electric light from the rail track. It was as if some modern-day Moses – and who could have blamed him? – had stretched out his strong hand toward the sky to spread a palpable darkness over the land of Germany. Surely it was time to let the Israelites leave, or at least to release them from their bondage.

I was almost on the stairs when, from under the arches, I heard the sound of a struggle. I stopped for a moment, looked around and as a cloud shifted lazily off the moon I got a *son et lumière* view of a man attacking a woman. She was lying on the ground trying to fight him off as, with one hand over her mouth, he fumbled under her skirt. I heard a curse, a muffled scream and then my own footsteps as they clattered down the stairs.

'Hey, leave her alone,' I yelled.

The man appeared to punch the woman and as he stood up to face me I heard a click and caught a glimpse of the blade that was now in his hand. If I'd been on duty I might have been carrying a firearm but I wasn't and as the man came toward me I shrugged the bread bag containing the food cans off my shoulder and swung it hard like a medieval ball and chain as he came within range. The bag hit him on his extended arm, knocking the blade out of his hand, and he turned and fled, with me in half-hearted pursuit. The moonlight dimmed momentarily and I lost sight of him altogether. A few moments later I heard a squeal of tyres from the corner of Motz Strasse and, arriving in front of the American Church, I found a taxi with its door open and the driver staring at his front fender.

'He just ran out in front of me,' said the driver.

'You hit him?'

'I didn't have a chance.'

'Well he's not here now.'

'He ran off I think.'

'Where did he go?'

'Toward the cinema theatre.'

'Stay where you are; I'm a police officer,' I told the driver and crossed the street, but I might as well have looked inside a magician's top hat. There was no sign of him. So I went back to the taxi.

'Find him?'

'No. How hard did you hit him?'

'I wasn't going fast, if that's what you mean. Ten or fifteen kilometres an hour, like you're supposed to do, see? But still, I think I gave him a good old clunk. He went right over the hood and landed on his head, like he was off some nag at the Hoppegarten.'

'Pull into the side of the road and stay there,' I told the driver.

'Here,' he said. 'How do I know you're a cop? Where's your warrant disc?'

'It's in my office at Alex. We can go straight there if you like and you can spend the next hour or two making out a report. Or you can do what I say. The fellow you knocked down attacked a woman back there. That's why he was running away. Because I chased him. I was thinking you might take the lady home.'

'Yeah, all right.'

I went back to the station on Nollendorfplatz.

The girl who'd been attacked was sitting up and rubbing her chin between adjusting her clothes and looking for her handbag.

'Are you all right?'

'I think so. My bag. He threw it on the ground somewhere.'

I glanced around. 'He got away. But if it's any consolation a taxi knocked him down.'

I kept on looking for her bag but I didn't find it. Instead I found the switchblade.

'Here it is,' she said. 'I've found it.'

'Are you all right?'

'I feel a bit sick,' she said, holding her jaw uncomfortably.

I wasn't feeling very comfortable myself. I didn't have my beer-token and I had a bag full of canned food that, within the limited purview of a uniformed bull, would have marked me out as a black-marketeer, for which the penalties were very severe. It was not uncommon for *Schmarotzers* to receive death sentences, especially if these also happened to be people who needed to be made an example of, like policemen. So I was anxious to be away from there; no more did I want to accompany her to the local police station and report the matter. Not while I was still carrying the bread bag.

'Look, I kept the taxi waiting. Where do you live? I'll take you home.'

'Just off the Kurfürstendamm. Next to the Theatre Centre.'

'Good. That's near me.'

I helped her along to the taxi, which was where I'd left it, on the corner of Motz Strasse, and told the driver where to go. Then we drove west along Kleist Strasse with the driver telling me in exhaustive detail just what had happened and how it wasn't his fault and that he couldn't believe the fellow he'd collided with hadn't been more seriously injured.

'How do you know he wasn't?'

'He ran off, didn't he? Can't run with a broken leg. Believe me, I know. I was in the last war and I tried.'

When we got to Kurfürstendamm I helped the girl out of the car and she was promptly sick in the gutter.

'Must be my lucky night,' said the taxi driver.

'You've got a funny idea of luck, friend.'

'That's the only kind that's going these days.' The driver leaned out of the window and slammed the door shut behind us. 'What I mean is, she could have been sick in the cab. And that Fritz I hit. I could have killed him, see?'

'How much?' I asked.

'That all depends on whether you're going to report this.'

'I don't know what the lady will want to do,' I said. 'But if I were you I'd get going before she makes up her mind.'

'See?' The driver put the taxi cab in gear. 'I was right. It is my lucky night.'

Inside the building I helped the girl upstairs, which is when I got a better look at her.

She was wearing a navy-blue linen suit with a lace-cotton blouse underneath. The blouse was torn and a stocking was hanging down over one of her shoes. These were plum-coloured like her handbag and the mark under one of her eyes from when she'd been punched. There was a strong smell of perfume on her clothes and I recognized Guerlain Shalimar. By the time we reached her door I had concluded she was about thirty years old. She had shoulder-length blond hair, a wide forehead, a broad nose, high cheekbones, and a sulky mouth. Then again, she had a lot to feel sulky about. She was about 175 centimetres tall, and against my arm felt strong and muscular: strong enough to put up a fight when she was attacked but not strong enough to walk away without help. I was glad about that. She was good-looking in a catlike way with narrow eyes and a

54

tail that seemed to have a whole life of its own and made me want to have her on my lap for a while so that I could stroke it.

She found a door key and fumbled for the lock until I caught her hand and steered the key into the Abus and turned it for her.

'Thanks,' she said. 'I'll be all right from here, I think.'

And but for the fact that she started to sit down on the floor I might have left her there. Instead I gathered her up in my arms and swung her through the door like an exhausted bride.

Advancing into the barely furnished hall I encountered the house guard dog: a barely dressed woman of about fifty with short, bottle-blond hair and more make-up than seemed strictly necessary outside of a circus tent. Almost at once and with a voice like Baron Ochs she started to reproach the half-conscious girl I was carrying for bringing disrespect upon her house, but from the going-over the landlady's eyebrows were giving me much of that seemed to be directed my way. I didn't mind that. For a while it made me feel quite nostalgic for my Army days when some ugly sergeant would chew my ear off for nothing but the hell of it.

'What kind of house do you think I'm running here, Fräulein Tauber? You should be ashamed to even think of coming back here in such a state as this, with a strange man. I'm a respectable woman. I've told you about this before, Fräulein Tauber.

I have my rules. I have my standards. This is not to be tolerated.'

All of this told me two things. One was that the woman in my arms was Fräulein Tauber. And the other was that I was hardly through protecting her from attack.

'Someone tried to rape her,' I said. 'So you can either help or you can go and put on some more make-up. The end of your nose looks like it could use some red paint.'

'Well, really,' the landlady gasped. 'There's no need to be rude. Raped, you say. Yes, of course I'll help. Her room is along here.'

She led the way down the hall, found a key from the bunch in the pocket of her sagging dressing gown, opened a door, and, switching on the ceiling light, illuminated a neat, well-furnished room that was cosier than a cashmere-lined leather glove, and about the same size.

I laid Fräulein Tauber down on a sofa of the kind that was only comfortable if you were wearing a whalebone corset, and kneeling at her feet I started to slap some life into her hands and face.

'When she started working at the Golden Horseshoe I told her something like this might happen,' said the old woman.

This was one of the few remaining nightclubs in Berlin and probably the least offensive, so the chain of causation that was being suggested was hardly obvious to me; but, containing any argument because I'd already been too rough on the woman, I asked her, politely, if she could fetch a cold compress and a cup of strong tea or coffee. The tea or coffee was a long-shot, but in an emergency there's no telling what Berlin women can come up with.

Fräulein Tauber started to come around again and I helped her to sit up. Seeing me she smiled a half-smile.

'Are you still here?'

The smile must have been painful because she flexed her jaw and then winced.

'Just take it easy. That was quite a left hook he handed you. I'll say one thing for you, Fräulein Tauber, you can take a punch.'

'Yeah? Maybe you should manage my fights. I could use a big purse. How'd you know my name, anyway, Parsifal?'

'Your landlady. She's fetching a cold compress and a hot drink for that eye of yours. It's just possible that we can stop it from going blue.'

Fräulein Tauber glanced over at the door and shook her head. 'If she's fetching me a hot drink you must have told her I was dying.'

The landlady returned with the cold compress and handed it to me. I laid it carefully on Fräulein Tauber's eye, took her hand and laid it on top.

'Keep some pressure on it,' I told her.

'There's tea on the way,' said the landlady. 'I had just enough left for a small pot.' She shrugged and gathered her dressing gown closer to a chest that was bigger than the cushions on the sofa.

I stood up, stretched a smile onto my face and offered the landlady one of my American cigarettes.

'Smoke?'

The old woman's eyes lit up like she was looking at the Koh-i-noor diamond.

'Please.' She took one tentatively, almost as if she thought that I might snatch it away again.

'It's a fair exchange for a cup of tea,' I said, lighting her cigarette. I didn't smoke one myself. I hardly wanted either of them thinking I was Gustav Krupp.

The old woman took an ecstatic puff of her cigarette, smiled and went back into the kitchen.

'And here was me thinking you were just Parsifal. Looks like you've got the touch. Healing lepers is easier than raising a smile on her face.'

'But I get the feeling she disapproves of you, Fräulein Tauber.'

'You make that sound almost benign. Like my old schoolmistress.' Fräulein Tauber laughed bitterly. 'Frau Lippert – that's her name – she hates me. If I was Jewish she couldn't hate me more.'

'And what's your name? I can't keep calling you Fräulein Tauber.'

'Why not? Everyone else does.'

'The man who attacked you. Did you get a good look at him?'

'He was about your height. Dark clothes, dark eyes, dark hair, dark complexion. In fact everything about him was dark on account of the fact that it

58

was dark, see? If I drew you a picture he'd look exactly like your shadow.'

'Is that all you can remember about him?'

'Come to think of it he had nice fruity breath. Like he'd been eating Haribos.'

'It's not much to go on.'

'That all depends on where you were thinking of going.'

'The man was trying to rape you.'

'Was he? I guess he was.'

I shrugged. 'Maybe you should report it. I don't know.'

'To the police?'

'I certainly didn't mean the newspapers.'

'Women in this city get attacked all the time, Parsifal. Why do you think the police would be interested in one more?'

'He had a knife, that's why. He might have used it on you.'

'Listen, mister, thanks for helping me. Don't think I'm not grateful because I am. But I don't much like the police.'

I shrugged. 'They're just people.'

'Where did you get that idea? All right, Parsifal, I'll spell it out for you. I work at the Golden Horseshoe. And sometimes the New World, when they're not closed for lack of beer. I make an honest living but that won't stop the cops from thinking otherwise. I can hear their patter now. Like it was a movie. You left the Horseshoe with a man, didn't you? He'd paid you to have sex with him. Only you took his money and tried to dodge him in the dark. Isn't that what really happened, Fräulein Tauber? Get out of here. You're lucky we don't throw you in Ravensbrück for being on the sledge.'

I had to admit she had a point. Berlin cops had stopped being people when they married into the Reich Main Security Office – the RSHA – and joined a Gothic-looking family that included the Gestapo, the SS and the SD.

'Anyway,' she added, 'you don't want the police buzzing in your ears any more than me. Not with your American cigarettes and all those cans in that bag of yours. No, I should think they might ask you some very awkward questions, which you don't look able to answer.'

'I guess you do have a point there, at that.'

'Especially not wearing a suit like that.'

Her visible eye was giving me the up and down.

'What's wrong with it?'

'Nothing. It's a nice suit. And that's the point. It doesn't look like you've been wearing it very much lately. Which is unusual in Berlin for a man with your accent. Which makes me think you must have been wearing something else. Most likely a uniform. That would explain the cigarettes and your quaint opinions about the police. And the tin cans, for all I know. I'll bet you you're in the Army. And you've been in Paris, if that tie is what I think it is: silk. It matches your pre-war manners, Parsifal. Manners are something else you can't get in Berlin any more. But every German officer gets to behave like a real gentleman when he's stationed in Paris. That's what I've heard, anyway. So, you're not a professional blackie. Just an amateur blackie, making a little money on the side while you're home on leave. This is the only reason you're naïvely talking about the police and reporting what happened to me this evening.'

'You should have been a cop yourself.' I grinned.

'No. Not me. I like to sleep at night. But the way things are going, before very long we're all going to be cops whether we like it or not, spying on each other, informing.' She nodded meaningfully at the door. 'If you know what I mean.'

I didn't say anything as Frau Lippert came back carrying a tray with two cups of tea.

'That's what I mean,' added Fräulein Tauber in case I was too dumb to understand her the first time.

'Drink your tea,' I said. 'It'll help keep that eye down.'

'I don't see how.'

'This is good tea,' I told Frau Lippert.

'Thank you, Herr—?'

'That is, I don't see how it can help a blue eye.'

I nodded, appreciating the interruption: it was Fräulein Tauber's turn to help me. It wasn't a good idea to tell Frau Lippert my name. I could see that now. The old woman wasn't just the house guard dog; she was also the building's Gestapo bloodhound.

'Caffeine,' I said. 'It causes the blood vessels to constrict. You want to reduce the amount of blood that can reach your eye. The more blood that seeps out of the damaged capillaries on that lovely face of yours, the bluer your eye will get. Here. Let me have a look.'

I took away the cold compress for a moment and then nodded.

'It's not so blue,' I said.

'Not when I look at you, it's not.'

'Mmm-hmm.'

'You know, you sound just like a doctor, Parsifal.'

'You can tell that from mm-hmm?'

'Sure. Doctors say it all the time. To me, anyway.'

Frau Lippert had been out of this conversation since it started and must have felt that it lacked her own imprimatur. 'She's right,' said the old woman. 'They do.'

I kept on looking at the girl with the cold compress in her hand. 'You're mistaken, Fräulein. It's not mm-hmm your doctor is saying. It's shorter, simpler, more direct than that. It's just Mmm.'

I drained my tea cup and placed it back on the tray. 'Mmm, thank you.'

'I'm glad you liked it,' said Frau Lippert.

'Very much.'

I grinned at her and picked my bag of canned food off the floor. It was nice to see her smile back.

'Well, I'd better be going. I'll look in again sometime just to see you're all right.'

'There's no need, Parsifal. I'm all right now.'

'I like to know how all my patients are doing, Fräulein. Especially the ones wearing Guerlain Shalimar.'

CHAPTER 4

The Pathological Institute was at the Charité Hospital just across the canal from Lehrter Station. With its red-brick exterior, its Alpine-style wooden loggias, its clock and distinctive corner tower, the oldest teaching hospital in the city was much the same as it had always been. Inside, however, things were different. Within the main administrative building, the portraits of more than a few of the Charité's famous physicians and scientists had been removed. The Jews were Germany's misfortune after all. These were the only spaces available in the hospital and if they could have put some beds on the walls they would have done it. The wards and corridors – even the landings outside the elevators – were full of men who had been maimed or injured on the front.

Meanwhile the morgue in the Institute was full to overflowing with dead soldiers and the still unidentified civilian victims of RAF bombings and blackout accidents. Not that their problems were over. The Army Information Centre wasn't always very efficient in notifying the families of those serving men who had died; and in many cases the Army felt that the responsibility fell on the Ministry of Health. But however the deaths were caused, the Ministry of Health believed responsibility for dealing with deaths in Berlin lay properly with the Ministry of the Interior, which, of course, was only too willing to leave such matters to the city authorities, who themselves were inclined to dump this role on the police. So, you might have said that the crisis at the morgue – and that's exactly what it smelled like – was all my fault. Me and others like me.

It was, however, with the hope of taking advantage of this bureaucratic incompetence that I went there in search of Geert Vranken's corpse. And I found what was left of it sharing a drawer in the cold room with a dead prostitute from Lichterfelde and a man from Wedding – most likely a suicide – who had been killed in a gas explosion. I had the mortuary attendant lay out the Dutchman's remains on a slab that looked and smelt worse than it ought to have done, but with an extreme shortage of cleaners in the hospital – not to mention carbolic soap – the dead assumed less and less of the hospital's dwindling resources.

'Pity,' grumbled the attendant.

'What is?'

'That you're not from the State Labour Service so I can get rid of him.'

'I didn't know he was looking for a job.'

'He was a foreign worker. So I'm waiting on the paperwork that will enable me to send his remains down to the incinerator.'

'I'm from the Alex, like I said. I'm sure there are jobs there that could be done by dead men. My job, for example.'

For a moment the morgue attendant thought of smiling and then thought better of it.

'I'll only be a minute,' I said and took out the switchblade I had found on the ground under Nolli Station.

At the sight of the long blade in my hand, the attendant backed off nervously. 'Here, what's your game?'

'It's all right. I'm trying to establish if this knife matches the victim's stab wounds.'

Relaxing a little, he nodded at Vranken's remains. 'Least of his problems I should have thought: Being stabbed.'

'You'd think so, wouldn't you? But before a train ran him over—'

'That would explain a lot.'

'Someone stabbed him. Several times.'

'Evidently not his lucky day.'

I slid the blade into one of the more obvious wounds in the dead man's pale torso. 'Before the war you used to get a proper lab report with photographs and descriptions so that you didn't have to do this kind of thing.'

'Before the war you used to get beer that tasted like beer.' Remembering who and more particularly what I was, he added quickly, 'Not that there's anything wrong with the beer now, of course.'

I didn't say anything. I was glad he'd spoken out of turn. It meant I could probably avoid filling out the morgue's paperwork – Commissioner Lüdtke had told me to drop the case, after all – as a quid pro quo for ignoring the attendant's 'unpatriotic' remark about German beer. Besides I was paying nearly all of my attention to the knife in the stab wound. I couldn't say for sure that it was the murder weapon, but it could have been. It was long enough and sharp enough, with just one edge and a blunter upper side that matched the wound almost perfectly.

I pulled the blade out and looked for something to wipe it with. Being a fussy type, I'm particular about the switchblades I keep in my coat pocket. And I figured I'd already encountered enough germs and bacteria just walking through the hospital without squirrelling away a private cache of my own.

'Got anything to wipe this with?'

'Here,' he said, and taking it from me he wiped it with the corner of his lab coat.

'Thanks,' I said.

I could see that he was anxious to get rid of me and when I suggested that there was probably no need to bother with the paperwork, he agreed with alacrity.

'I don't think he'll tell, do you?' said the attendant. 'Besides, I don't have a pen that works.'

I went outside. It was a nice day so I decided to walk back to the Alex and eat lunch at a counter I knew on Karl Strasse, but that one was closed because of a lack of sausage. So was the one on Oranienburger Strasse. Finally I got a sandwich and a paper at a place near the Stock Exchange, only there was even less of interest in the sandwich than there was in the paper, and probably in the Stock Exchange, too. But it's foolish to give up eating bread because you can't get the sausage to put in it. At least I was free to still think of the bread as a sandwich.

Then again, I'm a typical Berliner, so maybe I'm just hard to please.

When I got back to the Alex I had the files on all of the summer's S-Bahn murders sent up to my office. I suppose I wanted to make doubly sure that Paul Ogorzow was the real killer and not someone who'd been made to measure for it. It wouldn't have been the first time that a Kripo run by the Nazis had done something like that. The only surprise was that they hadn't already tried to pin the murders of Wallenstein, Baldur, Siegfried and Cock Robin on some hapless Jew.

It turned out that I wasn't the first to review the Ogorzow files. The Record Memo showed that the Abwehr – military intelligence – had also looked at the files, and recently. I wondered why. At least I did until I remembered all the foreign workers who had been interviewed during the course of the investigation. But Paul Ogorzow had been a German railway-worker; rape and a violent hatred of women had been his motive; he hadn't stabbed any of his victims, he had battered them to death. There was no telling if Fräulein Tauber's attacker would have battered her or stabbed her after he'd finished raping her, but from the blow he'd given her face there could be no doubting his dislike of women. Of course, lust murders were hardly uncommon in Berlin. Before Paul Ogorzow, there had been other violent, sometimes cannibalistic killers; and doubtless there would be others after him.

Much to my surprise I was impressed at the thoroughness and scale of Commissioner Lüdtke's investigation. Thousands of interviews had been conducted and almost one hundred suspects brought in for interrogation; at one stage male police officers had even dressed up as women and travelled the S-Bahn at night in the hope of luring the murderer into an attack. A reward of ten thousand Reichsmarks had been posted and, finally, one of Paul Ogorzow's workmates – another railway employee – had fingered him as the murderer instead of one of the many foreign workers. But among those foreign workers who had been interviewed was Geert Vranken. I shouldn't have been surprised to discover his name on the list of those who had been interviewed; and yet I was. I read the transcript with interest.

A science graduate from the University in The

Hague, Vranken had been quickly eliminated from Lüdtke's inquiry when his alibi checked out; but, hardly wanting to rely on this alone – after all, his alibi relied on other foreign workers – he had been at pains to adduce evidence of his good character, and to this end he had offered the name of a German whom he'd met before the war, in The Hague. Lüdtke's team of detectives, several of whom I knew, had hardly needed to take up this reference because, a week or so after Vranken's interview, Paul Ogorzow had been arrested. The certainty – on my part – that for once the right man had been sent to the guillotine at Plotzensee, in July 1941, gradually gave way to a feeling of pity for Geert Vranken and, more particularly, the wife and baby he had left behind in the Netherlands. How many other families, I wondered, would be similarly destroyed before the war was over?

Of course, this was hardly normal for me. I'd seen plenty of murder victims in my time at the Alex, many of them in even more tragic circumstances than these. After Minsk I suppose my conscience was easily pricked. Whatever the reasons, I determined to find out if, as Commissioner Lüdtke had said it would, the State Labour Service had yet informed Vranken's family that he had met with a fatal accident. Thus it was that I spent a fruitless hour on the telephone being rerouted from one bureaucrat to another before I finally gave up and wrote a letter myself, this to an address in The Hague that was in Vranken's work book and which, prior to its issue by the State Labour Service, was where previously he had been employed. In my letter I made no mention of the fact that Geert Vranken had been murdered, only that he had been hit by a train and killed. His being stabbed six times was more than any family needed to be told.

CHAPTER 5

I had an office in the Police Praesidium, on the third floor – a small room on the corner underneath the tower and overlooking the U-Bahn station on Alexanderplatz. The view out of the window on a late summer evening was the best thing about it. Life didn't look quite so dismal at that kind of altitude. I couldn't smell the people or see their pale, undernourished and sometimes just plain hopeless faces. All the streets came together in one big square just the same as they had done before the war, with trams clanging and taxis honking their horns and the city growling in the distance the way it always did. Sitting on the windowsill with my face in the sun, it was easy to pretend there was no war, no front, no Hitler and that none of it had anything to do with me. Outside there wasn't a swastika in sight, just the many varieties of specimen in my own favourite game of girl spotting. It was a sport I was always passionate about and at which I excelled. I liked the way it helped me tune in to the natural world, and because girls in Berlin are visible in a way that other Berlin wildlife is not, I never seemed to grow tired of it. There are so many different girls out there. Mostly I was on the lookout for the rarer varieties: exotic blondes that hadn't been seen since 1938 and fabulous redheads wearing summer plumage that was very nearly transparent. I'd thought about putting a feeder on my window-sill but I knew it was hopeless. The climb up to the third floor was simply too much for them.

The only creatures that ever made it up to my office were the rats. Somehow they never run out of energy, and when I turned back to face the room with its awful portrait of the Leader and the SD uniform that was hanging in an open closet, like a terrible reminder of the other man I'd been for much of the summer, there were two of them coming through the glass door. Neither of them said anything until they were seated with their hats in their hands and had stared at me for several seconds with preternatural calm, as if I were some lesser being, which of course I was, because these rats were from the Gestapo.

One of the men wore a double-breasted navy chalk-stripe, and the other, a dark grey three-piece suit with a watch-chain that glittered like his eyes. The one wearing the chalk-stripe had a full head of short, fair hair that was as carefully arranged as the lines on a sheet of writing paper; the other was even fairer but losing it on the front almost as if his forehead had been plucked like one of those medieval ladies in a rather dull oil painting. On their faces were smiles that were insolent or self-satisfied or cynical but mostly all three at the same time and they regarded me and my office and probably my very existence with some amusement. But that was okay because I felt much the same way myself.

'You're Bernhard Gunther?'

I nodded.

The man with the chalk-stripe suit checked his neatly combed hair fastidiously, as if he had just stepped out of the barber's chair at the KaDeWe. A decent haircut was about the only thing in Berlin that was not in short supply.

'With a reputation like yours I was expecting a pair of Persian slippers and a calabash.' He smiled. 'Like Sherlock Holmes.'

I sat down behind my desk facing the pair and smiled back. 'These days I find that a three-pipe problem's just the same as a one-pipe problem. I can't find the tobacco to smoke in it. So I keep the calabash hidden in the drawer alongside my gold-plated syringe and some orange pips.'

They kept on looking, saying nothing, just sizing me up.

'You fellows should have brought along a black-jack if you were expecting me to talk first.'

'Is that what you think of us?'

'I'm not the only one with a colourful reputation.'

'True.'

'Are you here to ask questions or for a favour?'

'We don't need to ask favours,' said the one with

the basilica skull designed by Brunelleschi. 'Usually we get all the cooperation we require without having to ask anyone a favour.' He glanced at his colleague and did some more smiling. 'Isn't that right?'

'Yes, that's right.' The one with the neat hair was like a thicker-set version of von Ribbentrop. He had no eyebrows to speak of and big shoulders: I didn't think he was a man you wanted to see taking off his coat and rolling up his sleeves in search of answers. 'Most people are only too willing to help us and it's rare we are ever obliged to ask for something as quaint as a favour.'

'Is that so?' I put a match in my mouth and started to chew it slowly. I figured that as long as I didn't try inhaling it, my lungs would stay healthy. 'All right. I'm listening.' I leaned forward and clasped my hands with an earnest reverence that bordered on the sarcastic. 'And if it persuades you to come quickly to the point then this is me looking all ready and willing to help the Gestapo in any way that I can. Only do stop trying to make me feel very small or I'll start to question the wisdom of letting you sit in my office with your hats in your hands.'

Chalk-stripe pinched the crown of his hat and inspected the lining. For all I knew it had his name and rank written there just in case he forgot them.

'You know my name. So why don't you introduce yourselves?'

'I'm Commissar Sachse. And this is Inspector Wandel.'

I nodded politely. 'Delighted, I'm sure.'

'How much do you know about the Three Kings? And please don't mention the Bible or I shall conclude that I'm not going to like you.'

'You're talking about the three men who came to Berlin from Czechoslovakia in early 1938, aren't you? I'm sorry, Bohemia and Moravia, although I'm never quite sure of the difference and anyway, who cares? The Three Kings are three Czech nationalists and officers of the defeated Czech Army who, having conducted a series of terrorist attacks in Prague – it is still called Prague, isn't it? Good. Well then, having orchestrated a campaign of sabotage there they decided to bring their war here, to the streets of Berlin. And as far as I know, for a while they were quite successful. They planted a bomb at the Aviation Ministry in September 1939. Not to mention one in the doorway here at the Alex. Yes, that was embarrassing for us all, wasn't it? No wonder the Press and radio didn't mention it. Then there was the attempt on Himmler's life at the Anhalter Railway Station in February of this year. I expect that was even more embarrassing, for the Gestapo, anyway. I believe the bomb was placed in the left luggage office, which is an obvious place and one that should certainly have been searched in advance of the Reichsführer-SS's arrival in the station. I bet someone had a lot of explaining to do after that.'

76

Their smiles were fading a little now and their chairs were starting to look uncomfortable; as the two Gestapo men shifted their backsides around, the wagon-wheel backs creaked like a haunted house. Chalk-stripe checked his hair again almost as if he'd left the source of his ability to intimidate me on the barbershop floor. The other man, Wandel, bit his lip trying to keep the death's head moth of a smile pinned to his delinquent mug. I might have stopped my little history there and then out of fear of what their organization was capable of, but I was enjoying myself too much.

I hadn't considered the concept of suicide by Gestapo until now, but I could see its advantages. At least I might enjoy the process a little more than just blowing my own brains out. All the same, I wasn't about to throw my life away on some small-timers like these two; if ever I did decide to blow a raspberry in some senior Nazi's face I was going to make it count. Besides, it was now plain to me that they really were after a favour.

'You know, the word here in Kripo is that the Three Kings get a kick out of embarrassing the Gestapo. There's one particular story doing the rounds that one of them even stole Oscar Fleischer's overcoat.'

Fleischer was head of the Gestapo's Counter-intelligence Section in Prague.

'And that the same brazen fellow won a bet that he could cadge a light for his cigarette off Fleischer's cigar.'

'There's always a lot of gossip in a place like this,' said Sachse.

'Oh sure. But that's how cops work, Herr Commissar. A nudge here. A wink there. A whisper in a bar. A fellow tells you that someone else says that his pal heard this or that. Personally I've always put a vague rumour ahead of anything as imaginative as three pipes' worth of deductive reasoning. It's elementary, my dear Sachse. Oh yes, and didn't these Three Kings send the Gestapo a complimentary copy of their own underground newspaper? That's the gossip.'

'Since you appear to be so well informed—'

I shook my head. 'It's common knowledge, here on the Third Floor.'

'—Then I dare say you will also know that two of the Three Kings – Josef Balaban and Josef Masin – have already been arrested. As have many other of their collaborators. In Prague. And here in Berlin. It's only a matter of time before we catch Melchior.'

'I don't get it,' I said. 'You caught Josef A in April; and Josef B in May. Or maybe it was the other way round. But here we are in September and you still haven't managed to shake the third King out of their sleeves. You boys must be going soft.'

Of course I knew this couldn't be true. The Gestapo had moved heaven and earth in search of the third man, but mostly they'd employed a more infernal sort of help. Because there was

78

another rumour around the Alex: that the Prague Gestapo had enlisted the services of their most notorious torturer in Bohemia, a sadist called Paul Soppa, who was the commander of Pankrac Prison in Prague, to work on the two Czechs in his custody. I didn't give much for their chances but, in the light of the continued liberty of Melchior, the certainty that neither man had talked was proof positive of their enormous courage and bravery.

'There are different ways of approaching every problem,' said Wandel. 'And right now we should like you to help us with this problem. Colonel Schellenberg speaks very highly of you.'

Walter Schellenberg was close to General Heydrich, who was Chief of the whole RSHA, of which Kripo was now one part.

'I know who Schellenberg is,' I said. 'At least, I remember meeting him. But I don't know what he is. Not these days.'

'He's the acting chief of foreign intelligence within the RSHA,' said Sachse.

'Is this problem a foreign intelligence matter?'

'It might be. But right now it's a homicide. Which is where you come in.'

'Well, anything to help Colonel Schellenberg, of course,' I said, helpfully.

'You know the Heinrich von Kleist Park?'

'Of course. It used to be Berlin's botanical garden before the Botanical Gardens were built in Steglitz.'

'A body was found there this morning.'

'Oh? I wonder why I haven't heard about it.'

'You're hearing about it now. We'd like you to come and take a look at it, Gunther.'

I shrugged. 'Have you got any petrol?'

Sachse frowned.

'For your car,' I added. 'I wasn't proposing that we burn the body.'

'Yes, of course we have petrol.'

'Then I'd love to go to the Park with you, Commissar Sachse.'

Kleist Park in Schöneberg had something to do with a famous German Romantic writer. He might have been called Kleist. There were lots of trees, a statue of the goddess Diana, and, on the western border of the park, the Court of Appeal. Not that Hitler's Germany had much use for a Court of Appeal. Those who were convicted and condemned in a Nazi court of first instance usually stayed that way.

On the southern border was a building I had half an idea might once have been the Prussian State Art School, but given that the Gestapo was now headquartered in the old Industrial Art School on Prinz Albrechtstrasse, there seemed to be little or no chance that anyone was being taught how to paint someone's portrait in the Prussian State Art School; not when they could more usefully be taught how to torture people. It was a fact that the Gestapo had always taken its share of the city's best public buildings. That was to be expected.

But lately they'd started confiscating the premises of shops and businesses that had been abandoned as a result of the shortages. A friend of mine had gone into the Singer Sewing Machine salesroom on Wittenberg Platz looking for a new treadle-belt only to discover that the place was now being used as an arsenal by the SS. Meyer's Wine Shop, on Olivaer Platz, where once I'd been a regular customer, was now an SS 'Information Bureau'. Whatever that was.

In the centre of the park was a curving promenade where you could walk, or perhaps sit, but only on the grass, since all of the city's many wooden park benches had been taken away for the war effort; sometimes I imagined a fat Wehrmacht general conducting the siege of Leningrad while warming his hands over a brazier that was fuelled with one of these. On the eastern edge of this promenade, and bordering Potsdamer Strasse, was an area of shrubs and trees that had been closed off to the public by several uniformed policemen. The dead body of a man lay under a huge rhododendron that was in late flower, but only just, since he was covered with red petals that looked like multiple stab wounds. He was wearing a dark blouson-type jacket, a lighter brown pair of flannel trousers, and a pair of severely down-at-heel brown boots. I couldn't see his face as one of my new Gestapo friends was blocking the sun, as was their habit, so I asked him to move and, as he stepped out of the way,

I squatted down on my haunches to take a closer look.

It was a typical mortuary photograph: the mouth wide open as if awaiting the attentions of a dentist – although the teeth were in remarkably good condition and certainly better than mine – the wide eyes staring straight ahead so that, all things considered, he looked more surprised to see me than I was to see him. He was about twenty-five with a small moustache, and on the front of his left forehead below the line of his dark hair a contusion that was the shape and colour of an outsized amethyst and which more than likely was the cause of death.

'Who found the body?' I asked Sachse. 'And when?'

'A uniformed cop on patrol. From the Potsdamer Platz station. About six o'clock this morning.'

'And how is it that you picked up the order?'

'The duty detective from Kripo telephoned it in. Fellow named Lehnhoff.'

'That was clever of him. Lehnhoff's not usually so quick on his toes. And what did this Fritz have in his pocket that marked him out as your meat? A Czech passport?'

'No. This.'

Sachse dipped into his pocket and then handed me a gun. It was a little Model 9 Walther, a palm-sized .25 calibre automatic. Smaller than the Baby Browning I had at home for when I wasn't expecting visitors, but quite accurate.

'A bit more lethal than a set of door keys, wouldn't you say so?' said Sachse.

'That will open a door for you,' I agreed.

'Be careful. It's still loaded.'

I nodded and handed the gun back to him.

'This makes it a Gestapo matter.'

'Automatically,' I said. 'I can see that. But I still don't see how this connects him with the Three Kings.'

'One of our officers from the Documentation Section looked over his papers and found some discrepancies.'

Wandel handed me a yellow card with the dead man's photograph in the top left-hand corner. It was his Employment Certificate. He said, 'Notice anything wrong with it?'

I shrugged. 'The staples in the picture are a bit rusty. Otherwise it looks all right to me. Name of Victor Keil. Doesn't ring any bells.'

'The impression of the rubber stamp on the corner of the photograph can hardly be seen,' said Wandel. 'No German official would have permitted that.' Then he handed me the dead man's identity card. 'And this? What do you make of this, Herr Commissar?'

I rubbed the document in my fingers, which drew a nod of approval from Sachse.

'You're right to check it that way first,' he said. 'The forgeries just don't feel right. Like they're made of linen. But that's not what gives this one away as a fake.'

I opened it up and took a closer look at the contents. The photograph on the ID card had two corner stamps, one on the top right-hand corner and the other on the top left, and these both looked clear enough. The two fingerprints were similarly clear, as was the police precinct stamp. I shook my head. 'Beats me what's wrong with it. It looks completely right.'

'The quality is actually quite good,' admitted Sachse. 'Except for one thing. Whoever made that can't spell "forefinger".'

'My God, yes, you're right.'

Sachse was starting to look satisfied with himself once more.

'All of which prompted us to investigate further,' he said. 'It seems that the real Victor Keil was killed during a bombing raid in Hamburg last year. And we now know, or at least we strongly suspect, that this man isn't a German at all, but a Czech terrorist by the name of Franz Koci. Our sources in Prague tell us that he was one of the last Czech agents operating here in Berlin. And he certainly fits the last description we had of him. Until October 1938 he was a lieutenant in a Czech regiment of artillery that was deployed to the Sudetenland. After the capitulation of the Benes government at Munich, he disappeared, along with many others who subsequently worked for the Three Kings.'

I shrugged. 'It sounds like you know everything about him,' I said. 'I can't imagine why you need me to look at his fingernails.'

'We don't know who killed him,' said Wandel. 'Or why. Or even how.'

I nodded. 'For the how you'll need a doctor. Preferably a doctor of medicine.' I smiled at my joke, thinking of the American, Dickson, and his aversion to the doctors of deceit at the Ministry of Propaganda. But it wasn't a joke for sharing, especially with the Gestapo. 'As for the who and the why, maybe I could take a closer look.' I pointed at the body. 'Do you mind?'

'Be my guest,' said Sachse.

I took out my handkerchief and then laid it neatly beside the body. 'Somewhere to lay any evidence I find. You see I intend going through the dead man's pockets.'

'Help yourself. But all of the useful evidence has already been collected.'

'Oh, I don't doubt that. If there's anything of value that the uniforms and Inspector Lehnhoff have left behind, I'll be pleasantly surprised.'

Sachse frowned. 'You don't mean—'

'Cops in this city are just as crooked as anyone else. Sometimes they're even as crooked as the crooks. These days most of them only join so they can steal a man's watch without getting caught.'

I lifted the dead man's left arm by way of illustration. There was a tan mark on his wrist, only the watch that might have made it wasn't there.

'Yes, I see what you mean,' said Sachse.

'The body's a little stiff, which means that rigor is setting in or passing off. It takes about twelve

85

hours to get established, lasts about twelve hours and takes another twelve hours to pass.' I tugged at the dead man's cheek. 'It starts in the face however and this fellow's face is soft to the touch, which probably means the rigor is passing off. You understand that all of this is very crude but I'd say your man has been dead for at least a day or so. Of course, I might be wrong, but I've seen plenty of dead men who would say I'm probably right about that.'

I undid the buttons on the blouson and then pulled open the shirt to inspect the torso. 'This man took a hard fall. Or received a substantial impact. There is substantial bruising on the left-hand side of his body.' I pressed hard directly on the bruise and the lowest part of the ribcage. 'Feels like one of the ribs has separated from the chest wall. In other words, it's broken.'

I took out my pocket knife, unfolded it carefully and, starting at the cuff I began to cut up the length of the dead man's trouser leg, but only because I didn't want to start unbuttoning his fly buttons. Generally speaking, I prefer to know a man a little better before I will do that. On the left thigh there was another heavy bruise that matched the broken rib and the contusion on the head. I was trying not to appear nervous, but on top of the bad feeling I had most of the time I now had a bad feeling about the dead man, too. The distance between Kleist Park and Nollendorf Platz was about a kilometre, and even a man who had collided with a taxi on the corner of Motz Strasse might have staggered to the park in less than thirty minutes. This wouldn't have been the only traffic accident in Berlin that night but it was almost certainly the only one likely to have gone unreported.

'You want to know what I think?'

'Of course.'

'This man has been involved in a road traffic accident. Of course that's hardly uncommon what with the blackout and Berlin drivers.'

I was quite certain I was looking at the man who had attacked Fräulein Tauber and who had collided with the taxi. A hundred different thoughts started to run through my mind. Did the Gestapo know that already? Was that what this was all about? To see how I would react when presented with the dead body, like Hagen's treachery uncovered when he stands beside Siegfried's bier? No. How could they know? None of the other parties involved – Fräulein Tauber, Frau Lippert, the taxi driver – even knew I was a cop, let alone my name. But for a moment my hand started to shake. I folded the knife and returned it to my coat pocket.

'Anything wrong, Gunther?'

'No, I like working with the dead. On most nights when I'm not contemplating cutting my own throat you can catch me down at the local ceme-tery with my good friend, Count Orlok.' Biting my lip I steeled myself to go through the dead man's pockets.

'We've searched his pockets,' said Sachse. 'There's nothing important left in them.'

From the dead man's pocket I took out a packet of Haribos and showed them to the two Gestapo officers.

'I don't know what that tells us,' objected Wandel.

'It tells us that the man had a sweet tooth,' I said, although it told me a lot more than that. Any doubts that this was the man who had attached Fräulein Tauber were now removed. Hadn't she mentioned the smell of Haribos on his breath?

'Apart from the false documentation,' said Sachse, 'and the gun, of course, all we found was a money clip, a door key, and a pocket diary.'

'May I see them?'

I stood up. The money clip was silver and in its fold was about fifty Reichsmarks in twenties and ones, but it was loose on the notes and made me think that it had held more money than was now present; and it was all too easy to suppose that the policemen who had stolen Franz Koci's watch had also relieved him of at least half of his cash. That would only be typical. The door key was on a steel chain that must have been attached to his belt: it was a key for an old mortise lock made by the Ferdinand Garbe Lock Company of Berlin. The diary was the most interesting item. It was a red-leather Army pocket diary for 1941 that they handed out to German officers: there was a little wallet at the front and at the back there was a useful guide to recognizing German army ranks and insignias. As a boy I'd had a diary with a similar guide for recognizing the footprints of animals – almost invaluable in a big city like Berlin. I turned to the current week and noted the only entry for the last forty-eight hours: 'N.P. 9.15 p.m.' It had been nine-thirty when I had interrupted Franz Koci's attack on Fräulein Tauber, which was time enough for them to meet on Nolli at nine-fifteen.

But why would a Czech terrorist intent on avoiding the attention of the police risk carrying out a sexual assault on someone at an S-Bahn station? Someone he had arranged to meet there. Unless the person he had arranged to meet hadn't turned up and, in frustration, he had attacked the girl. But that made no sense either.

I handed the diary back to Sachse. 'These diaries are even more useful to spies than they are for our men, don't you think? They tell the enemy who's worth killing and who's not.'

'I imagine he must have stolen it,' said Wandel, redundantly. 'Our intelligence suggests that some of these Czechos are damn good pickpockets.'

I nodded. That sounded fair enough to me considering that we had just stolen their country.

I had a lot of thinking to do and I decided to do it at the Golden Horseshoe. That was probably against the rules. Anyone with a thought in his head wouldn't ever have gone to the Golden

Horseshoe so I figured a man with my chequered history was worth a discount.

It was a big round room with small round tables around a big round dance floor. The floor was mostly given over to a mechanical horse on which the club hostesses and female customers were invited to take a musical ride and, in the process, flash a stocking-top or something more intimate. If you'd had a lot of beer it was possibly a lot of fun, but in the middle of Berlin's drought, a quiet game of cribbage had it beat.

One of the hostesses was perhaps the last black woman in Berlin. Her name was Ella. She sat at a table playing Solitaire using a pack of cards featuring photographic portraits of our beloved Nazi leaders. I joined her and watched for a while and she said that it improved her luck so I bought her a glass of lemonade and talked out the right cards for her; and when I gave her one of my precious American cigarettes she was all smiles and offered to ride the horse for me.

'For fifty pfennigs you can see my thighs. For seventy-five you can see the mouse and everything in its mouth. I'm not wearing any underwear.'

'Actually I was rather hoping to see Fräulein Tauber.'

'She doesn't work here any more. Not for a long time.'

'Where does she work now?'

Ella took a lazy puff of her cigarette and remained silent.

I pushed a note across the table. There were no pictures on it like the ones on the backs of the cards but she hardly minded about that. I let her reach for it and then put my finger on the little black eagle in the corner.

'Is she at the New World?'

'That dump? I should say not. She tell you that she works there?' She laughed. 'It means she doesn't want to see you again, darling. So why don't you forget her and watch me ride that pony.'

The Negress was tapping Morse code on the other end of the bill. I let it go and watched it disappear into a brassiere as large as a barrage balloon.

'So, where *does* she work?'

'Arianne? She runs the cloakroom at the Jockey Bar. Has for a while. For a girl like Arianne, there's plenty of money to be made at the Jockey.'

'In the cloakroom?'

'You can do a lot more in a cloakroom than just hang a coat, honey.'

'I guess so.'

'We got a cloakroom here, Fritz. It's nice and dark in there. For five marks, I could take real care of all your valuables. In my mouth, if you wanted.'

'You'd be wasting your time, Ella. The only reason they let me come back from the front was because I don't have any valuables. Not any more.'

'I'm sorry. That's too bad. Nice-looking fellow like you.'

Her face fell a little and, for a moment, seeing her sympathy, I felt bad about lying to her like that. She had a kind way about her.

I changed the subject.

'The Jockey,' I said. 'Sure I know it. It's that place off Wittenberg Platz, on Luther Strasse. Used to be a Russian place called Yar.'

The Negress nodded.

'I've only ever seen it from the outside. What's it like?'

'Expensive. Full of Amis and big-shots from the Foreign Ministry. They still play American jazz there. The real stuff. I'd go myself but for one rather obvious disadvantage. Coloureds ain't welcome.'

I frowned. 'The Nazis don't like anyone except Germans. You should know that by now, gorgeous.'

She smiled. 'Oh, I wasn't talking about them. It's the Amis who don't like coloureds in the place.'

From the outside, the Jockey Bar certainly sounded like the old Berlin from before the war with its easy morals and vulgar charms. Others thought so too. A small crowd of jazz fans stood on the sidewalk in the dark enjoying the music but unwilling to pay the prohibitive cost of going inside. To save paying the entrance fee myself I flashed the beer-token in my raincoat – a little brass oval that said I was police. Unlike most Berlin cops I'm not fond of trying to score a free one off an honest business, but the Jockey Bar was hardly that. Five marks just to walk down-stairs was little better than theft. Not that there weren't plenty of people already down there who seemed more than willing to be robbed. Most of them were smart types, with quite a few wearing evening dress and Party buttons. They say crime doesn't pay. Not as well as a job does at the Foreign Office or the Ministry of Propaganda. There were also plenty of Americans, as Ella had said there would be. You could recognize them by their loud ties and their even louder voices. The Jockey Bar was probably the one place in Berlin you could speak English without some fool in a uniform trying to remind you that Roosevelt was a gangster, a Negroid maniac, a warmonger in a wheelchair, and a depraved Jewish scoundrel; and the Germans who really disliked him had some even more unpleasant things to say.

At the bottom of the stairs was a cloakroom where a girl was filing her nails or reading a maga-zine and sometimes she managed to do both at the same time. You could tell that she was clever. She had dark hair and plenty of it but it was tied up like a velvet curtain at the back of her head. She was thin and she was wearing a black dress and I suppose she was good-looking in an obvious sort of way, which, lacking all subtlety, is the way I usually like my women; but she wasn't Arianne Tauber.

I waited for the girl to finish her nail or her

picture caption and to notice me and that seemed to take longer than it ought to have done with the lights on.

'This is a cloakroom, isn't it?'

She looked up, gave me the up and down and then, with a well-manicured hand, ushered my eyes to the coats – some of them made of fur – that were hanging on the rail behind her.

'What do those look like? Icicles?'

'From here it looks as if I'm in the wrong line of work. You, too, if I'm not mistaken. I had the strange idea that you're supposed to be the first line of welcome in this up-market shell-hole.'

I took off my coat and laid it on the counter and she stared at it with distaste for a moment before dragging it away like she was planning to kill it and then handing me a ticket.

'Is Arianne here tonight?'

'Arianne?'

'Arianne Tauber. That's Tauber as in Richard Tauber, only I wouldn't like to have him sitting on my lap.'

'She's not here right now.'

'Not here as in not working or not here as in she just stepped outside for a few minutes?'

'Who wants to know?'

'Just tell her that Parsifal is here. That's Parsifal as in the Holy Grail. Talking of which, I'll be in the bar if she does show up.'

'You and everyone else, I guess. There's the bar and then there's the bar, see? And if you get bored in there you can try the bar. That's bar as in Jockey Bar.'

'You were listening after all.'

I went into the bar. The place needed a coat of paint and a new carpet, but not as much as I needed a drink and a set of earplugs. I like music when I'm drinking. I even like jazz, sometimes, just so long as they remember where they left the melody. The band at the Jockey Bar was a three-piece trio, and while they knew all the notes of 'Avalon' these were in no particular order. I sat down at a table and picked up the drinks card. The prices felt like mustard gas on my eyeballs and when I'd picked myself off the floor, I ordered a beer. The waitress came back almost immediately carrying a tray on which stood a tall glass filled with gold, which was the nearest thing to the Holy Grail I'd seen since the last time I bought a forty-pfennig stamp. I tasted it and found myself smiling like an idiot. It tasted exactly like beer.

'I must be dead.'

'That can be arranged,' said a voice.

'Oh?'

'Take a look around, Parsifal. This louse house is jumping with important Nazis. Any one of these stuffed shirts could pick up the telephone and get you a seat on tomorrow's partisan express.'

I stood up and pulled out a chair for her. 'I'm impressed. That you know about the partisan express.'

The partisan express was what German soldiers

called the troop train that travelled between Berlin and the eastern front.

'I've got a brother in the Army,' she explained.

'That's hardly an exclusive club. Not any more.'

'Nor is this place. I guess that must be why they let you in.' Arianne Tauber smiled and sat down. 'But you can buy me a drink, if you like.'

'At these prices? It would be cheaper to buy you a Mercedes Benz.'

'What would be the point? You can't get the petrol. So a drink will do just fine.'

I waved the waitress toward me and let Arianne order a beer for herself.

'Got any more of those Ami cigarettes?'

'No,' I lied. Buying her a beer felt extravagant enough without throwing caution out of the window and giving her a smoke as well.

She shrugged. 'That's all right. I've got some Luckies.'

Arianne reached for her bag, and that gave me time to have another look at her. She was wearing a plain navy-blue dress with short sleeves. Around her waist was a purple leather belt with a series of shiny black or maybe blue lozenges that were arranged like the jewels on a crown. On her shoulder was an interesting bronze brooch of the Hindu goddess Kali. Her purple leather bag was round and on a long strap and a bit like a water-carrier, and out of it she took a silver cigarette box with three bits of inlaid turquoise that were as big as thrush eggs. On the side there was a little matching compartment for a lighter but which contained a roll of banknotes, and for a moment I pictured her lighting a cigarette with a five-mark note. As a way of wasting money that was only a little less profligate than buying a girl a drink at the Jockey Bar.

When she opened the little cigarette case I took one and rolled it in my fingers for a moment and passed it under my nostrils to remind myself that it was better to have America as a friend than an enemy before poking it between my lips and dipping my head onto a match from a book off the table that was in her scented hand.

'Guerlain Shalimar,' I said and puffed my cigarette happily for a second before adding, 'You were wearing it when I last saw you.'

'A gift from an admirer. Seems like every Fritz who comes back on leave from Paris brings a girl perfume. It's the one thing there's no shortage of here in Berlin. I swear I could open a shop, the amount of perfume I've been given since the war started. Men. Why don't they bring something useful like shoe laces, or toilet paper?' She shook her head. 'Cooking oil. Have you tried buying cooking oil? Forget it.'

'Maybe they figure you smell better wearing the perfume.'

She smiled. 'You must think I'm really ungrateful.'

'The next time I'm in Paris I'll buy you some paperclips and put you to the test.'

'No, really. The other night I didn't get a chance to thank you properly, Parsifal.'

'Skip it. You were in no state to be throwing me a cocktail party.' I took hold of her chin and turned her profile toward me. 'The eye looks fine. Maybe just a little bruised around the edges. Then again I always go simple for blue eyes.'

For a moment she looked bashful. Then she hardened again. 'I don't want you being nice to me.'

'That's all right. I didn't bring any perfume.'

'Not until I've apologized to you. For not being honest.'

'It's a national habit.'

She took a sip of her beer and then a kiss from her cigarette. Her hand was shaking a little.

'Really. There's nothing to apologize for.'

'All the same, I would like to explain something.'

I shrugged. 'If you want. Take your time. There's no one waiting for me at home.'

She nodded and then picked out another smile to wear. This one was looking sheepish.

'First of all I want you to know I'm not some joy-girl. Sometimes, when I'm in here, I'll let a man buy me a drink. Or give me a present. Like these cigarettes. But that's as far as it goes unless – well, we're all human, aren't we?'

'I certainly used to believe that.'

'That's the truth, Parsifal. Anyway, being the cloakroom girl in a place like this is a good job.

98

The Amis – even a few of the Germans – they tip well. There's nothing much to spend it on but I figure you still have to put something away for the bad times. And I've got an ugly feeling that there's plenty of those yet to come. Worse than now, I mean. My brother says so. He says—'

Whatever her brother had said she seemed to think better of telling me about it. A lot of Berliners were forgetful like that. They would start talking, then remember a little thing called the Gestapo and just stop, mid-sentence, and stare into the distance for a minute and then say something like what she said next.

'Skip it. What I was saying. It wasn't anything important.'

'Sure.'

'What's important is you know I'm not selling it, Parsifal.'

'I understand,' I said, hardly caring if she was selling it or not. But I was keen to hear her out, although I was still wondering why she felt obliged to explain herself at all.

'I hope so.' She picked a piece of tobacco off her tongue and her fingers came away red from her lipstick. 'Okay. Here's what happened that night. Household, building, contents, everything because I figure I have to tell someone and I get the feeling you might be interested. Say if you're not and I'll just shut up. But you were interested enough to come down here and look for me, right?'

I nodded.

99

'And as a matter of fact it's in here that the story starts. It was during my break. Magda – she's the girl you met, in the cloakroom – was behind the desk and I was in the bar. When we have our break we're supposed to come in here and have a drink with the customers. Like you and me are doing now.'

She tried on another smile. This one looked wry.

'Some break. Frankly it's not a break at all. The Fritzes here are generous with their drinks and their cigarettes, and usually I'm glad to get back to the cloakroom to have a rest and try to clear my head.' She shrugged. 'I was never much of a drinker but that kind of excuse really doesn't work in here.'

'I can imagine.'

I glanced around and tried not to grimace. There's something obscene about a nightclub in wartime. All of those people having a good time while our boys are away fighting Popovs, or flying sorties over England. Somehow it didn't feel right to have a photograph of the English film star Leslie Howard on the Jockey Club wall. For a while, after the outbreak of war, the Nazis had been sensitive enough to ban all public dancing, but following our early victories that ban had been lifted and now things were going so wonderfully for the German Army that it was thought to be fine for men and women to let down their hair and throw themselves around on a dance floor. But I didn't care for it at all. And I liked it even less when I

100

thought about the Fridmann sisters in the apartment beneath my own.

'Sometimes when I go home I can hardly walk I'm so heavy with the stuff.'

'I can see I'm going to have to come here again. This must be the only bar in Berlin where the beer still tastes like beer.'

'But at a price. And what a price. Anyway, I was going to tell you about this fellow called Gustav and how I came to be hanging around Nollendorfplatz in the dark the other night.'

'Were you?'

'Come on Parsifal, pay attention. A few nights ago when I'm in here I start talking to this Fritz. He said his name was Gustav but I have my doubts about that. He also said that he was a civil servant on Wilhelmstrasse. And that is what he looked like, I suppose. A real smooth type. Thin prick accent. Gold bird in his lapel. Silk handkerchief and spats. Oh yes, and he had this little gold cigarette holder that he brought out of a little velvet box every time he wanted a smoke. Just watching him was kind of fascinating in an irritating way. I asked him if he did that in the morning, too – I mean, if he used the little gold holder – and he said he did. Can you imagine that?'

'I'll give it a go.' I shook my head. 'No, I can't. He sounds like a fish in a glass case.'

'Good-looking though.' Arianne grinned. 'And rich. He was wearing a wristwatch and a pocket

101

hunter and both of them were gold, just like his cufflinks and his shirt studs and his tie pin.'

'Very observant of you.'

She shrugged. 'What can I tell you? I like men who wear gold. It encourages me. Like a red rag to a bull. But it's not the movement. It's the colour. And the value, of course. Men who wear a lot of gold bits and pieces are just more generous, I suppose.'

'And was he?'

'Gustav? Sure. He tipped me just for lighting his cigarette. And again for sitting with him. At the end of the evening he asked me to meet him the following evening at the Romanisches Café.'

I nodded. 'Just down from Wittenberg Platz.'

'Yes. At eight o'clock. Anyway he was late and for a while I thought he wasn't coming at all. It was nearer eight-twenty-five when eventually he showed up. And he was sweating and nervous. Not at all the smooth-as-silk type he'd been when we were in here the previous night. We talked for a while but he wasn't listening. And when I asked him why he seemed so out of sorts, he came to the point. He had asked me along to the café because he had a job for me. An easy job, he said, but it was going to pay me a hundred marks. A hundred. By now I was shaking my head and telling him I wasn't on the sledge just yet, but no, he said, it wasn't anything like that, and what did I take him for? All I had to do was wait under the station at Nolli at nine-fifteen

102

and give an envelope to a man who would be humming a tune.'

'That's nice. What was the tune?'

'"Don't say Goodbye, only say Adieu".'

'Zarah Leander. I like that one.'

'He even hummed it for me to make sure I knew it. I had to ask the man for a light and then his name and if he said it was Paul I was to give him the envelope and walk away. Well, I could tell there was something peculiar about all this, so I asked him what was in the envelope and he said it was best I didn't know, which didn't make me feel any better about doing it. But then he put five pictures of Albrecht Dürer on the table and assured me that it would be the easiest hundred marks I'd ever earned. Especially in the blackout. Anyway I agreed. A hundred marks is a hundred marks.'

'Mmm-hmm.'

'So I rode the S-Bahn one stop east to Nolli and waited under the station just like Gustav had told me to do. I was early. And I was scared, but the five Alberts felt good inside my stocking top. I had time to think. Too much time, perhaps, because I got greedy. That's a bad habit of mine.'

'You and the Austrian corporal.'

'I kept on thinking that if I had been given a hundred from Gustav for showing up with an envelope then I might make at least another ten or twenty from Paul for handing it over. And when eventually he turned up that's what I suggested.

But Paul didn't like that and started to get rough with me. He searched my coat pockets for the envelope. And my bag. He even searched my underwear. Took my hundred marks. And that's when you showed up, Parsifal. You see he wasn't trying to rape me. He was only trying to find his damned envelope.'

'Where was it? The envelope?'

'I didn't have it on me when I tried to brolly him. Well, that would have been foolish. I'd already hidden it in some bushes near the taxi rank.'

'That was clever.'

'I thought so, too. Right up until the moment he punched me.'

'Where is it now?'

'The envelope? When I went back the next day to look for it, the envelope was gone.'

'Hmm.'

She shrugged. 'Now I really don't know what to do. I'm scared to go to the cops and tell them. Naturally I'm worried about what was in that envelope. I'm worried that I've landed myself in the middle of something dangerous.' She closed her eyes. 'It seemed so easy when we were in the Romanisches Café. Just hand it over in the blackout and walk away. If only I'd done that.'

'This Gustav. Have you seen him in here since?'

'No.'

'Does anyone else know him?'

'No. It turns out that Magda thought his name

was Josef, and that's all she remembers. Am I in trouble, Parsifal?'

'You might be. If you went to the police and told them about this, yes, I think you would be.'

'So you don't think I should tell them.'

'With a story like yours, Arianne, the police – the real police – are the least of your worries. There's the Gestapo to consider.'

She sighed. 'I thought as much.'

'Have you told your story to anyone else?'

'God, no.'

'Then don't. It simply never happened. You never met anyone called Gustav or Josef in this place. And no one ever asked you to be a cut-out for them at the S-Bahn on Nollendorf Platz.'

'A cut-out?'

'That's what you call it when someone wants to give something to someone else without actually meeting them. But that's all right, too, because there was no something. No envelope. You don't even have a hundred marks to show for it, right?'

She nodded.

I sipped the beer and wondered how it and the cigarette could taste so good and how much truth there was in what Arianne Tauber had told me. It was just about possible that Franz Koci had taken a hundred marks out of her underwear, although he'd been carrying only half as much when the cops had found him in Kleist Park. Of course, they could easily have helped themselves to half his cash. And it was just about possible that some

Foreign Office type who had an envelope for a Three Kings agent might have been spooked off a meeting and subcontracted the job to a money-hungry girl from the Jockey Bar. Stranger things had happened.

'But I have a question for you, angel. Why are you telling me all this?'

'In case you didn't know, Parsifal's not exactly a common name around here.' She bit her thumbnail. 'Look, in spite of what I told you, about getting all that perfume, I'm not the most popular girl around town. There are a lot of people who don't like me very much.'

'Sounds like we have a lot in common, angel.'

She let that one go. She was too busy talking about herself. That was good, too. To me she looked like a more interesting subject than I was.

'Oh, sure, I'm attractive to look at. I know that. And there are a lot of men who want me to give them what men usually want women to give them but, beyond a cigarette and a drink and a tip, and maybe the odd present or two, I don't want anything from anyone. You should know that about me. Maybe you've worked that out already. You seem bright enough. But what I'm trying to say is that I don't have many friends and certainly none that are possessed of what you might call wisdom and maturity. Otto – Otto Schulze – the Fritz who runs this place, I couldn't tell him. I can't tell him anything. He'd tell the Gestapo, for sure. Otto likes to keep in with the Gestapo. I'm almost certain he pays them off with information: Magda, too, I think. And you've met Frau Lippert. So there's no one else, see? My mother is old and lives in Dresden. My brother is on active service. But frankly he wouldn't know what to say or do. He's my younger brother and he looks to me for advice. But you, Parsifal. You strike me as the type who always knows what to say or do. So, if you're interested, there's a part-time job going as my special counsel. It doesn't pay very much but maybe you can think of me as someone who is in your debt.'

'Suddenly I feel every one of my forty-three years,' I said.

'That's not so old. Not these days. Just look around, Parsifal. Where are the young men? There aren't any. Not in Berlin. I can't remember the last time I spoke to someone less than thirty. Anyone my age is on active service or in a concentration camp. Youth is no longer wasted on the young because it's wasted on the war instead.' She winced. 'Forget I said that. I shouldn't have said that. They're fighting for their country, aren't they?'

'They're fighting for someone else's country,' I said. 'That's the problem.'

Arianne looked sly for a moment, as if she'd outsmarted me in a game of cards. 'It's not healthy putting your head under a falling axe, Parsifal. You could get into trouble.'

'I don't mind a little trouble, when it looks like you, angel.'

'That's what you say now. But you haven't seen me throwing crockery.'

'Volatile, huh?'

'Like my boiling point was on the moon.'

'Smart, too. I'm not sure I'm qualified to be your special counsel, Fräulein Tauber. I don't know the boiling point on the moon from my own shoe-size.'

She glanced down at my feet. 'I'll bet you're a forty-six, right?'

'Mmm-hmm.'

'Then, for a lot of liquids with higher vapour pressures, the boiling point and your shoe-size are probably the same.'

'If that's true then I'm impressed.'

'Before the war I was a chemistry student.'

'Why did you stop?'

'Lack of money. Lack of opportunity. The Nazis like educated women almost as little as they like educated Jews. They prefer us to stay home polishing the hearth and stirring the pot.'

'Not me.'

She tugged my wrist toward her and checked the time on my watch. 'I have to go back to the cloakroom in a minute.'

'I could wait but I might need to telephone the Reichsbank to arrange a loan.'

'It might be worth it, Parsifal. I finish at two. You could walk me home if you like. Better still you could drive me, if you have a car.'

'I have a car. I just don't have any petrol. And I'll gladly walk you home. But I don't think Frau Lippert would approve, do you?'

'I said you could walk me home, not up the stairs. But if ever you did walk me up the stairs it's actually none of her business. And she knows that, too. The other night, she was just mouthing off. If I hadn't had that sock on the jaw I might have told her to shut up and mind her own business and she would have done. Up to a point. There's nothing in our agreement that says I can't have gentlemen friends in my room for a little quiet conversation. It's hard to hear everything you say in a place like this. You need to speak up. I'm a little deaf.'

'Now you tell me.'

'That's because last year I was near Kottbusser Strasse when a tame Tommy went off.'

A tame Tommy was what Berliners called an unexploded bomb.

'It blew me through the air. Fortunately I landed in some bushes that broke my fall. But, for a few glorious moments, I thought I was dead.'

'Why glorious?'

'Haven't you ever wanted to be dead? I have. Sometimes life is just so much trouble. Don't you think so?'

I nodded. 'Yes. I've wanted that, too. Quite recently as a matter of fact. I go to bed wanting to blow my brains out and wake up wondering why I didn't do it. I guess that's why I'm here.

You make a very diverting alternative to the idea of self-slaughter.'

'I'm glad about that, Parsifal. Hey, I don't even know your name. And I should know something about you if I'm going to let you walk me home, don't you think?'

'My name is Bernhard Gunther.'

She nodded and closed her eyes as if she was trying to visualize my name in her mind's eye. 'Bernhard Gunther. Hmm. Yes.'

'What does that mean?'

'Sssh. I'm trying to connect with it. I'm a little bit psychic, you see.'

'While you're there see if you can't get a fix on where I've left my Postal Savings Bank Book. There's five hundred marks in there I'd like to get my hands on.'

She opened her eyes. 'That's a solid name, Bernhard Gunther. Dependable. Honest. And wealthy with it, too. I can do a lot with five hundred marks. This is looking good. Tell me, what kind of work does Bernie Gunther do?' She pressed her hands together in supplication. 'No, wait. Let me guess.'

'It's better that I tell you.'

'You don't think I can't guess? I'm certain you were in the Army. But now, I'm not sure. If you were on leave then it's been quite a long one, hasn't it? So maybe you were wounded. Although you don't look like a man who was wounded. Then again maybe you got injured in the head. And that

110

might be why you say you're suicidal. A lot of boys are these days. I mean a lot. Only they don't put that kind of thing in the newspapers because it's bad for morale. Frau Lippert had another lodger who was a corporal in a police battalion and he hanged himself off a canal bridge in Moabit. He was a nice boy. You know, I might say you were a civil servant but you're a little too muscular for that. And the suit – well, no civil servant would ever wear a suit like that.'

'Arianne. Listen to me.'

'You're no fun at all, Gunther.'

'I don't want you to get the wrong idea about why I'm here.'

'What does that mean?'

'It means I'm a cop. From the Police Praesidium at Alexanderplatz.'

The smile dried on her face like I'd poured poison in her ears. She sat there for a moment, stunned, immobile, as if a doctor had told her she had six months to live.

I was used to her reaction and I didn't blame her for it. There wasn't anyone in Berlin who wasn't deeply afraid of the police, including the police, because when you said 'police' everyone thought about the Gestapo and when you started to think about the Gestapo it was soon hard to think of anything else.

'You could have mentioned that earlier,' she said, stiffly. 'Or is that how it works? You let someone talk themselves into trouble. Give them enough rope so that they can hang themselves, like my friend.'

'It's not like that at all. I'm a detective. Not Gestapo.'

'What's the difference?'

'The difference is that I hate the Nazis. The difference is that I don't care if you say Hitler is the son of Beelzebub. The difference is that if I was Gestapo you would already be in a police van and on your way to number eight.'

'Number eight? What's that?'

'You're not from Berlin, are you? Not originally.'

She shook her head.

'Number eight Prinz Albrechtstrasse. Gestapo headquarters.'

I wasn't exaggerating. Not in the least. If Sachse and Wandel had heard even half of her story, Arianne Tauber would have been sitting in a chair with her skirt up and a hot cigarette in her panties. I knew how those bastards questioned people and I wasn't about to condemn her to that. Not without being damned sure she was guilty. As it happened, I believed at least half of her story, and that was enough to prevent me from handing her over to the Gestapo. I thought she was probably a prostitute. An occasional one. To make ends meet a lot of single women were. You could hardly blame them for that. Any kind of a living was hard to come by in Berlin. But I didn't think she was a spy for the Czechs. No spy would have volunteered so much to a man in a club she hardly knew well.

'So, what happens now? Are you going to arrest me?'

'Didn't I already tell you to forget all about what happened? Didn't I tell you that? There never was an envelope. And there was no Gustav.'

She nodded silently, but still I could see she was unable to grasp what I was telling her.

'Listen to me, Arianne, provided you take my advice, you're in the clear. Well, almost. There are only three people who could possibly connect you with what happened. One of them is this fellow Gustav. And one of them is Paul. The man who attacked you. Only he's dead.'

'What? You didn't tell me that. How?'

'His body turned up in Kleist Park a day or so after that taxi hit him on Nolli. He must have crawled there in the blackout and died. The third person who knows about this is me. And I'm not about to tell anyone.'

'Oh, I get it. I suppose you want to sleep with me. Before you hand me over to your pals in the Gestapo you want to have me yourself. Is that it?'

'No. It's not like that at all.'

'Then what is it like? And don't tell me it's because you think I'm special, Parsifal. Because I won't believe you.'

'I'm going to tell you why, angel. But not here. Not now. Until then you think about everything I've said and then ask yourself why I said it. I'll

113

be waiting outside at two. I can still walk you home if you want. Or you can walk home by yourself and I give you my word you won't be woken up at five a.m. by men in leather coats. You won't ever see me again. All right?'

CHAPTER 6

I went back to the Alex for a while and sat at my desk and wondered if there might be a way of finding Gustav without involving Arianne Tauber. She and only she could have identified him and, for that reason alone, it seemed unlikely that he would ever go back to the Jockey and risk seeing her again. Especially if he was what it seemed he was – almost certainly a spy. More than likely he'd lost his nerve about meeting his Czech contact on Nolli. Possibly, he thought he was already being shadowed by the Gestapo, but if they had been tailing him, then surely they'd have picked her up when she met Gustav at the Romanisches Café. If he was under surveillance then the Gestapo would never have risked allowing him to pass information to her. It seemed more likely that Gustav had lost his nerve. In which case, who better than a joy-lady to deliver something to his Czech contact? Most of the prostitutes I'd ever known were resourceful, courageous, and, above all, greedy. For a hundred marks there wasn't a silk in Berlin who wouldn't have agreed to what Gustav had asked. Handing over an envelope in the dark was a lot easier and quicker and, on the face of it, safer than sucking someone's pipe.

'Working late?'

It was Lehnhoff.

'Victor Keil, aka Franz Koci,' I said.

'The Kleist Park case. Yeah. What about it?'

'The uniformed fairy that found him under the bushes. Sergeant Otto Macher. Do you know him well?'

'Well enough.'

'Do you think he's honest?'

'Meaning what?'

'It's a straightforward question, Gottfried. Is he honest?'

'As far as it goes these days.'

'In my book it goes all the way to the altar.'

'There's a war on. So maybe not as far as that.'

'Look, Gottfried. We're both in the shit-house age-group. And I certainly don't want to cause any trouble for you and Sergeant Macher. But I need to know if our dead Czecho was carrying more than just the fifty marks we found on him.'

All of the lavatories at the Alex had three numbers on the door, of which two were always '00'; and the phrase 'shit-house age-group' was used to indicate anyone born before 1900 and therefore over the age of forty.

'If you say you're in the shit-house then I believe you,' said Lehnhoff. 'But from what I've heard around the factory you're here not because you're

116

ready for your pension, but because you've got vitamin B.'

He meant that I had connections with senior Nazis who would keep me better nourished than other men.

'With Heydrich,' he added.

'Who told you that?'

'Does it matter? That's the splash on the men's porcelain.'

'The Czecho's watch was gone. It wasn't at his apartment when we searched it, and there wasn't a pawn ticket. But I really don't care about that. I'm guessing he had at least five Alberts on him when he was first found in the park. There were only fifty on him by the time I made his acquaintance. I need to know if I'm right about that. You don't have to say anything. Just nod or shake your head and we'll say no more about it.'

Lehnhoff's head remained still. Then he grinned. 'I can't help you. I just don't know. But even if I did, what makes you think I'd tell you?'

I stood up and came around the desk. 'I don't like threatening other men with my vitamin B. I much prefer it if people pay attention to my natural authority. Me being a Commissar'n all.'

'That won't work either. Sir.'

Lehnhoff was still grinning as he left my office.

I picked up my coat and followed him out onto the landing. Cool air was drifting up the enormous stairwell. Down on the ground floor there were raised voices, but that was normal in the Alex.

Even at the best of times the place was like a zoo full of all kinds of wild and noisy animals. But up on the third floor things were quieter. The blackout curtains were drawn and most of the lights were off. At the other end of the landing was an abandoned floor polisher. It looked a lot like me. Then the raised voices on the ground floor became a little more urgent and someone cried out with pain. Someone was working overtime and it gave me an idea.

'Hey Gottfried,' I said, catching him up. 'You know what they used to say about this place?'

Lehnhoff stopped at the top of the stairs and looked at me with open contempt. 'What's that?'

'Be careful on the stairs.'

I hit him in the stomach, hard enough to bend him in two and fold him over the balustrade so that he could empty his fat gut into the stairwell. If it was my lucky day some Nazi would slip on Lehnhoff's soup and break his collarbone. Holding him by the collar, I pushed him down so that his feet tipped off the shiny floor and then slammed my forearm across one of his kidneys. He yelled out with the pain of it but that was fine because nobody ever paid much attention to the sound of pain at the Alex. It was one more background noise, like the sound of a typewriter or a telephone ringing in an empty room. I could have slugged Lehnhoff all night until he was groaning for his pastor and it would have been just another night at police headquarters to anyone's ears.

'Now,' I said, bending close to Lehnhoff's waxy ear. 'Do I get an answer to my question or would you like to go downstairs? Three flights at a time?'

'Yes, yes, yes. Okay. God. Please.' His subsequent answers sounded exactly like a cry for help. 'We took a hundred marks off him. Me and Macher. Sixty for me and forty for him. Please.'

'In twenties?'

'Yes. Yes. Twenties. Yes. Pull me up, for God's sake.'

I pulled him back off the balustrade and dumped him on the linoleum, where he lay curled and twitching and whimpering as if his mother had just delivered him onto the Alex floor. He gasped:

'What the hell—'

'Hmm? What's that?'

'What the hell difference does it make to you, anyway? A hundred fucking marks.'

'It's not the money. I don't care about that. It's just that I didn't have the time or even the inclination to wait until you were ready to answer my question. You know something? I think I've been affected deeply by working in an environment where, within the context of a police interrogation, violence is now endemic.'

'I'll get you for this, Gunther. I'll make a fucking complaint. Just see if I don't.'

'Hmm. I wouldn't rush into that, if I were you. Remember. I've got vitamin B, Gottfried.' I twisted the hair on his scalp so that I could tap the back of his skull against the balustrade. 'I can see in the dark. And I can hear everything you say from a hundred miles away.'

The jazz lovers outside the Jockey Bar had called it a night and several smart-looking Mercedes cars were parked out front with drivers who were impatient to take their masters home in comfort and safety – or as safe as could be managed with most of your headlights taped up. There was a rumble in the sky but it wasn't the RAF. I could feel a breeze in the air and the breeze had an edge of moisture that was the vanguard of something heavier. Minutes later it started to rain. I moved into an inadequate doorway and buttoned my coat tight against my neck, but it wasn't long before it started to feel more like a shower curtain and I cursed my stupidity for not bringing along the nail-brush and the shard of soap that I kept in my desk drawer. But an umbrella would probably have been better. Suddenly, walking a prostitute home, even a pretty one, looked like a bad idea in a whole novel full of miserable ideas by some miserable French writer. The sort of novel that gets turned into an even more miserable movie starring Charles Laughton and Fredric March. And, reminding myself why I was there – she was the only person who had met Franz Koci, whose homicide I was supposed to be investigating – I pulled my hat down over my ears and pressed myself hard into the doorway.

Ten minutes went by. Most of the cars drove away with their passengers. It was two-fifteen. A kilometre to the west of where I was standing, the Führer, purported to be a bit of a night owl, was probably putting on his pyjamas, combing his moustache, and cleaning his teeth before sitting down to write his diary. At around two-twenty, the door of the Jockey Bar opened and, for a brief moment, an obtuse triangle of dim light fell on the patent-shiny sidewalk – long enough for me to see a woman wearing a raincoat and a hat and carrying a man's umbrella. She looked one way and then the other before glancing at her watch. It was Arianne Tauber.

Abandoning my inadequate refuge I walked quickly forward and presented myself in front of her.

'You look like a widow's handkerchief,' she said.

'It's only what happens when air turns back into water. You're a chemist. You should know that.'

'And you should know I changed my mind about letting you walk me home.'

'Looks like I got wet for nothing then.'

'That's precisely why I've decided to walk you home, copper. All that water dripping off your hat. If we move your head the right way we can probably fill a couple of glasses. So it's probably lucky that I managed to steal a half-bottle of Johnnie Walker to go with it. That's the only reason I'm late. I had to wait for the right moment to lead the raiding party on Otto's bar.'

'With a pitch like that I might just allow you to walk me home and then up the stairs.'

'Well, we can hardly drink it in the street.'

It's quite a walk from Luther Strasse to Fasanenstrasse and it was fortunate that the rain eased soon after we began; even so, we were obliged to stop a couple of times and take a nibble off her bottle. Amundsen wouldn't have approved of breaking into our supplies so soon after setting off from base camp, but then he had sled dogs and all we had were soaking wet shoes. By the time we reached my apartment, the half-bottle of Johnnie Walker was only a third, which is probably why we took off our clothes and, it being wartime when these things seemed to happen a little more quickly than of old, we went straight to bed and, after a few minutes of animal magic to remind us both of happier times before God got angry with the people who stole the fruit of his favourite tree, we resumed our earlier conversation with small glasses in our hands and, perhaps, a little less front. It's pointless trying to maintain a persona concealing one's true nature from the world when your damp clothes are lying in a hurried heap on the floor.

'I never slept with a cop before.'

'How was it?'

'Now I know why cops have big feet.'

'I hate to sound like a cop so soon after—'

'You *are* going to arrest me.'

'No, no.'

'I won't come quietly.'

'So I noticed. No, Arianne, I've been thinking about your job at the Jockey Bar and wondering if you should give it up or not. In case Gustav does go back there looking for you.'

'And what did you conclude, Commissar?'

'That if the Gestapo had arrested him and brought him back to the bar to look for you, then you'd be in trouble.'

'True. But even if I did leave the club, they wouldn't have a problem finding me. Otto has all my details. My work book number, my address, everything. No, if I left there, I'd also have to leave my room and go underground. Which is impossible. That sort of thing takes money and connections.'

'That's the very same conclusion I came to myself. As I see it, there are two other possibilities. One is that he assumes you handed over the envelope, as agreed, and never comes back at all. He gave you that envelope to give to Paul because he was scared to give it to Paul himself; and that could mean he's too scared ever to return to the club and ask you anything more about it. The other possibility is that he does come back, and if he does, then you find an excuse to telephone me at the Alex and then I come along and arrest him.'

'Conveniently leaving me out of it, right?'

I nodded and drank some more of the Scotch. It was the first proper liquor I'd tasted since coming back from the Ukraine. Normally I don't drink Scotch. But this tasted just fine. Like some fiery drink of the gods that might have been

123

gathered from a hive of immortal bees. My own sting was gone, at least for the moment. But after the defilement of my flesh, I was beginning to feel divine again.

'Conveniently leaving you out of it.'

'You said Paul was found dead in Kleist Park. But you didn't say any more.'

'No, I didn't.'

'How do you know it was him? I was as close to him as I am to you now and I'm not sure I would have recognized him again.'

'It was him all right. His injuries were those of a man who'd been hit by a car. And it's not like there were any other unreported traffic accidents in that area that night.'

'So who was he?'

'Do you really want to know?'

'I'm not sure. Maybe. Maybe not. Maybe you should decide, Gunther.'

I asked myself how much she ought to know, and when I told her it was mainly because I wanted to see how she would react. Despite our being in bed together – maybe because of it – I wasn't yet satisfied that she was as innocent as she had led me to believe. But even if she did turn out to be rather more culpable than I had previously supposed I couldn't imagine myself serving her up cold to the Gestapo.

'The man you were paid to meet at Nolli, he was really a Czech called Franz Koci who was working for the Three Kings.'

'You mean those terrorists who were in the news-papers earlier this year?'

'Yes.'

'Now I am scared.' She closed her eyes and lay back against the pillow, then sat up abruptly and stared at me with wide eyes. 'You know what that means, don't you? It means that Gustav must be some sort of spy. For the Czechs.'

'I'd say that was a pretty good guess.'

'What am I going to do?'

'You might try to remember some more about Gustav. And if that doesn't happen, I might tie you over a table and beat it out of you myself. Like the Gestapo.'

'Do they really do that? I've heard stories.'

'All of them are true, I'm afraid.'

'Maybe I should go underground, after all.' She shook her head and shivered. 'It must be bad enough to have someone hurt you to make you tell them something you know; but to have someone hurt you when you've got nothing you can tell them. That doesn't bear thinking of.'

'And that's precisely why I want you to tell me all about Gustav. Once again. From the very begin-ning. Everything you remember and everything you might have forgotten. Your best chance of disappearing from this picture is to paint another. Of him.'

There's a little red warning card with a hole in the middle that the Ministry of Propaganda likes you to slip over the tuning dial of your radio.

125

'Racial comrades!' it says. 'You are Germans! It is your duty not to listen to foreign radio stations. Those who do so will be mercilessly punished!' Now me, I'm a good listener. A lot of being a good detective is knowing when to shut up and let someone else do the talking. Arianne liked to talk – that much was obvious – and while she told me nothing new about Gustav she told me quite a lot about herself, which was of course the main point of the exercise.

She was from Dresden, where she'd gone to university. Her husband, Karl, also a student from Dresden, had joined the German Navy in the summer of 1938 and had been killed on a U-boat in February 1940. Three months later, her father, a commercial traveller, had been killed during a bombing raid while on a business trip to Hamburg.

Naturally I checked up on all of this later. Exactly as Arianne had described, her fiancé's boat, U-33, had been sunk by depth-charges from a British minesweeper in the River Clyde, in Scotland. Twenty-five men, including Karl and the boat's commander, were lost. Her younger brother, Albrecht, had joined the Army in 1939 but now he was with the military police. Her father had worked for the pharmaceutical works in Dresden and often did business with E.H. Worlée, another chemical company, in Hamburg. Soon after Herr Tauber's death Arianne had come to Berlin to work for BVG – the Berlin Transport Company – as a secretary to the director of Anhalter Railway

126

Station. But she had quit this job – a good job – because, she said, he couldn't keep his hands off her.

His was a predicament with which I strongly sympathized. I couldn't keep my hands off her either.

CHAPTER 7

Planting evidence was hardly uncommon at the Alex. For a lot of detectives lacking the skills or the patience to do the job properly, it was the only way they could ever secure a conviction. I'd never done it myself but there's a first time for everything and, in the absence of the evidence that was legally held by the Gestapo in the death of Franz Koci, I decided to 'find' some new evidence that hitherto was held only by me. But first I had to make Lehnhoff's earlier on-the-scene inquiry seem like what it was: incompetent, only more so, and when I reviewed his case notes I discovered that no fingertip search of the area in Kleist Park where Koci's body was discovered had ever been conducted. So I telephoned Sachse at Gestapo headquarters to prick his ears with this new 'information'.

'I thought you told me that all of the evidence at the scene of the crime had been collected.'

'I did. It was.'

'Like hell. With a homicide, especially an important homicide like this one, it's standard practice to have ten or fifteen police officers on their hands

128

and knees in a line to comb the general area. Or at least it was while this department had real police working here. Real police who did real police work. But there's no record of a fingertip search of the ground where Koci's body was found.'

'But looking for what?'

'Evidence. What evidence, I don't know. I can't tell you what it might be. But I think I'd recognize it when I saw it.'

'You really think that park's worth another look?'

'Under the circumstances, yes I do. Between you and me, Inspector Lehnhoff – the first investigating detective – is lazy and dishonest, so it wouldn't have been your fault if the ground wasn't properly searched. I suppose you just took his word for it that things had been done properly.'

I was saying half of this in case Lehnhoff decided to say anything about my assaulting him.

'Well, yes, I did.'

'I thought so. All right. You weren't to know. But under the circumstances you'd better organize a search yourself. Commissioner Lüdtke has told us all that budgets at the Alex are tight. I don't want him coming down on my neck about the cost of this.'

'I'll organize it immediately.'

'Good. Please let me know if they find anything.'

Of course I knew exactly what they were going to find in Kleist Park. I knew because I'd already put it there myself. And when later on that same day Sachse appeared in my office with a plastic bag containing a switchblade, I made a big show out of looking surprised.

'This is made by Mikov,' I said, examining the switchblade carefully. 'That's in Czechoslovakia, isn't it? I mean Bohemia and Moravia.'

'Yes.'

'That would fit with our friend Franz Koci, wouldn't it?' I leaned back in my chair and frowned a frown that could have made it big in silent movies. 'I wonder.'

'What?'

I made another big show of thinking hard. I walked around my office, which contained several filing cabinets, a lot of empty ashtrays, and on the wall a nice picture of Adolf Hitler. The picture had been put there by the previous occupant and while I hated it, for me to have taken it down would, in the eyes of the Gestapo, have made me look like Gavrilo Princip.

I opened one of the filing cabinets. This was as full as the Prussian State Library and contained unsolved cases and reports going back years. Very little of what was in there had anything to do with me, and for all I know, Philipp Melancthon's report to the Diet of Worms was one of the older files at the back of the drawer. But I knew what I was looking for. I forced a gap and tugged out a grey folder with Geert Vranken's name on the corner.

'Geert Vranken. Aged thirty-nine, a foreign railway worker from Dordrecht, in the Netherlands. Educated at the University of The Hague. Murdered earlier this month. His body, what remained of it, was found on the railway line just south of Jannowitz Bridge after being struck by a train to Friedrichshagen.'

'What about it?'

Sachse sat down on the corner of my desk, folded his arms and then checked his hair. This was still as neat as a field of wheat and approximately the same colour, and I briefly wondered if it ever looked any different in a high wind or underwater. Probably not. His head could have been found on the roof of the Pintsch factory, like Vranken's, after a train had gone over his neck and there wouldn't have been a hair out of place.

'I was the investigating officer, that's what. And while it's not uncommon for people to get hit by trains in the dark it is uncommon to find that they had already sustained multiple stab wounds. I examined the torso myself and I seem to remember that the contour of the wounds was not unlike the shape of this Bohemian switchblade.'

'How can we find out for sure?'

'Got a car?'

'Of course.'

'Good. You can drive me out to the Charité. Let's hope that they haven't incinerated the body.'

Sachse pulled up at the corner of the Charité opposite the Lessing Theatre where Ida Wust was playing in a show called *The Main Point is Happiness*. I couldn't disagree with that.

'How about it, Werner? Shall I go in and get us a pair of tickets while we're here?'

Sachse smiled thinly and shook his head.

'Not an Ida Wust fan, huh? You surprise me.'

'That old trout? You must be joking. She reminds me of my mother-in-law. But the other one's all right. Jane Tilden.'

'She's a bit too wholesome for my taste.' I opened the car door but Sachse stayed put. 'Aren't you coming in?'

'You don't need me in there, do you?'

Sachse was already looking a little green, and after hearing me relate my favourite but strictly after-dinner anecdotes from the gay world of forensic science, I couldn't blame him for not wanting to come in to the Pathological Institute. This, of course, was the intention behind these gruesome stories. I hardly wanted the mortuary attendant asking me any awkward questions in front of Werner Sachse about why I was back there with the same knife to check the same wounds in the same body.

'Strictly speaking,' I said, 'there should always be two officers present when a body is examined; however, on this occasion, perhaps that won't be necessary. Nothing ever quite prepares you for the sight of a body that's been chewed up by a railway locomotive.'

Sachse nodded. 'Thanks, Gunther. You're all right.'

Chuckling sadistically – the idea of a squeamish

Gestapo man just struck me as funny – I went into the hospital and along to the morgue, where I found the same attendant and, having established that Vranken's dismembered body was still safely stored there, informed him that the investigation was now a Gestapo matter and that in no circumstances was the body to be released for burial or incineration without first clearing it with me.

As always, mention of the Gestapo worked an almost magical effect, akin to uttering 'Open sesame', and the attendant signalled his total compliance with a nervous bow. Of course there was no need to see or examine Vranken's body again. I already knew what I was going to tell Werner Sachse: that Franz Koci had murdered Geert Vranken. And feeling pleased that I had managed to reopen what was now a proper murder case, I made my way back to the car.

A good humour never lasts long in Berlin. The smell of the war wounded in that hospital was asphyxiating. Dying men lay in dusty wards like so much left luggage, while to walk through a hallway or public corridor was to negotiate an obstacle course of rickety old wheelchairs and dirty plaster casts. And if all of that wasn't bad enough, I came out of the hospital and encountered a little squad of Hitler Youth marching down Luisenstrasse – most likely from a trip to see the National Warrior's Monument in the Invaliden Park – their throats full of some stupid warlike song and quite oblivious of the German warrior's true fate that was to be found in the not-so-glorious charnel house nearby. For a moment I stood and watched these boys with a kind of horror. It was all too easy to think of them as carrying the infection of Nazism – the brown-shirted bacilli of death and destruction and the typhus of tomorrow.

Feeling more sombre than before, I tapped on the window of the Horch-built Audi. It's a useful courtesy to observe with a man sleeping in his own car when he happens to be carrying a loaded automatic.

Sachse sat up straight, lifted the tip of his black felt hat, and opened the passenger door.

'Any luck?'

'Yes. If you can call it that. The Dutchman was stabbed by the Czech all right. Franz Koci's knife fitted those stab wounds like they'd been cut for it by a good tailor.'

'Well, you're the expert.'

'The question is, why? Why would a Czech spy stab and kill a Dutch railway worker?'

CHAPTER 8

After this 'breakthrough' – that's what Sachse called it, anyway – the investigation stalled again, the way investigations usually do. I wasn't too worried about that. Detective work is almost always a long game, unless the newspapers get involved, and then it's still a long game only you have to pretend that it's not. This job isn't only a matter of paying attention to detail, it's also about knowing what to ignore and who, as well. It's about reading the newspapers and staring into space and learning to be patient and to put your trust in your experience, which tells you that something nearly always turns up. Yes sir, the investigation is going very well. No sir, there's nothing we could be doing that we haven't done already. Good morning, anything new on the Franz Koci case? No new leads as yet. Good night. Collect your pay, go home, and do your best to forget all about it, if you can. A lot of police work is police idle, police baffled, police at breakfast, police at lunch, police drinking coffee – if there is any coffee – and always police staring out of the window, assuming there is one. And it all adds up to the same thing: that mostly, being a detective is about coping with boredom and the huge frustration of knowing that it isn't ever like it is in books and movies. Other things have to take place before something else can happen. Sometimes these are other crimes. Sometimes they're things other than crimes. And sometimes it's hard to know the difference – for instance, when a new law is passed, or when a top policeman is promoted. That's jurisprudence for you, Nazi style.

The new law was the yellow star, which made a big difference when it finally came into practice on 19 September. The day before, there were just people on the streets of Berlin. Ordinary people. You might say they were my fellow Berliners. The next day, there were all these people wearing yellow stars, which made me realize just how many Jews were living in Berlin and, at the same time, what a terrible thing it was to treat our fellow citizens in this way. Now and again there were even small demonstrations against the wearing of the yellow star. Not by Jews but by gentile Germans in favour of the Jews. People talked about 'the yellow badge of honour', and the stoic way the Jews endured their fate did not fail to impress even the most fanatical of Nazis. Except of course the fanatical Nazi who had signed this new police law into being; and he was in my mind a great deal after Saturday 27 September when he was promoted Reichsprotector of Bohemia and Moravia. There was no way that the man who was my boss, Reinhard Heydrich, would ever have been impressed with the way Jewish-Germans conducted themselves.

When I heard that Heydrich was on his way to Prague, I was glad – although not, of course, for him. I was glad he was to be gone from Berlin where there always existed the possibility that he might hand me some special task, as had happened at least twice before. And, for a day or two, I even managed to relax. I took Arianne to the Lido at Muggelsee and then to a show at the Schlosspark Theatre, in Steglitz. Somewhere in the day I even managed to ask her about Geert Vranken.

'Never heard of him.'

'He was a foreign worker from Dordrecht, in the Netherlands.'

'Dordreck? No wonder he came to Berlin.'

'Not Dordreck. Dordrecht.'

'Why ask me?'

'Because I think he may have been murdered by your friend, Paul.'

'Who?'

'Franz Koci. The Czecho that Gustav asked you to meet on Nolli Platz.'

Arianne rolled her eyes. 'Oh, him. I'd only just managed to forget all about that business.' She uttered a profound sigh and smacked the wicker beach chair we were sharing with her fist. 'What happened to him? This Dutchy.'

I told her how Geert Vranken had died; and I told her about Franz Koci's switchblade.

'That's really awful. And you mean to tell me that the poor man is still lying in the mortuary at the Charité like last week's one-pot dinner?'

I nodded.

'What about his family?'

'I wrote to his wife, telling her what had happened.'

'That was big of you.'

'I didn't have to do it. In fact I was almost ordered not to do it. But I thought someone should. Like you, I felt sorry for her. Besides, I was hoping that his wife might write back, with some more information. Something that would help me to find her husband's murderer.'

'You didn't tell her—'

'No, no. I just said there'd been an accident. And that because of wartime regulations, it was impossible for his body to be sent back. But that I'd see to it, personally, that he got a decent burial.'

'And will you? I mean, that sounds expensive.'

'As a matter of fact I'm hoping to persuade the Gestapo to pay for it.'

'How are you going to do that?'

'By lying. I shall tell them that the mortuary needs the space, which is true; and also that it's best Vranken's remains are not cremated, in case we need to examine the body again, which is not. Something like that. I'm really quite a good liar when the occasion demands it.'

'I don't doubt it, Gunther. And the widow? Have you heard back from her?'

'Not yet. And I probably won't. Would you write to some Nazi bastard who was occupying your country?'

We were both silent for a while the way you are on a beach. On the blue water there were lots of little white boats that looked as if they were made of paper. We watched the boats and we watched children building sandcastles and some girls playing volleyball. The beach was crowded with people who, like us, figured it was maybe the last day of summer and who were worried we might be in for another hard winter, like the last one when the temperature fell as low as minus twenty-two degrees centigrade. This, of course, was just one of many things we Berliners had to worry about following the overthrow of Kiev. The German High Command had issued a victory communiqué announcing that the Army was now in charge of 665,000 Soviet prisoners. This seemed like a fantastic figure, and there were some who thought it meant that the war in the East was all but won; but there were many others, like myself, who thought that there were probably a lot more Soviet soldiers where those 665,000 men came from.

Eventually, Arianne said:

'I've been thinking of going back to Dresden. To visit my mother.'

'Good idea.'

'You could come with me if you like. It's only two hours on the train. I'll probably stay there for a couple of weeks but you might like to stay

139

for the weekend.' She shrugged. 'You'd enjoy Dresden. It's not like Berlin where there's no room. My mother has a huge apartment in Johann Georgen Allee, overlooking the park. And of course it's much safer than Berlin. I don't think there's ever been an air raid.'

She was wearing a blue Lastex swimsuit that was like a dress and showed off her legs, which looked lovely to me. I was trying to keep my eyes on her face as she talked, but it was difficult when all I wanted to do was lay my muzzle on her lap and have her play with my ears and pull my tail.

'I am supposed to be investigating a murder,' I said, eventually. 'Two murders, if you count Geert Vranken. However, neither one of them is paying out right now; and I am owed some leave. So, maybe, yes, I could use a holiday. Only I'm going to have to clear it with the Commissioner. He worries when I'm not around. I'm the last real cop in Berlin. When I go, it's just the two sentries out front of the Alex and the cleaning lady. So I'll let you know, angel. Tomorrow, probably.'

CHAPTER 9

'I'm afraid that's quite impossible, Bernie.'

I shifted uncomfortably in Lüdtke's office. I felt about ten years old, a schoolboy again, in trouble with his headmaster.

'Would you mind telling me why, sir?'

'I was about to. I've just had a telephone call from an SS major called Doctor Achim Ploetz.'

'Never heard of him.'

'In Prague.' Lüdtke grinned. 'Yes, I thought that would shut you up. Major Ploetz is the Chief Adjutant to General Heydrich. It seems that your presence is required in Bohemia and Moravia. Or perhaps it's just Bohemia. I'm not sure.' He shrugged. 'Whichever one Prague is in is where you are requested to go.'

I felt a sudden chill on the back of my neck as if I'd run my finger along the edge of the blade of the falling axe at Plotzensee. Heydrich had that effect on people, which was probably why he was nicknamed 'the Hangman'.

'Did Major Ploetz explain why I'm needed in Prague, sir?'

'It seems that the General is planning some sort of weekend with friends, at his country house outside Prague. To celebrate his appointment as the new Reichsprotector of Bohemia. I had no idea that you and General Heydrich were on such cordial terms, Bernie.'

'No sir. Nor had I.'

'Oh, come now. You might not wear a scary badge on your lapel but everyone at the Alex knows you've got vitamin B. Even the footballs handle you with care.'

Many Gestapo officers were fond of wearing leather coats and hats; and since many of them were also better fed than the rest of us and hence fatter, too, they were known as 'footballs'. But sadly, kicking one was not an option.

'Perhaps I'll have my own adjutant telephone the General's adjutant and inform him that I will have to decline the invitation,' I said.

'You do that.'

'What about the case I'm working on? This Czech spy who got himself killed.'

'You told me it was a traffic accident, didn't you? Happens every day. And spies are apparently no exception.'

'Yes, but I'm pretty sure that he murdered that Dutch foreign worker, Geert Vranken. You remember. The fellow who got himself hit by a train after receiving multiple stab wounds.'

'I'm sure he'll be waiting for you when you get back from your weekend with the General.'

142

Lüdtke looked like he was enjoying my discomfort. He knew the truth about my dislike for the Nazis but it didn't stop him from savouring my dilemma: for me not to be a Party member and yet still in such apparent high favour with Heydrich was amusing to him. It amused me, too, which is to say it stopped me from thinking about much else.

'Doctor Ploetz, you say?'

'Yes.' Lüdtke leaned back in his chair and folded his hands behind his head as if he was about to surrender. 'I hear Prague's very nice at this time of year. I've often fancied going there with the wife. She collects glass, you know. And there's a lot of glass in Prague.'

'That should keep the Nazis happy. They like smashing glass. Here, maybe you should go instead of me.'

'Oh no.' Lüdtke smiled. 'I wouldn't know what to say to a man as important as the Reichsprotector of Bohemia. My God, I should be surprised if he even knew I existed.'

'Any man who can persuade Berlin detectives to wear women's clothes in order to catch a murderer is certain to have been noticed upstairs.'

'It's kind of you to say so, Bernie. But of course I had lots of help. Remember Georg Heuser?'

'Yes.'

'Georg Heuser was one of my best detectives on the S-Bahn murder case. Good man, is Georg. Of course, he lacks your subtlety and experience, but he's a promising young policeman. And of more use here than where he is now.'

'And where is that?'

'In a Special Action Group somewhere in the Ukraine.'

I didn't reply. Suddenly going to Prague didn't seem so bad after all. Not when they were still sending 'good' men to Special Action Groups in the Ukraine. Just thinking about Georg Heuser and what he was probably going through in Minsk, or Pinsk, or Dnipropetrovsk, or any one of a hundred Jew towns where innocent people were being murdered in their thousands, made me feel that I was much better off than I realized. And all talk of an S-Bahn murderer seemed laughable when one of our own investigating detectives now seemed likely to chalk up more victims in twenty-four hours than Paul Ogorzow had managed in one murderous year.

Lüdtke played with the rocker blotter on his desk for a moment as if trying to measure something.

'You hear stories,' he said, finally. 'About what is happening out east. In Ukraine and Latvia, for example. The Police Battalions. Special Action Groups and what have you. You were there, Bernie. What is the truth about what's happening? Is it true what they're saying? That people are being murdered? Men, women and children. Because they're Jews?'

I nodded.

'My God,' he said.

'I think you once said that whenever I came in here it was like rain coming in at the eaves. Now you know why. Since I came home there hasn't been a day when I didn't feel ashamed. And the nights are worse.'

'My God.'

'That's the third time you've mentioned God, Friedrich-Wilhelm. And I've been thinking that there must be a God because after all, the Leader is always mentioning Him and it's inconceivable he could be wrong about that. But what we've done to the Jews, and what we're still doing to the Jews, and, I think, what we seem intent on doing to the Jews for a good while longer, well, He's not going to forgive that in a hurry. Perhaps not ever. In fact, I've a very terrible feeling that whatever we do to them He's going to do to us. Only it'll be worse. Much worse. It'll be much worse because He's going to get the fucking Russians to do it.'

'I hear Prague is very nice at this time of year. I've often wanted to go there.' Arianne shook her head. 'I really can't imagine why I haven't been already. After all, Prague is only a couple of hours on the train from Dresden. And my Mama's a German-speaking Czech from Teplitz. Did I tell you that? She moved to Dresden when she met my Papa. Not that she ever really thought of herself as a Czech. Nobody does in Teplitz. At least that's what my Mama says.' She paused. 'Maybe I could go and see my brother. His unit is stationed near Prague.'

We were at Kempinski's Vaterland on Potsdamer Platz, a department store of cafés and restaurants that described itself as 'the jolliest place in Berlin' and which was as ersatz as the coffee we were drinking in the Grinzing Café, which with its diorama of Old Vienna and the Danube River was itself pretty ersatz. Of the several bars and cafés in Vaterland, Arianne much preferred the Wild West Bar's log-cabin walls, American flags, and the picture of Custer's Last Stand, but, immediately outside its door was an amusement machine with a light-gun on which you could shoot at pictures of aircraft, and the city's young anti-aircraft gunners were fond of using it for their boisterous practice. This particular form of entertainment was too like the real thing for my money and so we sat in the Grinzing and hugged each other fondly in sight of a *trompel'oeil* of the Austrian capital city with miniature bridges, mechanical boats, and an electric train-set while a little orchestra played Strauss waltzes. It was like being a giant or a god, which, in Germany, usually amounts to the same thing. Arianne was smaller than me by a head, and while that didn't make her Freia to my Fasolt, she was very much a goddess of feminine love. I'd seldom had a lover as expert as Arianne and, after the depressing horrors of the Ukraine, which, whenever possible, I was keen to put out

146

of my mind, perhaps I was falling for her. Hell, I had fallen for her. Since meeting her I hadn't thought about killing myself. Not once. I knew she was riding for herself but I could hardly blame her for that. The whole damned country was addicted to its own selfish pursuits. So I heard her out as she made her play and probably smiled a fond, indulgent sort of smile as she went about it. Because while there was a part of me that still didn't trust her, there was an even larger part that simply didn't care. Not any more. I was in Gaza, bound with new ropes and fresh bow-strings, with my hair in knots and my head in her lap. Sometimes it just happens that way.

'Have you got a passport?'

She nodded. 'When I was working for BVG my boss told me to get one so I could accompany him on a business trip to Italy. I knew what I was in for and if we'd ever actually got there I might have let him sleep with me, only his wife found out that I was going and then I wasn't going, and then I was out of a job. It's a very common story.'

'You'd need a visa, of course.'

'Sure. From the Police Praesidium on Alexanderplatz. Isn't that convenient, you working there and everything?'

'I don't know. It's possible you might need to produce some certification concerning the military importance of your journey. In which case – well, there is no military importance, angel. Not unless we count the restoration of my own morale. But somehow I don't see them buying that one.'

Arianne shook her head. 'No, you only need that kind of certification if you're planning to take the express train.' Smiling, she added, 'You forget. I used to work for BVG. I know all the rules and regulations that affect the railways. No certification of a journey's relevance is required for any other train. If we take the regular service between Anhalter Station and Jan Masaryk Station, there won't be a problem. I could probably remember the timetable if I put my mind to it.'

'I don't doubt it. But look, angel, I'm not sure where I'll be staying or what I'll be doing. You might find yourself on your own for longer than you'd like. For longer than I'd like, if it comes to that. It could even be dangerous.'

'I'll go and see the sights when you're not around. That shouldn't be too difficult to do. German's now the official language in Prague. And it's not like I'll be wearing a uniform. So I can't see how I'm likely to get into any trouble. Or how it could possibly be dangerous.' She frowned. 'I think you're just saying that because you don't want me to come with you.'

'I wasn't thinking about the danger you might be in from the Czechos,' I said. 'Frankly, they're the least of our problems. No, there's something far more dangerous in Prague than the damned Czechos.'

'And what's that?'

'The new Reichsprotector of Bohemia and Moravia, that's what. General Reinhard Heydrich.'

Someone once said there's no fool like an old fool in love. But middle-aged fools aren't any less foolish. I walked home and thought some more about taking Arianne with me to Prague. No matter how smart you are, sometimes you just have to sit down and lay out a balance sheet to help you decide on something. On the credit side Arianne was a potential liability; and on the debit side, she gave me a lot of pleasure, and not all of it horizontal. They say that if, in every transaction, you can identify what you received, where it came from, and what it cost, then you have debits and credits mastered. But what they don't say is that sometimes you just figure the world owes you a little bit extra and to hell with the consequences. In truth, that's how most people handle life's book-keeping. If you believe Prince Hamlet, conscience makes cowards of us all; but I can attest that it's just as likely that conscience, especially a guilty one, can make you just a little bit reckless.

CHAPTER 10

I got down to Berlin's Anhalter Station about an hour before the train was due to depart so that I could meet Arianne and make sure that we both got a seat in a compartment. The newspaper vendors were shouting about the greatest victory in all military history at Kiev, and now and then about some smaller Italian air success against the British at Gibraltar. A squadron of pigeons up in the rafters of the station roof must have been listening because they flew south across the station concourse in formation, as if in honour of our wonderful armed forces and their brave Italian allies.

The station was busy with people. Nowadays, Anhalter was always busier than Lehrter or Potsdam: Germans were not travelling west toward RAF targets like Hamburg and Cologne if they could help it. South was better and south-east was better still. Even the pigeons knew that much.

The train filled. Among the other passengers with a seat in our compartment was an old Jew, easily identified by the yellow star recently sewn onto the left breast pocket of his suit. Nothing else about him was Jewish according to the filthy caricature of a Jew you saw in the newsreels or on the front of *Der Stürmer*, and prior to the nineteenth of September and Heydrich's new police law I should have assumed the old man was just another Berliner. Except that he was without question a brave one: the Knight's Cross with oak leaves he wore on a ribbon around his neck was eloquent proof of that, and probably a clever way to offset the stigma of the yellow star.

By now people were standing in the corridor and a man wearing the uniform of a Labour Corps leader loudly demanded that the old man give up his place to 'a German'. From his substantial girth, his relationship with real work looked tenuous to say the least.

Normally I didn't interfere in these matters; maybe it was the sight of the Knight's Cross around the old man's neck – maybe it was just that like a lot of other Berliners I didn't like the yellow star – but I was feeling more querulous in the face of Nazi bullying.

'Stay where you are,' I told the Jew and stood up to face down the Labour leader.

His face reddened like a Muscovy duck as he tried and failed to lift his chest above the polished brown belt around his waist.

'And who the hell are you to interfere?'

It was a fair question. I wasn't in uniform. That was in my suitcase and, for once, I was almost regretting not wearing it. But I had the next best thing in my pocket: my warrant disc. I showed it to him in the palm of my hand and it had the usual effect of cowing the man and the rest of the carriage into respectful silence.

'Do you see a sign that says this carriage is forbidden to Jews?'

The Labour leader glanced around, redundantly. There was a small printed panel that read *Attention! The Enemy is Listening!* but nowhere was there an anti-Semitic sign of the kind you sometimes saw on park benches or at public baths. Even I was surprised about that.

He shook his head.

I pointed at Arianne. 'This woman worked for BVG until about a year ago.'

'That's right,' she said. 'I was secretary to the director himself.'

'Is there anything in the BVG railway rules and regulations that says a Jew must give up his seat to a German?'

'No. There isn't.'

'So there,' I said. 'Let that be an end of it. Go away and keep your ignorant mouth shut.' I might also have mentioned the decoration around the old Jew's neck, but I didn't want anyone in that compartment thinking that this was the only reason I was interfering on his behalf.

There was a murmur of approval as the Labour leader barrelled his way out of the compartment and down the carriage. I sat down.

'Thank you, sir,' said the old man, tipping his hat.

'Don't mention it,' I said and tipped my own in return.

Someone else said, quietly, 'No one likes that yellow star.'

By now the old man was looking thoroughly bewildered, as well he might be, and he could reasonably have asked any of us how it was, if none of us cared for the yellow star, we had allowed Heydrich's police order to happen. If he had, I might have suggested a better question: how had we allowed Heydrich to happen? There was no easy answer to a question like that.

The old man got off the train in Dresden, which was a relief to everyone. The sight of the word 'Jew' emblazoned on a man of such obvious valour made all of us feel thoroughly ashamed of ourselves.

Despite what had been said about the yellow star, no one in our compartment – no one at all – talked about the war. The injunction on the wooden wall that the enemy might be listening was more effective than might have been imagined. And since there was little else but the war on anyone's mind, this meant that none of the other passengers in our compartment said very much. Even Arianne, who liked to talk, was silent for most of the journey.

The train travelled north of the Elbe until Bad Schandau, where it passed over a bridge onto the south bank, then east and south again until Schöna, where it halted to allow several customs officers to board. Everyone – myself included, until I flashed my beer-token – was obliged to leave the train and have their luggage searched in the customs shed. None of my fellow passengers protested. After eight long years of Nazism, people knew better than to complain to authority. Besides, these officers were backed by twenty or thirty SS who stood thuggishly on the platform ready to see off any trouble.

The customs officers themselves were surprisingly courteous and polite. They did not bother to search Arianne or her bags when I informed them that she was travelling with me. If they had, I wonder what they might have found.

While the rest of the passengers were in the customs shed and we were alone in the compartment, she looked at me strangely. 'You're an odd one, Parsifal. I can't figure you out.'

'What do you mean?'

'The way you stuck up for that old Jew back there. Jesus, I thought you were supposed to be a Nazi.'

'Whatever gave you that idea?'

'I don't know. Maybe it's the company you keep. We don't see much of General Heydrich in my circle.'

'He's not an easy man to disappoint.'

'I can imagine.'

'Can you? I wonder. I wasn't always his creature. Even before the Nazis took over, I was out of the police, because of my politics. Which is to say that, like most people who supported the old Republic,

I didn't really have any politics except I wasn't a Nazi and I wasn't a Red. But that was no good, see? Not in the cops. So I left; but they'd have kicked me out anyway. Then, in 1938, not being a Nazi made me seem like good police again. I wasn't about to chalk someone up for a crime just because they were Jewish. That was useful to Heydrich and so he ordered me back into Kripo. And I've been stuck there ever since. Worse than that, if I'm honest. Suddenly, when war was declared, if you were in Kripo you were also in the SS; and when we attacked Russia—'

I shook my head. 'Well, from time to time I'm useful to him in the same way a toothpick might be useful to a cannibal.'

'You're worried he might eat you, too. Is that it?'

'Something like that.'

'Perhaps if more people stood up to Heydrich, the way you stood up to that fat Labour leader?' She shrugged. 'I don't know.'

'You don't know Heydrich. People don't ever stand up to Heydrich for very long. Most often, they end up standing in front of a firing squad. If they're lucky.'

'You're a bit like Faust, I suppose. And Heydrich is your Mephistopheles.'

I nodded. 'Except that I haven't had any of the pleasures of the world out of the deal. I didn't even get to seduce a beautiful and innocent girl. Gretchen, isn't it?'

'No. Arianne.'

'You're hardly innocent.'

'But I am beautiful.'

'Yes. You are beautiful, angel. There's no doubt about that.'

CHAPTER 11

An hour later we were moving again and quickly through Bohemia, although, from the number of Nazi flags and banners and German troops we saw, you would scarcely have been aware of this. And almost every Czech town we passed through had a new German name, so that it felt less like visiting a foreign country, or even an autonomous territory – which, strictly speaking, is what a 'protectorate' amounts to – and more like a colony.

We reached Prague in the late afternoon. According to my 1929 Austrian Baedeker – for some reason this edition included a section on Prague, as if it was still a city in the old Austro-Hungarian Empire – the hotel was just around the corner from Masaryk Station, so we decided to walk there and, holding Arianne's bag and mine, I led the way through a tall archway and short colonnade of Doric pillars into a square entrance hall with a glass roof and a peeling maroon and gold plaster architrave that resembled something out of an abandoned villa in Pompeii. The hall was full of field-grey uniforms, some of which eyed

Arianne hungrily, like wolves. I didn't blame them in the least. She had a figure like a snake charmer's pipe. Arianne herself was not unconscious of this effect and, smiling happily, she put an extra couple of notes into the swaying and seductive melody of her walk.

It was less than a hundred metres to the end of the street where the Imperial Hotel was situated. The outside of the building was grey and quite unremarkable, but inside the place was a shrine to art nouveau. On the face of it this seemed at odds with the hotel's obvious popularity with the German Army, which isn't well known for its interest in art except of course when it's stealing it from some poor Jew for Göring's personal collection. On the walls of the small but impressive entrance-lobby was a creamy-coloured ceramic relief featuring six classically dressed ladies exercising their pet lions. I knew they were classically dressed because they were wearing little gold circlets with asps on their heads and because they had bare breasts – a fashion of which generally I approve.

The breasts of women are a little hobby of mine; and while I know why I enjoy looking at them and touching them, it continues to elude me why I seem to like looking at them and touching them so much.

As soon as I saw the hotel entrance-lobby and the huge café with its temple-tall mosaic pillars I thought of the Ishtar Gate at Berlin's Pergamon

Museum, and I suppose this might have been one reason the Imperial was a local favourite with the German Army. Then again, it might just have been because the hotel was also expensive. The Wehrmacht likes expensive hotels and, if it comes to that, so do I. Since I first worked as the hotel detective at the Adlon, I have come to realize that I am very easily pleased: usually the best is good enough. Either way, the Imperial's café was full of soldiers and their off-duty laughter, their off-colour jokes, and their better-quality – better than Berlin – cigarette smoke.

Our fifth-floor corner-room had two windows. From one side there was a fine view of the south-east of Prague, which was mostly spires and smoking chimneys; from the other, to the west, you could see the rooftop immediately opposite, which had one of those pepper-pot domes made of oxidizing copper. It looked like a large green samovar.

Almost immediately we went to bed, which seemed like the sensible thing to do, as I had no idea of how soon Heydrich would summon me to his country house or for how long, and strenuous sex was something that had been on our minds ever since the train had left Berlin – although, to be more precise, it had probably been on my mind more than hers. Either way she didn't have to be persuaded, very much. It was love, or at least a good imitation of it, on my part at least.

And then there was life, which of course is love's

nemesis, sliding under the door in the shape of a brown envelope.

I rolled off Arianne's naked body and walked across the room to collect it.

Arianne rolled onto her belly, lit only her second cigarette of the day and watched me read the note.

'Mephistopheles?'

'I'm afraid so. His driver will collect me first thing tomorrow morning, in front of the hotel.'

'That certainly gives us plenty of time to do all kinds of things. Who knows, we might even find time to see the sights. I hear the Charles Bridge is worth a look.'

'Is that what you'd like to do?'

'Not right now.' She blew smoke at the ceiling and then gave me a narrow-eyed look. 'Right now I just want some more of what I came for.' She put down her cigarette and, lying back on the bed, opened her arms and then her thighs. 'Everything else, you know, is just tourism and I can do that on my own.'

I threw Heydrich's note aside, climbed back onto the bed and crawled between her thighs.

'But for this,' she said. 'I need help.'

CHAPTER 12

The General's driver was an SS sergeant who told me his name was Klein. He was a large, heavy man with fair hair, a high forehead and an expressionless face. I soon learned he was also tight-lipped. Working for the Reichsprotector of Bohemia and Moravia, there was a lot to be tight-lipped about.

The car was a dark green Mercedes 320 convertible, and with its less than discreet number plate – SS-4 – it was what Klein drove when Heydrich was not on official or state duties. For those, I soon learned, there was a larger model, a Mercedes 770. The 320 had an extra spotlight mounted on the front fender in case the General had to stop and interrogate someone at the side of the road. There was no flag on the wing but that hardly made me feel any less obvious or insecure. Both of us were in uniform. The top was down. There was no armed escort. We were in enemy territory. To me it felt like visiting an Indian Thuggee village wearing a red coat and whistling 'The British Grenadiers'. And noting with some amusement my obvious discomfort, Klein explained

161

that the General scorned any escort as a sign of weakness, which was why he preferred him to be driven around Prague with the top down.

'And how often do you drive him around Prague?'

'Between Prague Castle and the General's country house? Twice a day. Regular as sunrise.'

'You're joking.'

'Nope.'

'With one of the Three Kings at liberty, that seems unwise to me.'

We set off and I shrank back into the front passenger seat as a tall man standing beside the road snatched off his battered felt hat out of respect for who – but more probably what – we were. There was a lot of that in Prague. Because the Nazis liked this kind of thing. But I didn't like it at all, any more than I liked driving around with a three-colour target painted on my chest; and taking out my pistol, I worked the slide and dropped it into the leather pocket on the inside of the car door, from where it might be easily and quickly retrieved in an emergency.

Klein laughed. 'What's that for?'

'Just ignore me, Sergeant. I was in the Ukraine until the end of August. In the Ukraine there are lots of Ivans who want to kill Germans. I assume the same holds true for almost any conquered country. Except perhaps France. I never felt unsafe in France.'

'So why feel unsafe here?'

'To my ignorant ears at least, the Czech language sounds a lot like Russian. That's why.'

'Then let me reassure you, sir. To attack this, or the General's other car, SS-3, would be to risk the most severe retribution. That's what the General says. And I believe him.'

'But what do you think?'

Klein shrugged. 'I think this is a fast car and the General likes me to drive fast.'

'Yes, I noticed.'

'I think you'd have to be damned lucky to ambush this car. And that, in the long run, would be very unlucky for the Czechos.'

'And for the General, I'd have thought. Possibly you, too, Sergeant. Really yours is not much of a threat, because it seems to me as if their bad luck is predicated on yours. It's like saying that if you drown you'll make sure you take them with you. When they're dead, so are you.'

We drove about fifteen kilometres north-east of the city centre to a small village called Jungfern-Breschan. The Czechos called it Panenske-Brezany, which is probably Czech for a very quiet village that's surrounded by a depressingly featureless landscape – just a lot of flat, recently ploughed and very smelly fields. The village itself was rather more quaint and picturesque as long as your idea of what was quaint and picturesque included a few checkpoints and the odd detachment of motor-ized SS. Anyone foolish enough to have attacked Heydrich's car would have discovered that the countryside afforded them little cover from these soldiers. A team of assassins at Jungfern-Breschan would have been caught or killed within minutes. Even so, I had to wonder why Heydrich had chosen to live out here, in the middle of nowhere, when he had at his disposal in the centre of Prague a castle the size of the Kremlin, not to mention a handful of elegant Bohemian palaces. Maybe he was worried about defenestration. There was a lot of that kind of thing in Prague. I wouldn't have minded pushing Heydrich or any number of Nazis out of a high window myself.

We turned off the main highway and Klein steered the Mercedes down a gently sloping road that wound around to the right and then the left. There were trees now and the air was strong with the smell of freshly mown grass and pine-needles, and after the grey misery of Prague this felt like a place where it might be easier for Heydrich to escape from the cares of the world, even the ones he himself had inflicted or was planning to inflict. At Jungfern-Breschan, he might get away from it all, just as long as he didn't mind the several hundred SS stormtroopers who were there to protect his privacy.

A handsomely baroque pink stucco house came into view on our right. Behind a gated and guarded archway I counted six windows on the upper floor. It looked like a hunting lodge but I couldn't be sure. I'd rarely been hunting myself, and never for anything more elusive than a missing person, a murderer, or an errant wife, and it was hard to comprehend how anyone wanting to shoot a few pheasants also needed a matching Russian Orthodox chapel and a swimming pool in the grounds to be able to do it. Of course, it's always possible that if I'd prayed a bit more and learned to swim a bit better I might have bagged the odd snipe or two myself.

'Is that General Heydrich's new house?'

'No. That's the Upper Castle. Von Neurath continues to live there. For the moment, anyway.'

Konstantin von Neurath had been the Reichsprotector of Bohemia until Hitler decided he was too soft and gave the job to his blond butcher; but before that von Neurath had been the German Foreign Minister – a job now held by the most unpopular man in Germany, Joachim von Ribbentrop.

'There's an Upper Castle and a Lower Castle,' explained Klein. 'Both of them were owned by some Jewish sugar merchant. But when the Jew bastard took off in 1939 the estate was confiscated. The main house is the Lower Castle, further down the hill. It's a nicer house.'

'Doesn't the General mind? That the place used to be lived in by Jews?'

'Sir?'

'You've seen the propaganda films,' I said. 'Those people carry diseases, don't they? Like rats.'

Klein shot me a look as if he wasn't quite sure if I was serious, and decided, wrongly, that I was. To be fair to him, my sarcasm had a cautious

165

ambivalence about it since coming back from the Ukraine.

'No, it's all right,' he insisted. 'This merchant, he only owned the house since 1909. Originally, the house was owned by a German aristocrat who lost the place to the bank, who sold it to the Jew at a knock-down price. And before either of them, the estate was owned by Benedictine monks.'

'Well, you can't be less Jewish than a Benedictine monk, now can you?'

Klein grinned stupidly and shook his head.

I was toying with the idea of asking how a man with a name like Klein got to be in the SS at all, let alone driving for Heydrich, when the larger gates of the Lower Castle came in sight. In front of the gate posts were a pair of stone statues that would have given any animal-lover a moment's pause. One statue depicted a bear being torn to bits by a pair of hunting dogs; and the other, a similarly beleaguered wild boar. But you could see how that sort of thing would have been appreciated by Heydrich, who was certainly the incarnation of Nature red in tooth and claw.

Beside the wild boar an SS soldier stepped out of his sentry box and came smartly to attention as our car turned into the gateway. At the end of a drive about fifty metres long was the Lower Castle itself. It was a modest little place, but only by the standards of Hermann Göring, or Mussolini, perhaps.

This 'castle' was actually a late nineteenth-century French-style chateau, but no less impressive for that, with sixteen windows on each of two well-proportioned floors, front and back. Unlike the pink stucco Upper Castle, the Lower Castle was canary-yellow with a red roof, a square-tower portico painted white, and a central arched window that was about the same size as a U-Bahn tunnel. On the immaculate lawn was yet another piece of stone statuary: an enormous stag and two deer who were running away from the house. I took one look at the number of SS patrolling the grounds and felt like galloping away myself. With a couple of females in season for frolicsome company I might even have made it over the high wall.

Klein drew up at the front door and switched off the 320's three-litre four-stroke engine. As it cooled, it ticked away like there was a family of mice living underneath the 2½-metre-long hood.

For a moment I just sat there looking up at the house, listening to the soothing coo of some pigeons and, it seemed, to the sound of someone not too far away who was shooting at them.

'Executions?' I said, retrieving my pistol from the door pocket.

Klein grinned. 'Hunting. There's always something to shoot around here.'

'Something, or someone?'

'I can get you a gun if you'd care to go out and

bag something for the pot. We eat a lot of game here at the Castle.'

'Well, I always say, if you can't play the game properly, eat it. That reminds me. Who do I give my food coupons to?'

The Lower Castle didn't look like a food coupon sort of place, but I said it anyway, just for the fun of it.

'You can forget about that sort of thing for a while. This is not like Berlin. There are no shortages of anything. The General lives very well out here in the countryside. Cigarettes, booze, chocolate, vegetarian. Anything you want. Just ask one of them.'

Klein nodded in the direction of an approaching SS valet wearing a white mess jacket who opened my door and came smartly to attention.

'I'm beginning to see why he lives here. We're not just outside Prague. We're outside what counts as normal as well.'

I stood up, returned the Hitler salute, and followed the valet inside the house.

The main hallway was two storeys high with a wrought-iron gallery and a large, ornate brass chandelier that looked like Dante, Beatrice and the Heavenly Host of Angels waiting around for an appointment with Saint Peter. Behind the heavy oak door was a long-case clock the size of a beech tree and which I quickly learned was about as good at keeping time. There was a big round walnut wood table with a bronze of a mounted

168

Amazon fighting a panther. The panther was wrapped around the horse, which looked like a mistake when you took into account the Amazon's breasts. Then again, the Amazon had a spear in her hand, so maybe the panther knew what he was doing. There are some women who, no matter how good-looking they are, it's best to leave well alone.

Across the hall and down a short flight of marble steps was a large room with tie-side Knoll sofas and a hardwood coffee table that might once have been a small Caribbean island. The only reason you might have assumed this was a room was if you also assumed that somewhere further than the human eye could see there were more walls and windows and a door or two. There was a big empty fireplace with brass firedogs and a cast-iron screen that belonged on the door of a gaol. Above this was a mantelpiece with a muscle-bound Atlas at each corner and on the mantel itself several framed photographs of Hitler, Heydrich, Himmler, and a strongly featured blonde I assumed was Heydrich's wife, Lina. In another picture she and Heydrich were wearing Tyrolean costume and playing with a baby; they all looked very German. And it was difficult not to think of those Atlases as two poor Czechs groaning under the burden of their new masters. Above the mantel there was a large and unnecessarily well-painted portrait of the Leader, who seemed to be staring up at the Lower Castle's gallery as if he was wondering when on earth someone was going to come down and inform him exactly what he was doing there. I had exactly the same feeling myself.

As my eyes gradually adjusted to the size of the place I saw, in the distance, a set of French windows and through them a lawn, some shrubberies and trees, and the clear blue sky that was the inevitable and very pleasant corollary of having no neighbours.

A tall butler wearing a tailcoat and a wing collar glided silently into the hall and bowed, giving me time enough to get a good look at his hair, which, like the deferential expression on his face, seemed to have been painted on his head. The Iron Cross first class ribbon on his coat lapel was a nice touch, reminding everyone wearing a uniform that he, too, had done his bit in the trenches. He had a thick, jowly face and an even thicker beef-soup of a voice.

'Welcome sir, to Jungfern-Breschan. I am Kritzinger, the butler. The General presents his compliments and asks you to join him for drinks on the terrace at twelve-thirty p.m.' He lifted one arm in the direction of the French windows, as if he had been directing traffic on Potsdamer Platz. 'Please let me know if there's anything I can do to make your stay here more comfortable. Until then, if you'll come this way, I'll show you to your quarters.'

My room, in the north wing, was larger and better appointed than I'd been expecting. There was a good-sized bed, a secretaire desk with three ebonized drawers for the clothes I had brought from the Imperial, a table-chair and a leather armchair that stood next to a fireplace that was laid but not lit. In the window was a folding tray-table with a princely range of alcoholic drinks, chocolate, newspapers and American cigarettes, and as soon as Kritzinger had made himself scarce, I set about throwing away my Johnnies and filling my cigarette case. With a drink in my hand and a decent cigarette in my mouth I inspected my principality in more detail.

On the desk was a Brumberg table lamp with a parchment shade, and on the floor a dull maroon Turkish kilim. There were some towels on the end of my bed and the door had a key and a bolt, for which I was grateful. Absurdly so. When you're in a house that's already full of murderers it's perhaps foolish to think that locking your door is going to keep you safe. There were bars on the lower-floor windows but not on those of the upper floor. The window in my room, which had some sturdy brass bolts, had a fixed windowpane and two casements that opened out onto the back garden. There was a roller blind for summer and some thick red curtains for when the weather turned colder, which, in that part of the world, it always does.

I poked my head outside. The ground was about five or six metres below the window ledge. In the centre of a circular bed of flowers a sprinkler was a whirling dervish of water and rhythm. Beyond that was a gravel path lined with neatly trimmed bushes and then a thick clump of trees. And on the lawn was another stone group of escaping deer that was perhaps a pair to the one in the front garden.

I lay on my bed and finished my drink and smoked my cigarette. These did little to calm me. To be under the same roof as Heydrich made me nervous. I got up and poured myself another drink, which helped, but only a little. Whatever he wanted, I knew it wouldn't sit well with my conscience, which was already badly bruised, and I resolved that when eventually he got around to explaining what this was, I would tell him, as politely as I could, to go to hell. There was no way I was ever going back to the Ukraine to perform some loathsome act of genocide and it really didn't matter if that meant being sent to a concentration camp. I wasn't the same as any of those other bastards in uniform. I wasn't even a Nazi. Perhaps they needed reminding of that. Perhaps it was time I repeated my allegiance to the old Republic. If they were looking for an excuse to throw me out of the SD then I would hand them one. Arianne was surely right: if more people stood up to Heydrich the way I'd stood up to the Labour leader on the train then, maybe, things would change. More people would be dead, too, including myself, but that couldn't be helped. Lately that didn't seem so bad. That's what I told myself, anyway. It might have been the schnapps. And of course I wouldn't know for sure until the time came. But I knew it was going to take some courage on my part because I was also afraid. That's the only way I know that you can distinguish being brave from being stupid.

'That's rather beautiful, don't you think?'

I was looking at a dazzling modern picture of a dark-haired *femme fatale*. She was wearing a fabulous long dress that seemed to be made of golden Argus eyes, all set against a radiantly primordial golden background. There was something terrifying about the woman herself. She looked like some remorseless Egyptian queen who had been made ready for eternity by a group of economists who were slaves to the gold standard.

'Unfortunately it's a copy. The original was stolen by that greedy fat bastard Herman Göring and is now in his private collection, where nobody but him can see it. More's the pity.'

I was in the Lower Castle library. Through the window I could see the back garden where several SS and SD officers were already collected on the terrace. The officer speaking to me was about thirty, tall, thin, and rather effete. He had white blond hair and a duelling scar on his face. The three pips on his black collar-patch told me he was an SS-Hauptsturmführer – a captain, like me; and the monkey swing of silver braid on his tunic – properly called an aiguillette, but only by people who knew their way around a dictionary of military words – indicated he was an aide-de-camp, most likely Heydrich's.

'Are you Doctor Ploetz?' I asked.

'Good God, no.' He clicked his heels. 'Hauptsturmführer Albert Kuttner, fourth adjutant to General Heydrich, at your service. No, you'll know when you meet Ploetz. It will feel like someone left a freezer door open.'

'Cold, huh?'

'I've met warmer glaciers.'

'How many adjutants does he have?'

'Oh, just the four. A man for each season. There's myself. Captains Pomme and Kluckholn. And Major Ploetz, who's the Chief Adjutant. You'll have the great pleasure of meeting them all while you're here.'

'I can't wait.'

Kuttner smiled a knowing smile, as if he and I were already occupying the same forbidden radio frequency. 'And you, I assume, must be Captain Gunther.' He shook his head. 'The Berlin accent. It's quite unmistakable. By the way, the General doesn't go in for the Hitler salute very much, while we're here at the castle.'

'That suits me. I don't go in for Hitler salutes much myself.'

'Yes. The General likes to keep things very informal. So mess rules apply. No belts worn.' He nodded at my crossbelts. 'That kind of thing.'

'Thanks,' I said, unbuckling the crossbelt I was wearing.

174

'Also, it's fine to introduce yourself with your SS rank but, after that, do try not to use SS ranks when describing yourself or a brother officer. Army ranks or surnames save time. The General's very keen on saving time. He often says that while we delay time does not and that lost time is never found again. Very true, what?'

'He's always been very quotable, the General. You must try to write some of these sayings down. For the sake of posterity.'

Kuttner shook his head. It seemed he wasn't quite on my own frequency after all.

'That wouldn't do at all. The General hates people writing down what he says. It's an idiosyncrasy he has.'

I smiled. 'It's evidence, that's what it is.'

Kuttner smiled back. 'Yes, I see what you mean. Very good. Very good.'

'I guess that's why he has four adjutants,' I added. 'To help keep everything off the record.'

'Yes, I hadn't thought of that. But you could be right.'

I turned back to the golden picture in front of us. 'Who is she, anyway?'

'Her name is Adele Bloch-Bauer and her husband, Ferdinand, used to own this house. A Jew, which makes you wonder why Göring likes her so much. But there it is. Consistency not his strong suit, I'd say. It's a nice copy of course but I think it a great pity that the original isn't in the house, where it truly belongs. We're trying to persuade the

Reichsmarshal to give it back, but so far without much success. He's like a dog with a bone when it comes to paintings, I believe. Anyway, one can easily see why he likes it so much. To say that Frau Bloch-Bauer looked like a million marks hardly seems to do her portrait justice. Wouldn't you agree?'

I nodded and allowed myself another look, not at the painting but at Captain Kuttner. For a man who was Heydrich's adjutant, his free and frank opinions seemed to veer toward the dangerous. A bit like my own. It was clear we had more in common than just a uniform and a keen appreciation of modern art.

'It's different,' I allowed.

'Superficially stylish, perhaps. But somehow even a copy is deeper than the gold paint, which seems almost to have been spilled onto the canvas. Eh?'

'You sound like Bernard Berenson, Captain Kuttner.'

'Lord, don't say that. At least not within earshot of the General. Berenson's a Jew.'

'What happened to her anyway?' I lit a cigarette. 'To the golden lady in the picture?'

'Sad to say, and rather ingloriously given how she looks in this painting, the poor woman died of meningitis in 1925. Still, that might turn out to be just as well, when one considers what is happening to Jews in this country. And in her native Austria.'

'And Ferdinand? Her husband?'

'Oh, I've no idea what happened to him. And I don't much care, quite frankly. He sounds like your typical grasping Jewish merchant and he quite wisely cleared off the minute we walked into the Sudetenland. But I do know that the artist – another Austrian named Gustav Klimt – died at the beginning of the influenza epidemic in 1918, poor fellow. But he was a frequent guest here, I believe. Adele was rather fond of old Klimt, by all accounts. Perhaps a bit too fond. Funny to think of them all here, isn't it? Especially now that General Heydrich owns the house. *O quam cito transit gloria mundi.*'

I nodded but said nothing. While the eccentric young adjutant seemed to be a cut above the average SD automaton, I wasn't in the mood to mention the loss of my own wife to the influenza epidemic: if Klimt had been an early victim, my wife had been one of the very last to die of flu, in December 1920. Besides, there was something just a bit unpredictable about Captain Kuttner that made me wonder how someone like Heydrich could tolerate him. Then again, the General also managed, somehow, to tolerate me, and that spoke either of his enormous toleration – which seemed improbable – or his enormous cynicism.

Kuttner tried and failed to stifle a yawn.

'The General working you late, is he?'

'Sorry. No, actually I'm just not sleeping very well. Hardly at all, if I'm honest.'

'He has the same effect on me. I've hardly slept

177

a wink since I received his kind invitation to Prague. And it's not from excitement, either.'

'Really?' Kuttner sounded surprised.

'Really.'

'You surprise me. Actually he's been very understanding of my situation. Very understanding. He even referred me to his own doctor. He gave me something called Veronal, which is quite effective. For sleeping. Although you have to be careful not to mix it with alcohol.'

'Then I'd better make sure I never take any.' I grinned. 'I'm usually very careful never to let anything stand in the way of my drinking. But what I meant was that the General's reputation goes before him. He's not exactly Mohandas K. Gandhi, is he? And I might sleep a little better knowing exactly why the hell I'm here. I don't suppose you can shed any light on that, can you? In the same thoughtful and well-informed way that you have illuminated this picture for me.'

Kuttner scratched the duelling scar on his cheek. He seemed to do it when he was nervous, which was often.

'It was my understanding that you and the General were friends.'

'If you mean like a friend in need is a friend to be avoided, then yes we're friends. But I guess the friends we have are probably the friends we deserve.'

'You do surprise me, Commissar Gunther.'

'Well, maybe you've put your finger on it, Captain. Maybe I'm supposed to be the licensed jester here, to make everyone else but the General feel uncomfortable. Knowing Heydrich as I do, I can easily see how that might amuse him.'

'I can assure you that what you say simply cannot be the case. Most of the people here this weekend are the General's most intimate friends. And he's gone to considerable trouble to make sure that everyone enjoys themselves. Good food, excellent wine, fine brandies, the best cigars. Perhaps it's just you who is supposed to feel uncomfortable, Commissar.'

'That is always possible. The General always did like what the English call a Roman holiday. Where one man suffers for the pleasure of others.'

Kuttner was shaking his head. 'Please let me reassure you, Gunther. I was joking, just now. Your fears are entirely without foundation. The General was most anxious that you should be comfortable. He chose your quarters himself. He chose everyone's quarters. Including my own. I've known the General for quite a while now, off and on, and I can attest to his generosity and thoughtfulness. He's not at all the capricious cruel man that you seem to know. Really.'

'Yes, I'm sure you're right, captain.' I nodded at the *femme fatale* in gold. 'All the same, I wonder if the unfortunate sugar merchant's wife would agree with you.'

It was one of those early October afternoons that made you think winter was just a word and that there was no earthly reason why the sun should ever stop shining. The flowers in the Lower Castle's well-tended beds were mostly pink dahlias, white asters and red marigolds, providing a riot of autumn colour – which was the only kind of riot that the SS was likely to tolerate. The lawn was as green and smooth as a python's eyeball. Crystal glasses clinked, heels clicked, and somewhere someone was playing a piano. A soft breeze in the trees sounded like an enormous silk dress. They had turned off the sprinklers but there was strawberry cup with real strawberries and delicious Sekt so I managed to get nicely wet all the same.

About eighteen of us went in for lunch. With only another four we could have tossed a coin for kick-off. The white tablecloth was as stiff as a sail on a frozen schooner and there was enough silver on it for an army of conquistadores. Otherwise things were informal, as Captain Kuttner had promised, and I was glad we had abandoned crossbelts as the food was as spectacular as it was plentiful: pea soup with real peas and bacon, liver dumplings with real liver and real onions, Holstein Schnitzel with real veal, a real egg and real anchovies served with a real Leipziger Everything. I hardly had room for the real strudel and the real cheese that followed. The wines were equally impressive. There was a box on the table for food coupons, but no one was paying any attention to that and I figured it was just for show. I looked at it and wondered about the two Fridmann sisters in the apartment beneath mine back in Berlin and how they were getting on with the canned food I'd given them, but mostly I just kept on filling the hole in my face with food and wine and cigarette smoke. I didn't say much. There wasn't much need to say anything very much. Everyone paid close attention to Heydrich's table talk, which was the usual Nazi twaddle, and it was only when he started talking about the stupidity of trying to turn Czechs into Germans that I gave my jaws a rest and let my ears take over:

'People of good race and good intentions, they will be Germanized. Those we can't Germanize and educate to think differently from the way they think now, we'll have to put up against the wall. The rest – that's potentially at least half the population of Bohemia and Moravia – they will have to be moved out and resettled in the East where they can live out their miserable days in Arctic labour camps. However, whenever we can we must act with fairness. When all is said and done, the Czechs should be made to see the advantages of cooperation over opposition. And when the current state of emergency has ended, I will increase the local food ration and do everything in my power to hunt down black-market profiteers.'

There was a lot more of this guff, and I looked at the fat faces of my fellow officers to see if anyone felt the same way about it that I did, but I saw only consent and agreement. Probably they looked at me and thought the same thing.

Among these faces there was only one, apart from Heydrich's long, thin witch-doctor's mask, that I recognized and this was the former Foreign Minister and ex-Reichsprotector, Konstantin von Neurath. At almost seventy, he was the oldest person at the table and easily the most deserving of respect. Not that his ambitious young successor, Heydrich, accorded him much of this. From time to time he would pat the old man on the hand like a pet dog and speak to him in a louder voice, as if the Baron were deaf, although it was quite plain to anyone who had talked to him that there was nothing at all wrong with his hearing. I suspected that von Neurath was only present to make the new Reichsprotector's triumph complete.

Heydrich avoided conversation with me until well after we had risen from the table and were out on the terrace again with brandies and cigars – or in my case, coffee and cigarettes. It was there that he caught my eye and, having walked me down the Upper Castle's back garden, finally explained the point of my being there.

'You remember our conversation at my office in Berlin, the day we defeated the French. In June 1940.'

'I remember it very well. How could I forget the day when Germany defeated France? So that's what this is all about.'

'Yes. Again, someone is trying to kill me.'

I shrugged. 'Any number of Czechos must want you dead, sir. I assume that we're not discussing one of them.'

'Naturally.'

'Has there been a recent attempt on your life?'

'You mean, am I imagining this?'

'All right then. Are you?'

'No. There was an attempt made to kill me just days ago. A serious attempt.'

'When, where and how?'

'At the Wolf's Lair. Hitler's own field headquarters, in East Prussia. Yes, I thought that would surprise you. As a matter of fact I was surprised myself. It was September 24th. I had been summoned to Rastenburg to be told by Hitler that he was appointing me as von Neurath's successor, here in Bohemia. Well that's the when and where. The how is that someone tried to poison me. Toxicologists in the SD's laboratories are still trying to isolate the particular substance that was used. However, they're inclined to believe that it may have been a protein-based toxin called botulinum. From Latin *botulus*, meaning sausage.'

'That sounds especially lethal, for a German.'

'It's a bacterium that often causes poisoning by growing in improperly handled meat. I might have assumed it was just a simple case of food poisoning were it not for the fact that some of our SS doctors have been trying to synthesize it and other antibiotic compounds such as sulphanilamide. As a means of treating wound infection. But also as a compound neurotoxin. Or to put it another way, as a poison.'

'Perhaps it was a simple case of food poisoning,' I said. 'Have you considered that possibility?'

'I've considered it. And I've rejected it. You see mine was the only food that was contaminated. Fortunately I wasn't hungry and didn't eat. Instead I fed the food off my plate to Major Ploetz's dog, which subsequently died. Obviously the Leader could not have been the target because he is vegetarian. Naturally, all inquiries that could be made without alarming the Leader were made; and all of the foreign workers at the Wolf's Lair were replaced, as a precaution. But so far, nothing has been discovered that sheds any light on who was responsible for the incident. And there I feel we have to leave the matter. At least as far as Rastenburg is concerned. As I say, I have no wish to alarm or embarrass the Leader. But here in Prague I am able to take other precautions. You, Gunther, are to be one of these precautions, if you agree.'

'So you want me to do what? Be your food taster?' I shrugged. 'You should have mentioned this before lunch. I'd have sat beside you.'

Heydrich shook his head.

'Keep a lookout for someone who might be trying to kill you? Is that it?'

'Yes. In effect I want you to be my personal bodyguard,' said Heydrich.

'You mean you have four adjutants and no bodyguard?'

184

'Klein, my driver, is quite capable of pulling out a gun and shooting at some witless Czecho. As am I. But I want someone around me who understands murder and murderers, and who can handle himself, to boot. A proper detective who is trained to be suspicious.'

'The Gestapo isn't known to be naïve in my experience.'

'I want someone who is usefully suspicious as opposed to officious.'

'Yes, I see the difference.'

'And since I can't offer the position to Hercule Poirot naturally I thought of you.'

'Hercule Poirot?'

Heydrich shook his head. 'A fictional detective created by an English lady novelist. It doesn't matter. You're obviously not a reader. He's very popular. And so is she.'

I shook my head. 'You know that most bodyguards are supposed to care about what happens to their employers, don't you?'

Heydrich grinned. This didn't happen very often, and when it did his youngish, beaky face looked more like a nasty schoolboy's.

'Meaning you're not qualified, is that it?'

'Something like that.'

'I can get any number of "yes" men from the SD,' said Heydrich. 'The trouble is, will they be honest with me? Will they tell me unpalatable truths? What I need to know? And can I trust them?'

'It's true, sir. Without a gun in my hand you're not an easy man to contradict.'

'You, I've known for five years. I know you're not Himmler's man. I know you're not even a Nazi. I know you probably hate my guts. But while you almost certainly dislike me I don't believe you would actually murder me. In other words, I can trust you, Gunther; trust you not to kill me; and trust you to tell me those unpleasant truths that others would shrink from. That seems to me to be essential for what I need from a bodyguard.

'Of course, in many ways you're a fool. Only a fool would continue to remain in the police without joining the Party. Only a fool would remain sentimental about the Weimar Republic. Only a fool could fail to see that the new Germany cannot be resisted. But I have to admit, you're a clever and resourceful fool. I can use that. Most important of all, you're a damned good policeman. If you become my detective you'll have a room here at the Lower Castle; your own car; and an office at Hradschin castle, in the city. From time to time you'll even get to see that charming little whore you brought with you from Berlin. What's her name? Arianne, isn't it?'

That surprised me, although I suppose it ought not have done; there wasn't much that happened in Prague that Heydrich didn't know about.

'Frankly I'm not at all sure what she sees in you. The sort of woman who goes to the Jockey Bar is usually looking for someone with a bit more vitamin B than you have, Gunther. Of course, that particular disadvantage will be quickly remedied if you agree to take this position. Suddenly your status will be improved. You'll forgive me for saying so, but this is an important job.'

Throughout our conversation Heydrich's long thin pianist's hands were deep in the pockets of his uniform's riding breeches and this seemed to make his horseman's bandy legs even more U-shaped than normal. Now he pulled them out and from the pocket of his fart-catcher – an SD service tunic that was covered with so many gold and silver badges it looked more like a priest's reliquary – he produced a small silver cigarette case and offered me one. 'Smoke?'

'Thank you, sir.'

Finding a match, I lit us both.

'So what do you say?'

'Just how honest do you want me to be, General? Imprudently honest? Unflinchingly honest? Or just brutally honest? And what's in it for me apart from some more vitamins in my otherwise lousy diet? One of those opinion reflectors on your breast pocket if I manage to keep you alive? Or a one-way ticket on the partisan express if I don't?'

'Whenever we're alone you can say what the hell you want. At least on matters concerning my personal security. In fact I'm counting on it. On everything else – politics, government, racial policy – your stupid Republican opinions are of no interest to me and you'll have to keep your trap shut. As for what's in it for you, I should have thought that was obvious. You'll have free board and lodging, of course. And look around. We Germans live well here in Bohemia. Better than in Berlin. Good food, good wine, plenty of cigarettes and women – should your tastes run to more than one woman at a time. I know mine do. It's all to be had here in Prague. And if I am unlucky enough to be murdered by our own side, all I ask is that you present the evidence to Arthur Nebe or Walter Schellenberg. Between them they'll find some way of putting it in front of Martin Bormann.'

'All right, General. But here's my price. That you have to listen, now, to some of those stupid Republican views that you mentioned. The ones regarding politics and government and racial policy you said are of no interest to you. I'll say my piece and you listen. And when I've done, I'll do what you ask. I'll be your detective.'

Heydrich's eyes narrowed. I preferred his profile. When you saw his profile it meant he wasn't looking at you. When he looked at you it was only too easy to feel like the helpless prey of some deadly animal. It was a face without expression behind which some ruthless calculation was in progress. He flicked away his half-smoked cigarette and glanced at the Rolex on his wrist.

'All right. You've got five minutes. But it won't do any good, you know. When the panzers have finished doing their work in Russia what you say now will seem quite irrelevant. Even to you,

Gunther. Even to you. We'll make a Nazi of you yet.'

After lunch Heydrich and Generals Frank, Henlein, Hildebrandt and von Eberstein, a couple of colonels, and three of the adjutants convened a meeting in the castle library, leaving me and some others to amuse ourselves. Which is probably overstating what I was likely to do.

I was feeling tired, which was a combination of good wine and the adrenalin that was still in my blood after telling Heydrich what I really thought about his aim of Germanizing the Czech population, as well as several words on what was happening in the Ukraine. True to his word Heydrich listened for exactly five minutes, after which he walked silently back to the house leaving me feeling like a novitiate toreador who has just taunted his first bull. Perhaps I was still a little suicidal. It's the only possible explanation for what I'd done.

For a while I contemplated returning to my room and having a sleep; I also contemplated returning to the Imperial Hotel and spending what remained of my life with Arianne, but I was unable to find Klein or anyone who could organize me a car and, mindful of the warm sunshine, I went for a walk in the castle grounds instead.

Naturally, I was unnerved by how much Heydrich already seemed to know about Arianne. But, more importantly, I was already regretting my candour with him, which I attributed to the amount of alcohol I had consumed during lunch. And I asked myself how long it would be before a couple of SS guards came and fetched me for execution at some pit that was even now being dug in the adjacent forest. That was surely one advantage of living in the countryside: there was always plenty of space to bury a body.

Half-convinced that this was to be my fate, I found myself heading out of the front gates, smiling a nervous smile at the stone-faced sentry, and then setting off up the fairy-tale road in the general direction of the Upper Castle. This wasn't exactly an escape but I needed to be away from my so-called colleagues.

Thinking about escape I got to wondering about Ferdinand Bloch-Bauer, the Jewish sugar merchant whose estate this had once been. Had the statues been placed at the gates by him, or the aristocrat who had owned the house before? And where was he now? England? America? Switzerland? Or was he one of those unfortunate Czech Jews who'd fled to France thinking it was safe there only to find it overrun with Nazis in 1940? Time would tell who had been luckier – Ferdinand or his late wife, Adele.

Further along the quiet road I came in sight of the Orthodox chapel, and as I rounded the bend I saw the matching pink gateway of the Upper Castle and, walking toward me, another SS officer – a General whom I recognized from lunch but whose name eluded me. I wasn't wearing a cap or belts and neither was he, which meant I was able to forgo a salute. All the same I came to attention as he got nearer. I'd irritated enough SS generals for one day.

Even in uniform this General was a poor example of the master race. A bespectacled Himmler type with thinning hair, a wide mouth and a double chin, he was one of those pale, bloodless Nazis that reminded me of a very cold fish on a very white plate. Nevertheless, he smiled and stopped to talk, rippling his fingers in the air as though he was playing the upper register of a church organ as he tried to remember who I was.

'Ah yes, now you're—'

'Hauptsturmführer Gunther, sir.'

'Yes. Now I have it. You're the Police Commissar from Berlin, are you not? The Kripo detective.'

'That's right, sir.'

'I'm Jury, Doctor Hugo Jury. No reason why you should remember me either, especially after a lunch like that, eh? I'll say one thing for our new Reichsprotector, he knows how to entertain. That's the best lunch I've eaten in God knows how long.'

Jury was an Austrian, his accent – or rather his vocabulary – unmistakably Viennese.

'Walk with me for a while if you will, Captain. I'd like to hear more about the exciting life of a real Berlin detective.'

'If you like, sir. But there's not much to tell. I'm forty-three years old. I got my school certificate but didn't go to university. The war got in the way and then there didn't seem to be much call for a degree when there was a more urgent call to make a living and earn some money. So I joined the police and got married to a woman who died almost immediately afterward. Influenza they called it, but these days I'm not so sure. A lot of different illnesses got swept into that bin by a lot of overworked doctors and by some who were maybe not so much overworked as just inexperienced or even incompetent.'

'And you'd be absolutely right to have doubts. I should know. You see, I'm not one of these legal doctors we seem to be overrun with these days. I'm a medical man. I took my degree in 1911 and the chances are that I was one of those overworked, inexperienced and very possibly incompetent doctors you were talking about. During the influenza epidemic I remember sleeping for less than four hours a night. Hardly a recipe for good medical care, is it? Throughout the Twenties I was a specialist in tuberculosis. TB's one of those infectious diseases that present a lot of symptoms that are common to influenza. Indeed, I've sometimes thought that what we thought was a flu virus was actually pneumonia brought on by a massive outbreak of TB. But that's another story.'

'I'd like to hear it sometime.'

'If I may ask: How old was she? Your wife?'

'Twenty-two.'

'I'm sorry. That's young. Very young. And you've never remarried?'

'Not so far, sir. Most women don't seem to find my being a Berlin detective as exciting as you.'

'I've been married for almost thirty years and I can't imagine what I'd have done without my wife, Karoline.'

'You'll forgive me for saying so, sir, but I can't imagine you're an SS general because you're a doctor, sir.'

'No. I'm the District Leader of Moravia. And head of the Party Liaison Office in Prague. Before the war I was deputy leader of the Nazi Party in Austria. And if all of that sounds important, well, it isn't. Not any longer. Not since General Heydrich took over. I had hoped to persuade the Leader to break up the Protectorate in order that Moravia could become a separate state. Which is really what it's always been. But that isn't going to happen. Or so I've been told. I had also hoped to be able to discuss the matter with Heydrich, but one of his minions told me that this wouldn't be possible. Which leaves me rather wondering why I bothered to come along on this little weekend. In the circumstances, I'm surprised that I was asked at all.'

'That makes two of us, sir. General Heydrich and I were never what you might call close. Then again, one hesitates to decline such an invitation.'

'Quite so.'

By now we were about halfway back down the road to the Lower Castle and during our stroll no traffic had passed us, not even a man on a bicycle or a horse. Somewhere in the distance shots were being fired; presumably one of Heydrich's guests was trying to bag something for the pot. There were certainly plenty of pheasants about. Up ahead we saw Captain Kuttner standing in the Lower Castle gateway; and seeing us, he threw down his cigarette and ran toward us.

He was light on his toes; but there was also something vaguely girlish about the elbows-out way he ran.

'I loathe this little bastard,' murmured Doctor Jury. 'This is the cunt who told me I wasn't going to be able to have any time with General Heydrich.' Jury let out a sigh. 'Just look at him. Little fucker.'

'Hmm.'

'Like all of the General's henchmen he's a bit of a golem. Except that he's a German, of course. The original Golem of Prague was—'

'Jewish. Yes, I know.'

'Like his master.' Doctor Jury smiled. 'Rabbi Loew that is. Not General Heydrich.'

Kuttner clicked his heels and bowed a curt little bow. 'General,' he said. 'Captain. I regret I forgot to inform you both that for security reasons if you leave the grounds of the Lower Castle you will need a password to get back in.'

'And that is?' asked Doctor Jury.

'Lohengrin.'

'Very appropriate.'

'Sir?'

'The new king has assembled all of the German tribes in order to expel the Hungarians from his dominions,' said Doctor Jury. 'That's the plot of Wagner's opera. Or at least, that's how it begins.'

'Oh. I didn't know. Unlike you, sir, I don't go to the opera very often. In fact, hardly at all.'

'Hmm. Waste of a life.'

'Sir?'

'You seem to be as ignorant as you are stupid,' said Jury. Then he smiled at me, bowed slightly, and said: 'Nice talking to you, Captain Gunther.'

He walked quickly down toward the sentry box and then, having uttered the password, passed through the gate leaving me alone with Captain Kuttner.

'Bastard,' said Kuttner. 'Did you hear what he said? How unbelievably rude.'

'I wouldn't let it bother you, Captain. I don't much like opera either. Especially Wagner. There's something about Wagner that's just too piss-German, too fucking Bavarian for a Prussian like me. I like my music to be every bit as vulgar as I am myself. I like a bit of innuendo and stocking top when a woman's singing a song.'

Kuttner smiled. 'Thanks,' he said. 'But the real reason why Doctor Jury likes opera so much is every bit as vulgar as you describe. Rumour has it that he's been having an affair with a young singer at the Deutsches Oper in Berlin. Rather an attractive creature by the name of Elisabeth Schwarzkopf. And that would be vulgar enough were it not for the fact that she's also singing a duet with Doctor Goebbels. At least, that's what General Heydrich says.'

'Then it must be true.'

'Yes, that's what I thought.'

'General Heydrich always knows our dirtiest little secrets.'

'Oh God, I hope not.'

'Well, he certainly knows mine,' I said. 'You see, after lunch we went for a short walk in the castle grounds and I made the mistake of reminding him exactly what they are, just in case he'd forgotten.'

'I hardly think that can be true. Not if he's appointed you as his new bodyguard.' Kuttner lit a cigarette. 'Is it true? That you're going to be his detective?'

'I had thought I might have been arrested by now. So it would seem so.'

'Congratulations.'

'I'm not so sure about that.'

'You're right, it won't be easy. But he's fair, you know. And a good man to have on your side. I don't know what would have happened to my SS career if he hadn't taken me on. By the way, how's your stomach for flying?'

'Not good.'

'What a pity. The General insists on flying himself to Berlin and Rastenburg. Frankly, I'm always terrified. He thinks he's a much better pilot than he really is. He's had several crashes.'

'That's a comforting thought.' I shrugged.

'Perhaps we'll get lucky and end up in Scotland. Like Hess.'

'Yes. Quite.' Kuttner laughed. 'Still, I hate to think what would happen if we ever flew into some real trouble.'

'As a matter of fact that's what I was doing just now. Looking for trouble. I thought I'd get out of the house and scout the area.'

Kuttner winced, noticeably.

'The lie of the land, so to speak,' he said.

'Yes. Generally, trouble sort of comes looking for me, so I don't have to venture too far. I've always been lucky that way.'

'Quite a few of us in the SS have been lucky that way, don't you think?' Kuttner sighed a faint sigh of regret. 'With trouble. Frankly, I've had a bit of a rough summer.'

'You've been east, too, huh?'

Kuttner nodded. 'How did you know?'

I shrugged. 'I look at you and maybe I see something of myself.'

'Yes. That must be it.'

'Where were you posted?'

'Riga.'

'I was in Minsk.'

'How was that?'

'Loathsome. And Riga?'

'The same. And really quite unnecessary, a lot of it. You go to war, you expect to kill people. I was almost looking forward to it; to being in action. When one is young one has such romantic

197

ideas of what war is like. But it was nothing like that, of course.'

'No. It never is.'

Kuttner tried to smile, but the part he needed inside himself to make the smile work properly was broken. He knew it. And I knew it.

'It's an odd state of affairs, don't you think, when a man feels guilty for doing his duty and obeying orders?' He took a sharp drag of the cigarette he was smoking as if he hoped it might suddenly kill him. 'Not that guilt even begins to cover the way I feel.'

'Believe me, Captain, I know exactly how you feel.'

'Do you? Yes. I can see that you do. It's in your eyes.'

'And that's the reason you're not sleeping?'

'Can you?' Kuttner shook his head. 'I don't think I'll ever sleep, properly, again. Not ever. Not in this life.'

'Talk about it now, if it makes you feel any better.'

'Does it make you feel any better? To talk about it?'

'Not much. I talked about it once, quite recently, to an American journalist. And I felt a little better about it. I felt that it was at least a start.'

Kuttner nodded and then dredged up something from his memory. I didn't have to wait long.

'When you mentioned scouting the area, it made me think of something. Something awful. We were on our way through Poland. This was before our assignment in Riga. We had stopped at a town called Chechlo. It's a broken-down, shit-on-your-shoes, nowhere sort of place with a lot of drooling peasants whose tongues are too big for their mouths. But I don't suppose I shall ever forget it now; not for as long as I live. We had been burning down Polack villages for no real reason that I could see. Certainly there was no military necessity in it. We were just throwing our weight around like brutes. Some of my men were drunk and nearly all of them were animals. Anyway, we came across a troop of Polish boy scouts. The oldest of them couldn't have been more than sixteen and the youngest perhaps as young as twelve. And my commanding officer ordered me to put all of them up against a wall and shoot them. Shoot them all. They were in uniform, he said and we have orders to shoot anyone in uniform who hasn't surrendered. I said they were just schoolboys who didn't know any better because they didn't speak German, but he didn't want to know. Orders are orders, he said, get on with it. I remember their mothers screaming at me to stop. Yes, I'll always remember that. I wake up sometimes still hearing them beg me to stop. But I didn't. I had my orders. So I carried them out, you see. And that's all there is to it. Except it isn't, of course. Not by a long way.'

After several stiff drinks I can talk to anyone, even to myself. But mostly I was drinking so that I could talk to Heydrich's other guests. I like to talk.

199

Talking is something you need to do if you're ever going to encourage a man to talk back at you. And you need a man to talk a little if he's ever going to say something of interest. Men don't trust other men who don't say much, and for the same reason they don't trust men who don't drink. You need a drink to say the wrong thing, and sometimes, saying the wrong thing can be exactly the right thing to say. I don't know if I was expecting to hear anything as romantic as a confession to an attempted murder, or even a desire to see Heydrich dead. After all, I felt that way about him myself. It was just talk, a little bread on the water to bring the fish around. And the alcohol helped. It helped me to talk and to anaesthetize myself against the more revolting chat that came my way. But some of my colleagues were just revolting. As I glanced around the library it was like looking at a menagerie of unpleasant animals – rats, jackals, vultures, hyenas – who had sat for some bizarre group portrait.

It's hard to say exactly who was the worst of the bunch, but I didn't speak to Lieutenant Colonel Walter Jacobi for very long before I was itching all over and counting my fingers. The deputy head of the SD in Prague was a deeply sinister figure with – he told me – an interest in magic and the occult. It was a subject I knew a little about, having investigated a case involving a fake medium a few years back. We talked about that and we talked about Munich, which was where he was from; we talked about him studying law at the universities of Jena, Tübingen and Halle – which seemed like a lot of law; and we even talked about his father, who was a bookseller. But all the time we were talking I was trying to get over the fact that with his Charlie Chaplin moustache, his wire-framed glasses and his praying-mantis personality, Jacobi reminded me, obscenely, of what might have resulted if Hitler and Himmler had been left alone in the same bedroom: Jacobi was a Hitler–Himmler hybrid.

Equally unpleasant to talk to was Hermann Frank, the tall thin SS general from the Sudetenland who'd been passed over to succeed von Neurath as the new Reichsprotector. Frank had a glass eye, having lost the real one in a fight at school in Carlsbad, which seemed to indicate an early propensity to violence. It was the right eye that was fake, I think, but with Frank you had the idea he might have changed it around just to keep you guessing. Frank had a low opinion of Czechs, although as things turned out they had an even lower opinion of him: five thousand people filled the courtyard of Pankrac Prison in the centre of Prague to see him hanged the old Austrian Empire way one summer's day in 1946.

'They're a greedy barbarous people,' he told me candidly. 'I don't feel in the least bit Czech. The best thing that ever happened to me was to be born in the German-speaking part of the country, otherwise I'd be speaking their filthy

Slavic language now, which is nothing more than a bastardized form of Russian. It's a language for animals, I tell you. Do you know that it's possible to speak a whole sentence in Czech without using a single vowel?'

Surprised at this startling display of hatred I blinked and said, 'Oh? Like what, for example?'

Frank thought for a moment and then repeated some words in Czech which might or might not have had some vowels only I didn't feel like looking inside his mouth to see if he was hiding any.

'It means "stick a finger through your throat",' he said. 'And every time I hear a Czech speak, that's exactly what I want to do to them.'

'All right. You hate them. I get the picture. And losing your eye at school like that must have been pretty tough. It explains a lot, I guess. I went to a pretty tough school myself and there are some boys I might like to get even with one day. Then again, probably not. Life's too short to care, I think. And now you're in such an important position, sir – the police leader in Bohemia, effectively the second most powerful man in the country – well, that's the part I don't understand at all, sir. Why do you hate the Czechs so much, General?'

Frank straightened absurdly. It was almost as if he was coming to attention before answering – an effect enhanced by the fact that he was wearing spurs on his boots, which seemed an odd affectation to me, even in Heydrich's country home, which had stables, with horses in them. Pompously, he said:

'As Germans it's our duty to hate them. It was the failure of the Czech banks that helped to precipitate the financial crisis that brought about the Great Depression. Yes, it's the Czech bankers we can thank for that disaster.'

Resisting my first instinct, which was to shiver with disgust as if Frank had vomited onto my boots, I nodded politely.

'I always thought that was because our economy was built on American loans,' I said. 'And when they came due our own German banks failed.'

Frank was shaking his head, which was full of grey hair combed straight back so that the top of his head seemed to be in a line with the tip of his longish nose. It wasn't the biggest nose in the room so long as Heydrich was around, but at the same time you wouldn't have been surprised to see it pointing out the way at a crossroads.

'Take it from me, Gunther,' he said. 'I do know what I'm talking about. I know this damnable country better than anyone in the fucking room.'

Frank spoke with some vigour and he was looking at Heydrich as he did, which made me wonder if there was not some grudge he nursed for his new master.

I was glad when Frank walked away to fetch himself another drink, leaving me with the impression that spending an eternity with men like

Heydrich, Jacobi and Frank was the nearest thing to being in hell that I could think of.

But the Knight's Cross with Oak Leaves and Berries – for that matter the whole damned tree – for the curling turd of the evening went to Colonel Doctor Hans Geschke, a 34-year-old lawyer from Frankfurt on the Oder who was chief of the Gestapo in Prague. While studying in Berlin, he'd seen my name in the newspapers, and in spite of our differences in rank, this was a good enough reason for him to try to make common cause with me. Which is another way of saying he needed someone to patronize.

'After all,' he explained, 'we're both policemen you and I, doing a difficult job, in very difficult circumstances.'

'So it would seem, sir.'

'And I like to keep abreast of ordinary crime,' he said. 'Here in Prague we have to deal with more serious stuff than some Fritz slicing his wife up with a broken beer bottle.'

'There's not so much of that around, sir. Beer bottles are in rather short supply in Berlin.'

He wasn't listening.

'You should come in and see us very soon, at the Pecek Palace. That's in the Bredovska district of the city.'

'A palace, eh? It sounds a lot grander than the Alex, sir.'

'Oh no. To be quite honest with you it's hard to see how it was ever a palace except in some dark corner of Hades. Even the executive rooms have very little charm.'

Geschke's was a waxwork's expressionless face. Captain Kuttner had said that at the Pecek Palace Geschke was known as 'Babyface', but this could only have been among people who knew some very frightening babies with duelling scars on their left cheeks. Geschke was one of those factory-manufactured Nazis they turned out like unpainted Meissen porcelain: pale, cold, hard, and best handled with extreme care.

'I haven't seen much of the city yet,' I said. 'But it does seem rather infernal.'

Geschke grinned. 'Well, we do our best in that respect. So long as they fear us, they do what they're told. We mustn't let these Czechos make fools of us, you see. We have to be the master in our own house, so we can't afford to overlook any wrong. We really can't. You let them get away with one thing, there will be no end to it. But tell me, Gunther. In the Weimar Republic, when you had a suspect at the Alex and he refused to cooperate, what did you do? How on earth did you manage?'

'We never hit anyone, if that's what you're driving at, sir. We weren't allowed to. The Prussian Police Regulations forbade it. Oh, some cops smacked a suspect around now and then, but the bosses didn't like that. We got results because we got the evidence. Once you have the evidence it's hard for a man not to sign a confession. Find the evidence and everything else follows. We were good at that:

finding evidence. The Berlin Detective Service was, for a while, the envy of the world and its backbone was the police commissars.'

'But weren't you at all frustrated by the stupidities of Prussian justice? Sometimes it seemed to be absurd that penal servitude for life rarely ever lasted longer than twelve years. And that so many criminals deserving of their death sentences were reprieved by the Prussian government. For example, those two Jews, Saffran and Kipnik. Remember them?'

I shrugged. 'Honestly? I can think of many others I'd like to see under the falling axe before those two. Why, just a few months ago there was the S-Bahn murderer case. Fellow named Paul Ogorzow who killed six or seven women and tried to kill as many more again. Now, *he* deserved his fate.'

'Is it true that he was a Party member?'

'Yes.'

'Unbelievable.'

'Lots of other people thought so, too. That's probably why it took so long to catch him. But what you were saying is absolutely right. We can't afford to overlook any wrong. Especially when it's a wrong committed by our own, don't you think?'

'Ah, now there speaks a true policeman.'

'I like to think so, sir.'

'Well, if there's anything I can do to help you, Gunther, in your new capacity as the General's personal detective, then please let me know.'

Geschke raised his glass and bowed. 'Anything to help General Heydrich and keep him safe for the new Germany.'

'Thank you, sir.'

I glanced around the room and tried to picture which, if any, of the General's guests might actually try to poison him and found that in the new Germany it wasn't so hard. In a room full of murderers anything seemed possible.

About halfway through this unforgettable evening Major Dr Ploetz, Heydrich's First Adjutant and number one myrmidon, turned on the library radio so that we could listen to Hitler's speech from the Sports Palast, in Berlin.

'Gentlemen, please,' he said, while the radio was warming up. 'If I could ask you to be silent.'

'Thank you, Hans-Achim,' said Heydrich, as if he and not the Leader had been at the microphone. And then solemnly, as the sound of the Sports Palast crept into that room, he intoned: 'The Leader.'

It was typically thoughtful of Heydrich. I suppose he thought it would be a treat for those of us who were feeling a little homesick. And it was: a bit like hearing my mother reading the old story of how the bad boy Friedrich terrorized a lot of animals and people. It remained to be seen if the Third Reich's ranting answer to bad Friedrich might yet be bitten by the same dog that had eaten the naughty boy's sausages but, for me at any rate, there was always the hope that he would be. It was hard to think of a treat half as enjoyable as the idea of the Leader being bitten by a greedy dog. His own, perhaps.

In the corridor outside the library a man was on the telephone, and I poked my head out of the door to see who among Heydrich's guests had dared to make or take a call in the middle of Hitler's speech. Whoever he was I certainly didn't blame him. Even at the best of times the Leader was always too loud for me. Probably he'd honed his oratorical skills in the trenches, during bombardments.

Not that you couldn't have heard every rasping word of the broadcast in the corridor. The radio was an AEG Super Orchestra as big as a Polish peasant's barn, and with the speech playing at full volume there was no chance of not hearing it almost anywhere in the house. Probably you could have heard the speech at the centre of the earth.

'No, you did the right thing in calling me here, Sergeant Soppa.'

The man speaking was Oscar Fleischer, head of the Gestapo's Resistance Section in Prague – the same man who had been taunted so infamously by one of the Three Kings.

'All right, I'll be there in half an hour. Just don't let the bastard die until I get there. He did? So it was him after all.'

Fleischer caught my eye and turned his back on me.

'No, no, I'm perfectly certain he'll want to know. Yes, of course I'll tell him. I'll do it right now. Yes. Goodbye.'

Fleischer replaced the telephone and, grinning excitedly, scribbled something on a piece of paper before handing it to Captain Pomme and then running upstairs, two steps at a time.

I lit a cigarette and drifted out into the corridor next to Captain Pomme.

'Good news?' I asked.

'I should say so,' said the adjutant and went back into the library without further eludication.

I was about to follow when I glanced out the window above the telephone and had a good view of Heydrich's other adjutants – Kuttner and Kluckholn – standing under the flagpole on the front lawn. Although the window was open, I couldn't hear what was said – not with the radio in the library so loud – but it was plain that a heated argument was in progress, indeed that the two men were on the edge of exchanging blows. I was about to go outside and play Saturday night policeman when Kuttner strode angrily up the drive toward the gatehouse. A moment later Fleischer, wearing belts and his cap, galloped downstairs again and went straight out the front door as a car drew up and then took him away in a furious spray of gravel.

A little disappointed that I was not going to break up a fight between two SS officers, I turned my attention back to what was being broadcast in the library.

Hitler's speech was the traditional opening of the Winter Relief Campaign. This was the Nazi Party's annual charitable drive to provide food and shelter for the less fortunate during the coming winter months and was as near as it ever got to real socialism. Failure to donate was not an option. People who forgot to donate were quite likely to find their names in the local newspaper. Or sometimes, worse.

Hitler's oratorical style for the Winter Relief speech was calculated to impress rather more than the actual content and usually it wasn't so much what he said as the way he said it. But my normal reaction was that it was a little like listening to Emil Jannings recite a bit of cudgel verse, Caruso singing a song from a Silly Symphony or Mark Antony eulogizing a dead cat. This year it was different, however, as it soon became clear that there was more at stake than a few fat Germans going hungry in January. As well as the more predictable bromides about the glory of giving and being generous – something that was second nature to us Germans, of course – the Leader proceeded to make an announcement concerning the beginning of 'the great decisive battle of the coming year', which would be devastating to the enemy.

Now many of us in that library and in the country at large were already under the impression that 'the great decisive battle' was already as good as won. We had certainly been told as much by

Doctor Goebbels on several previous occasions. But here was Hitler more or less admitting that he'd bet the family silver on what was yet to happen, that he'd gambled all of our futures on something that was not a cast-iron certainty; and the upshot was that anyone listening to him now was left inescapably with the distinct idea that things in the East were not going entirely to plan for our hitherto invincible armed forces.

When the speech and the thunderous applause that greeted it in the Sports Palast had finally concluded and the AEG radio was, at last, turned off by Major Dr Ploetz, it was immediately apparent that there were several others in that library who had the same thought as me: someone in the government – Hitler himself, perhaps? – had woken up to the painful reality of just what Germany had undertaken to do in Russia. And this being the Third Reich of course, which was based on lies, it meant that things were probably much worse than we had been told.

Our sombre faces told the same grim story. Indeed, General von Eberstein, who was some big noise in the SS general staff, may actually have muttered some desperate imprecation to a God who was certainly some place else, if anywhere at all. General Hildebrandt, who was Heydrich's equivalent rank in Danzig, merely hurled his cigarette into the fireplace as if he was as disgusted with it as he was with everything else.

This might have been what prompted Heydrich

to say a few words, to resurrect our visible lack of enthusiasm. More likely it was Fleischer's handwritten note that Captain Pomme had handed him a few minutes earlier. Heydrich himself was grinning like he'd just eaten the last slice of honey-cake.

'Gentlemen,' he said. 'If I could have your attention for just a few more minutes. I've been given a note by Criminal Commissar Fleischer of the Gestapo, which contains some excellent news. As most of you know, since May of this year we've had two of the Three Kings – Josef Balaban and Josef Masin – in custody at Pankrac Prison, here in Prague. These are, of course, two of the three leaders of Czech terrorism here in Bohemia. However, the third king, Melchior, as we like to call him, has eluded us. Until now. It seems that one of our two prisoners – I don't know which, but somehow I feel sure that his name must be Josef – has agreed to cooperate with our inquiries and, finally, has revealed that Melchior's real name is Vaclav Moravek, formerly a captain in the Czech Army. We have already begun a search for him here in Prague and at his home town of Kolin, near Losany, and it is now expected that we shall shortly make an arrest.'

I felt oddly sick. It seemed that while we'd been stuffing ourselves with Veal Holstein and Leipziger Everything, a brave man had been tortured into revealing the name of the most wanted man in the Third Reich.

'Bravo,' said one of my brother officers, an Abwehr major named Thummel.

Others also present applauded this news, which seemed to please Heydrich no end, and there he might, and perhaps should, have left the matter. But full of his own importance, Heydrich continued to talk for several more minutes. He was not, however, a public speaker. Self-conscious and calculating, he lacked Hitler's common touch and rhetorical flourish. His voice was pitched too high to inspire men; worst of all, he used a string of big German words where one or two smaller ones would have worked better. Of course, this was typical of the Nazis, for whom language was often used to mask their own ignorance and stupidity – which they possessed in an inexhaustible supply – as well as to give their words the placebo effect of authority; like a doctor who has an impressive Latin name for what is wrong with you, but sadly not a cure.

Fortunately for everyone present, Captain Kuttner and Kritzinger the butler appeared with champagne and a tray of Bohemian glass flutes, and before long there was something of a party atmosphere in that library. I drank a glass without much pleasure and, when I thought I was un-observed, I slipped away onto the terrace and smoked a cigarette in the darkness. It felt like somewhere I belonged – a crepuscular world of creatures that hooted and howled and where one might hide to avoid larger predators.

After a while I glanced through the leaded library window and seeing no sign of Heydrich, I decided I might sneak off to bed. But I had not reckoned on Heydrich's study being immediately at the top of the first flight of stairs; the doors were open and he was seated behind his desk signing some papers under the cold bespectacled eye of Colonel Jacobi. Insouciantly I headed toward the north wing corridor and my room; but if I had hoped not to catch the General's eye I was quickly disappointed.

'Gunther,' he said, hardly looking up from his signature file. 'Come in.'

'Very well, sir.'

Entering Heydrich's study in the Lower Castle at Jungfern-Breschan I had the distinct feeling that I was in a smaller, more intimate version of the Leader's own study at the Reich Chancellery, and this would have been typical of Heydrich. Not that there was very much that was small or intimate about that room. The ceiling was about four metres high and there were marble relief columns on the walls, a fireplace as big as a Mercedes, and enough green carpet on the floor for a decent game of golf. The refectory-style desk had more glass protecting its smooth oak surface than a good-sized shop window. On this were a marble-urn lamp, a couple of telephones, a leather blotter, an ink-stand, and a brass model of a plane – quite possibly the same Siebel Fh 104 he used to fly himself to and from Berlin. In the arched window was a bronze bust of the Leader, and behind a throne-sized desk chair was a green silk wall-hanging with a gold German eagle holding onto a laurel wreath enclosing a swastika, as if it was something worth stealing.

Heydrich put down his fountain pen and leaned back in the chair.

'That girl back at your hotel,' he said. 'Arianne Tauber. Have you called her to tell her you won't be coming to see her tonight?'

'Not yet, sir.'

'Then don't. Have Klein drive you into Prague. I think I will be safe enough tonight, don't you?'

'If you say so sir.'

'Oh no. In future it's for you to say so. That was rather the point of your appointment. But I'm sure you'll get the hang of it. Meet me at Pecek Palace tomorrow morning at ten o' clock. I have a meeting there to coordinate the arrest of this Moravek fellow.'

'Very well, sir. And thank you.'

I may even have clicked my heels and bowed my head. Working for Heydrich was like being friendly with a vicious tom cat while you were looking around for the nearest mouse hole.

CHAPTER 13

Arianne was pleased to see me, of course, although not as pleased as I was to see her, in our bed, alone, naked and willing to use her body to help divert my thoughts from Heydrich, Jungfern-Breschan, the Three Kings and Pecek Palace. I told her nothing of my worries. Where Heydrich was concerned, it was best to know very little, as I was beginning to discover myself. What did I tell her as, exhausted by our love-making, we lay intertwined like two primitive figures carved from the same piece of antler-horn? Only that my duties kept me out of Prague, in Jungfern-Breschan, otherwise I should certainly have visited her at the Imperial Hotel before now.

'That's all right,' she said. 'Really, I'm quite happy here on my own. You've no idea how nice it is just to sit and read a book, or to walk around the city by myself.'

'I do,' I muttered. 'I can imagine, anyway.'

'I left a message for my brother. And there are plenty of other Germans in Prague I can talk to. As a matter of fact, this hotel is full of Germans. There's a very beautiful girl in a suite on the same floor as us who's having an affair with some SS general. And she's a Jew. Doesn't that sound romantic?'

'Romantic? It sounds dangerous.'

Arianne shrugged that off. 'Her name is Betty Kipsdorf and she's utterly sweet.'

'What's his name?'

'The general? Konrad something. He's more than twice her age but she says you really wouldn't know it.' She laughed. 'On account of the fact that he used to be a gymnastics teacher.'

I said I didn't know who that could be. And I didn't. I wasn't exactly on first-name terms with any SS generals, even the ones I knew.

'He's very vigorous, apparently. For a general. Me, I always say that if you want a job done and done properly it's a captain you want. Not some effete flamingo with clockwork heels.'

Flamingos were what the ranks called officers of the General Staff, a reference to the red stripes on their trouser legs.

'What do you know about flamingos?'

'You'd be surprised who we get through the doors of the Jockey Bar.'

'No. But I'm still surprised that you'd prefer a captain to one of them.'

'And perhaps a little suspicious.'

'That's probably no fault of yours.'

'We'd get on like a house on fire if you weren't a cop, don't you think so, Parsifal?'

'These are the times we live in, I'm afraid. All

217

sorts of things make me suspicious, angel. Two aces in a row. Double-sixes. A sure thing for the state lottery. A kind word or a compliment. Venus rising from the sea. I'm the kind of Fritz who's apt to look for a maker's mark on the scallop shell.'

'I might get insulted if I knew what any of that was about. After all, there's a little part of you that's still in me.'

'Now it's my turn to get insulted.'

'Don't be, Gunther. I enjoyed it, a lot. I think that maybe you underestimate yourself.'

'Perhaps. I might even call it an occupational hazard except that, so far, it's helped to keep me alive.'

'Is staying alive so very important to you?'

'No. Then again I've seen the alternatives, and at close quarters. In Russia. Or twenty years ago, back in the trenches.'

She gave me a little squeeze, the kind that feels like a wonderful sort of conjuring trick and that doesn't need any limbs. Whenever a woman holds me tight like that it's the best argument there is against the solipsistic idea that one can be truly certain only of the existence of one's own mind.

'How much more suspicious would you get if I said I'd fallen for you, Gunther?'

'You'd have to say it a lot for me to believe it might be true.'

'Maybe I will.'

'Yeah. Maybe. When you've said it the first time

we can review the situation. But right now it's just a hypothetical.'

'All right, I—'

She paused for a moment, uttering a sigh that was as unsteady as a whippet's hind leg as I nudged up deep against the edge of her latest thought.

'Go on. I'm listening.'

'It's true, Parsifal. I'm falling for you.'

'You're a long time in the air, angel. By now anyone else would have hit the ground.' I nudged into her again. 'Hard.'

'Damn you, Gunther.'

Her breath was hot in my ear except it sounded cold and erratic, like someone laughing silently.

I prompted her a little more and said, 'Go on. Let's hear what it sounds like.'

'All right. I love you. Satisfied?'

'Not by a long way. But I will be, if this keeps up.'

She hit me on the shoulder but there was pleasure on her face. 'You sadistic bastard.'

'I'm a Nazi. You said so yourself. Remember?'

'No, but you're also rather wonderful, Gunther. All the more so because you don't realize it. Since Karl, my husband, there have been other men. But you're the first man I've cared anything about since he died.'

'Stop talking.'

'Go ahead and make me.'

I didn't say anything. Conversation between us had become unnecessary. We didn't need speech to act out a story that many others had told before. It wasn't original but it felt like it was – an almost silent film that seemed both familiar and new. We were still performing our own highly stylized homage to German expressionism when the telephone rang on the bedside table.

'Leave it,' I said.

'Is that wise?'

'It sounds like trouble.'

It stopped ringing.

When our own motion picture finished, she got up to fetch one of my cigarettes.

I rolled onto my back and stared out of the window at the little pepper-pot dome on top of the building opposite.

The telephone started to ring again.

'I told you,' I said. 'It always rings again when it's trouble. Especially first thing in the morning, before breakfast.'

I picked up the receiver. It was Major Ploetz, Heydrich's first adjutant. He sounded shaken and angry.

'A car is coming to pick you up and bring you back here, immediately.'

'All right. What's up?'

'There's been a homicide,' said Ploetz. 'Here, at the Lower Castle.'

'A homicide? What kind of homicide?'

'I don't know. But you should be outside your hotel in fifteen minutes.'

And then he hung up.

For one glorious moment I allowed myself to hope it was Heydrich who was dead. That one of those officers and gentlemen of the SS and the SD, jealous of Heydrich's success, had shot him. Or perhaps there had been a machine-gun attack by Czech terrorists while Heydrich was out for his early morning ride in the countryside around Jungfern-Breschan. Perhaps even now there was a horse lying on top of his lifeless body.

And yet surely if it had been Heydrich who was dead, Ploetz would have said so. Ploetz wouldn't ever have used the phrase 'a homicide' for someone as important as his very own general. The victim had to be someone of lesser importance or else Ploetz would have said 'Heydrich has been murdered' or 'The General has been murdered' or 'There's been a catastrophe, General Heydrich has been assassinated.' A homicide didn't begin to cover the lexicon of words that would probably be used by the Nazis if ever Heydrich was unfortunate enough to meet with a well-deserved but premature death.

'Is it?'

'Is it what?' I answered her absently.

'Trouble,' said Arianne.

'I have to go back to Jungfern-Breschan, immediately. There's been a death.'

'Oh? Who?'

'I don't know. But I'm sure it's not Heydrich.'

'Some detective you are.' She shrugged. 'Well, it certainly won't be the gardener who's dead if they want you to go back immediately. It must be someone important.'

'I can dream, I suppose.'

Fifteen minutes later I was washed and dressed and standing outside the Imperial Hotel as a black sedan drew up. The driver wearing an SS uniform – it wasn't Klein – stepped smartly out of the car, saluted, opened the door, and pulled down the middle row of seats because there were two men wearing plain clothes who were already seated in the back.

They were well-fed, hefty types, probably the kind who couldn't run very fast but who could hand out a beating without breaking the skin on their knuckles.

'Commissar Gunther?'

The man who spoke had a head as big as a stonemason's bucket but the face carved on the front of it was small, like a child's. The eyes were cold and hard, even a little sad, but the mouth was a vicious tear.

'That's right.'

A grappling iron of a hand came across the back of the seat.

'Kurt Kahlo,' said the man. 'Criminal Assistant to Inspector Willy Abendschoen, from Prague Kripo.'

He looked at the other man and grinned, unkindly.

'And this is Inspector Zennaty, of the Czech

Police. He's only along for the sake of appearances, aren't you, sir? After all, technically speaking this is a Czech matter, isn't it?'

Zennaty shook my hand but he didn't say anything. He was thin and hawklike, with shadowy eyes and a hair style that looked like an extension of a short stubbly beard.

'I'm afraid our Czecho friend doesn't speak much German, do you, Ivan?'

'Not very much,' said Zennaty. 'Sorry.'

'But he's all right, is our Ivan.' Kahlo patted Zennaty on the back of the hand. 'Aren't you, Ivan?'

'Very much.'

'Mister Abendschoen would have attended himself,' said Kahlo, 'but almost everyone in Prague is now looking for this Moravek fellow. General Heydrich has made his apprehension the number one police priority in the whole of the Protectorate.'

I nodded. 'So who's dead? They didn't say.'

'One of General Heydrich's adjutants. A captain named Kuttner, Albert Kuttner. Did you know him at all, sir?'

'I met him for the first time yesterday,' I said. 'How about you?'

'I only met him a couple of times. To me, one adjutant looks like another adjutant.'

'I'd expect this one might look a bit different now, don't you?'

'Good point.' Kahlo's eyebrows were almost

permanently at an angle, like a sad clown's, but somehow he managed to raise them even higher up his forehead.

'How about you?' I asked Zennaty politely. 'Did you know Captain Kuttner?'

'Not very much,' said Zennaty.

Kahlo grinned at this, which helped persuade Zennaty to stare out of the window. It was a kinder view than Kahlo's sneering, ugly mug.

We drove east for a while, to Kripo headquarters in Carl Maria von Weber Strasse, where Zennaty briefly left the car and Kahlo informed me he had gone to fetch an evidence box. He and Zennaty had been across the river at the Justice Ministry when Abendschoen, Kahlo's boss, had telephoned telling him to pick me up and then go to Jungfern-Breschan.

After a few minutes Zennaty returned and we drove north again.

To see Prague in the autumn of 1941 was to see a crown of thorns with extra points, as painted by Lukas Cranach. A city of church spires it certainly was. Even the spires had smaller spires of their own, the way little carrots sometimes grow bigger ones. These lent the unfeasibly tall Bohemian capital an unexpectedly sharp, jagged feel. Everywhere you looked it was like seeing a Swiss halberd in an umbrella stand. This sense of medieval discomfort was accentuated by the city's omnipresent statuary. All over Prague there were statues of Jesuit bishops spearing pagans, heavily muscled Titans stabbing each other with swords, agonized Christian saints horribly martyred, or ferocious wild animals tearing each other to pieces. To that extent Prague appeared to suit the cruelty and violence of Nazism in a way Berlin never did. The Nazis seemed to belong here – especially the tall, spindly figure of Heydrich, whose austere pale face reminded me of a flayed-alive saint. The red Nazi flags that were everywhere looked more like blood dripping down the buildings that they hung on; the polished bayonets on German rifles at sentry points across the city glittered with an extra steely edge; and goose-stepping jackboots on the cobbles of the Charles Bridge seemed to have a louder crunch, as if beating down the hopes of the Czechs themselves.

That was shameful if you were a German but worse if you were a Czech, like the impotent Inspector Zennaty. Worst of all if you were one of Prague's Jews. Prague was home to one of the largest communities of Jews in Europe, and even now there were still plenty of them left for the Nazis to kick around. Kick them around they duly did; and it remained to be seen if the legendary Golem that was reputed to dwell in the city's Old New Synagogue would, as legend supposed, emerge from the attic one night and climb down the outside wall to avenge the persecution of Prague's Jews. Part of me hoped that he had already put in an appearance at Jungfern-Breschan and that Captain Kuttner's unexplained death was just the beginning. If things were anything like the silent movie called *The Golem* I'd seen not long after the Great War, then we Germans were in for some fun.

Twenty minutes later the car stopped outside the front door of the Lower Castle and we went inside.

Kritzinger, the butler, ushered Kahlo, Zennaty and me upstairs to Heydrich's study, where he was waiting, impatiently, with Major Ploetz and Captain Pomme. Heydrich and Pomme were wearing fencing jerkins and it was clear from their flushed and still-perspiring faces that they had not long finished their absurd sport.

Since I was the only one wearing uniform I saluted and then introduced Kahlo and Zennaty.

Heydrich looked coldly at Zennaty. 'You can wait downstairs,' he told the Czech policeman.

Zennaty nodded curtly and left the room.

'You took your time getting here,' said Heydrich, sourly.

The remark appeared to be directed at me so I glanced at my watch and said, 'I received the call from Major Ploetz in my hotel just forty-five minutes ago. I came as quickly as I could, sir.'

'All right, all right.'

Heydrich's tone was testy. There was a cigarette in his hand. His hair looked dishevelled and uncombed.

'Well, you're here now, that's the main thing. You're here and you're in charge, d'you hear?

You're the experienced man in this situation. Incidentally, I don't want that fucking Czech involved at all. D'you hear? This is a German matter. I want this thing investigated quickly and discreetly, and solved before it can reach the ears of the Leader. I've every confidence in you, Gunther. If any man can solve this case, it's you. I've told everyone that you enjoy my complete confidence.'

'Thank you, sir,' I said, although this wasn't at all how I felt or indeed what he meant. I wasn't about to enjoy Heydrich's confidence for any longer than he took to say it.

'And that I expect everyone to cooperate fully with your inquiry. I don't care what you ask and who you upset. D'you hear? As far as I'm concerned everyone in this house is under suspicion.'

'Does that include you, sir?'

Heydrich's blue eyes narrowed, and for a moment I thought I'd gone too far and that he was going to bawl me out. I was relieved he wasn't holding a sword. I had gone too far, of course, and it was clear the two adjutants thought so too, but just for now, neither man was prepared to protest my insolence. Unpredictable as always, Heydrich took a deep breath and nodded, slowly.

'I don't see why not,' he said. 'If it helps. Anything that will get this sorted out as quickly as possible, before my tenure in this position descends into farce and I become a fucking laughing stock in Berlin.'

He shook his head and then stubbed out his cigarette, irritably.

'That this should happen now when we're just about to put paid to UVOD.'

'UVOD?' I shook my head. 'What's that?'

'UVOD? It's the Central Leadership of Home Resistance,' said Heydrich. 'A network of Czech terrorists.'

He leaned down on the desk with both fists and then hammered the glass surface hard enough for the model plane to shift several centimetres nearer the lamp. 'Damn it all.'

I lit a cigarette and drew down a lungful of smoke and blew it back at him hard, hoping it might help to distract him a little from what I was about to say and the way I meant to say it.

'Why don't you take it easy, General? This isn't helping me and it's certainly not helping you. Instead of beating up the furniture and biting my head off why don't you or whoever else has the best grip on the story tell me exactly what happened here? The whole once-upon-a-time in a town called Hamelin. And then I can do what I do.'

Heydrich looked at me and I sensed he knew I was taking advantage of him. Everyone else was looking at me too, as if surprised that I should dare to speak to the General in this way; but just as surprised that he should continue to hold off shouting me back into my shell. I was a bit surprised about that myself, but sometimes it can be interesting just how wide the door can open.

For a moment he bit his fingernails.

'Yes. You're absolutely right, Gunther. This isn't getting us anywhere. I suppose, well, it's a great shame that's all. Kuttner was a promising young officer.'

'Yes, he was,' said Pomme.

Heydrich looked at him strangely and then said, 'Why don't you fill in some of the details for the Commissar?'

'Yes sir. If you wish.'

'Mind if I sit down?' I said. 'Like any copper I listen better when I'm not thinking about my feet.'

'Yes, please gentlemen, be seated,' said Heydrich.

I picked a chair in front of the Leader's bust and, almost immediately, regretted it. I didn't care for Hitler staring at the back of my head. If ever he learned about what was at the back of my mind I was in serious trouble. I reached into my fart-catcher's pocket and took out my officer's diary. It was more or less the same kind of diary the Gestapo had found on Franz Koci's dead body in Kleist Park.

'If you don't mind,' I said to Pomme, 'I'll make some notes.'

Pomme shook his head. 'Why should I mind?'

I shrugged. 'No good reason.' I paused. 'Whenever you're ready, Captain Pomme.'

'Well, Albert, that's to say Captain Kuttner, was supposed to awaken me at six o'clock this morning. As usual. He awakens me, or Major Ploetz, or Captain Kluckholn, because it's our job to awaken the General at six-thirty. I suppose that's just the pecking order. Him being the fourth adjutant, you understand. However, this was no longer a satisfactory arrangement. Kuttner was never a good sleeper, and lately he's been dosing himself with a sleeping pill, which meant he started to oversleep in the morning. This made me late, and that made the General late. This morning was fairly typical in that respect. And anticipating some sort of a problem, I managed to awaken myself at six and then went to see if Kuttner was awake. He wasn't; or so it seemed at the time. I knocked on the door several times, without success. Again, that wasn't so very unusual. When he's taken a pill it can be a while before he can be roused. But after ten minutes I was still knocking without a reply and, well, I suppose I began to worry a little.'

'Couldn't you just have gone in there and shaken him awake?' I asked.

'I'm sorry, Gunther, I didn't make myself clear. He always locked his door. He was quite a nervous person, I think. Something to do with what happened to him in Latvia, he said. I don't know. Anyway, the door was locked and when I bent down to take a look through the keyhole I saw that the key was still in the lock.'

Pomme was a handsome little martinet, not much more than thirty years old, lugubrious, with a wide but narrow-lipped mouth. In his white fencing jerkin he resembled a nervous dentist.

'Having failed to awaken Kuttner I quickly

230

awoke the General and then went to find Herr Kritzinger, to see if there was perhaps some other means of gaining entry to Kuttner's room.'

'What time was this?' I asked.

'It would have been about six-forty-five,' said Pomme. He glanced at the butler, who was the only man in the room who remained standing, for verification.

The butler looked at me. 'That is correct, sir,' he said. 'I went to find the spare key. I keep spare keys for all of the doors in my safe. I noticed the time on the clock on my mantelpiece when I was opening the safe. I went back upstairs with the room keys, but I was unsuccessful in using the spare to push the key out of the lock so that I could open Captain Kuttner's door from the outside.'

I considered telling him about the key-turners we'd used at the Adlon Hotel for just such a situation but it hardly seemed relevant now.

'I then instructed one of the footmen to go and find the gardener,' said Kritzinger, 'and have him fetch a ladder to take a look through the window and perhaps open it from outside the house.'

'Meanwhile I resumed knocking on the door,' explained Pomme. 'And calling Captain Kuttner's name. And by now I was late for my fencing bout with the General.'

Heydrich nodded. 'Every morning I fence with one of the adjutants before breakfast. Kuttner was the best – he was outstanding with the

231

sabre – but, of late, he had too much on his mind to be competitive. This morning when I arrived at the gymnasium there was no sign of Pomme, so I went to look for him and met the footman who'd been sent to fetch the gardener. When I asked him if he'd seen Captain Pomme he explained the situation. That would have been around six-fifty-five. So I went to see if I could assist and found Pomme still knocking on Kuttner's door. It was now seven o'clock. I suppose I also became a little concerned for Kuttner's safety. The fact is, he'd been rather depressed of late. And I ordered Pomme and Kritzinger to break down the door. Which they proceeded to do.'

'That can't have been very easy,' I said. 'The doors here are thick.'

Instinctively Pomme rubbed his shoulder. 'It wasn't. It took us all of five or ten minutes.'

'And when the door was open what did you see?'

'Very little,' said Pomme. 'The curtains were drawn and the room was quite dark.'

'Was the window closed or open?'

'Closed, sir,' said Kritzinger. 'The General ordered me to pull back the curtains so that we could see and I noticed then that the window was closed and bolted.'

'Then I called Kuttner's name,' said Heydrich. 'And hearing no reply I approached the bed. It was immediately clear to us all from his position that something was very wrong. He was still wearing his uniform and his sleep seemed abnormally sound to me. What with the sound of the door coming down and our voices, it didn't seem right that he shouldn't even stir. So I pressed my fingers on the side of his neck to look for a pulse and I noticed straight away that his skin was cold to the touch. Colder than it ought to have been. And then I noticed that there was no pulse. No pulse at all.'

'Have you been trained to take a pulse like that?' I asked.

Heydrich frowned. 'Why do you ask?'

'It's a straightforward question, sir. You'd be amazed how many dead men turn up fit and well after someone has taken their pulse and pronounced them dead.'

'Very well, yes, I have. During my Luftwaffe training at the Werneuchen Aerodrome, in 1939, I received basic training in first aid. And again in May 1940. That was in Stavanger.' He shook his head. 'There's no question about it, Gunther. The man was quite dead. That would have been at approximately ten minutes past seven.'

Kritzinger was nodding.

'What happened next?' I asked him.

'The General ordered me to telephone for an ambulance.'

'Where did you call?'

'The Bulovka Hospital is the nearest,' he said. 'It's on the north-east outskirts of Prague, about ten kilometres away.'

'I drive past it every morning,' said Heydrich.

'A Czech doctor called Honek attended,' said Kritzinger. 'In fact he's still downstairs.'

'And what did you do?' I asked Pomme.

'General Heydrich told me to go and fetch General Jury right away.'

'Why?'

'Because he's a doctor, too,' said Pomme.

'Yes, I remember now. He was a specialist in tuberculosis, I believe. Before he joined the SS.' I nodded. 'So, you went to fetch him. What happened then?'

'I'm afraid he was feeling rather the worse for wear after last night. It was at least another fifteen minutes before he was dressed and on the scene.'

I looked at Heydrich. 'Meanwhile, sir, you were still in the room with Kuttner, isn't that right?'

'Yes.'

'What did you do while you were waiting for Doctor Jury?'

'Let's see now. I opened the window, to get some air. I was feeling a little queasy for some reason. No, that's not fair. He was a friend of mine. I lit a cigarette, to calm my nerves. But I tossed the end out of the window when I was finished. The crime scene is substantially uncontaminated.' He shook his head and then ran a thin hand through his short hair. 'I can't think of anything else. After a while Doctor Jury turned up with Pomme. The doctor was, as Pomme says, very hung over. But not so hung over that he was incapable of pronouncing poor Kuttner dead. After that I had

234

Ploetz call you and the local police right away. At approximately seven-thirty.'

'Where's Doctor Jury now?' I asked.

'In the library, sir,' said Kritzinger. 'With Doctor Honek. He asked for a pot of strong black coffee to be brought to him there.'

'Has Doctor Honek examined the body?'

'No,' said Heydrich firmly. 'I decided that there was no urgency about doing so. I thought it might be better if he waited until you had had a chance to examine the body yourself.'

I nodded. 'I'll do that now, if I may.'

'Of course,' said Heydrich.

'Mister Kritzinger,' I said. 'Would you ask Doctor Jury to join us in Captain Kuttner's room?'

'Yes sir.'

'Captain Pomme? Perhaps you'd like to lead the way.'

I stood up and looked at Kahlo, the Criminal Assistant from Prague Kripo. 'You'd better fetch the evidence kit that Zennaty brought,' I said.

'Right you are, sir.'

'General? If you'd care to join us?'

Heydrich nodded. 'Major Ploetz? You'd better inform the rest of my guests of what has happened. And that they will be required to answer the Commissar's questions before anyone is allowed to leave. And that includes everyone at the Upper Castle.'

'Yes sir.'

★　★　★

Kuttner's room was on the same floor as mine, but it was in the south wing and overlooked a little glass winter garden. On the pink-papered walls were some pictures of English hunting scenes that made a welcome change from the Czech ones with which I was more familiar. The fox, who appeared to be smiling, must have believed he stood a good chance of escaping from the hounds, and that was all right with me. Lately I'm the kind of antisocial type who cheers when the fox makes a clean getaway.

Before I looked at the body I made my way around the room, noting a large pile of books by the bed and a bottle of Veronal beside a water carafe on the desk. The screw cap was still off the bottle. There were several pills on the floor but, oddly, the bottle was upright. Kuttner's belts and the holster containing his Walther automatic were hanging on the back of his chair.

Heydrich saw me pick up the open bottle of Veronal. 'Until I realized the true nature of his injuries I assumed that the Veronal was the culprit,' he said. 'It was only when Doctor Jury opened the tunic of his uniform to examine Captain Kuttner that we realized he'd suffered a lethal wound to his abdomen.'

'Mmm hmm.'

Kuttner lay at an angle across the bed, as if he'd collapsed there. His eyes were closed. One of his arms lay neatly alongside his torso; the other was sticking straight out at right angles to the rest of his body, like a dead Christ. Well, half of a dead

Christ anyway. But both hands were unscathed and empty. There were four buttons on his captain's fart-catcher tunic with three of them unbuttoned from the top. He was wearing a white collarless shirt, unbuttoned at the neck, and no tie. It was easy to see how anyone could have missed the fact he'd been shot. It was only when you lifted the flap of the tunic that you could see the blood covering the shirt. He was still wearing his riding breeches, and just one boot. The monkey-swing – his adjutant's braided rope – was off his top button but still attached to the right epaulette. He looked like a man who had been shot while he was still undressing.

'Has anyone been over the floor yet?' I asked Heydrich. 'To look for evidence?'

'No,' said Heydrich.

I nodded at Kahlo who, without complaint, dropped onto his hands and knees and began to look for a bullet-shell, or perhaps something as yet unimagined.

I collected the P38 from Kuttner's holster, sniffed the barrel and then checked the magazine. The gun was dirty and not well maintained, but clearly it hadn't been fired in a while.

'Your conclusions?' asked Heydrich.

'Beyond the fact that he was shot in the torso and that it hardly looks like a suicide I don't yet have any,' I said.

'Why do you think it doesn't look like a suicide?' asked Pomme.

'It's unusual to shoot yourself and then neatly replace the weapon in the holster,' I said. 'Especially when you weren't being neat about so much else. If you were going to shoot yourself, you would take off both boots, or neither of them. Quite apart from that his own pistol has a full magazine and hasn't been fired in a while.'

I shrugged.

'Then again there is no other gun in the room. But all the same it's hard to imagine that he was shot, returned to his room, locked the door, lay down on the bed, took off one boot, and then quietly died. Even if that's what it looks like.'

'What I can't understand,' said Heydrich, 'is why nobody seems to have heard a shot.'

'Well, we don't know that until we ask everyone,' I said.

'I can ask around, if you like,' offered Pomme.

'What I mean,' Heydrich said firmly, 'is that the sound of a shot would surely have raised the alarm. Especially here, in a house full of policemen.'

I nodded. 'So the chances are that somehow the shot was muffled. Or someone did hear the shot and either chose to ignore it, or thought that it was something else.'

I went to the open window and put my head outside.

'Today I can't hear anything,' I said. 'But yesterday when I arrived here, at around the same time, someone was out there shooting birds. Rather a lot of birds.'

'That would have been General von Eberstein,' said Captain Pomme. 'He likes to shoot.'

'But not this morning,' I observed.

'This morning, he has a hangover,' said Pomme. 'Like General Jury.'

Kahlo stood up. 'Apart from all of these pills, there's nothing on this floor, sir,' he said. 'Not so much as a bloodspot.'

'What, nothing at all?' I frowned.

'No sir. I'll organize a more thorough search, after the body's gone. But this floor is clean, sir.' He shook his head. 'It's a mystery. Maybe he shot himself, threw the gun out of the window, closed it again, and then collapsed on the bed and died.'

'Good thinking,' said Heydrich, sarcastically. 'Or maybe Captain Kuttner was just shot by a man who could pass through solid walls.'

'You'd better check outside, anyway,' I told Kahlo.

He nodded and left the room.

Heydrich shook his head. 'That man is an idiot.'

'How well do you know this house, General?'

'You mean, are there any false walls and secret passages?'

'Perhaps.'

'I haven't the faintest idea. I've not been here for very long at all. Von Neurath had the house before I did. He knows this place much better than me, so you'd better ask him that.'

Absently I drew open Kuttner's drawers and found several shirts, a toilet bag, some underwear,

239

a shoe-cleaning kit, some *Der Führer* magazines, a clay pipe, a book of poems, and a framed picture of a woman.

'Can I ask von Neurath something like that?'

'As I told you already, Gunther, I expect everyone to cooperate. No matter who or what they are.'

'Thank you, sir.' I smiled. 'Do I have to be polite? Or can I just be myself?'

'Why change the habit of a lifetime? You're the most insubordinate fellow I know, Gunther, but sometimes that yields results. It might however be a good idea if, while you were conducting your investigation, and practising your habitual impertinence, you wore civilian clothes. So that you can't be accused of something that would get you court-martialled in a uniform. Yes. I think that might be best. Have you any civilian clothes with you?'

'Yes sir. They're in my room.'

'Good. And that reminds me, Gunther. You'll need a suitable space from which to conduct your investigations. You can use the Morning Room. See to it will you, Captain Pomme?'

'Yes, Herr General.'

'Pomme will be your liaison officer for the inquiry. For SD, SS, Gestapo or military matters, go through him. Anything else speak to Kritzinger. Come to think of it, he's the real Lower Castle expert, not von Neurath.'

Kritzinger bowed his head in Heydrich's direction.

General Jury appeared in the doorway, breathing

heavily. He was perspiring and looked pale, as if he really did have a severe hangover. He closed his eyes for a moment and let out a sigh.

'Ah, Jury, you're here.'

Heydrich was trying to keep the smirk out of his voice but without success; it was obvious that he was enjoying the other general's hangover as another man might have taken pleasure at watching someone slip on a banana skin.

'What else would you like to know about the Captain?' Jury asked biliously. 'Beyond the fact that he's dead and that there appears to be a gunshot wound in his abdomen, I can tell you very little, without examining his body in the morgue. And it's been many years since I did that kind of thing.'

'What made you think it was a gunshot wound?' I asked. 'Rather than a knife wound?'

'There's what looks like a neat bullet hole in his shirt,' explained Jury. 'Not to mention a neat hole on his body. And yet there's very little blood on the Captain's torso. Or for that matter, elsewhere. It's rare in my experience that a man who is stabbed doesn't bleed more. I saw no blood on the floor or the bed. But it was only an educated guess. And I could yet turn out to be wrong.'

'No, I think you're right,' I said. 'He was shot all right.'

'Well then, Commissar,' he said stiffly. 'I fail to see the need for the question. Indeed, I'm inclined to consider it impertinent. I am a doctor, after all.'

I decided to let Jury have it between his oyster eyes. In his present, crapulous state – assuming it was for real – he was weak and vulnerable and it might take a while to find him like that again. Besides, I thought it important that I make a very early test of Heydrich's declaration that I enjoyed his full confidence and that he didn't care what I asked or indeed who I upset, just as long as I solved the case. If Heydrich stood by and let me bully General Jury then it would surely send out an early message to other senior officers in the Lower Castle that I was to be taken seriously.

'All right,' I said. 'You're a doctor. But that doesn't mean you didn't kill him. Did you kill him?'

'I beg your pardon.'

'You heard me, Doctor Jury. Was it you who shot Captain Kuttner?'

'If that's your idea of a joke, Commissar Gunther, then kindly take note of the fact that no one in this room is laughing. Including myself.'

This wasn't quite true. Heydrich was smiling, almost as if he approved of me putting Jury on the spot in this way, which at least told me he was serious about my investigating the murder.

'I can assure you it's no joke, sir. Yesterday afternoon, when we talked on the road up to the Upper Castle, you told me that you hated Captain Kuttner.'

'Nonsense,' spluttered Jury.

'You told me you thought he was a cunt. And

that you detested him. That was before you went on to describe Captain Kuttner as General Heydrich's golem.'

Jury coloured with embarrassment.

'Golem,' said Heydrich. 'That's an interesting choice of words. Remind me, Gunther. What exactly is a golem?'

'A sort of creature created long ago by a local Jewish mystic called Rabbi Loew, sir. To do his bidding on behalf of Prague's Jews.'

Jury was still protesting his innocence, but, for the moment, Heydrich ignored him.

'If Captain Kuttner was the golem, then I suppose that makes me comparable to this Jewish mystic. Rabbi Loew.'

'That was certainly my impression, sir.'

'General Heydrich, sir,' said Jury. 'I can assure you that I meant nothing of the sort. Commissar Gunther is entirely mistaken. In no way did I mean to compare you to – that person.'

'Leaving that aside for a moment,' I said, roughly. 'Why did you detest Captain Kuttner?'

Jury advanced on Heydrich. Though I was the one asking the questions, all of his answers were directed, a little desperately, at the Reichsprotector.

'It was an entirely private matter,' he insisted. 'And nothing at all to do with the Captain's death. It's true I did dislike the man. However, if the Commissar is suggesting that it was a reason for killing him then I really must protest.'

'A man has been murdered,' I said. 'An officer

of the SS, in circumstances that compel investigation, regardless of personal feelings. I'm afraid there is no such thing as a private matter in a situation like this, General Jury. You know that as well as anyone else. This is now a criminal investigation and I'll decide if your reason was sufficient reason to kill him.'

'And who made you judge and jury, Captain?' demanded the doctor.

'I did,' said Heydrich. 'Commissar Gunther is one of the most competent detectives in Kripo, with an admirable forensic record. He is only doing the job that I have asked him to do. And doing it rather bravely, I think.'

'Can I see your gun, Doctor Jury?'

'What?'

'Your pistol, sir. I notice you're wearing it, this morning. May I examine it, sir?'

Jury glanced at Heydrich, who nodded firmly.

'I'm not sure why I put on my belts this morning,' he muttered. 'I suppose it was because I was suddenly roused from sleep by Captain Pomme. I mean, I wouldn't normally—'

He unbuttoned his holster and handed over the Walther P38, standard issue for most SS officers unless, like me, they were anything to do with the criminal police, in which case they were given the PPK. He checked the safety, ejected the magazine quickly, and placed both in my hands. It was an impressively competent display for a man who was a doctor and an SS bureaucrat.

I inspected the breech, which was empty, sniffed the barrel, and then glanced at the single-stack magazine in the palm of my hand.

'Only three rounds,' I said. 'And it's been fired. Recently.'

'Yes. I did some shooting practice with my gun yesterday afternoon. In the woods near the Upper Castle. It was just to keep my hand in. It's my belief that one cannot be too careful, what with all these Czech terrorists from UVOD running around.'

'And are you a good shot, sir?'

'No. Not good. Competent, perhaps.'

I nodded at Kuttner's body. 'Obviously we won't know the kind of gun that was used to kill the Captain until a post-mortem has been performed. However, I'm afraid I will have to keep your weapon for now, sir.'

'Is that really necessary?'

'Yes. I may need to try to match the bullet that killed Captain Kuttner with a bullet fired from your gun. What were you using for target practice yesterday?'

'Songbirds. Pigeons.'

'Hit anything?'

'No.'

'Did anyone see you? Baron Neurath perhaps?'

'I don't know. You'd have to ask him, I suppose.'

'I will.'

'I didn't kill Captain Kuttner,' he repeated.

I said nothing.

'But I think that perhaps I could explain my opinion of him to you and the General in private.'

'I think that's an excellent idea, Hugo,' said Heydrich. He glanced at Kritzinger and Pomme. 'Gentlemen. If you would excuse us for a moment, please.'

The butler and the Captain left the bedroom. I closed the door as best I could given the fact that it had been broken in. I stayed there for a moment, running my fingers over the splintered wood and broken brass-work while Jury blustered his way through an explanation of why he had disliked the dead man.

'The matter is a delicate one, involving a lady I know. She is a woman of probity and reputation, you understand. However, the other day I overheard Captain Kuttner talking about her in a way I considered extremely distasteful. I'm sure you'll understand if I don't mention her name or the specific details of the scurrilous gossip that was being relayed.' Jury cleared his throat nervously, removed his glasses and started to polish the lenses with a handkerchief. 'But I can assure you it was not the sort of thing one would expect to hear from an officer and gentleman.'

'It's true,' admitted Heydrich. 'Kuttner had an unfortunate tendency to be indiscreet. Even outspoken. I had occasion to speak to him about this.'

I nodded. 'Exactly who did Kuttner tell about your affair with this little opera singer?' I asked him bluntly.

'Well, I really must protest.' Jury proceeded to give me a look as if he wished it was me lying on the bed with a bullet hole in my torso.

'What was her name again? Elizabeth something. Elizabeth Schwarzkopf, wasn't it?'

'Suppose we just leave her name out of this,' said Jury.

'All right. Suppose we do. Only that's going to make it a little difficult to try to clear your name, General. You see I'll need to speak to this other officer that Kuttner was speaking to. About your girl friend. Who was he?'

Jury bit his lip. This took some doing given how thin it was. 'Major Thummel,' he said.

'And by the way, you were right,' I said. 'Captain Kuttner was a gossip. He told me the same thing. About you and Fräulein Schwarzkopf and Doctor Goebbels. Kuttner seemed to think that there might be some other reason behind the Minister's patronage than just her singing.'

'You are impertinent, Captain Gunther.'

'There's no question about that, sir. The question is what else was said. And whether any of that is enough of a motive for murder.'

'Need I remind you that you are speaking to a general?'

'You can sit on the highest branch if you want, sir. But it certainly won't stop me from shaking the tree. And I can shake it quite hard if I have to. Hard enough to dump you on your backside.'

'I'm afraid Gunther is right, Hugo,' said Heydrich. 'This is really no time to be sensitive. I must have this situation cleared up as soon as possible if I am to avoid any embarrassment. That's embarrassment to me and my office, you understand, not to you, Hugo. I can't allow anything to get in the way of an early conclusion to this unfortunate matter. Even if that does mean us riding roughshod over your feelings and quite possibly your whole future, too, if you refuse to cooperate with the Commissar's inquiry.'

Heydrich looked at me now.

'The fact is, Gunther, that Captain Kuttner heard this story from me. It was I who told him about General Jury's affair with Fräulein Schwarzkopf. I'm sorry, Hugo, but everyone in Berlin knows what's been going on. Except perhaps the Leader, and your wife, Karoline. Let us hope that she above all people can remain in ignorance of all this.

'But, Herr Commissar, I think that the part of the story at which poor General Jury will have taken most offence relates not to her talents in the bedroom, which I assume are considerable, but to her talent as a singer. I'm afraid it's true, Hugo. If the Fräulein was really any good as a soprano she'd be singing with the Berlin State Opera and not the German Opera. And you may not know it for sure but the Commissar is quite right that she has been sharing her sexual favours with the Minister of Propaganda. I have the incontrovertible proof of that, which at some future stage I would be happy to show you. So there's no need to get on your high horse about all of this. You've both been fucking her and that's all there is to it. I mean, how else do you think she was made a principal soprano so soon after joining the chorus? It was Goebbels who fixed that for her. In return for services that she rendered to him horizontally.'

Jury's cheeks were now quite red and his hands were fists. I wondered if that showed a man who was angry enough to kill a brother officer in cold blood.

'I don't care for your manners, General Heydrich,' said Jury.

'That is of small account to me, Hugo.' Heydrich paused. 'Well, how about it? Did you kill Captain Kuttner?' He paused. 'If you did then I promise that we can arrange things so as to avoid too much of a scandal. You can resign, quietly, and go back to your loyal wife, Karoline. Perhaps you can even pick up your medical career again. But I can promise that if you deny it and it turns out to be you after all who murdered the Captain, then it will go very hard for you. We have plenty of filthy prison cells in Terezin Castle where even a distinguished man such as you can be forgotten for years, right up until the moment when I sign his death-warrant and have him hanged the old

Austro-Hungarian way. By strangulation from a pole.'

'I didn't kill him,' insisted Jury and then, with a short click of his heels and a bow of the head, he left the room abruptly.

'I hope you enjoyed that capricious demonstration of your new powers,' said Heydrich. 'I know I did.'

A few seconds later there was a knock on the open door. It was Kurt Kahlo.

'I searched underneath the window, sir,' he told me. 'Nothing. But I found this lying on the floor further down the corridor. I marked the spot, so don't worry.'

He placed a small brass object in my hand.

'What is it?' asked Heydrich.

I held the object up in my fingers. It looked like a metallic cigarette end.

'Unless I'm very much mistaken, sir, it's a shell case from a Walther P38.'

Heydrich tossed the shell case back to me.

'Well, Gunther. Much as I should like to stay and observe you destroy the character of another of my guests, I do have urgent business to attend to. The rather more urgent matter of finding Vaclav Moravek.'

'Yes, of course, sir.'

'I've told Major Ploetz that no one is to leave until you've had a chance to question him. No one, apart from him and me and Klein, my driver.'

250

'Thank you, sir.'

'I shall see you this evening when you can tell me of the progress you've made.'

'All right, sir.'

When he was gone I opened Captain Kuttner's tunic and pulled up his bloody shirt to inspect the bullet wound and was surprised to find not one but two holes, both in the centre of his chest and each about the size of the nail on a man's little finger. Kahlo was searching the floor again. I didn't say anything about there being two gunshot wounds. After a minute or so I turned the dead man onto his side so that I could inspect his back.

'There's no exit wound,' I said, carefully using the singular. I rubbed my hand up and down the dead man's back. 'But sometimes you can find the bullet just underneath the skin. I've seen bullets just fall out of people who'd been shot, after which they can end up just about anywhere. But I think this poor sonofabitch is still carrying metal.'

I pushed Kuttner onto his back again and stood up.

'Show me where you found that shell case.'

Kahlo led the way out of Kuttner's bedroom and in the corridor outside he pointed to a box of matches on the floor that he'd used to mark the spot where he'd discovered the shell casing.

'All right,' I said. 'You cut along to the Morning Room and make it look as much like an interview room as possible. On second thought, no. Leave it as it is. But we'll need pencils and paper, a jug

251

of water, some liquor, some glasses, a fresh pot of coffee every hour, a telephone, some cigarettes, and a typewriter.'

'Yes, boss.'

'And tell Doctor Honek that the ambulance men can remove the body to the hospital. And have him arrange an autopsy, will you? Today, if possible.'

'Yes, boss.'

I glanced back to Kuttner's door, about twenty metres away, and once Kahlo had gone, dropped onto my hands and knees and made my way slowly along the corridor. After a few minutes a door opened and out of a bedroom stepped the only officer in the Lower Castle who wasn't a member of the SS or the SD. He was wearing the uniform of a major in the German Army.

'You look how I feel,' he observed.

'Hmmm?'

'Last night. I drank far too much. But on top of all that there was the champagne, which never agrees with me at the best of times. Still, under the circumstances I didn't want to turn it down. We were celebrating after all, weren't we? All the same I do regret it now. Woke up with a bit of a head this morning. I felt like I wanted to curl up and die.'

'You have to be alive to feel like that, I suppose.'

'What's that? Oh, yes. I heard one of the adjutants got Stalin's greatcoat. A terrible business.'

Stalin's greatcoat was a coffin.

'Which one was he? All of these adjutant fellows sort of look the same to me.'

I found what I was looking for: the second shell casing. I stood up and found myself facing a man of about the same age as me.

'Captain Kuttner.'

He shook his head as if he couldn't remember him. 'And you're the detective fellow, from Berlin, aren't you? Gunther, isn't it?'

'That's correct, sir.'

'I suppose that accounts for why you're crawling around the place on your hands and knees.'

'I do quite a lot of that anyway, sir. Even when I'm not hunting for evidence. I like to drink, you see, sir. That is, when I can get it.'

'There's no shortage of it here, Gunther. If this keeps up I shall need a new liver. Major Paul Thummel, at your service. If there's anything I can do to help, just let me know. Major Ploetz says that you want to interview everyone who was staying here last night. Fine by me. Just say when. Always glad to help the police.'

I pocketed the little shell casing. 'Thank you, sir. Perhaps we could speak later on. I'll have Captain Pomme contact you to arrange a time.'

'Sooner the better, old man. Ploetz says that none of us can leave the house until we've given a statement. Frankly it all sounds a bit excessive. After all, it's not like any of us is going to run away, is it?'

'I think it has rather more to do with remembering details that might seem unimportant anywhere else. In my experience, it's always better if you can interview witnesses as close to the crime scene as possible.'

'Well, you know your job, I suppose. Just don't interview people in alphabetical order that's all. You'll find that puts me last, I think.'

'I'll certainly bear that in mind, sir.'

Investigating the murder of one young SD officer who had almost certainly participated in the murders of hundreds, perhaps thousands of Latvian Jews, Gypsies and 'other undesirables' struck me as absurd, of course. A mass murderer who'd been murdered. What was wrong with that? But how many had I killed myself? There were the forty or fifty Russian POWs I knew about for sure – nearly all of them members of an NKVD death squad. I'd commanded the firing squad and delivered the *coup de grâce* to at least ten of them as they lay groaning on the ground. Their blood and brains had been spattered all over my boots. During the Great War there had been a Canadian boy I'd put the bayonet into when it was him or me, only he'd died hard, with his head on my shoulder. God knows how many others I'd killed when, another time, I'd taken over a Maxim gun and squeezed the trigger as I pointed it at some brown figures advancing slowly over No Man's Land.

But it seemed that Albert Kuttner's death mattered because he'd been a German officer and a close colleague of General Heydrich's. That was supposed to make a difference, only it didn't. At least not to me. Investigating a murder in the autumn of 1941 was like arresting a man for vagrancy during the Great Depression. But I did what I was told and started to go through the motions the way a proper policeman would have done. What choice did I have? Besides, it kept my mind off what I knew was happening out there, in the East. Most of all it kept my mind off the growing sense that I'd been to the worst place on the planet only to realize that the worst place of all was inside me.

'I've prepared a list of everyone who stayed at the Lower Castle last night and therefore who you will want to interview,' said Major Ploetz.

He handed me a sheet of neatly typed, headed notepaper.

'Thank you, Major.'

We were in the Morning Room. With its greenish silk Chinoise wallpaper, the room felt like an extension of the garden and a little more natural than the rest of the house. There were a couple of big sofas facing each other like very fat chess-players across a polished wooden coffee-table. In the window was a grand piano and in the fireplace there was a fire that cheered the room. Either side of the marble fireplace was a mosaic of picture frames featuring Heydrich and his family. Kahlo was inspecting these, one at a time, as if looking to judge a winner. Now wearing my civilian clothes, I was seated on one of the sofas, smoking a cigarette.

'Here is your mail, Commissar, forwarded from the Alex in Berlin. And here is a copy of Albert Kuttner's SD personnel file. The General thought it might help you to get a better sense of the man and what he was like and – you never know – perhaps why he was killed. The personnel files of everyone staying here this weekend are being sent over from Hradschin Castle this morning.'

'That's very efficient of you, Major.'

It was easy to see why Ploetz was Heydrich's Chief Adjutant. There was no doubting his efficiency. With his lists and memoranda and facts and figures Achim Ploetz was a real electric Nazi. Before the war I'd been to a town called Achim. It was near Bremen in a nice part of the country that, in its natural state, is mostly moorland. But there was nothing natural about Achim Ploetz, and in that respect at least, Doctor Jury was right: all of Heydrich's adjutants were a bit like the golem of Prague.

Outside the Morning Room window a Mercedes drew up and Heydrich's driver got out and opened the passenger door expectantly.

Ploetz saw him out of the corner of his eye.

'Well, I'd better go and tell the General that our car is here,' he said. 'If there is anything you want, just ask Pomme.'

'Yes. I will.'

Then he was gone and Kahlo and I were standing

at the window peering around the heavy drapes like two comedians getting ready to take a curtain call. The convertible's top was down and the engine was purring smoothly like some green metal dragon. Ploetz climbed aboard first and sat in the rear. Heydrich sat up front with the driver as if that might help him to control the car despite the fact someone else was at the wheel. He was just like that, I guess. As we watched them drive away there was no sign of an armed escort.

'So, what do you make of it, sir?'

'Bloody fool,' I muttered.

'How's that, sir?'

'Heydrich. The way he drives around the city like he's invulnerable. Like Achilles. As if daring the poor bastards to come and have a go.'

'The Czechos are just mad enough to do it, too.'

'You think so?'

Kahlo nodded.

'How long have you been in Prague?'

'Long enough to know that the Czechos have got guts. More than we like to give them credit for.'

'Kurt, isn't it?'

Kahlo nodded.

'Where are you from, Kurt?'

'Mannheim, sir.'

'How did you become a cop?'

'I'm not exactly sure. My dad was a car-worker at the Daimler-Benz factory. But I never much fancied being stuck in a factory myself. He wanted me to become a lawyer, only I wasn't clever enough, so becoming a cop seemed like the next best thing.'

'So what do *you* make of it?'

'It's a puzzle, sir. A man is found shot dead inside a first-floor bedroom that's locked from the inside. The windows are bolted and there's no murder weapon present. Down the corridor there's a spent nine-millimetre Parabellum round on the floor, so clearly a gun was fired at some time between the hours of midnight and, say, five o'clock this morning. And yet you'd also expect someone to have remarked on that, because a P38 wasn't picked as the Army's choice of firearm because it's so bloody quiet. They can't all have been so pissed they didn't hear anything. The staff weren't pissed. Not with Kritzinger in charge. Why didn't they hear something? And not just a gunshot, either. I can't imagine Kuttner standing on the landing upstairs and saying nothing as someone is about to shoot him. Me I'd have shouted "Help" or "Don't shoot", or something like that.'

'I agree.'

'Kuttner was under the influence of a sleeping pill,' he said. 'Maybe he didn't realize quite how much peril he was in. Maybe it was dark and he didn't see the gun. Maybe he was shot outside and because he was drugged he didn't realize the severity of his injury. So he comes back in the house, goes back to his room, locks the door, lies down, and dies. Maybe.'

I shook my head. 'You've got more maybes there than Fritz bloody Lang.'

'I know,' he said. 'Frankly, I wouldn't know where to start with this one, sir. However, I'm keen to learn from someone who does, such as you. That is, if General Heydrich is to be believed. Anyway, you have my full cooperation, sir. Just tell me what to do and I'll do it, with no questions asked.'

'Questions are good, Kurt. It's obedience I have a problem with. In particular, my own.'

Kahlo grinned. 'Then I think yours should be an interesting career, sir.'

I opened Kuttner's SD file and glanced over the details of the dead man's short life.

'Albert Kuttner was from Halle-an-der-Saale. Interesting.'

'Is it? I can't say I know the place.'

'What I mean is, Halle is where Heydrich is from.'

'So he could be taking this personally.'

'Yes. True. Kuttner was born in 1911. That makes him seven years younger than Heydrich. His father was a Protestant pastor at a local church. But instead of pursuing a career in the Church, or in the Navy – like his boss—'

'Heydrich was in the Navy? I didn't know that.'

'It's said he got kicked out of it for conduct unbecoming when he knocked up some admiral's daughter. But don't tell anyone I said so.'

'This admiral's daughter. Is that the present Frau Heydrich?'

'No. It's not.'

'So he is human, after all.'

'I wouldn't go that far.'

'Kuttner studied law at the Martin Luther University of Halle-Wittenberg and the Humboldt University of Berlin, where it seems he was a brilliant student. He received his doctor of laws in 1935 and worked for the ministries of justice and the interior before joining the SD.'

'So far, so predictable.'

'Hmm. Near the top of his class in officer school. Highly praised by everyone who assessed him; he was being groomed for one of the top jobs in Berlin. In May this year he was transferred to the Einsatzgruppen and ordered to Pretzsch, where he was assigned to Group A and sent east. Nothing unusual about that. Lots of decent men have been sent east. Decent men and some lawyers. On June 23rd he and the group were ordered to proceed to Riga, in Latvia, to help with "the resettlement of the indigenous Jewish population".'

'Resettlement. Yes, I know what that entails.'

'Good. It will save me having to explain the distinction between "resettlement" and "mass murder".'

'Am I to assume that your appreciation of the distinction is based on personal experience, sir?'

'You are. But please don't assume that I did a good job. There are no good jobs out east. Albert Kuttner didn't take to his work any more than I did. Which is why he felt guilty. Like me. And why he wasn't sleeping.'

'Thus the Veronal in his room.'

I turned the page in Kuttner's file and read on a little before speaking again.

'That guilt appears to have manifested itself for the first time just three weeks into his tour of Latvia when he put in for a transfer to the Army. But the request was refused by his commander, Major Rudolf Lange. Well, that hardly surprises me. I knew Rudolf Lange when he was with the Berlin police. The cat never stops catching mice. He was a bastard then and he's a bastard now. Reason given for refusal of request for transfer: personnel shortages. But a week later he puts in for another transfer. This time he's given an official reprimand. For conduct likely to damage morale.'

'It's a dirty job so someone has to do it, right?'

'Something like that, I suppose.'

I turned another page in Kuttner's file.

'By August however, Albert is back in Berlin facing a disciplinary inquiry. It seems he threatened a superior officer with a pistol – it doesn't say who, but I hope it was Lange, I've often wanted to stick a gun in that fat fucker's face. Kuttner's placed under close arrest, but not close enough because he then attempts suicide. No details on that either. But he's sent back to Berlin for that disciplinary inquiry. A so-called SS court of honour. Only the disciplinary inquiry is suspended. No reason given.'

'Do you think Heydrich might have pulled some strings?'

'That's what it looks like, because the next thing is that Albert is on the General's staff in Berlin. Lighting his cigarettes, booking seats at the opera, and fetching coffee.'

'Now that is a good job,' said Kahlo.

'You don't strike me as an opera fan.'

'Not the opera. The cigarettes.' His eyes were on my cigarette. 'The tobacco ration being what it is.'

'Sorry.' I opened my cigarette case. 'Help yourself.'

Kahlo took one, lit up and then puffed with obvious satisfaction. Holding the cigarette in front of his eyes, like a rare diamond, he grinned happily.

'I'd forgotten how good a cigarette can taste,' he said.

'There's a page missing from this file,' I said. 'In my own SD file there's a page headed "Personal Remarks". I've only ever seen it upside down but it's full of things my superiors have said about me like "insubordinate" and "politically unreliable".'

'You read good upside down.' Kahlo grinned. 'I'm a bit of a beefsteak Nazi myself, sir. Brown on the outside but red in the middle. Although I'm not as rare as my old dad. Being a car-worker he was red all the way.'

'Mm hmmm.'

I handed Kahlo the file.

'It's not much to go on,' he said, flicking through it. 'Let's see what we can find out for ourselves.'

I picked up the telephone and asked the Lower Castle switchboard to connect me with the Alex in Berlin. A few minutes later I was able to speak with the Records Division. I asked them if they had a file on Albert Kuttner. They didn't. So I had them run a check on his address, which was always something you could do in Berlin because it wasn't just individuals who generated records in Prussia, it was places, too. The Prussian State Police were nothing if not thorough. And a few minutes later Records called back to tell me that Flat 3, 4 Pestalozzi Strasse, in Charlottenburg was home to another man besides Albert Kuttner.

And when I had the Records people check him out, I started to believe I had something.

'Lothar Ott,' I said, reading aloud my notes of these several telephone conversations. 'Born Berlin February 21st 1901. Two convictions for male prostitution, one 1930, the other 1932. Not only that but his previous address was number one Friedrichsgracht, near Berlin's Spittelmarkt. That won't mean much to a cop from Mannheim but to a bull from Berlin it means a lot. Until 1932, number one Friedrichsgracht was a notorious homosexual club called the Burger Casino. Either the late Captain Kuttner was very tolerant of homosexuals or—'

'Or he was maybe a bit warm himself.' Kahlo nodded. 'I mean, you wouldn't live with someone like that unless you were, would you?'

'What do you think? You met him.'

'You're asking if Kuttner struck me as the type?

263

I dunno. A lot of officers strike me that way. It's possible, I suppose. He could have been the type. You know, a bit fastidious. A bit too careful about his appearance. A bit too much Cologne on his hair. The way he walked. Now I come to think of it, yes, I can see it. When he shrugged it looked just like my brother's daughter.'

'I agree.'

'Someone ought to give this other fellow, Ott, a knock and see how he takes the news that Kuttner's dead.'

'That's an idea.'

So I telephoned the Alex again and explained Kahlo's idea to an old friend in Kripo called Trott, who promised to go and see Lothar Ott and give him the bad news in person and then report back on the show.

As soon as I replaced the receiver, the telephone rang. Kahlo answered it.

'It's Doctor Honek,' he said, handing me the candlestick. 'Calling about the autopsy.'

I took the phone.

'This is Gunther.'

'I managed to find someone to perform an autopsy on Captain Kuttner,' said Honek. 'Today. Like you asked me, Commissar. In view of the circumstances, Professor Hamperl, from the Pathological Institute of the German Charles University in Prague, has agreed to carry out the procedure at four o'clock this afternoon. He's most distinguished.'

'Where?'

'At the Bulovka Hospital.'

'All right. We'll be there at four.'

After I hung up, Kahlo said, 'We? What's this "we"? You don't want me there, do you?'

'You said you were keen to learn, didn't you?'

'Yes, but well, the thing is, I've never seen an autopsy before.'

'There's nothing to it. Besides, we have a distinguished professor to perform the autopsy.'

'I don't know,' he said, anxiously. 'I mean, dead people. I don't know. They look like they're dead, right?'

'It's best that way. When they look alive it puts the pathologist a bit off his knife.' I shrugged. 'It's your choice. Now let's have a look at that list of names that Major Ploetz gave us. I think some of them look like they're people.'

Those present at the Lower Castle on the night of 2nd/3rd October 1941 included the following:

SS Obergruppenführer Reinhard Heydrich
SS Obergruppenführer Richard Hildebrandt
SS Obergruppenführer Karl von Eberstein
SS Gruppenführer Konrad Henlein
SS Gruppenführer Dr Hugo Jury
SS Gruppenführer Karl Hermann Frank
SS Brigadeführer Bernard Voss
SS Standartenführer Dr Hans Ulrich Geschke
SS Standartenführer Horst Bohme

SS Obersturmbannführer Walter Jacobi
SS Sturmbannführer Dr Achim Ploetz
Wehrmacht Major Paul Thummel
SS Hauptsturmführer Kurt Pomme
SS Hauptsturmführer Hermann Kluckholn
SS Hauptsturmführer Albert Küttner
SS Unterscharführer August Beck

Staff

SS Sturmscharführer Gert Kritzinger	Butler
SS Oberscharführer Johannes Klein	Chauffeur
SS Unterscharführer Hermann Kube	Chef
SS Rottenführer Wilhelm Seupel	Assistant Chef
SS Rottenführer Walther Artner	Senior Footman
SS Stürmann Adolf Jachod	Senior Footman
SS Stürmann Kurt Bauer	Footman
SS Stürmann Oskar Fendle	Footman
SS Helferin Elisabeth Schreck	Secretary to Heydrich
SS Kriegshelferin Siv Elsler	Assistant Secretary to H.
SS Kriegshelferin Charlotte Teitze	Maid

SS Kriegshelferin Rosa Steffel	Maid
SS Kriegshelferin Liv Lemke	Maid
Bruno Kopkow	Head Gardener
Otto Faulhaber	Assistant Gardener
Johannes Bangert	Assistant Gardener

Upper Castle Personnel

SS Gruppenführer Konstantin von Neurath	
The Baroness von Neurath, Marie Auguste Moser von Filseck	
SS Hauptsturmführer Eduard Jahn	
SS Oberscharführer Richard Kolbe	Butler
SS Rottenführer Richard Miczek	Chef
SS Sturmmann Rolf Braun	Footman
SS Kriegshelferin Anna Kurzidim,	Maid
SS Kriegshelferin Victoria Kuckenberg	Maid

For obvious reasons it is recommended that you conduct your interviews at the Lower Castle in strict order of seniority. For reasons of security and confidentiality, please confine all interviews to the Morning Room. Interviews at the Upper Castle should be conducted by arrangement with

*the Baron's adjutant, SS Hauptsturmführer
Eduard Jahn. A safe will be provided for your
use in the Morning Room. All documents
pertaining to this inquiry should be placed in
it when not in use for reasons of confidentiality.*

Signed SS-Major Dr Achim Ploetz,
Adjutant to SS Obergruppenführer
Heydrich

My eyes slid off the page and landed on the floor
with a loud sigh.

'If one were to assume that anyone at the Lower
Castle might have had the opportunity and the
motive to kill Captain Kuttner,' I said, 'that leaves
us with thirty-one suspects.'

'Christ,' muttered Kahlo. 'That's at least one for
every day of the month.'

'Thirty-nine including the personnel at the
Upper Castle with von Neurath. It's only a short
walk from there to the Upper Castle, so I don't
see how they can be excluded.'

'And God knows how many if we include all of
the SS up at the guard house.'

I grunted.

'Do you want to include them?'

'How many are in the garrison?'

'At least two hundred.'

'I don't want to include them, no. No. But I
hardly see how I can exclude them given the possibility that Albert Kuttner may have been warm.

268

A bit of rough trade with an enlisted man in the woods might have been just his beer. The first thing we have to do—'

'You mean apart from interviewing the senior ranks.'

I paused.

'So far no one's complained about being kept waiting by you,' said Kahlo. 'But it won't be long.'

I nodded. 'All right. While I start with the formal interviews, the first thing you have to do is to try and speak to everyone informally and get a sense of Kuttner's movements last night. Who was the last person to see him alive and at what time? That kind of thing. Now, I saw him at about nine o'clock when he was having a fairly heated discussion in the garden with one of the other adjutants – Captain Kluckholn, I think. Then about half an hour later, after Heydrich had made a speech, he appeared in the library with some champagne. So you might start with that in mind. I want times and places. And see if you can't get a plan of the house. That way we can start plotting his various positions.'

'Yes, I suppose that might help.'

'Any suggestions of your own will be gratefully considered.'

'Then a clairvoyant with a crystal ball couldn't do any harm. Strikes me that's the only way we're going to find a murderer who walks through locked doors and shoots people without making a sound.'

'You make me begin to wonder what I'm doing here, Kurt.'

'By the way, sir, if you don't mind me asking. What *are* you doing here? What I mean is: all this damned cauliflower. It's like a market garden in this house.'

He was referring to the oak-leaf collar patches that distinguished SS generals, brigadiers, and colonels from lesser mortals.

'What's it all about? What's the reason for it?'

'You ask some pretty good questions for a man who promised to work for me, no questions asked.'

'So what's the answer?'

'I believe General Heydrich wanted a quiet weekend with friends to celebrate his appointment as the new Reichsprotector of Bohemia.'

'I see.'

'You sound surprised. But not as surprised as I was to be asked along on this jaunt. The General and I, we've grown apart, you understand. Schiller once wrote a pretty good poem to his friends. When I was at school we were obliged to learn all five verses. I used to think he said all there was to say about what friendship means in Germany. Only I don't remember a verse covering the kind of friend I have in General Heydrich. Goethe did it better, I think. You know? What happens when Mephistopheles invites you over for real coffee and American cigarettes.'

Even as I said it Arianne came into my mind; it was she who had made the comparison between Heydrich and Mephistopheles on the train from Berlin, and ever since then I'd been wondering just how long I had to work for Heydrich before my soul was forfeit.

'Oh yeah,' said Kahlo. 'Temptation. And temptation like real coffee and American cigarettes. Well that's very tempting.'

'I figure that the alternative is worse. I can't answer for why all the cauliflower is here, but that's why I'm on board. Because the General asked me to dance. Because he doesn't like it when you say no.'

'All right. I'll buy that.'

'Good. Now let's see what we can do about getting a bead on the invisible man.'

SS Obergruppenführer Richard Hildebrandt was the Higher Police Leader in Danzig and commander of a large unit of SS that was stationed in West Prussia. In the event of the citizens of Berlin rising up against Hitler, Hildebrandt would be in charge of suppressing that particular revolution.

Born at Worms in 1897, he was an old friend of Heydrich's. Smooth, neat, fastidious, and of only average height, he had the look and manner of a prosperous businessman. Certainly he had the best tailoring of any officer who was staying at the Lower Castle. On his left breast pocket he wore a Knight's Cross of the War Merit Cross with Swords – a silver Nazi medal that had nothing to do with the proper Knight's Cross, and everyone who'd seen proper combat thought of this decoration as a substitute Iron Cross; but I suppose a general has to have some kind of furniture on his tunic if ever people are going to listen to him. But the gold Party badge he wore next to the *faux* Knight's Cross was the real hallmark of his sterling Nazi status and near-untouchability. That little gewgaw occupied pride of place on his uniform and was the cynosure of anyone who knew what was what in Nazi Germany.

He sat down on the sofa opposite me, lit a cigarette and crossed his legs. 'Will this take long, Commissar?'

'Not long, sir.'

'Good. Because I have some important paperwork I need to get through.'

'How well did you know Captain Kuttner?'

'I didn't know him at all. Until I arrived here the day before yesterday I had perhaps spoken to him twice, and only on the telephone.'

'How did you find him?'

'He struck me as efficient. Well educated. Diligent. As one might expect of an officer working for a man like General Heydrich.'

'Did you like him?'

'What kind of stupid question is that?'

'A fairly easy one, I'd say. Did you like him?'

Hildebrandt shrugged. 'I did not dislike him.'

'Can you think of any reason why someone would want to kill him?'

'No, and my own opinion is that a Czech must have committed the crime. There are Czechs working here, in the house and grounds. My advice, Commissar, would be to start by questioning them, not senior generals in the SS.'

'My apologies, Herr General. I was led to believe by Major Ploetz that I should conduct these interviews in strict order of seniority, so as not to keep anyone important – such as yourself – hanging around.'

Hildebrandt shrugged. 'I see. My apologies, Commissar.'

I shrugged back.

'However, I still fail to see why senior ranks should be questioned at all. In my opinion my word should be good enough.'

'And what word is that, sir?'

'That I had nothing at all to do with this man's death, of course.'

'I don't doubt it, sir. However, it is not the point of this interview to find out if you murdered Captain Kuttner. The immediate purpose of this inquiry is to build a detailed picture of the man's last few hours. And having done so, to identify some genuine suspects. You do see the difference.'

'Of course. Do you take me for an idiot?'

I didn't answer that. 'You were with us all, in the library, to listen to the Leader's speech, were you not?'

'Naturally.'

'And then to hear Heydrich's speech.'

Hildebrandt nodded, impatiently. He took a last puff of his cigarette and then extinguished it in a heavy glass ashtray that lay on the table between us.

'Do you remember Captain Kuttner bringing in some champagne after that?'

'Yes.'

'Did you stay celebrating very long?'

'Yes. I confess I drank rather too much, I think. Like everyone else I have a bit of a headache this morning.'

'Yes sir. Only I have a bigger one. I have to solve this murder. That won't be easy. You do see that, don't you? At some stage it's possible I'm going to have to accuse a brother officer of killing Kuttner. Perhaps even a senior officer. I think you might try to be a little more understanding of my position, sir.'

'Don't tell me my duty, Commissar Gunther.'

'With the scary badge in your lapel? I wouldn't dream of it, sir.'

Hildebrandt glanced down at his gold Party badge and smiled. 'You mean this, don't you? I've heard that's what some people call it. Although I can't imagine why anyone would be scared of this.'

'It means that you joined the Party very early on, doesn't it?'

'Yes. In my case it was 1922. The following year I took part in the Munich putsch. I was right behind the Leader as we left the beer hall.'

'You must have been very young, sir.'

'I was twenty-six.'

'If you don't mind me asking, what happened to you, sir? After the putsch failed.'

His eyes misted over for a moment before he answered.

'Things were difficult for a while. Very difficult.

274

I don't mind telling you. Apart from the harassment I received at the hands of the police, I was short of money and I had little choice but to go and work abroad.'

He seemed relieved to be talking about something that was nothing to do with Kuttner; relaxed even, which, momentarily, was my intention.

'Where did you go?'

'America. There I tried my hand at farming for a while. But after that failed I became a bookseller, in New York.'

'That's quite a switch, sir. Did you fail at being a bookseller, too?'

Hildebrandt frowned.

'Or did you come back to Germany for another reason, sir?'

'I came back because of the wonderful things that were happening in Germany. Because of the Leader. That was 1930.'

'And you joined the SS when, may I ask?'

'1931. That is when I first met Heydrich. But I don't see what any of this has to do with the death of Captain Kuttner.'

'I'm coming to that, if you'll bear with me. I suppose you must have a high regard for the standards of the SS, having joined as early as 1931.'

'Yes, I do. Of course I do. What kind of a question is that?'

'Do you suppose that Captain Kuttner lived up to those standards?'

'I'm sure he did.'

'Are you sure he did, or do you suppose he did?'

'What are you driving at, Gunther?'

'If I told you that Captain Kuttner was a practising homosexual, what would your reaction be?'

'Nonsense. General Heydrich would never have tolerated such a thing. I've known him long enough to be quite sure of that.'

'What if General Heydrich didn't know about it?'

'There are no secrets from Heydrich,' said Hildebrandt. 'You should be aware of that. And if you're not, you soon will be. What he doesn't know, probably isn't worth knowing.'

'Would it surprise you if I told you that there are some things even Heydrich doesn't know?'

'Nonsense,' he repeated. 'This whole line of questioning is nonsense, Commissar. Kuttner was artistic, at worst. But we don't condemn a man for enjoying good music and appreciating good paintings.'

'With respect, I don't think it is nonsense, sir. Kuttner was living with a man in Berlin. A man with convictions for male prostitution. A man who used to frequent a notorious homosexual bar called the Burger Casino, dressed in a schoolboy sailor-suit, and who used to take his clients to a nearby pier on the river in order to have sex with them.'

'Rubbish. I just don't believe it. And I think it very poor taste on your part to malign a fellow officer who is no longer in a position to defend himself from that kind of defamation.'

'Let us assume for one minute that I'm right about this.'

'Why?'

'Please, sir. Indulge me for a moment.'

'Very well.'

'What would your opinion be of a man like that?'

'My opinion?'

'Yes, sir. What do you think of an SS captain who shares his bed with a male prostitute?'

Hildebrandt's smooth face darkened. The lips tightened and the jaw turned pugnacious.

'I mean, sir, it's said it was Ernst Röhm's homosexuality that was one of the reasons the Party turned on him, why he was executed.'

'That's probably true,' admitted Hildebrandt. 'Röhm was a degenerate. As were some of the others. Edmund Heines. Klausener. Schneidhuber. Schragmüller. They were loathsome specimens and richly deserved their fate.'

'Of course they did.'

I wasn't sure they had deserved their fate, not all of them. Erich Klausener had been the leader of the police department at the Prussian interior ministry in Berlin and not a bad fellow at all. But I wasn't there to debate with Hildebrandt.

'Do you think that sort of thing should be tolerated in the SS?'

'Of course it shouldn't. And it isn't tolerated. Never has been.'

'Do you think it brings dishonour to the SS? Is that why?'

'Certainly it brings dishonour to the SS, Commissar Gunther. What a fucking question. It's obvious. If the man was, as you say, homosexual – although I still don't believe Kuttner was – then I'd go further than that. Such a man should be put in front of a firing squad. Like Röhm and those other queers. It's the pansies and the Jews who almost destroyed Germany during the Weimar Republic.'

'Oh, surely,' I said.

'Who continue to threaten the moral fibre of our country. We are cultivating increasingly healthy blood for Germany and it must be kept pure. As the father of three children myself, two of them boys, I say it quite emphatically. If such a man was under my command I should not hesitate to denounce him to the Gestapo. Not for a minute. No matter how serious the consequences.'

'Well, of course,' I said, 'I know it's illegal under paragraphs 174 and 175 of the Criminal Code. But I thought that homosexuals could only be sent to prison for up to ten years. So, let me get this straight. There are extra punishments that apply to such people in the SS, is that right? Like being shot, as you say. I assume you would know, sir.'

He lit another cigarette.

'As a matter of fact I do know. And in the strictest confidence I will tell you what happens. In the SS we have about one case of homosexuality a month. When they are uncovered, by order of the Reichsführer-SS himself they are degraded, expelled, and handed over to the courts; and following completion of the statutory punishment, which you mentioned, they are then sent to a concentration camp, where they are most often shot, while attempting to escape.'

'I see.'

'Personally, I can't see the need for the camp. If it was up to me, it would be the commanding officer who would shoot such a man. Summarily.'

'So, let me get this straight. If you had absolute incontrovertible proof that Captain Kuttner was a homosexual, and he'd been your junior officer, you'd have shot him yourself. Is that right?'

'Absolutely.'

'Thank you, General. That will be all, sir. I do appreciate your candour in this matter.'

Hildebrandt paused. 'Are you playing games with me, Commissar?'

'I was merely testing a theory, sir.'

'And what theory is that?'

'Only that it's quite possible he wasn't murdered by a Czech after all, as you insisted earlier. But by another German. I dare say you're not the only man who thinks Kuttner was probably murdered by a Czech. It's a common enough prejudice we Germans have: a suspicion of other lesser races. Take Berlin's S-Bahn murderer, this summer. Paul Ogorzow. Remember him?'

'Yes.'

'Before he was caught everyone thought the murderer was a foreign worker. But Paul Ogorzow was a German. Not only that, but he was a Party member. Not as early a member as you, sir, but

I think he joined well before Hitler became Reich Chancellor.'

I shrugged. 'When it comes to murder, I like to keep an open mind.'

Hildebrandt got up to leave. He straightened his immaculate riding-breeches, which were the expensive kind – with the suede inside legs, as if he actually went riding – and moved toward the Morning Room door.

'By the way, sir. How did you find living in America?'

'I beg your pardon?'

'Did you enjoy living in America, sir?'

'Yes. I did.'

'I'd love to work in a foreign country. So far it's been France, Bohemia and the Ukraine. And I didn't much like the Ukraine. And I certainly didn't like the work.'

Hildebrandt remained silent.

'Neither did Captain Kuttner,' I said. 'Did you know that?'

'No.'

'Yes. He told me that himself. It bothered him. A lot. Made him feel disgusting.'

'There's no doubt that it's difficult work,' said Hildebrandt. 'Not everyone is suitable for this kind of duty. However, there's no shame in that, I think. No shame for you anyway, Commissar.'

'Thank you, sir. I'll try to bear that in mind.'

I had about thirty minutes before my next appointment in the Morning Room so I went upstairs to search Kuttner's room. I wanted to do this without anyone else looking over my shoulder just in case I found something interesting that I had to show Ploetz or Heydrich or whoever else took it upon themselves to scrutinize my work.

But Kuttner's bed had already been stripped. The sheets and blankets lay in a heap on the floor. The window had been opened wider than before and the room was full of the scent of freshly cut grass. The gardener at Jungfern-Breschan was forever tending the lawns. Outside the window the motorized lawnmowers were already at work.

Seated on the end of Kuttner's bed was a girl of about twenty-five. She had blond hair and a hand-kerchief in her hand and was wearing a sleeveless grey pinafore and a regulation SS black dress – the one with the big floppy collar trimmed with white piping. She was an SS Helferin: a helper and, in this case, a maid.

I watched her silently from the doorway for several minutes. And not noticing me she didn't move except, now and then, to press the handkerchief to her nose as if she had a head cold. Finally my curiosity could no longer be contained and, clearing my throat, I advanced into the dead man's room.

Abruptly the Helper stood up and looked the other way – at least she did until I caught hold of her arm.

'I'm sorry, sir,' she said. 'I didn't mean any harm coming in here. Mister Kritzinger sent me to strip the bed and I was just overcome for a moment, at the thought of that poor man being murdered.'

She was older than I had first supposed and not particularly good-looking – too thin and highly strung for my taste. Her skin was clear as tissue paper and you could see the little blue veins at the side of her forehead like the maker's mark on good porcelain. The mouth was wider and sadder than it ought to have been perhaps, but it was her big eyes I was really interested in because they were red and full of tears.

'I'm Commissar Gunther.'

'Yes sir. I know who you are. I saw you when you arrived here, yesterday.'

She gave a little curtsy.

'I'm investigating Captain Kuttner's murder.'

She nodded. She knew that, too.

'Did you know him?'

'Not really, sir. We talked a few times. He was kind to me.'

'What did you talk about?'

'Nothing really, sir. Nothing important. It was just incidental talk, you might say. Idle conversation about nothing very much.'

'It's all right. I'm not going to tell anyone. I'm just trying to get the handle on what kind of a fellow he was. Maybe when I've done that I'll have a better grip on why someone killed him.' I pointed at the bed where she'd been sitting. 'Can we sit down and talk? Just for a minute.'

'All right.'

She sat down and I sat beside her.

'Albert was a very sweet, gentle man. Well, he was more of a boy, really. Such a handsome boy. I can't imagine anyone wanting to hurt him. Let alone kill him. He was thoughtful and considerate, and very sensitive.'

'You liked him then.'

'Oh, yes. Much more than some of these other officers. He was different.'

'He certainly was.'

Thinking I might have sounded insincere, I added, 'I liked him, too.' Even as I said this I realized for the first time since hearing about Kuttner's death that I really had liked him. Probably it was mostly the fact we had both shared a terrible experience in the East; but more than that, I had also liked his wit and candour, which bordered on the indiscreet.

To that extent at least Kuttner reminded me of me, and I wondered if I had started to take his murder a little more personally than seemed appropriate.

'Go on.'

She shook her head. 'I don't want to get in any trouble.'

'I can promise you that you won't. But if there's anything you know that sheds any light on what happened here last night then I think I need to know about it, don't you? General Heydrich is very determined that I find out who murdered the Captain. And the only way that is going to happen is if I persuade people like you to have confidence enough in me to tell the truth.'

'All right, sir.'

'Good. What's your name?'

'Steffel. Rosa Steffel.'

'Well, Rosa, why don't you tell me what happened?'

'Last night,' she said, 'when all of the officers started to go to bed, he insisted on helping me collect up the glasses, even though I could see he was dead tired.'

'That was kind of him,' I said. 'What time was that?'

'It must have been after one o'clock. I heard the clock chime in the hall. Some of the cauliflowers were still up, of course, swigging brandy in the library. And one or two were drunk. One in particular. I wouldn't like to say who he was but he got a bit too familiar with me, if you know what I mean. You see, there's something about this uniform. When some of the cauliflowers get drunk they think we're little better than camp-followers and they take liberties with us. This particular officer touched my breasts, and he tried to put his hand up my dress. I didn't care for it and told him so; but he's my senior officer and it's not easy trying to put a man in his place when he's a general. It was Captain Kuttner who came to my assistance. Rescued me, if you like. He told the General off, in so many words. The General was furious and swore a lot at the Captain and told him to mind his own effing business. But Captain Kuttner was wonderful, sir. He ignored the General and escorted me back below stairs before the General could touch me again.'

I shook my head. 'Some of these SS generals are loathsome,' I said. 'I've just come out of a rather rough meeting with General Hildebrandt. And he really put me back in my shell. Was it he who touched you?'

'No.'

I sighed. 'Rosa. Please. I'm in a real spot here. One of these men – yes, maybe even one of these cauliflowers – murdered a man in cold blood. Right here in this room. The room was locked from the inside and the window was bolted, which means that this investigation is already difficult. Don't make it impossible. You need to tell me who it was who touched you last night.'

'It was General Henlein.'

'Thank you.'

'What happened when Captain Kuttner escorted you below stairs, Rosa?'

'We talked a bit. Like we usually did. About nothing much, really.'

'Tell me one of the things you used to talk about, Rosa.'

She shrugged. 'Prague. We talked about Prague. We both agreed that it's very beautiful. And we also talked about our home town.'

'You're not from Halle-an-der-Saale, too?'

'Sort of. I'm from Reidesburg, which is just outside Halle.'

'It seems as though everyone but me is from Halle. General Heydrich is from Halle, do you know that?'

'Of course. Everyone knows about the Heydrichs in Halle. Someone else here is from Halle, too; at least that's what Albert told me, but I'm afraid I don't remember who that is.'

'What else did he tell you?'

'That he went to the same school as the General. The Reform Real-gymnasium. My brother Rolf went there, too. It's the best school in town.'

'Sounds like they had a lot in common. Albert and the General.'

'Yes. He said things had been difficult for him, lately. But that the General had been very kind to him.'

The idea of Heydrich being kind was not something I felt like contemplating. It was like hearing that Hitler liked children, or that Ivan the Terrible had owned a puppy.

'Did he elaborate on any of that? On why things had been difficult? On exactly how the General had been kind to him?'

Rosa looked at her handkerchief as if the answer lay crushed inside its sodden interior.

'Albert made me promise not to tell anyone about it. He said that people in the SS were not supposed to talk about such things. And that it might get me into trouble.'

'So why was he telling you about it?'

'Because he said he had to tell someone. To get it off his chest.'

'Well, he's dead now and so is that promise, I think.'

'I suppose so. But do *you* promise not to tell anyone that I spoke about this with you?'

'Yes. I promise.'

Rosa nodded. And hesitantly, she gave voice to what Kuttner had told her.

'He said he was in our Latvian provinces during the summer and that Germany had done terrible things there. That lots of people, thousands of people, had been killed for no other reason than that they were Jews. Old men, women and children. Whole villages full of defenceless people who had nothing to do with the war. He said that, at first, he carried out his orders and commanded the firing squads that murdered these people. But after a while, he'd had enough and refused to have anything more to do with these killings himself. Only this landed him in trouble with his superior officers.' She shook her head. 'It seemed unbelievable to me, but when he talked about it he started to cry and so I couldn't help but believe him, at the time. I mean a man – especially an officer – he doesn't cry for nothing, does he? But now, I don't know. Do you really think it can be true what he told me, Commissar Gunther? About the killings?'

'I'm afraid it's true, Rosa. Every word of it. And not just in Latvia. It's going on everywhere east of Berlin. For all I know it's even going on here in Bohemia. But he was wrong about one thing.

Within the SS and the SD, it's an open secret what's been going on in the eastern territories. And just to put your mind at rest, I'm almost certain it wasn't his talking about this that got him killed, but something else.'

Rosa nodded gratefully. 'Thank you, Commissar. I was worried about that.'

'Tell me something. When Captain Kuttner intervened on your behalf, with General Henlein, you said the General swore at Albert.'

'That's right.'

'Did he threaten him?'

'Yes.'

'Can you remember his exact words?'

'Perhaps not exactly. As well as a lot of horrible words I don't want to repeat, the General said something along the lines of "I'll remember you, Kuttner, you worthless little coward." And "I'll make you pay for this, just see if I don't."'

'Did anyone else hear that besides you, Rosa?'

'Mister Kritzinger. General Heydrich. They must have heard it. And I suppose some of the others too, but I don't remember their names. In their uniforms they all look the same to me.'

'I have the same problem. And that's partly why I took mine off. Sometimes, when I'm playing detective, it's necessary to put myself apart from everyone else. But frankly I hope I never have to put the uniform on again.'

'You're beginning to sound a lot like Albert.'

'I suppose that's why I liked him.'

'You're a strange one, too, Commissar. For a policeman.'

'I get a lot of that. Remember that wild kid they found walking around Nuremberg during the last century? The one who claimed he'd spent his early life alone in a darkened cell?'

'Kaspar Hauser. Yes, I remember. He ended his days in Ansbach, didn't he? Everyone knows that old story.'

'The only difference between me and Kaspar is that I have a terrible feeling I'm going to end *my* days in a darkened cell. So, for that reason alone, it might be best if you made me a promise not to tell anyone that we've had this conversation.'

'I promise.'

'All right, you can run along now. I'm going to search Albert's room.'

'I thought you already did.'

'What do you mean?'

'I mean that the other two adjutants, Captains Kluckholn and Pomme, were here already when I came in to strip the bed. They'd emptied the drawers into some cardboard boxes and took them away.'

'No, that was nothing to do with me. However, they probably wanted to collect Albert's personal effects to send back home to his parents. The way your pals do when you catch the last bus home.'

'Yes, I expect so.'

289

But Rosa Steffel didn't sound any more convinced of this than I was.

On the way back to the Morning Room I found Kritzinger winding the long-case clock. I looked at it and checked my wristwatch but the butler was shaking his head.

'I wouldn't ever set your watch by this clock, sir,' he said. 'It's running very slow.'

'Is that well-known in the house?' I was thinking of the approximate times that had been given to me in Heydrich's study earlier on.

'Generally, yes. The clock urgently needs to see a clockmaker.'

'There must be plenty of those in Prague. This city's got more clocks than Salvador Dali.'

'You would think so, sir. But so far my own inquiries have revealed that all of them seem to be Jews.'

'A Jew can't fix a clock?'

'Not in this house, sir.'

'No, I suppose not. That was naïve of me, wasn't it? This is an interesting time we live in, wouldn't you say? Even if it is always the wrong one.'

I glanced at the gold pocket watch in Kritzinger's hand.

'How about your watch, Herr Kritzinger? Can that be relied upon?'

'Yes sir. It's a Glashütte and belonged to my late father. He was a station master, on the railways in Posen. A good watch is essential for a

290

railwayman in Prussia, if the trains are to run on time.'

'And did he? Get the trains to run on time?'

'Yes sir.'

'Me, I always thought it was the Leader who did that.'

Kritzinger regarded me with polite patience. 'Was there something I could help you with, sir?'

'According to that Glashütte of yours, Kritzinger, what time did the party in the library fold last night?'

'The last gentlemen went up to bed just before two, sir.'

'And they were?'

'I believe it was General Henlein and Colonel Bohme.'

'I believe General Henlein made himself a late-night snack out of Captain Kuttner. Is that right?'

'I'm not sure what you mean, sir.'

'Sure you do. The General cut the Captain off at the tops of his boots, didn't he?'

'I believe the General might have said something to the Captain, yes sir.'

'Didn't he threaten him?'

'I wouldn't like to say, sir.'

Kritzinger snapped the lid shut on the gold pocket watch and dropped the timepiece into his vest pocket. It was an impatient action, quite at odds with his general demeanour, which was always to be of service even when it was in the

291

face of the provocation I offered, like asking him apparently frivolous or trivial questions that bordered on the impertinent or the unpatriotic.

'I can understand that. Nobody likes a *Petzer*. Especially when the *Petzer* is the butler. In relation to their employers and perhaps their guests, too, good butlers are expected to behave like the three wise monkeys, right?'

Kritzinger's head bowed almost imperceptibly. 'That describes my position vis à vis my superiors, only up to a point, sir. As you suggest, I am obliged always to observe. But I never judge. One must always guard against such unnecessary distractions in service.'

'Particularly now, I'd have thought. Working for General Heydrich.'

'I really couldn't say, sir.'

'Herr Kritzinger? I respect you. And I wouldn't ever try to bully a man who wears an Iron Cross ribbon in his lapel. The way I figure it, you probably won yours the same way I won mine: in hell. Fighting a real war against real soldiers who fought back, most of them. So you'll know that I'm not likely to be a man who makes idle threats. But this is a murder inquiry, Kritzinger, and that means I'm supposed to behave like a very nosy fellow and take a peep between the pots on everyone's window ledge. I don't like doing it any more than you do, but I will do it even if I have to throw every fucking pot through your window. Now what did General Henlein say?'

The butler stared at me for a long moment,

blinking with silent disapproval, like a cat in an empty fishmonger's.

'I can assure you, I do appreciate your position. There's no need for profanity, please, sir.'

I sighed and thumbed a cigarette into my mouth.

'I think there's every fucking reason for profanity when someone is murdered. Profanity helps to remind us that this isn't something that happened politely and with good manners, Kritzinger. You can polish the silver on this all you want, but a man was shot last night, and every time I put a cigarette near my mouth I can still taste his blood on my fingers. I see a lot of bodies in my line of work. Sometimes it looks like I brush it off, but "fuck" is what I still say to myself every time I see some poor bastard with a leaky hole in his chest. It helps to focus on the true profanity of what happened. Do I have to swear more loudly and twist your face in my hand while I'm doing it or are you going to heave it up? What did General Henlein say to Captain Kuttner?'

Kritzinger coloured and then glanced around nervously.

'The General did threaten the Captain, sir.'

'With what? A blanket bath? A kiss on the cheek. Come on, Kritzinger, I'm through dancing with you.'

'General Henlein had taken a fancy to one of the maids, sir. Rosa. Rosa Steffel. She's a good girl and she certainly did not encourage him. But the General had consumed a little too much alcohol.'

'You mean he was drunk.'

'That's not for me to say, sir. But I do believe he was not quite himself. He made a pass at Rosa, that left the girl embarrassed, and I would have intervened had not the Captain done so first. This earned him a reprimand from General Henlein. More than just a reprimand, perhaps. He was abusive. But I recall it wasn't just General Henlein, sir, who spoke so violently. Which is another reason, perhaps, I did not interfere, sooner. Colonel Bohme had something to say as well, and between them they straightened the unfortunate Captain's tie for him.'

'Give me some verbs, here, Kritzinger. What were they going to do to him when they were sober?'

'I do believe that the General called the Captain a filthy coward and said he'd make him pay for his damned interference. Then the Colonel came in with his two pfennigs' worth. He accused Captain Kuttner of insubordination and of being a Jew lover.'

'What did Captain Kuttner say to that?'

'Mostly nothing at all, sir. He just took it as you might have expected given their difference in ranks.' Pointedly, he added, 'The way a butler might have to take abuse from one of his employer's more uncouth and loutish house guests.'

That made me smile. It was easy to see how Kritzinger had won his Iron Cross.

'Colonel Bohme also mentioned something

294

about sending Captain Kuttner to the eastern front where his cheek and insubordination would receive short shrift from his commanders. Captain Kuttner replied – and I believe I'm quoting him here – that "it would be a privilege and an honour to serve with real soldiers in a real army commanded by real generals".'

'He said that?'

'Yes sir. He did.'

'Good for him.'

'I thought so too, sir.'

'Thank you, Herr Kritzinger. I'm sorry if I was loutish with you.'

'That's all right, sir. We both of us have jobs to do.'

I glanced at my wristwatch again and saw that I had five minutes before I was supposed to see General von Eberstein in the Morning Room.

'One more thing, Kritzinger. Did you see Captain Kuttner before he went to bed?'

'Yes sir. It was after two. By my watch. Not this clock.'

'How did he seem?'

'A little depressed. And tired. Very tired.'

'Oh?'

'I remarked upon it. And wished him a good night.'

'What did he say to that?'

'He gave a bitter sort of laugh, and said that he thought he'd probably had his last good night for a long while. I confess this struck me as an unusual thing to say, and when I asked him what he meant he said that the only way he would sleep would be if he were to take some sleeping pills. Which he intended to do.'

'So you had the impression that he hadn't yet taken them?'

Kritzinger paused and thought about this. 'Yes. But as I say, he certainly didn't look like a man who needed sleeping pills.'

'Because he looked so tired already?'

'That's right, sir.'

'Did you see him drink very much last night?'

'No. He hardly drank at all. He had a glass of beer in his hand before he went to bed, but now I come to think of it that was all I saw him drink the whole evening. He seemed to be a most abstemious sort of person, if I'm honest.'

'Thank you. By the way I should like to have a plan of the house, with an indication of who was in each of the bedrooms. Is that possible?'

'Yes, sir. I'll see to it.'

'All right, Kritzinger. That'll be all for now.'

'Thank you, sir. Will you be lunching with everyone, sir?'

'I really hadn't thought about it. But I missed breakfast and now I find I'm ravenously hungry, so yes, I will.'

SS Obergruppenführer Karl von Eberstein was chatting with Kurt Kahlo when I came into the Morning Room. He was a genial type for an aristocrat.

'Ah, Commissar Gunther, there you are. We were beginning to think you'd forgotten me.'

He was early and he knew it, but he was also a general and I wasn't yet ready to start contradicting him.

'I hope I haven't kept you waiting for long, sir.'

'No, no. I was just admiring General Heydrich's grand piano. It's a Blüthner. Very fine.'

He was standing right in front of the instrument – which was as big and black as a Venetian gondola – and touching the keys, experimentally, like a curious child.

'Do you play, sir?'

'Very badly. Heydrich is the musical one. But of course it runs in that family. His father, Bruno, was something of a star at the Halle Conservatory. He was a great man and of course a great Wagnerian.'

'You sound as if you knew him, sir.'

'Bruno? Oh, I did. I did. I'm from Halle-an-der-Saale myself.'

'Someone else from Halle. That's a coincidence.'

'Not really. My mother was Heydrich's godmother. It was me who introduced the General to Himmler and set him on his way.'

'Then you must feel very proud of him, sir.'

'I do, Commissar. Very much so. He's a credit to his country and to the whole National Socialist movement.'

'I had no idea that you and he were so close.'

Von Eberstein came away from the piano and stood beside me in front of the fire, warming his backside with conspicuous enjoyment.

He was in his late forties. On his grey tunic was an Iron Cross first and second class, indicating he'd been given it twice, no small feat, even for an aristocrat. Still, there was a pious air about him – a bit like a hypocritical priest.

'I like to think of him as my protégé. I'm certain he wouldn't mind me saying that.'

The way he said this made me think that Heydrich just might mind him saying that.

'How about Captain Kuttner?' I asked. 'He was from Halle, too. Did you know him well?'

'Well enough. His father I know rather better. We were in the Army together. During the last war. Pastor Kuttner was our regimental chaplain. But for him I'm not sure I'd have fared as well as I did. He was a tremendous comfort to us all.'

'I'm sure.'

Von Eberstein shook his head. 'It's a great pity that this happened. A great pity.'

'Yes. It is, sir.'

'And you're quite certain it was murder and not suicide?'

'Of course we'll have to wait for the autopsy this afternoon to be completely sure. But I'm more or less certain, yes.'

'Well, you know your business, I suppose.'

'Why do you mention suicide?'

'Only because of what happened to Albert in

298

Latvia. He tried to kill himself there. Or at least threatened to kill himself.'

'Exactly what did happen? I'm still a little unclear about that.'

'I believe he suffered a nervous breakdown brought on by the difficulty of his war assignments. I mean, of course, the evacuation of the Jews in the eastern territories. Not everyone is equal to the tasks that have been set before us as a people.'

'I wonder if you might be a little more specific, sir. Under the circumstances I think I should know all there is to know.'

'Yes, I agree with you, Commissar. Perhaps you should.'

Von Eberstein proceeded to explain, using words and phrases that made the whole filthy business of murdering thousands of people sound like an engineering job, or perhaps an exercise in crowd control after a large game of football. It was typical of the Nazis that they should call a spade an agrarian implement; and as I listened to one weasel word after another, I felt I wanted to slap him.

'Responding to fundamental orders issued in Berlin, Lieutenant Kuttner was assigned the task of tactically coordinating the activities of a special detachment of SS that was made up of units of Latvian auxiliary police. Throughout the summer this same detachment carried out many extensive special actions in and around the Riga area. Principally, Kuttner's function was to perform a rudimentary census for the purpose of apprehending communists as well as identifying provincial Jews. After the census, Jews were ordered to assemble at a given location and from there they were evacuated. It was later found that some of these evacuations were carried out with unnecessary brutality, and this seems to have occasioned feelings of guilt and depression in poor Kuttner. He started drinking heavily, and following one protracted bout of drinking he threatened a superior officer with his pistol. Subsequent to that, he tried but was prevented from shooting himself. Because of these incidents he was sent home to face a court martial.'

'Well, that's clear enough,' I said and watched Kahlo cover the smile on his face with a hand and its cigarette.

'Yes, it was an unfortunate business and might have severely blighted what was a very promising career. Albert was a brilliant young lawyer. But the Reichsführer is not an insensitive man and fully understands the problems that are sometimes provoked by these special actions. I talked it over with him at some length—'

'I'm sorry, sir,' I interrupted. 'To clarify what you said just now. You mean you discussed Lieutenant Kuttner's case with Reichsführer Himmler, on an individual basis?'

'That's right. He and I agreed that it should not be held against a man that he was too sensitive for such psychologically arduous duties. Given his legal talents it was a waste of a fine mind just to allow him to be cashiered without a second chance to redeem himself. Consequently, Heydrich agreed to take Kuttner onto his personal staff; and if he had not, then I would certainly have done so. Captain Kuttner was far too able an officer to let go.'

'You were referring to Lieutenant Kuttner, sir. This is only a few weeks ago and now he is a Captain. Am I to understand that not only was there no court martial, but that Lieutenant Kuttner was promoted Captain upon joining General Heydrich's staff?'

'For reasons of administrative efficiency it's usually best if adjutants are all of an equal rank. It saves any petty bickering.'

'If you don't mind me saying so, sir, but Kuttner was lucky to have that kind of vitamin B. I mean, to have two patrons who can count the Reichsführer-SS as a friend.'

'Yes. Perhaps.'

'How long have you and Reichsführer Himmler been friends, sir?'

'Oh, let's see now. I joined the Party in 1922. And the SS in 1925.'

'That explains the gold Party badge,' observed Kahlo. 'It seems as if you've been part of the movement since the very beginning, sir. If I'd had the good sense you had then I might be something better than a Criminal Assistant now. No disrespect intended, sir.'

'Oh, I wasn't always so resolute in my devotion to the Party.'

'Go on, sir.' Kahlo grinned.

'No, really. There was a time – after the failure of the Beer Hall putsch and despairing of our cause – when I even left the Party.'

Von Eberstein wagged a finger at Kahlo.

'So, you see, we all make mistakes. For three years I was—'

He paused and looked thoughtful for a moment.

'Well, I was doing other things.'

'Like what, sir?'

'It doesn't matter now. What matters now is that we find the person who murdered Captain Kuttner. Is that not so, Commissar?'

'Yes sir.'

'Have you any ideas on that score?'

'I've got plenty of ideas, sir. We Germans have never been short of those. But mostly what I know is limited by the terms in which the mind can think, which means it's probably best I don't try to explain what those ideas are. Not yet, anyway. What I can tell you is that not everyone liked the young Captain as much as you and General Heydrich. And I'm not talking about the Czechs, sir. I figure that given half a chance they'd shoot any one of us wearing a German uniform. No, I'm talking about—'

'Yes, I know what you're talking about.' Von Eberstein sighed. 'No doubt you've heard about that unfortunate incident in the library last night. When General Henlein spoke with unnecessary harshness to Captain Kuttner.'

'I'm not saying it demonstrates a motive for

302

murder, but when you've seen men murdered for no motive at all, as I have, it gives pause for thought. Henlein was drunk. He was armed. Clearly he didn't like Kuttner. And he certainly had the opportunity.'

'All of us had that, Commissar. You've a difficult job to do here and no mistake. But I've known Konrad Henlein ever since I was the Police President of Munich. And I can tell you this: he's no murderer. Why, the man used to be a teacher in a school.'

'What kind of teacher?'

'A gymnastics teacher.'

'So he's the one,' I said, thinking of the girl in the suite at the Imperial Hotel – the one Arianne had spoken to.

'What?'

'I was just thinking. The gym teacher at my school was a regular sadist. Now I come to think of it, I can't imagine a man who was more likely to murder someone than him.'

Von Eberstein smiled. 'I'm sure that Henlein isn't like that. Indeed I'm confident that none of the senior ranks here in Heydrich's own house could have committed such a heinous crime.'

But I didn't share his confidence.

'When this is all over, Commissar; when you have – as I'm sure you will – solved the crime, I believe we'll find that the solution is much less remarkable than we might suppose right now. Isn't that usually the case?'

'I might agree with you, except for the very singular circumstances of this particular case. Most murders are simple, it's true. Simple, sordid, violent crimes of passion, greed, or most likely alcohol. This isn't anything like that. There appears to be no love interest here. Nothing was stolen. And if the murderer was drunk then he was an unusually thoughtful drunk who was very careful not to leave a trace of his presence in Captain Kuttner's room. It's only an opinion at this stage, however I have the feeling that someone is playing a game here. Possibly to embarrass General Heydrich.'

'It's true there are those who are jealous of Heydrich,' admitted von Eberstein.

'Possibly to embarrass all of you.'

'In which case I wonder that you can write off the Czechs as possible culprits quite so quickly, Commissar. Perhaps you've forgotten how fond the Three Kings were of teasing the local Gestapo. One of them even left a provocative and embarrassing message in poor Fleischer's coat pocket. And it strikes me that this is just the sort of stunt they might pull. Especially now, when their organization is under threat. If I were you I'd be trying to examine the backgrounds of the house staff in closer detail. They may be in the SS but some of them have a German–Czech background. I wouldn't be at all surprised if that throws up something that wasn't found when they were checked the first time.'

'General von Eberstein's got a point, sir,' said Kahlo. 'It could be them thumbing their noses at us. Just like before. And nothing would give those bastards more pleasure than to have us chasing our own tails.'

I grinned. 'That's what it feels like, doesn't it?'

'I don't believe it,' said Kahlo. 'Krautwickel. I thought that was it after the potato soup. That had real bacon in it. And real potatoes, too. But this is even better. I haven't had Krautwickel since the war started. If this keeps up, sir, I might just have to kill someone myself just so that we keep this investigation going for a good while longer.'

'That's as good a motive for murder as any I've heard today,' I said. 'I may even have to put you down on my list of suspects after that remark.'

We were in the Dining Room, but with Heydrich and Ploetz and some Gestapo officers away in pursuit of Vaclav Moravek, there were fewer of us for lunch at the Lower Castle than there had been for dinner. At my direction, Kahlo and I were seated at the opposite end of the table from everyone else; not because I disliked their company – which of course I did – but mostly because I wanted to avoid discussing the case with any of them. Besides, I hoped that our position at the table would set us apart and help to remind the cauliflower that a murder investigation was being conducted. Doubtless that suited Doctor Jury very well, and probably General Hildebrandt too, who, following their interviews, now regarded me as they would have regarded a large and verminous dog.

Another reason I wanted to sit apart from the SS cauliflower was to give me a chance to get to know Kurt Kahlo, who to my surprise I liked more than I had ever expected to like anyone at Heydrich's house.

'Why do they call Mannheim the chequerboard?'

'Because it's the most regularly built city in Germany, that's why. The city centre is divided into one hundred and thirty-six neat squares and the blocks of houses are only distinguished by letters and numerals. My dad used to live at K4. He was a factory foreman at Daimler but he got hit hard by the inflation. Me and my brother had to go to work to help supplement the family income and so that we could stay on at school, if that doesn't sound like a contradiction.'

'You married?'

'Five years, to Eva. She works at a local hotel.'

'Which one?'

'The Park.'

'Any good?'

'Too pricey for me.'

'I was in the hotel business for a while. I was the house bull at the Adlon.'

'Nice.'

'How does Eva like the hotel business?'

'She likes it. The guests can be a bit much sometimes. Especially the English, at least when they were still coming to Germany. They used to try it on a bit, and give themselves airs, you know?'

'Sounds a lot like this place.'

'Yeah.' Kahlo looked sideways at the cauliflower. 'How'd you come to know General Heydrich?'

'The way you know a dangerous dog. Most of the time I just cross the road or walk the other way when I see him coming. But sometimes he corners me and I have to humour him or end up badly bitten. Really, I'm like one of those four animals on his way to the town of Bremen. A donkey, probably. And like the donkey I'd just like to live without an owner and become a musician.'

'What instrument do you play?'

'Nothing, of course. Whoever heard of a donkey that could play a musical instrument? But I seem to be in the robbers' house, all the same; just like in the story.'

Kahlo grinned. 'It's not what you'd call a relaxing place, is it? Some of these bastards would frighten Himmler himself.' He shook his head. 'I almost feel sorry for Captain Kuttner.'

'Almost?'

'I met him, remember?'

'What did you think of him?'

Kahlo shrugged. 'Hardly matters now, does it? He's dead.'

'If you think that's going to save you from telling everything to your barber, you're wrong.'

'All right. I thought he was an arrogant little prick. Like all these fucking adjutants, he thought he was more than just his master's voice. He turned up at Kripo headquarters here in Prague a few days ago demanding this and that and as soon as possible. My boss, Willy Abendschoen, had to deal with him and that meant to some extent I did, too. A right little cunt he was.'

'A few days ago?'

'Monday. Heydrich wanted a report on something.'

'Specifically?'

'OTA transmission intercepts. OTA is the code-word for all the intercepts.'

'You mean radio broadcasts to the British, by the Czechos.'

'No, no. That's what made this interesting. The Czechos were *receiving* broadcasts, and what's more, from somewhere in the Fatherland. Intelligence tip-offs. Abendschoen reckoned that the Czechos were sending the information on, to Benes, in London, so that he could boost his standing with Churchill and the Tommy intelligence community.'

'A Czech spy in Germany.'

Kahlo shook his head. 'No, a *German* spy in Germany. As I'm sure you know, there's nothing worse than that. I'm not entirely privy to all of this, you understand, sir; it goes well above my pay grade. But here in Prague the word on the cobbles is that there's a high-level traitor in Berlin who's behind the OTA transmissions; who's been feeding the Czechos with top-grade information about Reich policy on a number of things. Heydrich wanted everything we had on OTA so that he could hand it all over to a special search group he's setting up inside the SD. The Traitor X Group it's called, or VXG, for short. Catching Moravek, the third of the Three Kings, is just half the game. You catch him then you stand a better chance of identifying traitor X.'

'Yes, I see. I think I'm going to need to know more about Kuttner's movements in the days leading up to his death.'

'Very good, sir. But right now all I've got are his movements in the hours leading up to his death.'

'Let's hear them.'

We sat back in our chairs as the SS waiters cleared away. Kahlo found his notebook and flicked through several pages until a wet thumb found his place. He was about to read when the waiters returned with dessert. Kahlo's eyes were out on stalks.

'That's Mish-Mash,' he said, groaning with anticipated pleasure. 'With real cherry-sauce.'

I tasted the sauce. 'Actually, it's cranberry,' I said.

'No,' he breathed.

'I'll eat while you talk.'

Kahlo looked at his shredded pancake pudding, licked his lips and hesitated. 'You won't finish all that sauce, will you, sir?'

'No, of course not. Now, let's hear it.'

309

Reluctantly, Kahlo started to read out his notes.

'Yesterday lunchtime you know about because you were here. According to Elisabeth Schreck, Heydrich's secretary, at three p.m. Kuttner made a couple of telephone calls. One to Carl Maria Strasse – sorry, sir, that's Kripo HQ – and one to the Pecek Palace: Gestapo HQ. At around four, you saw him again, sir, on the road to the Upper Castle. At five he spent an hour in General Heydrich's office. I don't yet know what that was about. Then he went to his room: Kritzinger saw him go through the door. At eight o'clock there were drinks in the library and then all of you listened to the Leader's speech on the radio. Fleischer's telephone call from Gestapo head-quarters was put through just after nine, and that's when you saw Kuttner outside, having an argument with Captain Kluckholn. Do you know what that was about, sir?'

'Not yet.'

'Kuttner helps to bring some champagne into the library after the speech and after that things are understandably vague. Just after one a.m. there is some sort of altercation between Kuttner and General Henlein and Colonel Bohme. I'm not quite sure what that was about.'

'General Henlein made a pass at one of the maids. Her name is Rosa Steffel. Kuttner was her champion.'

'I see. Then he's in Heydrich's office for a while with the General and Colonel Jacobi.' Kahlo lowered his voice. 'He's the one who I find to be the most sinister of the lot.'

'Then Kritzinger sees Kuttner just before two and wishes him a good night. Says he seemed dog-tired.'

Kahlo made a note of that and then continued reading his notes.

'At six o'clock this morning Kuttner fails to awaken Captain Pomme, as arranged. Nothing new there. He often overslept because he was taking sleeping pills. At six-thirty Pomme says he's still knocking on Kuttner's door, trying to awaken him. At six-forty-five Pomme goes to fetch Kritzinger to see if there's some other means of opening the door, which is locked from the inside. There isn't. Kritzinger tells one of the footmen to go and fetch a ladder and see if he can't get in from the outside.'

'And did he?'

'Yes. But the ladder was locked up and the footman had to go and fetch the gardener, so it was seven-fifteen a.m. by the time he brought it around to the window. Coming back a bit, though: at seven a.m. Heydrich is also outside Kuttner's door, and that's when he tells Pomme and the butler to break it down. Entering the room they find Kuttner dead and Captain Pomme is dispatched to fetch Doctor Jury. Jury arrives in the room just as the footman arrives with the ladder.'

'We shall want to speak to that footman. Maybe he saw something.'

'His name is Fendler, sir.'

'Then at seven-thirty I get the call from Ploetz in my room at the Imperial. And at eight-thirty we viewed the scene of the crime.'

'What were you doing at the Imperial anyway? Why weren't you staying here in your room, sir?'

'I was sleeping. What do you know about Veronal?'

'It's barbital. Sleeping pills. Take too many and you don't wake up. That's about it really.'

'Ever use them yourself?'

'The wife did. She'd been working nights at the Park and couldn't sleep in the day. So the doctor gave her some Veronal. But she didn't care for the stuff at all. They always left her feeling like she'd been coshed.'

'Strong then.'

'Very.'

'Kuttner goes to bed at around two a.m. having told the butler that he intended to take some sleeping pills. Nobody sees him enter his room.'

'I'm not sure if I'd take sleeping pills knowing I had to be up at six,' observed Kahlo. 'Then again, you do get used to them, so it's possible he didn't see that as a problem.'

'Which may be why he doesn't undress for bed. He's still dressed when we found him.'

'Looked like he took one boot off and then got tired. Or dead. So then maybe he was shot before he entered his room.'

'In the corridor.' But I was shaking my head

even as I said it. 'Sure. After he's shot – and by the way nobody hears the shot—'

'Perhaps the murderer used a sound suppressor.'

'For a P38? Hasn't been invented yet. So, after he's shot in the corridor and no one hears anything, he staggers along to his room without mentioning it to anyone or shouting for help, locks the door carefully behind him, as you do when you've just been shot, lies down on the bed just to get his breath back, removes a boot, and then dies sometime between two and five-thirty a.m.'

'It's a mystery, isn't it?'

'No, not really. I solve this kind of case all the time. Usually in the penultimate chapter. I like to keep the last few pages for restoring some sort of normality to the world.'

'You know what I reckon, sir? I reckon that if you solve this case Heydrich will probably promote you.'

'That's what I'm worried about.'

'And then you won't ever get to Bremen to live there without an owner.'

'Shut up and eat your Mish-Mash.'

Kahlo's mention of the Traitor X Group and a top-level spy in Germany who had been transmitting information to the Czechos got me wondering about Arianne and her friend Gustav, the man she claimed to have met in the Jockey Bar.

A smooth type with a thin prick accent and spats. Or so she had described him. A civil servant with a gold cigarette holder and a little gold eagle in his lapel. A man whose nerves had prevented him from meeting Franz Koci, a former lieutenant of Czech artillery and possibly one of the last members of the Three Kings group operating in Berlin – at least he had been until a collision with a taxi cab in the blackout had terminated his career as a spy.

Was it possible that Gustav and Heydrich's traitor X were one and the same person?

Arianne struck me as an unlikely sort of spy. After all, hadn't she confessed to being Gustav's unwitting courier *before* I had told her that I was a cop? And, having told her I was a Commissar from the Alex, what kind of spy was it who, instead of disappearing the very next day, chose to begin a relationship with someone who very probably ought to have seen it as his duty to inform the Gestapo about her? What kind of spy was it who was prepared to risk so much for so little? After all, I was privy to no secret information she could have passed to anyone. Surely she was just what she seemed to be: a good-time girl with a dead husband and a brother who was a kennel hound with the Field Military Police. I'd checked him out, too. What else did she want but a chance to see a bit of what life had to offer before the Nazis turned her into yet another dutiful little German wife producing children for her first-class rabbit medal – the Honour Cross for the German Mother?

All the same, now that I knew about the local SD's VXG, it had become very obvious that bringing Arianne along to Prague for my own pleasure had helped put her in considerable danger; and it seemed imperative that she return to Berlin as soon as possible.

It was while I was deciding to send Arianne back to Berlin that I remembered Major Ploetz had given me a letter forwarded from the Alex. Sitting in the Morning Room with a coffee and a cigarette awaiting the next senior officer on my list, I read it.

The letter was from a girl I knew in Paris; her name was Bettina and she worked at the Lutetia Hotel. I'd stayed there during my posting to the French capital. I had fixed her up with a better job at the Adlon and she was writing to thank me and to tell me that she would be coming to Berlin before Christmas. She hoped to see me then. She wrote a lot of other things besides, and since I didn't get many letters, least of all from attractive girls, I read it again. I even passed it under my nose a couple of times, as it seemed to be scented – then again, that might have been my own imagination.

I was reading the letter a third time when Kahlo ushered General Henlein into the Morning Room.

Henlein wore round metallic-framed glasses that flashed in the firelight like newly minted coins. His hair was dark and wavy but the wave was on the ebb-flow. His mouth was sulky, and facially he was not unlike Doctor Jury. It was hard to connect this 43-year-old from Maffesdorf and the leader of the Sudeten German Movement with the vigorous gymnastics teacher described by Arianne's girl friend at the Imperial.

Kahlo handed me the plan of the house that Kritzinger had given him, and while Henlein made himself comfortable I glanced over it briefly and, for the moment, noted only that Henlein had occupied the room immediately next to Captain Kuttner's.

Kahlo sat down on the piano stool. Henlein, seated on the sofa opposite me, picked some fluff off his breeches, checked the cutlery on his tunic lapel – another War Merit Cross with swords – and smiled nervously several times. He had good teeth, I'll say that for him; they were the only vigorous-looking thing about him.

'Let me say something before we go any further.' He spoke quietly, as if he was used to being listened to. 'It's no secret that I was blue last night. I think we all were, after the Leader's speech and the good news about the Three Kings.'

He paused for a moment, as if waiting for me to agree with him; but I didn't say anything. I just lit another cigarette and let him hang there.

Momentarily discomfited, he swallowed notice-ably and then continued:

'Toward the end of the evening I believe I may have made certain remarks to the unfortunate Captain Kuttner that I now regret. They were spoken in the heat of the moment and under the influence of alcohol. I have never been much of a drinker. Alcohol does not agree with my constitution. I try to keep myself fit, you understand, as all of us should who are in the SS. It is an elite, after all, and a higher standard is expected of us. Not just physically, but in matters of behaviour, too. Consequently, it seems to me that my own behaviour was not all that it could have been. And in retrospect the poor Captain was quite right to remonstrate with me. Indeed, it is very much to that officer's credit that he did so.

'Of course when I heard what had happened I was shocked and saddened. I deeply regret this brave young officer's passing and also the fact that I was unable to apologize to him in person. In my own defence I should like to reiterate that it is quite out of character for me to behave in such an inappropriate fashion. But the circumstances of his death being what they are, I feel it is incumbent on me to state, upon my word as a German officer, that I did not shoot Captain Kuttner. Nor do I have any knowledge of his death. After returning to my own room at around two o'clock this morning, I have very little knowledge of anything except that I went to bed and awoke with a filthy hangover. It was after nine when Major Ploetz informed me of what had happened and explained that you were handling the official inquiry at the request of General Heydrich. And let me assure you, Commissar

Gunther, that I will cooperate with your investigation in any way I can. I'm sure that this can't be easy for you.'

'I appreciate your candour.'

Almost to my amusement, Henlein got up to leave. I let him get as far as the door before throwing a grappling hook after him.

'However, there are a few questions I should like to ask you.'

Henlein smiled again. This time the smile was sarcastic.

'Do I take it that you intend to cross-examine *me*?'

You would have thought he was Hitler himself the way Henlein pronounced that personal pronoun.

I shrugged. 'If that's what you want to call it. But look here, I'm only taking you at your word. You just offered to cooperate with my investigation in any way you can. Or am I mistaken?'

'I know what I said, Commissar Gunther,' he said, crisply, his glasses flashing angrily as his head moved with jerky indignation. 'I assumed that my word as a German officer – and not just any German officer – would suffice.'

He straightened a little and put his fists on his hipbones as if challenging me to knock him over. I wouldn't have minded punching him on the nose at that, if only to find out for myself how vigorous he really was.

'You're quite right, sir.' I paused to achieve the full amount of mockery that was implied in my next remark. 'That was an assumption, I'm afraid. And it isn't correct. As you also said yourself, General Heydrich has authorized me to handle an official inquiry, and that does necessitate my asking a lot of questions, some of which might very well sound impertinent to a man of your high standing. But I'm afraid that can't be helped. So, perhaps you'd like to sit down again. I'll try not to keep you too long.'

Henlein sat down and regarded me with some disfavour.

'According to a plan I have here of all the officer accommodations in the Lower Castle, which has been prepared by Herr Kritzinger, you were in the room right next door to Captain Kuttner.'

'What of it?'

I smiled, patiently. 'Whenever a man is murdered I usually go and speak to his neighbours to ask if they heard or saw anything suspicious, that's what of it.'

Henlein sighed and then leaned back against the cushion and made a little steeple out of his fingers, which he tapped together with a pedant's impatience.

'Weren't you listening? I already said. I went to bed, drunk. I saw nothing and heard nothing.'

'You're sure about that?'

Henlein tutted loudly. 'Really, this is too much. I had assumed Heydrich had chosen you because you were a detective. Now I find you're nothing but a stupid policeman.'

I was getting tired of all this. I was tired of a lot of things, but being made to feel I was lucky to breathe the same air as the regional governor of the Sudetenland was close to the top of the whole tiresome heap. I decided to take Heydrich at his word and dispense with good manners; for me this was never particularly difficult, but when I let go I took even myself by surprise.

I sprang to my feet and coming around the back of the sofa Henlein was sitting on I pushed my jaw into his face.

'Listen, you pompous shit-curl, a man was murdered in that room. And in case you'd forgotten while you were sitting behind your nice desk on that lazy fat arse of yours, guns make loud noises when you pull the trigger.' I clapped my hands hard in front of his nose. 'They go "bang" and "bang" and "bang", and other people are supposed to do something about that noise when they hear it.'

Henlein was colouring now, lip quivering in anger.

'So don't give me "What of it?" and make like you were a hundred miles away with a cast-iron alibi. You were right next door to a man you had earlier threatened in front of several witnesses. That's just a brick's width away from being in the same room with him, see? So, you may be a senior officer, you might even be a gentleman for all I know, but you're also a goddamn suspect.'

'How dare you speak to me like that, Commissar Gunther?'

'Ask me that again,' I snarled back.

'How dare you speak to me like that?'

He stood up with the look of a man who was about to challenge me to a duel.

'I've a very good mind to punch you on the nose,' he said.

'I suppose that counts as brave coming from a man with that kind of tinfoil on his chest.' I pointed at his War Merit Cross. I said, flicking his Party badge with my forefinger, 'Well, I'm not scared.'

'I am going to make a point of breaking you, Commissar. I am going to take great pleasure in making sure that by the time this weekend has ended you will be directing traffic on Potsdamer Platz. I've never been insulted like this in all my years as a German officer. How dare you?'

Henlein walked toward the Morning Room door.

'That deserves an answer, General. I'll tell you how. You see, I know all about your little friend on the top floor of the Imperial Hotel. Betty, isn't it? Betty Kipsdorf? Apparently you and she get along very well. And why not? She's a real sweet girl, from what I hear.'

Henlein had stopped in his tracks as if commanded to do so on a parade ground by a particularly tough drill sergeant.

'I haven't seen her myself but my source tells me she thinks you're very vigorous. Somehow I doubt she means that you and she like to go for energetic walks in the countryside. And I do wonder how our host will greet the news that dear Betty is a Jew.'

He turned slowly and then sat down on a chair by the door, like a man awaiting a doctor's appointment. He took off his glasses and turned several shades of white before settling on the colour of a goat's cheese that seemed to reflect the greenish wallpaper.

'Yes. Sit down. Good move, General.'

'How did you find out?' he whispered.

For one glorious moment I thought I was about to hear a confession of murder.

'About the girl.'

'You idiot, I'm a cop not a brass monkey. If you're going to keep a joy-lady in a hotel then make sure she's the kind of girl who can keep her peep shut.'

It was good advice. I hoped I was paying attention to it myself.

The spectacles in his hand were trembling. Four years later, while being held by the Americans at the military barracks in Pilsen, Konrad Henlein would use the glass in those spectacles to cut open his veins and kill himself. But for now they were just a pair of harmless, trembling specs. Then he started to cry, which was tough because I'd put him through all of that without the least suspicion he'd shot Captain Kuttner. You get a feel for these things: Henlein was a lot of things – a pompous ass, a Nazi agitator, a womanizer – but he wasn't a murderer. It takes a lot of nerve to pull the trigger on a man in cold blood, and if his tears proved anything, it was that he didn't have what it takes.

'Relax. We're not going to tell anyone, are we, Kurt?'

I went over to the piano and offered Kahlo a cigarette. He took one, stood up and lit us both.

'No sir,' he said. 'Your little secret is quite safe with us, General. Provided of course that you cooperate.'

'Of course. I'll do anything you want. Anything. But I am telling you the truth, Herr Commissar. I didn't kill the Captain. It's as I told you. I was drunk. I went to bed around two. Even that's a blur, I'm afraid. I'm only aware of what I said to the unfortunate Captain because one of my brother officers drew it to my attention this morning. I feel terrible about what happened. But the first I knew that Captain Kuttner was dead was when Major Ploetz came and told me this morning. I'm not the type of person to kill anyone. Honestly. I'm almost a vegetarian, like the Leader, you know. It's true I do have a gun. It's in my room. But I am certain it's never been fired while it's been in my possession. I can fetch it now if you like and then perhaps you can check for yourself. I believe that we have scientists in police laboratories who can determine such things.'

Somewhere during the course of Henlein's miserable, pleading speech I stopped listening. I stared at the keys of the piano for a moment and then I stared out of the window, all the while wondering what the hell I was doing with my life. At least the cigarette tasted good. I'd reacquired a taste for good tobacco, and I told myself that when this was all over and Heydrich had Kuttner's murderer I was probably going to have to get used to the ration line again, and three Johnnies a day. Because I had the strong feeling that finding Kuttner's killer was going to impact upon my becoming Heydrich's bodyguard after all. I couldn't see how I was going to keep a job like that when I'd finished insulting all of his closest colleagues; at least, that was my earnest hope.

Then Kahlo was talking again and Henlein was answering him and it was another moment or two before I realized that the subject had changed. We were no longer speaking about Captain Kuttner or even Betty Kipsdorf but something entirely different.

'Your friend Heinz Rutha,' said Kahlo. 'The furniture designer. He hanged himself in prison, didn't he? In 1937, wasn't it?'

'Yes,' said Henlein.

'Because he was queer, too.'

'I wouldn't know about that.'

'Is that why you decided to work for Admiral Canaris and the Abwehr? Because of what happened to your friend? Because you held the Nazis responsible for that?'

'I don't know what you're talking about.'

'But maybe not just Canaris, eh? Maybe because of that you went to work for the British.

Maybe you're a British spy. Maybe you've always been a British spy, General Henlein. You help to destabilize the Czech Sudetenland for Hitler while all the time you're really working for the Tommies. Good cover, I'd have thought. I mean it doesn't get better than that, does it? Frankly I can't really say that I blame you. The way you were passed over first by Frank and then by Heydrich, you've every reason to feel aggrieved, haven't you, sir? So, how about it? Are you spying for the Tommies?'

'Please.' Henlein looked desperately at me. 'I really don't know anything about this.'

'Neither do I,' I said.

'I'm no more a spy than I am a murderer.'

'Says you,' said Kahlo.

'That's quite enough,' I told Kahlo.

'Suppose we let the Gestapo find out,' persisted Kahlo. 'Suppose we were to hand you over to Sergeant Soppa. You've heard of him, haven't you, General? He's the specialist they brought in to question the Three Kings. I haven't seen him in action myself but apparently he uses this technique he calls the Bascule. They strap you onto a wooden board, just like the one they use on a guillotine—'

'Thank you General Henlein, that will be all for now, sir.'

Kahlo was still speaking, only now I was talking over him. Not only that but I had Henlein by the arm and I was steering him out to the door of the Morning Room.

'If there's anything else you think we need to know then please don't hesitate to contact me, sir. As for your friend at the Imperial, my advice would be to get her out of there. Find somewhere else for your trysts. An apartment, perhaps. But not a hotel, General. If I know about Betty, it won't be long before someone else does, too.'

'Yes, I understand. Thank you, Herr Commissar. Thank you very much indeed.'

Henlein glanced uncertainly at Kahlo and then he was gone.

I closed the door behind him and, for a moment or two, Kahlo and I faced each other in awkward silence.

'What the hell was all that about?'

'You heard.'

'I guess I did at that.'

'You had him on the ropes.' Kahlo shrugged. 'It seemed a pity not to take advantage of that, sir. I thought that there might never be a better opportunity to ask him some questions that needed asking.'

'It's those questions that I'm interested in, Kurt. You see, I thought I was supposed to kick the ball. Only it turns out that you're allowed to pick it up and run with it. That makes me wonder what kind of game we're playing here.'

Kahlo looked sheepish. 'We're on the same side, sir. That's all that matters, isn't it?'

'Actually I wonder about that, too. This VXG. The Traitor X Group you mentioned. The one

326

that Heydrich was setting up to find the high-level spy who's been giving information to the Czechos. You wouldn't be part of that group, would you, Kurt?'

'Didn't I say?'

'You know you damn well didn't.'

'I should have thought it was obvious after what I told you over lunch about the VXG. About how Captain Kuttner came down to Kripo HQ to brief us about it. How would I have known about those OTA radio intercepts if I wasn't part of the group? That stuff is highly sensitive. By rights I shouldn't have told you about that at all.'

'So what else haven't you told me?'

'Frankly, I thought that enjoying General Heydrich's confidence as you do, you knew about traitor X yourself. That you knew that and that you knew—'

'What?'

'That everyone in this house is under suspicion.'

'Of being traitor X?'

'Yes sir. I assumed you would certainly know that much, at least.'

I shook my head. 'Let me get this straight. Everyone in this house is suspected of being a spy for the Czechos.'

Kahlo nodded. 'I don't think you are. And I know I'm not. And I'm damned sure Heydrich isn't. Or his three adjutants. Everyone else, well there's a question mark against everyone else, yes.'

He shrugged. 'I'm sorry, sir. I really thought you knew about all this.'

'I didn't.'

'Well that's hardly my fault is it? I just do what I'm fucking told. It's up to Heydrich what he tells you, not me. I'm just a Criminal Assistant.' He kissed his cigarette and continued: 'Maybe it slipped his mind. Maybe he assumed that I would tell you. Which I have.'

'When we were discussing a possible motive for someone murdering Captain Kuttner—'

'No sir,' he said firmly. 'You never discussed that with me. You discussed that with General Henlein.'

'Well, don't you think you might have mentioned it before now? In passing? I mean, if someone suspects you of being a spy, then that would be a pretty powerful fucking motive for murder, don't you think? Maybe Kuttner was onto someone in this house. Maybe that's why he was killed. But why should I have to know about that? I'm just the investigating detective. Jesus, I feel like a parrot with a cloth over my cage.'

'Try to look at it from my point of view, Commissar. Kuttner turns up at Prague Kripo on Monday. Several of us are picked out to join Heydrich's Traitor X Group. But Kuttner tells us that on no account are we to talk about this to anyone. It's all top-secret, he says. Anyone opens his pie hole about this group to anyone, the reward is a ticket on the partisan express. Then he gets killed and you're in charge of the investigation.

Heydrich's clever dick. That's what Ploetz says. Christ, that's what everyone says. And the way you speak to the General. Like you had a special licence. How am I to know that you're not fully in the picture, sir? I'm used to being told this but not that, see? I'm just a foot-soldier, sir. All this fucking cauliflower, I'm not familiar with it. And I'm certainly not used to hearing them getting roughed up by a mere captain like you.'

'Everyone in the house?' I repeated dumbly.

'More or less. Like I said, it's everyone except me and you and the adjutants. And Heydrich, of course. There's a list, see. Of suspects. I haven't got a copy myself, but I can remember who was on it. And Henlein's name was certainly one of them.'

I poured myself a cup of coffee and sipped it thoughtfully.

'Hildebrandt?'

Kahlo nodded.

'But he's an old friend of Heydrich's,' I said. 'To say nothing of the fact that he's an old friend of Hitler. Von Eberstein? What about him? Is he suspected, too?'

Kahlo nodded again.

'But how? How can they be under suspicion? That little gold Party badge is supposed to mean something.'

'I only know what I've been told. And that's not everything. Hildebrandt is a suspect because for two years, from 1928 until 1930, he was in

America. While he was there he went bankrupt as a farmer but someone paid off all his debts and then helped to set him up as a bookseller in New York. The suspicion in the SD is that it was the British Secret Service. And that it was them who persuaded him to return to Germany and join the SS in 1931 to spy for the British.

'Von Eberstein was a banker after the war and a bit of a weekend Nazi, if you know what I mean. He actually quit the Party after the putsch, which automatically makes him suspect. For three years he had no Party affiliation at all. And during this time he goes from being a banker with the Commerce and Private Bank to running his wife's factory in Gotha; but when that goes belly up his debts are paid off anonymously and he starts a travel agency. That business takes him to London for much of 1927 and 1928. But by 1929 he's back in the Party again. So did the Tommies set him up with the travel agency and train him to operate a radio while he was in London? That's the sort of thing Heydrich wants to know.'

Kahlo grinned and wagged his finger.

'You see how easy it is to fall under suspicion? And it doesn't matter who you are, or how high up in the Party you have flown. Doctor Jury is a suspect because before he joined the Austrian Nazi Party in 1932 he attended several medical conferences in Paris and London. While he was in Paris he had an affair with a woman who also had an affair with a French colonel in their intelligence service. Also his friendship with Martin Bormann automatically makes him a suspect in Himmler's eyes, since it seems Himmler would love to discredit any friend of Bormann's in the eyes of Hitler.

'General Frank is a suspect because of something his ex-wife Anna has told her new husband, Doctor Kollner. He succeeded Frank as the deputy governor of the Sudetenland and he has made certain allegations based on what Anna Kollner told him about his loyalty to the Leader. And also because his new wife, Karola Blaschek, is suspected of having contact with several Czech resistance figures. She comes from the local town of Brux and there's a suspicion that some of her friends and relations in that town may have been part of UVOD. The Home Resistance.'

'What about von Neurath? Not him, surely. He was the Foreign Minister for Christ's sake.'

'Konstantin von Neurath is suspected of being recruited as a British spy as early as 1903, when he served as a diplomat at the German Embassy in London; or possibly when he was at the German Embassy in Denmark in 1919. While he was German Ambassador to London in 1930 he came under the suspicion of the Abwehr but he was cleared after an investigation; but in 1937 the Abwehr was burgled by a special SS team and certain papers were removed that showed the whole investigation to have been a sham. Subsequent to this, von Neurath joined the Nazi Party for the first time, as a sign of his loyalty. As if he suddenly needed to underline his loyalty. Instead of which it seems to have put him under suspicion.'

Kahlo stubbed out his cigarette and helped himself to coffee. But he wasn't yet finished.

'And that's possibly the reason Major Thummel is suspected of being the traitor X. He was in charge of the Abwehr section that was supposed to have investigated von Neurath. He may be a friend of Heinrich Himmler and he may wear a gold Party badge, but he's also a close friend of the Abwehr's boss, Admiral Canaris, who is Himmler's most bitter rival. Heydrich's too.

'Let's see now. Who else was on that list? Brigadier Voss? He commands the SS Officer School at Beneschau. Until 1938, he was in charge of the officers' training school at Bad Tolz where there's a powerful radio transmitter. When officers from that school were mobilized for the invasion of Czechoslovakia in 1938, someone tipped off the Czech Intelligence Service about it. Voss was one of only a handful of people who knew the invasion was about to happen. He's also a keen amateur radio enthusiast. Who better to broadcast secrets to the Czechos? He even speaks the language.

'Walter Jacobi was dismissed from the SD in 1937 by his then boss, General Werner Lorenz. I'm afraid I don't know why. In the spring of 1938, he took a holiday in Marienbad, in the Sudetenland. Coincidentally perhaps, or perhaps not, one of the other guests taking the cure at the Spa was a retired British naval commander who is currently believed to be the head of an operational Czech section within the British SIS. After his holiday, Jacobi rejoined the SD.'

'Guilt by association.'

'Possibly.'

Kahlo nodded.

'Henlein – well, you heard what I said to him. And Fleischer's been under suspicion for a while now because of his failure to arrest the third of the Three Kings. You probably know as much about that as I do. It's common knowledge that the Czechos were making a fool of him for a while. The rest of the cauliflower, I really don't remember or I don't know. Your guess is as good as mine.'

'I doubt that very much,' I said. 'And by the way, what happened to "I'm keen to learn" and "You have my full cooperation" and "It's a puzzle, sir"?'

'You don't think it's a puzzle?'

'Of course it is. I just don't much like the fact you've had one of the pieces in your trouser pocket all along.'

'And I don't suppose you've ever kept your mouth shut about something?' Kahlo shook his head. 'Come on, sir. We both know that saying one thing and thinking another is what this job is all about. Tell me it's not like that for you. Go on.'

I found myself silent.

'Tell me that you've told *me* everything. That there's something you're not keeping from me.'

Still I didn't answer. How could I when Arianne was back at the hotel? If I'd told him less than half of what I knew about Arianne Tauber there was no telling what might happen to her.

Kahlo grinned. 'No, I thought not. You see, when it comes right down to it, Commissar, I reckon your piss is just as yellow as mine.'

I sighed and fetched myself a brandy from the decanter. Suddenly I felt very tired and I knew the brandy wasn't going to help.

'Maybe you're right.'

'Look, sir. You want to know what I think? I think we should go through the motions of trying to find Kuttner's killer, just like you were told to do. We ask the right questions, we do our duty, right? Like regular cops. That's all we can do and it's pointless thinking we can do any more than that. But when it comes right down to it, what does it fucking matter, eh? You tell me. Who cares who killed the bastard? Not me, not you. From what I heard, he did his own fair share of murder out east. And the chances are he had it coming. Probably we all do. But what's one more murder, eh? One tiny drop in a very tall glass of beer, that's what it is. Take my advice, sir. Don't sweat it. Enjoy the free forage and the booze and the cigarettes. For as long as we can, eh?'

'Maybe.'

'That's the spirit, sir. And who knows? Maybe we'll get lucky. Even a blind chicken finds the corn now and again.'

I needed a walk and some fresh air after all that information, although it might have been the brandy and the Mish-Mash. I went around the house to the little Winter Garden that Kuttner's room looked out on. Inside the glass house was a fountain shaped like a shrine with a water nymph's head spouting water and above him a bronze statue of a centaur with a winged cherub on his back. On either side of the fountain was a veritable jungle of sago palms and geraniums. It seemed an odd place to find a centaur, or a cherub, but I wasn't surprised at anything any more. The water nymph could have told me my fortune lay in farming guinea pigs and I wouldn't have batted an eyelid. Anything looked like a better bet than being a detective in Jungfern-Breschan.

A ladder lay on the ground, and assuming that this was probably the one Kritzinger had ordered Fendler, the footman, to fetch around to Captain Kuttner's window, I spent the next ten minutes propping it up against the wall of the house. Then I climbed up to take a look at the window ledge. But that told me only that the glass roof needed cleaning, that the sun was still strong for the first week in October, and that I was not at all certain to kill myself cleanly if I threw myself from the top. I descended the ladder and found one of the footmen waiting at the bottom.

'Fendler, sir,' he said, unprompted. 'Herr Kritzinger saw you were out here and sent me to see if I could be of any assistance, sir.'

He was not far off being two metres tall. He wore a white mess jacket with SS collar patches, a white shirt, a black tie, black trousers, a white apron, and grey over-sleeves, as if he might have been cleaning something before receiving his order from the butler to wait on me. He was lumpish in appearance, with an expression that suggested he was none too bright, but I'd gladly have changed places with him. Polishing silver or removing the ash from a fireplace looked like more rewarding work than the domestic task I had been set.

'You're the one who Kritzinger told to fetch the ladder to look in Captain Kuttner's window, are you not?'

'That's right, sir.'

'And what did you see, when eventually you got up there? By the way, what time was that, do you think?'

'About a quarter past seven, sir.'

I tugged my shirt off the sweat on my chest.

'I was about to ask you why it took so long to fetch a ladder and prop it up against the window, but I think I know the answer to that already. It's heavy.'

'Yes sir. But it wasn't in the Winter Garden like it is now, sir.'

'That's right. It was locked up, wasn't it?'

'Bruno, the gardener – Bruno Kopkow – he helped me carry it around here and prop it up.'

'How did you know which window to choose?'

'Kritzinger told me it was the room overlooking

336

the Winter Garden, sir. And to be careful I didn't drop it on the glass roof, sir.'

'So, you prop the ladder up against the window. Then what? Tell me everything you saw and did.'

Fendler shrugged. 'We – Kopkow and I – we heard a loud bang, sir, and then just as I was stepping on the lowest rung, sir, General Heydrich looks out of the window, and seeing me and Bruno tells us that there's no need to bother coming up now as they had just broken down the Captain's bedroom door.'

'And what did you say? If anything?'

'I asked him if everything was all right and he said that it wasn't, because it looked as if Captain Kuttner had probably killed himself with an overdose.'

'Then what did you do?'

'We took the ladder down and left it where you found it, sir, just in case anyone decided they needed it again.'

'How did he seem? The General.'

'A bit upset, I suppose. Like you would be, sir. He and the Captain were friends, I believe.' The footman paused. 'I knew he must be upset because he was smoking a cigarette. Usually the General doesn't smoke at all in the morning and never before he fences, sir. Mostly he only smokes in the evening. He's very disciplined that way, sir.'

I glanced up at the window of Kuttner's room and nodded. 'I don't doubt it.'

'Will there be anything else, sir?'

'No. That's all, thank you.'

I went back to the Morning Room. Kahlo was waiting for me.

'Police Commissar Trott telephoned while you were out, sir. From the Alex. He said to tell you that he went to see Lothar Ott at Captain Kuttner's apartment in Petalozzi Strasse and told him that the Captain was dead. Apparently Ott wept like a baby. The Commissar's exact words. That would seem to confirm it, wouldn't you say? That the Captain was warm?'

I nodded. It only confirmed what I already knew.

'Who'd have thought it?' said Kahlo. 'I mean, the fellow seemed quite normal in a lot of ways. Like you or me, really.'

'I guess that's the point. That maybe they are just like you or me.'

'Speak for yourself, sir.'

'I used to think like you. But the Nazis have taught me to think differently. I'll say that for them. These days I say live and let live, and if we can learn to do that, then maybe we can behave like a civilized country again. But I suspect it's already too late for that.'

I glanced at my wristwatch. A cheap Bulova, it had two ways to remind me that we had an autopsy to view at the Bulovka Hospital at four and that only one of them was the time.

'Come on,' I said to Kahlo. 'We'd better get

going. You're about to discover just how like you and me Albert Kuttner really was.'

Sergeant Klein had returned from Hradschin Palace in Prague to drive us out to the hospital. He'd read the Leader's Sports Palast speech in the morning newspaper and, instead of depressing him, Hitler's 'facts and figures' had left him feeling optimistic about our prospects in the East.

'Two and a half million Russian prisoners,' he said. 'No country could ever recover from losing that many men. If that was all, it would be enough; but as well, fourteen thousand Russian planes have been shot down and eighteen thousand of their tanks destroyed. It's hard to imagine.'

'And yet the Leader still believes we have a fight on our hands,' I remarked.

'Because he's wise,' insisted Klein. 'He's saying that so as not to raise our hopes in case the impossible should happen. But it's obvious, the Ivans are as good as beaten, that's what I think.'

'Let's hope you're right,' said Kahlo.

'I hate to think what we're going to do with two and a half million Russian prisoners if he's wrong,' I said. 'If it comes to that I hate to think what we're going to do with them if he's right.'

I paused for a moment before adding what was sometimes called 'the political postscript' – something that was usually said for the purposes of self-preservation.

'Not that I expect him to be wrong, of course.

And I don't doubt that the Leader will be delivering a victory speech in Moscow before very long.'

Then I bit off the end of my tongue and spat it onto the road, only I did it subtly so that Klein didn't notice.

Set on a hill overlooking the north-east of the city, Bulovka Hospital was a four- or five-storey building made of beige-coloured stone with a red mansard roof and a greenish little bell-tower that stuck up in the air like an infected finger. Built before the Great War, the hospital was surrounded with lush gardens where recuperating patients could sit on wooden benches, enjoy the many blooms in the flower beds and generally appreciate the democratic ideals of the sovereign state of Czechoslovakia; at least they could have done when there had still been a sovereign state of Czechoslovakia. Like every other public building in Prague the hospital was now flying the flag of the least democratic European state since Vlad the Third impaled his first Wallachian Boyar.

Klein drew up in front of the entrance. Two men wearing surgical gowns were already waiting for us, which only seemed excessively servile until you remembered Heydrich's reputation for obsessive punctuality and ruthless cruelty. One of the men was Honek, the Czech doctor who had attended the crime scene at the Lower Castle earlier that day. He introduced the other man, a handsome German-Czech in his early forties.

'This is Professor Herwig Hamperl,' said Honek,

'who is most distinguished in the field of forensic medicine. He has kindly agreed to take charge of this autopsy.'

'Thank you, sir,' I said.

Swiftly, as if he wanted us to be gone and out of his hair as quickly as possible, Hamperl muttered a curt 'good afternoon' and led the way upstairs and along a wide bright corridor with walls that showed the grimy blank squares where signs and posters written in Czech had been displayed until German became the official language of Bohemia. Hamperl might have been a German Czech, but I soon discovered he was no Nazi.

'Has either of you two gentlemen attended an autopsy before?' he asked.

'Yes,' I said. 'Many.'

'This is my first,' said Kahlo.

'And you're feeling nervous about it, perhaps?'

'A little.'

'Being dead is like being a whore,' said Hamperl. 'You spend most of your time on your back while someone else – in this case, me – gets on with the business in hand. The procedure can seem embarrassing, sometimes even a little preposterous, but it is never disgusting. My advice to anyone who hasn't witnessed an autopsy before is to try to see only the lighter side of things. If it starts to seem disgusting then that's the cue to leave the room before an accident occurs. The smell of a dead body is usually quite bad enough without the smell of vomit to cope with. Is that clear?'

'Yes sir.'

Hamperl unlocked a wooden door with smoked windows and led us into an autopsy suite where a stout-looking body lay under a sheet on a slab. As Hamperl started to draw back the sheet to reveal Kuttner's head and shoulders I saw Kahlo's eyes widen.

'Jesus,' he muttered. 'I don't remember his stomach being that big.'

Hamperl paused.

'I can assure you it's not big with fat,' he said. 'The man might be dead but the enzymes and bacteria in his belly are still very much alive and feeding on whatever still remains in his stomach. Probably last night's dinner. In the process, these enzymes and bacteria produce gas. Here, let me demonstrate.'

Hamperl pressed hard on the sheet still covering Kuttner's stomach which caused the body to fart, loudly.

'See what I mean?'

Hamperl's behaviour was a piece of crude theatre that seemed intended to make us feel uncomfortable. In a way I didn't blame him for this at all. The Nazis were past masters at making others feel uncomfortable. Doubtless, the Professor was just paying us back, in kind. A fart from a dead Nazi was as eloquent a comment on the German presence in Czechoslovakia as I was ever likely to hear, or indeed smell. But Kahlo winced noticeably, and then bit his lip as he tried, vainly, to steady his nerves.

Hamperl collected a long sharp curette off a neatly prepared instrument table and held it at arm's length, like a conductor's baton. The light from the abbey-sized windows caught the flat of the curette and it glittered like a bolt of lightning. Instinctively Kahlo turned away, and noting his discomfort at the symphony of destruction he was about to begin, Hamperl grinned wolfishly, exchanged a meaningful look with Doctor Honek, and said:

'There's one thing you can say about the dead, my dear fellow. They have an extraordinary ability to deal with pain. Any pain. No matter how bad it might seem to you. Believe me, this poor fellow won't feel a thing as I seem to do my absolute worst. Much worse than perhaps you have ever seen inflicted on any human being before. However, do try not to let your imagination run away with you. The most terrible thing that could happen to this man happened several hours before he arrived in this hospital.'

Kahlo shook his head and swallowed loudly, which sounded as if a very large frog had taken up residence in his throat.

'I'm sorry, sir,' he said to me. 'I just can't do this. I really can't.'

He covered his mouth, and left the room quickly.

'Poor fellow,' said Hamperl. 'But probably it's just as well he's gone. We need all our attention for the task that now lies before us.'

'Surely, that was your intention,' I said. 'To scare him off.'

'Not at all, Commissar. You heard me try to reassure him, didn't you? However, it's not everyone who can witness this procedure with a cool head. Are you sure about yourself?'

'Oh, I have no feelings at all, Professor Hamperl. None whatsoever. I'm like that curette in your hand. Cold and hard. And best handled with extreme care. Just one slip would be most unfortunate. Do I make myself clear?'

'Quite clear, Commissar.'

Hamperl threw back the remainder of the sheet covering Kuttner's body and went quickly to work. Having photographed the two entry wounds on the dead man's chest, and then probed them both, first with his finger and then with a length of dowel, he made a Y-shaped incision from Kuttner's porcelain-pale shoulders, across his hairless chest and down to the pubic area which, unusually, appeared to have been shaved, and recently, too.

Hamperl remarked upon this.

'Well, you don't see that every day. Not even in my profession. I wonder why he should have done this.'

'I've a good idea,' I said. 'But it will wait.'

Hamperl nodded. Then he was cutting through subcutaneous fat and muscle, and the speed of his scalpel was something to behold, with the flesh swiftly shrugged off the bone like the skin of a very large snake; and within only a few minutes there was just a mess of intestines and prime rib that might have been the envy of any good Berlin butcher. Especially in wartime.

'There appears to be something lodged at the top of the oropharynx,' said Hamperl. He looked up at me and added, 'That's the part of the throat just behind the mouth.'

He collected a small white object, flicked it off his fingers' ends into a kidney dish and then held it up for our joint inspection.

'It appears to be a troche, perhaps,' he said. And then: 'No, this was not designed to dissolve in the throat, but in the stomach. It has hardly dissolved at all. A pilule. A tablet, perhaps.'

'He was taking Veronal,' I said. 'A barbiturate.'

'Is that so?' Hamperl's voice was dripping with sarcasm. 'Well then, that is probably what it is. Only it could not have affected him very much in the condition you see it in now. Although this would be quite consistent with a case of overdose where someone has swallowed several pills all at once. Doctor Honek said there was initially some suspicion that this might have been a barbiturate overdose.'

'That's right,' I said. 'Until I found the bullet wounds.'

'Quite.'

At an almost imperceptible nod from Professor Hamperl, Doctor Honek stepped forward with a set of surgical bolt cutters and began to cut the ribs, which, under the steel jaws, snapped loudly like thick twigs, one by one, in order to expose the chest cavity. But there was one he hesitated to cut.

345

'One of these ribs looks damaged, don't you think so, sir?' asked Honek.

Hamperl bent down to take a closer look. 'Chipped,' he said. 'Like a tooth. But not from a Veronal pilule. Most probably from a bullet.'

Honek went back to work. He was even quicker than the Professor and within a couple of minutes Hamperl was slicing through the remains of the diaphragm and reflecting back the whole chest-plate, like the top of a boiled egg, to expose the dead man's heart and the lungs.

'Quite a lot of blood has pooled inside the diaphragm,' he murmured.

By now Albert Kuttner was hardly recognizable as a human being. His intestines – most of them – were resting on the upturned palm of his own hand as if, like the perfect aide-de-camp he had possibly hoped to become, he might assist even in the process of his own dissection.

Hamperl placed the chest-plate on a nearby table where it remained like the remains of a Christmas goose.

I cleared my nose, noisily.

'Commissar? Are you all right?'

'I'm just trying to see the lighter side of things that you were talking about earlier, sir.'

'Good.'

But the Professor sounded almost disappointed that I was not yet lying on the floor.

'Cutting the pulmonary artery,' he said to Honek. 'Checking for blood clots. Which we have. Probably a post-mortem blood-clot.' He slashed some more of the lungs and then squeezed the heart. 'Feels like something hard in here. A bullet probably. See if you can find it, will you, Doctor Honek?'

He handed the heart to the other man and got to work with the scalpel again, slashing at the flesh holding what looked like a shiny red football.

'The liver, is it?' I asked.

'Very good, Commissar Gunther. The liver it is.' Hamperl laid the liver in another dish before removing the spleen as well.

'Looks like this got hit, too,' he said. 'It's almost in pieces.'

I went over to the table where Honek was still palpating the heart to isolate the bullet, and glanced briefly at the spleen.

'It's a mess all right.'

'That certainly covers all of what's in the medical dictionary,' observed Hamperl.

Honek had isolated the bullet. He cut it out and laid it in a separate metal tray like a gold-prospector putting aside a precious nugget. This was easier on the eye than watching Hamperl clamp Kuttner's small intestine so that he could haul it out in one block. I'd seen one too many of my comrades in the freezing cold of the trenches with their steaming guts hanging out of their tunics to view that particular sight with any equanimity.

So far we had been there for less than thirty minutes and already the kidneys were being removed.

The second bullet was lodged deep in the spine and took several minutes to gouge out.

When that was done Hamperl asked, 'Do you wish me to remove the brain?'

'No. I don't think it will be necessary.'

'Then that would appear to be that, for now.' He shrugged. 'Of course, it will take a while to analyse the organs, the haematology, and the contents of the stomach. Naturally I will test the quantities of Veronal present then.'

'At this moment in time I must ask you both not to make any verbal reference to a second bullet,' I said. 'As far as anyone else is concerned, just the one shot was fired.'

'Am I to understand that you plan on using this subterfuge as the basis for some incriminating piece of cross-examination?' said the Professor.

'Yes,' I said. 'I am. You can mention your real findings in your written report, of course.'

'Very well,' said the Professor. 'It'll be our little secret until you say otherwise, Commissar.'

When both bullets were lying in a tray I took a closer look. I'd seen enough spent lead in my time to recognize metal from a thirty-eight when I saw it.

'Right now, I'd be grateful if you were to indulge me with your first thoughts, sir.'

'All right.'

Professor Hamperl sighed and then thought for a moment.

'Both shots seem to have been fired at fairly

close range,' he said. 'Of course I should have to check the shirt for powder burns to give you an accurate distance, but the size of the entry wounds persuades me, strongly, that the shooter could not have been more than half a metre away when these shots were fired. The angle of the entries would seem to indicate that the person who fired the shots was immediately in front of him. The grouping of the shots was tight, as if the two shots were fired in very quick succession before the victim moved very much.'

'If the shooter fired at only half a metre's distance, why didn't the slugs go straight through him?'

'One clipped the rib and lost most of its velocity before it penetrated the heart, I shouldn't wonder,' Hamperl said thoughtfully. 'And the other lodged deep in the spine, as you saw. That's why.

'As I say, we'll have to see how much barbiturate was absorbed by his organs but on the basis of the organ damage and the amount of blood that was in the diaphragm, I'd say it was the shots that killed him, not the Veronal.'

'What do you know about that stuff?'

'Barbital? It's been around for a good while. Almost forty years. It was first synthesized by two German chemists. Bayer sells the stuff as a soluble salt or in tablet form. Ten to fifteen grammes would be a safe dose; but fifty or sixty could be lethal.'

'That's not much of a margin for error,' I said.

'Of course for someone using it regularly, they

would soon develop a tolerance of the drug and possibly require a higher dose, which they might easily accommodate without any mishap. But if they left off taking it for a while, it'd be a mistake to start again with a high dose. Possibly a lethal one.'

'So it has to be handled with care.'

'Oh yes. It's powerful stuff. My own sleep would have to be very disturbed to want to take it myself. All the same it's a lot better than its predecessor: bromides. There's no unpleasant taste with Veronal. In fact, there's not much taste at all.'

'Any side effects?'

'It would certainly affect the heart rate, the pulse, and the blood pressure. And of course that would substantially affect the bleeding. Perhaps there would have been more blood exiting from the wounds if this man hadn't sedated himself. As it is, most of the blood from the wounds was in the diaphragm.'

'Anything else?'

'You wouldn't want to mix the stuff with alcohol. It reacts badly in the stomach. I've seen cases of people who mixed it and were choked to death when they vomited in their sleep.'

'Thank you.'

'Will there be anything else?'

'I believe there's a way that you can find out if he was homosexual.'

Hamperl didn't bat an eyelid.

'Ah, yes, I see. The shaven pubic area. Yes, it is

unusual for a man to shave himself down there. It might indicate an effeminate inclination, yes. I see what you mean. Intriguing, isn't it?'

'There were other things that make me think he might be homosexual,' I added. 'Things I can't tell you about. But I would like to know for sure.'

'Sometimes,' agreed Hamperl, 'in a habitual sodomite the anus becomes dilated. It loses its natural puckered orifice and develops a thicker, keratinized skin. Or even becomes like an open shutter on a camera. I assume you're referring to that. Would you like me to take a look?'

'Yes.'

Doctor Honek, would you help me to turn the cadaver over, please?'

The two men wrestled the gutted body onto what there was of its front and spread the dead man's buttocks.

After a moment or two Hamperl started to shake his head.

'The anus looks all right to me. Of course, the fact that there has been no apparent interference doesn't indicate that he wasn't homosexual. But I could always swab the anus for semen when I do some of the other tests. And swab his penis for traces of faecal matter.'

'Please do that.'

Hamperl was trying to conceal a gleeful, triumphant smile. 'An SS officer who was homosexual. Perhaps that's why he was murdered. I can't imagine this sort of thing goes down well in Berlin.'

Hamperl exchanged a look with Doctor Honek, who was looking equally amused.

'Of course one hears things. About Berlin and transvestitism.'

I nodded. 'All the same, if I were you I wouldn't mention this either. The SS doesn't have much of a sense of humour about that sort of thing. It would be a shame to find that out the hard way.'

'You'll have my histological report on the organs and my pathological diagnosis in forty-eight hours, Commissar.'

'Thanks, again.'

The Professor escorted me to the door.

'So, Commissar, will you be leaving your own body to science do you think? For medical students to use in the anatomy lab.'

I glanced at the shambles that was a man I had been speaking to about a painting by Gustav Klimt at Jungfern-Breschan just twenty-four hours earlier.

'No, I don't think I will.'

'Pity. A man as tall as you must have a fine skeleton. I sometimes think that the real fun stuff for our bodies doesn't start until we're dead.'

'I'm already looking forward to it.'

Kahlo apologized again as Klein drove us away from the hospital.

'You get used to it,' I said.

'Not me. Not ever. It was the smell of the ether that really got to me I think. Reminded me of when my mother died.'

'Bad huh?' said Klein.

Kahlo shook his head, but his expression told a different story and seeing it in his rear-view mirror Klein reached into the leather pocket on the inside of the driver's door and took out a silver flask.

'I keep this for cold days,' he said and handed it to me.

'It doesn't get much colder than that,' I said. 'Not for Captain Kuttner, anyway.' I took a bite off the flask, which was full of good schnapps, and handed it back to Kahlo.

'That bastard.' Kahlo upended the flask. 'That bastard Professor was enjoying it, too. My discomfort. Did you hear him, sir? The way he started laying it on. I thought, fuck this. I'm off. He's having a laugh at my expense.'

'That he was,' I said. 'But a man has to take pleasure in his work where and when he can. Especially in this country.'

I bent forward to the floor of the car, lit a cigarette and handed it back to him.

'There was a time when *I* took pleasure in my work, too. When I was good at it. Those were the days when the Berlin Murder Squad was the best in the world. When I was a real detective. A professional. What I didn't know about the science of murder wasn't worth knowing. But now.' I shook

353

my head. 'Now I'm just an amateur. A rather quaint and old-fashioned amateur.'

It was five-thirty in the afternoon, and back in the library at the Lower Castle irritation and disappointment hung in the air like mustard gas ready to contaminate the lungs of all who were unfortunate enough to breathe it in. SS and Gestapo officers shook their heads and smoked furiously and looked around for someone to blame. Opinions were offered and rejected angrily and offered again until voices were raised and accusations made. There appeared to be several of them in the library, and while ultimately there was only one man whose opinion counted there were others who were determined not to be held responsible for 'the failure'.

Kahlo and I had crept into the Morning Room so as to avoid being drawn into these recriminations; but we left the door wide open so that we could hear and increase our strength, for a wise man is strong and a man who listens at doors increases his strength.

'We let him slip through our fingers,' raged Heydrich. 'We have at our disposal the most powerful police force ever seen in this city and yet we don't seem to be able to catch one man.'

'It's too early to give up hope, sir.' This sounded like Horst Bohme, the head of the SD in Prague. His Berlin accent was instantly recognizable to me. 'We're continuing to conduct house-to-house searches for Moravek and even now I'm certain that something will turn up.'

'We know his name,' said Heydrich, ignoring him. 'We know what he looks like. We even know he's somewhere in the city and yet we can't find him. It's a total bloody failure. An embarrassment.'

'Yes sir.'

'An opportunity thrown away, gentlemen,' stormed Heydrich. 'However, I suppose I shouldn't really be all that surprised, given what happened here in May. At the UVOD safe house in – what was the name of that dumb Czecho street, Fleischer?'

'Pod Terebkov Street, sir,' said Fleischer.

'You had them all in your fucking hands,' yelled Heydrich. 'They were trapped in that damned apartment. And still you managed to let two of them escape. Jesus, I should have you shot for incompetence or for being complicit in their evading capture. Either way I should have you shot.'

'Sir,' protested Fleischer. 'With all due respect they were thirty metres off the ground. They used a steel radio aerial to slide out of the window thirty metres down to that courtyard. It was covered in blood when we found it. A man's fingers were on the ground.'

'Why didn't you have men in the courtyard? Is there a shortage of SS and Gestapo here in Prague? Well, Bohme? Is there?'

'No sir.'

'Fleischer?'

'No, Herr General.'

'So this time you would think we could get it right. This time we have a photograph of Vaclav Moravek. We know the safe house he's been using for the last five months. And what do we find? A note, addressed to me. Remind me of what Moravek's note said, Fleischer.'

'I'd rather not, sir.'

'It said "Lick my arse, General Heydrich". It's even written in German and Czech, as the law says it ought to be, which is an especially insolent touch, don't you think? "Lick my arse, General Heydrich". It would seem that I'm an even bigger prick than you are, Fleischer. You're already a laughing stock after that incident in the Prikopy Bar.'

'On that particular occasion you mention, sir, the man was wearing a Party badge in the lapel of his jacket.'

'And that makes all of the difference, does it? I wish I had ten marks for every bastard wearing a Party badge I've had to shoot since 1933.'

'Someone tipped him off, sir. Moravek must have been told we were coming.'

'That much is obvious, my dear Commissioner. What isn't fucking obvious is what we're doing about finding the traitor who might have told him. Major Ploetz?'

'Sir?'

'Who is liaising with the special SD squad that I ordered to be set up? The VXG.'

'It was Captain Kuttner, sir.'

'I know who it was, Achim. I'm asking who it is now.'

'Well, sir, you haven't said.'

'Do I have to think of everything? Apart from my children, who incidentally will be arriving here in less than forty-eight hours, nothing, I repeat nothing, is more important than finding the man behind the OTA transmissions; traitor X, or whatever you want to call him. Nothing. These are the Reichsführer's own orders to me. Not even Vaclav Moravek and the Three Kings and the UVOD Home Resistance network are as important as that, do you hear?'

Another voice spoke up, but it was one I didn't recognize.

'Frankly, sir, I don't wish to speak ill of the dead, but Captain Kuttner was not a good liaison officer.'

'Who's that speaking?' I asked Kahlo.

He shook his head. 'Don't know.'

'The fact is, Kuttner was arrogant and rude, and often quite unpredictable; and he managed to piss off the local Kripo and Gestapo in double-quick time while he was here.'

'Like I said,' murmured Kahlo. 'He was a prick.'

'He did not serve you well, General,' continued the same voice. 'And now that he's gone, might I suggest, sir, that I handle the liaison with the VXG.

I can promise you I'll make a better job of it than he did.'

'Very well, Captain Kluckholn,' said Heydrich. 'If Captain Kuttner was as bad as you say he was—'

'He was,' insisted another voice. 'Sir.'

'Then,' said Heydrich, 'you had better get yourself over to Pecek Palace and then Kripo and try to smooth over any ruffled feathers and make sure they know what they're supposed to be doing. Clear?'

'Yes sir.'

I heard a chair move, and then someone – Kluckholn, I imagined – clicked his heels and left the room.

'Talking of ruffled feathers, sir.' This was Major Ploetz. 'Your detective, Gunther, has already managed to upset the whole chicken coop. I've already had several complaints about his manner, which leaves a great deal to be desired.'

I nodded at Kahlo. 'True,' I said. 'Too true.'

'I agree with Major Ploetz, sir.' This was Colonel Bohme, again.

'I suppose you think I should have picked you to handle this inquiry, Colonel Bohme.'

'Well, I am a trained detective, sir.'

Heydrich laughed cruelly. 'You mean you once went on the detective-lieutenant's training course at the Police Institute, in Berlin-Charlottenburg, don't you? Yes, I can easily see how that might make anyone think he was Hercule Poirot. My dear

Bohme, let me tell you something. We don't have any good detectives left in the SD or in the Gestapo. Within the kind of system that we operate we have all sorts of people; ambitious lawyers, sadistic policemen, brown-nosing civil servants, all, I dare say, good Party men, too; sometimes we even call them detectives or inspectors and ask them to investigate a case; but I tell you they can't do it. To be a proper detective is beyond their competence. They can't do it because they won't stick their noses in where they're not wanted. They can't do it because they're afraid of asking questions, they're not supposed to ask. And even if they did ask those questions they'd get scared because they wouldn't like the answers. It would offend their sense of Party loyalty. Yes, that's the phrase they'd use to excuse their inability to do the job. Well, Gunther may be a lot of things but he has the Berlin nose for trouble. A real *Schnauz*. And that's what I want.'

'But surely Party loyalty has to count for something, sir,' said Bohme. 'What about that?'

'What about it? A promising young SS officer is dead. Yes, that's what he was, gentlemen, in spite of your own reservations. He was murdered and by someone in this house, I shouldn't wonder. Oh, we can pretend that it might have been some poor Czecho who killed him, but we all of us know that it would take the Scarlet Pimpernel to get past all these guards and to walk into my house and shoot Captain Kuttner. Besides, I flatter myself that if a Czecho did take the trouble to penetrate our security, he would prefer to shoot me instead of my own adjutant. No, gentlemen, this was an inside job, I'm convinced of it and Gunther's the right man – my man – to find out who did it.' He paused for a moment. 'And as for Party loyalty, that's my job, not yours, Colonel Bohme. I'll say who is loyal and who isn't.'

I'd heard enough, for the moment. I stood up and closed the door to the Morning Room.

'Hardly a ringing endorsement,' said Kahlo. 'Was it, sir?'

'From Heydrich?' I shrugged. 'Don't knock it. That's as good as it gets.'

I sat down at the piano and fingered a few notes, experimentally. 'All the same, I get the feeling I'm being played. And played well.'

'We're all being played,' said Kahlo. 'You, me, even Heydrich. There's only one man in Europe who has his mitts on the keyboard. And that's the GROFAZ.'

The GROFAZ was a derogatory name for Hitler.

'Maybe. All right. Who's next on our list? I have a sudden desire to ruffle some more feathers.'

'General Frank, sir.'

'He's the one with the new wife, right? The wife who's a Czech.'

'That's right, sir. And believe me, she's tip-top. A real sweetheart. Twenty-eight years old, tall, blond, and clever.'

'Frank must have some hidden qualities.'

'Yes sir.'

'Or better still some hidden vices. Let's find out which it is.'

'Did you know Captain Kuttner very well, General Frank?'

'Not very well. But well enough. Ploetz, Pomme, and Kluckholn and Kuttner—' Frank smiled. 'It sounds like an old Berlin tailor's shop. Well, they all sort of merge into one, really. That's what you want from an adjutant, I suppose. Me, I wouldn't know, I don't have an adjutant myself. I seem to manage quite well without one, let alone four. But if I did have an adjutant I should want him to be as anonymous as those three are. They are efficient, of course. Heydrich can tolerate nothing less. And being efficient, they stay out of the limelight.

'I knew Kuttner slightly before his Prague posting. When he was at the Ministry of the Interior. He helped me in some administrative way, for which I was grateful, so when he turned up here I tried to help him out. Consequently he shared a few confidences with me. Which is why I know what I'm talking about.

'Kuttner was the latest addition to Heydrich's stable of aides-de-camp. And that meant that he and Heydrich's third adjutant, Kluckholn, were never likely to get on very well, since the first principle of doing the job well is, I imagine, to make your superior redundant. So Kluckholn resented Kuttner. And feared him, I shouldn't wonder. Well, that's understandable; Kuttner was a clever man. Much cleverer than Kluckholn. He was a brilliant lawyer before he went east in June. Kuttner, on the other hand, felt that Kluckholn tried to keep him in his place. Or even to put him down.'

For a moment I picture the two men arguing in the garden the previous evening. Was that what I had witnessed? Kluckholn trying to put Kuttner in his place? Kuttner resisting it? Or something more intimate perhaps.

'Was Heydrich aware of this rivalry?'

'Of course. There's not much that Heydrich's not aware of, I'll say that for him. But he likes to encourage rivalry. Heydrich believes it persuades people to try harder. So it wouldn't have bothered him in the least that these two were vying with each other for his favour. It's a trick he's learned from the Leader, no doubt.'

'No doubt.'

General Karl Hermann Frank looked almost ten years older than his forty-three years. His face was lined and furrowed and there were bags under his eyes, as if he was another Nazi who didn't sleep very well. He was a heavy smoker, with two of the fingers on the hand holding his cigarette looking like he'd dipped them in gravy, and teeth that resembled the ivory keys on an old piano. It was difficult to see what a beautiful 28-year-old woman saw in this thin, stiff-looking man. Power, perhaps? Hitler might have passed him over to succeed von Neurath but, as SS and Police Leader of Bohemia and Moravia, Frank was effectively the second most important man in the Protectorate. More interesting than that, perhaps, was why a beautiful Czech physician should have married a man who, by his own admission, hated Czechs so much. The hatred I'd heard him articulate about the Czechos the day before was still ringing in my ears. What, I wondered, did Mr and Mrs Frank talk about after dinner? The failure of the Czech banks? Czech-language sentences that didn't use any vowels? UVOD? The Three Kings?

'Sir, when you say there was no love lost between Captains Kluckholn and Kuttner, do you mean to say they hated each other?'

'There was a certain amount of hatred, yes. That's only natural. However, if you're looking for a man who really hated Captain Kuttner – hated him enough to kill him, perhaps – then Obersturmbannführer Walter Jacobi is your man.'

'He's the SD Colonel who's interested in magic and the occult, isn't he?'

'That's right. And in particular, Ariosophy. Don't ask me to explain it in any detail. I believe it is some occult nonsense that's to do with being German. For me, reading the Leader's book is enough. But Jacobi wanted more. He was forever badgering me to become more interested in Ariosophy until I told him to fuck off. I wasn't the only one who thought his interest in this stuff to be laughable. Kuttner, whose father was a Protestant pastor and no stranger to religious nonsense himself, thought that Ariosophy was complete rubbish, and said so.'

'To Colonel Jacobi's face?'

'Most certainly to his face. That's what made it so very entertaining for the rest of us. It happened when they were both at the SS officer school in Prague. That was last Sunday, the 29th of September. The day after Heydrich arrived here in Prague. The school asked him to come to a lunch in his honour and, naturally, his adjutants accompanied him. Someone, not Kuttner, had asked Colonel Jacobi about the death's head ring he was wearing – a gift from Himmler, apparently. One thing led to another and before very long Jacobi was talking balls about Wotan and sun worship and the masons. In the middle of this, Captain Kuttner burst out laughing and said he thought all of that German folk stuff was "complete poppycock". His exact words. For a moment or two there was an embarrassed silence and then Voss – he's the officer in charge at Beneschau and one of the guests here at the Lower Castle, and, I might add, an idiot – Voss tried to change the subject. But Kuttner wasn't having any of it and said some other stuff and that's when Jacobi said it.'

Frank frowned for a moment.

'Said what?'

'I'm trying to think of his exact words. Yes. He said something like "If it wasn't for the fact that you are wearing an SS uniform, Captain Kuttner,

I would cheerfully kill you now, and in front of all these people."'

'You're quite sure about that, sir?'

'Oh, yes. Quite sure. I'm sure Voss will confirm it. Come to think of it, he didn't say "kill", he said "shoot".'

'What did Kuttner say to that?'

'He laughed. Which didn't exactly defuse the situation. And he made some other remark that I didn't understand at the time but which relates to the fact that there was already some previous bad blood between them. Apparently they knew each other at university. And they were enemies.'

'I thought Jacobi was from Munich, sir,' said Kahlo.

'He is.'

'And that he studied law at Tübingen University,' Kahlo added. 'At least that's what it said on his file.'

'Oh, he did. But he also studied law at the Martin Luther University in Halle. The same as Kuttner. He might not look like it, but Jacobi is only a year or two older than Kuttner was. According to Heydrich, they even fought a duel. While they were students.'

'A duel?' Kahlo guffawed. 'What, with swords?'

'That's right.'

'About what, exactly?' he asked.

'They were in a duelling society. It doesn't have to be about anything at all. That's the whole point of being in a duelling society.'

'So it might even have been Jacobi who put the *Schmisse* on Kuttner's face?'

'It's possible. You should certainly ask him.'

'Given that Jacobi was Kuttner's superior,' I said, 'then surely Kuttner was being grossly insubordinate when he said what he said. Surely there would be repercussions of saying something like that. Why wasn't Kuttner put on a charge?'

'For one thing, this was the mess and it wasn't a formal occasion. As you may know, there is supposed to be a certain amount of leeway in what officers can say to each other upon these occasions. Up to a point. But beyond that, well, that wasn't a problem either because Kuttner had vitamin B, of course.'

'You mean with Heydrich.'

'Of course with Heydrich.'

Frank lit a cigarette with a handsome gold lighter before crossing his legs nonchalantly, affording us a fine view of his spurs. Maybe his Czech wife, Karola, liked the dashing cavalry-officer look. This was certainly better than Frank's natural look, which was that of a man recently released from a prison. His bony head, drawn features, strong fingers, sad smile and chain smoking were straight out of a French novel.

'What you also have to understand,' said Frank, 'is that after Kuttner's breakdown in Latvia, and because it was Heydrich and von Eberstein who saved the young man from being cashiered, his brother officers were already cutting him quite a

366

bit of slack. And for Jacobi to have pressed the matter through official channels would have meant taking on Heydrich. And since Heydrich is now the source of all advancement in Bohemia, you would only do that if you were prepared to park your career in the toilet. Jacobi might be a cunt and a complete waxed moustache but he's not entirely stupid. No, not entirely.'

'But is he a killer?' I said. 'To shoot a fellow officer in cold blood, that does seem stupid.'

Frank's tired eyes tightened, and a few seconds after that a smile arrived on his lean face, like a winning card. 'And I thought you were supposed to be a detective.'

'It's Jacobi who's keen on the occult, sir, not me. And generally, I question witnesses because, more often than not, it turns out to be more reliable than a crystal ball, or a set of Tarot cards.'

Leaning forward in a way that made him seem almost simian, Frank played with a ring on his right hand for a moment and kept on smiling as he enjoyed the superiority of knowing something I didn't, at least for a few seconds longer; it was obvious to both of us that he was going to tell me, eventually, exactly what this was.

'Heydrich thinks highly of you, Gunther. But I'm not so sure.'

'To some coppers that might seem like a crushing blow, sir, but I'm sure I'll get over it, with a drink or two.'

'I don't mind if I do.'

Frank glanced at Kahlo, who went over to the drinks tray.

'Yes sir? What'll it be?'

'Brandy.'

'Me, too,' I said. 'And have one yourself, why don't you?'

I waited until we were all holding a glass and then toasted the General.

'Here's to getting over our superiors not thinking as highly of us as we'd like.'

Frank knew that was meant for him – that of course he might have been the new Reichsprotector of Bohemia and not Heydrich if the Leader had thought more of him. To his credit Frank took the jab on his chin without blinking, but he took the drink even better, like he was swallowing a baby's cordial. I'd seen men drink like that before and it helped explain how we were both the same sort of age but with different maps on our faces. Mine was all right, I guess, but his looked like the Ganges Delta.

'I think we'd better have the decanter over here, Kurt,' I said.

'Good idea,' said Frank.

When there was a fresh glassful in his fingers Frank studied it carefully for a moment and said, 'Usually there's a payoff for a good informer, isn't there?'

'Sometimes,' I said. 'But with all due respect, you don't look like a man who's going to be happy with five marks and a cigarette.'

'A favour, Commissar. More than one favour perhaps.'

'What kind of favour?'

'Information. You see, since being passed over for the top job here in Bohemia – as you were kind enough to remind me – I don't hear as well as I used to.'

'And you'd like us to be your ear-trumpet, is that it?'

Frank looked critically at Kahlo. 'I don't know about him. But you'll do for now.'

'I see.'

'I just want to be kept in the loop, that's all. Right now I'm the last to know everything. It's Heydrich's little way of reminding me he's in charge. You saw the way he dealt with von Neurath the other evening. Well, I get the same treatment.' He shrugged. 'It's not like I'm asking very much, Commissar. After all—' He poured the second brandy on top of the first and then licked his lips loudly. 'It's not like I'm a spy or anything.'

Kahlo and I exchanged a swift look.

Smiling, I poured myself another drink. 'Are you sure about that, sir?' I kept on smiling, to make him think I might be joking and to keep him listening without taking offence. 'Let's look at it logically. A man with an axe to grind like you. I think you'd make a pretty good spy.'

Frank ignored me. 'Don't change the subject. Not now when we're making progress. Just tell me this: do we have a deal?'

'To trade information now and in the future? Yes, I think so. I could use a few friends in Prague. Right now I don't have any. Come to that, I don't have any at home either.'

Frank nodded, his eyes glistening.

'All right,' he said. 'You first. Some information. A sign of good faith.'

'Yes. If you like.'

'What's the name of this bit of mouse that Henlein has got stashed in the Imperial Hotel? I hear you know all about her.'

'Her name is Betty Kipsdorf.'

'Is it now?'

'Now tell me why you want to know.'

'Maybe I just wanted to see if you were prepared to keep your end of the bargain before I told you about Lieutenant Colonel Jacobi's interesting past.'

'What, more interesting than fighting a duel with my murder victim? And threatening to shoot him?'

'Oh this is very much more interesting than that, Commissar. That was merely an appetizer. Here is the main dish.

'Jacobi joined the SA in 1930, while he was still a law student in Tübingen. Nothing unusual about that, of course, but I would suggest that there are not many law students who get themselves arrested for murder in the same week that they graduate.

'Yes, I thought that would catch your breath. In 1932, Jacobi murdered someone in Stuttgart, which is only twenty kilometres from Tübingen. The victim was a KPD cadre, although it seems that might not be the real reason the boy was killed. There was it seems some suspicion he was queer and that this was the real motive for the murder. Now I don't have to tell you of all people what things were like in 1932. In some ways von Papen's government was every bit as right-wing as Hitler's. The Stuttgart prosecutor's office was rather slow in putting together a case against Walter Jacobi. So slow, in fact, that the case was never actually brought because, of course, in January 1933 the Nazis were elected and nobody was interested in bringing a case against a loyal Party member like Jacobi any more. All the same it's no wonder he joined the SS and then the SD soon afterward; it was probably the best way of staying out of jail. And of course one of the very first things he did when he achieved a certain position of authority within the SS was to have the papers in the case destroyed. That almost got him kicked out of the SD, in 1937; but Himmler stepped in and pulled his nuts out of the nosebag.'

'And you were thinking that a good detective might have found that out for himself, sir?'

'Something like that.'

'You overestimate me, General. Then again there's only so much I can find out in less than twelve hours. That's how long I've been on this case. And of course there's a limit to how much I can ask my superior officers without bringing down a charge of gross insubordination on my head.'

Frank laughed. 'We both know that's not true.'

He laughed again in a way that made me think that there were probably a lot of things he found funny that I would have felt very differently about.

'We both know that it suits General Heydrich to have you humiliate us all. Especially at this particular moment as he becomes Reichsprotector of Bohemia. It becomes an object lesson in power for us all. Perhaps to test our loyalty. Hitler admires Heydrich because he suspects everyone of every-thing. Me included. Me especially.'

'And why would he suspect you, General?'

Frank looked at Kahlo almost as if he knew it had been Kahlo who told me about the VXG.

'Don't pretend to be naïve. I'm married to a Czech woman, Commissar. Karola. My first wife, Anna, hates my guts and is married to a man who affects to look like the Leader and now makes it his business to tell lies about me and my new wife. Just because she's German Czech. Between them they have already turned my two sons against me. And now they're doing their best to allege that the only reason my wife married me was because she is a Czech spy and that when I go home at night she persuades me to part with state secrets. Well, it's simply not true. And it's why I didn't think your joke was funny. I'm loyal to Germany and the Party, and one day I hope that I will have the opportunity to demonstrate to the whole world just how devoted to the Leader and the cause of National Socialism I really am. Until then I hope

I can count on your help – yes, both of you – to put paid to this baseless innuendo.'

He stood up and I shook hands with him and, in my defence, so did Kurt Kahlo. It was Frank's idea that we should, not mine, and at the time I thought nothing of it – a handshake seemed like a small price to pay for some important information about a potential new suspect. It was another eight or nine months before I realized I'd shaken hands with the man who had ordered the destruction of the small town of Lidice and the murder of everyone in it, in reprisal for the assassination of Reinhard Heydrich.

I glanced at my watch. It was seven o'clock.

'If I wasn't confused before,' admitted Kurt Kahlo, 'I'm certainly confused now. Every time we speak to someone we find out a little bit more. The only trouble is that it leaves me a little bit less enlightened. It's curious, really. You might even call it a paradox. Even as I think I'm getting a proper grip on this case I find there's something interrupting my thoughts, as though someone had built a wall between the two halves of my brain. Just as I find a big enough chair to stand on and look over at the other side, I forget what I'm supposed to be looking for anyway. And then, before you know it, I've even forgotten why I'm standing on the chair in the first place.'

Kahlo sighed and shook his head ruefully.

'Sorry, sir, that's not helping, I know.'

Even as Kahlo spoke I was trying to put up a fight against the rampaging contagion of his utter confusion. In my mind I seemed to hear a lost chord and see some words underneath the palimpsest. An elusive fragment of real insight flashed like a pan of magnesium powder inside the dark chamber that was my skull and then all was black again. For a brief moment everything was illuminated and I understood all and I was on the cusp of articulating exactly what the problem was and where the solution might lie and didn't he, Kahlo, know that what he was describing was precisely the intellectual dilemma that afflicted every detective? But the very next moment a grey mist descended behind my eyes and, before I knew it, this same thought that looked like an answer was slowly suffocating like a fish landed by an angler on a riverbank, its mouth opening and shutting with no sound emerging.

I told him I needed to get away from the Lower Castle so that I might order my own thinking. That's what I also told myself. I'd had enough of them all for one day and suddenly that included Kahlo, too. I decided that I wanted to go back to the hotel and devote my energies to Arianne for a while and that we could spend our last night together before I sent her home in the morning.

'Ask Major Ploetz to find a car that will take me back into Prague,' I said.

Kahlo looked sad for a moment, as if

disappointed I was not ready to be honest with him about where I was going.

'Yes sir.'

I did not have long to wait before a car became available but I was less than pleased to discover that I was to share a ride with Heydrich himself.

'Now you can tell me what conclusions you've come to,' he said as Klein steered us left out of the Lower Castle's infernal gates and onto the picture-postcard country road.

'I haven't any, yet.'

'I was rather hoping you would have everything wrapped up by this weekend. Before my wife, Lina, gets here.'

'Yes. I know. You told me that before.'

'And before my guests are obliged to leave. They do have duties to perform.'

'Mmm-hmm.'

'I must say I find it rather odd than you think you can just take the evening off while a murderer remains at liberty in my house. Perhaps I didn't make myself clear this morning. It is urgent that this case is solved before news gets back to Berlin.'

'No, you made that perfectly clear, sir.'

'And yet you're still going to see that whore of yours.'

I nodded. 'Tell me something, sir. Do you play chess?'

'Yes. But I don't see what that has to do with this. Or your whore.'

'Well then you might know that in major

tournaments it isn't uncommon for players to get up and leave the board between moves. Reading, sleeping, or indeed any pleasant distraction can refresh the human mind, enabling the player to perform at a higher intellectual level. Now, while I don't expect to do any reading this evening, I do expect my lady friend will provide some very pleasant distractions, after which it's perfectly possible that I may get some sleep. All of which is a long way of saying that I need some time away from you and your house in order to try to make sense of everything I've discovered today.'

'Such as?'

Reaching the main road at last, Klein stepped hard on the accelerator leaving Jungfern-Breschan behind, and we sped toward Prague at almost eighty kilometres an hour, obliging me to raise my voice to answer the General.

'I know of at least three people who are staying at the Lower Castle who hated Captain Kuttner. Henlein, Jacobi and Kluckholn. I can't yet say if they hated him enough to kill him. They hated him for a variety of reasons that mostly come down to the fact that Kuttner was insubordinate and clever and perhaps a bit conceited and really not quite the senior officer's toady that a good adjutant ought to be. But there were other reasons, too – probably more important reasons – that might have got him murdered. Principally the fact that he was your liaison officer for the SD's Traitor X Group. If he'd found out something concerning the identity of the traitor, that would have been a pretty good reason for someone to kill him. You might have told me about that yourself, General.'

'When?'

'This morning. When we were in your office. When you handed me this case.'

'I hardly wanted to broadcast the news about the existence of such a squad in front of my own butler. Besides, I had assumed your Criminal Assistant would inform you about that. Major Ploetz tells me Kahlo is part of the VXG.'

'He assumed it was a secret. I've only just found out about it.'

'Well, you know now.'

'Is everyone who has been invited to your house under suspicion?'

'Until the traitor is apprehended? Yes. Of course. What a ridiculous question. Oddly enough, Gunther, traitors have a habit of turning out to be the people we trusted most. It would be foolish to assume that there are some people who are simply above suspicion merely by virtue of a long acquaintance with the Leader or me, or their continuing demonstration of Party loyalty. A Czech spy would be no good if he was suspected of being a Czech spy, would he? However, I do agree that this might conceivably have been the reason why Kuttner was murdered. Which makes it all the more imperative that we catch the bastard as soon as possible, wouldn't you agree?'

'I have another reason why he might have been murdered.'

'I'm listening.'

'Captain Kuttner was homosexual.'

'Nonsense. Whatever gave you such a ridiculous idea? Let me tell you, I knew Kuttner for more than a decade. And I would have known. It's impossible that I wouldn't have known such a thing.'

'Nevertheless it's a fact.'

'You'd better have some damned good evidence for an assertion like that, Gunther.'

'I'll spare you the details, sir, but you can take it from me that I would hardly have told you in front of your butler; and I wouldn't mention it now, in front of your driver, unless I was damned sure about what I'm saying. Moreover I think we can agree that being homosexual, especially in the SS, is, in these enlightened times that we live in, more than enough reason to get you killed. I suspect any number of SS officers would feel entirely justified in shooting that kind of man. Equally, I suspect one or two would have felt quite justified in having Kuttner shot for – what shall we call it, sir? – his dereliction of duty with that Special Action Group in Latvia.'

'That's something you should know quite a bit about yourself, Gunther. Perhaps you have asked yourself why you were allowed to leave your own police battalion in Minsk so easily. If you have not done so already then perhaps you should.'

378

I nodded. 'Arthur Nebe said something to me at the time, by way of an explanation.'

'And Nebe takes his orders from me. Wouldn't you agree?'

'Yes sir.'

'You remind me of someone, Gunther. A rather stubborn Belgian by the name of Paul Anspach. He used to be President of the International Fencing Association. After Belgium was defeated, in June 1940, Anspach, who had acted as a military judge advocate, was arrested for alleged war crimes and put in prison. After he was released I had him summoned to Berlin, where I ordered him to surrender the Presidency to me. He refused. I can't tell you how irritating that was; however, I admired his courage and sent him home.'

'Not even you can always get what you want, General.'

'I can actually. With the help of the Italian President of Fencing, I managed to have him stripped of the International Presidency anyway. It's pointless being stubborn with me, Gunther. I always get what I want in the end. You should know that by now. That it's not wise to oppose me. In case you didn't understand, that's the point of the fucking story.'

'I've never believed it was wise to oppose you,' I said, 'even when I was doing it. No more than I think it's wise for you to drive without an escort in an open-top car. You are an invitation to any would-be Gavrilo Princip to have a go. In case you had forgotten, the Archduke Franz Ferdinand of Austria also travelled in an open car.'

Heydrich laughed, and although such a thing seemed almost impossible, I found I disliked him even more than before.

'If I should ever gain the impression that my conduct in this respect was wise or ill-considered – if ever someone were to attack this car – I would not hesitate to respond with unheard-of violence. I suspect that the population of Prague is well aware of this fact. And while your concern is touching, Gunther, I think it unlikely that I will ever need to take your advice about this.'

'Oh, I don't mean to sound like I care what happens to you, sir. Any more than I mean to sound touching. What I mean to say is what your detective ought to say. Your bodyguard. Whatever it is you choose to call me. I don't know a hell of a lot about fencing, but if it's anything like boxing, then a fighter is told to protect himself at all times. That's not weakness, General. Any more than it's weakness to look out for a fellow officer from Halle-an-der-Saale who went to the same school with you.'

'It's clear to me by now that not everyone agreed with that.'

'Tell me, sir, was Kuttner any good at his job?'

'In so far as it went.'

'Meaning?'

'I have three other adjutants, all of whom are

quite competent. I had thought that one more wouldn't make any difference. One is enough for most people, of course. Of course I am not most people. However, the only reason I have four adjutants – correction, three adjutants – is to remind me to delegate more. I have a great problem trusting people to carry out my orders.

'Ordinarily there's nothing any of them do that I couldn't do better myself. But seeing them at my every beck and call reminds me that there are other more important tasks that require my attention. Having three adjutants makes me more productive, more efficient. Frankly, however, I can't stand the sight of any of them. Kuttner was at least someone I thought I liked. But adjutants are a necessary evil for a man in my position. Much like yourself.'

'I'm flattered.'

'That certainly was not my intention.'

'Your father knew Kuttner's father. Is that right?'

'Yes. But, since you ask, what is more relevant, perhaps, is that my mother gave Albert Kuttner music lessons.'

'Is that how you met?'

'I think it must have been. I seem to recall seeing him when I was back on leave from the Reichsmarine. I couldn't have been more than twenty at the time. Kuttner was much younger, of course. I may even have tried to talk Albert into joining the naval academy, just like me. After all, he went to the same school that I did. But his father was less of a nationalist than my own, which might be why he chose to pursue a legal career instead. Not that any of this is relevant.'

'I disagree. Finding out everything there is to know about a man who has been murdered and a lot more besides is, in my opinion, always the best way to discover why he was murdered. And once I find out why, it's often a very simple matter to discover who.'

Heydrich shrugged. 'Well, it's your business. You know best in these matters. You must do what you think fit, Gunther.'

About halfway between Jungfern-Breschan and Prague the road ran between recently ploughed fields. It was a desolate scene with little in the way of other traffic until, nearing Bulovka Hospital, we encountered an ambulance and, further on, a tram grinding up the hill that led to the city suburbs. Crossing Troja Bridge the car slowed and rounded a corner, and a man snatched off his cap and bowed as he caught sight of a German staff car.

It was easier to hear Heydrich now that we weren't going quite so fast, and once again I tried to question him about Albert Kuttner.

'Did you like Albert Kuttner?'

'Is that your way of asking if I killed him?'

'Did you?'

'No. And to answer your other question, no, I didn't like him. Not any more. Once I did. A while ago. But not lately. He was a disappointment to me. And to some extent he was becoming something of a liability. Since you mentioned Colonel Jacobi, I assume you know the details of what happened there. The quarrel they had. To be frank, Gunther, I am not at all sorry that Kuttner is dead. But my conscience is clear. I gave the man every opportunity to atone for his inadequacies. At the same time I can't have people murdering my staff just because they don't like them. Christ, if you and I were to murder all of the people back at the Lower Castle I didn't like, then we should have hardly anyone left in the local SD: Jacobi, Fleischer, Geschke, von Neurath. I wouldn't shed a tear if any of them caught a bullet.'

'That's straightforward enough, I suppose.'

'Henlein and Jury are particularly awful, don't you think? Cunts. The pair of them.'

'When first we talked, sir. In the garden, yesterday. You mentioned an attempt on your own life. Do you think Kuttner's murder might be related? A case of mistaken identity, perhaps? Kuttner was tall and blond, much like you. His voice and accent were not unlike yours either.'

'You mean, high?'

'Yes sir. In the dark, who knows? The killer might simply have shot the wrong person.'

'The thought had occurred to me, of course.'

'In which case I might very well be wasting my time looking for one of our colleagues with a good reason to murder Captain Kuttner, when my energies might be better spent looking for one of them who badly wants you dead.'

'Interesting idea. And of my dear friends and esteemed colleagues back at my new home, which of them would you say has the best reason to want me dead?'

'You mean, apart from me?'

'You have an alibi, don't you? You weren't actually in the house at the time when Kuttner was murdered.'

'Thoughtful of you to have provided me with one,' I said.

'Isn't it?'

'I should have thought that Frank or von Neurath have the best reasons, from a professional point of view. Von Neurath might like to be revenged on you for the sake of it. Although he doesn't strike me as a murderer. But Frank does. With you dead, Frank probably gets your job.'

'This is intriguing. Anyone else?'

'Henlein and Jury probably hate you too, don't you think?'

'Almost certainly.'

'And I wouldn't trust Jacobi as far as I could kick him.'

'He does make the flesh creep, does he not?'

'Geschke and Fleischer are hardly my idea of good friends, either.'

'Not friends, perhaps. But colleagues. And good Nazis. And since we are discussing those among my staff who might hate me, there's Kritzinger, too. I'm not suggesting that he might kill me, but I shouldn't be at all surprised if he hates me. He's an Austrian, from Vienna, and before the war he worked for the Jew who used to run the estate.'

'Ferdinand Bloch-Bauer. Kuttner told me.'

'After the Anschluss he and his master fled here from Vienna hoping to escape the inevitable before Bloch-Bauer finally took off for Switzerland, in 1939.'

'But Kritzinger is in the SS. Most of the staff are in the SS, aren't they?'

'Of course. But very few of them were in the SS until the Reich acquired the Lower Castle.'

'I thought that's why they were hired. Because you knew you could trust them.'

'They are all in the SS because it means the Reichsprotector doesn't have to pay them out of his own pocket, Gunther. Otherwise I should never be able to keep a house as big as that, not on my salary.'

That made me sit up a little: Heydrich had never struck me as mean with money; mean-spirited, yes, but not an embezzler. And to be so honest about it, too! Of course, I knew he'd never have told me if Himmler didn't know about it and approve. Which meant that they were all in it. The whole rotten crew. Living high on the hog while the ordinary Fritz went without his beer and his sausage and his cigarettes.

'Oh, I'm sure Kritzinger is a good German,' continued Heydrich. 'But it has to be faced, he was devoted to the Bloch-Bauers.'

'Then why on earth do you keep him on?'

'Because he's an excellent butler, of course.

Good butlers like him don't grow on trees, you know. Especially now that we're at war. I wouldn't expect someone like you to understand what that means, but Kritzinger puts his professional duties as a butler ahead of his own personal opinions, always. He sincerely believes that it is his duty to provide good service and concentrate only on that which lies within his realm, as a butler. If you were to question him he would probably tell you that he wouldn't care to say, or something else that was courteously evasive.'

'And yet you said that he might hate you.'

'Of course. I have to recognize that it's a possibility. It would be stupid not to consider it. Doing what I do, Gunther, it's wise not to trust anyone. All I ask of people is that they do their duty, and in that respect at least, Kritzinger is beyond reproach.' He looked impatient for a moment. 'That may be too subtle a distinction for a man like you, but there it is. Such are the dilemmas that afflict everyone who finds himself in a position of great authority.'

'All right, General. Whatever you say.'

'Yes. It had better be.'

When we were still several blocks east of the Imperial Hotel, Klein drew up outside an apartment building with massive, fierce-looking atlantes, Jugendstil windows, and a roof like a Bavarian castle. The portal was covered in mosaic and topped with a decorative filigree balcony. The building looked as if it had been designed by someone whose architectural influences were Homer and the Brothers Grimm. But the address was chiefly remarkable for the absence of any SS or even regular Army sentries, and it was immediately clear to me that this was not an official building.

'What's this place?' I asked.

'The Pension Matzky. A brothel run by the Gestapo for the entertainment of important Czech citizens. It's staffed by twenty of the most beautiful amateur courtesans in all of Bohemia and Moravia. You need a password just to get through the door.'

'I bet that keeps the tone up.'

'Occasionally I visit the place myself. Or when I wish to reward the men who work for me with something special. And everything at the Pension Matzky is special.'

As we were sitting there a furtive-looking man went through the front door; but he was not so furtive that I didn't recognize him. It was Professor Hamperl, the man who had carried out the autopsy on Captain Kuttner.

'Who's he?' I asked. 'One of these important citizens of Prague?'

'I really have no idea,' said Heydrich. 'But I expect so. Incidentally, the password is Rothenburg. Now ask me why I told you that, Gunther.'

'Why did you tell me that?'

'So that you'll be thinking about what you're missing when you see that whore you brought from Berlin. I ask you, Klein, with the thousands

387

of very willing girls there are in this town, can you imagine such a thing?'

Klein grinned. 'No sir.'

Heydrich shook his head. 'That's like taking an owl to Athens.'

'Maybe I just like German owls.'

Heydrich smiled his wolf's smile, stepped out of the car and went inside the Pension without another word.

'Oh, good. You're back. Now we can go out somewhere.'

It was seven-forty-five, but a short while later when I looked at my watch it seemed like it was nine o'clock. With her head in shadow, Arianne was just a naked torso lying on the bed like a piece of marble sculpture. Dominated by light and form, she herself was almost secondary and not a person at all, so that I was reminded, a little, of what I'd seen during my time at the Bulovka Hospital.

I sat down on the edge of the bed and laid my hand on the curving white ski-slope that was the summit of her behind, descending the broad field of her thigh to her near-invisible knee.

'It's not that I don't want you here.'

'I know you want me, all right,' said a disembodied voice. 'You've made that perfectly clear. All you do is fuck me.'

'It's no longer safe for you here in Prague. I told you. There's a special group of SD that's been set up to look for Gustav. If they had any idea you'd actually met him, no matter how innocently – well, you can't imagine what would happen. At least, I hope you can't imagine what would happen. You're in danger, Arianne. Real danger. That's why you urgently have to go back to Berlin. First thing tomorrow. For your own protection.'

'And you. What will you be doing?'

'I'll be going back to Heydrich's house in Jungfern-Breschan.'

'Is that his car? The Mercedes you went away in yesterday morning?' She paused. 'I followed you downstairs to say goodbye and changed my mind when I saw those other men in the car.'

'Yes. That's his car. One of them anyway.'

'What are you doing there, anyway? At Heydrich's house. You don't tell me anything.'

'There's nothing to tell. Not yet. I had a couple of rather boring meetings with some very boring generals.'

'Including him.'

'Heydrich is a lot of things but he's never boring. Most of the time I'm much too afraid of him to be bored.'

Arianne sat up and put her arms about my neck.

'You? Scared? I don't believe it, Parsifal. You're brave. I think you're very brave.'

'To be brave you first have to be scared. Take my word for it. Anything else is just foolhardy. And it's not bravery that keeps people alive, angel. It's fear.'

389

She started to cover my head and neck with kisses. 'Not you,' she said. 'I don't believe it.'

'I'm afraid of him, yes. I'm afraid of all of them. Afraid of what they might do to me. Afraid of what they might do to Germany. But right now I'm afraid of what they might do to you. That's why I went to the Masaryk Station before I came here and bought you a ticket back to Berlin.'

Arianne sighed and wiped a tear from her eye.

'Will I see you again?'

'Of course.'

'When?'

'Soon, I hope. But right now everything is confused. You've no idea how confused.'

'And sending me back to Berlin makes things simpler?'

'Yes. But I told you, that's not the reason you have to go back home. All the same I'll sleep a lot sounder knowing you're all right.'

She stroked my head for a moment and then said: 'On one condition.'

'No conditions.'

'That you tell me you love me, Parsifal.'

'Oh, I love you all right. As a matter of fact I love you very much, Arianne. That's why I have to send you away. It was a mistake bringing you here, I can see that now. It was selfish of me. Very selfish. I did it for me and now I have to do this for you, see? I don't in the least want you to go home. But because I love you I really do have to send you away.'

Maybe I did love her at that. Only it didn't matter very much one way or another. Not now that she was leaving Prague. And somewhere inside me I knew that I couldn't ever see her again. So long as she knew me she would be in danger because of who and what I was. After she had gone home she would be safe because I was the only person who could connect her with Gustav and Franz Koci. I knew I was going to feel bad about losing her, but this was nothing to how I knew I would feel if ever being with me put her into Heydrich's cold white hands. He'd gut her for information the way Hamperl had gutted poor Albert Kuttner on the slab at Bulovka.

'I'll always love you,' I said, for effect.

'And I love you, too.'

I nodded. 'All right. Let's go and find some dinner.'

CHAPTER 14

I couldn't sleep that night, but Arianne had very little to do with that, although she didn't sleep well either. Sometime before dawn I must have slept a little because I dreamed I had returned to an almost preternatural time and place that was before the Nazis. But this was a recurring dream for me.

We made a desultory attempt at intimacy but our spirits were not in it, hers even less than mine. We washed and dressed and ate some breakfast in the mosaic café downstairs. She seemed depressed and spoke very little, almost as if she was already on the train back to Berlin; but then again, I wasn't exactly gabby myself.

'You seem very quiet this morning,' she said.

'I was thinking the same of you.'

'Me? I'm fine.' She sounded defensive. 'I didn't sleep very well.'

'You can sleep on the train.'

'Yes. Perhaps I will.'

Pushing aside the salt and pepper cellars, I tried to take her hand but she pulled it away.

'Don't pretend, Bernie. You look like you can't wait to get rid of me.'

'Let's not go over this again, Arianne.'

'As you like.'

We walked toward the elevator. The boy opened the double doors to admit us to his little vertical world, but just as I was about to follow Arianne inside the hotel clerk appeared in front of us and handed me a sealed envelope. As the car groaned its way up the shaft I read the note that it contained.

'What is it?' asked Arianne.

'I just lost my ride to the Jungfern-Breschan.'

She frowned.

'Oh? Why?'

'Heydrich reminding me who's boss, probably.'

'You mean you've got no car?'

'That's right.'

'Well, how will you get there? It's fourteen kilometres.'

'Apparently I will have to walk over to Hradschin Castle and beg a lift there.'

The elevator car arrived on the top floor, where we got out.

'That's quite a walk from here,' she said. 'To the castle. I did it yesterday. At least forty minutes. Maybe more. You should telephone them and make them send a car.' She smiled uncertainly. 'Then you could spend some more time with me.'

I shook my head. 'Believe me, I'm in no hurry to get there. Besides, it's a nice day. And the walk will do me good. It will give me some time to think. Now I can see you off at the station.'

'Yes. That would be lovely.'

On our way along the floor she went into the bathroom; and I went back to the room. I lit a cigarette and lay down on the bed and waited for her.

Arianne was quite a while, although this wasn't unusual. She was always well dressed and well groomed, which was one of the reasons I liked her. There's something very sexy about disassembling something that has taken so long to put together: belt, dress, shoes, suspenders, corselette, brassiere, stockings, panties. But when she returned after at least fifteen minutes, she seemed even stiffer than before, as if the paint she had applied to her lovely face was meant not just to enhance her beauty but also to cover her true feelings.

'Actually,' she said, a little breathlessly, as she came through the door, 'I'd rather you didn't come to the station if you don't mind. I've just done my make-up and I know I'll cry if you're standing on the platform waving goodbye. So, if you don't mind, darling, let me go on my own. It's only five minutes' walk. My bag isn't heavy. And I can manage perfectly well on my own.'

I didn't protest. Clearly her mind was made up.

And that was it. When I walked out of the hotel and turned right and west to walk to the Charles Bridge and the Castle that lay beyond it, I never expected to see Arianne Tauber again, and it was as if a great load had been lifted off my shoulders. I felt if not carefree then certainly a profound sense of liberation. Strange how wrong we can be about so much. Being a detective, even a bad one, I should have been used to that: being wrong is an important part of being right, and only time can tell which it turns out to be.

In the Old Town Square, I took a moment to remind myself of that. A few tourists, mostly off-duty German soldiers, had assembled in front of the town hall's astronomical clock to witness the hourly medieval morality lesson involving Vanity, Delight, Greed and Death which took place in two little windows above the elaborate astrolabe. The off-duty soldiers took lots of photographs of the clockwork figures and checked their wristwatches, but none of them looked like they were learning much. That's the thing about morality lessons. Nobody ever learns anything. We were face to face with the past, but none of us seemed to understand that we were also face to face with an allegory of our future.

I got back to the Lower Castle at around ten o'clock and found Kurt Kahlo waiting patiently for me in the Morning Room.

'Captain Kluckholn was just here,' he said.

'What did he want?'

He handed me a sheet of paper.

'It's a list of Kuttner's personal effects,' he said. 'Apparently these are available for our inspection in Major Ploetz's office.'

I glanced over the list.

Kahlo handed me a brown envelope and, smiling, shook his head.

'He's also given us two tickets each for the circus next Wednesday evening.'

'The circus? What the hell for?'

Kahlo nodded. 'Prague's Crown Circus. I hear it's very good. Everyone's invited. Even me. It's an outing for the SD and the SS and the Gestapo. Isn't that nice? Mr and Mrs Heydrich are going. And so are Mr and Mrs Frank. Apparently your lady friend, Fräulein Tauber, is also invited. Whoever she is. I didn't even know you had a lady friend here in Prague.'

'I don't. Not any more. Right now she's on a train back to Berlin.'

'God, I wish I was.'

'Me too.'

'Now I understand why you wanted to get away last night. At the time I thought you were headed for the Pension Matzky.'

'You know about that, do you?'

'More than you might think. A mate of mine in the local vice squad had to interview the girls. Heydrich set the place up even before he became Reichsprotector.'

'He never struck me as the type to pimp for his fellow officers.'

'Oh, he's not. The place is a honey trap. It's equipped with listening devices so that he can eavesdrop on important Czechos or the top brass when they come down from Berlin. My mate reckons he's blackmailing half of the General Staff. Apparently he's got a similar place planned in Berlin. In Geisebrechtstrasse. If I were you, sir, I'd keep away from both.'

'Thanks for the tip. I think I will.'

'Don't mention it.'

'Anything else?'

There was a second envelope in Kahlo's hand. He handed it over. In the envelope was a letter from Geert Vranken's father in the Netherlands, thanking me for contacting his daughter-in-law – she was too upset to write herself – and for informing them of his son's 'accident'; he also asked me to keep him informed of exactly when and where his son's remains were eventually interred.

'News from home?'

'Not exactly.' I put the letter and the circus tickets in my pocket. 'Who's our next witness?'

'Brigadier Bernard Voss.'

'Remind me who he is.'

'In charge of the SS Officer School at Beneschau. And everything you'd expect from the commandant of an officer training school: a real stiff prick. Very probably you could use some uglier words than that. Especially if you're a Czech. In November 1939 some students from the local university organized a demonstration during which Frank's driver was injured. He shouldn't have been there at all, but that's another story. Anyway, twelve hundred students were arrested and Voss commanded the firing squads that shot several of them. As an example to the rest.'

I pulled a face. It was easy to despise a man who'd done something like that. I knew because I'd done something like that myself.

'And Voss once met Hitler,' added Kahlo, 'which is not so unusual in this house. However, when you talk to him it seems to have been the most important day in his life.'

It was easy to believe this after just ten minutes in Voss's company. Hitler he regarded as the modern equivalent of Martin Luther; and maybe he wasn't so far wrong: Luther was another hugely deluded German I regarded with more than a little distaste.

Fortunately for my inquiry it seemed Voss was just as happy to talk about the incident at Beneschau involving Kuttner and Jacobi as he was about the day he met Hitler.

'Captain Kuttner was a highly intelligent young officer and I was surprised that he should have said what he did. However, I was not at all surprised that Colonel Jacobi should have answered him in that way. But then, that's Jacobi for you.'

'Where was General Heydrich when this happened?'

'In the dining hall at Beneschau we have a long refectory-style table. I was right next to Jacobi. But Heydrich was at the opposite end of the table.'

'Why didn't he sit next to you, sir? Surely that would have been customary.'

Voss shrugged. 'The General was late. Delayed by some official business.'

His voice was about as thick as a recently tarred road.

'Why weren't you surprised that Jacobi should have said what he said?'

Voss shrugged again. He wasn't as tall as he should have been; these days you don't have to look commanding to be in command. But he did look tough for a man of almost fifty, which is about the number of stitches it must have taken to sew up the *Schmisse* on his left cheek, and you couldn't argue with an Iron Cross first class or the courageous even foolhardy way he smoked, like every cigarette was his last.

'It's no secret that he and I don't agree on a number of issues. Still there was no excuse for young Kuttner to be insubordinate like that. That was a surprise. I always thought him a very polite, courteous young man. Always. Ever since I first met him several years ago.'

'So you knew him before he came to Prague?'

'Oh yes. He was a cadet-officer at the SS Junker School in Bad Tolz when I was the commander there.'

'When was that?'

'When I was the commander at Bad Tolz? Let's see now. July 1935 until November 1938. Kuttner was one of the best young officers that was ever produced there. He graduated at the top of his class. As you might have expected. After all, he was a law graduate of some brilliance. And great things were expected of Kuttner. He was certainly being groomed for one of the top jobs in the SS. Yes, it's true he had important connections. But he had considerable ability of his own. If only things hadn't gone wrong for him in Latvia he'd have been a major by now. With an important desk job in Berlin.'

Voss shook his head.

'Of course, he's not the first SS officer that this sort of thing has happened to. I know because I keep up with a lot of the young men who passed through my hands at Bad Tolz. Men like Kuttner. The work is too much to expect anyone to carry out without it having some effects on morale and character. They're only flesh and blood, after all.'

It was odd how the same did not seem to apply to the victims of 'the work' that Voss described.

'A new approach is needed to the work of evacuation and resettlement. A different solution to the Jewish problem. A better solution. And I've told Heydrich as much. Something is needed that takes into account the humanity of the men we ask to carry out these special actions.'

He sounded so reasonable I had to remind myself that he was talking about mass murder.

'After Bad Tolz, when you next saw Kuttner again – which was when?'

'At the luncheon where the incident we were talking about took place.'

'When you saw him again, would you say that he'd changed?'

'Oh yes. Very much. And the change was obvious. To me he looked a nervous wreck. Which is what he was, of course. But still highly articulate. And likeable. Yes, I still liked him. In spite of everything. It's a great shame this has happened.'

After I finished with Brigadier Voss, Captain Kluckholn appeared in the Morning Room and explained that Major Thummel had to be back in Dresden that evening and, with their agreement, he had leapfrogged the list of witnesses ahead of Geschke, Bohme and Jacobi.

'Is that all right with you, Gunther?'

'Yes. But now that you're here, Captain, I have a couple of quick questions I'd like to put to you.'

'To me?'

'To you, yes. Of course. And by the way thanks for the circus tickets.'

'Don't thank me. Thank the General.'

'I will.' I opened my cigarette case and offered him one.

Kluckholn shook his head. 'Don't smoke.'

'Hermann, isn't it?' I lit my nail and whistled down the smoke.

He nodded.

'Which adjutant are you? First, second, or third? I never can remember.'

'Third.'

Kluckholn folded his hands at his back and waited politely. He was the tallest and most

401

distinguished of Heydrich's remaining three adjutants. He was also the leanest. His hair was dark and worn slightly longer than most other officers in the SD, which added an almost glamorous, film-starrish aspect to the way he looked. A uniform suited him and he knew it. There was a second-class Iron Cross ribbon worn from the second buttonhole on his tunic and the right angles on the flares of his riding breeches looked like they'd been put there by Pythagoras. The Spanish-cut top-shaft boots were polished like horse brass and had almost certainly been supplied by an expensive dressage company like König. I had half an idea that if Heydrich ever accused him of being improperly dressed, Kluckholn would have hanged himself with his own aiguillette.

'Tell me, Hermann. The night before Captain Kuttner was found dead. What did you two argue about?'

'I'm afraid you're mistaken. We never argued.'

'Oh, come on. I saw you in the front garden. While the Leader was on the radio telling us how wonderfully things were going for our armies in Russia, you two were at each other's throats, like one of those stone sculptures on the front gate.'

'I'm sorry to contradict you, Gunther. You may have seen what you assumed to be an argument but if you had been privy to our conversation you would have heard something quite different from an argument.'

'So what was it?'

'A gentlemanly discussion.'

'Clenched fists. Gritted teeth. Face to face like a couple of boxers at a weigh-in. I think I recognize an argument when I see one.'

'Are you calling me a liar, Captain Gunther?'

I let my lips tug at my cigarette for a long second before I answered him.

'No, not at all. But all the same I'm still wondering if the gentlemanly conversation you had that was very different from an argument makes you a suspect in a murder. You hardly liked the man, after all.'

'Who said so?'

'You did. Yesterday afternoon when General Heydrich was biting everyone's ears in the library. I couldn't help but hear your handsome eulogy of Captain Kuttner. I would say I was eavesdropping except that I imagine your boss left the door open and meant me and some others in the house to hear exactly what was said. There's not much he does that hasn't got a damned good reason behind it. Incidentally, I'm not the only one who's wondering if you were up to putting a bullet in adjutant number four. Some of the other officers aren't exactly slow when it comes to casting aspersions on the characters of their fellow officers. Are they, Kurt?'

'I'm afraid so. But it is disappointing, sir. I thought that among brother officers of the SS and the SD there would be a greater sense of honour and camaraderie. To be honest, there have been times in the last couple of days when this room seemed more like the school principal's office, the number of tales that have been told in here.'

'So how about it, Hermann?'

Kluckholn shook his head. 'Whatever you heard, Captain Gunther, I can assure you I did not murder Captain Kuttner. Perhaps my language was a little intemperate yesterday, in the library. But I had a better opinion of him than perhaps you heard me say.'

Kluckholn spoke as if his voice was being recorded on a gramophone disc.

I looked at Kahlo. 'Kurt. Would you please close that door?'

Kahlo moved away from the piano and closed the door behind him quietly.

'What are you hiding, Hermann?'

Kluckholn shook his head. 'I can assure you, I'm not hiding anything.'

'Sure you are, Hermann.' I shrugged. 'Everyone in this damned house is hiding something or other. Small secrets. Big secrets. Dirty secrets. And you're no exception, Hermann.'

'I would rather you did not call me Hermann in that familiar way. I prefer Kluckholn, or Captain Kluckholn. And your suggestion that I'm hiding something is not only nonsensical it is also insulting.' Colouring with irritation and injured pride, Kluckholn moved toward the closed door.

404

'And I am not going to remain here to endure your insinuations.'

'Yes, you are, Hermann.'

I nodded at Kahlo, who quickly turned the key in the lock and then pocketed it.

Meanwhile Kluckholn looked as if I had just stood on his corn.

'You really are a most vulgar, tiresome fellow, Gunther. Has anyone told you that?'

'Many times. It must have something to do with all the vulgar murders I've investigated. Not to mention all the murders that I myself have been obliged to commit. Of course that hardly makes me unusual in this house. But like Captain Kuttner I found there was something about it I didn't like. Which is the reason I'm here now, speaking to you instead of carrying on the good work out east with all the special action boys. By the way, how was it that you escaped that particular tour of duty, Hermann?'

'I'm ordering you to unlock that door,' Kluckholn told Kahlo.

Kahlo folded his arms and looked sad, as if disappointed that he couldn't obey the order. I didn't doubt that he was more than equal to the task of dealing with Kluckholn if the third adjutant decided to try and get tough with him. Kahlo looked tougher. Kahlo would have looked tough in a bath full of Turkish wrestlers.

'Maybe you had vitamin B, too,' I said. 'Better still perhaps you had vitamin A. What's the big name in Berlin that's been helping you to keep your nice polished boots out of the murder pits of Minsk and Riga, Hermann?'

Kluckholn stood immediately in front of Kahlo and held out his hand. 'As your superior officer I am ordering you to hand over that key.'

'Why don't you sit down and tell us what you're hiding, Hermann? For example, why don't we talk about this list of Captain Kuttner's personal effects? It was you who compiled that, wasn't it?'

'Open that damn door, or you'll regret it.'

'The trouble is, I'm afraid, that you left some items off the list. And I don't like it when people try to deceive me. You see I conducted a very swift search of the room before you tidied up. Which is how I know that this list doesn't include those copies of *Der Führer* magazine that were in Kuttner's drawer.'

I felt Kahlo frown at me.

'They're not quite what you think,' I told Kahlo. '*Der Führer* is or rather was a homosexual magazine. Used to be quite popular with some of Berlin's warmer boys. So were the others in that drawer. *Der Kreise* and *Der Insel*. Lots of naked men playing with medicine balls or doing press-ups on top of each other.' I shook my head. 'You see the corrupting things I've had to deal with in my career as a police officer, Kurt? It's a wonder I'm not in the cement myself, some of the filth I've seen.'

'Lots of bums, was it, sir?'

'Lots. Collector's items now, on the Berlin black market, pornography being so hard to obtain these days. Expensive stuff. For connoisseurs of that kind of thing, you might say.'

Kahlo pulled a face that was a pantomime of disgust.

'It's a dirty job, sir. Being a detective.'

'Don't tell anyone, Kurt. Not in this house. They'll all want to do it.'

Kluckholn had calmed down a bit and was looking a little less inclined to fight Kahlo for the key to the Morning Room door.

But another minute passed before he turned away and sat down on the sofa.

'Of course,' said Kahlo, 'it's possible the Captain here took those dirty magazines off the list not because he wanted to deceive you, sir, but because he wanted to keep them for himself.'

'No,' said Kluckholn, loudly.

'I never thought of that, Kurt. Good thinking.'

Kahlo grinned, enjoying himself. There wasn't much licence to insult senior officers in the Gestapo and SS, and he was going to take full advantage of it now.

'Of course,' I said. 'He took them to use while he was rubbing his own pipe.'

'No,' insisted Kluckholn. 'No. I was merely trying to safeguard Kuttner's reputation. Not to mention the reputation of the squadron.'

The squadron was what nice well-bred people like Kluckholn called the SS.

407

'Kuttner wasn't like that, I'm sure of it. He liked women. Those filthy magazines must have belonged to someone else. Perhaps they were already here when the house was taken over. Perhaps they belonged to the Jews who owned the place before von Neurath. After all, as far as I could tell, they were hardly recent copies.' He shook his head. 'Anyway, I talked it over with my own conscience and I decided that it was best to burn them. It was obvious they had no bearing on the case.'

'You burned them?'

'Yes, I burned them all. It was quite bad enough that Kuttner should be murdered, but we hardly wanted you questioning his reputation as an officer and a gentleman.'

'We? You mean you and Ploetz burned them?'

'Yes. And we certainly didn't want those filthy magazines being sent to his parents in Halle, along with all his other personal effects.'

'That much I can understand.'

'I doubt that, Gunther. I really do.'

'What makes you think he liked women, Hermann?'

'Because he talked about a girl he'd met. A girl here in Prague. That's why.'

'This girl have a name?'

'Grete. I don't know her surname.'

'She wouldn't be the woman in the framed photograph that's still listed among his possessions?'

'No, that's his mother.'

'Maybe this Grete was just his black face,' I said.

'To help persuade you that he was as normal as the rest of you.'

'Or maybe,' offered Kahlo, 'he was just dipping his toe into the water, to see if he liked it.'

'Or maybe Hermann here is just making it up,' I said. 'To make his fellow adjutant seem like less of a queer in our eyes than he really was.'

'Perhaps he's a bit warm himself, sir. Perhaps he has to give Kuttner an alibi so he can have one, too. Could be that's what they were arguing about. A lover's tiff.'

Kluckholn stood up and stared angrily at Kahlo. 'I don't have to take that from you.' He turned to glare at me. 'I don't have to take it from either of you.'

'Sit down,' I said. 'Before I make you sit down.'

Kluckholn remained standing.

'By the way,' I said. 'What other evidence did you destroy when you were burning Kuttner's puppy mags?'

Kluckholn shook his head and sat down. 'Nothing,' he said. 'Nothing at all.'

'A diary, perhaps, Some love letters? Photographs of the two of you on a nice trip to Rügen Island with all the boys?'

I wasn't interested in any of these, although I might have been if I had ever supposed that they had been among his possessions. There was however one more thing I was interested in; something I knew had been in his drawer because I had seen it.

'What about the pipe?'

'What pipe?'

'There was a broken clay pipe in his drawer. What happened to that?'

'I didn't see a clay pipe. But I fail to see what relevance a broken old pipe might have to anything.'

'That all depends,' I said. 'Doesn't it, Kurt?'

'Depends on what?' Kluckholn asked.

'Depends on what he smoked in it,' Kahlo said. 'Tobacco. Marijuana. Opium. They say a clay is best for opium, don't they, sir? Clay keeps the heat better.'

'That's right,' I said. 'Opium or marijuana might be just the thing for a man who was having trouble sleeping. Or just to ease the conscience of a man who felt very guilty about what he'd done in Riga.'

'Of course,' added Kahlo, 'you would only throw it away if you suspected that's what it had been used for. You wouldn't throw it away if you thought he'd only used it to smoke tobacco.'

'Good point,' I said. 'Of course, if we still had it we could have tested it in the lab. They might have cleared him of any suspicion on that score. But now we'll never know.'

Kluckholn was about to say something and then seemed to think better of it. For a moment his brown eyes met mine pleadingly, as if he wanted me to stop and he really did have some secret he couldn't bring himself to reveal. He took hold of his fist in the palm of his other hand and started to squeeze it, trying to stop it from punching me, almost as if Belshazzar had managed to get hold of the disembodied hand that was interrupting his famous feast.

'Go ahead,' I said. 'Punch me on the nose. Then we'll have all the excuse I need to beat it out of you. Won't we, Kurt?'

'Just say the word, sir. I'd love to smack this bastard.'

Kluckholn regarded us with real hatred before he seemed to shrink into a silence and then a shape that made me think we really would have to beat anything else out of him.

Which effectively meant that the interrogation was over.

'Back at the Alex, when a suspect won't talk, we put him down in the cells to think it over. That's what I'd do with you, Hermann, if we weren't doing this in a nice country house with a good piano and some choice works of art. That's what we'd do if we were doing this back in Berlin. We'd lock you up for the night, if we were doing this the proper police way, not like some bullshit scene in a crappy detective novel by that English lady novelist Heydrich seems to admire so much.'

I flicked my cigarette into the fireplace, where it smashed against the chimney wall in a hail of tiny sparks.

'You can go,' I said. 'But I shall certainly want to speak to you again, Hermann. You can depend on it.'

411

Kluckholn stood up and, without uttering another word, he made straight for the door, which Kahlo then unlocked with a deliberate insolence that reminded me strongly of myself.

When the Captain was gone, Kahlo went over to the coffee table where I'd left my cigarette case and helped himself.

'Guilty conscience, do you think?' he asked.

'Around here? I'm not sure what that might look like.'

'The bastard was shaking like a rice pudding. If he didn't do it, or knows who did it, then I'm a Blue Dragoon.'

The Blue Dragoons was the nickname of an Army punishment battalion stationed on the peat-bog moors of the Ems River region. They said that if the damp didn't kill you, the labour – digging peat in all weathers – was certain to do it.

'That's probably what he's worried about,' I said. 'Being sent there. Or whatever the SS equivalent of the Blue Dragoons might be. Some lesser circle of hell, probably.'

'A firing squad looks like a better bet, if you ask me. He destroys evidence and won't say what he and Kuttner were arguing about? Fuck off. Not to mention his declared dislike of the man. If it was me, I'd arrest him now and tap it out of him with a small hammer.'

Kahlo took a fierce drag of his cigarette and then bared his teeth like he was enduring pain.

'And you know something, sir? Kluckholn might

be just as good as it can get for us. In fact, I think he's perfect for it.'

'Meaning what, exactly?'

'Only that he's standing right in front of your box camera with a name and number chalked on a piece of board. No, really. You could just as easily snap him for this murder as anyone else.'

'You sound so like the Gestapo sometimes that I wonder why I like you, Kurt.'

'You're the one with Heydrich's breath in your ear. When you've got a suspect who's suspicious it's foolish to go and look for someone with a kind face and a good alibi. Come on, sir. Every bull does it now and then, even when they don't have to. And if you ask me, you have to.' He paused. 'We have to.'

I grinned. 'It's quite like old times, working with you. You remind me of why I left the police the first time.'

'It's your funeral.' Kahlo shrugged. 'I just hope that I'm only the chief mourner.'

'You needn't worry. I'm not about to reach up and pull you in the grave beside me.'

'It's not just that.'

'What then?'

'I need to get on. In the job. I can't stay being a Criminal Assistant for the rest of my bloody life. Unlike you, I've got a wife to support. The only way I'm going to get a promotion is if you deliver someone's head for Kuttner's murder, or if I join one of those SS police battalions in Russia. Come on, sir, you've been there. Everyone says it's the holiday in hell.'

I nodded. 'That it is.'

'It sent Kuttner over the edge. We know that. I don't want that happening to me. I want kids. I want to be able to look them in the eye when they go to bed at night.'

'Yes, I can understand that.'

'Right then. So far I've managed to avoid all that resettlement shit. But I don't know how much longer I can do it. I can't afford for you to fuck this case up because you're a bit squeamish about sewing someone into the bag for this, sir.'

'So, you admit you don't actually think he did it, then?'

'It doesn't matter what I think. What matters is if it will stand up in front of General Heydrich.'

'Well, I don't think it will. I agree, Kluckholn's keeping something from us. But if you remember, he said that Major Ploetz was party to the decision to burn those puppy mags. For all we know he knew about the pipe, too. You can't put a man in front of a firing squad just because he tries to sidestep a few awkward questions.'

'No? This is Germany, sir. Remember? It happens every day. Someone has got to go down for this and if you ask me it might as well be him. Besides, adjutant or not, he's only a fucking captain and it's going to be a lot easier pinning a charge on him than on any of the cauliflower. There's not one of these bastards that doesn't have a supply of vitamins that goes all the way to the top.'

He had a point. I didn't like it but what he was saying made a lot of sense.

'Am I interrupting you?'

An officer in Army uniform put his head around the door, and for a moment I failed to recognize him.

'Only Captain Kluckholn said he was going to try to get me bumped up your list but – peculiar fellow – he wouldn't answer me when I asked him just now if that was all right with you. Seemed rather upset about something. Had a face like thunder.' He paused. 'Well, is it? All right, I mean? I can come back in a few minutes if you'd prefer, only I was rather hoping to catch this afternoon's train to Dresden. There's quite a lot of work waiting on my desk. The Admiral – that's Admiral Canaris – he keeps me pretty busy these days, I can tell you.'

'I'm sorry. Major Thummel, isn't it?'

'That's right.'

'You'd better come in.'

'Good of you,' he warbled.

Paul Thummel advanced into the Morning Room. He moved with flat-footed nonchalance, like a golfer approaching a putt he expected to sink without any trouble, and sat down on the sofa recently vacated by Hermann Kluckholn.

'All right here, am I?' He smoothed his hands along the silk cushions like a schoolboy and then leaned back, comfortably. 'I haven't been in this room,' he added, looking around. 'Very cosy. Although maybe a bit too feminine for my taste. Not that I have any. At least that's what my wife says. She gets to choose the wallpaper in our house, not me. I just pay for it.'

Thummel was about forty. He had dark hair which, like almost everyone wearing a German uniform, he wore very short at the sides so that what was on top of his skull resembled a little cap. His face was sharp and he had a very pronounced hook nose that looked as if it was trying its best to meet halfway his equally prominent chin. He was friendly and as smoothly confident as you might have expected of a man wearing a gold Party badge, a first-class Iron Cross, a decent cologne, and a silver wedding band.

'Any suspects yet?'

'It's still a little early for that, Major.'

'Hmm. Bad business all round. Leaves an unpleasant taste in the mouth to think that some fellow sitting next to you at dinner might have murdered some other fellow you knew in cold blood.'

'Have you anyone in mind?'

'Who me? No.' Thummel crossed his legs, took hold of the shin of his boot and hugged it toward him like an oar in a two-man scull. 'But fire away with your questions, Commissar, all the same.'

'Are you feeling better today?'

'Hmm?'

'The hangover?'

'Oh, that. Yes. Fine thanks. I'll say one thing for Heydrich, he keeps a spectacular cellar. Himmler will be jealous when I tell him.'

That was a little heavy-handed, I thought. Just as he was doing so well creating an easygoing impression of himself he had to go and spoil it by mentioning Himmler, with whom he was quite probably familiar. I looked at Kahlo who rolled his eyes eloquently as if to suggest that in comparison to Kluckholn I was wasting my time – that Thummel was one of the people with a kind face and a good alibi he had been talking about.

'Nevertheless, I shan't be at all unhappy to go back to Dresden. I don't feel at all comfortable here in Bohemia. Nothing to do with the Reichsprotector's hospitality, of course. But there's something about this country that makes you feel as if you might get your head bashed in on your way to church, like poor old King Wenceslas. Or that one might be defenestrated by a bunch of malodorous Hussites. Awkward, stinky mob, the Czechos. Always were. Right the way through history. Always will be. If you ask me the General's got his work cut out with these bastards. You were in Paris before this, I hear.'

'That's right, sir.'

'Well, I don't have to tell you how different Prague is from Paris. The Frenchies are nothing if not pragmatic. They know what side their bread is buttered on, for now. But the Czecho is a very

417

different kettle of fish. He's a real festering sore is your average Czecho. You mark my words, Commissar, there's going to be a lot of blood spilled here if we're ever going to hold on to this country.'

He frowned.

'Sorry. Rattling on like a milkmaid as usual. You want to talk about poor old Captain Kuttner, don't you? Not my opinion of the Czechos.'

'I found a spent cartridge on the landing in front of your door. From a P38. Which would seem to indicate that a shot must have been fired in that vicinity. On the morning of the murder did you hear a shot fired?'

'You mean in the house. Not outside. Seems to me there's always someone shooting something out there. No, I didn't hear a thing. Mind you, that night I slept like a pickled marmot after all the booze I'd consumed. Slept right through until about – let's see now – well, it must have been about seven o'clock in the morning when I heard a couple of loud bangs. I got up to see what the commotion was about and Captain Pomme, I think, explained to me that he and the butler had been obliged to batter down Kuttner's door, on account of how they thought he must have taken an overdose of barbitol. At least that's what I think he said. So I wandered along to see if I could help and heard Dr Jury say that the poor fellow was dead. There was nothing I could do, of course, so I went back to bed. Stayed there until just about

418

nine. Had a wash, dressed, came out my door again, and there you were, crawling around on the floor looking for that bullet casing. Frankly, I've been racking by brains ever since for a reason why anyone would have killed him. Not to mention how. The room door was locked and bolted from the inside, wasn't it? Window bolted? And no murder weapon yet found. A regular mystery.'

I nodded.

'I even had a look about the dead man's bedroom last evening, in search of some inspiration. I'm not trying to show the hen how to lay an egg and all that but while I was there I found several floor-boards underneath the rug that were loose. Loose enough to pull them up. There was a good space underneath them. Easily big enough for a decent-sized man to have hidden there. And it occurred to me that the murderer, with a sufficiently cool head, might have been lurking in there all the while that you were all in the room, on top of him, so to speak. Of course, he would have to have devised a means of replacing the floorboards on top of his place of concealment and then pulling the rug back. With a couple of lengths of fishing line, perhaps. Yes, that's what I'd have used if it had been me in there. With a couple of strategically-placed nails on the skirting-board, you could have wound the rug in as easily as a venetian blind.'

I looked at Kahlo, who shrugged back at me.

'Sorry.' Thummel smiled ruefully. 'I just sort of thought you ought to know. Really, I wasn't trying to make you look a fool or anything, Commissar Gunther.'

'Actually, sir, I seem to be managing that particular task perfectly well on my own.'

I sighed and stared up at the ceiling where, immediately above, Kuttner's room was situated.

'Why didn't I think of that?'

'You can't think of everything. Such an investigation as you are trying to conduct in this house would try the patience and ingenuity of any mortal man. And look here, I am not saying that is where the murderer was hiding. I am merely suggesting it as a possibility, although not a strong one, I think.'

He shrugged.

'However, I will say this. In the Abwehr we are constantly impressed by the resourcefulness and imagination of the enemy. Especially the Tommies. Desperation is the father of innovation, after all.' He sighed. 'I do not say that is how it was done, Commissar. I say only that is how it could have been done.'

I nodded. 'Thank you, sir.'

'Don't mention it, Commissar. I certainly won't. If you receive my meaning.'

'We had better go up there and take a look for ourselves.'

We all three stood up and moved, simultaneously, for the Morning Room door.

'By the way, Major Thummel,' I said, remembering the letter I had received from Berlin that morning.

420

'Does the name Geert Vranken mean anything to you?'

'Geert Vranken?' Thummel paused for a moment and then shook his head. 'No, I don't think so. Why, should it?'

'There was a murder investigation in Berlin this summer. The S-Bahn murderer? Vranken was a foreign worker on the railways who was interviewed by the police as a potential suspect and he mentioned a German officer who might be prepared to stand as a character witness for him.'

'And you think that was me?'

'I just received a letter from his father in the Netherlands and he said that his son had met a Captain Thummel, in The Hague, before the war, in 1939.'

'Well, there you are, Commissar. It must be another officer called Thummel. Last time I was in The Hague was 1933. Or maybe thirty-four. But certainly not in 1939. In 1939, I was stationed in Paris. You know, Thummel is not an uncommon name. The maître d' at the Adlon Hotel is called Thummel. Did you know that?'

'Yes sir. I do know that. You're right, it must be another officer called Thummel.'

Thummel grinned cheerfully. 'Besides, I'm hardly in the habit of giving guest workers a character reference.' He nodded upstairs. 'But I don't mind showing you those loose floorboards, Commissar.'

*   *   *

After Thummel had left Kuttner's bedroom, Kahlo climbed into the space in the floor and waited patiently while I replaced the boards. Then I took them up again.

Kahlo climbed out, covered in dust.

'Well, it's possible, all right,' I said. 'But hardly probable.'

'Why do you say that, sir?'

'The amount of dust on you. If someone had been hidden there on Friday morning I'd have expected a little less dust than there is in there now. Or at least, was, until you got in there.'

I handed Kahlo the clothes brush I'd picked up from the top of the dresser.

'Lucky it's not a good suit,' I said.

Kahlo growled an obscenity and began to brush off his jacket and trousers.

'Depends on how much dust there was down there before, doesn't it?' he muttered.

'Maybe.'

'And with all of the cauliflower still pissed in their rooms, any one of them might have hidden himself in there and no one would have been any the wiser.'

'I've looked at the rug, too, and I can see no means whereby someone drew the rug back over the boards while he was hidden down there. No fishing line; no nails on the skirting.'

'Perhaps,' said Kahlo, 'the murderer has been back in here and removed them.'

'Perhaps. Anyway, if the murderer did manage

to conceal himself down there, that puts Kluckholn in the clear. Immediately after the murder, he was here in the room, remember? With you and me.'

'Pity. But I still like him for it. And like you said yourself, it's hardly probable, is it? That the killer would have hidden in here.' Kahlo shook his head. 'No, you're right. Kluckholn must have done it some other way. It might just be that he turned himself into a bat.'

I grinned and shook my head. 'He couldn't have done it that way, either. The window was closed, remember?'

'So the General says. We all assume that because he's the General his evidence is one hundred per cent. What if he made a mistake about that? What if the window was open after all?'

'Heydrich doesn't make mistakes about things like that.'

'Why not? He's only human.'

'Whatever gave you that impression?'

Kahlo shrugged.

'It'll be lunchtime soon,' he said. 'You could ask him then.'

'Why don't you ask him yourself?'

'Yeah sure. I meant what I said about that promotion, you know.'

He handed me the clothes brush and then turned around.

'Do you mind, sir?'

I brushed the worst of it off his jacket and thought of Arianne brushing off my own jacket the previous day. I liked that she had been so particular about my appearance, straightening my tie, adjusting my shirt-collar, and always picking my trousers off the floor and tucking them under the mattress so that they might keep the crease. It was a caring touch I was missing already. By now she was probably across the Bohemian border and back in Germany and a lot safer than she was in Prague. I knew what Thummel had been talking about; there was something about Prague that I didn't care for at all.

'I'm looking forward to lunch,' said Kahlo. He was sniffing the air like a big hungry dog. 'Whatever it is smells good.'

'Everything smells good to you.'

'Everything except this case.'

'True. Look, you go ahead, to lunch. I'm going to stay here for a while.'

'And do what?'

'Oh, nothing much. Stare at the floor. Listen to that crow outside the window. Shoot myself. Or perhaps pray for some inspiration.'

'You're not going to miss lunch, are you?'

Kahlo's tone made this sound as serious as if I really was planning to shoot myself. Which wouldn't have been so very far from the truth.

'Now I come to think of it, that's a good idea,' I said. 'Eating has a habit of interfering with my thinking. In that respect it's almost as bad as beer. If I fast for a while maybe I'll be given a vision as to how this murder was done. Yes, why not? Maybe if I starve myself like Moses for forty days and nights then perhaps the Almighty will just come and tell me who did it. Of course he might have to set the house on fire to get my full attention, but it'll be worth it. Besides, I'm pretty sure I have a head start on Moses in one respect.'

'Oh? What's that?'

I opened my cigarette case. 'A smoke. A very small burning bush from whence a great deal of wisdom can be imparted. I reckon any one of those saints could have saved themselves a lot of time and discomfort with a simple cigarette.'

After Kahlo had left me alone with my angst I sat on the edge of Kuttner's mattress and lit one, and when I'd had enough of looking at my cigarette's little mystic trail of holy inspiration I decided to take a look around the house. With more or less everyone now gathered in the Dining Room I was able to go where I pleased without having to furnish an explanation of what I was doing. Besides, I wasn't sure there was an explanation for what I was searching for. All I knew was that I needed to have an idea – any idea – and to have one fast.

Hearing a loud cheer downstairs in the Dining Room gave me my first idea. It wasn't much of an idea but it had at least the merit of being practical. An experiment. An empirical test of an assumption I and everyone else had made right from the very beginning of the case.

I went along to my own bedroom and fetched

the Walther PPK from my bag. Back in Kuttner's room, I closed the door as best I could, racked one bullet into the chamber, fired the weapon twice in quick succession and then sat down to wait for whatever was going to happen. But if I had expected the shots to summon the arrival of a concerned group of officers in Kuttner's room, I was wrong. A minute passed, then two; and after five minutes I was quite certain that no one was coming because no one had heard the shots. Of course this told me only that Kuttner might easily have been shot without anyone hearing or bothering to investigate the shots, but that still felt like something. It was one assumption I'd made that could easily be proved to have been false. And where there was one, there might easily be another.

I went back to my room and replaced the gun in my bag before heading out and along the landing with its blackamoor figures, the hunting-style leather chairs, the decorative Meissen and the less decorative framed photographs of Hitler, Himmler, Goebbels, Goering, Bormann and von Ribbentrop. It was a home from home if you lived at the Berghof.

I was familiar with the more attractive parts of the Lower Castle, including the Library, the Dining Room, the Billiard Room, the Winter Garden, the Conference Room and the Morning Room; but there were other parts of which I knew nothing or which felt forbidden. Heydrich's study certainly felt like it was out of bounds, even to someone who was supposed to be Heydrich's detective. Outside the door I paused for a moment, knocked, and then, hearing no one and expecting to find the door locked, I turned the thick brass handle. The door opened. I went inside. I closed the heavy door behind me.

The room – one of the largest in the house – was quiet and cool; it felt more like a sepulchre than a study. I walked around for a good minute before I was retracing my footsteps, which, like a ghost's, were completely silent in that room, as if I hardly existed at all. Heydrich could have arranged that, of course, and only too easily. As easily as emptying out the crystal ashtray on the desk which looked very clean and brightly polished. One of Kritzinger's duties, perhaps?

I don't know that I expected to find anything. I was just being nosy, but like any detective I felt I had the licence to indulge this tendency, which only feels like a vice when it is accompanied by something more venial like envy or greed. There was nothing in there I really coveted, although I had always wanted a nice desk with a comfortable office chair, but maybe this furniture was a little too grandiose for my purpose. All the same I sat down, spread my hands along the Reichsprotector's desk, leaned back in his chair, glanced around the room for a moment, handled some of the books on his shelves – mostly popular fiction – looked over his many photographs, inspected the blotter for some recent correspondence – there wasn't any – and then decided I was very glad I wasn't Reinhard Heydrich. Not for all the world would I have changed places with that man.

The leather desk diary was full of appointments and not much else. There were many previous meetings at the Wolf's Lair in Rastenburg, at the Berghof, at the Reich Chancellery; and future evenings at the circus – strangely, that was under-lined – a day at Rastenburg, a weekend at Karinhall, a night at the Deutsches Opernhaus, Christmas at the Lower Castle, and then a December confer-ence at an SS villa in Grosser Wannsee. As Heydrich's detective would I be required to go to all of these places? Rastenburg? The Reich Chancellery? The thought of actually meeting Hitler filled me with horror.

I searched the wastepaper bin underneath the desk and found only a sock, with a hole in it. There were no office drawers for me to search. If Heydrich had secret files they were certainly kept somewhere secret. I looked around the room.

The safe I decided at last was behind the portrait of Hitler; and so it proved; but I wasn't about to try and open it; even my impertinence had its limits. Besides, there were things I really didn't want to know. Especially the secret things that Heydrich knew.

The heavily lined curtains looked like they belonged in a theatre and might easily have afforded me a hiding place if someone came into the study. The big windows were as thick as my little finger and quite possibly bullet-proof, too. At the back of the curtains were a couple of machine pistols and a box of grenades; Heydrich wasn't leaving much to chance. If anyone attacked him in his house he clearly intended to defend himself to the last.

But did I want him or one of his adjutants to catch me in there? Perhaps. Being thrown out of his office might also have resulted in my being thrown off the case and sent back to Berlin in disgrace, which seemed like an outcome devoutly to be wished. But it didn't happen and finally, after I'd been in there for almost fifteen minutes, I got up and went out onto the landing, still unobserved.

The next door along from Heydrich's study was a suite of rather more feminine rooms – doubtless these had been set aside for Lina Heydrich – where, among the rose-patterned sofas, elegant chairs, and long mirrors, was a dressing table as big as a Messerschmitt.

I went downstairs and managed to creep un-noticed past the open door of the Dining Room, which was full of cauliflower; nearer the back garden I put my head around the door of a Play Room, and then a Nursery.

As yet I had no knowledge of the extensive serv-ants' quarters in the basement, so I descended a narrow flight of stairs and walked along a dimly lit corridor that seemed to serve as the spine and nervous system of the house. Even on a sunny day like this one, the stone-flagged basement corridor felt more like the lock-up at the Alex, although it smelled a lot better. Kahlo was right about that.

In the big kitchen several cooks were hard at work preparing the next course of lunch, which was being served by waiters whose faces were more familiar. They regarded me with suspicion and alarm. Fendler, the footman I'd spoken to earlier, who happened to be smoking a cigarette near the back door, came over and asked me if was lost. I said I wasn't of course, but a little deterred by the horrified looks I was getting, I was about to return upstairs and get some lunch after all when, at the furthest, dimmest end of the corridor, a door opened and an SS sergeant whom I was certain I'd never seen before came out, closed the door carefully behind him, and then went into the room opposite.

In the moment before the door closed I saw a brightly lit, busy room containing what looked like a telephone switchboard, and thinking that this was as good a time as any to introduce myself in person – there was another call to the Alex I wanted to place – I went along the corridor and opened the door.

Immediately, a burly-looking SS corporal jumped up from a wooden bench, threw down his newspaper, and blocked my way. At the same time he kicked another door shut behind him, but not before I caught a glimpse of several large

430

tape-recorders and, seated in front of them, some more SS men wearing headphones.

'I'm sorry, sir,' said the corporal, 'but I'm afraid you can't come in here.'

'I'm a police officer.' I showed him my warrant disc. 'Commissar Gunther, from the Alex. General Heydrich has given me the run of the house to investigate a murder.'

'I don't care who you are, sir, you can't come in here. This is a restricted area.'

'What's your name, Corporal?'

'You don't need to know that, sir. You don't need to know anything about what happens in here. It doesn't concern you or your particular investigation.'

'My *particular* investigation? That's my call, Corporal. Not yours. What is this place anyway? And what happens behind that door? It looks like Deutsches Grammophon in there.'

'I'm afraid I'm going to have to insist that you leave, sir. Right now.'

'Corporal, did you know that you're obstructing a police officer in the execution of his duty? I have no intention of leaving until I have a full explanation of what's going on in here.'

By now voices were raised, my own included, and there had been a certain amount of chest-on-chest pushing and shoving. I was angrier at myself than at the corporal – frustrated at having missed finding the loose floorboards before and now irritated to discover what looked to me like a listening post for eavesdropping on the house guests – only the corporal didn't know that, and when someone appeared behind me in the door I had just come through and I turned around to see who this was, the corporal hit me. Hard.

I didn't blame him. I didn't blame anyone. Like raising your voice and arguing and pointing, blaming people is not something you can do when you're heading down through the black hole that suddenly appears underneath your shoes. Doctor Freud didn't give it a name and, strictly speaking, you only know what being unconscious really means if a thug with a hardwood fist like a Zulu's knobkerrie has used this same lethal object to hit you expertly on the back of the neck, as if trying to kill a large and argumentative and rather gullible rabbit. No, wait, I did blame someone. I blamed myself. I blamed myself for not listening to the eavesdropping SS corporal in the first place. I blamed myself for missing the trick with the floor-boards in Kuttner's bedroom. I blamed myself for taking Heydrich at his word and thinking I really did have the run of the house to pursue my investigation. But mostly I just blamed myself for thinking it was even possible to behave like a real detective in a world that was owned and run by criminals.

I don't suppose I was unconscious for longer than a couple of minutes. When I came to I could have wished it had been a lot longer. Another thing you can't do when you're unconscious is feel sick or have a splitting headache or wonder if you should dare to move your legs in case your neck really is broken. Ignoring the severe pain of opening my eyelids I opened my eyelids, and found myself staring down the blunderbuss-barrel of a large brandy balloon. It was a big improvement on a real blunderbuss, or the pistol that these circumstances usually produce. I took a deep, heady breath of the stuff and let it toast my adenoids for a moment before taking the glass from the hand that was holding it in front of me and then pouring all of the contents carefully – tipping my head meant moving my neck – down my throat.

I handed the glass back and found it was Kritzinger who took it from me.

I was in a neat little sitting room with a window onto the basement corridor, a small desk, a couple of easy chairs, a safe, and the chaise-longue I was lying on.

'Where am I?'

'This is my office, sir,' said Kritzinger.

Behind him were two SS men, one of whom was the corporal who had argued with me a few minutes before. The other was Major Ploetz.

'Who hit me?'

'I did, sir,' said the corporal.

'What were you trying to do? Make a bell ring?'

'Sorry about that, sir.'

'No, don't apologize. Kritzinger?'

'Sir?'

'Give this boy a piece of sugarloaf. I reckon he won it fair and square. The last time I got hit like that I was wearing a pointy hat and sitting in a trench.'

'If only you'd listened to me, sir,' said the corporal.

'It looked to me as if that's exactly what you've been doing.' I rubbed the back of my neck and groaned. 'To me and everyone else in this house.'

'Orders are orders, sir.'

Ploetz put his hand on my shoulder. 'How are you feeling, Captain?' He sounded oddly solicitous, as if he really did care.

'Really, sir,' insisted the corporal. 'If I'd known it was you, sir—'

'It's all right, Corporal,' Ploetz said smoothly. 'I'll handle things from here.'

'Sure, doc, sure,' I said. 'You can pretend there's a perfectly innocent explanation for all that recording equipment and while you're at it, I'll pretend I'm a proper detective. Right now the only thing I am absolutely certain of is the quality of that brandy. Better pour me another, Kritzinger. I pretend better when I've had a drink.'

'Don't give him any,' Ploetz told Kritzinger. And then: 'Your tongue is quite loose enough as it is, Gunther. We wouldn't want you to say something to your own detriment. Especially not now you're in the General's good books.'

I ignored this. It didn't sound right. Clearly the

434

blow on the back of my neck had affected my hearing.

'That's right, doc. We've got to be careful what we say. What is it that the sign says? Attention! The enemy is listening. Well, they are. And they're pretty good at it, too. Aren't you, boys? What were you listening to anyway? And don't tell me it was the Leader talking about the Winter Relief. Something in the Meeting Room? Something in the bedrooms? Maybe you've got a recording of Kuttner getting shot. That might come in useful. For me, anyway. Something in the Morning Room? Me, perhaps. Only what would be the point in that? I don't mind calling you all crooks and liars to your ugly faces. Just see if I don't.'

Ploetz moved his head in the direction of the door and the two SS men started to leave.

'Look, Gunther,' Ploetz said, 'I think it might be better if you returned to your room and had a lie-down. I'll inform the General of what's happened. Under the circumstances, he'll want to know you're all right.'

At this moment a lie-down looked very appealing.

Ploetz went outside while Kritzinger helped me to my feet.

'Are you all right, sir? Would you like me to help you back to your room?'

'Thanks no, I'll manage. I'm used to it. It's an occupational hazard for a policeman, being hit. It comes of sticking my nose in where it's not wanted. I should know better by now. It used to be that a detective could turn up at a country house, question everyone, find some recognizable clues, and then arrest the butler over chilled cocktails in the library. But it hasn't worked out like that, I'm afraid, Kritzinger. I'm afraid you won't be getting your big moment when everyone realizes what a clever fellow you've been.'

'That is disappointing, sir. Perhaps you would care for another brandy after all.'

I shook my head. 'No. I expect Doctor Ploetz is right. I do talk too much. It comes of not having any answers. I don't suppose you know who shot Captain Kuttner.'

'No, sir.'

He smiled a fleeting smile and then scratched the back of his head, awkwardly.

'Pity.'

'You understand, sir, that there are lots of things in this house I prefer not to hear, but if these things had included a shot, or perhaps a snippet of conversation that might shed some light on his unfortunate death, then I should certainly tell you, Commissar. Really I would. However, I am certain there's nothing I can tell you.'

I nodded. 'Well, that's very good of you to say so, Kritzinger. I really think you mean that. And I appreciate you saying it.'

'Really?' The smile flickered on again for just a second. 'I wonder.'

'No, I do.'

'I flatter myself that perhaps I know your own

436

independent cast of mind. One can't help but hear things in a house like this.'

'So I noticed.'

'Consequently, I know you believe that I think in a certain way only, for what it's worth, I don't. I never have. I am a good German. Like you, perhaps, I don't know what else to be. But unlike you, I am not a courageous man, if you follow me.'

'That Iron Cross ribbon in your buttonhole says otherwise, Mister Kritzinger.'

'Thank you, sir. But that was then. I think things were simpler in that war, were they not? Courage was perhaps easier to recognize not only in oneself but in others as well. Well, I was younger then. I have a wife now. And a child. And long ago I concluded that the only practical course of action available to me was simply to do as I'm told.'

'Me, too.'

I headed for the stairs a little unsteadily. It had been a very German conversation.

As I passed the dining room I noticed that lunch was finishing. Seeing me, Heydrich made his excuses to the other cauliflower and, smiling, nodded toward the Drawing Room.

It wasn't every day that Heydrich smiled at me. I followed him, and he led me to the French windows and out onto the terrace where he offered me one of his cigarettes and even condescended to light it for me. He did not smoke one himself. And he seemed oddly cheerful considering that

Vaclav Moravek continued to elude the Gestapo. I had only ever seen him like this once before, and that had been in June 1940, after the French capitulation.

'Major Ploetz told me what happened to you below stairs,' he said, almost apologetically. 'I should have informed you about the SD listening station but really, I've had so much on my plate. As if I didn't have enough to do here in Bohemia with the Three Kings and UVOD and the traitor X. Reichsmarshal Göring has tasked me to submit to him a comprehensive draft as to how we can sort out the way the Jews are being handled in all new territories under German influence. Well, I'm sure I don't have to tell you what things are like in the East. It's nothing short of chaos. But that's hardly your concern.

'But to come back to the traitor X: as you know, all of the guests in this house were under suspicion in that respect. However, by a simple process of elimination our intelligence analysts had narrowed down the search for the traitor's identity to one of six or seven officers. Consequently everything these men said on the least of subjects was of interest to us. Which is why some of the rooms in the Lower Castle have concealed microphones, just in case one of them should let something important slip.'

'You mean, like the Pension Matzky.'

Heydrich nodded. 'You know about the microphones, do you?' He grinned. 'Yes, like the Pension Matzky.'

438

'And do these rooms here include the Morning Room?'

'Yes, they do.'

My stomach turned over for a moment; not for my own sake – as far as Heydrich was concerned, I was a hopeless case – but for Kurt Kahlo's, and I started to rack my brains for anything he had said that might have been interpreted as evidence of his disloyalty.

'So you've heard everything that was said in there?'

'No, not me personally. But I've read some of the transcripts.'

'Kuttner's room?'

'No. My fourth adjutant was hardly important enough to have rated that level of surveillance.' Heydrich made a face. 'Which is a pity, because if he had been, then of course we would now know who it was who pumped two bullets into his chest.'

I let out a weary sigh and tried to put some sort of tolerant, understanding face on what had just been revealed to me.

'In my book, a traitor is a traitor. I can easily see why you should wish to employ every method at your disposal in order to catch him. Including secret microphones. But I just hope you'll excuse some of my Criminal Assistant Kahlo's looser talk in the Morning Room. You can blame me for a lot of that. He's a good man. I'm afraid I've been a bad influence on him.'

'On the contrary, Gunther. It's thanks to you

and your unconventional, not to say insubordinate methods, that the traitor has now been revealed. In fact, everything has worked out exactly as I had hoped it would. You, Gunther, have been the catalyst that changed everything. I don't know who to congratulate more: me for having the inspiration of bringing you here in the first place, or you for your own stubbornly independent cast of mind.'

I felt my face take on an expression of disbelief.

'Yes, it's quite true. It seems that we owe you everything in this matter, Gunther. Which makes it all the more unfortunate that your immediate reward should have been to be knocked unconscious by one of our more robust colleagues in the SD. For which, once again, I offer my sincere apologies. You were after all merely doing your job. A job well done. For even as we speak the traitor is under close arrest and on his way to Gestapo headquarters in Prague.'

'But who was it? The traitor.'

'It was Major Thummel. Paul Thummel, of the Abwehr.'

'Thummel. He's a man with a gold Party badge, isn't he?'

'I did say it would turn out to be someone who was apparently above reasonable suspicion.'

'But he's also a friend of Himmler.'

Heydrich smiled. 'Yes. And that is something of a bonus. The acute embarrassment that this particular association will cause the Reichsführer will be a great pleasure to behold. I can't wait to see Himmler's face when I tell the Leader. For that same reason, however, it's by no means certain that we'll make any of this stick against Thummel. We shall, of course, do our best.'

I nodded. 'I'm beginning to understand. It has something to do with that letter I received this morning from the Netherlands, doesn't it?'

'It does indeed. You asked Major Thummel if he was the same Captain Thummel who was in The Hague in 1939. He denied it, of course. Now why? Why would that be of any interest to you? But this was a lie. It was a matter of only a few minutes to check through a record of his military service. When Thummel was a captain in 1939, he passed through The Hague on his way to Paris. We know he was in The Hague because he visited our military attaché at the German Embassy. But while he was in The Hague we also think he met secretly with his Czech controller, a man named Major Franck. Franck and Thummel shared a Dutch girlfriend named Inge Vranken. I shall want to see your letter of course, but it rather looks as if Inge Vranken was your friend Geert's little sister.

'We suspect Thummel has been spying for the Czechos since as early as February 1936. For a long time he was using a radio transmitter to send messages here, to Prague. As you are aware we were intercepting some of that radio traffic; what we called the OTA intercepts. The Czechos called him A54. Don't ask me why. Call sign probably.

441

The radio messages were forwarded by courier to the Czech government in exile in London. That went on for quite a while. But then Thummel began to get scared. He stopped using the radio transmitter altogether. And to all intents and purposes it looked as if he had closed up shop, thus narrowing our chances of getting him.

'We suspect that UVOD despaired of having lost their best agent. Not least because his material had put the exiled Benes government in London in very good odour with Winston Churchill. No more intelligence meant no more operational scraps from the top table. So the UVOD people set out to re-establish contact with him in Berlin, in person; and for a while that did the trick. But with the net closing in, he lost his nerve for that, too. Frankly I think he's been expecting this for a while.'

'But why? Why would an old Party comrade – a man with the confidence of Hitler – why would such a man spy for the Czechos? Why spy at all?'

'That's a good question. And I'm afraid I don't yet know the answer. He's still denying everything, of course. It's likely to be several days before we have any idea of the reason behind his treason, or even the full extent of his treachery.'

Was it possible that Thummel had been Gustav? For a moment I pictured Thummel in the hands of the local Gestapo and wondered how long it might take them to beat 'the full extent of his treachery' out of the man.

442

'Surely it won't take your people that long.'

Heydrich shook his head. 'Actually it will. As I said, Thummel has vitamin B. We shall have to question him quite carefully. Himmler would never forgive me if I had him tortured. In the short term at least we can but hope that close interrogation will find holes in his story.'

'I understand.'

Heydrich nodded, silently.

'Well,' he said. 'Good work, Gunther. As my personal detective you are off to a flying start, I think.'

He was heading back through the French windows when I spoke again.

'What I don't entirely understand, General, is why you murdered Captain Kuttner.'

Heydrich stopped and turned slowly on the heel of his shoe.

'Hmm?'

'It was you who killed your own adjutant. That I am certain of. I know how you did it. I just don't know why you did it. I mean why bother to murder him when you had ample opportunity to have him court-martialled? No, I don't understand that. Not entirely. And I certainly don't understand exactly why you had me go to all the trouble of investigating a murder that you yourself had committed.'

Heydrich didn't say anything. It seemed he was waiting for me to do some more talking before he said anything. So I did. It felt like I was talking

443

my own neck into a noose, but it was hard to imagine it being any more painful than it was now.

'Of course, I have a few ideas on that score. But first, if you'll permit me, sir, let me deal with how you killed him.'

Heydrich nodded. 'I'm listening.'

'I see you haven't denied it.'

'To you?' Heydrich laughed. 'Gunther, there are about three people in the world to whom I ever need to justify myself, and you're not one of them. Nevertheless, I should like to hear your explanation of the solution to the crime, as you see it.'

'On the night before he was murdered, you gave Kuttner a dose of Veronal, which unwittingly he drank in a glass of beer. It was the only thing Kuttner drank that night, as he knew to avoid mixing the drug with alcohol. But I bet you persuaded him to have just the one. Everyone else was celebrating, after all. And what an honour to be served by you. I should have thought beer was perfect for your purposes. It wasn't so alcoholic that he might refuse. And of course beer is bitter, so Kuttner wouldn't ever have tasted the significant dose of the drug with which you'd doctored it.

'But doctor it you certainly did. Kritzinger reports seeing Kuttner looking very tired at around two. So the drug was already working its effect. But Kuttner didn't know that, so when he got back to his room he took his regular dose of Veronal and actually passed out with one of

444

the pills still in his throat. Which accounts for how he only had one boot off. My guess is that you wanted him to sleep extra soundly, although why you didn't just do him in with an overdose, I'm not sure. Possibly you wanted to make sure he was indeed dead and there is, as you must know, always something uncertain about an overdose. It's amazing just how much people can swallow without dying. But a bullet is much more certain. Especially when it's fired point-blank to the heart.

'In the morning, you let Captain Pomme and Kritzinger try to rouse him before making sure that you were on the scene to authorize them to break down the door. And being a General, naturally you were first into the bedroom, which meant you were also the one who was able to take charge and examine Kuttner's drugged body and pronounce him dead. Naturally, they took your word for it, General. You're not an easy man to contradict, sir.

'Judging by his appearance, of course, it hardly looked at all probable that he was still alive. He was half dressed from the night before, and there was an open bottle of Veronal on the bedside table, so everyone assumed that the obvious explanation was the correct one: Kuttner had taken an overdose, possibly intentionally – after all, most of his fellow officers were aware he'd had some sort of breakdown – and was dead. No one suspected that he had been shot because the fact is he hadn't

445

been shot. Not at that moment. At that moment he was only unconscious.

'Having ordered Kritzinger to call an ambulance and Captain Pomme to fetch Doctor Jury, you were now alone in the room with the Captain's unconscious body. Doctor Jury's room is in the other wing of the house, so you knew Pomme would take several minutes to return with him. Apart from the telephone in your office, the nearest telephone is on the ground floor, so Kritzinger was far away, too. All the same, you probably waited a few minutes just to make sure that no one was around before closing the door as best you were able. There was now plenty of time for you to produce a gun from inside your fencing jerkin, pull aside his tunic and coolly fire two shots in rapid succession into Kuttner's body at close range, killing him instantly. Because he was still wearing his tunic, the gunshot wounds were not immediately obvious to anyone who had already seen the body. Moreover these wounds didn't bleed much either because Kuttner was lying on his back. Not to mention the convenient effect that the extra Veronal would have had on the dead man's blood pressure.'

Heydrich listened patiently, still denying nothing. Folding his arms he placed a thoughtful finger across his thin lips. He might have been considering some plan for the evacuation of Prague's Jews.

'You put the gun back inside your jerkin. Then

you opened the window, just to help ventilate the room a little more, just in case someone caught a whiff of the shots. When you opened the window, that's when you saw the footman, Fendler, with the ladder; you told him that the ladder was no longer required; that poor Kuttner was dead of an overdose, because after all, you were obliged to pay lip service to what at that moment everyone else believed.

'Then you did a quick search on the bed and the floor for the spent brass. You wanted to pick this up so that you could help to muddy the waters and add to the mystery that was bound to attach to a murder in a room locked from inside. That might have taken a while. They're elusive things when you need to find them in a hurry. Of course, if someone had entered the room you would have given some excuse about looking for clues. After all, there were pills on the floor. You were just picking them up. You are a policeman, after all. Maybe it was you who chucked them there for effect. Set dressing, so to speak. But to me it never seemed right that the Veronal bottle remained upright on the table when there were pills on the floor.

'Having found the two spent brass cartridges, you flung them along the corridor, lit a cigarette to help conceal the smell of the two shots – although, as I discovered for myself a little while ago, it isn't particularly noticeable, and certainly no more noticeable than the noise of two shots. I fired my own pistol in Kuttner's room while you were all eating lunch and, of course, no one noticed a thing. Most people assume a noise like that is something else, something a little less dramatic. A car backfiring. A vase of flowers knocked over. A door slammed by a careless footman. Of course you already know that. I'll bet you even conducted a similar experiment yourself when you were planning this whole thing.

'It was about then that Captain Pomme and Doctor Jury arrived in the room. Doctor Jury was a good choice. For one thing Jury was possibly still drunk, and at the very least badly hungover, and he probably didn't even notice that the dead man was still bleeding, only that he'd been shot. Again no one was about to suspect your own first version of events. Besides, there was now an even bigger mystery in front of everyone's eyes, which is how a man could be found shot dead in a room locked on the inside with no murder weapon on the scene. It's a useful thing, mystery. Any stage conjurer knows the value of misdirection. You draw attention to what one hand is doing while the other hand does the dirty work.

'People do love a good mystery, don't they? You included, General. Perhaps you more than most. On your bookshelves I found a well-read copy of a detective novel by that writer you mentioned to me when I arrived here: Agatha Christie. It's a novel called *The Murder of Roger Ackroyd*. And I only had to flick through it for a few minutes to see that the book contains certain similarities with this case. A body in a locked room. Only that person, Roger Ackroyd, isn't dead at all; not in the beginning; and it's the person who supposedly finds the body – Doctor Sheppard, isn't it? – who turns out to be the murderer. As indeed you are. In fact, I wouldn't mind betting that's where you got the idea in the first place.

'But my neck and my head hurt and I just can't figure out why. Why would you murder your mother's favourite piano pupil? It couldn't be that, could it? Jealousy? No, not you. That would be much too human of you, General Heydrich, sir. No, there has to be some other reason. Something much more important than personal revenge.'

I paused and lit another cigarette.

'Well, don't stop there,' said Heydrich. 'You're doing so well and I have to confess I'm actually quite impressed. This is more than I had expected of you, Gunther.' He nodded firmly. 'Keep going. I insist.'

'For old time's sake, you'd rescued Albert Kuttner's career. That was oddly sentimental of you. And quite out of character, if you don't mind me saying so, sir. Or perhaps you did it at someone else's request. Kuttner's father. Your mother, perhaps.'

'You'd best leave my mother out of this, Gunther, if you don't mind.'

'Gladly. You'd rescued Albert Kuttner's career only to discover that, as you told me yourself, he was a disappointment. More than just a disappointment, he'd become something of a nuisance, even an embarrassment. Kuttner was insubordinate. For example, there was that scene at the Officers' Training School with Colonel Jacobi. And what was worse, you had found out he was quite possibly homosexual, too. After what happened to Ernst Röhm and some of his warmer friends in the SA, that was too much. Did you worry that you might be tainted with an association like that? I wonder. In Germany it's one thing to be suspected of being a Jew, as you are, and quite another to be suspected of being soft on homosexuals. Even then, however, you could have sent Kuttner quietly back to Berlin. To one of those nice private clinics in Wannsee where top Nazis go to dry out or be weaned off drugs. Some of them even claim they can cure you of homosexuality. So you must have had an important reason to murder him in cold blood like that. There must have been some sort of gain in it for you. But what?'

'Excellent. You're almost there.'

Heydrich lit a cigarette and looked very amused, as if I was telling him a very funny story. It made me suspect that he had a better punch-line than the one I had written myself. But I was in too far now to stop.

'Everything you do has a reason, doesn't it, General? Whether it's murdering Jews or murdering your own adjutant.'

Heydrich shook his head. 'Don't get sidetracked,' he said. 'Keep to the point.'

'But why have me investigate the murder? At first I assumed it was because you thought I wasn't up to the job; that you wanted me to screw up; but that was too obvious. You could have picked anyone for the job. Willy Abendschoen from the local Kripo is a good man, I hear. Clever. Efficient. Or you could have picked someone more pliable than either of us. Unless of course that was exactly what you wanted. Someone who doesn't care about his future in the SD. Someone who is just pig-headed enough to ask the difficult questions that the cauliflowers might not care to answer. Someone for whom advancement and promotion is not an issue. Me. Yes, that must be it. You picked me to handle the investigation of Kuttner's murder because you really wanted me to search for your spy. You used the murder of Kuttner as a pretext for a secret spy hunt.'

'Now you're on to it,' said Heydrich.

'You couldn't risk some flat-footed idiot questioning all of your spy suspects about being the traitor X, or A54, or whatever he's called; not without putting them on their guard. But if I questioned them all about something else, something serious that necessitated their being detained here, then all of them might relax, more or less, since each knew he was innocent of murder. And of course my conversations with them were being recorded, transcribed, picked over by your own

451

SD analysts for something small, an inconsistency, perhaps. A clue. Real evidence. You didn't know exactly what it was, but you thought you would recognize it when you saw it. And you're right. That's all a clue really is. I have to hand it you, sir; it's clever. Utterly ruthless, but clever.'

Heydrich clapped his hands three times. To me it sounded almost ironic, but there was it seemed some genuine appreciation in his congratulations.

'Well done. I underestimated you, Gunther. I've always assumed that as a policeman you were the more muscular type. Tough, resourceful, and irritatingly dogged, but hardly intellectual. It seems I was wrong about that. You have a much better brain than I gave you credit for. I had hoped you might uncover the spy, it's true. But I did not expect you would also solve the murder. That has been a real bonus. But now I really am intrigued. I want to know. I must have made a mistake. Exactly how did you conclude that it was me who shot Captain Kuttner?'

'Sorry to disappoint you. It wasn't anything clever, at all.'

'Oh, come on. You're being unnecessarily modest.'

'Actually you told me yourself. Just a few minutes ago. Only I and the doctor who carried out the autopsy knew that Kuttner had been shot twice. Even Jury didn't notice that. And I kept it secret in the hope that eventually the real killer would mention two shots when everyone else believes that it was just the one shot that killed him.'

Heydrich frowned. 'Is that all?'

To my delight he sounded disappointed.

'What else is there? I'm not one for crossword puzzles, General. Or detective novels. Actually I really can't stand them. Me, I'm just a plain, old-fashioned cop. And you described me rather well a moment ago when you said I was irritatingly dogged. I don't have the better brain you gave me credit for. These days I wouldn't know what to do with it. You see, sir, most murders aren't complicated. People just think they are. The same goes for the detection process. There are no great scenes of revelation. There's just the small stuff. And that's where I come in. Really, if detective work was as difficult as it seems in the books, then they wouldn't let cops do it.'

'Yes, I take your point.' Heydrich sighed. 'But now I have another question. And perhaps you should answer this one more carefully.'

I nodded.

'What do you think you're going to do about it?'

I didn't answer. I didn't know. What could I do against a man of Heydrich's standing and authority?

'What I mean is: are you intending to try to arrest me, perhaps? To make a scene.'

'You murdered someone, General.'

'You're right, of course. And I did regret having rescued Kuttner's career. I could have lived with his behaviour in and after Latvia. What happened to him there is by no means unusual – which is of course why Reichsmarshal Göring has charged

453

me with finding a better solution to this problem. I could even have lived with his behaviour to Colonel Jacobi. The two of them have some history, it seems; however, Jacobi is a prick and frankly anyone who gets the better of that man is to be admired rather than condemned.

'But I was shocked when Berlin's Gestapo informed me that my own adjutant was probably homosexual. Not that he was very obvious about it; indeed I was so sceptical that I sent him along to Pension Matzky, where I'm afraid to say he disgraced himself with a girl called Grete. When he failed to perform with her, unfortunately she mocked his inadequacy and earned herself a beating. He was very apologetic about it afterwards; he even sent her some flowers by way of compensation; most bizarrely he then seems to have adopted an entirely opposite opinion of the poor girl and decided that he felt some romantic attachment for her. I'm sure there are medical explanations for his mental state. But if there are, I have no time for them. That was when I decided to get rid of him. I dislike men who are violent to women almost as much as I dislike men who are unreliable.

'Anyway, if I had sent him back to Berlin in disgrace it wouldn't have been long before he disgraced himself again and, more importantly, disgraced his family in Halle. I couldn't have that. I am very fond of those people. Fond enough to want to spare them any further pain. So I thought it was better for him to be quietly murdered by me in a way that can be easily hushed up rather than allow his family to endure the public disgrace that would follow his being sentenced to some SS punishment battalion. Indeed, it already seems to me much more probable that at some stage in the hopefully not too distant future Captain Kuttner will become an unfortunate victim of Vaclav Moravek, and heroically shot by him while trying to assist in the Czech terrorist's arrest. We may even have to award him a posthumous decoration. That's a story that should play well at home, don't you think?'

'Why not? He is as good a Nazi hero as any others I can think of.'

Heydrich smirked. 'Yes, I thought you might approve. You were wrong about one thing, however. I couldn't ever have risked wasting so much time searching for my spent brass on the floor of Kuttner's room. So, I had the gun inside a sock, so that it could be fired without any of the spent brass being ejected onto the floor or the bed. It all stayed safely inside the sock. Until as you say, I threw it into the corridor. Anyway, having decided to kill him – it was as you say *The Murder of Roger Ackroyd* that gave me the idea of how to do it – I then wondered if I might put his death to some useful purpose. If I could rely on you to be your usual awkward self and pose a lot of awkward questions to people like Henlein, Frank, von Eberstein, Hildebrandt, Thummel and von Neurath, whom we've had our doubts about for some time. And you came up trumps. Nothing you've said can spoil what I'm feeling now. And you'll no doubt be pleased to discover that you will have advanced my reputation even further. The apprehension of the traitor X will put me in very good odour with the Leader. Ever since the invasion of Poland, the traitor has been a thorn in our side. No more. And my triumph will be complete just as soon as the third of the Three Kings is in my hands. You see, now that I have Thummel, it can't be very long before everything is neatly wrapped up.'

'Hardly,' I said. 'I'm not about to let you get away with murder, General.'

'We're getting away with it every minute,' murmured Heydrich. 'I thought you knew that.'

'Kuttner had it coming for all I know, but even in the SS there are standards that have to be adhered to. Military discipline. Due process. Probably it will cost me my job. Even my life, but I can at least try to bring you down.'

'You're a fool if you think you can bring me down. But then I think you know that already, don't you? It's certainly true, you can cause a bit of trouble for me, Gunther. Himmler won't thank me for exposing Paul Thummel; and naturally the investigation will have to be entirely above reproach. Very possibly that will involve you. In which case I can hardly have you shot or sent to a concentration camp. No, I can see I'm going to have to provide you with a better, more urgent reason than your loyalty to me, one that will make sure you keep your mouth shut about all of this.'

I shook my head. 'I don't think that's going to happen, sir. Not this time.'

'Do try to be sporting about this, Gunther. At least let me try.'

'If you like.'

Heydrich threw away his cigarette and glanced at his wristwatch.

'We'll go straight to Gestapo headquarters. There, if you wish, you can make out your own report, in as much detail as you like. Pecek Palace is the proper place to bring charges against me. That is, if I can't provide you with a better reason than simple self-preservation.'

'I dare say you have people there who can persuade anyone to do anything.'

'Oh, you misunderstand me, Gunther. You weren't listening, perhaps. I said I was going to give you a much better reason to keep your mouth shut than self-preservation, and I meant it. You're quite safe from that sort of thing, I can assure you. I'm going to give you something much more compelling than violence against your person, Gunther. Shall we?'

I nodded, but something told me that I had already lost. That this was one murderer who was almost certain to get away quite unscathed.

It was three-thirty in the afternoon when Heydrich and I got into the Mercedes with Klein and started

457

out for the centre of Prague. No one said very much but it was obvious that Heydrich was in a good humour, humming a pleasant-sounding melody that was the very opposite to the threnody playing inside my own thick skull.

Nearing the railway line that led west to Masaryk Station, we overtook a horse-drawn hearse headed south, for the Olsany Cemetery. The mourners walking behind looked at Heydrich with baleful eyes as if somehow they held him responsible for the death of the person they were escorting to church. For all I knew that was true, and the sight of his distinctive SS car must have been like catching a glimpse of the grim reaper himself. You could feel the hate following us like X-rays and despite Heydrich's overbearing confidence that he was invincible, it was clear to me that the hatred directed at him could just as easily have been a hail of machine-gun bullets. An ambush was the best way to kill Heydrich, and once you were in that car, anything might happen. If it had happened right then and there, I wouldn't have minded that much.

By the time we reached the outskirts of the city what little confidence I had of making something stick to Heydrich had faded. Optimism has its limits. I was an idealist and ahead of me lay an unpleasant, possibly painful, even fatal demonstration of just where idealism could get you. A jail cell. A beating. A train ride to the concentration camp being built around the fortress of Terezin.

A bullet in the back of the head. Heydrich might have assured me I was safe but I had little confidence in his assurances; and thoughts of my own peril overpowered any other ideas of just what the man sitting in front of the car – whose own mind seemed more preoccupied with Schubert and his trout – had in store to deflect me from any attempt to bring charges against him.

So we drove on to what promised to be some sort of final reckoning between us.

Pecek Palace, formerly a Czech bank, was part of a government area that was home to several tall and rusticated grey buildings any one of which could have been Gestapo headquarters. But the real HQ was easy to spot at the end of the street, surrounded as it was with checkpoints and bedecked with two long Nazi banners. It was a grim, granite edifice that was a near-copy of the Gestapo's central HQ in Berlin's Prinz Albrechtstrasse, with huge cast-iron lamps that belonged on an ogre's castle, and a Doric-columned portico that might have seemed elegant but for several SS men who were grouped out front, easily recognizable with their leather coats, pork-knuckle faces and pugilist's manners. None of them looked as though they would have turned a short hair to see a defenestrated Czech crash onto the black cobbles in front of their cold eyes. Five storeys above the street the balustrade featured stone vases that resembled giant funeral urns. Certainly it wouldn't have surprised the Czechs to have been told that this was what these were used for. After three years of occupation the Gestapo at Pecek Palace had the most fearsome reputation in all of Europe.

Klein stopped the car at the entrance and the guards came to attention. I followed Heydrich through the wrought-iron doors and up a short, shiny limestone staircase that was lit by a large brass chandelier. At the top of the stairs were some glass double-doors lined with green curtains and in front of these were two SS guards, a pair of Nazi flags, and between them a portrait of the Leader – the one by Heinrich Knirr that made him look like a queer hairdresser. To the left was a reception area where I presented my identification and endured the awl-like scrutiny of the uniformed NCO on duty.

'Tell Colonel Bohme to come and fetch us,' Heydrich told the NCO. And then to me: 'I'm lost in here.'

'A common experience, I imagine.'

'Bohme is the one who thought he could solve Kuttner's murder,' said Heydrich.

'Are you going to tell him or shall I?'

'Oh, I know you find it hard to credit, but I take a lot of vicarious pleasure in your solving Kuttner's murder. I mean I can admire it as a piece of reasoning. And I'm very much looking forward to seeing the expression on his stupid Saxon face.'

'I'd been kind of looking forward to that myself. Bohme was the other officer who straightened

Kuttner's tie after your speech the other night. When he rescued the maid, Rosa, from Henlein's clumsy drunken pass. I shall miss the opportunity of making him feel like he had something to hide.'

'You're a natural contrarian, Gunther,' observed Heydrich. 'I think your problem is not with the Nazis, it's with all authority. You just don't like being told what to do.'

'Maybe.'

I glanced around.

'Major Thummel's here?' I said.

'Yes.'

'Is Bohme questioning him?'

'Abendschoen is leading the interrogation. He's much more agile than Bohme. If anyone can trip Thummel up without breaking skin, it's Willy Abendschoen.'

A minute or two passed before we heard footsteps coming up the broad stairs.

Bohme arrived at the top of the stairs and marched smartly across the hall and into the reception area. He saluted in the usual Nazi way, and under the circumstances I didn't bother returning the compliment; but Heydrich did.

'Let's go and see the prisoner, shall we?' said Heydrich.

Bohme led the way back across the hall and downstairs. At the bottom of the stairs we walked on through a warren of unpleasant smelling and dimly lit corridors and cells.

'I hear it's down to you, Captain Gunther, that we found Thummel was the traitor,' Bohme told me. 'Congratulations.'

'Thank you.'

Bohme paused outside a cell door. 'Here we are.'

'Not only that but he has also solved the murder of Captain Kuttner,' said Heydrich.

'Then you've really covered yourself in glory, haven't you?' said Bohme. 'So who did it?'

I glanced at Heydrich.

'What's the game, General?' I said. 'If you've got a card to play here, then you'd better play it, only don't treat me like an idiot.'

'In spite of all that, an idiot is what you are,' said Heydrich. 'A very clever idiot. Only a clever man could have deduced who murdered Captain Kuttner, how and why. But only an idiot could have behaved as you did.'

Heydrich pushed open the door to a large interrogation room that was complete with stenographer, several wooden chairs, some chains hanging from the ceiling, and an en suite bath. Besides the stenographer there were two largish men in the room and a naked woman.

'Only an idiot could have been so easily duped by the Czechs,' said Heydrich. 'By her.'

He pointed at the girl.

It was almost as well he identified her because she was nearly unrecognizable.

The naked girl was Arianne Tauber.

★   ★   ★

462

As soon as I saw Arianne I moved to help her and found myself solidly restrained by Bohme and another largish man who'd been standing, unseen by me, behind the heavy wooden door of the interrogation room; restrained and then, on Heydrich's order, searched for a non-existent weapon and quickly manacled on a length of chain to a cast-iron radiator as big as a mattress, safely out of harm's way.

I hauled at the chain attached to my wrists and swore loudly, but no one was paying much attention to me. I was like a dog that had been safely kennelled, or worse.

Heydrich laughed, and that was the cue for the others to do the same. Even the stenographer, a young hatchet-faced woman in SS uniform, shook her head and smiled as if she was genuinely amused by my threats and bad language. Then she straightened the little forage cap she was wearing and adjusted the grip that kept it on her head. She must have sensed me wishing I could have smacked it onto the floor.

I glanced around the windowless room. It was as big as a chapel in a disused church. The walls were tiled in pea-green. Dusty bare light bulbs hung from the heavily cobwebbed ceiling. The floor was covered with pools of water. There was a slight smell of excrement in the cold air. I hauled some more upon my chain, to no effect. It seemed my situation was as helpless as Arianne's seemed hopeless.

She did not move. Her battered purple eyes remained closed like sea anemones. Her wet hair was coiled around her face like dark yellow snakes on the head of a dead Medusa. There was blood in her nostrils and she appeared to have lost some fingernails, but she was not dead. The edges of her bare breasts shifted a little as breath entered and left her body; she could not move because she was strapped onto a wooden bascule. She was not, however, about to be guillotined, although that was the point of the bascule: to restrain the body and transport the head of a condemned person smoothly through a lunette so that he or she might be quickly decapitated by the falling axe.

Arianne was strapped onto the bascule for an altogether different but almost as unpleasant reason.

The bascule was positioned precipitously over the end of a bath full of pinkish-brown water so that it worked very like a lever. One of Arianne's torturers had his foot on the end of the bascule just under her bare feet and all he had to do to allow the wooden board carrying her body to tip forward on the fulcrum that was the lip of the bath was to move his black boot a few centimetres; then she would fall head first into the water and remain there until either she drowned or her torturers decided to lift the bascule up again. It was ingeniously simple, and although the bath was smeared with blood, as if the bascule sometimes fell awkwardly – and perhaps that explained the several contusions on her eyes, cheeks and forehead – it was obviously effective.

At the end of my chain I was at least a metre away from everyone and this seemed to suggest that others before me had stood where I was, chained to the same radiator and obliged to watch friends being tortured. I couldn't even kick the edge of the stenographer's neat little corner-table with its typewriter, pencil, notebook, magazine, coffee-cup and nail-file; but I promised myself that if the bitch started filing her nails while Arianne was being tortured, I would take off my shoe and throw it at her.

Looking at Arianne, it was impossible to believe she was the same woman I had left behind at the Imperial Hotel that morning. Somehow Heydrich, or the SD or the Gestapo had discovered something about Arianne that had persuaded them to arrest her. But what? Only she and I knew about Gustav and the envelope he had asked her to give to Franz Koci. Nobody else knew anything. Nobody but Gustav. And even if Paul Thummel was indeed Gustav, it seemed impossible that her arrest could be connected with his. Not yet. They had to have picked her up at the station *before* I had identified Paul Thummel as traitor X.

'Has she talked?' Heydrich asked Bohme.

The other man pulled a face. 'Well, of course, sir. What a question.'

'You think so? What about Masin and Balaban?

465

You couldn't get them to talk, could you? You had those two Czechos for five months before you managed to get anything out of them.'

'They were exceptionally strong and determined men, sir.'

'Well, I'm not surprised, now that I've been in here. To me this hardly looks like torture. Somehow I imagined something much worse. Back at my gymnasium in Halle we used to do this sort of thing to other boys just for sport.'

'With all due respect, sir, there's not much that's worse than the water bascule. Short of death itself, which would hardly be to the purpose, no other torture quite persuades as much that you are surely about to die.'

'I see. So, what has she told us?'

Bohme approached the stenographer, who handed him a few sheets of typed paper; these he passed to Heydrich and, while the Reichsprotector glanced over what was written there, one of Arianne's tormentors slapped her bruised cheeks to bring her out of a faint.

With the sleeves of their striped civilian shirts rolled up above their substantial biceps and their collars removed, Arianne's tormentors looked ready for work. The man with his foot on the bascule was examining his knuckles, probably inspecting them for damage. His blond hair was almost white and he seemed indifferent to Arianne's suffering. The other man was smoking a cigarette that stayed in his mouth while he was slapping her.

'Come on,' he said, almost kindly, like a father speaking to a child who was lagging behind on a Sunday afternoon walk in the park. 'That's it, Arianne. Wakey-wake. Say hello to our important visitors.'

Arianne retched bath water and some vomit that was part blood and then coughed for almost a minute.

'Come on. Open your eyes.'

She started to shiver, probably from shock as much as the cold, but still she didn't open her eyes; at least not until her fatherly interrogator sucked at his cigarette for a second, peeled it off his lower lip and then touched her breast with it.

Arianne opened her eyes and screamed.

'That's the girl,' said the man who had burned her.

It was odd how sorry he looked, I thought; almost as if he regretted hurting her; as if he wouldn't have hurt anyone by choice; right up until the moment he smiled a smile that was as thin as a razor and then burned her breast a second time, for the pleasure of it. I could see that now. He enjoyed giving pain.

Arianne screamed again and started to weep invisible tears.

'Please, stop this,' I pleaded.

Heydrich ignored me. He finished reading the transcript of the interrogation and handed the pages back to Bohme.

'Is this really all that she knows, do you think?' he asked.

Bohme shrugged. 'That's a little hard to say, sir. We've only had her for a few hours. At this stage there's no telling how much she knows about anything.'

So it was true; her arrest had preceded Paul Thummel's; in which case they couldn't be connected.

'Sergeant Soppa, isn't it?' Heydrich was looking at the very blond man whose foot was on the water board.

'Sir.'

'I believe you are something of an expert in matters like this. It was you who got Balaban to talk, wasn't it?'

'Finally. Yes sir.'

'What is your opinion?'

Sergeant Soppa shifted his feet a little but still managed to keep Arianne's head aloft. She looked like a human torpedo that, at any moment, he might launch into the water.

'In my experience they always keep something back to the end, sir,' he said ruefully. 'There's always one important thing that they'll hold onto until the last. For their own self-respect, you might say. And they figure you'll miss it because they've already told you absolutely everything else. It's only when they're begging to tell you something they think you don't know – anything – that you can be sure you've got everything there is to be had out of them. Which means that it's always best to keep the interrogation going for longer than seems decent.'

Heydrich nodded.

'Yes,' he said. 'I see what you mean. So then, I think we shall have to know if she knows something that we don't yet know.'

Heydrich nodded at Sergeant Soppa, who immediately took a step back so that the bascule carrying Arianne's naked body tipped forward and hit the water with a splash, head first.

There was a horrible gurgling sound, like a drain trying to clear itself. Arianne was swallowing water. Her hands and feet flailed helplessly under their restraints like the fins of a landed fish. Then Soppa picked up a length of thick rubber cable that was lying on the wet floor and started to beat Arianne hard, the way no living creature, not even a stubborn mule, should ever be beaten. Each blow of the cable snapped loudly on her flesh and sounded like a dangerous electrical short-circuit.

I watched her beautiful body endure this for several seconds. I remembered the exquisite pleasure we had given each other just a few hours before in the hotel room back at the Imperial. That seemed a very long time ago now. More than that, it seemed like another life, in another place where cruelty and pain did not exist. Worse than this, the body I had known and kissed so tenderly already seemed like a different one from the one I was looking at now.

Why had I agreed to bring her to Prague? I could easily have refused her request to accompany me. Surely this was all my fault. I had perhaps foreseen something like this happening, only not quickly enough.

Her hair floated and twisted in the water like yellow seaweed. There was only so much of this kind of treatment she could take. That anyone could take. I told myself I had to do something and I hauled on the chain with all my strength but I was helpless to help her. At this realization, I felt an unpleasant sensation and taste arrive in my mouth from my gut and I spat it out onto the wet floor. If I'd thought, I might have spat it at Heydrich.

'For Christ's sake, you're killing her,' I yelled.

'No,' said Soppa's smiling colleague. 'Not at all.' His tone was scoffing. 'You might say that we're the ones keeping her alive. Believe me, you have to know what you're doing to take someone right to the edge like this. To almost kill them, and then not kill them. That's the skill, sir. Besides, this little bitch is a lot tougher than she looks. She might panic a bit if ever she was to go swimming again. But, no, we won't kill her.' He glanced at Heydrich. 'Not unless he tells us to do it.'

Arianne's head stayed under the water but Sergeant Soppa stopped beating her for a moment, wiped his brow and nodded. 'That's right. We've been helping people to take the waters in Prague

470

like this for a while now. Just like Marienbad, it is, this place. Or Bad Kissingen.'

He grinned at his own attempt at humour. Then he started beating her again.

After a few seconds I turned my face to the wall and closing my eyes against the edge of my vision, I pressed my forehead against the cold, hard tiles. These felt like Heydrich's conscience. I might have closed my eyes but I could hardly close my ears, and the awful combination of sound that was Arianne drowning while she took a dreadful beating continued for another fifteen long seconds before I heard the ghastly dripping creak of the bascule being lifted out of the bath and the banshee rasp of her trying, painfully, to drag air into lungs that were already bloated with water.

By now I was absolutely certain that Colonel Bohme was right: there was not much that was worse than the water board. Just listening to it seemed bad enough. And when I looked again I saw Arianne was just a few centimetres above the surface of the water, dripping wet, trembling uncontrollably, her body galvanized with the spasms that were her agonized attempts to breathe and covered with fresh, livid welts. Sergeant Soppa had thrown aside his cable and had the heel of his hand on the edge of the water board, ready to do exactly the same thing again the very second that Heydrich or Bohme gave him the order.

Soppa's colleague tossed away his cigarette and

turned on a tap to pour some more water into the bath. Had she swallowed that much? Or had it just spilled onto the floor? It was hard to tell. Then he lifted Arianne's head by the hair, shook it like a handbell, and spoke into her ear.

'Is there anything you want to tell us, darling?' he asked. 'Something close to your heart. Next time we'll fucking drown you, if we have to. Won't we, Sarge?'

'Sure,' said Soppa. 'And I'll fuck her while she's drowning.' He stroked Arianne's bare behind with lascivious intent and then patted it fondly.

'Ask her – ask her if she knows where Vaclav Moravek is hiding,' said Heydrich.

Soppa's colleague repeated the question into Arianne's ear.

She gulped loudly and whispered, 'No. I've told you everything I know. I've never heard of Vaclav Moravek. Please. You have to believe me.'

She swallowed another painful breath, belched and tried to say something else, but her previous answer drew a sneer and then a nod from Heydrich which was the cue for another ducking. And this time her head banged against the side of the bath as she fell into the water. Her body struggled against the leather straps and the buckles which cut cruelly into her skin so that a thin trickle of blood ran down her shoulders and dripped into the turbulent bath water.

I held my own breath at the same time as she went under the water so that I could at least

472

experience some small part of her ordeal. But this time they kept her under for much longer than a minute and when, with my lungs bursting, I realized I could hold my own breath for no longer I let it out with a yell, even as Arianne's struggles appeared to have ended for good. Her hands and feet stopped moving. The water calmed. All was still. Including my heart.

'Pull her up, you bastards.'

'Is she dead?' asked Heydrich.

'No,' said Soppa. 'Not by a long chalk. Not to worry, sir. We've brought people round who were under the water for much longer than that.'

He and the other man lifted Arianne out of the bath and proceeded to use a combination of smelling salts, slaps, brandy and massage to try to put some life back into her.

'Leave her alone,' I pleaded. 'For God's sake. She hasn't done anything.'

'You think so?' said Heydrich. 'I'm afraid that you're wrong about that, Gunther. At least, that was the impression I gained from Colonel Bohme, on the telephone, just before lunchtime.'

He turned and faced the stenographer.

'Read the Captain what she's already told us, please.'

'Yes, sir.'

'Just the salient points if you will.'

'Yes sir.'

The stenographer picked up her transcript and

read entirely without emotion, like someone announcing the arrival or departure of a train.

Question: What is your name and address?

Answer: My name is Arianne Tauber and I live in a room at Flat 6, 3 Uhland Strasse, Berlin, which is owned by Frau Marguerite Lippert. I have lived there for ten months. I work at the Jockey Bar on Luther Strasse, where I am employed to be the cloakroom attendant.

Question: You are a Berliner?

Answer: No, originally I am from Dresden. My mother still lives there. She lives in Johann Georgen Allee.

Question: So why are you here in Prague?

Answer: I am on holiday. I came here with a friend. I was staying at the Imperial Hotel.

Question: What is the name of that friend?

Answer. Kripo Commissar Bernhard Gunther. From the Police Praesidium at Berlin Alexanderplatz. I am his mistress. He will vouch for me. He works for General Heydrich. Clearly there has been some mistake here. I spent the weekend with him and I was going home to Berlin when I was arrested.

Question: Do you know why you were arrested at the Masaryk Station this morning?

Answer: No. Clearly there's been some sort of mistake here. I've never been in any trouble before. I am a good German. A law-abiding citizen. Commissar Gunther will vouch for me. So will my employers.

Question: But aren't you also working for UVOD?

Answer: I don't know what you mean by that. What is UVOD? I do not understand.

Question: UVOD is the Home Resistance Network here in Prague. We know you are working for UVOD. Why?

Prisoner refused to answer the question.

Prisoner refused to answer the question.

Prisoner refused to answer the question.

Answer: Yes, I am working for UVOD. Following the deaths of my husband and my father in February and May 1940, for which I held Adolf Hitler ultimately responsible, I decided to work for a foreign government against the National Socialist government of Germany. Since I am from Dresden and my mother is Czech, it seemed logical that this foreign government should be Czech.

Question: How did you go about establishing contact with UVOD?

Prisoner refused to answer the question.

Heydrich interrupted the stenographer. 'Perhaps I did not make myself entirely clear, my dear young woman,' he said patiently. 'I asked you to read out only the salient points. What I meant was that it will save a great deal of time if you omit all mention of when the prisoner refused to answer a question.'

The stenographer coloured a little. 'I'm sorry, sir.'

'Now continue.'

'Yes sir.'

Question: How did you go about establishing contact with UVOD?

Answer: I made contact with an old friend from university called Friedrich Rose in Dresden, a

475

Sudeten German communist, who put me in contact with a Czech terrorist organization that is part of the Central Leadership of Home Resistance – UVOD. I am part Czech myself and I speak a little Czech and I was pleased when, having investigated my background, they accepted me into their organization. They said a native German could be very useful to their cause. Which is all that I wanted. After my husband died on a U-boat all I wanted was for the war to be over. For Germany to be defeated.

Question: What did they ask you to do?

Answer: They asked me to leave Dresden and to undertake a special mission on their behalf. In Berlin.

Question: What was this mission?

Prisoner refused to—.

'Sorry, sir . . .'

After a short pause, while she tracked down the transcript with a well-manicured fingernail, the stenographer started reading again.

Answer: At the request of UVOD I joined the Berlin Transport Company in the autumn of 1940 and worked for the BVG director, Herr Julius Vahlen, as his personal secretary and sometime mistress. It was my job to monitor Wehrmacht troop movements through Berlin's Anhalter Station and to report on these movements to my Czech contact in Berlin. This I did for several months.

Question: Who was your contact?

Answer: My contact was a former Czech German Army officer I knew only as Detmar. I didn't know his surname. I would give him a list of the troop movements on a weekly basis. The troop movements were passed on to London, I think. Detmar would give me some more instructions and some money. I was always short of money. Living in Berlin is so much more expensive than Dresden.

Question: What else did Detmar tell you to do?

Answer: At first I had to do very little. Just give him the troop movement reports. But then in December 1940 Detmar asked me to help the Three Kings organization in Berlin to plant a bomb in the station. This was much more important work and much more dangerous, too. First of all I had to obtain a plan of the station building; and then, when the bomb was ready, I had to prime it and put it in a place where it had been decided it would cause the most damage.

Question: Who taught you how to prime a bomb?

Answer: I am a qualified chemist. I studied Chemistry at university. I know all about handling difficult materials. It's not difficult to prime a bomb. I'm better at that than I was as a stenographer.

Question: What was the purpose of that bomb?

Answer: The purpose of the bomb at Anhalter Station was to cause panic, to demoralize the population of Berlin; and to disrupt troop movements in and out of the city.

Question: Wasn't the real reason for planting that bomb altogether different? Wasn't the real reason that you had inside information about the train belonging to the Reichsführer-SS, Heinrich

Himmler, that was due to be leaving the station? And that the bomb was meant to kill him?

Answer: Yes. I admit that this bomb was really designed to assassinate the Reichsführer-SS, Heinrich Himmler. I planted the bomb in the left luggage office in February 1941. This is right by the platform where Himmler's train was to leave from; and, even more importantly, the office is also beside the place on the platform where Himmler's personal carriage was usually located. The assassination was unsuccessful because the bomb was not powerful enough. It was meant to bring down a joist on top of the train and it didn't.

Question: Then what happened? After the failed assassination?

Answer: With the war in Europe more or less won, it was decided by my controller that troop movements in Germany were of less importance to UVOD; and a few months afterwards I left the BVG's employment. I was not unhappy about this as my boss, Herr Vahlen, was besotted with me and something of a nuisance. Thereafter I worked in a series of night-clubs. Especially the Jockey Club, where I was supposed to befriend Germans from the Foreign Ministry in order to sleep with them and get information useful to the Czech cause. I did this. Again I was short of money and sometimes I was obliged to sleep with some of these men in the Foreign Ministry for money so that I could keep myself. I also worked for UVOD as a courier. Then in the summer of 1941 my contact Detmar was replaced by another Czech called Victor Keil. I do not know what happened to Detmar and I don't know Victor's real name. But we were very uncomfortable comrades. Victor was a very demanding man to work for and I did not like him at all. He was not brave like Detmar. He was fearful and he did not inspire much confidence. He didn't understand my situation at all, how difficult it was for me in Berlin. And we often quarrelled. Usually about money.

Question: Tell me what Victor asked you to do for him.

Answer: He gave me a gun and asked me to shoot someone for UVOD. I don't know the man's name. All I had to do was meet the man and shoot him. I didn't want to do this. I was worried the gun would attract too much attention and I'd get caught. So Victor gave me a knife and ordered me to use that instead. Again I refused. I am not a murderer. So Victor murdered the man himself at a railway station in Berlin where I had arranged to meet him. He was a foreign worker, Dutch I think, and all I had to do was ask him for a light and distract him and Victor would commit the murder. Which he did. But it was horrible. And I said I couldn't ever do something like that again.

Question: What station was this?

Answer: The S-Bahn station at Jannowitz Bridge.

Question: What else did he ask you to do?

Answer: Victor had come into possession of an important list of Czechs who were working for the Germans in Prague. I don't know where he got this list. He was intending to return to Prague with it.

Leaving me on my own. Which greatly alarmed me as I suspected he wasn't planning to come back. He was scared he was being followed and so, temporarily, he gave me the list to look after until he was sure he wasn't being shadowed by the Gestapo. Then Victor and I quarrelled, again about money. I was broke and I said that if I was going to stay on in Berlin and do important jobs for UVOD like help to kill people I wanted more money to cover my expenses. We'd arranged to meet at the station in Nollendorfplatz, in the blackout, but as he went away there was an accident and Victor was knocked down and killed by a taxi. Which was a disaster.

Question: So what did you do then?

Answer: I was in real shit here. Without a contact in Berlin I had no way of getting the list of traitors to our people in Prague. And no way of getting more money. So I resolved to try to go there myself and make contact with someone from UVOD. But it was dangerous and, of course, I was still very short of money. Not to mention a suitable cover story to get myself down to Prague.

Question: So how did you do this?

Answer: After Victor's fatal accident I had become intimate with a police officer called Bernhard Gunther, who was investigating Victor's death. When I met him I didn't know he was a policeman; but when he turned up at the bar one night I got a bit suspicious and searched his coat pockets in the cloakroom and found his Kripo identification disc. At first I thought he was suspicious of me so I decided that the best

480

thing to do would be to seem to take him into my confidence. And to throw myself on his mercy and persuade him that I was simply a joy-girl who had made a bad mistake. When I told him this he didn't know that I knew he was a cop.

Anyway I told him that a man I'd met in the Jockey Bar who I knew only as Gustav had hired me to give an envelope to a stranger on a railway station in return for a hundred marks. I told Gunther that I got greedy, which is why the transaction went wrong. And I also told him I had no idea what the envelope contained as I'd since lost it.

Question: Which station was this?

Answer: The S-Bahn station at Nollendorfplatz.

Question: Tell us about Gustav.

Answer: There never was a Gustav. In fact it was Victor who had given me the envelope. And I didn't mention anything about a list of Czech agents who were working for the Gestapo. I just told him about the envelope and that I'd been looking to make an easy hundred marks. Subsequently Gunther revealed he was a policeman and told me that he believed Victor had been working for the Czechs and that I was in danger. I think it flattered him that he could help me; and I allowed a relationship to develop. An intimate relationship.

Question: Tell me more about your relationship with Bernhard Gunther.

Answer: After Victor was killed, I had no one to help me in Berlin. I thought of returning to Dresden but then the idea of developing Gunther as an unwitting source of intelligence presented itself to me. I knew he was a senior detective in Kripo. So I began a relationship with him. I told him I loved him and he believed me, I think. It was dangerous but I felt the possible benefits were worth taking that kind of risk. And when he told me he had been posted to Prague, I saw a way of travelling there in comparative safety and comfort: as Gunther's mistress. This seemed a fantastic opportunity that was too good to ignore. After all, what better cover could I have for travelling to Prague than as a Kripo Commissar's bit on the side? He even paid for my ticket and arranged my visa at the Alex. In all respects he was very kind to me.

Question: Did Commissar Gunther know of your involvement with UVOD?

Answer: No, of course not. He suspected nothing except perhaps that I had been a whore. Or very stupid. Or both. Either that or he didn't care to ask very much. Perhaps it was a bit of both. He was in love with me and he liked sleeping with me. And, of course, also he was too busy with his own work.

Question: Did he talk about his work?

Answer: No. It was very hard to get any information out of him. He said it was safer for me that way. It took me a while to find out that he was working for General Heydrich and that he was coming to Prague to work at Heydrich's country house. But he didn't say what he was doing there.

Question: What happened when you arrived in Prague?

Answer: We arrived in Prague and stayed at the

Imperial Hotel. We spent the first day together. For most of the next day Gunther was away on official business. He turned up at night to sleep with me. Which suited me very well as I had the rest of the time to myself. I had heard Detmar talk about what to do if he and I ever lost contact. The places to go for help. There was a man in Prague, a UVOD agent called Radek. I should go to these places myself and try to make contact with this man. And I decided to go to these places and ask around for Radek. It was taking a risk but what choice did I have?

Question: What were these places you went to?

Answer: Elektra. It's a café on Hoovera Ulice, next to the National Museum. And Ca d'Oro, a beer restaurant on Narodni Trida, in the same building as the Riunione Adriatica di Sicurta. Detmar had given me some instructions in how to go about this: I should take a red rose wrapped in an old copy of Pritomnost and leave it on the table while I ordered something. Pritomnost is Presence, the weekly review that Masaryk helped to found. I could buy a copy on the black market quite easily. That's what happened. And having made contact with Radek in the Elektra – I do not know his last name – I handed over the list of traitors.

Question: Was it Radek who came up with the plan to kill General Heydrich this morning?

Answer: No, it was someone else Radek introduced me to. I'd told them about Gunther and how he was working at the Lower Castle in Panenske-Brezany. How a car from Gestapo HQ with just a driver would come and pick him up and drive him there. A plan was quickly conceived – the opportunity appeared too good to miss. Two men from UVOD would hijack Gunther's SS car and sit on the floor behind the seats so that they might get into the grounds of the castle, walk in and shoot everyone and anyone they could. Hopefully Heydrich would be one of these casualties.

Question: By which time you would be safely on a train back to Berlin?

Answer: Yes. That was the plan.

Question: And Gunther?

Answer: He was also to be shot by the two UVOD assassins. But the plan went up in smoke when Gunther's car from Pecek Palace was cancelled and the poor fool had to walk to the Castle and requisition a car from there. After that, there seemed little or no choice but to get on the train as arranged. I'd done all I could. What will happen to me, please?

'That's a very good question,' said Heydrich.

He turned to me.

'And at the present moment in time, as you can see for yourself, things are not looking so good for your lady friend. But I think it answers your earlier remark, Gunther: that she hadn't done anything. Now you know. She tried to murder Himmler. She planned to murder me, and as many of my guests as possible. And she planned to murder you. That's quite an achievement. It looks as if she played you for a fool, wouldn't you say?'

I didn't say anything.

'It's fortunate for you I'm still feeling grateful

that you helped us catch Paul Thummel, otherwise you yourself might now be facing what undoubtedly lies ahead of this deeply misguided young woman.'

While the stenographer had been reading, Arianne had recovered consciousness and was at least alive; but she had fainted again and while I could see no way of saving her from execution, or at best a concentration camp, I did think there was a way of preserving her from further suffering on the water bascule. Much of what I'd heard made sense to me, but it was obvious that she was still concealing things from her torturers; and it was equally obvious that I was now in a position to tell Heydrich exactly what I knew and thus save Arianne from herself, even if that meant putting my own head in the Gestapo's lunette.

It was clear that it was me who'd been betrayed by her; and yet, as I started speaking, it somehow felt as if it was Arianne who was being betrayed by me.

I guess it made it easier that I despised myself so much, not for what was said now but for what hadn't been said before – in the Ukraine, and immediately afterward. I hardly counted the short lecture I had given Heydrich on my first day at the Lower Castle. I had tried to believe that in spite of all that I had seen and done in the East I was a person like her, with a sense of moral purpose and values. As a matter of fact I had no such qualities; and I didn't blame her in the least for wanting to kill me. In Arianne's eyes, I deserved to be shot, like everyone wearing an SS or SD uniform, and I couldn't argue with that. Whatever happened now or in the future, I had it coming to me. We all did. But if my plan was going to work – if I was to prevent her from further suffering – I had to make certain Heydrich understood what I said in the only way he could understand it: not out of pity for Arianne but out of loathing and contempt for her, and a desire for revenge. A sense of my true feelings for Arianne would only have caused her more harm. And for her sake I had to kill any love I had for her, and kill it quickly, too. I had to harden my heart until it was made of iron. Like a true Nazi.

I fished out my cigarettes and lit one to give myself some puff for what I was about to do. It wasn't easy with my hands manacled to a chain. Nothing about what I was doing was easy. I blew some smoke at the ceiling for nonchalant effect and leaned back against the wall. How much Arianne heard of what I said next, I don't know. None of it, I hope.

'It looks like I've been had all right.' I sighed. 'Well, it wouldn't be the first time a fellow like me got given the slow trot around the Tiergarten by a pretty girl. Only it's been a while since I was dummied as well as she managed it. Christ, at my age I should know better, of course, but since I stopped believing in Santa Claus I don't get many presents that are as nicely wrapped as this little half-silk.' I shrugged. 'I'm not making excuses, General. That's just how it is for a man who likes to think he's still in the game. And I don't sleep so well on my own any more. The same as Captain Kuttner. She was my version of Veronal. A lot easier to swallow. But probably just as lethal.'

I allowed myself a wry smile.

'So, she tried to send me upstairs, did she? Bitch. And after all I tried to do for her. That really sticks a hole in my sock. Go ahead and wash her hair again, Sergeant, why don't you? I'm all through pulling my chain about it. Hell, now I can see why she was jumpy when she got out of bed this morning. I thought she was sad because she had to go back to Berlin. Because we were to be parted. What a chump I've been. She's quite a liar, I'll say that for her. It strikes me that you fellows have got your work cut out there, with or without the water board. You could send her to the guillotine and the head on that little cunt would still talk its way out of the basket. And, by the way, make sure you send me a ticket. That's one party I wouldn't want to miss. Who knows? Maybe I can help to put her there myself. Because you know, it strikes me that the ration is short on that story of hers, and that maybe I can make up the weight. In fact, it would be my pleasure.'

Heydrich gave me a narrow-eyed look as if he was trying to estimate the distance between what

I was saying and what he believed. It was like facing a suspicious parent and, moreover, one who was such a practised liar himself that he knew precisely what to look for in establishing what was true and what was not. An art expert with a picture of uncertain provenance could not have been more thorough in the way he studied the brushwork and checked the signature on the contrary picture I had painted for him.

'Such as?' he said, coldly.

'Such as Victor Keil's real name was Franz Koci.' I flicked my cigarette into the bathwater as if I hardly cared that Arianne's head might yet be ducked in it. 'I know that because I was the cop who investigated his death; and at the special invitation of your friend Colonel Schellenberg. He was found dead in Berlin's Kleist Park. After the collision she mentioned, with the taxi on Nollendorfplatz, he must have staggered down Massen Strasse. We found him under a big red rhododendron bush with the knife he'd used on the Dutchman, Geert Vranken, still in his possession.

'I've been thinking about the letter I received from Vranken's father, in the Netherlands. And how Paul Thummel was the character reference Geert gave the police when he was a potential suspect in the S-Bahn murders. Well, because Thummel had had some sort of relationship with Vranken's sister, he must have found out from her, I suppose, that Vranken was working on Berlin's railways. That must have been the reason the

Abwehr asked to see the files on the S-Bahn murders; which they did; and in particular the interviews with all the foreign workers. The official excuse was that they were on the lookout for spies; but in reality, Thummel must have been on the lookout for Geert Vranken. He was the only person in Germany who could connect him with his Czech controller in The Hague. And when he saw Vranken's statement, which mentions knowing a German officer who might vouch for him, Thummel must have panicked. Most likely Vranken was killed by Franz Koci at Paul Thummel's specific request.'

Heydrich was nodding now. 'Yes, that makes sense, I suppose.'

'Either he radioed the request to UVOD here in Prague or, as seems more likely, he told Arianne. Probably she was the cut-out between Thummel and Franz Koci, who she knew better as Victor Keil.'

Heydrich continued nodding. This was a good sign. But an even better one was to come.

'Horst.' Heydrich waved at Colonel Bohme. 'Release him.'

A little reluctantly – he still hadn't forgiven me for being a better detective than he was – Bohme produced a key from the pocket of his riding breeches and unlocked my manacles.

I rubbed my wrists and muttered a thank you. I didn't say anything about Arianne, who remained strapped to the bascule balanced over the bath of water. It was crucial that Heydrich believe that his revelation about her part in the plot to kill me meant I was now indifferent to her immediate fate; and it was equally crucial that my story was both plausible and authoritative, even though a lot of it was based on sheer guesswork, so that it would seem there was little real point in torturing Arianne any more; at least for the present.

To my enormous relief he now came to this conclusion.

'Take the woman back to her cell,' he told Sergeant Soppa.

'Yes sir.'

Soppa and the other man laid the bascule down on the wet floor and started to unstrap Arianne. She groaned slightly as the buckles were released, but it was hard to tell if her heavily bruised eyes were open, so I had no way of knowing if she saw me.

Either way, it was certainly the last time I ever saw her.

'Let's continue this conversation in your office upstairs, Horst,' said Heydrich. 'Gunther?' Now he was ushering me out of the interrogation cell, ahead of him.

I walked toward the door. My heart was on the floor alongside Arianne's bedraggled, half-drowned body, twisting over and over like a dying trout.

Heydrich held my arm for a moment and then smiled a sarcastic smile. 'What? No fond goodbyes for your poor lover? No last words?'

I didn't turn around to look back at her. If I had he'd have seen the truth in my face. Instead I met Heydrich's chilly, wolf-blue eyes, turned a deep sigh into a wry laugh and shook my head silently.

'To hell with her,' I said.

It was, I thought, the only place Arianne and I were ever again likely to meet up with each other.

In a large office on an upper floor of the Pecek Palace, Heydrich told an orderly to bring us schnapps.

'I think we all need one after that ordeal, don't you, gentlemen?'

I couldn't argue with this. I was desperate for a drink to put a little iron in my soul.

A bottle arrived. A proper one containing real liver glue but none of the deer or elk blood that Germans sometimes said it contained. That was just a story like the one I was getting ready to tell Heydrich and Bohme. I drank a glassful of the stuff. It was ice-cold, the way it's supposed to be. But I was colder. Nothing's been invented that's as cold as how I felt at that moment.

I went and sat on the windowsill and looked out at the old medieval city of Prague. Somewhere, under one of those dark, ancient roofs, was a fatal creature of death and destruction that was exactly like my own twin brother. Indeed, if the Golem had looked in my eye at what was elusively called the soul, he might well have concluded that I was a man to be shunned, just as people in the street below avoided the Pecek Palace front door like it was a Jaffa pesthouse. Given the wicked, monstrous, inhuman events that I'd just witnessed in the basement, they weren't so far wrong.

Unbidden, I fetched the bottle and poured another glass of the embalming fluid that helps make Germans like me more German than before and I lit a cigarette half-hoping that it might set fire to my insides and turn me to ashes like everything else that was almost certain to be turned into ashes in due course.

'I expect you're wondering how we got onto her,' said Heydrich.

'No, but I would have got around to it before long.'

'The list of Czechs working for the Gestapo here in Prague was hardly complete. One of the people Arianne Tauber approached in that other café she mentioned – I can't remember what it was called – he was ours.'

'The Ca d'Oro,' said Bohme. 'It was the Ca d'Oro, sir. The head waiter is a French fascist who's been working for the Gestapo since the Spanish Civil War. As soon as he saw her sitting there with the flower inside the magazine he contacted us.'

'After that,' added Heydrich, 'it was only a question of having her followed around the clock. She led us to Radek, about whom Bohme already had his suspicions, didn't you, Horst?'

'That's right, sir.'

Bohme grinned and taking the bottle from my windowsill, he refilled my glass again and helped the General and then himself.

'That's why your car didn't turn up this morning, Gunther. We arrested the two assassins around the corner from your hotel. And the girl when she arrived at the railway station a little later on. We had hoped there would be someone there from UVOD to see her off, but there wasn't, so we picked her up and put her in the bag with the two killers.' He shrugged. 'Not that I think there was ever much danger of either one of you being killed. It was a pretty desperate, spur-of-the-moment sort of plan. And the chances are they'd have been shot by the sentries at the Lower Castle before they got very far.'

'All in all,' said Heydrich, smugly, 'it's been an excellent day's work. We have the traitor. We have some more terrorists. It can only be a matter of time before we catch up with Vaclav Moravek.'

'Yes, congratulations, sir,' said Bohme, toasting him. 'Tell me, what are your orders regarding Arianne Tauber? Do you want her questioned again?'

Heydrich was still thinking this over when I said, 'I expect I can fill in the rest of the gaps in her story for you.'

'Yes, why don't you tell us again how you met,' said Heydrich. 'In detail.'

I gave him the whole story, more or less; from the circumstances in which I had first met her at

493

Nollendorfplatz Station, to my own middle-aged infatuation; there seemed little point in hiding anything other than my true motive for telling him.

'Paul Thummel was obviously this fellow Gustav she told me about back in Berlin. She might have denied he exists downstairs but there can be no doubt about that now. I expect that's the one thing she was keeping back from Sergeant Soppa. He was right about that. I also expect that when Thummel sees her again he'll fold like a picnic table. Especially when he sees the state you've left her in.'

I lit a cigarette and swung my leg carelessly.

'As far as I can gather, it was Paul Thummel who gave her the list of agents to pass on to Franz Koci. As a major in the Abwehr he was well placed to know exactly who they were. But when she met up to hand them over to Franz Koci, they quarrelled about money, just as she said, and he must have thought she was holding out on him. Maybe she was, too. I expect he demanded that she give him the list and when she wouldn't – at least not until her complaints had been addressed – he got rough with her and decided to search her underwear.

'That was when I saw her for the first time. I assumed, wrongly, that he was attempting to rape her. Or worse. As you know, there's been a lot of that in the blackout this summer. Women attacked and murdered in and around railway stations. I guess it was still on my mind a lot. So naturally I went to her assistance.'

'Very gallant of you, I'm sure,' said Heydrich.

'Koci and I fought but he got away and ran into the blackout. The next day I was looking at his dead body under a bush in Kleist Park.'

'At the request of Walter Schellenberg,' said Heydrich.

'That's right. The Berlin Gestapo guessed he was a Czech agent, but they had no idea how he'd met his death. Who killed him, or why. I agreed to help. And soon enough I was able to connect Franz Koci with Geert Vranken.'

'But you decided to leave the girl out of it.'

I nodded.

'So you could take advantage of her, I suppose.'

It hadn't been like that; but it was no good saying that I had honestly believed her to be more innocent than she turned out to be. I needed to give Heydrich the kind of cold and clinical reason he could understand. The kind of reason he would have acted upon himself, no doubt.

'Yes. That's true. I wanted to fuck her. I had the idea she was just a dupe, but that was always me. Of course as soon as I started sleeping with her I stopped seeing what was right under my nose. That she was in it all the way up to her pretty neck. But it was such a pretty neck.'

'The rest of her is not bad either,' said Bohme.

'About that neck, Gunther,' said Heydrich. 'I won't be able to save it. You know that, don't

495

you? The fact that she was involved in a plan to kill me, well, that's of no real consequence. But an attempt to kill Himmler is a different story. The Reichsführer takes any assault on his personal safety rather more personally than I do.'

I shrugged as if I cared nothing now for what happened to her. And I shrugged because I knew Heydrich was right. Nothing could save Arianne now. Not even Heydrich.

'The real question here is what happens to you, Gunther. In many ways you're a useful fellow to have around. Like a bent coat hanger in a toolbox, you're not something that was ever designed for a specific job, but you do manage to come in useful sometimes. Yes, you're an excellent detective. Tenacious. Single-minded. And in some ways you'd have done a good job as a bodyguard. But you're also independent, and that's what makes you dangerous. You have standards you try to live up to but they're your standards, which means that ultimately you're unreliable. Now that I'm where I am in the scheme of things, I can't tolerate that. I had hoped I might be able to bend you to my will and use you when I could. Like that coat hanger. But I can see now I was wrong. Yes, it's difficult to turn a woman over to the Gestapo, especially a good-looking woman like Arianne Tauber. Some can do it and some can't and you're just the type who can't. So, I have no further use for you. You've become an unfortunate liability, Gunther.'

This sounded like the best thing he'd ever said to me; but I was through opening my mouth like that for a long while. Perhaps permanently. He hadn't yet finished telling me my own fate.

'You will return to your desk in Kripo and leave Germany's destiny in the hands of men like me who truly understand what that means.'

He smiled his paper-knife smile and toasted me silently.

I toasted him back but only because, perhaps for the last time, I was hoping to point out a long hair in his chicken soup.

'And the attempt on your life, sir? The poisoning, at Rastenburg? I accept that you no longer wish to have me act as your bodyguard. But am I to take it that you no longer wish me to investigate the recent attempt to kill you?'

He stared at me for a moment and, with a quiet surge of pleasure, I realized he had forgotten all about this incident.

'There never was such an attempt,' he said defiantly. 'I made it up so that I might have a plausible reason to invite you to Prague with the rest of them.'

I nodded meekly, a little surprised that he'd admitted such a thing; and I wondered where the actual truth was to be found: if there really had been an attempt to poison Heydrich at Rastenburg after all.

'Besides, as the most powerful man in Bohemia and Moravia, I think I'm quite safe here, wouldn't you agree, Horst?'

So that clinched it, for me; he *was* lying.

Bohme smiled an obsequious smile. 'Absolutely, sir. You have Prague's SS and SD at your immediate disposal; not to mention the Gestapo and the German Army.'

'You see?' crowed Heydrich. 'I have nothing to worry about. Especially not in Prague. The day the Czechs try to kill me – really try to kill me, not that half-baked attempt we had today, although you mark my words that will have its own repercussions – the day they try to kill me will be the very worst day in the history of this country and will make the defenestrations of Prague look like a childish prank. Isn't that right, Horst?'

'Yes sir. In a long line of crazy Czech ideas that would be the craziest idea of all.'

I had my doubts about that. I hadn't been in Bohemia for very long but from what little I knew about the country it seemed only appropriate that the idea of the Bohemian – a type of fellow not easily classified and who never acted in a conventional or predictable way – had got started in Prague. In Prague throwing someone out of a window *was* just a childish prank. A bit of harmless fun. But I didn't expect a Roman Catholic German from Halle-an-der-Saale to understand this. And if I really had been as single-minded and independent as Heydrich said I was, I would probably have told him he was wrong: murder – even political assassination – is rarely ever committed by people who are anything else but crazy; and, over the centuries, one way or another, a lot of crazy things had happened in Prague.

So I nodded and told Heydrich he was right, when I knew he wasn't.

And that is what makes anyone dangerous.

I moved back to the Imperial Hotel and waited for my Berlin rail warrant to arrive. Heydrich liked to keep most people waiting and I waited for several days. So I saw the sights and tried not to think about what might be happening to Arianne. But of course that was impossible. I preferred to believe that she hadn't actually condoned my murder but that she had felt obliged to go along with it as part of the general plan to kill Heydrich; and after all, when you're shooting Germans it's hard to know who is a Nazi and who isn't. It's a dilemma I understood very well.

Finally my travel papers came through, and on my last night in Prague I remembered my ticket for the Circus Krone, and decided to go along.

It was a cold autumn evening with a clear sky and a full moon, and people were already wearing their warmest winter coats. I sat well away from the rest of my SS colleagues but I had a good view of all of them in the front row of seats and I confess I paid more attention to Mr and Mrs Heydrich and Mr and Mrs Frank than I did to the clowns and the animals.

I hadn't seen Lina Heydrich before. She was handsome rather than beautiful. She wore black with a thick fur stole and a little black pillbox hat. Mrs Frank wore a wool overcoat with wide lapels and a brown fedora. The two wives sat beside each other and next to them sat their husbands, who were wearing civilian clothes, like everyone else in the SD and Gestapo who was at the circus that night. Frank wore a plain gaberdine coat with a white shirt and a patterned silk tie. Heydrich wore a thick double-breasted overcoat and held a black trilby on his lap. And he also wore a pair of horn-rimmed glasses that I'd never seen on him before.

Like anyone else, these four marvelled at the trapeze and laughed at the clowns and they appeared to enjoy themselves. Like anyone else. That was what struck me most of all. Out of uniform, Heydrich and Frank looked just like anyone else, although even as they sat there a security crackdown was already under way in the city. Later on, I learned that the mayor of Prague, Otokar Klapha, had been executed and on the very same day that Arianne was arrested. Hundreds of UVOD collaborators were being rounded up and buildings right across the city were covered with posters listing the names of many others sentenced to death. You wouldn't have known any of that if you'd watched Heydrich at the circus, shaking with laughter as three clowns behaving like the sort of simpletons the Nazis would probably have murdered for reasons of racial purity fell off chairs and soaked each other with buckets full of water.

Two days later, Heydrich announced that the deportation of all the Jews in the Protectorate – some ninety thousand of them – was to begin at the end of the year. To where, he didn't say. Nobody did. Me, I had a pretty good idea, but by then I was back in Berlin.

CHAPTER 15

It felt good to be in Berlin again. At least it felt good for an hour or two. Soon after arriving back at my apartment in Fasanenstrasse I discovered to my disappointment that the two Fridmann sisters from downstairs had been deported to some shithole in Poland. Behnke, the block warden, who knew these things, insisted that it was a nice town called Lodz and that they'd be happier there 'living with their own', instead of with 'decent Germans'. I told him I had my doubts about this but Behnke didn't want to hear them. He was more interested in learning Russian so that he would be able to speak to his peasants when eventually he met them. He really thought he was going to get some of that living space in Russia and the Ukraine that Goebbels was forever ranting about. I had my doubts about that, too.

It grew cold. Wind tore the leaves off the trees and hurried them east in their thousands. The water on the Spree looked like corrugated iron. The cold felt like barbed wire. There was one thing to be done before the snows arrived, a sentimental gesture that meant nothing to anyone I had ever met; but I suppose I wanted to feel better about myself. I organized the release of Geert Vranken's remains from Berlin's Charité Hospital and paid for them to be buried in a zinc-lined wooden crate – just in case, after the war, his family wanted to dig it up and take his remains home to the Netherlands.

There was one other person at the funeral: Werner Sachse from the Gestapo. With his black leather coat, his black hat and black tie, he looked like a proper mourner. The short service was conducted by the pastor of St John's Church, in Plotzensee, and when it was over Sachse told me he admired the thought if not the practice.

'Where would we be if policemen paid for every foreign worker who gets killed in an accident?' he asked.

'It wasn't an accident,' I reminded him.

Sachse shrugged as if the correction I'd offered hardly mattered. The fact remained that the dead man wasn't German and therefore his death was of little or no account.

For a moment I wondered if telling him why I was doing it was a mistake; and then I told him anyway.

'I'm doing it so that somewhere, someone who isn't German will have a better opinion of us than we deserve.'

Sachse pretended to be surprised about that, but before we parted we shook hands, so I knew he wasn't.

CHAPTER 16

Commissioner Friedrich-Wilhelm Lüdtke was known as Stop-Gap Lüdtke on account of his name and because no one had expected him to survive in the job because he wasn't a Party member. But he did what he was told, and when someone told him to put me on night duty that's what he did. Not that I minded very much. Being on nights kept me out of sight and out of mind. At least it did until early on the morning of Monday 17 November. I mention the murder I investigated that night only because it was Heydrich himself who had me taken off the case. I expect he was worried that I might actually solve it.

It was about five o'clock in the morning when I got the telephone call from Kriminal Inspector Heimenz at the police station in Grunewald. There had been a murder at one of those fancy modern villas in Heerstrasse. He wouldn't say who it was on the telephone; all I knew was that it was someone famous.

One of the good things about being on nights was that I had access to a car, so I was at the address in less than half an hour. And it was easy to find. There were several police cars parked outside, not to mention a huge silver Rolls-Royce. As soon as I stepped through the elegantly modern front door I guessed whose house it was. But I hardly expected that he was also the victim.

General Ernst Udet was one of the most famous men in Germany. At the age of just twenty-two he had survived the Great War as Germany's highest-scoring air-ace. Only Manfred von Richthofen had more victories than he did. After the war he'd made several movies with Leni Riefenstahl and was a stunt-flier in Hollywood. The house was full of film posters, flying cups and photographs of aeroplanes. A polished wooden aircraft propeller hung on one wall and it was several minutes before I could tear myself from all of Udet's memorabilia to look at his dead body. He wasn't very tall, but then you don't need to be tall to fly aeroplanes, especially when these are experimental: Udet was the Director-General of the Luftwaffe's developmental wing. He was also a close friend of Hermann Göring. Or at least, he had been a close friend until someone shot him.

The body was naked. It lay in the middle of an enormous double bed, and surrounded by empty brandy bottles, most of them good-quality French brands. There was a neat hole in his forehead and a hammerless Sauer .38 in his right hand. For a small man – he couldn't have been more than one sixty – he had an enormous penis. But it wasn't

505

any of these details that drew the eyes. Not even the telephone line that was coiled around one of his muscular arms like a Jew's tefillin. It was what was written on the headboard in red lipstick that tugged at my eyeballs and made me think I had walked in on a major scandal.

REICHSMARSHAL, WHY HAVE YOU FORSAKEN ME?

I suppose the choice of words was meant to make you think of Jesus Christ, nailed to the cross, and abandoned by God the Father. But that wasn't what I thought of; and it wasn't what Inspector Heimenz thought of, either.

'This is one homicide I'm happy to leave to you boys at the Alex,' he said.

'Thanks. Let me tell you, he looks how I feel.'

'Cut and dried, isn't it?'

'So *you* take the case.'

'Not me. I want to sleep at night.'

'You're in the wrong job for that.'

'The Grunewald is not like the rest of Berlin. This is a quiet district.'

'So I see. Who found the body?'

'The girlfriend. Name of Inge Bleyle. She claims they were on the telephone when she heard the shot. So she drove straight over here in that modest little car you saw parked outside and found him dead.'

'That Rolls is hers?'

'So it would seem. Apparently Herr Udet had been drinking heavily all week.'

'From the look of things, Martell and Rémy Martin are going to be inconsolable.'

'It seems that he and the Air Ministry had had their differences concerning the success of the air war against the British.'

'You mean the lack of it, don't you?'

'I know what I meant to say. Perhaps you'd better speak to Fräulein Bleyle yourself, sir.'

'Perhaps I had. Where is she now?'

'In the drawing room.'

I followed him downstairs.

'Hell of a place isn't it, sir?'

'Yes.'

'Hard to imagine anyone who owned a place like this shooting himself.'

'Is that what you think happened?'

'Well, yes. The gun was in his hand.'

I stopped on the stairs and pointed to one of the many photographs covering the wall: Ernst Udet and the actor Bela Lugosi, posing on a California tennis court.

'Looks to me as if Ernst Udet was a lefty,' I said.

'So?'

'The gun was in his right hand. I don't know about you, but if I was going to shoot myself – and believe me I've considered it, seriously, these past few months – I'd probably hold the gun in my stronger hand.'

'But the words written on the headboard, sir. Surely that was meant to be some sort of suicide message.'

'I'm only sure that's what it's meant to look like. Whether it is or not we'll only know when a doctor gets him on the slab. You'd expect a powder burn on the skin if he really did press the gun to his forehead, and I didn't see one, that's all.'

The inspector nodded. He was a small man with small hands and a small way about him.

'Like I said, this is one homicide I'm glad to leave to the Alex.'

Inge Bleyle had stopped crying. She was about thirty years old, tall – much taller than Ernst Udet – and good-looking in an understated way. She was wearing her fur coat and there was a drink in one hand and a cigarette in the other, neither of which looked like she'd paid much attention to them since they came her way.

I found an ashtray, held it under her cigarette and tapped the back of her hand. She looked up, smiled ruefully and then put out the cigarette in the ashtray while I continued holding it.

'I'm Commissar Gunther. From the Alex. Feel like talking?'

She shrugged. 'I guess so. I guess I have to, right? I mean, I found him, and I made the call, so someone has to start the ball rolling.'

'I believe you told the other detective that you were on the telephone with Herr Udet when the shot was fired. Is that correct?'

She nodded.

'What had you been talking about?'

'When I first got to know him, well before the

war, Ernst Udet was the life and soul of the party. Everyone liked him. He was a real gentleman. Kind, generous, impeccably well-mannered. But you couldn't imagine he was even related to the Ernst Udet of recent memory. He drank, he was short-tempered, he was rude. He'd always drunk a lot. Half of those Great War pilots drank just to go up in those planes. But he always seemed like he could handle the drink. But lately he started drinking even more than usual. Mostly he drank because he was unhappy. Very unhappy. I'd left him because of his drinking, you see. And he wanted me back. And I didn't want to come back because it was obvious that he was still drinking. As you have no doubt seen for yourself. It looks like a one-man house party in there.'

'Why was he drinking? Any particular reason? I mean, before you left him.'

'Yes, I understand. He was drinking because of what was happening at the Air Ministry. That Jew, Erhard Milch, was trying to undermine Ernst. All of the people in his department had been fired and Ernst took that very personally.'

'Why were they fired?'

'Because that bastard Göring didn't have the guts to fire Ernst. He figured that if he fired all of Ernst's people then Ernst's sense of honour would compel him to resign. He blamed Ernst for the failure of our air attacks on Britain. That's what he said to Hitler, to save his own skin. Of course it wasn't true, not a damned word of it,

509

but Hitler believed him anyway. But that was just one reason he was depressed.'

I groaned, inside. After Prague I needed this case like I needed a pair of silk stockings of the kind Inge Bleyle was wearing on her lovely legs.

'And another reason?'

She shrugged. Suddenly she was looking evasive, as if it had dawned on her that she was talking to a cop.

'What with the war in Russia, well that was getting him down too. Yes, he was depressed and drinking too much. Only – well, he wasn't long back from a clinic in Bühlerhöhe. They'd dried him out. He did that for me, you know. Because he wanted me back and I'd made that a condition of our getting back together. But I wanted to wait a little, see? Just to see if it took – the cure.' She sipped her whisky and grimaced. 'I don't like whisky.'

'In this house? That's not unusual.' I took the glass and put it on the table between us.

'Then, a couple of days ago, something happened to him. I don't know what, exactly. Ploch, his chief of staff at the Ministry until Milch had him fired, had just returned from Kiev. He went to see Ernst and told him something. Something awful. Ernst wouldn't say what it was, just that it was something happening in the East, in Russia, and that no one would ever believe it.'

I nodded. You didn't have to be a detective to know what Ploch had probably told him. And it wasn't anything to do with aeroplanes.

510

'Because of that, Ernst had telephoned Göring to ask him about it and they'd argued. Badly. And Ernst threatened to tell someone at the American Embassy what Ploch had told him.'

'He said that?'

'Yes. He had a lot of American friends, you see? Ernst was very popular. Especially with the ladies. The late ambassador's daughter – I mean the American ambassador's daughter, Martha Dodds, she was a very close friend. Perhaps more than just a friend. I don't know.'

She paused.

'And he told you all of this on the telephone?'

'Yes. We were talking. Ernst was crying some of the time. Begging me to come and see him. One thing I do remember him saying. It was that he could no longer believe in Germany; that Germany was a wicked country and deserved to lose the war.'

The more I heard about Ernst Udet, the more I started to like him. But Inge Bleyle felt obliged to disagree; anyone would have felt the same.

'I didn't like it that he was saying such things. I mean, that kind of talk is not good, Commissar; even if you are a decorated hero like Ernst. I mean, you hear stories about the Gestapo. People being arrested for unpatriotic talk. I told Ernst to be quiet and to keep his mouth shut in case he got us both into trouble. Him for saying such things and me for listening to them without ringing off. That's what you're supposed to do when you hear

511

those things. You understand, the only reason I stayed on the line was that I was concerned for his state of mind.'

I nodded. 'I understand.'

'Then I heard the shot.'

'Had he talked about killing himself?'

'Well, no. Not in so many words.'

'Did you hear anything else? Voices, perhaps? Footsteps? A door closing?'

'No. I put the telephone down and drove straight over here. I live only a short distance away in the West End. When I got here all the lights were on. And I still had my key so I let myself in. I shouted his name a couple of times and then went upstairs and found him dead, as you saw. I came back downstairs and used the telephone in the study – it's a different line – to call the police. I didn't want to touch the one in his hand. That was an hour ago. I've been here ever since.'

'Do you think he killed himself?'

She opened her mouth to say something; checked herself – the way you do – and said: 'It certainly looks that way, doesn't it?'

Sensible girl. No wonder she was driving a Rolls-Royce. They don't hand those cars out to just anyone.

After that two fellows from the Air Ministry showed up: Colonel Max Pendele, who was Udet's adjutant, and another officer. That was at eight a.m. Then someone from the Ministry of the Interior turned up as well. That was at nine.

At about eleven o'clock I drove back to the Alex to type out my report.

After I'd done this Lüdtke asked me to come up to his office, and when I got there, he told me I was off the case.

I didn't ask why. By then I hardly needed to. It was plain that someone important didn't want me asking any awkward questions, and there were plenty that could have been asked about the death of Ernst Udet; and it was only after Heydrich's death that I learned it had been he who told Lüdtke to take me off the case.

Five days later they buried Udet. It was a state funeral. They carried him out of the Air Ministry in a casket covered with a Nazi flag, placed him on a gun carriage and then processed up to Invaliden Cemetery, where they buried him close to his old pal the Baron von Richthofen. Of course, state funerals were for heroes, not suicides or enemies of the state, but that was okay because the story released by the authorities – and this was the reason behind my removal, since of course I knew different – was that Udet had been killed testing an experimental fighter plane.

Hermann Göring delivered a eulogy; the nine-centimetre flak gun in the Tiergarten fired a salute that had many Berliners running for an air-raid shelter thinking that the RAF was back in our skies. A few days later they were back, although not to drop any bombs.

It was as well I was off the case. Being a detective

has made me unreasonably suspicious. I see connections and conspiracies where other people see only the need to look the other way and keep their suspicions to themselves. Another air ace, Werner Mölders, was killed flying back to Germany for Udet's funeral, from the Crimea; and around the Alex there were whispers that there was a lot more to his death – the Heinkel on which he was a passenger crashed as it tried to land in Breslau – than had been allowed to meet the eye.

Certainly the British thought so, for the RAF dropped leaflets over Germany alleging that, like Ernst Udet, Werner Mölders had been opposed to the Nazi regime. And that he had been murdered.

Six days later, Mölders was also given a state funeral and he was buried alongside his great friend and confidant Ernst Udet in the Invaliden Cemetery.

In retrospect both of those two state funerals felt like dress rehearsals for what followed six months later in June 1942.

It was six a.m. I was on my way home after a night at the Alex when I received a telephone call to go and see Arthur Nebe in his office at RSHA headquarters in Prinz Albrechtstrasse. It was a summons I had been dreading. I knew of the attempt on Heydrich's life: on 27 May, a group of Czech terrorists had thrown a grenade into his open car as it drove through the streets of Prague. Heydrich had been seriously injured but, as far as anyone

514

knew, he was making a strong recovery. It was only what you might have expected of such a brave hero; at least that's what the newspapers said.

Nebe had already dispatched two senior detectives from the Alex – Horst Kopkow and Dr Bernhard Wehner – to Prague, to help with the investigation. The assailants were still at large and throughout Bohemia and Moravia a huge security operation was under way to catch them; everyone in Kripo – myself included – believed they would soon be arrested.

Nebe, who was now back in Berlin after murdering tens of thousands of Jews in the Ukraine, looked wearier than usual. But it looked as if these efforts had been appreciated: there were even more decorations on his tunic than I remembered, and in this respect at least he was beginning to resemble a South American Generalissimo. His long nose had turned a little purple, no doubt a result of the heavy drinking that was required to complete our historic German tasks, and there were bags under his eyes; he was smoking almost continuously and there were patches of bad eczema on the backs of his hands. The hair on his head was almost silver now but his eyebrows remained dark and overgrown, like the forest of briars in *The Sleeping Beauty*, shielding the enchanted castle that was his soul from the discovery of the outside world.

He came straight to the point.

'Heydrich died at four-thirty this morning.'

'He picked a nice day for it.'

Nebe permitted himself a wry smile.

'Is that all you've got to say?'

'Yes. I warned him to be more careful. But he wasn't the careful type, I guess.'

'I'm flying to Prague in an hour's time. I'll be part of an SS honour guard that will bring his body home to Berlin.'

'I think you'll find he was born in Halle, Arthur.'

'While I am there I shall also be reviewing progress in the investigation. As a matter of fact, there isn't any progress. It's fucking chaos down there. Chaos of catastrophic proportions. The local Gestapo is arresting everyone.'

'That's one way of catching the murderers, I suppose.'

'I need my own man. Someone whose abilities I respect. That's why you're coming with me, Bernie. To find some truth.'

'Truth? You're not asking for much, are you?'

'We can argue about it in the car on the way to the airport. Anything you need while you're there, you can buy.'

We drove straight to Tempelhof Airport where a Heinkel was already fuelled and waiting for us. We climbed aboard and took off immediately. From the air, Berlin still looked good. Flying over it was probably the best way to see the city, which looked green and natural, a decent place to live, like the old Berlin of my youth. You couldn't see the corruption and the savagery from up there.

'You'll observe what's going on. Nothing more than that. Observe and report directly to me.'

'Bernhard Wehner won't like that. As a commissioner he outranks me, Arthur. From the way he behaves I think he outranks Hermann Göring.'

'Wehner's not a detective, he's a bureaucrat. Not to mention a cunt.'

'Is he in charge?'

'No. Frank thinks he's in overall charge. And so does Daluege. The criminal inquiry is being handled by Heinz Pannwitz.'

'I'm beginning to understand the problem. What's Dummi doing there?'

Kurt 'Dummi' Daluege was the chief of Germany's uniformed regular police.

'Apparently he was in Prague for medical treatment.' Nebe grinned. 'Not a well man, it seems.'

'What's wrong with him?'

'Nothing trivial, I hope.'

'Heinz Pannwitz. I don't know him.'

'He's a Berliner, like you and me. And capable up to a point. But a bit of a thug, really. He's been with the SD in Prague since 1940, so he has a fair bit of local knowledge.'

'I wonder why I never met him.'

'Yes, I heard you were down there last October.'

'I had hoped never to go back.'

'Rough, eh?'

'Not for me. Not particularly. But there was a girl. Arianne Tauber. It was very rough for her.'

'She's the one who tried to blow up Himmler, right?'

'Yes. The assassination attempt that no one talks about. Do you happen to know what happened to her?'

'No, but I could probably find out. In return for your help in Prague.'

I nodded. 'Fair enough. There was another fellow. The spy. Paul Thummel. What happened to him? Do you know?'

'Difficult case,' said Nebe. 'You have two sides to that story. The Abwehr says that Thummel only ever pretended to spy for the Czechs so that he could obtain information about UVOD's London contacts. The SD, however, insists he was the genuine Esau. And nobody wants to put him on trial so they can prove the case one way or the other. That would be embarrassing for someone important, either way. So Thummel stays in an isolation cell at the fortress in Terezin, under a false name, the poor bastard.'

When we arrived in Prague we found things were even more chaotic than Nebe had described. The streets were empty of everyone except lots of SS troops, who were reportedly trigger-happy, while the cells at Pecek Palace and the prison at Pankrac were full after the arrests of almost five hundred Czechs, nearly all of them innocent, of course. But the situation at Hradschin Castle was nothing short of laughable. Daluege was working on the assumption that the assassination was the beginning of an organized Czech uprising; he had called in police reinforcements from Dresden and declared a nine p.m. curfew. Most of the Czechs arrested had simply fallen foul of Daluege's curfew.

Pannwitz and Frank were jointly of the opinion that the ambush was the work of a team of British parachutists, and these two had set in train a painstaking search of every single house in Prague in the hope of uncovering the assassins' hiding place.

As soon as they saw Arthur Nebe, Kopkow and Wehner complained that there was little hope of catching anyone so long as revenge appeared to be the only order of the day, for as well as the five hundred Czechs who had been arrested, it seemed that the Gestapo had already shot more than one hundred and fifty men and women who were suspected of working for UVOD, including two witnesses to the actual assassination. Which hardly helped their investigation.

Nebe and I viewed the damaged car, the scene of the crime and other evidence, including a bicycle used by one of the assassins, and the coat he had been wearing; these were on display to the public in the window of a popular shoe store in the centre of Prague. Then we went to Bulovka Hospital to view Heydrich's dead body and found the autopsy was still in progress. This was conducted by Professor Hamperl – who had also handled Captain

Kuttner's autopsy eight months earlier – and Professor Weygrich, who was also from the German Charles University in Prague.

Nebe, who had no taste for hospitals, left me there to speak to the two professors while he went to the Pecek Palace for a meeting with Frank and Pannwitz.

I did not enter the operating theatre. Although the whole floor was guarded by several SS-men – to me this looked like covering the well after the child had already fallen in – I could easily have entered the theatre itself; Nebe made that clear to the NCO in charge of the guard detail. But I didn't go in to the autopsy theatre. Perhaps I just didn't trust myself not to tell Heydrich that if he had listened to me then he would have been alive. Perhaps. But I think it's more likely that I wanted to avoid finding the least bit of sympathy in myself for that truly wicked man. So I sat on a wooden bench outside the doors and waited for good news, like an expectant father.

When the autopsy finished, Hamperl was first out of the operating theatre, and he greeted me like an old friend.

'So, he's really dead, is he?' I asked.

'Oh, yes.'

I lit a cigarette. I never much cared for big cigars.

We walked along the landing.

'Tell me,' asked Hamperl. 'Did you ever catch that poor Captain's murderer?'

The official record showed that Kuttner's murder

remained unsolved. Hamperl probably knew that. It was just his way of teasing me. I was hardly about to tell him that he'd just finished dissecting Kuttner's murderer. Somehow that didn't seem appropriate. Besides, as well as the SS guards there were several Gestapo men hanging around the floor.

'No,' I said. 'We never did.'

'We? You were in charge of that case, weren't you, Commissar Gunther?'

'I thought that, too. But it turned out I wasn't really.'

'Who was?'

I nodded back at the autopsy theatre. 'He was. Heydrich.'

'I expect he's why you're here now. Yes?'

'It's not because I like this place.'

'No, indeed. Well, it was good to see you again, anyway.'

'No, don't go away. I've come all the way from Berlin to talk to you, Professor.'

'I've got nothing to say.'

'Come on, Professor. Help me out here.'

'It'll be a day or two before Professor Weygrich and I have finished our report,' said Hamperl. 'You can read it then. Now, if you don't mind, Commissar, I have a lot of work to do in the lab.'

I followed him downstairs.

'All I want from you is your probable assessment. And then I'll leave you alone.'

'No. I can't help you there. My report is for the

eyes of General Frank only. Until he authorizes its release, I can't discuss the case with anyone. That's what he told me. And I wouldn't care to disappoint that man. He's in a mood to do harm to this city. To the whole country, perhaps.'

I ran ahead a few steps and then stopped in front of Hamperl.

'I can appreciate that. But I really must insist.'

'Don't be ridiculous, Commissar. You're in no position to insist on anything. The report must remain private for now. Now get out of my way.'

I stayed where I was. 'Would it make a difference if I said the word "Rothenburg", sir?'

Hamperl did not reply.

'I'm sure you know what I'm talking about, Professor Hamperl. The Pension Matzky.'

'I was visiting a patient,' he said. 'In my capacity as a doctor, you understand. That is why I was there.'

'Of course. I understand perfectly. What you don't know perhaps is that nothing that happens there is private. Nothing at all.'

Hamperl's fixed jaw slackened a little.

'What do you mean?'

'There were hidden microphones.'

'I see.'

'All I'm asking is that you give me a few minutes of your time, Professor. In private. Do you have a car here, sir?'

'Yes. Why?'

'Perhaps you could give me a lift back into the

centre of Prague, sir. We might talk a little during the journey.'

'Yes. I don't see why not. We could certainly do that. A good idea. Follow me.'

That evening I met Arthur Nebe at the Esplanade Hotel where both of us were staying, and over an excellent dinner I told him what I had learned that afternoon from Professor Hamperl.

'It seems that Heydrich was making a strong recovery until yesterday lunchtime. He'd just finished a meal cooked specially for him by his wife, Lina, when he collapsed and lost consciousness.'

'I hope you're not going to tell me she poisoned him.'

Nebe grinned and poured himself a glass of wine. He was doing his best to enjoy himself in spite of everything that had happened, and some of the wariness that was almost always in his narrow eyes was gone. Probably it was just the wine. Nebe was especially fond of good wine and good restaurants. He put his long nose into his wine glass and breathed deeply.

'Do drink up, Bernie. This is a superb claret.'

'It wasn't her that poisoned him. But—'

He put down his glass and watched my face for some sign of humour.

'You're not serious.'

'Professor Hamperl is scared, Arthur. He'd like the autopsy to report that Heydrich died from anaemic shock.'

'The man lost his spleen, didn't he? Anaemic shock would be a fair conclusion to that sort of injury.'

'However, Professor Weygrich wishes to mention the presence of organ damage resulting from an infection. A bacteria or poison.' I shrugged. 'Well, again, you might expect infection to result from bomb splinters.'

'Certainly.'

'However.'

'Ugh. That word again.'

'Hamperl would prefer not to mention this inflammation of the tissues at all. Mediastinitis, he called it.'

'I fail to see the need for two ominous howevers. Infection is common in such situations.'

'After the patient was making a strong recovery?' I shook my head. 'Listen, Arthur. On Tuesday Heydrich had a temperature of one hundred and two degrees Fahrenheit. But yesterday his temperature was down and his wound was draining freely. That is until midday, when the infection suddenly returned. A complete reversal of his condition.'

'So what are you saying, Bernie?'

'I'm not saying anything. Hamperl is saying it. And frankly he's not likely ever to say it again, to anyone. I had a hard enough job getting him to say it the first time. And here's another thing, Arthur. I'm never going to say any of this again, either. If you ever ask me about this I'll just say I don't know what you're talking about.'

'All right.' Nebe nodded. 'So, let's hear it.'

'Hamperl believes the infection was introduced long after the wound was sustained. That Heydrich was infected by a bacterium introduced by an outside agency. In other words, he *was* poisoned.'

'Good God. You are serious.' Nebe grabbed his glass and drained the contents. 'Who did it?'

'He won't say. But I checked through the medical records myself and they show that Heydrich was initially under the care of Himmler's personal physician, Professor Karl Gebhardt.'

'That's right,' said Nebe. 'As soon as he heard Heydrich had been injured Himmler ordered Gebhardt to come to Prague and take charge of Heydrich's treatment.'

'But later on, Hitler's own doctor, Dr Karl Brandt, arrived on the scene and, having examined Heydrich himself *he* recommended that Heydrich be treated with an anti-bacterial sulphonamide. Gebhardt refused however, on the basis that the drug isn't particularly soluble and, crystallizing in the kidneys, sulphonamide can cause a certain amount of pain. You wouldn't want to prescribe it to someone who wasn't eating or drinking.'

'But you said that Heydrich was eating and drinking normally.'

'Exactly,' I said. 'And if he was taking liquids, any pain from sulphonamides would have been considerably lessened.'

'So what are you saying? That Gebhardt poisoned Heydrich?'

525

'I'm saying it's a possibility. When I was last in Prague, Heydrich told me that SS doctors were experimenting with sulphonamide compounds, as a way of treating wound infections. Doesn't it seem odd that Heydrich of all people should have been prevented from taking advantage of a drug newly synthesized in SS laboratories?'

'Yes, it does,' admitted Nebe.

'At least until you remember that Heydrich already suspected Himmler of trying to kill him.' I shrugged. 'Who better than a doctor to finish the job started by the British parachutists? And here's another thing that I found out at the Bulovka Hospital. After her husband died Lina Heydrich had some sort of altercation with Dr Gebhardt and actually accused him of killing her husband. It seems that she had to be restrained from hitting him.'

'Jesus Christ. I never knew this.'

'Apparently she told Major Ploetz, Heydrich's adjutant, that she won't be accompanying your SS guard of honour back to Berlin.'

'What?'

'You heard me. It seems she herself believes that her husband's death is not exactly as advertised.'

'Himmler will be furious. Hitler, too.'

'There is that possibility.'

Nebe rubbed his jaw anxiously.

'You're right, Bernie. We never had this conversation.' He toasted me with his glass. 'I might have known you'd discover a very different culprit from the ones I was hoping to find. I think we'd best leave it there, don't you?'

'I already did. When I get back to Berlin I'm going to deny I was ever here. As I discovered last October, being in Prague can be damaging to your health. Even fatal.'

Nebe uttered a grim-sounding sigh.

'About your girl friend, Arianne Tauber. It's not good news, I'm afraid. I wish I could give you some good news, but I can't. I'm sorry.'

'Good news I wasn't expecting, Arthur. I just want to know for sure what happened to her.'

'They sent her to a concentration camp near Krakow.'

I nodded.

'Well, that's not so bad. People have survived concentration camps before.'

'Not this one. This is a new kind of concentration camp. Only part of it is a true concentration camp of the kind that you and I know about. You know, like Dachau or Buchenwald. Mostly this is a special new sort of concentration camp. Much bigger than those others. It's called Auschwitz.'

That was the first time I ever heard the name Auschwitz. While I was eating a good dinner and enjoying a fine bottle of wine in an expensive restaurant. It seems astonishing now that the name did not stay with me longer, but within a few days I had more or less forgotten it. Years later, I heard the name again, and this time it stayed with me. It stays with me always now, and whenever I think of it I know I can put at least one face and name to the several millions of people who died there.

AUTHOR'S NOTE

The Three Kings were Josef Masin, Josef Balaban and Vaclav Moravek. Balaban died in Prague's Ruznye Prison on 3 October 1941; Vaclav Moravek was killed in a shoot-out with the Prague Gestapo on 21 March 1942; Josef Masin was executed in May 1942, as part of the Nazi retaliation for the attack on Reinhard Heydrich.

On 9 June 1942, a special train carrying one thousand Jews left Prague for Auschwitz. The train bore a sign which read ATTENTAT AUF HEYDRICH (Assassination of Heydrich). On the same day, General Karl Hermann Frank ordered Horst Bohme to destroy the Czech village of Lidice, north-west of Prague, because it was vaguely suspected of having harboured some of Heydrich's assassins. One hundred and ninety men over the age of sixteen were executed, summarily. One hundred and eighty-four women were sent to Ravensbrück; eighty-eight children were sent to Lodz. On 1 July 1942 Eichmann ordered the women and children to be sent to Chelmno, where they were all gassed in specially converted gas vans. The village itself was razed to the ground.

On 16 June 1942 Karel Curda walked into Pecek Palace and gave away the names and addresses of many prominent UVOD resistance workers, among them the Moravec family (no relation). Marie Moravec poisoned herself rather than be taken alive by the Gestapo. Her son, Ata, was captured and tortured. His interrogators showed him his mother's severed head before dropping it into a fish tank. Ata Moravec broke down and revealed the hiding place of the Heydrich assassins; this was the church of St Cyril and St Methodius in Resolva Street. The Germans called this church Karl Borromäus.

Hiding in the crypt of St Cyril's (a Russian Orthodox church – not a Roman Catholic one, as might have been supposed) were Jan Kubis, Adolf Opalka, Jaroslav Svarc, Josef Gabcik, Josef Bublik, Josef Valcik and Jan Hruby – all members of an assassination team trained by the British Special Operations Executive for a mission called Operation Anthropoid. A pitched battle ensued during which all six men were killed or committed suicide. The bodies were identified by 'the traitor' Curda. The entire families of all these brave heroes were sent to Mauthausen Concentration Camp, where they were executed on 24 October 1942.

On 3 September 1942, the officials of the Resolva Street church of St Cyril's were tried in the conference hall of the Pecek Palace in Prague. The trial lasted three and a half hours. On 4 September, Bishop Gorazd, Jan Sonnevend, Vladimir Petrek and Vaclav Cikl were hanged.

Adolf Hitler gave Lina Heydrich the Lower Castle at Jungfern-Breschan (the Czech name for this place is Panenske-Brezany) in gratitude for her husband's 'heroic work'. Heydrich's eldest son, Klaus, was killed in a traffic accident outside the gates of the house in October 1943. The boy is buried in an unmarked grave in the grounds of the house. In January 1945 the Heydrichs left the house for good.

Paul Thummel was released and rearrested on several occasions. In February 1942 he broke down under questioning and admitted he was a spy. He was imprisoned in the fortress at Terezin (Theresienstadt) under the false name of Dr Paul Tooman. There he remained for three years. In August 1944 he was divorced by his wife Elsa, which was the last time he saw her. In April 1945 he 'committed suicide' in Terezin.

Karl Hermann Frank was captured in 1945, tried by the Czechs, found guilty and executed outside Pankrac Prison on 22 May 1946. The whole execution may be found on the internet for those who are inclined that way at http://www.executedtoday.com/2009/05/22/1946-karl-hermann-frank/

It's only my opinion but he died rather bravely, for what it's worth.

SS-Standartenführer Dr Walter Jacobi was arrested by the Americans in September 1945. He was executed in Prague on 3 May 1947.

SS-Obergruppenführer Richard Hildebrandt was hanged for war crimes in Poland on 10 March 1952.

SS-Obergruppenführer Karl von Eberstein testified for the prosecution at the Nuremberg trials. He denied knowledge of and responsibility for Dachau Concentration Camp, which fell under his authority as the Higher SS and Police Leader for Munich. He died in Bavaria on 10 February 1979.

SS-Gruppenführer Konrad Henlein was captured by the Americans and committed suicide in May 1945. However, he may actually have been a spy for the British.

SS-Gruppenführer Dr Hugo Jury committed suicide in May 1945.

SS-Brigadeführer Bernard Voss was hanged in Prague on 4 February 1947.

SS-Standartenführer Dr Hans Ulrich Geschke was most probably killed during the Battle of Budapest in February 1945. He was declared dead in 1959.

SS-Standartenführer Horst Bohme was killed at the Battle of Königsberg in April 1945. Declared dead, 1954.

SS-Sturmbannführer Dr Achim Ploetz. Fate unknown to the author.

Konstantin von Neurath was tried at Nuremberg and sentenced to fifteen years in prison. Released in 1954, he died aged eighty-three in August 1956.

General Kurt Daluege was hanged by the Czechs in Prague in October 1946.

Lina Heydrich died on 14 August 1985. She always defended her husband's name.

The portrait of Adele Bloch-Bauer by Gustav Klimt remained in the possession of the Austrian State Gallery in Vienna until 2006, when an Austrian court determined that it and three other pictures were the rightful property of Ferdinand Bloch-Bauer's niece, Maria Altmann, to whom he had left them in his will, following his impoverished death in Zurich in November 1945. Klimt's portrait of Adele Bloch-Bauer was one of four paintings sold at Christie's, New York, in November

2006. It fetched eighty-eight million dollars and may be viewed today at the Neue Galerie in New York City.

The author visited the house at Panenske-Brezany in February 2011. It is closed to the public, however, and mostly derelict. Under the old communist government of Czechoslovakia, the house was a secret weapons research facility.

According to a Prague newspaper in March 2011, Heider Heydrich, aged seventy-six, Heydrich's surviving son, offered to 'find finances' for the restoration of the house at Panenske-Brezany. The story caused a furore in the Czech Republic. It is, however, the author's opinion that the son is not the father and that this once beautiful house is worthy of restoration. I imagine he would like to find the grave of his elder brother.